La Famiglia

SIENNA MYNX

DEDICATION

La Famiglia is the fourth book in the Battaglia Mafia Series. There are many blessings, trials and tribulations within family. As I the author delved into the Battaglia's family history I could not help but to reflect on my own. I dedicate this installment to my wonderful, complicated, and often times loving family. Thanks to your faith and unwavering support I can conquer all.

Villa Mare Blu – 1972
Mondello Beach/Palermo - Sicily

Near Palermo, Sicily crystal blue waters nestled between two mountains washed over the beaches of a seaside town called Mondello. It was indeed a beautiful vacation spot for both Sicilians and tourists, under a Mediterranean sun that bloomed hot and bright in the sky no matter the season. The Battaglia family owned a portion of the beach at the foot of Mt. Gallo with homes called Villa Mare Blu. Many violent and unexpected events occurred during their holiday visits to Sicily. Often these events were centered on who Giovanni's father was. Most were resolved without alerting the authorities because of the unshakable relationship Don Tomosino Battaglia had with Don Marsuvio Mancini. However, violence came and went without explanation in Giovanni's young life.

Tonight would be more of the same.

"Svegliati! Wake up boy!" Tomosino bellowed.

The foot of Giovanni's bed was kicked. Hard. Startled out of his sleep Giovanni sat upright with his hands flat at his sides. He struggled to capture his breath. At times Patri Tomosino's angry orders dispelled the tranquility in Villa Mare Blu. But those moments were reserved for the adults who followed him. His father's arrival in Giovanni's room at the late hour was unsettling. Only recently were Giovanni and his mother released from captivity outside of Chianti. Eve had been banished as punishment for running away with the Don's only son when he was barely twelve years of age. Rumor had it soon after his mother's return that she was with child again. A new baby would explain his father's generosity to bring them out of isolation and back to Sicily.

Giovanni didn't care what his mother and father's issues were. He was glad to have returned to this life, his friends, and the family. For him things were back to normal, except for the unexpected nighttime visit.

1

"See to him!" Tomosino leveled his pointer finger at Giovanni. "He will be your responsibility until your mother wakes."

"Patri? I don't underst—" Giovanni began.

Tomosino shoved a little kid forward. The boy looked to be no older than five or six. He was thin, frail, covered in bruises. A dark puffy swell had closed his left eye. The child shivered. Made the center of attention, he bowed his head in fright. He wore no shoes, only a pair of stained, soiled underwear.

"Who is he, Patri?" Lorenzo asked with evident disgust. Giovanni cast his line of vision to the other side of the room. There his cranky cousin, who often slept through most anything, was awake. Apparently Lorenzo could smell the stench off the child, for his nose wrinkled and his brow furrowed with disgust.

Tomosino stared down at the little boy. He seemed perplexed. Didn't he know the origin from which the boy came? "Tell them your name," his father said.

Slow and timid a small voice replied. No one in the room could hear what the child had whispered.

"Speak up!" Tomosino barked.

La picoletto lifted his head and turned his chin upward to answer. "My name is... Dominic Antonio Esposito, signor," he replied.

Giovanni thought he recognized compassion on his father's face. It was fleeting. After the introduction was had his father gave no further instruction. He turned and walked out. Alone in the room with Giovanni and Lorenzo the little boy wept silently.

"The kid smells like pig shit, Gio," Lorenzo pinched his nose with one hand and pointed with the other. "Look at him. Did Patri dig him out of the trash?"

"Can't you see he's scared?" Giovanni replied. "Stop making fun of the boy."

Dominic kept his gaze trained on the floor. Giovanni pushed up to his feet. He walked over to the kid, but had to kneel to earn his attention. Lorenzo was right. The boy smelled like he crawled through sewage, or lived in it.

"Ciao, Dominic Esposito. Sono Giovanni." He touched his chest during the introduction and then pointed to his cousin. "And that there big mouth is Lorenzo. Tutto va bene—everything's fine."

The boy nodded he understood.

"Are you hungry?" Giovanni asked.

The kid peeked up at him and his swollen eye nearly opened. "Sí, Giovanni, very much."

"Oh no! No!" Lorenzo shot to his feet. "Wake your mother, or I'll wake mine!" Lorenzo huffed. "Have them take him out of here. They can feed him and clean him. I want to go to sleep and the little stinker isn't climbing in bed with me," Lorenzo said.

"Christo!" Giovanni shouted.

The last of his patience had expired. He'd shut Lorenzo up if he had to. He and Lorenzo were both the same height and weight. Giovanni had lost a few fights to Lorenzo in the past, but that was before he spent two years in Ireland fist to elbows fighting every dirty bastard who called his mother a whore and him a half-breed. The demand for his cousin's obedience weighed between them as the silence in the room lengthened. And then he went unchallenged.

"Ignore him. Fresh clothes and a bath is what you need." Giovanni looked around the room. He walked over to his chest of drawers. In his bottom drawer he found an old pair of shorts and a t-shirt he had been able to wear several years ago. It would be too big for the child but he imagined it could do for the night. He took Dominic's hand and pulled him along. Silent and obedient Dominic went without complaint. He was a good learner, a good follower.

"How old are you?" Giovanni asked.

Dominic shrugged his small shoulders.

Giovanni stopped. He stared down at the kid. "You don't know how old you are?"

The boy shook his head no in response.

"You look five or six to me, maybe younger." Giovanni decided.

Dominic smiled.

Where did his father find this kid, Giovanni wondered? How could he not know his age? Confused and a bit alarmed Giovanni set aside his concern and continued down the dark hall. At the opening to the bathroom he reached in and turned on the light. "You do know how to bathe yourself? Right?" Giovanni ran the water. He proceeded to strip the little boy of his soiled underwear and then tossed the wretched pair into the small trashcan near the toilet. He picked up Dominic who weighed nothing and set him in the water. The dirt on the kid looked to be imbedded into the cells of his skin. After watching the child struggle with a large bar of soap to cleanse himself, Giovanni took control. He had to release the dirty water and run it fresh from the tap to truly get to the business of cleaning him. It took over thirty minutes, and his arms hurt from the scrubbing.

"Look at you," Lorenzo teased from the bathroom door. "Will you fix him a bottle or give him your tit to suck next?"

Giovanni sighed. He loved Lorenzo. However tonight was not the night for his bullshit. Whenever Patri's presence or actions stirred them in the middle of night, out came his couin's bravado. Lorenzo constantly wanted to prove his toughness Giovanni supposed. What Lorenzo failed to understand was that Patri didn't bring the kid to their room to annoy them. He did it so Giovanni could make the child appear less scared and traumatized before the women saw him. In particular his mother who was known to be sensitive to the violence that followed his father. Cleaning the boy was an important job and his father trusted him to do it.

"Christo! Look at the bathwater," Lorenzo continued. "I don't care that you've cleaned him, he sleeps on the floor!"

"Go back to bed!" Giovanni threw the sponge at the wall and got to his feet. "Porca miseria! Go before I knock you on your ass!"

He challenged Lorenzo to say another word. After a tense stare off, Lorenzo mumbled a few curses and stalked off. He glanced back and saw terror in the kid's eyes. The boy had put his back to the wall as if he thought Giovanni would turn his anger on him next. His good eye was stretched so wide it bulged and his breathing looked labored in his skeleton thin chest.

"Are you afraid of me?" Giovanni asked.

The child whimpered. He shut his eyes and began to tremble.

"Don't be afraid, Domi. Can I call you Domi? That's a good name for you. Eh?"

Fat tears coursed down Dominic's chubby cheeks. Even the bruised eye swollen shut appeared to bleed tears. The child's bottom lip quivered. Giovanni attempted to cheer the kid up with a goofy face. He made two or three of them consecutively, and then he laughed to alleviate the kid's fear. "I'm not going to hit you, and Lorenzo is a jackass but I'm not going to hit him either. Come here. We're done with the bath."

Dominic shook his head no.

Giovanni faced a new problem. If his mother woke and found the scared boy she'd go crazy and his father would surely be enraged. He couldn't lose control of the situation. Giovanni thought it over for a minute.

"I guess you haven't had a good slice of pie in a while? Have you?"

"Pie?" Dominic asked. His tiny chest looked caved in from starvation.

"Yes, pie. Do you want some? How about a meat sandwich? We have some of the sweetest goat's milk. Fresh."

4

Dominic nodded. "Sì."

"Come here."

Dominic pushed off the wall and extended his arms. Giovanni retrieved a large towel and picked the child up. He dried and dressed him. The kid was quite cute when the dirt was scrubbed from him. He had a head full of dark curly hair and round brown eyes ringed in dark lashes. Giovanni decided to carry him out of the bathroom. Quiet, they ventured into the kitchen. And he made good on his promise. They ate. Dominic devoured the pie, the sandwich, the milk, the grapes, and cheese too. He'd never seen a kid so small eat so voraciously.

When he finished Dominic grinned up at Giovanni. "Tante grazie," Dominic wiped his mouth with the back of his hand.

Giovanni leaned forward. "Where is your mama? Your papa?"

The question was greeted with silence.

"Do you know?" Giovanni pressed him.

Dominic didn't answer.

"Tomorrow mio madre will come for you. Her name is Eve. She is very kind. She will take care of you. But she and the other women, my aunts, will want to know where you came from, who your parents are. Why you have the bruises you have. You are not to tell them. We wait until Patri tells us what to do and what to say. Do you understand? This is very important to remember."

Dominic nodded.

"I need you to answer me, Domi. You trust me now, right? Say the words."

"I understand, Gio," he replied in the meekest voice.

"Good. Now let's find you a place to sleep." Giovanni stood.

"Can I stay with you?" Dominic asked alarmed.

The request threw Giovanni. "I have school in the morning. I need my rest. Don't you want your own bed? We have one just across the hall." For the past few months his father insisted they live in Mondello because of his business affairs in Palermo with the Mancinis. Both he and Lorenzo attended school. Dominic looked a bit worried. He glanced around the kitchen and then back to Giovanni with his good eye. "Per favore? Can I stay with you?"

"You can sleep with me tonight. How's that?" Giovanni replied.

The kid nodded his head with eager approval to the offer. For the moment the sleeping arrangement would stand. Giovanni hoped his father would give them instruction soon. Suddenly he cared for the kid and feared for him as well. Whomever beat the boy this way *wanted to end his life. Of this Giovanni was sure. He cleaned off the table and took Dominic back into his arms. He carried him to the room he shared with Lorenzo and put him in his bed. Lorenzo watched them but remained silent. As soon as the kid was under the blankets he was asleep. For the remainder of the night Giovanni stared up at the ceiling—lost in thought. Dominic was his responsibility. He would take care of him to the best of his ability. And then a new truth dawned on Giovanni. His father had saved Dominic's life. That made his father a hero. Giovanni smiled.*

A week later –

"Why go alone?" Lorenzo asked. "And with him? Do you have a fever in your brain?"

"I can handle it," Giovanni grunted.

"Take us with you, Gio. The little shit is up to something," Lorenzo said.

Giovanni walked across the freshly mowed lawn with his books thrown over his shoulder in his bag. Santo kept pace at his right side and Lorenzo to the left. Carlo remained a few paces behind them, his arm thrown over the shoulder of a girl. She looked trapped by Carlo's advances and walked stiffly with her head bowed. Carlo whispered what Giovanni guessed were obscenities in her ear. Nothing would deter Giovanni from his mission. He and Armando Mancini had a deal and he didn't need or want the rest of them to know the specifics.

"You sure about this, Gio? You will owe me," Armando said underneath a snicker. He appeared from nowhere and now walked boldly with Giovanni and his crew. "Or do you need your cousin to hold your hand?"

"Let's do it," Giovanni answered. Armando was smug in front of the parochial school because he was Don Mancini's son. Even Giovanni and his clan had to respect him. But down at the beaches it was neutral territory and war constantly raged between the young teens in both their gangs—privately.

Giovanni went for his bike. He ignored the barb, the questioning glare from his cousin and friends, the little voice in his head that warned caution. Armando and Giovanni were rivals from birth. However, Giovanni made a bargain with a devil for a single favor. And even in his young years as Don Tomosino's son he understood why the devil was often necessary. He dropped his books in the basket to the front of his bike and hopped on.

"Gio! Wait!" Lorenzo insisted.

Fast as the wind, Giovanni began to pedal away. He glanced back once to see Lorenzo and his friends watching in stunned silence. He had only an hour before Del Stavio closed his jewelry shop. Biking through the small village and along the rocky narrowed cobblestone streets that led into Palermo proved to be a bit of a challenge. He, however, managed the excursion against the tailwind of his nemesis, who had made the trip so many times before. Armando knew of the short avenues to bring them there in thirty minutes as opposed to fifty.

Excited and a bit apprehensive, he set the bike against the store once they arrived. He looked over to Armando who cut him a deceptive smile. Giovanni wasn't sure if his rival would hold up his part of the deal. He half expected to see Armando's crew descend on him for a savage beating as punishment for traveling out of Mondello and into their territory. But Armando dropped the kickstand on his bike and went for the door of the jewelry store. Giovanni followed.

"Ciao! Armando and Gio! You're here!" Del Stavio chuckled. "I am ready for you as promised." He twisted his long mustache at the ends and then wiped his hands down the front of his apron.

"Can I see it?" Giovanni's gaze bounced around the jewelry display case.

"Of course!" Del Stavio said grandly. "Armando asked that I do this in a hurry. I have it here." He walked over to the counter and opened a dark purple velvet cloth. "St. William the patron saint of orphaned children. Here he is."

Giovanni gazed upon a small ¾ inch sterling medallion with a beautifully crafted portrait of the saint stamped in the center of the medal. The medallion rested on a stainless steel chain. He touched the length and lifted it to the sparse light. The small silver disc gleamed and sparkled as it swayed from a length perfect for a boy or young man. Giovanni couldn't afford gold from his allowance. But he imagined he couldn't afford this as well. Del Stavio was the best jeweler and friend to men like his father. However, a custom piece could only be requested by one of the Five Dons of Sicily or their progeny. Thus, Armando had to commission it. After paying his allowance as bounty to Armando, the smug bastard agreed. However, a single favor to be asked at any time for this privilege was now expected of Giovanni.

He cut his eyes over to Armando. He understood the full cost of

7

this sacred piece. And then he remembered the little boy who needed it so desperately. He lowered the medallion on the cloth and nodded. "Mille grazie—thank you very much. It's what I wanted. I'll take it, Del Stavio," Giovanni said.

"Prego! Before I let you accept this, you must tell me if you understand the meaning," the old jeweler chuckled.

Giovanni nodded. "Of course. St. William was orphaned as a child and raised by strangers who became family, who taught him how to survive."

"And?" Del Stavio asked. His eyes sparkled under an arched bushy brow.

Armando cut in. He smirked at Giovanni sharing the rest of the tale. "At fifteen St. William decided to dedicate his life to God. He built a monastery on Mount Vergine and performed many miracles. He had only a wolf and staff as his protection. With the hand God dealt him he became stronger, became a man of worth, and a helper to those who needed him. Like little orphan boys with a murdered mommy and daddy."

Del Stavio's smile dimmed, but brightened as he tried to make light of what Armando insinuated. "Basta. It is yours, Gio. Take it."

"Grazie, Del Stavio," Giovanni said. "Tanto grazie."

Del Stavio waved off the payment offered to him by Armando. "I know of the boy you will give this to. Go with God's blessing. I hope it brings la piccoletto peace."

It was of no surprise to Giovanni that many had heard of Dominic. Tomosino was questioned by the local officials the day after he took the abused boy into his home. All Giovanni and Lorenzo were able to discern was that Dominic's father was dead. Murdered. They heard their mothers whisper that Dominic's madre was a poor village girl who spent a tortured existence at the hands of her husband, until her death shortly after giving birth to the little boy. Dominic had been an instrument of abuse from the day he entered the world. But the kid was strong, alive, and now his brother. He would take care of him.

"Grazie!" Giovanni accepted the wrapped gift. "Grazie!"

Once outside he dropped the package in the basket on his bike and climbed on.

"Oooh Gioooo?" Armando sang.

"Not now. I must get home." Giovanni quipped.

"Now," Armando said, he stepped before Giovanni and blocked his escape. "The favor I want. I intend to collect next week. Meet me tomorrow after prayer behind the rectory to discuss the details."

"What is this favor?" Giovanni frowned.

"Not a what—a who?" Armando grinned. The request pinched the last nerve Giovanni had on reserve for tolerance. He hated the smug superiority the cowardly young Mancini wielded from being Don Mancini's son. But a deal was a deal.

"I hear Tomosino killed that kid's father you have hidden in Villa Mare Blu. I hear he made the boy watch too. Papa told me that our men had to find what was left of Micheli across the fields of his farm. Do you want to know why he did it? No? Because I assure you it wasn't for any noble reason you may think."

In Giovanni's heart he wanted to believe his father had rescued Dominic. That Patri was a hero. But he believed differently after hearing the whispers of the nuns today in school. Nothing Don Tomosino did was without self-reward.

"Out of my way," Giovanni said.

Armando snickered. "Meet me tomorrow," he yelled after him. "We have a deal!"

Giovanni pedaled away, fast. He arrived home much later than he hoped. This time the bike ride took him over an hour and his legs felt as if they were made of jelly when he got off. As soon as he approached the front of the villa he could see Dominic grinning from the top window with his hands and face pressed against the pane. Giovanni waved. Dominic waved back.

His mother greeted him at the door.

"Where have you been? Lorenzo arrived two hours ago," she asked with a stern look of disapproval. Though his father's men were powerful, they were in Mancini territory and the Mafioso only tolerated the clans of the Camorra. Danger was a way of life. And Giovanni could easily become a target for ransom if his father fell out of Don Mancini's graces.

"Sorry, Madre. I had to stop and get something. Is Patri home?"

"No. Inside! Now."

Giovanni started past his mother but she grabbed his arm and delayed him. "Dominic has been in that window since you left for school. He's been waiting for your return, Gio. Every time I drag him from the room to eat, bathe, do his lesson, he finds a reason to return."

This Giovanni already knew. Dominic followed him around the house. He mimicked him at every turn. It irked Lorenzo, but Giovanni accepted it as something the kid needed to do. He didn't mind.

His mother continued. *"I want him baptized. That nasty man who was his father never bothered. You talk to Dominic and explain it to him, what the sacrament means."*

"I'll go see him," he said. He turned on is heel and stumbled. Dominic had appeared right behind him. He had to hold on to the boy's small shoulders to keep from tripping. Dominic grinned up at him. Giovanni chuckled. *"Come with me, Domi. I have something for you. That's why I was late today."*

"Get him cleaned up, he's been out in the gardens with Zia. Dinner is in another hour," his mother said. She shook her head causing her long scarlet red hair, held from her face by a blue silk ribbon, to sway about her shoulders as she walked away. He glanced back to see her hand to her stomach and the swell that was very prevalent in the dress she wore. He hadn't believed the rumor when they said she was pregnant again. But the truth was there for all to see. She grew larger every day. Patri was very excited over the promise of a new child. He doted on Eve. And Giovanni had even seen his mother smile a few times when his father was around. It was progress. They were a family again. Their time in Ireland was done.

Dominic was pulled along by Giovanni's hand. Giovanni took him to the sitting room and closed the door. *"Here, sit here."* He led him to the sofa seat and joined him. He reached in his pocket and removed the tiny box that Del Stavio had given him. He opened it for Dominic.

"This here is the patron saint of orphans. St. William. See here, this is the wolf at his side. The one who protects and helps those that can't help themselves. This will make you stronger. You wear it, and St. William's wolf will be there to protect you always. No more nightmares. Okay? Do you understand?"

Dominic nodded. *"Si. No more nightmares, Gio."*

Giovanni put the necklace around Dominic's tiny neck. *"This means we are brothers, Dominic. Always."*

"Always," Dominic said with a nod. He knew the kid took the commitment seriously. He kind of liked having a little brother of his own to mentor. Dominic stared at the medallion then turned it over. *"What does this mean?"* he asked of Del Stavio's insignia.

"The jeweler who made this has been blessed by the Pope. He is the private jeweler to the Five Dons of Sicily. Any man, woman or child who wears this insignia is covered by God's grace." Giovanni recanted with a smile.

"God has blessed me?" Dominic asked, and for the first time Giovanni sensed that the boy believed him.

"Sí. No more waiting on me, Dominic, no more worry about tomorrow. You have a family now."

"Mio famiglia," Dominic threw his arms around Giovanni's neck. He hugged the boy and then shoved him off. If Lorenzo caught them embracing he'd tease them both the rest of the night. "Ma-ma is having a baby. She let me touch and I felt it move in her belly." Dominic smiled. "It will be a girl. That's what I think," Dominic grinned wider. "Pretty with red hair like Ma-ma."

Giovanni's brows lowered. "Well don't say that to Patri. He wants a boy I'm sure." What took Giovanni most by surprise was that Dominic called Eve 'Ma-ma'. That had to be progress. Giovanni smiled a little. "No matter if it is a boy or a girl you will be a big brother soon, like me. You will have to protect the baby. Can you make this vow to me?"

"Sí. I will." Dominic nodded. "I will protect the baby always. It will be my baby too."

"I believe you, Domi," Giovanni smiled. Despite his ego he embraced the boy again. Silently he vowed to protect Dominic always. "Let's go find Madre and see what she has on the stove."

June 16, 1992 – Sorrento, Italy

A shot fired. Like a cannon blast the echo thundered each time Mira pulled the trigger. Birds took flight from the branches of tall trees. Insects were startled into silence and adrenaline pumped through every chamber of her heart. Mira held tight to the weapon, breathing through her nose. She concentrated on the task before her.

"Bravissima! Again." Giovanni clapped.

Mira raised the gun steady with one hand firm on the trigger and the other on the grip used for support. What Giovanni didn't acknowledge was the recoil interfered with her aim. She found greater success when she aimed a fraction lower than her intended target. Before her were six cans and two jars lined up. She fired three more times shattering one jar and missing two cans. Giovanni stepped over. He moved his cigar in his jaw, and she frowned when he exhaled smoke that reached around to tickle her nose. She was pregnant for Christ's sake, and still he wouldn't let go of his damned cigars.

First his hands went down her hips and next she felt him press into her backside. Not for arousal, though contact this way made her heart flutter faster than the wings of a trapped butterfly. He touched her, oblivious of her excitement, intent on calming her. And then his arms lifted, extended and covered hers. He kept his hands on her wrist to level the direction of the shot.

"I should do it the way I feel comfortable," she protested. *How was she supposed to concentrate this way?* Giovanni's presence almost always had an affect on her. And lately it was hormonal. If she wasn't hungry, or horny, she was a crying bundle of nerves. She needed space. "Giovanni, I'm serious. I want to do this on my own."

He lifted his hands from her wrist and stepped to her side— granting her wish. She peeked over at him and then quickly returned her gaze to the target.

"Renaldo, remove the cans and put a target for Bella on that tree," he ordered.

Mira rolled her eyes. She lowered the gun and waited for the target change. *So he's going to make it harder because I don't need him babying me?* Once Renaldo completed the task Mira leveled the gun with the most plausible aim. Giovanni too stared straight ahead. Removing the cigar from his mouth he put the burning end out with his thumb. "*Concentrare, Bella*, you empty the clip until there is nothing standing. You kill every time you pull the trigger."

She nodded. "*Sì*. I know. I know."

"On my mark," he said. Again he returned and stepped behind her. He eased his hands around to hold the swell of her round belly and allow her to rest her weight against him.

"Gio—" she began to protest.

"Shh..." he kissed her cheek. "You need me, Bella, for now. And when you don't I won't hold on so tight anymore. I promise."

Mira smiled. There would be no escape from his instruction until he determined it necessary. At six months pregnant she found she was swollen everywhere. People who saw her always guessed her to be eight months at the very least. The twins weighed like bowling balls in her uterus. But she managed. And due to his love and encouragement she made it through many difficult weeks. For Mira, the joy of being the wife of Giovanni Battaglia was rooted in his unwavering devotion. She would need his protection always, no matter what weapon she wielded in her hands.

"*Ti piace questo?*" he asked in a voice that stilled her heart and warmed her between her thighs. If he touched her below she wouldn't mind. Mira shook off the naughty pangs of desire and concentrated on her goal.

"*Ti piace questo?*" he asked again.

"It feels nice," she admitted. *Of course it felt nice, he was her husband and it always felt nice.* She blinked twice and again her desires stirred when they shouldn't. No wonder there was never peace in their bed. She was on him every night or vice versa.

"Steady. That's my girl. Hold her gently. She's your baby, Bella." He kissed her cheek. "You can do this."

Whom he spoke of was the Berretta 9000 he gifted to her a few days ago. Very light in her hand, she was told by Giovanni it was designed for 'civilian sensibility'. *What the hell did that mean?* She asked. He laughed and said it was a woman's gun. It held a 12 round magazine so she had very few shots left. Maybe three. And from the moment the stainless steel semi-automatic was given to her she feared it, loathed having to own and handle it. But today not so much. Today she felt a sense of control.

Giovanni brushed his lips against her inner ear. "So sexy, when you touch her this way," he said beneath the soft groan in his throat. With his warm breath against her temple next, he made her feel far too vulnerable to level an accurate shot.

Mira rolled her eyes. "I can't believe you're turned on because I'm holding a gun?" she chuckled.

"I'm turned on by you period." He sounded amused.

Mira pulled the trigger. Giovanni didn't flinch as the recoil from every shot fired pushed her harder into his protective embrace. She released the clip, picked up the next one from the folding table before her, and shoved it up into the gun with swift speed. She then opened fire. This time she hit the target dead center and she didn't stop until she shredded the tree bark. She smiled at her accomplishment. A quick glance behind her confirmed he too was impressed.

Giovanni chuckled, white teeth showing between his sensual lips. "Bella is a better shot than Leo when properly motivated," he proclaimed. "Maybe she should watch over him."

The other men chuckled over the joke, but Leo's smile seemed forced to cover a flushed look of embarrassment. Mira shoved her elbow into her husband playfully and he hugged her in return. Giovanni bit her cheek and the act was more pleasure than pain.

"Very well done, *cara*. You make me proud. Now if only you will allow my swim lessons."

"Maybe. Some day. One step at a time, Giovanni. Okay?"

"Understood." Giovanni let her go.

"Boss? *Mi scusi.*"

Mira glanced back. Giovanni obstructed her view but she could see who had joined them. Santo stood with several other men off to the side. She lowered the gun and frowned as Giovanni drew away.

Why had Lorenzo left?

Why did Giovanni insist on doing business with this man?

Neither of these questions she dared ask, but they plagued her constantly. Santo removed his dark sunglasses and their eyes met. Mira felt her hand go tighter on the gun involuntarily. His dark stare lingered a moment longer then shifted away. She tried to shake the shiver that went through her. Maybe she should tell her husband how uncomfortable the man made her? But what would be her reason? And more importantly, what would be Giovanni's reaction? For now she ignored the feeling and remained cautious.

The more pressing matter was the burn to her arms and how her wrist ached. Today's lesson was over. She'd been at it all week. She knew how to fire and reload like the rest of them. She may not be a perfect shot but she'd take down someone threatening her or her children. Of that much she was assured. Still it troubled her that gun lessons were a necessity in her marriage, her life.

Giovanni was engrossed in the news Santo brought. Typically a visit like this would mean he'd have to travel out to Napoli or even worse to Genoa. She prayed not. Dominic and Catalina were supposed to arrive in two days. They'd all make the trip together in a week to the infamous Mondello Beach, Sicily she had heard so much about.

"Bella! Change of plans. We leave for Mondello in the morning. Make yourself and Eve ready for travel," Giovanni announced.

Mira whirled around, stunned. "We can't. What about—"

He stalked off with Santo at his side. Neither man bothered to glance back. Mira sighed. She wiped her hand across her brow to clear it of sweat. It felt like her twins were baking in her oven. She was hot all over. The noonday sun burned hotter, and appeared closer to earth than normal.

"*Donna?* May I?" Leo asked. He reached for her weapon. Giovanni told her to name her gun but she thought it silly. She handed it over to Leo and he smiled. She had grown fond of his shadow and didn't understand why Gio and the men constantly teased him.

"I'll return it to you after it is cleaned and—" Leo began.

"No need. Just put it away, I don't want Eve to see the thing," Mira said.

Leo frowned.

Mira clarified. "I have a small army to follow me around every day. I have you. Exactly when do you think I will need the gun?"

"The boss wants you to keep it," Leo answered. "Forgive me, *Donna,* but I have my orders."

"For heaven's sake!" Mira tossed her hands up. Leo continued to stare at her. "Put it in my room, and lock it in the cabinet."

Leo looked relieved. Mira shook her head and started back toward the trail to her home. She moved a bit slower but the walk always made her feel stronger. She could see her husband ahead. He stopped, said a few words and then dismissed Santo and his crew. His violet blue eyes turned on her. When angry those eyes were clear as crystals. Eve had the same trait. Would her sons?

Mira smiled, and tried to walk a little faster. Of course it provoked the response she wanted. Giovanni hurried to her side to offer aid. He immediately put his arm around her waist and she leaned into him for support.

"Why today? Can't we wait for Catalina to return from Milano?"

"No, Bella. It's tomorrow." He kissed the top of her forehead "Soon you won't be able to make the trip."

They continued on the path. Mira felt a bit winded but she didn't say why. The doctor said she should exercise. During her frequent visits she often felt the doctor held back on her condition. He and Giovanni were always there to reassure her it wasn't true.

"Am I fat, Gio?" Mira asked. That morning she realized she could no longer see her feet.

Her husband let go a sharp peal of laughter. "Of course you are fat, Bella."

Mira hit him, and he laughed harder. He had to restrain her from hitting him again. And it took several deep breaths to stop his laughter.

"Calm down," he said as he grinned. "You're carrying my boys. Sons. The best blessing God could have given us. You American women and your fascination with weight is ridiculous. A real man wants to see his woman grow with life, feel the swell of her thighs, her belly," he said in earnest.

It was true. As much as she was aroused by his physique, he expressively showed her he desired hers as well. From the first moment she gave her body to him Giovanni knew every curve and seemed to be pleased with her body changes. They had mastered the perfect positions for lovemaking to get around her girth.

"Giovanni?"

"Yes," he said as they strolled slower with his men flanked behind them.

"Where's Lorenzo?" she asked.

He didn't answer.

"It's been four months. Did you two have a disagreement? Tell me," she probed.

"He's in Europe. We speak often. He will be back after the boys are born," Giovanni replied.

Mira smiled. She eased her arm around his waist. When the doctor told them that she was carrying boys it was a non-event for Giovanni. He was so certain of the babies' sex that he'd already made the announcement to the family.

Early on in her pregnancy she would question his confidence, his control, but day-by-day she accepted her husband for who he was to them all. Mira glanced up at Melanzana. Once they cleared the path the melon colored walls of their villa glistened, blocking out the sun. "What is Mondello like? Is it as beautiful as Sorrento?"

"More than beautiful. You will love our new home."

"How long will we stay?" she asked.

"Until the boys are ready to travel. A month or two after their birth. Is that okay?" he asked.

"Does it matter?" she chuckled. "You'll do what you wish either way."

Giovanni stopped. Mira glanced up at him and saw the scowl hardening the look in his eyes. He took her hands and kissed them. "Am I that bad, Bella?"

"Huh? No. It was a joke. Don't be silly." She tried to continue to walk. He stopped her. He forced a smile.

"I want you to love Sicily, to see it as our second home. I only push because… Sicily is a part of us both. More than you realize."

"Okay. If you say so." Mira shrugged.

"What do you want? Tell me? Name it and I will make sure you have it," Giovanni said.

Careful of her choice she decided on a simple request. "You. Tonight. I want just you, no business. Just you, me, and Eve for our last night in Sorrento. I saw Santo. Promise you won't leave with him."

"Done." He nodded his head like an eager to please child.

Mira touched his cheek. "I'm okay, Giovanni. I want to go to Sicily. It's where you spent a lot of your childhood. Our children will love it, and so will I."

"Ti amo, cara," he leaned forward and brushed his lips over hers. "I am truly a lucky man."

She lifted her arms to circle them around his neck and drew his mouth back down to hers. The kiss swept them both up in the familiar sensuous warmth of their passion. And soon he overpowered her, deepening the thrill. She inhaled every scent, from his rich cologne to the blue roses blooming around the trail. And she fell deeper in love with her husband.

La Dolce Vita...

This was indeed the good life.

1.

Giovanni entered his office short on patience. Mira's temperament stressed both his mind and his heart. She was much better today. In fact her mood was so light and jovial he had a hard time trusting it. Yesterday she broke down into a crying fit that left the entire family distressed. He was summoned from Napoli. Santo had to conclude his business affairs because Dominic tended to other matters concerning the Bonaduces in *his* triangle.

The reason for Bella's tantrum was of no importance, if she lost control he had to be there because only he could calm her down. The doctors said it was an imbalance with her hormones, and the mood swings were to be expected. But the problem was the diagnosis they received a few weeks ago. The truth that he kept secret from his wife could possibly mean an early childbirth.

The plans were finalized. He'd take her to paradise and find a way to force her to relax for the next few weeks. During her lesson with her new gun, Santo updated him on the turf dispute with two important clans within the *Camorra*. The Mottola clan was almost as powerful as Giovanni in the *Camorra*, and their involvement in the matter was troubling. Though Giovanni was impressed with how well Santo managed things up to this point, he now had reason to be worried.

As he bounded down the steps to head to his office Renaldo informed him of Rocco's arrival. His uncle had been avoiding him since the truth of Mira's paternity was uncovered. Almost four months. They had a huge fight and Rocco ordered Zia away from Melanzana as well. This hurt his Bella and he could never explain to her the true reason why.

Maybe Rocco had come around.

"What is it old man?" Giovanni asked. He decided to take the visit with him first.

Rocco paced. He looked at Giovanni, paused, and then began to pace again. With a heavy sigh Giovanni walked over to the sofa in his office and sat. He reclined back to spread his arms wide across the top. Though he could go for a glass of *vino*, he decided to keep a clear head. And he knew his cool demeanor made light of the tension between him and his *zio*. Though this discussion would happen he believed it could end on an unpleasant note.

"Is it true? Zia tells me before the babies are born you will take Mirabella to Sicily."

Giovanni gave a single nod. The side of his face rested between his thumb and trigger finger. His gaze honed in on Rocco's look of incomprehension.

"Why? It's too soon," he said in a tone uncharacteristically sharp. Rocco's arthritic hands, gnarled by age and hard work, were now clenched into white-knuckled fists. "Mancini knows you have his daughters. In the past few months he's been quiet. It's not like him. He's plotting something, Gio, and... I fear you have underestimated him."

"*Non importa*. He is of no threat to me or *mia moglie*—my wife. To expose himself weakens his bond with his son."

"I'm telling you that—"

"Marsuvio breathes through an iron lung and is on his deathbed. A shell of the man he used to be. He won't risk his legacy in the Mafia by challenging me for my Bella's affections. It has been three months since I delivered that warning and he's heeded it. *Va bene zio Rocco.* You worry for nothing."

"You told him. Didn't you? You told him that Tomosino ordered the death of Mira's mother."

Rage rose in Giovanni like a black tidal wave washing out the last of his patience. "Listen to me, *zio*! Never say those words again. Patri is dead and so is the past. Bella will never need to learn of my tie to her mother's death."

"It is not your lie, son. It's your father's sin. If it is in the past then you should tell her. Prepare her. Especially if you want to take her to *Sicilia*. You are not invincible, Gio!" Rocco pointed at him. "Dominic came to see me last month. You have started to deal with *Sacra Corona Unita* again. First the *'Ndrangheta* and now the *Mafioso* are circling? There are snakes in your pit and you opened the door! This is dangerous."

"*Balle!* In order to take this family forward I have to deal with enemies. Keep them close. Not run and hide to rot on a vineyard like you," Giovanni spat with disgust. "I know what I'm doing. I won't die in some stupid Mafia war. I won't waste away in prison and be forced from my wife and children. I won't run and hide when my enemies come for me. What I *will* do is take this family forward. Legitimize us, and invest in the clans of the *Camorra*, which I have made stronger!"

"Gio—"

"She is my wife!" he shouted to the top of his lungs. Like cannon blast his words boomed in the office. Rocco stepped back. "Mine! Even Mancini knows that my marrying Bella has changed everything between our families. And he will respect me." Giovanni leveled a finger at his uncle. "So will you."

Rocco cut his gaze away. Rocco was from a different era of men. Born out of the same traditions that Mancini and his father upheld. They lived by a code, tenets of the Mafia that ruled their choices. Therefore, Rocco would choose his words wisely. And Mancini would choose his actions against Giovanni with the same care. These were delicate times. His plans to legitimize some of their interests would mean he'd have to give over more control to the lower clans of the *Camorra*. He needed to ensure that the peace held between the *Mafioso* and the *Camorra* when he shifted control elsewhere. The `Ndrangheta continued to use the ports of Napoli and were closely watched by Santo's crew. Of course his hands would never be clean of some of their lucrative affairs, but drugs and human trafficking were not a business he'd be sullied by ever again.

"I will go with you. Zia and I will come to *Sicilia*," Rocco sighed. "I can be of use to you with Mancini. In case there is trouble."

"No." Giovanni stood. "You had your chance to stand with me. You chose not to for the past four months. You kept Zia away from Bella and forced me to make an excuse for your absence. You tried to manipulate me, old man. I'm not the nephew you have to tutor any longer."

Rocco blinked at the refusal. "Gio? You are not alone in this. I can help you."

Giovanni corrected his tone. "I run this family. I alone decide our fates and that's the way it has always been since Patri died. You can come after the babies are born. I know you have not shared with Zia who Bella is. Let's keep it that way."

"But Zia is why I returned She rides me over this disagreement between us. She wants to be with Mirabella and Eve. In fact she insists upon it."

"I said no. Bella and Eve need to get acquainted with Sicily. I need them to be relaxed not influenced. Santo will run things here for me. Dominic will travel between Sorrento and Mondello as needed. Bella… she's delicate. These last few months are critical."

"Is something wrong with the babies?" Rocco asked.

Giovanni hadn't told many about the depressive state his wife often slipped into. She had her highs where she smiled, and cared for the family, burden free. But there were dark moments that he managed to keep private behind closed doors. Tears for Fabiana would cripple her with grief. Stress and worry over the company she and Catalina loved to play with would have her on the phone pacing at all hours in the night. And the worst episodes were the fears that she would not be a good mother because of her own mother's abandonment.

Later in her pregnancy a new issue arose. There was blood in her urine. Often she'd find blood when she wiped. It scared the shit out of them both. He'd flown in the best perinatologist in Italy for high-risk pregnancies. He was currently doing casework out of Palermo and came highly recommended. Giovanni learned the real reason for her issues. Her diagnosis changed everything.

Rosetta and limited staff were allowed near her. Dominic said he should let her design clothes more to relax her, and he did. She and Rosetta worked on projects in her sewing room often. It made her happy. His *consigliere* also suggested she be allowed to make friends. Giovanni disagreed. She needed him, not strangers, to see her through this.

"Gio? Is there something I should know, son? Something that makes you worry for her health?" Rocco asked.

He smiled. "She's fine. No worries. We leave in the morning. I hear there have been some changes at the vineyard? No?"

Rocco nodded. "We've made a few."

"*Bravo!* No more worry about Mancini." Giovanni dropped his arm around Rocco's shoulders and started to walk him to the door. "For years the old *Don* knew that Bella was alive, *zio*. He let her go decades without making contact. He's a coward. *Un idiota.* No threat to Bella. We are going to Sicily to celebrate the birth of my sons. The best doctor for her is based out of Palermo. My sons will be born on Sicilian soil."

"And her sister? How do you plan to deal with her?" Rocco asked.

Giovanni didn't bother to answer.

Rocco shook his head. "I pray you know what you are doing."

Giovanni chuckled. "Don't I always?"

* B *

"Zia?" Mira stopped.

She put a hand to her joy filled heart that thundered crazily in her chest. She hadn't seen Zia in close to six weeks. When she called, and often she did, to ask her to return, Zia told her she was needed in Chianti and would try to see her soon. Mira was beginning to think Zia didn't want to visit. Giovanni was always dismissive of those fears.

"You're here!" Mira hurried over to the old woman and embraced her. The hug was awkward and stunted by her middle girth. But she grinned and held to Zia.

"*Ciao, bella,*" Zia stroked her back. She patted her back within their embrace. "I've missed you, Mirabella."

"I've missed you too. Wait until Eve sees you," Mira gushed, releasing her. She wiped away her tears.

"Eve's sleeping. I've already checked on her," Zia chuckled almost giddy with happiness. "She's so big, Mira. *Mama mia!* I've missed her so much!" Zia exclaimed.

When Mira stood tall she saw a young woman sitting quietly on the sofa. "Cecelia? Is that you?"

"*Sì. Ciao, Donna,*" Cecilia stood and bowed her head in her usual shy manner. She was such a demure beauty with short brown hair, olive skin, and large round eyes. She wore a white dress that belted at the waist and dropped neatly from her curvy hips. "I hope it is okay that I came."

Mira walked over with her arms extended. Cecelia hadn't returned to Melanzana since her unfortunate accident on Mira's wedding day. The young girl embraced her with what sounded like a deep sigh of relief.

"How are you?" Mira asked.

"I'm doing much better." Cecilia stepped back. She lifted her foot in her leather slipper. "See?"

"You sure are," Mira touched her hand. "I'm so sorry for the accident. Did you get the gifts I sent?"

"It was so generous of you, *Donna*. My mother told me to thank you. The money was such a help with our expenses."

"Good," Mira felt a little relief. Still the accident weighed heavily on her heart. Giovanni told her the fall could have broken Cecilia's neck. And Nico had been so worried over Cecilia's recovery.

22

"Zia asked that I return," Cecilia said. "She tells me that you will give birth to sons soon. It is a true blessing." Cecilia touched Mira's stomach. Mira beamed so hard with happiness she felt her face flush and her cheeks ache. The twins moved in response to Cecilia's touch and Mira chuckled when the young woman's eyes stretched in wonder.

"If I lifted my shirt you might even see a foot or elbow poke against my skin. My sons are constantly wrestling in my belly." Mira laughed.

"Mira?" Zia began. "I think Cecilia should stay and help you. With Eve and the babies on the way you need the additional hands. No?"

"Why can't you stay, Zia? I've been asking for you. Did Giovanni tell you I wanted you to come? I told him to call and convince you."

Zia forced a smile. "Rocco hasn't wanted me to leave the vineyard. I can't go against his wishes."

"What? Why?" Mira exclaimed.

"Shh, now. Gio's been very protective of you. He wants his time with you and Eve," Zia said.

"That's nonsense. He's off working half the time. Why would he want you to stay away?" Mira stopped herself. Giovanni's reasoning never made sense to her. Had he told Rocco to keep Zia away? Damn him. She tried not to let them see her irritation with his smothering. They would definitely have words on this later.

Before Zia could clarify Rosetta walked in. The young woman stopped and blinked in surprise at the sight of Cecilia. Rosetta's hair was swept up into a slender ponytail. She wore a blue jean skirt with a red and orange tank-top underneath an unbuttoned, oversized white shirt with thong sandals. Most days when Eve took her nap Rosetta spent her time in the sewing room completing a task Mira had assigned to her. She was a good pupil, an eager learner. In fact Mira considered sending her to Milano to work with Catalina instead of Mondello.

The two women, Cecilia and Rosetta, hadn't seen each other since the wedding. Truthfully, the apprentice work Rosetta did for Mira at times left Eve to Ana on some days. And soon Mira would add two more babies to the mix. She couldn't complain for assistance because Giovanni would then learn of how time consuming her side project of being Rosetta's teacher had become.

Mira smiled. Zia always knew her needs without her voicing them. "It would be great for Cecilia to return." Mira clapped. "We leave for Mondello tomorrow and I won't return to Sorrento until after the babies are born. Cecilia you can help us get the nursery ready."

"Ah, *ciao,* Zia," Rosetta went to her aunt to embrace her. She never took her eyes from Cecilia who held her stare. "What is this about? Sicily?" Rosetta asked.

"Giovanni informed me that we have to leave in the morning. So we have plenty of packing to do," Mira said.

"But... what about Catalina? She's returning from Milano. You said I might be able to go back with her."

Mira shrugged. "Don't worry about that. I'll work it out. You'll get your chance to work in Milano."

"Are you feeling okay, Mira?" Zia asked. "Not over-exerting yourself?"

Mira laughed. "How can I? Everyone around here watches me like a hawk, including your stubborn grand niece. Do you know the other day she grabbed my hand and forced me to sit down, imitating her father?"

Zia laughed. She put her arm around Mira's waist. "Let's go upstairs and look in on Eve. You can tell me how you keep your days. And tonight we can prepare a good dinner for the family."

Mira welcomed the comfort of Zia's embrace. Together they walked out of the room. She glanced back at Rosetta who paced. Cecilia sat on the sofa once more watching Rosetta. "You two come up in an hour and I can show you all the things we need to pack. Okay?"

"*Sì, Donna,*" said Cecilia.

"*Sì, Donna,*" said Rosetta.

After a few minutes Mira and Zia were out of earshot. It was only then that Rosetta turned her attention to Cecilia. If Cecilia ever told any of them what she'd done she didn't know what Mira or Giovanni would do to her. Cecilia stared up at her silently. Rosetta relaxed. Cecilia was just a simple country girl. Rosetta didn't see any malicious intentions in her silent stare. But she had to be sure that Cecilia remained quiet. She was so close to having everything she wanted.

Rosetta cleared her throat.

"If this is going to work you are to tell no one what happened the day you fell at the church," said Rosetta.

"The day you pushed me?" Cecilia asked.

"No one!" Rosetta narrowed her eyes. "If you think I pushed you, then what do you think I'll do if you accuse me?"

Cecilia lowered her gaze. Rosetta watched the courage drain from Cecilia's face.

"Catalina came to visit me soon after. She asked me," Cecilia glanced up. "She asked me if you had anything to do with my accident. You haven't fooled everyone, Rosetta."

Rosetta was stunned. Her relationship with Catalina had improved. She even thought they were friendly now. When exactly did she go to visit Cecilia?

"I told her nothing," Cecilia quickly added. "I didn't do it because I fear you. I don't want the *Donna* or Gio embarrassed by your behavior at their wedding." Cecilia took a step forward. Rosetta locked eyes with her and clenched her fists and teeth. "I told Catalina I slipped on the top step. Because I did slip, I let my guard down with you. That will be my one and only mistake."

"Really?" Rosetta smirked.

"Yes. I want no trouble with you, Rosetta, or the Battaglias. I only need a job to help feed my family. It's important."

Rosetta relaxed. She believed her. Cecilia was not a real threat. Not now that she had the *Donna's* trust, and apparently Catalina's. Let the stupid fool wipe Eve's butt and runny nose. Rosetta had bigger things to do. Satisfied that her message was clear she smiled. "Catalina works out of Milano and lives with Dominic in Napoli. So I am the one the *Donna* trusts. Do we understand?"

Cecilia nodded.

"Good. Welcome back. I'm sure Evie will be glad to see you." Rosetta turned and walked out. The smile she wore broadened. As long as their stay in Sicily was temporarily she could withstand the return trip home. Everything she's ever wanted was now within her reach.

* B *

"*Papa mangiare*—eat!" Eve hit Giovanni's hand and opened her mouth. In her free hand she held her pacifier away ready to be sucked. He lifted the fork from his plate with a small portion of gravy and pasta. He then fed her once more. The laughter at the table mixed with eager conversation about the return to Sicily. Most of the men in his *Camorra* clan were Sicilian. And since the tensions with Mancini were elevated he intended to take many of them on the visit. Tonight however, his attention was split between Eve and the business conflict Santo and Dominic were barely managing.

Eve grabbed the fork and tried to scoop more food. With his assistance she managed control. His little firefly was very independent like her mother in that regard. Giovanni kissed the top of her curly head after feeding her a mouthful. Once satisfied his daughter dropped back against his chest pushing her pacifier back in her mouth as she chewed.

She had grown an inch. Mira showed him her height marks on the inside of the door. The other day Giovanni learned she wore a thing called 'training bloomers' and could go to her little pink plastic toilet without soiling herself. When he arrived home early one evening she took his hand and led him to the toilet to show him. He was very proud.

Bella returned with Zia. His wife and aunt carried trays of fresh baked bread and meat for his men who ate with the family. He watched as she dropped several on their plates and joked with them. When her gaze lifted to his he winked and she flashed him the sweetest grin. Bella was in her best of moods today.

The evening would be perfect if all of the family were present. Lorenzo's absence was felt. Especially since he's had several intense arguments with his cousin because of his exile. Lorenzo had the balls to threaten to return. Under Dominic's advisement, Giovanni dispatched Carlo to ensure Lorenzo continued on the path agreed upon.

The empty chairs for Dominic and Catalina kept drawing Giovanni's attention. More and more lately they too had been absent and in his thoughts. Giovanni struggled with their independence and growth as a couple. Soon Dominic would press him for a date they could marry and he'd have to honor his word and grant it. How could he ever make them understand why it broke his heart that his brother and sister had chosen this path? Mira had begged him to open up and explain his confliction to her, but the words constantly failed him. For now he walked the tightrope of complacence and disgust.

The good news was Dominic handled his role as *consigliere* beyond Giovanni's expectations. Youth be damned, Dominic Battaglia was his left and right hand. A brother to him, a confidant, a constant in the turbulent waters of their joined lives.

And Mira often shared with Giovanni news of Catalina's achievements since they opened her design factory and boutiques in Milano. They were happy. Their happiness made his beautiful wife healthy, thus enough happiness for him.

"Papa?" Eve turned up her face. She said something that sounded to be a mix of Italian and English. He couldn't discern the meaning of her question. He gave her a nod as if he understood. Eve plucked her pacifier from his hand and stuck it in her mouth. She turned in his lap and he pulled her up against his chest so she could rest her head under his chin. The love of his *lucciola* was always so genuine and pure. And when he held her in this way a calm went through him unlike anything he's ever known outside of Mira's love.

Giovanni smiled.

Fatherhood had changed him. And it was all thanks to Mira. They were solid. Rocco's fears were unfounded. Mira vowed to him that their family would always be her first and only priority.

Three Months Earlier - March 2, 1992
Milano, Italy –

The enforcer stepped forward and unchained the locks to the entrance of the building Giovanni now owned. His name was Renaldo Cracchiolo. He was a silent lethal presence that shadowed Giovanni's life on every mission. Renaldo entered first but held the door open for his boss to pass.

"Careful of where you step, Bella," Giovanni said.

His hands held her gloved ones and he walked backward over the threshold to lead the way. She wore sharply pointed heeled boots and designer jeans that fit nicely around her shapely slender legs. It was the damn boots she wore that kept him nervous over each step she took. She was pregnant after all, and should probably dress more matronly for comfort. His wife would not be told what to wear. Period.

Underneath her magenta red leather blazer she wore a white button down blouse that clearly defined the gentle swell of her small round belly. It wasn't as profound at three months pregnant, but the baby bump, her enlarged breasts, and thick dark hair that dusted her shoulders enhanced her natural beauty. Around her eyes he tied a blindfold of the silk scarf she wore around her neck after their plane landed. She'd been bubbling with questions and a bit irritable over his secrecy. Giovanni loved to surprise his lady. But this secret was the only one he struggled to keep.

He let her hands go.

"Where are we?" she asked in that soft inquisitive voice of hers he loved.

"Guess?"

"How can I when I'm blindfolded?" she chuckled.

"Try and guess," he teased.

She removed her gloves and lifted her chin as if sniffing the air. The temperature inside was considerably warm. The place smelled of sawdust and fresh paint thanks to the round the clock workers sent in to prepare the building. The Nigerians who dealt in unsavory business behind the walls of his property had been eradicated. The entire building had been scrubbed clean. It felt pure enough for his wife's dreams.

"A new building. I smell paint, fresh paint," she said.

"Is that all?" he asked.

"Stop teasing me," she laughed. "I have no idea where we had to fly to and drive to that has new paint."

"You've been on me for weeks about this, and you can't guess?" Giovanni replied.

Her nose wrinkled. "What are you talking about? Guess what? For all I know you've bought another tower to keep me locked away in," she teased.

He laughed. Giovanni had noticed that he often laughed when it was just him and her. Giovanni's gaze swept the open space of the boutique. According to Dominic and Catalina the walls were to be stark white. This aided in making the workspace open, clean, and it inspired creativity. The floors were done in blood red Italian marble tiles, which was his idea. He liked the contrast.

The building had three floors above them and one beneath. Catalina assured him that the layout was similar to Mirabella's in New York. To confirm it he had the man, Theodore "Teddy" Tate, send him the floor designs for her American business.

"Well? Can I remove my blindfold? Let's stop with the games I have to pee," she said after a lengthy pause. Her tone and mood had shifted from excited delight to irritability.

Giovanni smiled, not the least bit affected by her aggravation. "Go on. Take it off."

She untied the knot to the back of her head. When the blindfold lowered and her gaze lifted the frown lines melted off her face. She blinked and turned in awe. Dress mannequins, clear racks for clothing to be hung, a changing room, and all the things that women would find appealing as furnishing for a high-end boutique awaited her.

"What have you done?" she asked.

He watched with Renaldo at his side as she walked around smiling, touching, and then laughing over one thing then another.

"Is it mine?" she asked.

"It's yours. And this isn't all."

Before he could anticipate her next move she flew into his arms. Giovanni was bowled back from the surge of excitement. His wife squealed with tears in her eyes. She hugged his neck so tight he felt choked and restrained. "Thank you! Oh my God! Thank you, Giovanni! I can't believe it. It's beautiful. When did you... how?" she let him go. She jumped up and down in her heels and he held her hips to keep her steady.

"Bella, calm yourself," he chuckled, but he meant it. The last thing he needed was for her to trip in those dangerously high-heels she wore.

"What's upstairs? Is upstairs ours... did you do this upstairs too... is it mine?" she queried.

"Yes... It—"

She grabbed his hand and started toward the elevator to the back of the boutique. Bella talked so fast he could barely catch on to what she was saying. She spoke of break down rooms typically used to do dress runs for her models before and after fashion shows. Offices needed for her staff and sewing rooms for the business of cutting, stitching, and weaving her designs in-house for special clients. All of it was information overload. But he nodded with a sly grin and let her have her fun.

They visited each floor and she pointed out how similar the layout was to her office in New York. When they reached the fourth floor it dawned on her how he had done this exactly in the fashion of her New York office.

"Catalina! You and Catalina did this. Didn't you? Did Teddy help? Was he involved?"

Giovanni had to hold her to slow her down. She felt soft, warm in his arms. "I told you, Bella. I am the man to make sure your dreams come true. Teddy did nothing. It was all me."

She shook her head. "Of course, honey, it was all you."

"You give up nothing for loving me. Right?" he boasted.

"Right," she reassured him.

"You will have everything you wish as we build our life together," he said.

She nodded. She hugged him with her face pressed against his chest. "This is what we dreamed of when we came to Italy—Fabiana and me. This is our dream. We were going to build our own fashion house in Italy. Start our lives together and then take over Europe. From Milano to Paris we'd leave our mark. We had so many plans. So many."

Giovanni lifted her chin. "It's time you've seen your final gift.

Your office."

"Really? So you designed that too huh?" Mira's mouth took on a decidedly sensuous curve. Those curious brown eyes of hers ringed in long thick lashes stared up at him with undiluted love.

"I do everything for you," he replied.

"And for you," she teased.

"Give me a kiss, my woman," he said, unable to resist her mouth so close to his.

"Why don't you take it, my husband," she whispered. She brought her lips just a centimeter away. "You know how, don't you?"

He caught the corner of her lower lip between his teeth. She released a silent cry of surprise over the sting of the nip. With a tiny sigh in her throat she returned his kiss. Letting his tongue glide deeper and sweep fully in her mouth, he enjoyed the melting sweetness of her tongue as it rolled over his own. The round hard swell of her tummy carrying the future of their family brushed his lower abdomen. Desire speared him—strong, seductively insistent. When she guided her hand to his groin and squeezed he had to force himself to let her go. Giovanni shook his head and smiled.

"Something wrong?" she teased.

He took her hand and walked her toward two glass doors. There had been a single request made to Dominic. One he wanted his consigliere to see to personally, and he was stunned by the execution and presentation of his gift. However, his surprise was no match for Mira. She walked into the office staring up at the portrait in silence. Three years ago just before they met, Mira had taken publicity photos for her debut in Milano. One in particular was of a very fetching, seductive pose of Mira and Fabiana back to back. Maybe it was done for fun, or to advertise their partnership. It was Theodore Tate who provided the still image to Dominic and Giovanni for them to have immortalized in a realistic portrait. Italy remained one of the greatest places to find talented artists and Salvatore Gilucci painted this personally for the Battaglia family. Today was the first time Giovanni had laid eyes upon the portrait.

Mira's slender figure was nicely defined in an alluring black dress that stopped mid thigh. She appeared both seductive yet professional in her pose. Her thick hair was straightened and reached just beyond her shoulders, tucked behind her ears to reveal teardrop black jeweled earrings. Her smoky dark eye shadow, and extended lashes made the side ways stare she gave the camera lens suggestive. Fabiana was just as striking in the portrait. Her scarlet red hair cascaded to her shoulders. She wore an identical sexy fitted dress but hers was white with matching stilettoes that only added to the beauty of her legs. She too cut the camera a sideways glance with a seductive smirk to her red lips. The yin and yang power team stood back to back with arms crossed. Both women were fiercely composed.

"I remember this. We took the picture two months before we... before we traveled to Italy." Mira put both hands to her brow. Giovanni remained close out of concern. When her shoulders shook he realized she was crying. He embraced her from behind.

"You two made quite a team," he said. He hoped she shed tears of happiness. That was the only emotion he wanted to evoke. Giovanni glanced up at the painting and was riveted by the artist's ability to capture his Bella the way he saw her. The portrait was seven feet tall and four feet wide. Against the stark white wall it commanded attention.

"I love you so much, Giovanni. For doing this. For doing all of this. For being my best friend and knowing what I need. I thought... never mind what I thought," she sniffed.

"You thought I wanted to change you. I do. But never for the worst, Bella, only for the good of our marriage and our family. We need you." He kissed her. "I want a wife, a mother to my kids. And for that to happen I want you to be whole. This is who you are." He glanced back up at the portrait. "Mirabella Ellison Battaglia. I don't fear that woman. I love her too."

Mira turned in his arms. There was so much emotion in her weepy eyes he couldn't discern which one she settled on. "I will keep my promise. Not a day before we are ready will I return full time to my career."

"And I promise to be ready when we decide you do," he smiled. He kissed her.

She ran her hands over his arms, up to his shoulders and neck. He dragged his mouth from hers to look into her face. Beneath her long lashes her pupils were large, her plump lips parted, she had that dazed look in her eyes when she wanted him to make love to her. "Ti amo," he whispered against her mouth.

"Ti amo," she breathed in response. The sexual tension they shared mixed nicely with the way her touch to his neck and the side of his jaw soothed him. After a moment of mutual reflection Mira eased her hands down his sides to circle his waist. Giovanni stole a glance behind him. Renaldo knew better than to enter unless summoned. No one was on the floor. The room was carpeted but emptied of furniture. Giovanni's gaze switched to the portrait. The first time he saw Bella she was as fiercely independent as that woman staring back at him in the photo.

"I want to celebrate, baby," she said and kissed his chin, beneath his neck. Her hands glided around his waist and rubbed up his back slowly. "Here."

"Now?" It was as much a question as it was a warning. She was still in a delicate way. The miscarriage scare was just under two months ago. They enjoyed sex regularly but always in a controlled manner, their bed. There he could reign in his desires and balance her comfort against his insatiable appetite.

"Yes. Now," she said. "Let's christen my office."

Mira shed her leather jacket. "You will have to undress me. I have trouble bending forward you know," she teased. She kicked her boot at him in a playful fashion.

After a deep intake of breath Giovanni walked out of her inner office to the front and closed the doors. The doors each locked from the inside. They would be alone. He returned to find Mira before the portrait. She ran her hand over the bottom of Fabiana's image as if touching the painting simulated touching her friend. He entered the room. Though they spoke often about Fabiana it occurred to him why his wife's torment was never-ending. Fabiana was her sister, family, the only family she had before she met him.

Giovanni felt a pang of guilt over the secret he carried. Surely his actions in separating his wife from Marietta weren't the same as the loss of Fabiana. Even if he introduced Mira to Marietta they wouldn't bond. The women were different. They had nothing in common. He reasoned that he did his wife a favor by sparing her the stress. But how long could he keep them apart?

"I really do love it. Fabiana was so beautiful. Wasn't she?"

"She was." Giovanni agreed.

"That's what I will name our Italian operations. Fabiana. We can keep the American company Mirabella and start a new one under her name. What do you think?" she looked back.

Giovanni removed his trench coat and tossed it. He began to shed his suit jacket. He tried to shake his guilt, conceal it from her. "I like the idea."

Mira grinned and turned to face him with a joyful clap. "I'm so happy! She will always be here."

When he looked up at the portrait again all doubt melted away. Mira came to him. He began to unbutton her shirt.

"Are you sure we won't be disturbed?" she asked.

"No one will dare," he replied. Her shirt opened. He kissed her brow and then lowered. His hand travelled down her left leg and captured the zipper at the top of her ankle boot. He ran the tab down and removed one boot from her foot and then the next. She aided him by bracing for balance by gripping the tops of his shoulders. He stood and immediately went for the buttons to her jeans. Her breasts were twice the size they once were. She swore the pregnancy swelled in her boobs instead of her belly. He had to agree. Lucky for him he was indeed a breast, ass, and thigh man.

"Catalina will love this. I can decorate the office from home. I have a ton of magazines to order from. You know? I can look through them and start ordering what I like."

"Sounds good to me," he said. She giggled with excitement. He lowered the zipper to her jeans and began to peel the fabric down her shaeply hips and thighs. She really was very, very, lovely—

The high-waist black lace panty trimmed her pussy. Giovanni ran his tongue along the seam. She gasped a breath. He could see it happen as if it occurred in his mind in slow motion. He'd undress her with care. Taste the pussy that was his. Fuck her. Fuck her again. Release the pent up desire that has cramped his dick since she emerged from the shower with her skin glistening with moisture, her hair poufy around her face, and her round ass and large breasts bouncing with each step she took.

He loved the body of his pregnant wife.

Giovanni removed her panties next. Mira tried to cross her arms and keep them lowered to cover her belly. The action offended him. She should never hide her beautiful curves. He knocked her hands away.

She talked of something related to the fashion business as she used his shoulders for balance to step out of her undergarments. His hearing dulled. Nothing she said registered. At his level the lovely smell of her fragrant skin had left his head spinning. All he could think of was having her.

Giovanni swiped a finger between the thick folds of her pussy. She silenced. She was wet. Her pussy felt warm and ready. For a moment he stroked her there as his eyes climbed the round curve of her stomach, the thick peaks of her dark nipples. And his gaze reached hers.

"Enough talking," he said. "My ears burn."

She blinked those round eyes of hers at him, and then smiled. She combed her fingers back over his scalp and stared down at him. "You trying to say I talk too much?"

He stood and this time it was he who had to look down on her.

He lifted her chin. "Tell me all about decorating later. Focus on me. Only. Now."

A spark flickered in her eyes, and to him it resembled obedience. His mouth found hers again and this time he devoured her sweet tongue and lips. Her silky tongue responded, stroking deeply. His lips suctioned softly. And her sweet sighs reminded him of all the other parts of her body he wanted to taste and suck the same way.

Mira's hands worked fast at undoing his buckle and lowering his zipper. She pulled her mouth away to focus on the task. He only wore sleeveless t-back undershirts and boxers. He removed his clothes.

"Down boy," she ordered.

His heart hammered fast, stricken by the primal surge of lust that seized his loins from the request.

Her steely gaze narrowed. "Now," she said.

It was difficult to breathe. The air he did manage to take in was hot and sultry. Giovanni went to his knees. He carefully brought her with him. She pushed hard on his bare shoulders for him to recline so she could straddle his lap. But he was too busy rubbing his lips across the fuzz of pubic hair around her pussy. She didn't shave and trim as much as she used to. He didn't bother to question why. He was a man not a boy. He preferred his wife with hair on her pussy. The urge to spread her out on the carpet and drive several inches of his dick through her tight core became his singular purpose. When the damp folds of her pussy brushed his dick he went back as she requested.

"Good, baby, let me take control." Mira cooed to him.

Giovanni put his hands behind his head, stretched out with his ankles apart. His male strength was hard and aroused when she fisted his dick and guided him to her opening. She decended. He slipped into bliss. His lids fluttered once her wet tightness sheathed his shaft. He heard her gasp for a breath. On instinct he shot his hips upward and encountered tight muscle. Urgent desire ripped through him and he gripped her hips for mercy. He thrusted slowly now, and aimed his dick with each push to what he knew would be her pleasure point. She countered his move with her own. Her soft thighs curved sensually around his hips as she rode his cock with a sweet rhythmic swirl of her hips back and forth.

"Ah, yes!" he grunted.

Giovanni was forced to rise to hold her, love her. In doing so he put her belly between them and felt the life they created. She was the woman of his dreams. She had given him more than he dreamed for. He captured a taut nipple in his mouth. He cupped her ass. He palmed both round cheeks and controlled her rise and fall on his dick. Mira's pussy muscles expanded and then tightened on his cock in synchronization with his bottom maneuvers. So demanding was the pleasure boiling him from the inside, he lost the ability for any coherent thought. His brain fired off commands to take more. Mira put down moves that owned him. Every feeling was raw and undiluted. Giovanni dropped back and gripped her hips to slam her pussy up and down on his dick, refusing to relinquish control. He ignored the sharp breaths escaping his woman. It got so good to him he shot up again and began to sink his teeth into the curve of her neck, sucking her skin in through his pursed lips.

"Owe! Damn it, Gio!" Mira wheezed. She held the back of his neck with one hand and rubbed down his back with the other as he put another mark of passion on her neck, then shoulder, and then left breast. She kept moving on his lap. She wasn't too big to flip her to the floor but he remained cautious all the same. He licked the sweat between her breasts, rolled his tongue over the slender curve of her neck, now bruised unintentionally, as she shivered and clung to him. Lately it took a lot more work on his part to make sure she reached her climax. But he was so fucking turned on he could not hold back.

"Do it, baby," she said as if hearing his inner thoughts, understanding his resistance. Giovanni bit into her shoulder for restraint and she tensed but clung to him, and he couldn't hold back any longer. With a final groan and grunt of surrender he gushed a release and crashed beneath her.

Afterwards she eased from his arms and he fell to his back. Mira lay at his side, turned on hers. Thankfully the floor in her office was carpeted and not the cool marble tile throughout the building. She put her arm around his waist. He kept her warm by running his hand up and down her skin for as far as he could reach. Her face rested against his chest. They both stared up at the portrait.

"It's still hard, even now, to believe all the changes in my life with Fabiana gone." Mira began. "But if none of it had happened I wouldn't have found you. Our love. And our children wouldn't exist. Things I never knew I wanted until you were mine." Mira kissed his chest. She half rolled on top of him. Her warm tummy pressed into his side and her moist pussy pressed against his thigh. "You continue to surprise me. The man you are that they don't know. The man I believe in." She touched his face. He turned his gaze to her and stared into her eyes, listening. "You're my best friend,

Giovanni. I trust you with my life. I'll do whatever is needed to protect what we have. No matter what. Always."

"You finished, sweetie?" Mira asked.

Giovanni snapped out of his thoughts. His wife reached for their daughter who lifted her arms for her mother. He opened his mouth to object but Mira put Eve on her hip with ease. Several more men had come inside and started to eat. How long had he been daydreaming?

"Zia has missed our Evie so much. I'm going to let Zia give her a bath." Mira came closer. "Maybe I'll give you one later," she whispered.

Giovanni smiled.

"Don't stay in Villa Rosso too late. Okay? After the girls are done packing I expect to see you."

"Girls?" he asked curiously.

"I hope you don't mind but Cecilia is coming to Sicily with us. She agreed to help me and Rosetta."

"Is that necessary?" Giovanni frowned.

"Yes." Mira said with a firm tone. "Especially since you've purposefully kept Zia from staying here. I know it was you."

Giovanni's brows lowered at the accusation. Apparently his wife was told of Rocco's refusal to let Zia return and the blame was cast his way.

"I can explain that," he began.

"Not the place. Right?" she glanced over to the others in the room. An unspoken rule between them held his tongue. They never disagreed in front of the family. It was always kept behind closed doors. She heaved Eve a bit higher on her hip. "Soon I will have three children under the age of two. I need all the help I can get. Cecilia is coming with us."

He smiled and nodded. "You're the boss."

Mira leaned in and gave him a kiss. "Not really, but I like when we pretend," she joked. He shook his head with laughter. Eve patted his cheek. "Say bye Papa," Mira said.

"Ciao, Papa!" Eve waved.

He winked at his daughter and watched them go. Giovanni reclined back in his chair. The family was good. Rocco worried for nothing. He had made the best choice for them all.

2.

The elevator made a slow climb. Pressed for time he checked his watch once more. His gaze switched back to the numbers blinking above. Dominic Battaglia exhaled the constricting breath of impatience caught in his lungs. At last he reached the fourth floor. The doors parted. The noise level hit him full force. Dominic shoved his hands down deeper in his pockets as he walked inside. It was a warm day but he wore a charcoal grey suit, with a black shirt. The men of the Battaglia family were always seen impeccably dressed in public. It was an unstated rule.

Fabiana's, a fashion house under Mirabella's company, catered to the privileged and famous. The new division within the company blossomed in the short three months since it's launching. On the fourth floor, one would find the nucleus of the operation. Below him was a high-end boutique that allowed Mirabella's collection to be purchased by appointment only. Today the offices bustled with activity. Staff and models hurried about as if uncertain of their destination. The ten million dollar operation he found in disarray in New York washed Battaglia money clean since Mira's resurrection.

Profits were good.

Today was a big day for his lady. Catalina had decided to do a store window fashion show on the lower floors for the Italian press and locals. Since the boutique wasn't open to everyone the crowds gathered for a peek of *Fabiana's* women's wear collection. It took him a full five minutes to push his way through the assembly. He thought the idea of a fashion collection display was far too premature, but Giovanni and Mira overruled his objections and gave Catalina her wish. It was a small project. Only sixteen handpicked couture outfits would be featured. But to Catalina it was the biggest venture she'd undertaken in her life. This meant his woman spent day and night with that French black designer who whined constantly. He struggled to be selfless. It was hard.

Dominic let his eyes do the seeking. He caught the lyrical sound of laughter and glanced left. Catalina stood between a tall black model named Zenobia and a slender man with a pink mohawk who he had never seen before. Catalina was beautiful in her business attire. She wore a very slimming nude colored mini dress with a bright red belt and heeled shoes. It was tastefully cut, and against her olive skin it flattered her curves. Her long chestnut brown hair was in a very curly style, which reached beyond her shoulders with bangs that covered her brows. When she spoke every eye went to her. He felt a swell of pride rise in his chest after witnessing her confidence. Dominic checked his watch and frowned. Time was short. He decided to give her the space she needed to conclude her business. He turned left and went to the office that would eventually be Mirabella's whenever she returned to this fashion world. Every time he entered the door of the office the picture of Mira and Fabiana standing back to back riveted his gaze. He approached the limestone white desk and picked up the phone. He made a quick call to check his service for messages. Again Lorenzo had left one. It was the fourth message he'd received that day. Carlo must not have made contact yet. That concerned him. Dominic hung up and dialed Lorenzo.

* B *

Golfe de Saint-Tropez —

Ring. Ring. Ring...

Marietta glanced over to the satellite phone. To her dismay it blinked yellow and rang louder. "Fuck this." Marietta snatched up the phone and turned it off.

Lorenzo had been in a sour mood. He woke up barking at her. He ranted about being ignored, castrated, and made a fool of by his stupid Mafia kingpin cousin. No matter how much they toured and enjoyed each other the dark moments with him sulking and brooding often came. She'd been able to tolerate his mood swings at first. Now she was sick of it. He was her man, and he needed to act like it. Always. Not some loser who needs to be part of some Mafia gang to feel important. It was stupid.

"Marietta? Was that the phone?" Lorenzo yelled.

"No, baby," she said sweetly, hiding a snide smile on her lips. She glanced up at her reflection in the overhanging microwave oven. The mischief she tried to swallow spread wider across her lips. She liked being bad. She liked bad boys. She was addicted to everything Lorenzo's dark life brought.

"You coming?" he yelled again. "What the fuck is taking so long?"

"Be right there!" she sang. Marietta picked up the portable radio with the new batteries tucked inside. It was time for his afternoon, before dinner treat. And then she'd feed and make love to him for the rest of the night. Four months into this with Lorenzo and she felt happier, more desired, more loved than she had in her entire miserable life. And she did love Lorenzo, deeply and completely. She would die for him. He was hers. When he confessed the trip was part business and pleasure she didn't mind. In fact she rarely saw him do business. He had a few meetings with people in London and Paris, but nothing that kept him from spoiling her daily. Her baby knew how to treat a girl.

Marietta climbed the lower deck stairs and emerged to the upper deck that faced the back of the yacht. The windows had a smoky grey tint that made it impossible to see inside but easy to see outside. She found Lorenzo as she left him, in a large leather lounge chair, with his shirt unbuttoned to reveal his nicely bronzed superman chest. How many times had she run her tongue over the hard definition? Damn she liked a man that was physically fit. Each morning when the sun rose he went for a swim. And it showed well in his tan and his physique. Lorenzo even had muscles in his dick. She felt lightheaded thinking about his cock coiled up under his long shorts. He punished her good.

He sat there staring at her. The side of his face rested against his palm. His gaze switched to the radio she carried and she could see a flicker of excitement in his eyes, despite the mean scowl he wore all day.

The first time she did a routine from her days as a stripper for him he acted like a madman. Surely he'd seen his share of strippers before. He claimed her routine was different, the music was different, and her moves were different. And he even made her vow to never dance or move like that for another man. Ever. It was for him only. After she figured out how much he liked it she decided to ration out these performances. When he slipped into a dark brooding mood and she saw their evening turning into a boring routine of his ranting about the injustices of being second best to his cousin, she gave him something special.

"For me?" he asked, with a single nod of his head directed at the radio. "I thought you were fixing my dinner?"

"Don't be so grouchy. You know you want this instead," she teased. She popped open the cassette player and dropped her mix tape from an American southern rap group called '2 Live Crew' inside.

Marietta glanced back over her shoulder. Before he was slumped in the chair as if bored. Now he sat forward with his elbows resting on his knees and his hands clasped together. He had the predatory look of a lion tracking a prized gazelle in his eyes. *Oh yes, he was going to wear her out tonight. Thank you lord!*

"*Dammelo*," he said.

"I intend to give it to you, baby. You know how I do it. You got to let me warm up. *Amore mio*."

Marietta pressed play. The sultry voice of a rhythm and blues singer set the mood. It began this way. By the time her man was fully aroused the song would switch to hardcore rap with her putting down sharp gyrations, bouncing of her butt cheeks, and seductive hip rolls would eventually bring her to his lap with him fucking her with wild excitement. He'd lick the sweat off the peaks of her nipples. His face would be buried between her thighs for what felt like hours. That was their game and she liked it just as much as he did.

With a smile to her lips Marietta turned and approached him. She stopped right in front of him so he had to sit upright and part his knees a bit so she could stand in between. Her gaze leveled on his. She untied her black silk robe that stopped mid-thigh. She was nude underneath. Except for the gold belly bracelet that circled her slender waist and connected to the diamond piercing in her bellybutton. She got the piercing and expensive waist jewelry when they visited Morocco. She never took it off. It turned him on to see her wearing it.

There was no need for a strip tease. Her man had barely enough patience for her to disrobe let alone remove a bikini. Besides she often sunbathed, swam, ate, and lounged on his yacht in the nude when they were parked out in the middle of the ocean or docked on the coasts of the French Riviera. And she liked to dance. She liked the way men desired her when she danced.

The music took over. Marietta danced in front of him. A slow circular whine of her hips and roll of her belly muscles with her hands pressed in front of her in mock prayer began the dance. She often started off his favorite routine like that of a belly dancer before she got raunchy. The working of the muscles in her mid section, rotation of her hips, and bounce of her breasts made him lick his lips with restraint.

40

The long wild curls of her hair fell over into her face. The long diamond hoops in her ears bounced against her jaw and her diamond bangles on her right wrist jingled, as did the charm bracelet he put on her ankle. And she worked it for him. The rhythm and blues switched to the hard thump of bass as hardcore rap lyrics spewed from the speakers and she pushed him back by the shoulders into the chair to gyrate with her body rubbing and gliding over his.

They barely got into her routine before they heard it. Actually Lorenzo heard it first. He seized her and threw her to the floor. He landed on top of her. Stunned she gasped for a breath. At first she thought it was his excitement. He was known to be rough when really turned on. She tried to kiss him, wrap her legs around his waist and ignore the pain to the back of her head and back that suffered the blunt of his force. He put a finger to her mouth, and in his eyes she read the warning. *Be silent, be still, someone's here.* That was the nature of their affair. Danger could present itself at any moment. Even out in the ocean. It's what Lorenzo warned her of constantly.

The rap music blared loudly. Lorenzo reached for her robe and put it against her chest. "Dress. Stay low."

Alarmed, Marietta agreed. Lorenzo's hand then reached for a gun he kept near his chair. He had guns all over the damn boat. They made him comfortable and her uneasy. But soon she heard it too, the sound of a boat approaching. *How the hell did he hear that over the music?*

In a crouched position he went for the door. In her heart she had always been afraid that someone from the Capriccio family would arrive and exact revenge for what was done to David. Lorenzo laughed off her concerns. *But was this the moment? Were they here for them?* Marietta wanted to go after him. She searched for the other gun, the one he kept in the cooler near the refrigerator. She found it and checked to make sure it was loaded. Nothing in her life came easy. She constantly worried that Lorenzo would be taken from her as abruptly as he had stormed into her life.

She eased on her robe.

She heard Lorenzo roar with laughter. It had to be his voice. Tying a knot to her robe she scrambled to the window with both hands on the weapon. She peeked out. Carlo boarded their boat from another and the men on the other boat tossed his luggage to him. Those men shouted at Lorenzo with friendly banter and he shouted back in Italian. She watched Carlo and Lorenzo embrace. Two months ago Lorenzo was drunk, so drunk she literally had to carry him to their room in Paris.

And it was then she learned of the dark secret he carried about his best friend.

Paris, France
April 12, 1992

"Asshole! Stop it. You're embarrassing me!" Marietta said in a hushed whisper. She nodded to the door attendant and forced him inside. Lorenzo slurred in Italian. He hugged her so tightly she was barely able to breathe from the pressure his strong arm applied on her side. They'd spent the day sightseeing and at first it was lovely. He was her funny sexy guide. And he bought her whatever she wanted. The driver behind them carried the haul from Chanel, Fendi, Yves St. Laurent. But as the day wore on he kept pulling her into one restaurant, café, or pub after another, to drink. And before long it became too much.

"You're so damned sexy. You know that?" he growled in her ear. Before she could respond he picked her up and put her over his shoulder. The guests of the hotel were shocked. A few ladies gasped. Several frowned and stepped back. Lorenzo carried her inside the elevator despite her pleas for him to put her down. The driver followed as if it was the most natural thing. Humiliated she fought him when the doors closed.

"Put me down damn it! I'm serious, Lorenzo! Enough of this shit!"

He slapped her ass and started pressing every button on the elevator panel. The elevator made its climb. The doors open and closed. She screamed at the top of her lungs to be released.

"You bastard! You asshole! You mean fucker! I'm serious."

When he didn't respond she threatened him in Italian. Sharp words of ripping his balls off, made him roar with laughter and deliver a few more hard smacks to her ass. She even bit his back to no avail. The doors to the elevator kept opening and closing and Marietta grew weak from the way he carried her. The blood rushed to her head. Infuriated she stopped struggling, screaming obscenities, and finally he did let her down, but only to drag her out of the open elevator on shaky legs.

"I'm so pissed with you!" Marietta seethed through clenched teeth. She glanced back to the driver. He lowered his gaze and followed them to their room with her bags. Marietta questioned her sanity and the rollercoaster ride that was their romance on days like

this. The unconventional ways they showed affection had to be unhealthy for them both. And Lorenzo's demons never let up on them, no matter how beautiful the city, and how wonderful the time they shared. What woman could put up with a man like him?

A woman who was just as emotionally crippled, she surmised. The door opened to their hotel suite and he staggered inside. She turned on the driver. "You're fucking useless." She spat at the man. "Leave the bags there and get the fuck out!" she shouted.

The man nodded quickly and made a hasty exit.

"Lorenzo! We need to talk. I'm so sick of this shit with—"

She walked into the en-suite and paused. Lorenzo sat on a white antique chaise. His face buried in his hands, his shoulders shook as if he were sobbing. Stunned Marietta froze. She'd seen him shit faced drunk before. Even had to force him off her when he got too amorous and hurt her during sex. Dealt with his wrath when she chastised him in public. But seeing him weak was something totally different.

"Lorenzo?" she said cautiously.

"Morte," he said in a hoarse voice etched with pain. "Morte."

"Death?" she asked. Lorenzo groaned deep. Through his suffering she heard frustration and regret that made the blood in her veins cool. "Who is dead, Lorenzo? What are you talking about?" It had to be about that sick mother of his and the cruel way she took her life on his birthday.

Marietta went to him. She got on her knees. "Baby? C'mon it's me. What is it, Lorenzo? Talk to me?"

He lifted his face from his hands and looked at her. Though the whites of his eyes were blood shot, and his face flushed, she saw no tears. Even in this tortured state the man refused to allow himself the release of tears. But it didn't mean he didn't feel. His suffering glistened in his irises and pooled around the brim of his lashes.

"Oh, baby, what is it? Tell me?" Unsure of what to do she did what she could. She took his face and kissed him. Hard at first, desperate to soothe him, and the kiss soon melted his resistance. Instead of the rough handling in the elevator, his response became gentle, almost clumsy and shy. He drew her up to him and Marietta straddled his lap. The chaise allowed for the position. Marietta tamed his passion with her darting tongue pursuing his. All the while she fought to release his belt and zipper. In a flurry of hand movements she got access to what she wanted—him. Marietta gushed a breath of sexual release when she eased down on his cock and took him deeply. Lorenzo helped her, buried his face in her

breasts as she began to move. To her surprise he was able to maintain control though he was clearly drunk. And she was sexually charged by his strength. Marietta bounced on his cock and took him deeper, in and out of her channel. Passion ruptured her heart and it felt as if the chambers exploded. She seized on him, arms tight to his neck, gasping and wheezing. Lorenzo made another deep grunt and stood.

Marietta gasped. He was such a giant of a man, holding her felt effortless on his part. He pulled her up by the waist and slipped out of her. She groaned in disappointment and locked her legs around his waist.

His mouth sealed over hers and he kissed her lovingly, carrying her without staggering to the bedroom. He forced her to release him and dropped her on the bed. She blinked up at him. Before she could challenge him for ending their lovemaking he dropped to the side of the bed on his knees. Lorenzo grabbed her by the ankles and she slid across to him. His face lowered between her forced apart thighs. Marietta clenched her teeth against the moans. His tongue licked at her pussy with long strokes, and did so over and over. To aid him, and open herself for more, she grabbed the tops of her knees and kept her legs apart. Lorenzo scooped her up by the ass and feasted on her clitoris. He sucked and applied more pressure with that amazing tongue of his before releasing her. Her head went back and she arched from the mattress. Marietta cried out unable to stop herself. His intent on pleasuring her below crushed her will without mercy. When his tongue pierced her channel then swiped out and up to tickle her clitoris she lost it. The climax was swift and punishing.

Her cries of pleasure and then weakening moans were the only noise to be heard in the room. Lorenzo peeked up at her from over her pussy with the most intensely focused stare. He pressed a kiss to the quivering lips of her sex to soothe her.

Marietta's lids fluttered shut. She knew he was undressing. Heard it. But instead of doing the same she rolled to her side and curled up with a smile. Next came the best part. She'd spend the night in his arms. She'd love him until all his problems with intimacy and self-loathing went away. She could do it. She was woman enough to do it.

Lorenzo's hands were on her. He unzipped the back of her dress. She straightened and went limp as he removed the silk garment, and bra. Marietta rarely wore panties with her man, per his request. Sometimes he just wanted to touch her. And he hated any barrier between her thighs. She giggled when he kissed her shoulder.

"I love you, Lorenzo," she exhaled. He didn't respond. It was okay. She knew he loved her too. He said it before. But he didn't use the word much. It made him uncomfortable, weak. She understood. Why else would he spend so much time with her, focused on her? He could have any woman he wanted and yet he chose her. More importantly she chose him.

The bedding slid with her. And her oversensitive nipples and stomach were dragged over the sheets as he pulled her to him and put her in position. Marietta got to her hands and knees. Her curly locks were in her face covering her eyes, reaching her nose. Her hair was thick and puffy with curls like that of a poorly groomed poodle. However, she could see herself and him in the mirror across from the bed. Marietta blew air upward from her bottom lip to make her bangs move so she could see more clearly. She intended to watch the show.

His knees pressed between hers with the intent of spreading her thighs. The front of his hairy thighs brushed the backs of hers. She could feel his spry pubic hair caress her ass. He smacked his cock against her pussy. It bounced up and brushed her clit. The touch, though brief, sent a tickle of pleasure through her. 'Daddy Long Dick', is the name she jokingly gave him.

He liked it.

And then he entered her without warning. Each time with Lorenzo felt like the first time. No man wielded the power of his dick so fiercely accurate. He thrust in and out of her with measured slow strokes so she could feel the muscled veiny strength of his cock. She lifted her head and watched them. Saw his face. The twist of desire and pleasure made his features hard, but he wore a smile, a beautiful satisfied smile that put one to her lips as well. She studied how her breasts swayed in time with his hard pounding. She watched how his muscular chest bulked with deep intakes of breath and went tight with each release. Lorenzo's gaze lowered to her ass. He was watching the tunneling of his cock deep between. She dipped her back to give him a better view. He went fast and strong now, urgent with his strikes.

Bam. Bam. Bam. Went the headboard. He thrust in and out of her pussy and her lashes fluttered before they shut. Marietta put her face into the mattress to keep from screaming out her bliss. She too moved with frenzied backward pushes to take him deeper. Oh how much she enjoyed when he went deep. He smacked her left butt cheek hard. Her head shot up and she glared at him.

"Bastard!" she said with a laugh.

"Keep watching, cara. Don't hide from me," he groaned in return.

She fixed her gaze on the mirror once more, breathing out of her mouth with deep pants. This time he stared at her too in the mirror. She held his gaze.

It amazed her that his big body, large hands, and thick dick carried such strength and yet he could manage to be controlled and loving while inebriated to keep from hurting her. Lorenzo gripped her by the neck. He forced her head to go back, and kept her steady with a hand to her hip. The slow rhythmic thrusts came harder, faster. His powerful control drilled her pussy. And she loved the mix of torture with her pleasure. Rapture tore through her slick spasming channel with each slam of his hips. It became a harsh smack sounding off in the room. And Lorenzo fucked her like a champion, her warrior.

God she loved him— Marietta could no longer look at him in the mirror. Though her neck stretched back and he now gripped her hair instead of the back of her throat. She closed her eyes and stayed the course; afraid it would end to soon.

"Oh yes!" she cried out. "Fuck me, baby! Yes, daddy, like that, fuck me," she wept.

Friction and heat sparked between them with his cock tunneling deeper. She knew for certain she couldn't stand much more.

"Che bella scopta!" he cried out with a hard grunt.

Marietta smiled and moved her hips in wild circles. Lorenzo's frenzied thrusts took over. He let go of her hair and held both of her shoulders as he slammed his seed deep inside of her. Exhausted she collapsed and he came on top of her. He soon moved to avoid hurting her and she rolled with him. Neither could speak. She captured air into her lungs. Soon she turned over, snuggled his sweaty chest, and started to drift asleep. Before she could the word 'morte' came to mind. He said death earlier. What did he mean?

Marietta lifted her head and looked at him. "Lorenzo?" she panted.

"Mmm?"

"What's wrong? Why did you say death? Earlier?" she asked.

"My fault," he mumbled. "I'm the bringer of death."

She knew of his torment about Tomosino's untimely demise. She felt such a pang of sympathy for how guilty he was. Her eyes began to tear. "Tomosino's death isn't your fault. You have to stop punishing yourself."

"Madre, Tomosino, Carmine... my fault... morte... because of me. I'm a murderer, cara. It's all I am."

Marietta froze. Her heart went still. She spent days watching Lorenzo help his best friend overcome his grief for young Carmine's death. Was this the same Carmine, Carlo spoke of? The one he mourned? She touched Lorenzo's cheek. "What did you do, baby? To Carmine?"

Lorenzo's eyes flashed open. He glared at her for a moment.

"I only meant—"she began.

He rolled her over. "Don't talk, Marietta. I need you to be silent. I need you to forgive me."

"I do," she said, not sure of which offense he spoke of.

"Come here." He turned her to her side and pulled her up against his chest so he could spoon her from behind. "Sleep. That's what I need. No more talk of death."

Marietta snuggled him and relaxed. "Whatever you say, baby," she replied.

Marietta watched Carlo and Lorenzo embrace from the window. They started toward the door and she stepped back. Going to the radio she turned off the music and brushed her curly hair back from her face. Lorenzo entered first and Carlo hung back.

"You decent, *cara?*"

"Yes," she said. Though she remained nude under her robe. He looked her over as if he had to be sure she met the standard to be around his friend and then called to Carlo to enter. When he stalked in as tall and as handsome as Lorenzo, Marietta tried to show no reaction. But she saw his. That razor sharp gaze of his focused intensely on her. It lowered to her legs and made the climb up. And that sly smile that was all him tilted the corner of his mouth.

"*Ciao, Carlo,*" Marietta said.

"*Ciao, bella,*" he answered.

Lorenzo walked over to Marietta and pulled her into his arms. He hugged her. "Carlo's going to stay for awhile. We'll sail into San Tropez and do some dancing tonight. You'll like that."

Lifted in his arms she embraced Lorenzo's neck and stared at Carlo from over his shoulder. "Yes. I think I will."

* B *

Catalina walked into Mira's office, which was hers for now. Behind the desk sat Dominic in a large wingback chair. The side of

47

his face rested between his thumb and index finger.

"Domi? I didn't know you were here."

She closed the door behind her. How long had he been sitting alone, waiting? She stared at him a moment. He devastated her with how handsome he was in his dark suit and tie. She and Mira joked that they should send the Battaglia men down the runway for her men's line. Dominic wasn't as tall as Giovanni and Lorenzo but he was by far sexier than any male model she'd seen.

"*Ciao, Domi*," she said with a smile. The day had been grueling and she missed him terribly.

"Why don't you use your own office, Catalina?" Dominic asked. He sat forward and clasped his hands on the tall desk he sat behind. He glanced left to right at the file folders and portfolios. "This is Mira's office." His gaze then lifted to hers.

"I do use mine. At times. But this one's bigger. I can hold meetings and stuff in here."

"And stuff? What stuff?" Dominic stared at her. She always felt nervous when he had that look. It was far worse than her brother's. Giovanni spoiled her. He rarely saw through her deception, until recently. However, since she was a kid Dominic knew when she was lying. She liked playing boss. And from Mira's office that is exactly how everyone treated her.

"Okay. The truth is I'm the boss around here. Even Carole listens to me. I thought I should conduct business in the boss's office, for appearances. Mira won't be back in that chair," she pointed to the chair Dominic sat in. "For two to three years. And you and I know it."

Dominic continued to stare at her.

Catalina smoothed her hands down her hips and tossed her hair from her shoulder. She approached him with an imposed air of confidence. "I know what this is about." She walked around the desk. "You think this... all of this... it's getting out of hand. We haven't seen each other in over a week, baby."

Dominic sat back in his chair. Catalina turned it sideways so he faced her. She leaned forward with her hands gripping both sides. "Everything I do for this company is out of love for the *famiglia*. This is our business too. Right?" She didn't bother to wait for an answer. She continued. "And I've got good news. I've finished early. We can leave whenever you're ready. I can't wait to get to Mondello."

A hint of a smile touched his face. Guilt filled her when she thought of her neglect. But she also battled such overwhelming excitement over her projects at *Fabiana's*. She'd been sketching her own designs. She was going to show them to Mira. She eased on to his lap and crossed her legs so they dropped in a very ladylike manner in her skirt over the right arm. Dominic initiated the kiss. It was a slow meticulous roll of his tongue over hers. Sweet yet uninhibited, she responded and controlled their passion while demanding more.

"Mmm," she released him. "I have missed you, honey. What time does our flight leave?"

"We won't be taking a flight. We'll catch the train to Rome then take the train and ferry to Sicily."

"What?" Catalina frowned. "That'll take over twelve hours."

"I got us a private car in first class." Dominic smiled. "It'll be romantic."

"Domi, that's such a waste of our time, besides I have—"

He put a finger to her mouth. "I want you alone. We need to talk before we see Giovanni. I intend to ask him for his blessing."

Her eyes stretched. Her heart leapt at the mere mention. "You plan to ask him to let us marry? Are you serious? So soon? He said we have to wait a full year."

"I have his confidence again. Besides, I want a wife, a mother of my children. Our future."

Catalina pressed her lips together. Yes, she wanted to be his wife. Since she was twelve years old she'd dreamt of it. But things had changed for her. So much had happened since their trip to America. Teddy said she was as talented as Mira and as business savvy as Fabiana. She was trying to convince him to return to Milano to work with her on some new ideas she had. And downstairs the press and people of Milano were in a frenzy over her fashion show.

"Maybe we shouldn't push Giovanni, Domi. Things are good between you and him. He's letting me work here and he's been really good about us living together in Napoli."

"So?" Dominic frowned. "You think I want to live in sin?"

"Sin?" Catalina nearly laughed. She knew better. "We sinned a long time ago, Domi. I just think we should take things slow."

"Do you want to be my wife?" he asked, and she caught an edge of concern in his tone.

Catalina touched his cheek. She kissed his lips. "Of course, sweetheart."

"Then it's settled. We will go to Giovanni and tell him the time has come."

"But, Domi…"

"No more discussion, Catalina. We will go to him and get his approval."

She sighed. "Why the hell do we have to go by train?"

"You know we can't have sex at Villa Mare Blu, a private train car is what we need," he smiled.

"Oh please," she rolled her eyes. "Are you saying we're going to stay in *Sicilia* for months and not have sex?"

"We cannot. It's Giovanni's rule. Now let's go," he patted her leg. "We have a train to catch."

Catalina eased off his lap and stood. She fixed her dress. "I have to close up around here."

"You said you were ready, all mine?" Dominic asked.

"Yes sweetheart, but if I'm going to be out of reach for over twelve hours on the biggest day of *Fabiana's* I need to put things in order. Right?"

Dominic drew back his sleeve. "You have an hour."

Catalina suppressed the urge to demand more time. Instead she blew him a kiss. "That's all I need." She walked out of the office and looked back through the glass door. Dominic paced. She sighed sadly. Disappointed.

3.

"Our sons are a good omen. Did you know twins built Rome? Their names were Romulus and Remus," Giovanni said.

"That's a myth."

"Myth! It's a legend, Bella. I've told the story to Eve," Giovanni said.

"Oh I've heard the story. Twins who were suckled by a she-wolf? Please!" Mira said under a light chuckle. "I think I believe the tale of Romulus and Remus more than she does. Try the old lady and the shoe, or Peter, Peter, pumpkin eater. She likes that one."

Giovanni scoffed. "Nonsense. Eve loves my fables." He touched his daughter's foot.

"Aha! See! It's a myth!" Mira laughed. "You just admitted it."

He smiled. "Naughty Mama doesn't know that Papa's fables are always rooted in truth," he said to his sleeping daughter. "Look at her, Bella. She's a good *bambina*. She's Papa's girl. Easy to please as long as she has her little suckie thing."

"Pacifier." Mira corrected him once more.

Giovanni rubbed his finger across Eve's cheek. "*Mia piccola lucciola*," he said. Calling her his little firefly in a tone of adoration that was so sweet. She was truly a child made from love. Mira had watched for months as the bond of love between father and daughter strengthened. For Eve the sun rose and set on the broad shoulders of Papa. And Giovanni basked in his daughter's attention, softened when she walked into a room on bowed legs. Woke her on nights he arrived home late and took her into his office to sit with him when he met with his men, something Mira only recently learned of.

"Do you think we can convince her to release the little plug she sucks on for good?"

Mira laughed. "I'd like to see you try."

"But isn't she too old?" Giovanni asked. "I think it stunts her. She should be talking more."

Mira looked down at her daughter with concern. "You may be right. I've never been around babies before Eve. I only gave her the thing because she cried so much when she was born. It helped her sleep. Now she won't let it go."

"Then we need to take it from her." Giovanni said.

"Let's take it one day at a time," Mira advised.

She cradled Eve against her. When she held her this close she felt a warm glow of happiness flow through her. On the plane the seating to the back was reserved for their entourage, Rosetta, Cecilia, Leo, Nico, and Renaldo. The front seating allowed for her to recline and gaze out of the window at the scattered clouds. Giovanni remained close. If she needed water he was the first to pour her a glass. Before she knew she was hungry he offered her a slice of kiwi, or the sweetest grapes she'd ever tasted. He whispered in her ear how pretty she was yesterday and today. Her husband found ways to touch her even with Eve sleeping against her breast.

This is what it felt like to be his love—she was spoiled because of her husband's devotion. Mira's head turned slightly in an effort to see him. She liked the physical changes in her husband too. He had started boxing more down in his secret room. His body was fit and his muscular form chiseled nicely under the fine dark threads of his tailored suit. He had grown some facial hair, a mustache goatee that made his mouth all the more tempting to her, especially when he gave her those half smiles when he was pleased. His thick dark hair was tapered neatly to his collar. He was a massive, self-confident presence that constantly drew the attention of others, men and women. And he smelled lovely. A manly scent hung over him. It spoke of power and control. She blushed over being caught staring. He only responded by kissing her cheek and ear once more.

Mira closed her eyes and relaxed. He was happy. She was happy. From the moment they boarded the plane he made the most wonderful promises to her. Their return to Sicily was as important to him as the day they exchanged their vows.

"Do you know what I think?" Giovanni asked. "I think our boys will be the greatest of all the men in my family and yours, I feel it don't you?"

She pop-kissed him in response. He drew her back in with a more seductive kiss, and when he released her she felt her heart lodged in her throat. "*Cara mia,*" he said softly. "Mother of my gladiators," he chuckled. "What would I have ever done if I never found you?"

"We found each other. And I'm more than the mother of your children. I'm your soul mate, and you're mine. We're destiny."

"*Destino*," he nodded.

Mira averted her gaze back to the window with a deep sigh. When he treated her so adoringly she felt foolish. Two days ago they had an awful fight. It started from nothing. That morning she had awoken with the deepest feeling of depression. It followed her throughout the day. While in her sewing room, opening a box of fabric samples sent by Carole and Catalina, she broke down in a screaming fit when she uncovered the poor quality of the material. Her rage was so intense and destructive to anything within her reach the staff notified his men and they sent for Giovanni to return from Napoli. He stormed through the doors of Melanzana and yelled at everyone to leave her to him when he found her pacing and crying in her room. He called her moody and irrational. She called him a bully and uncaring about her isolation. The argument ended with him forcing her to bed.

The doctor said she was hormonal and the depression was to be expected. But she knew Giovanni hid the truth of her issues. No matter what reasons he and the doctor fed her about her condition, the spotting of blood could not be normal. She never had blood when she wiped while carrying Eve. And even worse she feared her inability to control her emotions. The arguments between her and Giovanni were always away from the eyes and ears of the family, but left them both drained and disillusioned. She didn't understand why their life, her role as a mother and *Donna* to this family all of a sudden became insufferable on one day, and then the very next day a dream come true. She prayed Sicily, and his dedication to being at her side for the last trimester would alleviate her anxiety. She feared nothing would.

"Why are you quiet? What are you thinking?" he asked.

"Can't I own my thoughts privately?" she answered.

"Of course, Bella. I only asked because I love it when you share those thoughts with me," he teased.

She didn't bother to smile. Like the wind her mood shifted and again she felt a bitter resentment rise in her. "It's Sicily. You talk as if the place is better than Disney World."

Giovanni's brow creased.

"I'm excited," she quickly added. "It's our little adventure and I need a change of pace. Still the timing is so close to my delivery date feels rushed."

"It's well planned. Trust me, Bella. Everything I do for you and our family is planned."

The clouds cleared and she could see the island of Sicily. She was curious about his life as a boy and why Mondello, which was only a few miles outside of Palermo, was so important to him. "I still have questions."

"Ask them."

"Why? Why should I? You're not going to answer them," she sighed.

"Try me," he said.

She glanced over at him. He arched his brows. "Try me, Bella."

"Did you, Lorenzo, and Domi spend a lot of time here? Or were you mostly raised in Italy?"

A gust of laughter escaped him. As if he expected her to ask him the code of the Mafia. He was always on guard with the secrecy of his lifestyle. It became possible for him to hide many details about his past. "Yes, and yes, Bella," he answered. He kissed her cheek and just under her jawline. He took Eve's hand with his fingers and lifted it to press a gentle kiss to her tiny knuckles. Their daughter sucked a little harder on her pacifier but didn't wake.

"Domi's adopted. Right?" she continued. "I've always wanted to know his story. Like where did he come from?"

"He was hatched from an egg," Giovanni chuckled.

"Is he the son of a family member?" she ignored his joke. "Or did your mother convince your father to adopt? Which would be strange."

"Why?" he asked. She could hear a bit of impatience in his tone but she chose to ignore it as well.

"You said your father rejected his first wife because she couldn't have kids. He took your mother when she was young and kept her because she carried you. I saw the way the men acted when you announced we were having sons. If you are this happy to have your legacy I would think your father was even more traditional regarding the children he accepted as his own."

Giovanni scratched his brow. Mira felt his emotional retreat. When he struggled with intolerance his mood swing would be abrupt. She didn't want to ruin the pleasant moment they'd shared. But the more he held back the more she wanted to know his secrets. Being overprotective of her was one thing, but locking out parts of his heart and the secrets to why he was the man he was couldn't go on. "Tell me, baby. Can't I know about who Domi is to you? Where he came from? Your parents' adopting him is strange isn't it?" Mira pressed.

"No," he replied.

"Okay. Well how about the timing? Your mother had Catalina. But in between there's Domi? The age gap between you means your father adopted Domi right after you returned from Ireland. Right? I did the math. You and Eve were back from Ireland after being gone for two years. And then he adopts a son while she is pregnant with Catalina? He had the family he wanted. Why adopt another child?"

"Bella, let it go," Giovanni sighed.

"Oh good grief what's the big secret? You told me you would answer my questions. Answer them." She demanded.

"Why does it have to be a secret? If I don't want to talk about it then I just don't want to fucking talk about it." Giovanni sat back in his chair.

"Not good enough. I've had a history lesson on all your business associates. Zia said I needed to make sure I understood these 'clans' that are a part of your organization. But what about when it comes to Domi, Lorenzo, Carlo, Nico, Renaldo?"

"Let it go," Giovanni sighed.

"Leo, and Carmine—" she continued. "By the way we haven't seen Carmine in months? What happened there?"

"Carmine quit. I told you that," Giovanni grunted.

Mira rolled her gaze away from him. If they are the Mafia she doubted any man could up and 'quit'. But they weren't the Mafia. The Battaglias were something far worse according to the news reporters hawking her for an interview since her wedding. The meaning, history, and dirty dealings of the *Camorra* in southern Italy remained a mystery to her. She decided to let the Carmine disappearance go. Especially after a woman on her staff told her that Carmine had been killed and buried in a private memorial service that her husband attended. Secrets. Lies. They were a stain on her marriage and she pretended not to notice.

"All I'm saying is I've gotten an explanation of who these men are and I see how close you are to your inner circle. Ignorance isn't always bliss, Giovanni." She lowered her voice. "You can't put a gun in my hand one day and say beware of the boogie man and then deny he exists the next."

Her husband looked over at her. He then cast his gaze past her to the window as if considering her argument. "Domi's not the boogie man."

"You know what I mean," she said.

"I do. He's my brother. His biological father worked for a family acquaintance of Patri's in Sicily," he said. His voice was almost mournful. But she saw no sign of emotion on his face. She adjusted Eve in her arms and waited. If he wanted to tell her then he'd do so at his own pace.

"When Micheli Esposito died he left Domi an orphan. A scared little kid with no family, no compassion, he was in a bad state." She could hear the tightness in Giovanni's voice. She touched his hand to get him through it. "It's not so strange, Bella, that my father would want to help a kid like Domi. My father wasn't all evil. He had compassion in him."

"I never said—"

"My father always wanted sons. And Domi is his son." Giovanni insisted.

"I only meant—"

"I know your meaning!" Giovanni said, and his voice pitched high. Mira removed her hand from his. He expelled another deep breath. "Forgive me. I don't like thinking about those days of how we found Domi. How close Domi came to not existing."

"I'm so sorry," Mira said softly. "Your wounds are so deep, Giovanni. I'm your wife. I want to share your burden."

"You can't."

"I know," she said sadly. "And that's what troubles me."

They sat in silence for a moment and she spoke. "I think I'm crazy. Why do I keep crying? Why do we keep fighting? The doctor said it's normal but I wasn't like this with Eve. Not really. I cry all the time."

"Not all the time, only a few days," he said. "Look at me."

She did as he asked.

"I have a surprise for you," he said.

"You do?" she asked.

"Tomorrow we visit family, and I show you all the places I loved as a child. Tonight I make love to you under the stars, near the sea. So no more tears. Okay?"

Fleeting memories of their time at the blue grotto surfaced and she smiled. "Okay."

The pilot announced their approach. Everyone set their chairs upright. Mira repositioned Eve who woke. She looked around, confused. "Give her to me, Bella," he said.

Thankful that Giovanni took their daughter Mira was able to stretch in her chair. Soreness always centered in her pelvis and lower back when she sat too long. She gazed out at Sicily as they coasted and then skidded into a landing. All she saw were trees and tarmac. Her anxiety, as sharp and debilitating as it could be, had dulled to a barely noticeable ache in her chest. She was ready to understand the love affair her husband had with this island.

After the plane taxied to a stop Giovanni's top three men who shadowed them always, Leo, Renaldo, and Nico, stood with bowed heads beneath the low roof of the jet and exited the plane. Mira was helped from her seat and escorted down the ladder steps of the plane by Giovanni.

The first person she sought was her daughter. Nico held Eve. The enforcer was who her daughter reached for first if she couldn't have mommy or daddy. She hugged his thick neck and pressed her cheek to his as she sucked on her pacifier. The gentle giant of a man, with a mean brood, was serious over his role as guardian. He walked away carrying Eve in his arms. Before Mira could fully process her surroundings her husband swept her into his unyielding embrace and gave her a little spin.

"*Benvenuta all'Sicilia.*" He kissed her brow. She eased her arm around his waist to walk by his side to the awaiting car. The impression she had of Sicily at first was a bit underwhelming. Beyond the trees, the land was flat. In the distance she could see mountains with peaks so high they disappeared into the clouds. Nothing remarkable stood out. Sorrento was an oasis of beautiful cliffs and narrow cobbled lane streets. Sorrento was home.

A cooling wind swept her hair and bangs into her eyes. Mira eased off her sunglasses from the top of her head and slipped them on to withstand the glare of the afternoon.

Soon after she was ushered to the car waiting for them and they were driven away with two vehicles following. The freeway was congested with braided strands of traffic. The family travelled out of Palermo through one of the main arteries of town. Mira stared at the passing box shaped homes with antennas on flat roofs and laundry drying from the balconies. Locals drove motorbikes, or travelled in passenger vans. The city moved with one heartbeat—east.

"How far to Mondello?" she inquired.

"Not far. *Lucciola*, are you excited?" Giovanni asked their daughter.

Eve laughed when he reached over and tickled her. She was placed in her car seat between her parents. She played a continuous game of 'peek-a-boo' with her father. After a fit of giggles she careened her neck to look out of the window. Mira reached and removed the pacifier from Eve's mouth and for once her daughter didn't object. Eve began to talk fast in Italian, English and her own garbled baby language intermixed. Very few words could be understood. She leaned forward in her car seat and pointed at the window as if emphasizing a point. Giovanni smiled and reached to undo her restraints. Possibly he wanted to free her to see the city they drove out of.

"You know better," Mira said.

He grunted in defiance but obeyed her wishes. Eve kept talking and pointing. When her parents didn't give the proper response Eve began to buck in her restraints and cry to be freed. Mira caved and gave her the pacifier again.

The city soon retreated and the car drove along cliffs that dropped off to the sea.

"Are we close?" she asked after twenty minutes into their drive.

"You just asked me that," he chuckled.

"Oh," Mira said. "I guess I did."

"These cliffs stretch up to Monte Gallo. Our familiy's land is at the foot of the mountain. It's called Villa Mare Blu."

"Blue sea house?" Mira translated.

"The waters are clear as ice and the sands pure white, like snow. We also have our own private grotto. So much to show you and Evie," Giovanni boasted.

Before long they travelled alone on the road through lush emerald green cypress trees. A colorful splash of flowers in bloom could be seen from her window. The road branched off the freeway and steeped down to the bottom of Monte Gallo. The paved road of progress was replaced by the bumpy ride into private property. The trees inched in closer with wild flowers in bloom everywhere. The color purple sprinkled and touched every branch like the surreal beauty of a postcard.

"Now we're here," Giovanni announced.

Eve clapped. Giovanni clapped with her and their daughter kicked her feet with happiness.

The car came to a stop.

The driver opened the door for them. Giovanni was quick about freeing Eve. He pulled her out of her car seat to emerge from the car. Mira stepped out with the assistance of Rosetta who was the first to greet her. The smell of spring flowers and exhaust filled her lungs. She glanced to the villa at the end of a dirt-paved stretch of the road. Immediately Mira noticed three people standing under a stone archway before a palatial two story stone villa. Among them was a beautiful young woman who looked to be Mira's age. The woman stared directly at Mira with bold self-assuredness.

"Her name is Carmella," Rosetta whispered. "She once dated Giovanni when they were kids. Everyone thought they would marry when they were children. But Giovanni never chose a wife. That is until he found you, *Donna*," Rosetta clarified.

Mira's heart grew hot with envy. What the hell was Carmella doing here if she shared an intimate connection with her husband? She glanced to Rosetta who nodded as if she understood the unspoken question. "She lives here, *Donna*. With her mother and brother. Takes care of Giovanni when he visits Mondello," Rosetta added.

"Bella? Come," Giovanni extended his hand.

"Thank you, Rosetta," Mira said, keeping emotion from her voice. She left the side of the car, careful of the long hem of her green linen summer dress.

The short older woman with grey and black streaked hair came forward first. "*Bambina!* At last!" The woman exclaimed. She went straight for Eve with her arms outstretched. Eve was immediately alarmed. She turned her face away, clinging to her father's neck.

Giovanni embraced the woman as he would Zia—warm and friendly. He then handed over a protesting baby Eve. Sophia balanced Eve's resistance to be held and peppered her face with kisses. Mira repressed the urge to take her daughter and soothe her. But after a few soft whispers the toddler relaxed and stared at the stranger in confusion.

"*Mia moglie*—my wife," Giovanni gestured to Mira.

"*Ciao, Donna*," the old woman said. "*Benvenuta in Mondello*."

Mira glanced to Giovanni who nodded his head with encouragement. The woman had a calming spirit like Zia. And she did seem genuine with her excitement over their arrival. The old woman spoke so fast in Sicilian that Mira barely understood her. From a rough translation she gleamed that her name was Sophia and she and her family considered themselves caretakers of the place.

Mira nodded her head hello and locked eyes with Carmella. It wasn't until the woman's name was spoken by her mother did she approach them. And Mira disliked her approach immediately. Everything from her smile to the sway of her slender hips was directed toward Mira's husband. Her flawless olive skin glowed with pale gold undertones. The moistness of her full pouty lips spread into a seductive smile that only made her more attractive. Carmella was close to Mira's age apparently. But they differed in appearance in many ways. Her hair was cut in a short-cropped style with dark curls that framed her deep-set brown eyes. She had a cover model's figure. She wore a pair of jeans and a low cut shirt that revealed her tiny waist and uplifted double D sized breasts. Was this the kind of woman Giovanni dated? Did he find Carmella attractive? Mira looked to her husband who had what she considered a goofy smile on his face. She felt the urge to smack him.

"Giovanni, you've finally made it. We've been waiting. *Come è stato il tuo volo?*"

She asked about his flight. It was a very causal greeting. However, Mira didn't appreciate the familiarity between them. It was intimate, affectionate, and exclusive. She watched the woman touch her husband's sleeve. Carmella's fingers gathered around the material and gripped tightly. And then she moved in to offer a customary kiss to both of his cheeks while brushing his chest with her breasts. And the kisses landed too close to the corner of Giovanni's mouth. The harlot had to lift on her toes like a ballerina to do so. Giovanni aided by holding Carmella's elbows. Mira's eyes stretched when Giovanni had the nerve to return the kiss to Carmella's left and right cheek.

"I want you to meet my Bella," Giovanni said with a proud boastful voice. The woman turned her brown eyes toward Mira. "Carmella, this is—"

Carmella interjected with a smile. "I know who she is, Gio. The world does. You were a beautiful bride. We came to the wedding. You might not remember Mama and me."

"I don't," Mira replied.

The woman glanced over to Eve, as if Mira's response didn't matter. "And this is your *bambina*? Oh my! She has your eyes, Gio. She's adorable. *Ciao, bambina.*"

Eve blinked at the woman and sucked harder on her pacifier. Before long her daughter burst into tears over the unwanted attention from Carmella. Mira couldn't help but smile. *That's right, baby, tell the tramp to back off.* Giovanni took Eve from Sophia and she immediately stopped the crying.

Anthony was introduced next. He told the men to follow him with the luggage in Italian after greeting Mira with kisses to the cheek. He had to be fifteen or sixteen. Rosetta and Cecilia joined Mira. Carmella seemed to recognize Rosetta, but her greeting was less than friendly. Rosetta responded in the same cool detached manner.

"Everyone inside. *Prego!*" Sophia said.

She started off and the others followed. Giovanni extended his hand to Mira. It was expected that he be the one to escort her and their daughter into their family home. She made a point to refuse him. His brows lifted in surprise over the rejection. She continued on with Cecilia and Rosetta.

Tall trees with wide spread palm leaves made the afternoon sun less blistering for the short walk to the door. Villa Mare Blu was something to behold. Built entirely of ancient stone the front of the villa was a grand estate where citrus and olive trees grew all around. It reminded her of one of those great monasteries from the 1700s. At the very top of the flat roof was a distinctive tower that housed a cast iron bell inside. The stone architecture had a weathered charm with wild vines creeping up the walls, twisting around the second floor wrought iron balconies. A cobbled stone walkway, flanked by purple wildflowers on either side, had a smooth paved finish that made it easy for her to cross. Mira kept her gaze fiercely focused on Carmella. The woman glanced back at her once and the smile she gave was absent of warmth. In that brief exchange all of Mira's suspicions were confirmed.

Signorina Carmella was not happy to see the new *Donna* in the family.

Giovanni caught up with Mira. He forced his hand into hers. She squeezed it hard. He chuckled and brought her hand to his lips. He heaved Eve up in his free arm, unaffected by her cold aloof manner. As soon as they stepped inside he became her tour guide.

"My mother's heart went into the renovation of these floors. They're made from ancient terracotta coated with this Sicilian majolica. It's the kind of glaze you see on pottery that makes it look like glass. It's how the floors would have been hundreds of years ago in this region. She wanted to preserve the history of this place, and the influence of the different cultures on this island. Especially for the Baldamentis."

"Who?"

"The Battaglia family lineage traces back to the Baldamentis. They were the Sicilians who owned this region at one time. Very influential family on my father's, mother's side."

"Oh."

"Do you like the floors? Nice eh?"

"It's okay," Mira said. Giovanni pulled her closer. He forced her to wrap her arm around his waist and placed his across her shoulders. He kissed the top of her head as if she was the one that needed forgiveness. The man was willfully confused. They walked through the spacious halls and rooms of their new home. It was by far more charming than the place Lorenzo kept in Bellagio. The furnishing had an Indian and Moroccan feel to it—old and new mixed together in a comfortable arrangement of sofa chairs and hand carved end tables. And though it was only two stories, as opposed to four like Melanzana, the villa had huge open archways and rooms with wide windows. Natural light flooded in from every angle.

In Villa Mare Blu one room led straight to a zen garden. The flow of running water out of a marble carved fountain in the likeness of a Greek goddess was very calming. Mira wondered what happened when it rained. She figured the awnings with Spanish influenced shingles most likely kept any rain from pouring inside.

"Bella, there are two bedrooms down here. There's a sitting room that leads to the gardens, entertainment rooms, and a full dining room. There are six more rooms upstairs. Ours is the largest. In ours there is a belvedere off of our bedroom where we can dine alone if you want. And a large bathroom with a shower you will like."

"Mmhm," she replied.

"This is the kitchen. We only have one. See the brick oven for cooking the rolls you and Zia love to make?" Giovanni asked. Alone with him she shrugged off his hold and turned with her arms crossed.

"Who is Carmella?" she asked.

Giovanni's brows lowered with concern. He studied her as if she were crazy for even asking. He shifted Eve in his arms and turned as if he was going to dismiss her question.

"You heard me!" Mira said. "Is *she* the reason why you were so excited to come here? What is she to you? Your *goumada!*" Mira shouted. She yelled the accusation so loud her throat hurt under the strain. "I saw you. Embarrassing me in front of everyone by kissing her!"

"I don't have time for this shit!" he passed Eve off on her. To her surprise he walked out. Mira stood there unsure of her next move. Did she chase after him, or let him go? Mostly Giovanni tolerated her angry outbursts, but he rarely walked out on a fight. She started to go after him when Cecilia walked into the kitchen.

"*Donna?* Are you okay? I heard you yell."

Mira realized tears had slipped down her cheeks. She felt the burn of shame and tried to hide her face. "No. I'm not okay. I'm tired. I feel funny."

"Do you want me to go get—"

"Leave him alone," Mira said. She held Eve as best she could but her daughter felt as if she grew an inch on the flight. And Eve made the effort worse. She kept kicking Mira in her stomach as she fidgeted to be put down to explore her new surroundings.

"Here, let me take her." Cecilia reached for Eve who looked relieved to have her offer. "I can get her changed for lunch. Sophia told me to tell you she's prepared a nice meal for us."

Mira glanced around the kitchen at the covered dishes and

realized she was hungry. She'd go upstairs and splash water on her face. That usually calmed her. And then she'd find Giovanni and apologize for her outburst. "Where's my room?"

"I'd be happy to show you." Carmella volunteered. She had apparently been watching them silently from the door.

"No thanks," Mira replied.

The women stared. Mira didn't have the energy or tolerance needed to pretend at civility. She wanted Carmella out of her home immediately but first she needed some air. "I'll find the room myself."

"I know where it is. I've been here before," Rosetta volunteered. She too had appeared from the other entranceway into the kitchen. Mira felt a sense of relief. Rosetta was the best person next to Catalina that Mira trusted. She followed her to the stairs. She could hear Giovanni shouting at one of his men about something. She made sure to avoid her husband. She was too embarrassed. Had the entire villa heard her accusations? Maybe that's why Carmella, Rosetta, and Cecilia all stared at her the way they did. Thankfully the stairs were to the back instead of the front of the villa.

When she finally reached her room she was in tears. Something was wrong with her. She knew it. The crying wasn't the worst of it. Her anxiety consumed her. She was coming apart. Giovanni tried to make light of it but she knew they couldn't go on like this for much longer.

Mira sat on the bed. She missed Fabiana. With her best friend her anxiety attacks were only about the latest line of clothes she'd send down the runway, or Kei's pressure to marry. They'd sip wine and talk her through the stress. Her mood swings were blamed on an artist's temperament. Kei and Fabiana used to joke that she was worse than a toddler when stressed. It dawned on her that she'd felt this hopelessness before. She cried often and slipped into the black void of depression when she was pregnant with Eve. But that was to be expected since Fabiana was dead and she believed at the time that Giovanni was lost to her. Now the friendships she had with Kei and Fabiana had ended. And she felt so guilty over the loss. If she had never come to Italy maybe things would have been different.

New York, New York - 1988

"There! Right there! There he is!" Fabiana waved her hand above the heads of the others dining in Le Cheriee from their corner

table. She'd chosen a trendy sidewalk French cafe not far from their office, where ladies lunched, and businessmen cut deals. Mira hated the exposure. She cringed inwardly. Fabiana could always be counted on to make a scene, she thought with the cut of her eyes.

The hostess saw Fabiana's wave and started toward them. The young statuesque woman with dark Hershey brown skin wore a slimming tight black mini dress and a trendy auburn red pageboy haircut that made her quite striking. She strutted toward them on stilts for legs. Mira wondered if the young woman ever considered runway modeling. Teddy strolled behind the hostess, trailing drool. His gaze was glued to the young girl's ass. Mira shook her head.

"Teddy! Teddy! Over here!"

"Would you stop?" Mira grabbed Fabiana's arm and forced it down. Her best friend immediately snatched away with a tight grin. Mira knew that look. She couldn't chastise Fabiana like a child. She wouldn't tolerate it.

Mira tried to explain her concern in a calm manner. "I would appreciate it if you don't bring attention to our table. We're trying to be discreet," Mira said. They dined on the outside patio as many New Yorkers did on a lovely sunny day.

"Oh girl, no one recognizes you. Stop being so uptight." Fabiana tossed the words at her in such a dismissive manner that the truth stung. Her friend glanced up in that moment and read the anger Mira knew blazed in her eyes. Fabiana combed her fingers back through her scarlet red hair moving her bangs from her face. "I only meant you need to loosen up, Mira. Please. We haven't seen Teddy in weeks."

Mira thought to remind Fabiana of the two autographs she signed when they first arrived at the place, or the reporter eating inside of the restaurant from the New Yorker, but she decided not to. She was in no mood to argue. Theodore Tate was their attorney and closest friend and he was here after being abroad. They called him Teddy, or Teddy Bear. When they first met him they almost fired him before capitalizing on his talents. He had hit on both of them repeatedly. Now they knew it was just part of his playboy charm. Another reason she kept him and Kei apart. Kei had a jealous streak that could end the partnership in a flash. Considering Kei was a large investor in her company she had to defer to his wishes as her boyfriend and as a businessman. Thankfully Teddy had agreed to meet with them today. He'd just returned from Sicily, and Mira worried about how exhaustive the long flight was for him.

The young hostess stopped and gestured for Theodore to sit. He gave her a sly wink that made the woman blush before he took a seat.

"Sorry I'm late," Teddy said, in a smooth cool manner that was all him. "Hi beautiful. What's with the sunglasses?"

Before Mira could answer him Fabiana plucked the sunglasses from her face. "She's hiding and it's ridiculous!"

"Stop it, give them back," she hissed.

Fabiana put the pair in her purse, well out of reach.

"You're really working my nerves." Mira sighed in defeat.

Fabiana laughed, winked, and then sipped her pink martini.

Teddy chuckled.

Mira didn't share in the humor.

"Did I miss something?" Teddy asked Mira. "What has you in a mood?"

"Tell him. He's been in Sicily. He doesn't know. Tell him!" Mira insisted. Her heart hurt. Kei held her all night while she cried in his arms. Fabiana listened patiently as she paced the floor and ranted over the injustice. That bitch Susie Chu wrote a scathing review of her show during New York Fashion Week. She could barely lift her head. She felt like screaming.

"I already know about the review. And it wasn't that bad. In fact that's why I wanted to meet," Teddy said.

"Hear him out, Mira," Fabiana nodded.

"Wasn't that bad?" Mira asked, tears blurred her vision but she glared at Teddy and then Fabiana in disbelief. "She called my line, that I slaved on for a year, 'an amateurish rip off of the house of Gucci'." Mira used air quotes on the words as Susie Chu did in her write up. "Carole Montague said it was proof that originality is extinct in the industry as long as house of Mirabella's doors are open. Now, you tell me what designer comes out against a peer and demoralizes them in public? I'm humiliated. My work is nothing like Gucci. It's slander! I ought to sue both those bitches!"

"Oh please! Get off the cross. You aren't being persecuted here," Fabiana said. "This is business. Carole and Susie have an agenda. Every other critic salivated over your work. I already got a call in from Vogue, who want to run your couture line instead of Montague's."

It was the first time Mira had heard the news. She frowned at Fabiana who grinned in return. "Surprise!" Fabiana said. "You big baby!"

Mira put her hand to her mouth. "Seriously?"

"Yes girl! One critic gives you a scathing review and it

dismisses the others that loved you? Fuck them!" Fabiana said.

"Fabiana!" Mira glanced at the few people who now looked over at their table.

"FUCK THEM," Fabiana shouted with the toss of her hair. "Now. Stop your whiney-pity-party-anxiety-fit-bullshit. Teddy has news."

"Wait? That's not the good news?" Mira laughed.

Teddy and Fabiana stared at her. There was something else. Something big. When the two of them conspired together it always meant a big change for Mira. This is why she trusted them both with her life.

Mira sucked down a deep breath. She scanned the others around them. No one was staring. Hell no one cared. She felt foolish for her behavior over the past two days. Teddy reached across the table and touched her hand. "I do have news."

"Okay. What is it?" Mira asked

"Italy!" Teddy announced.

"What about Italy?" Mira asked.

"Milano is where a talent like yours needs to be. What you need is to be inspired. Free of entanglements. I know you and Kei are not seeing eye-to-eye. I know you want to cut off his financial backing and strike out on your own. Strike now. Move to Italy."

Stunned she sat back. She looked over to Fabiana and saw her face already flushed with excitement. "We can't move to Italy. It'll take us years to pay back what we owe Kei if we sever business with him. And I am in a relationship with the man. Or have you forgotten?"

"Tell her Teddy. Tell her the rest."

He nodded his head. "I met a man Mira. His name is Marsuvio Mancini. He's a fan of yours. He wants to sponsor a visa for you to open up a store in Napoli. And he's willing to put up capital."

Mira laughed. Fabiana glanced over to Teddy and they exchanged puzzled looks. "You want me to cut my boyfriend out of my business and get in debt with some strange man you met in Italy?"

"No. He's Sicilian, and he's no different than any other investor. His sponsorship will make you self reliant, open doors for you. And then we can branch out to Milano. Stand on your own two feet. Make Mirabella's a success your way."

Mira waved him off. "Kei and I have hit a rough patch. But we aren't breaking up. He's been more supportive lately."

"Forget Kei, Mira. This is about you. Us!" Fabiana said. "We

have a year to be ready. And we should. Italy is where it's at. Here's the plan. We do the Vogue shoot. Get a lot of good press going. We'll definitely get a top pick celebrity for the Oscars. I promise you that. And then we buy back Kei's shares. This is your way to be truly independent."

"I thought Paris is where it's at?" Mira said.

"You know this is good for us. Teddy and I will fly to Napoli and Milano to check everything out. We will meet with some attorneys there. I'll check out this Mancini guy too. Right, Teddy? Make sure he's legit. Nothing is guaranteed," Fabiana said.

"Mancini is a good business man. No worries there. I'll handle him personally." Teddy quickly interjected. "He has a lot of power in Sicily and influence with the Italian Parliament. This is a great idea."

Mira sucked down a deep breath. Lately Kei had started talking marriage again. Talk of marriage, kids, and domestic bliss made her nervous. They'd separated twice over arguing the future of their relationship and she knew if she rejected him again it was a deal breaker. How could she explain to him why she felt restless, trapped by his smothering love. She needed something to spark her confidence. She needed her independence.

"Okay. Go to Italy and check it out Fabiana. If you two can come back with a good plan I'll... consider it," she exhaled. "I need to think about Kei. I love him. I respect him. I owe him my success."

"Yay!" Fabiana squealed. She picked up her martini glass with the pink vodka sloshing over the rim. "To the future. Love, fashion, hot sexy Italian men, and Mirabella's."

"Cin, Cin!" Teddy laughed. He clinked his water glass to hers. Mira was the last to pick up her soda and join the celebration.

"This is where it began. We'll look back ten years from now and remember this meeting. Remember this day. When we decided to take Mirabella's to Italy," Mira smiled.

"Damn right!" Fabiana cheered. "I can feel it. This is the start of something big."

"Can I get you something?" a soft voice spoke.

Ashamed of her behavior and the tears on her cheeks Mira kept her gaze lowered when she shook her head no. She yielded to the compulsive sobs that shook through her. Fabiana was dead. Her sister was gone. She'd never have anyone as close to her heart again.

Rosetta walked over and sat next to her. "*Donna*, it's okay.

You will like it in Sicily."

"Oh yes. I know." Mira wiped away her tears and forced a smile. "I'm fine." She tried to wave off Rosetta's concern.

"I heard from Renaldo that Catalina will be here tomorrow. Isn't that great? She is going to give us all the updates on the latest in Milano."

Mira rubbed her temples. "That's great."

"Rosetta, *lasciare*," Giovanni said.

Mira glanced up at the sound of his voice. He stood there, filling the inside of the door with his hands in his pockets. Rosetta left without another word. Giovanni closed the door behind her. Though Mira didn't want to argue she forced herself to meet his stare and hold it. It was her husband who blinked first. He wiped his hand down his face in an effort to choose his words wisely. "*Che cosa*? The things you say to me, Bella—"

"I don't think it's wise that we talk right now," Mira said.

"*Che cosa desidera?* Why aren't you happy?" he demanded. "I've done everything in my power to make this special."

"I need a minute. Space!" she shouted.

"Mira." He pointed a warning finger at her. "Enough of this bullshit. You hear me?"

She wept.

Giovanni stood there watching. He didn't speak.

"I can't help it. I can't control it." She put her hands to her face. He walked over to her. She felt him standing in front of her. He stroked the back of her head. "I love you, Giovanni. You're the closest to me, the dearest to me, and you piss me off. I hate myself for these childish tantrums. It's not normal. My pregnancy is no excuse." She lifted her head and looked up at him. "Some days I just don't feel like myself."

"Everyone is ready to have lunch. Can we try civility with each other?" he asked.

"You forgive me?" she sniffed. "For being a bitch?"

"You're my bitch, so what's to forgive?" He lifted her chin and she looked up into his caring eyes. "I can take it, *bambina*. I'll give you a little space before we take a tour of our new home. We'll take a trip down to the beach. How does that sound?"

She blinked. He pinched her chin then let his hand fall away. Before he turned she tossed another question at him. "Who is *she* to you, Giovanni?"

"*Famiglia.* Carmella has been a part of this family for many years, Bella."

Mira held back the urge to challenge his answer. For all she knew the woman was family. He never wavered in his devotion to her. And she's weathered the glares, and snide comments from women outside of the family who didn't like the idea of his black American wife. But Carmella felt different.

He extended his hand. "Lunch? *Cara mia Mirabella*, you are the only woman for me."

"I'm better," she said softly. "It won't happen again."

"We need to celebrate not argue. *Per favore?*"

Tears blinded her eyes and choked her voice. She swallowed, and then forced a smile. "I feel better. Really."

He kissed her brow. "That's my girl."

They rejoined the family together. The meal was served out under the noonday sun on the terrace that faced a garden. The coastal winds flowing in over them kept the temperature of the day mild and cozy. Giovanni pulled out the chair for her. Mira's gaze swept all that were gathered. Carmella wasn't among them.

"Cin Cin!" Giovanni said with the raise of his glass. Everyone silenced for the announcement of a toast. Glasses rose. Giovanni turned his attention to her. "To my Bella, at last she returns to *Sicilia. Salute.*"

The toast felt odd as did his insistence on her loving Sicily. He acted as if the island, the culture, the people were a part of her. Why would that be so important to him? She had her own identity, and she was proud of who she was and where she was from. First he wanted her kids born here, and now he tried to force the same connection on her.

Mira smiled at her husband and blew him a kiss to appease him.

Sophia served them from the kitchen with the help of Rosetta. Before long Mira had all but forgotten her anxiety, and the ache in her heart for Fabiana subsided. She fed Eve and listened to Giovanni and the men swap stories of their childhood or family memories. Every man in Giovanni's inner circle was Sicilian or so they claimed. Mira had no real way of knowing.

After an hour of celebrating she felt the need to walk not sit. She scooted her chair back and stood to go help Sofia in the kitchen. She figured she'd make peace with Carmella being in the house. Besides the woman was of no threat. However, in the kitchen she found Sophia with Cecilia fixing pies. Carmella wasn't present. Sophia looked up and smiled. She came over to her. She wiped her hands on her apron and her eyes shifted from Mira to the door she entered.

"*Donna*? Do you need anything?"

"No. I just thought I'd offer to help," Mira said. Zia always encouraged Mira to join her in the kitchen. And when Zia left Mira oversaw every meal served to the family. Giovanni wouldn't eat unless she prepared his plate herself.

"*Perdono*. We will have the desert out in a moment," Sophia said. Mira liked the kindness in her eyes. But she sensed a tense weariness in Sophia's tone.

"Oh no worries. The men are still feasting on what you prepared. It's really good."

"Go join them," Sophia shooed her to leave. "We have it."

Mira turned to leave. She stopped and glanced back at Sophia. "Where's Carmella?"

Sophia refused to look at her when she answered. She busied herself at the stove. "Giovanni sent her back to Palermo. She's to not return while you're here."

"He said that?" Mira asked.

"*Sí. Non problemo*. She has work to do at home. I apologize if she did anything to offend to you." Sophia glanced up. So did Cecilia. The women stared at her, reading her discomfort. Mira felt a hot flash of shame raise the temperature in her neck and cheeks. She didn't mean to banish the woman. *Or did she?* When she pushed her husband he pushed back at anyone standing between them. She nodded her head at Sophia and walked out. When she returned to the table Giovanni was caught up in another tale again. She sat next to him and smiled. It was true, she felt better already.

* B *

To set aside his business responsibilities was not easily done. Upon his arrival to Sicily he received three requests from local men of importance to meet. Giovanni would see no one. It was customary that he pay a visit to the Mancinis. That tradition would be abandoned as well. He closed his mind to the matter. He was in Sicily to help his wife, and every sacrifice along the way was worth it. Helping her regain control of her emotions and to relax during the final stage of her pregnancy would be his top priority.

Time ticked on. Giovanni sipped his wine and stared out at the garden. The villa had settled into the calm that typically crept in over the island at sunset. Dark shadows stretched about him and he relaxed in the shade. He felt soul weary the past few weeks.

"I'm ready," she said from behind him.

Giovanni turned his gaze back over his left shoulder. She stood there smiling. She had changed into a maternity dress with soft pink, lavender, green, and yellow colors connecting in intricate designs. She made these dresses for him and her. The low cut front tied around her neck and separated her enlarged breasts, giving a lift to flatter her expanding curves. The hem was long but an opening along the right revealed thigh and leg when she moved.

Mira lifted a pair of flat thong sandals with one hand and fancy high-heel shoes in the other with a sweet smile. "Which one?"

He stood and pointed at the flats.

"I should have known you would make this choice. You don't like me to wear heels anymore."

"I want you comfortable. Those look comfortable. I'll be barefoot."

"Huh?" Mira laughed.

Giovanni kicked off his loafers. He knelt and folded his pants just above his ankles. "There! Now I'm comfortable!" He stood and threw up his hands.

Mira shook her head with a smile that melted his heart. It was too easy to get lost in her smile.

"I see."

"What do you see, Bella?" he asked.

"We must not be going far." She dropped her thong sandals before her feet and tossed the other pair of shoes aside. She eased her foot in one then the other. And then she extended her hands to him. He walked over and captured her hands, bringing them both up to his mouth to kiss.

"Where are we going? To the beach?" she asked.

"We're going somewhere more private," he replied.

"I guessed that," she chuckled.

"My wife is so smart."

"Yes I am, thank you very much. Plus you mentioned it earlier remember?"

"I did. Why did you pretend to not know?" he asked.

"To keep you on your toes. Besides you also mentioned making love under the stars. I figured we'd go somewhere to make that happen instead of the lumpy sand on the beach. You know I'm not as limber as I once was."

"Let me worry about how limber you can be. Come." He pulled her behind him with her hand in his. And he was careful of his pace. He'd learned to shorten his stride and choose his steps where she could follow him. They walked out of the east side of the villa. There was an open trail that went downward toward the gates of the property. He could see his men in the distance. He could hear the sea in the wind and the sea birds as they sailed across a sunset sky. He glanced back at her. She smiled with bright enthusiasm glittering in her eyes.

"This end of the beach is private. You want to take walks? Bring Evie out here, you can. I have men covering it," Giovanni boasted. He glanced back at his man posted. Maybe he'd bring in a few more of the men to ensure the beach stayed cleansed of Mancini vermin.

"This place is beautiful," she said.

He slowed so she could walk at his side. Once they passed Renaldo they started left. He felt her hesitation. *"Problemo?"*

"I thought we were going to—"

He stopped. She looked out of the clearing to what was before them.

"This is my surprise, Bella."

A wooden square shaped house with a flat roof. It stood three feet off the sand by the aid of wooden posts. The front of the beach house had a wide plank, which stretched out to the lapping waters of the shore.

"It's a beach villa?" she asked.

"My father and Rocco built it when they were kids. There are other smaller villas closer to Villa Mare Blu where the men will sleep. But this is the only one sitting on the edge of the sea. They used it as a fishing house. Lorenzo and I renovated it years ago. It's my escape."

"So it's abandoned?" she asked.

"Nothing we own is abandoned. It's ours for the night. I'll take you there next," he replied.

"Next?"

"Let's walk on the beach. Are you up for it?" he asked.

"Sure," she said.

They strolled for a moment before he pointed out to the ocean. "Look." The sun was a huge orange globe. She'd noticed it before. However, it now slowly neared the edge of the sea. Light faded from the sky. Darkness descended on them fast. The remaining light streaked across the heavens with vibrant colors of magenta and purple. Its reflection shimmered across the rolling waves of the ocean. The sun eased into the water and the day was extinguished.

"Wow. That is something. It's really beautiful," she said.

They continued to walk in the sand, feet sinking with each step. When they got as close to the waves to rush in over their feet he stepped behind her and held her belly with one hand while squeezing her breast with the other. The round cushion of her thick ass brushed up against his groin. He buried his face in her hair and inhaled her scent. He felt his arousal quicken over the touch and smell of her. He knew to reign in that urgent lust. "I'd come here with my mother and watch the sun set when I was a young boy."

"She liked this beach?" Mira asked. She moved his hand down from her breast so they both could hold her belly. Immediately he felt one or both of his son's kick. They stilled when he applied a little pressure like good babies. Mira relaxed into his frame. Sometimes at night he'd experience a little bump or tap to his back as she slept with her belly pressed into him. He'd turn over and touch her. Make her comfortable. He'd whisper to his sons to give her a break. And they always did. He relaxed and gave in to his deepest feelings for her.

I love this woman. A lifetime of bullshit and finally I have what I never wanted since the loss of my sweet mama. The purest love. What if I had never met her? What if our fathers hadn't commited their sins? I'd give it all up for her, for my children, without hesistation.

"Tell me about your mother. Why she liked this beach," she asked and his thoughts blew away with the sea wind. He was with her again. Focused on the moment and not the emotion. He had to firm his voice when he spoke to keep from her how enticed by emotion he was to be weak.

"My mother had two things in life that gave her happiness, her children and her faith. Here she believed she was closer to God." His hands slipped from her belly to her hips.

The sun was gone. There was barely light left in the sky. Giovanni took her hand and together they started toward the private beach villa. He helped her climb the five steps before he reached in his pocket to dig out the key. She waited patiently as he unlocked the door made of weathered wood, and he pushed it open with a loud creak that echoed their arrival.

"Aspetti un momento," Giovanni told her to wait. He entered first, which was customary.

Mira peeked inside as he went about turning on lights and checking the rooms. He wore a gun tucked to the back of his pants but he never removed it. She guessed the pre-search of the place was to make sure it was set to his liking.

"*Avanti, Bella,*" he called out from somewhere inside to tell her to come in.

The sweet smell of rosemary greeted her when she entered. The fragrance accompanied the polishing the beach cabin had undergone. Its mix made her light headed. She tried not to inhale deeply. The walls, floors, all were dark wood. The furnishings were simple. Most of the chairs were made of wicker with large cranberry red pillows for sitting.

"It's nice. I like it," she said.

"The door, it's the bedroom." He tilted his chin toward it. She knew his meaning. She walked over and pushed it open wider. The bed made her gasp with surprise. It wasn't high off the floor, which meant she would need help lowering to it and rising from it, but it was huge. It consumed the majority of the space in the room. A sheer white drape covered it from all corners. It hung like that of a tent from an iron chandelier with five pointed hooks. Disbelief and wonder seared through her. On the nightstands placed on either side of the bed sat lanterns. The tall flames flickered behind the murky casing. It's luminance provided a very romantic, golden candle glow. Giovanni walked over to the left. He waited for her to look his way before he pulled aside the curtain to reveal a wall of glass that gave an expansive view of the sea. He flipped on the outside light and Mira stepped forward. Giovanni released the latch to the center of the glass and she soon realized it wasn't a window but a door. He had to slide the left pane over to the far left, and the right glass pane to the right. In doing so the night air, and Mediterranean warmth custom to Sicily poured in.

All the beauty of this beach villa had coalesced into the serenity the scene before her brought. Mira walked out to the open deck and stopped before a long wicker lounge chair. It was huge enough for three to recline in. It too was cushioned with the same plush cranberry red pillows as the ones inside the beach house.

"I love it," she said and her gaze lifted to the stars. So many stars crowded the sky. She felt as if she were trapped in a planetarium under a dome view of celestial majesty. Mira had never seen a night so perfect. Her hand rested on the swell of her belly and she could feel her sons settle inside of her. She had a name for this beach house, for their special place.

"We should call this place Serenity."

Giovanni dimmed the outside light on the deck so the stars and sea could be seen with even more clarity.

"I like that name," Giovanni said.

She stood there with the wind in her hair, and closed her eyes.

"This is our place. No one can come here but you and me," Giovanni said.

"And Carmella? Did you share this place with her?" Mira asked.

To see his Bella jealous was a new experience. It never dawned on him that she would ever consider any other woman a rival. She was his wife. It went against everything he believed in, to forsake their vows, to be with a woman other than his wife. So he dealt with the situation. He sent Carmella away the moment he realized the reason for Mira's attitude change. What he shared with Carmella happened when they were kids and ended badly—thanks to Armando Mancini. He hadn't touched her since they were teens. Though he knew the rumors that reached all the way to Sorrento said differently.

"Carmella has never shared a bed with me in Villa Mare Blu or Melanzana. I won't lie to you, Bella. This place has seen a lot of my bad days. It wasn't built for 'serenity'."

"I understand, but she lives here," Mira said. "In Villa Mare Blu? By your request. Before me, she... was here to take care of you when you visited?"

"Ask the question you mean," he replied.

"You already know what I mean, Giovanni," she replied.

"I wouldn't disrespect you, or our marriage by bringing you around another woman I desired."

Mira stared at him with those round brown eyes he lost his soul to. A slow wry smile tipped the corner of her mouth and she nodded her head in agreement. At last the woman was completely reassured. *Great!* He tired of the matter and wouldn't discuss it further. Giovanni stepped back and his gaze swept her once more. He had made a good decision to bring her here, to give them this privacy. And that summer dress made her radiant. It tied at the back of her neck. The design of the dress kept the fabric cradling her breasts from drifting loose. So he decided to start there. Undressing her was always for his pleasure and his privilege.

"Vegna qui," he extended his hand and told her to come to him. She did. They faced each other. He needed to be inside of her. To have her soft thighs wrapped around him while he plunged every inch of his love into her sweet tightness. He needed to hear her call his name and swear at him when their loving became too much. Out of all the changes his Bella endured in her pregnancy her sexual desires had increased.

When he reached behind her neck Mira leaned in to brush a kiss over his collarbone. She rested her face on his chest. Time and space faded. They were simply husband and wife now. Her face lifted. Her gaze held his as he slowly untied the dress. The front bodice fell away to reveal her breasts. "I'm silly for being paranoid about her, huh? I just—"

He kissed her.

"Enough of that shit. She's gone. I don't want to discuss it anymore," he said.

"Okay." She rose on her toes and wrapped her arms around his neck. Love plucked his heart and his brief irritation with questions about Carmella subsided. She brushed her plump lips over his and they kissed. Her breath seeped into his mouth, sliding along a sigh. With a mastered tease she enticed his tongue to explore deeper. He sealed her mouth with his and stroked his tongue inside. The kiss felt surprisingly gentle. Ravishment of his Bella would be reserved for later in the evening. She tickled the roof of his mouth with the tip of her tongue. Her submission sent the pit of his stomach into a swirl. Giovanni worked the dress from her body and each layered piece drifted to her feet. There he stood in bare feet, and she naked with her sandy feet.

Sex had evolved into a careful exploration of good and better experiences between them. Bella's favorite was the leapfrog position, a name she gave it. Often she lowered to her knees with his help, and rested her elbows on the edge of the bed while he fucked her on his knees from behind. Strange as it was he had to agree he liked the rhythm and pace. There were several other positions. But his favorite is where they would start tonight.

He led her inside.

She began to unbutton his shirt.

"The wall, Bella," he whispered in her ear. He'd keep her pinned there for the rest of the night. She glanced back at the wall and then at him. Her hands stopped fiddling with the buttons. She placed them to her curvy hips. He looked at the line of her body and his gaze lingered on the beautiful perfection that was her breasts.

"The wall huh? We did that one the other day. And you bit me on the back of my shoulder."

"I always bite you," he pinched her nipple.

"What if I had another position in mind?" she stepped closer.

The wall position had her facing it with her hands pressed flat and legs spread. Though it required they remain on their feet through the act of sex she was fully open to him and able to move her ass to match his thrusts.

"It's my night after all," she reminded him.

"Is that so?"

Mira glanced back at the wall once more. When his pants were off the wait would be over. Bella should make up her mind quick. And she did. She walked around him to yank the throw blanket from the bed. Giovanni kicked off his pants. Mira wrapped the blanket around her shoulders and walked over to the light switch that illuminated the deck. The moonlight was bright enough. She tossed a challenging look back over her shoulder at him and then strolled out of the room to the deck that faced the sea. The temperature was warm enough for an adventure but cool enough for the blanket. "You know what I like," she said, and pointed to the chair.

Giovanni's smile deepened. He sat down upon the large wicker deck chair with the long plush pillows that extended his legs. He reached up to help her ease on to his lap. She gazed down at him with that soft dreamy look on her face that spoke to her innocence. Not in the literal sense. She was innocent to deception, manipulation; to the ways women often controlled their husbands. Their life was all about mutual love. And though she grew every day, and her temperament shifted with the wind, she always made time to please him. Make him feel honored to be her husband.

Bella accepted his help. She did so with a determined crease to her brow. Giovanni adjusted the blanket around her shoulders to cover her backside from the elements of the night. The moonlight reflected all around them. Mira rose on her knees with a hand braced to his shoulder for support. She fisted his erection. He gasped at how tight her hold was. He didn't complain. The determined set to her jaw and sideways bite of her tongue as she angled him looked so cute. Giovanni swallowed a smile; afterall his wife was not doing this for amusement. And when the delicious tingles hit the head of his cock as it brushed the damp folds of her pussy, he was reminded of that fact.

Without warning she sank on his dick and his mind went blank. All urgent sensation skyrocketed through his pelvis and seized the breath in his lungs. He lost all sensibility. Her cunt clinched around his shaft. Intense pleasure shivered down his spine. Thanks to the semi-recline of the deck chair and the sturdy wood it was made from, the balance and comfort was there. Her belly rested against his chest. Her thick nipples pointed at his mouth. He licked the circumference of one and then teased it into his mouth as he desperately tried to hold back a premature climax.

"Mmm, so good, baby," she stroked the back of his head and moved up and down on his dick. "You like that?"

"Yes… move that pussy," he groaned.

He gripped her hip and aided her rhythm. She had a mercilessly wet tightness that enslaved him. He clenched his jaw as pure ecstasy spasms rocked through his pelvis and gripped him by the balls. She rode him with a front to back and then up and down lap dance. Tension spiraled through his loins and it felt so good. He released her nipple to lick the sweat between her breasts. He buried his face between. He'd cum all over them if he had her in bed. They'd move the sex play there next.

"You feel so good, honey," Mira panted hard. It felt as if her lungs couldn't capture enough air to keep her heart beating. The blanket slipped from her shoulders and gathered to her hips. Every muscle in her vagina ached, and she twisted her hips to decrease the coiled knot of tension low in her pelvis. Giovanni gripped her by both buttocks. He helped with the frequency of her rise and fall on his dick. It felt like raw steel slammed up into her core. The cool ocean breeze washed over her feverish spine. But nothing could cool the friction of his pistoning cock ramming up in her with increased velocity. "Fuck! Oh fuck!" Mira gasped. She gripped the top of the chair for support.

A mistake.

When Giovanni was this caught up in their lovemaking, shoving her tender breasts in his face guaranteed painful consequences. And he went for them. She lowered her face and kissed his creased brow prompting him to suck and kiss her breasts harder. The sharp nips and sucks had her jerking and wheezing. The solid ridge of his penis pushed further up into her. "Yes, baby," she encouraged him. "Oh yes!"

He released a muffled groan, continuing to suck on her breasts. Giovanni pumped his dick up into her and rolled his hips to deliver each measured strike with precision. His powerful body, strong hands, and muscular chest forced her to take his cock the way he intended. Rapture devoured her gut.

"Gio, baby, please slow down!" she cried out.

He didn't slow the pace, and despite her plea neither could she. With each drive of his hips she felt her control shatter. She knew he was trying to prolong their pleasure before he came apart, but her bottom maneuvers increased and he lost the battle.

"Fuck yes!" he roared, after he released her breast.

He gripped both sides of her hips and raised her a fraction, holding her above. He then thrust upward in a slightly different angle and Mira's pussy spasms sent a seizure that strangled the breath from her lungs. Mira gasped. Her head dropped back. From his protective embrace he fucked her in a cherished way and nothing compared to the shared bliss of their joined release. A trillion stars gleamed as they'd done through the millennia. Wet heat exploded from her pussy and his glide in and out of her as he climaxed, spreading joy and pleasure all the way to her brain. She felt her mind melt. She felt her muscles go rigid. She felt herself drift and disappear.

★ B ★

"*Quando?* What time did he land?"

Armando stared across his desk at his *capu*, a short, long nosed fellow with a wicked scar on his chin, he was one of his most loyal enforcers. He went by the name of Mario. Often when you expected him to fuck up he didn't. And when you counted on Mario to deliver on the simplest tasks, he fumbled.

"Around noon today. He's returned to Villa Mare Blu. He and that wife of his."

If Giovanni came for a holiday it didn't explain the disrespect. Men in his world knew it was customary to reach out to the Mancinis when travelling or visiting their region of *Sicilia*. The thin truce between the Battaglias and Mancinis held strong because of common courtesy. Nearly six months ago Giovanni arrived for a visit and Armando's father was sick with rage afterwards. But no explanation of the reasons for the visit was shared with Armando. He closed his hand into a tight fist.

"Giovanni has about four of his top men with him. We believe—"

"The arrogant son-of-a-bitch is never unprepared. You don't know what he has." Armando spat the words with distaste. "Stay on top of the Battaglias' movements."

Mario nodded. There was no time for Armando to unleash his frustration. In fact he really had little time for Giovanni. He was deeply troubled by the one request his father was adamant he fulfill. Armando left his office and bounded up the stairs to his father's room. The Mancini estate had been in his family for nearly four hundred years. It had burned down in the 1920s and was rebuilt to a grand state. No matter how big and empty the villa was, Armando loved, protected, and lorded over it. Family and tradition were the bedrock of his devotion.

The hall was empty, dark, silent. He walked toward the room with a photo envelope in his hand. At the door he paused. It took him four long months to dig up the information his father needed. And still he was no closer to understanding the reasons why. He wanted answers.

Armando knocked.

"*Avanti*. Come in," rasped the elder Mancini.

Armando entered to find his father sitting on the side of the bed. The old man stared out at the gardens beyond his room window. The dinner that was served in his room sat cooling on the tray. He'd heard from his aunts that his father wasn't eating.

"What do you have for me, boy?" Mancini asked, without looking over to acknowledge him.

"Shouldn't you be on your oxygen, Papa?" Armando replied.

Mancini turned his cold glare toward him. Armando felt his courage shrivel under that withering stare. His father in his younger days could be cruel and punishing for the slightest infraction. Even now one look of disappointment from him and Armando felt like a six year old boy hiding in his room afraid of Mancini's belt. Throughout Marsuvio Mancini's illness he had moments of strength that reminded all of them that he was still *Don* of Palermo.

"What do you have for me?" Mancini asked again.

"I need answers, Papa. This has gone on far enough. I—" Armando cleared his throat. "Isabella is in Hong Kong. My sources say she's been there for two months. She's set to travel back to Sicily soon. I believe."

"Hong Kong." His father repeated the word slow as if trying to process the meaning.

"My question, Papa. You've asked me… You've put a hit on your own daughter. My sister."

Mancini gave a cruel, wicked smile. It was as if the accusation filled his father with pride instead of shame. "That *puttana* is not your sister or my daughter. And she will rot in a desecrated grave before I am dead."

"Why? You raised her, and she raised me when you went off to America and left me with Mama. She—"

"To hell with the whore! She's dead I say!" his father coughed, hacked, wheezed. He grabbed the oxygen mask and put it up to his mouth. Armando tossed the folder to the bed and hurried to turn up the dial on the tank that was out of his father's reach. The release of more air to fill his father's weak lungs stopped the coughing attack. Mancini nodded that he felt better. His father was the strongest man Armando had ever known. Even in his weakened state he believed in his father's strength.

Mancini reached for the folder. Armando watched him curiously and then spoke. "You wanted photos of the black woman Lorenzo has been with. We found them. I had a man take pictures of them in St. Tropez and it was expensive, Papa. Lorenzo Battaglia has been very hard to keep up with."

"Did he suspect?" Mancini shot his son a glare. "I told you to be discreet."

"He didn't suspect."

His father inhaled the oxygen with one hand to the mask pressed over his mouth and nose. He used the other shaky hand to remove the images from the folder. Armando studied his father's reaction. Mancini's eyes narrowed, the blood drained from his already pasty pale face. Armando lowered his gaze down to Lorenzo's woman. She was a black woman, with wild curly hair, probably American. Very pretty, if you were into that kind, and Armando wasn't. She wore a bikini on a boat. It looked like she danced with a glass of wine in her hand.

Mancini lowered the mask. "*Marietta? Bella mia,*" Mancini whispered to the image with affection.

"You know her?" Armando asked.

His father traced his finger over the woman's image. Armando thought he saw the makings of a smile on his face. "It's her. I see it. *Mama mia,* I see it." Mancini said. "I've found her. She's alive."

"Who is she?" Armando asked.

Mancini took his time. He shuffled through one image to the next. The last picture showed an excited Lorenzo Battaglia lifting the woman in his arms. She held to his neck and kissed him. That image alone dissolved the smile on his father's face. He actually glared with what Armando thought to be rage. It was only then the dots slowly connected. The day everything changed for his father. It was the day Giovanni visited and Isabella soon after. First Giovanni marries a black woman and now Lorenzo has a black one as a plaything. It was all connected to Isabella and his father somehow.

"Giovanni Battaglia is here. In Mondello?" Mancini asked.

"He and his wife have returned to Villa Mare Blu," Armando answered.

"He brought Mirabella here?" Mancini asked.

"Who? Is that her name? Mirabella?"

Mancini took a deep breath of oxygen before he answered. "Where is Lorenzo? Is he still in France?"

"Those pictures are a few days old. Now that we found him we are tracking him. He's still near France. Papa? You know both of their names. Who are these women to you and Isabella? You have to tell me what's going on."

"These women are the daughters of a friend of mine, from my time in America. And they are in danger with the Battaglias."

Armando listened.

"You find Isabella. And put a bullet in her after you bleed her out, cut her throat first." His father's gaze was leveled and unwavering with murderous intent. "I want Isabella to beg for her life before you end it. I want you to tell her it is on my order that she dies. Do you understand me? Make it your number one priority in life." Mancini looked to the image on the bed. "And then you will bring me Marietta and Mirabella," he smiled. "If Giovanni gets in the way you deal with him too."

"If that's what you want, Papa." Armando started for the door. He fumed silently. The time his father spent in America wasn't a total mystery to him. Isabella had shared things when he was young. She spoke of a black mistress his father had taken up with. Disrespected his mother and the family by making his whore his priority. She even showed him a picture she found in his father's office. He glanced back at Mancini who was again staring at the photos of Lorenzo and the one he called Marietta. If these women were the daughters of that American cunt who made his mother weep for years then he'd gladly kill them too. Armando smiled and left his father's room.

Mancini turned to his drawer. He pulled it open. Inside he found a leather binder, worn, tied together by a leather string. He'd had his sister Maria locate it with his things in the attic after he learned that Marietta was alive.

Carefully he untied the leather string and opened the binder. Inside he had a copy of the girls' original birth certificates. He even had their little feet stamped on the back as identification. Twin girls. His little brown baby girls. He also located the old and fading Polaroid of their mother.

"Lisa," he sighed.

November 1964 Philadelphia

"Awww! See that was painless! Now I have a picture of us to keep until you come back." Lisa smiled up at him. *Manny Cigars*

82

wiped the loose tears that glistened on her cheeks. He kissed her nose, her lips, and her brow. He captured her face in both hands and pressed his brow to hers, closing his eyes for strength. She dropped the Polaroid camera and photo. Her slender short arms wrapped around his neck. Her lips upon his restored his faith. It wasn't the end. He'd find a way to have her and honor his father's wishes. She tried to pull him down on her but he refused.

"I can't," Manny said.

The look of hurt over his rejection cut him to the core. What could he say to convince her that it also hurt him to leave? His pride wouldn't allow him to summon the words.

"Manny, why are you doing this?" He tried to turn away. She grabbed his sleeve and forced him to remain at her side. "Take me with you. I won't be any trouble, I promise. I'm clean. I don't use that poison anymore. You said you forgave me. If you go again I'll die."

"You won't. I've already gutted the fucker who put you on that shit."

"Manny—"

"Shhh..." he kissed her. "Stop pleading. The answer is no. I can't take you to Sicily and you know why."

He let her go. She moved off his lap and sat upright, fixed the front of her dress. She cried silently. He hated to see her cry. He pushed up from the sofa and stepped away. He couldn't be next to her. If he was next to her he was weak. And Manny Cigars was anything but weak. Not even for a woman.

Lisa stood. She wore a paisley dress and her round tummy was barely defined. Her hair was brushed smooth into a large dark afro puff situated behind her head. "Will you come back this time? Or is this it?" she asked. "For once can you please be honest?"

He wanted to hit something, gut something, crush bone and marrow. Release his frustration anywhere but here. She was backing him into an emotional corner and he hated it. Hated himself for failing her. Hated her for loving him. The situation was killing him. He had no control. "My father has summoned me. I'll go and see to his wishes. And then I will return. We will have twins. Baby girls. Do you think I will abandon my children? Abandon you?"

"I trust you," Lisa said in a sad hollow voice that drew his gaze her way. She stared down at her tummy, ran her hands over the swell. "You're all I have left, Manny. You and my babies. If you say I should stay then I understand. Gemma is going to move in with me. Capriccio will help us." Her gaze lifted to his and he was snared in the pools of love stirring like amber waves in her irises. "But you have to hurry, Manny. Promise me you will be back before our babies are born. Promise me and I will believe you. I'll stay clean. I'll wait for you. And we'll be a family."

He nodded his head. "I promise. With all my heart."

He didn't speak English with anyone but her. Never felt the need to. But with her he practiced and perfected a small vocabulary. He also taught her words of his own. Lisa walked over to him and he opened his arms. He held her and they stared out at the city. He kissed her again only to say goodbye. But with Lisa one kiss could never be enough. His love for her overwhelmed him and before long he was stripping her of her clothes and making love to her. She was so young when he corrupted her, forced his way into her life and made her his. By isolating her and filling her head with lies, something remarkable happened. She gave him her heart, and he discovered he gave her his.

Mancini made the young girl a woman, his woman and no other woman, not even his wife drove passion through him like Lisa. He needed to make love to her once more so he could remember the feeling of this moment. He would be gone for a couple of months. He swore it to himself as he pushed away all doubts.

Melissa woke. She felt her babies kick for the first time. When she turned over to tell Manny he was sleep. She stared at him for a long moment. The man who once scared her, who had caused her so much pain and shame in the past was now her deepest love. She had no future without him. The thought of him not returning was too much for her to bear. She feared her addiction. She feared for her children without his protection.

Melissa drew back the covers and kept her hand protectively over her stomach as she pushed up from the bed. Manny didn't wake. Naked, aching from the sexual healing he put on her heart she tip-toed out of the room.

She found the Polaroid. The one she convinced him to take. Manny didn't like having his picture taken. Most of the men like him didn't. She smiled at the image of them both. Lisa kissed it. She found his suit jacket and stuck it in the pocket. When he got to Sicily this time he wouldn't stay long. This time he'd come back to her and they'd have a normal life. She was clean, drug free, she was even thinking of doing some sewing again. Capriccio told her she could sew and design the costumes the girls who worked the clubs wore.

Her dream was to some day open her own dress shop and design clothes. Everyone told her she was good at it. Gemma especially.

The future had promise.

"What are you doing?" he said behind her.

Lisa looked back at him. "I'm getting your things ready for you. The sooner you leave, the sooner you will come back. Right?"

He stared at her. He didn't answer. She tried to act like it didn't matter. And then a smile broke on his face.

"Ti adoro, sì, nothing and no one will keep me from returning."

Mancini set the Polaroid of Lisa next to the picture of Marietta. He saw his beloved in his daughter clearly. All of these years he believed Marietta was dead. He suffered such guilt and shame for his actions. He abused everyone and everything he loved because of his loss of Lisa and their babies. The past was the past. There was little he could do about it. But he had every intention of changing the future.

He smiled.

"Marietta, I will meet you soon."

4.

Catalina pulled a fresh cotton white shirt down over her head and eased her arms into the sleeves. She then reached for her grey leggings to slip on. The private train car was unusually cold. She wished she had a pair of socks for her feet. The journey was half over. For Catalina there was only a small part of travelling by train that she enjoyed. When the train was disassembled and then rolled on a ferry to cross the Straits of Messina, and then put back together on the other side. It was how one travelled from Italy to Sicily.

When she was a little girl Dominic would be in charge of bringing her to Mondello after she was released for school break. Patri wanted her well learned at an all girls Catholic institution and her mother agreed. She suffered the strict discipline of the church while praying for the day Dominic would come and rescue her.

And he was so handsome too. Barely eighteen, Dominic's long lashes, piercing brown eyes, and boyish charm made Sister Clara smile when he arrived.

Sister Clara never smiled.

At twelve things changed. Catalina began to notice how his handsomeness affected others, especially girls her age. All her friends would gather by the window with her to wait for him to walk up the cobblestone streets and pass through the tall iron gates. It was innocent then. He was her brother. She liked the attention of being *la piccoletta* of the Battaglia family. She bragged to friends that her brothers, Giovanni, Lorenzo, Dominic, and Carlo, would bury anyone who defied her. And that Dominic was her guardian who treated her like a princess. She loved him as a brother, then. But soon it changed in her heart. She loved him as much more.

Often when vacation time came she and Dominic traveled separate from their parents to Mondello, Sicily. Always on a train. Dominic would wake her early in the morning once the train brought them out of Naples through the city of Rome. They would leave the train car and go up on deck while the ferry crossed the straits. It was a unique experience to watch the sunrise. And it might explain why he chose this method of travelling. The train held such sweet memories for them both.

Dominic sat near the window in nothing but his slacks. His jaw was tight and his lips pressed into a thin grim line.

"Domi?"

With no discernable emotion on his face he turned his gaze toward her. She smiled. A half smile crossed his lips to reassure her. Of course he said nothing. When Dominic was deep in thought he rarely shared those thoughts. Catalina put her hands to her hips and studied him further.

Should she force the conversation or give him some space?

Something was off with him. And it sure as hell wasn't their sex life. He nearly broke her back earlier by fucking her on that uncomfortable bunk. He was so full of lust and repressed passion thanks to their short separation. Catalina tolerated the demands he put on her body. The train car they traveled in was larger than most, but sex here felt awkward and impersonal. Dominic returned his gaze to the window. The tiny silver medallion of St. William gleamed from the stainless steel chain around his neck in the darkness, beneath his collarbone.

"*Dica?* You worried about something?" Catalina asked.

When he didn't respond she threw up her hands in defeat. She wouldn't press the issue further. In fact she had something of her own to discuss. The idea of pushing Giovanni for permission to marry had her on edge since they left Milano. It was too soon. She couldn't focus on being a wife when she had so many exciting things happening for her. But how could she explain this to Dominic?

"Come sit with me." Dominic gestured to the bunk he sat on. Catalina walked over and he took her hand to pull her down. She snuggled up against him.

"I'm worried about Gio and Mira," Dominic confessed.

Catalina sat upright. "You are? Why? Something wrong with the baby?"

"No. And it's babies remember?"

Catalina laughed. "How could I forget? Gio brags to everyone about the sons he will have."

Dominic gave a weak smile, and then he chuckled. "Yes. He's happy Catalina. But–"

"But what? Finish." Catalina insisted.

He closed his eyes and dropped his head back with a deep sigh.

"I can't get into it. Never mind it. You know me, I worry about the family constantly. Gio is so stubborn. It's hard to get him to see reason when it comes to his wife."

"But why worry now, Domi? We've been through so much. Now is the time to celebrate. Everyone is happy about the babies, and Mira has her company back. Why worry?"

"Because Gio is strongest when we all are." Dominic interjected. "Lately I've felt a disconnection in the family. We are cast to the wind now. You in Milano, Lorenzo gone, me splitting my time between the *Campania* and business in the triangle, this is not what's best for us." He brought her hand up to his lips and kissed her knuckles. "It's good that we will return to *Sicilia* and spend time with the family these next few months. We all need this."

Catalina measured her response. She knew her working away from him became tiring, but they were never apart for longer than a few days or weeks. "I understand. But, Domi we're changing. And that makes us strong." She touched the tiny silver St. William medallion he wore on his neck. She kissed it. "Don't worry. We're going to be okay because you always see to it."

Dominic nodded and returned his gaze to the night outside of the window. No matter how she tried to soothe him she knew he doubted her faith. Maybe now wasn't a good time to tell him she wanted to move to Milan. No. She'd keep that to herself for the time being.

* B *

Near Sainte Maxime, Southern France –

Lorenzo could not look away. Marietta danced across *Le Femme* with her eyes trained on him. She wore a bright tangerine orange mini dress. The low neckline to the front of the dress reached her navel and parted her voluptuous breast. The dress hugged her curvaceous figure and rose up her shapely thighs when she wound her hips. It revealed her flawless slender brown legs with diamonds sparkling off her left ankle. Above her light beams spun and cast red, yellow, and blue rays across the dancefloor. Flashes of color washed over the gyrating bodies on the dance floor. Smoke clouded the atmosphere of the club. A thick white curl of it rolled out of his nostrils after a drag of his cigar. All the while he never lost track of his Marietta.

She knew the rules.

At any club of her choosing Marietta could dance for as long as she pleased, but never with another man. He had no tolerance for that bullshit. And she wasn't the kind of woman to tease or push his buttons by flirting with others. Tonight she'd been quite happy. His femme fatale had chosen a dance club that played American rap and pop music. So he parked their yacht at *Sainte Maxime* and summoned a driver to take them to the nightspot. He and Carlo observed her from the corner of the discothèque. Marietta moved with the grace of a ballerina and the sexual tease of a street whore. It excited him when they were in private and irked him in public. But she was a free spirit that loved to dance. And he wasn't in the mood to fight with her about such trival bullshit.

"She's a wild one," Carlo said. He took a sip of his lager.

"She's tame with me. I can handle her," Lorenzo answered. His reply may not have been loud enough to be heard over the music. The song switched to a loud thumping techno beat and Marietta squealed. She jumped on her feet in high-heeled pointed shoes. The bounce of her breasts drew the eyes of many men. Lorenzo groaned. He would indeed have to end her dancing soon. Marietta flung her long dark curly locks from side to side like a rock star. Once she opened up to him, trusted him, he got to know a remarkable, exciting, vulnerable woman. A woman he could trust. Who he felt he could actually love.

"You sure about that?" Carlo chuckled.

"Sure about what?" Lorenzo frowned.

"You can handle her?" Carlo's gaze never left Marietta. He stared at her in a way that Lorenzo didn't appreciate.

A man stepped to Marietta and she pushed him away keeping up with her sexy dance moves. The guy leered. Lust and possibly alcohol made his body language clear of his intent. Lorenzo lowered his cigar and his gaze narrowed on the scene. The stranger tried to touch Marietta again and she slapped him hard. The guy was stunned by her sudden attack. He stumbled back into a dancing couple. Lorenzo tensed. Marietta pointed to his table when the man looked to make a move. The *bastardo* glanced his way. He hesitated. Lorenzo and Carlo stared back. They both waited for the man to decide. In a flash either of them would be happy to teach the stranger manners. The tense pause held and then broke. The man turned and walked off. Marietta began to dance again.

Carlo laughed. "She can take care of herself. Maybe I should put her out in the streets with Ringo, teach him how to never make the mistake of trusting a motherfucker like Carmine did."

Lorenzo smiled. He'd put an end to the night soon. Marietta had been drinking and if allowed to continue with her partying she could be a viper with her tongue. He'd hate to have to snap a man's neck for not understanding her charm. But first he needed to hear the answers he dreaded. *Why had Giovanni ignored him for so long? How was the family making it without him?* "Tell me what's going on with my cousin?"

"Gio has his concerns," Carlo answered.

"About me?" Lorenzo scoffed. "*Interessante.* The one sent on a fool's errand is indeed a fool. Why should he be concerned now?"

"He thinks you will defy him and return to Sicily, with her." Carlo tossed his chin upward toward the dancing temptress. "Why is that, Lo?"

"You know I can't speak on it," Lorenzo grumbled.

Carlo rubbed his jaw. He fished out his lighter and picked up his cigar to relight it. Lorenzo took another drag of his own and considered taking Carlo into confidence. He had to keep Marietta's identity a secret from her and the rest of the family. The secret kept her alive. But for how long was he expected to play this charade? And could he truly trust Giovanni to reunite the sisters? Especially when he had no motivation to do so.

"That's not all. Things are not good, Lo," Carlo began after a deep exhale. "In fact things are far worse."

"*Dica,*" Lorenzo said.

"It's Santo. He's the *capo bastone* now. Giovanni's left hand."

"Where the fuck is Domi?"

"Oh he's off trying to wash the blood from Gio's money. Santo keeps the peace with the clans. What Tomosino created is fractured, what Giovanni wants to instill is the Sicilian way. The clans of the *Camorra* don't like the power Giovanni has as *capo di tutti capi.* And now Gio's dividing territory we bled for? The other families war over the business we're dropping. Including the gambling houses."

"*Che cosa!* Did you say the gambling houses? Those are my fucking gambling houses in Napoli!" Lorenzo slammed his fist down on the table. "Giovanni can't give them up. It's a power move that the lower clans would seize and destroy. What of our men? What will they do?"

Carlo nodded his head in agreement. "We aren't in that business anymore. The men have other tasks assigned to them by Santo. Things that I have no insight into."

"The drugs I understand. The whores, I can live with his decision, but I don't agree. The gambling houses? He's fucking out of his mind! What is left?" Lorenzo shouted.

"Dominic and Giovanni have opened the *Donna's* company in Milano, it's called *Fabiana's*." Carlo added, staring hard to read his reaction.

"*Basta!* Are we going to be fucking women making dresses like his wife?"

The comment against their leader should bring about scorn or worse from Carlo. But they'd been best friends since childhood. With Carlo he could speak freely, to a point. He wiped his hand down his face. "The triangle. What goes on there? The `Ndrangheta won't give up Milano. No matter what Giovanni promises them. And I know the Bonaduces wait for a chance at revenge. He isn't blind to this. Is he?"

"Santo and Domi have talked Gio into furthering legitimate investments. A few more vineyards, a couple more properties, a few land deals up through Tuscany. A resort and vacation place for tourism in Florence. I believe Santo keeps peace for Giovanni with the `Ndrangheta by letting the fuckers grow their product on land in Genoa."

"Heroin?" Lorenzo asked.

Carlo nodded his head. "I hear the Nigerians are still sniffing around. I can't prove any of it. Santo's men are loyal."

"Then why say it to me if you can't prove it?" Lorenzo asked.

"There are rumors that Santo might start his own clan. But those rumors never reach Giovanni's ear, just mine," Carlo said.

Lorenzo considered the information. His cousin's trust of his inner circle was always a blind spot for manipulation. It's how Lorenzo was able to get fucked up with the Calderones and go undetected by Gio. It was also how he'd been able to hide his part in Tomosino's death from Giovanni for years. "If Santo played peacemaker with the `Ndrangheta without bloodshed then it stands to reason he's cut a side deal," Lorenzo said. "And we both know trafficking is all the `Ndrangheta cares about."

He released a tensed breath. "What do we still own?" Lorenzo asked.

"All of the sanitation in the *Campania*. We have sixteen hundred businesses that pay us to run their operations all the way to Chiaiano. It's mostly where I'm needed now. The export out of the bay is doing well. Everyone wants a piece of the action and Giovanni only allows a few. My boys and yours see to it. The factories are ours, legitimately so. Rocco's grape and olive groves produce and we have a distribution deal in the works for our product. The guns from the Irish import in and out of Napoli to West Africa. Business is the same there."

Lorenzo laughed. "So my cousin isn't really letting go of all his bad deeds, is he?" he shook his head. "The *Camorra* is not *la Cosa Nostra*. The family respect we earned from the other clan bosses is only as strong as our grip on their fucking necks. We cannot survive if we continue down this path. Dominic should be advising Gio better. What is he thinking?"

"Gio is distracted. He spends a lot of time with the *Donna*. Lovesick. Like you and her." Carlo chuckled. Lorenzo's gaze switched to Marietta who was now dancing in the center of the dance floor with several people cheering her on. He grimaced.

Carlo continued, "The other day the bosses from the other clans met to voice their grievances and Gio received a message that the *Donna* had an episode. Do you know he left the meeting to Santo to close? He let the bastardo sit in his chair and play *Don* as he raced back to Sorrento to hold his wife's hand. I hear she threw a bitch fit over some fabric she received out of Milano," Carlo chuckled.

"Gio did this?" Lorenzo frowned not seeing any humor in the news. He knew Giovanni was devoted to Mirabella, but no woman ever came before their business. Not even their mothers.

Carlo gave a single nod of his head.

Stunned, Lorenzo couldn't speak. To show fractured leadership was dangerous. Not only would they lose control within the *Camorra*, but become targets themselves. In their world weakness meant death. And death was the only way out of their destiny.

"We need you back. Giovanni needs you at his side not Santo, Lo. Think about it. You are the only one who can truly make him see what we stand to lose."

"What the fuck can I do from here?" Lorenzo snarled. "You came to tighten my leash! And you never backed me with Gio when I needed it so don't bitch to me now about the state of things."

"You've been secretive for months. No! For fucking years!" Carlo shouted over the blare of the music. "Do you think I'm a fucking idiot? I know you keep secrets! That's why Giovanni put a leash on your neck and I helped him tighten it because of your bullshit!"

Lorenzo glared but he held his tongue against the truth tossed in his face. Carlo had no idea how dark and dangerous the secrets Lorenzo kept were. Including his role in the assassination of

Carmine. Lorenzo sat back and pounded his fist on the surface of the table for restraint.

Carlo spoke loud and clear over the music. "I don't understand why the boss gives a fuck about your woman." He kicked the chair in front of him. "You want my loyalty," He pointed his finger at Lorenzo. And then his lethal gaze sliced away toward Marietta. "Explain her."

Marietta danced with a married couple. She had a fresh drink in her hand. She laughed and spun around, never missing a step.

"She's important. Trust me," Lorenzo grumbled.

"Explain her!" Carlo shouted. "How is she important? Since when does your dick matter to Giovanni? Why were you truly going after David Capriccio? Why is my brother dead over this bullshit?"

Lorenzo struggled with entrusting the truth to Carlo. Carlo had always been unpredictable with the ladies. But even more he was loyal to the code of their lives. Which version of the truth would secure Carlo's loyalty to him?

"What is it?" his best friend demanded.

"Look at her Carlo. Look at her again!" Lorenzo said.

Carlo's gaze returned to Marietta. He watched her with a curious frown. "I see nothing."

"Are you sure?" Lorenzo leaned in. "She's American, she's beautiful, she's black and the same age as Mirabella. Look at her. Who is she?" Lorenzo asked.

The furrow that creased Carlo's brow lessened and he saw the realization take hold of his friend. "The *Donna*? She's related to her? Cousins? What?"

"She's her twin sister," Lorenzo said.

Carlo's eyes stretched open. His gaze volleyed between Marietta and Lorenzo before settling on Lorenzo. "What the fuck? Are you sure?"

"Yes I'm sure. The Capriccios discovered the truth and tried to kill her. I stopped it. Saved her life. Carmine saved her life."

"Why?" Carlo's gaze returned to him. "Why did you fucking care? And why use my brother to protect her?"

"She's the daughter of Marsuvio Mancini. They both are."

"Not possible!" Carlo roared with laughter.

"It's true dammit!" Lorenzo shouted over his best friend's laughter. "Now do you see why Gio wants me to keep her away? Neither of the women know they have a Sicilian father. They were orphans, a junkie mother died and they were separated."

His friend gaped at Marietta. If one was to look at her and Mira side by side the resemblance was unmistakable. Though they differed in skin color and Marietta had more curves, she had the *Donna's* eyes, her smile, her manner in a way mirrored her sister. After digesting the truth his friend admitted he found it hard to unsee the similarities. Lorenzo settled on that answer. He'd rather end the revelation there, than to dig up his bloody connection to Tomosino, Giuseppe Calderone, and Carmine's death.

"How long have you known? Does Armando know? How the fuck does *Don* Mancini have twin daughters like them? And the *Donna*? Our *Donna*? She belongs to him?"

Lorenzo chuckled. "No. She belongs to Giovanni you ass. That's the point."

"Right. Right," Carlo nodded his head. "But Mancini's daughter? Not fucking possible! It can't be."

Carlo kept on with the questions. Lorenzo waited until Carlo ran out of steam to enlighten him. "Marsuvio knows. It's been a secret he kept for many years. Remember Fabiana?" Lorenzo asked. His chest went tight at the mention of Fabiana's name. He released a slow breath. "She was lured to Napoli by Mancini to bring Mirabella to Italy. He put them up in our building. Remember that?"

"Yes, I remember," Carlo said.

Lorenzo reached for his drink. He needed another. One big swallow and the burn in his heart lessened. "Gio met Mira and Mancini couldn't stop their affair without exposing himself and the secret he's kept for many years. Only Domi, Rocco, Giovanni and me know the truth. Giovanni wanted me to take Marietta away until Mira had the babies. He's paranoid because—" Lorenzo looked up at Carlo. "This you can never say, never speak of."

Carlo nodded.

He leaned forward so he wouldn't have to shout the forbidden truth over the blare of the music. "Because Tomosino is the one that killed their mother. Patri found out about their mother and went to Mancini's father for permission to put out the hit. *Don* Mancini agreed to have the black whore killed in America. It was done because of Tomosino's desire to bring Marsuvio to power and strengthen the families after the First Mafia War."

"Holy shit," Carlo said.

"Giovanni fears if Mira learns the truth she'd blame him. Abandon him. And that's the secret I carry," Lorenzo finished.

"He fucking should be worried!" Carlo said. "A fucking Mancini? He married a Mancini?"

"Shut the fuck up! Don't say it again," Lorenzo warned. "No

one can know. Especially Armando. He'd put a bullet in the sisters before he ever called them *famiglia*. And no fucking body lays a hand on Marietta or the *Donna*."

Carlo nodded his head in agreement. "I understand. You can't take her back to Italy or Sicily. Shit you're fucked." Carlo wiped his hand down his face. "To hell with it, Lo. Cut ties with her. Send her ass back to America. She and the *Donna* should never know the truth. I hear Mancini has one foot in the grave. Let the dirty secret die with him."

Marietta came over to the table. She put her drink down and dropped on Lorenzo's lap. Even her sweat smelled like the sexy scent of Shalimar she often wore. Lorenzo inhaled her and bit her neck. Marietta giggled. The soft round cushion of her ass pressed in on his groin. He could feel the sexual tension coil tight in his dick. He kissed her cheek. Marietta turned her face to force her tongue on him. She tasted of champagne. Her small hands rubbed over his chest and he chuckled at how excitable she could get when they had an audience. "Come dance with me, baby," she said between the kiss. He stopped her.

"I'm bored," she pouted.

"You've had too much to drink. No more dancing." Lorenzo admonished. "It's beginning to piss me off."

She cut her gaze over to Carlo. She frowned. "Why are you staring at me like that?"

Carlo sneered. He didn't answer.

"Go easy on him, Marietta. He's here to do us a favor. To be our witness," Lorenzo said.

"Witness to what? Forget him, take me to another club," Marietta whined.

Lorenzo moved her hair from her brow. He lifted her chin with one finger. "*Sei la mia rosa.* I've decided on something today. I want you in my life. *Per sempre.*"

"What are you talking about?" she half-laughed. When he didn't laugh in response her smile faded. "What do you mean? Forever?"

"I'm talking about marriage, *cara*. I want you to marry me."

Carlo choked on his lager. Marietta sat upright on Lorenzo's lap. She shoved him back against the chair with both hands pressed to his shoulders. She searched his face with her eyes stretched and mouth gaping. "Me?"

"Of course you." He smiled.

She touched her heart. "You? Me and you? Get married?"

"Is that yes?" he asked.

"Yes? Yes!" she screamed and crushed him with a tight hug to the neck. He glanced over at Carlo who stared on in disbelief.

"Welcome to la famiglia, Marietta," Lorenzo said, holding her close to him. He would do everything to get what he wanted, and Marietta was the key.

* B *

"Giovanni—stop," Mira gasped awake.

"Mmm, relax. Lie still… mmm, it's okay, just let me…" he said. *Ti voglio bene.*

Mira gripped the sheets. If he had warmed her up she would have been ready. Sometimes men could be beastly when it came to sex. Penetration, thick, slow, and measured felt at first invasive, and then glorious when he trapped her in his arms and pumped his hips. Her hips moved and her belly trembled.

"Yes, Bella, move for me…" he groaned in her ear.

Mira relaxed against his chest and let the sweet aches of their union take her under. He pushed deeper into her, breaching her body limits. Mira gripped the bed sheets. She could feel every generous inch of him. With a drag of his cock he thrust deep into her and his teeth sank into her shoulder. Mira winced. *Damn him and the biting!* Giovanni eased his hand lower to cup her pussy with his finger slowly slipping between the folds of her sex to stroke her clit. Mira bit down on her quivering bottom lip. The hand massage of her pussy as he rapidly thrust into her, made all the difference. She smiled as her husband's pelvis pumped against her ass and her body adjusted to the way he loved her. On her side with him holding her, he restricted her movements. His arm was across her waist. His leg looped over her thighs to keep them shut.

She gripped the mattress tighter and worked her magic below. She knew what her man liked. Her succulent pussy caressed his cock each time he buried deep after a long dick thrust. She clasped her inner walls tightly as his shaft pulsed in her. Giovanni kept going but his loud groans predicted his ending. Spirals of delicious heat travelled through her pussy. The babies shifted too far up and she struggled to breathe.

"It'll kill me, Bella, but if you need me to, I can…" he said in a coarse, strained voice. It was a lie. He must have sensed her tighten up. The babies shifted again and the discomfort passed. All she did was sigh in relief and he continued to move in and out of her. His thrusts increased in speed and he fucked her a little harder.

"Gio—" Before she could say anything more, rapture tore through her clitoris and nearly split her in half.

"*Tesora mia,*" he said. He kissed the back of her head and then dropped his forehead against it. Mira closed her eyes and rode the wave of pleasure seizing her pelvis. His withdrawal and reentry brought down her climatic ending. Giovanni's hand left her pussy and gripped her hip. He held her still and worked in and out of her at an angle that caused the babies to relax from the knotted position they found. She reached back and gently covered her hand over his to encourage him to continue. Sheer pleasure tore through her, and her body shuddered as he released inside of her.

She smiled when he went still. "Morning," she said.

Mira turned with his help to face him and lie on her side. She went into his arms. Holding his waist, placing her face against the hard definition of his chest with her belly resting against his hot and sweaty abdomen, she felt bliss. His heart hammered so fast she feared he'd go into arrest. But she held to him tightly and waited for both of them to settle into bliss.

"What do you want to do today?" he asked her, his voice unintentionally gruff.

"Today is mine again, huh? Anything I want, right?" she asked.

"Yes," he chuckled.

"Then I want to see everything. Take me on a tour of Mondello," she said.

"A tour? I had planned to take you into Palermo, Bagheria to see friends and family."

"Are your parents buried there? Bagheria?" she asked.

She felt him go stiff. She waited a beat and then lifted her head from his chest. He moved to give her room so he could look into her eyes. She tried to spare him her morning breath but she had to know. "Your father is buried there? Right? What about your mother?"

"My father is buried in the family plot. Yes. It's in Bagheria where he was born. My mother is buried here."

"What? Here? At Villa Mare Blu? Or in Mondello?"

He released her and turned over to his back. Mira lifted on her elbow to stare at him. "Why not bury her next to your father?"

"She wasn't his wife, Mira. I've explained this. Patri never divorced his wife. The church still sees him as married. His wife will be buried next to him. That is how it's done," he said.

"Oh, baby," she ran her hand over his chest. "I'm sorry. I know how important they both are to you. It must have been hard to separate your parents that way."

"I've learned to live with hard things, Mira. Mama loved Mondello. And I made sure she was laid to rest properly." His gaze dropped over and fixed on her. "She's at peace now."

"I want to meet her. For you and I to go visit her grave so I can pay my respects. Is that okay?"

"Why insist?" he asked.

"Why? She's the most important woman in the world to you that's why. She made you." Mira touched his face. "You're my husband. Shouldn't I meet your mother?" When he didn't respond she tried harder to explain. "Even in death I can feel her everywhere. Sorrento, here, I can see how she cared for your home and took care of this family. If I had any family I would want them to know you. I'd take you to Virginia and have you sit at the table so my granny could make some of her best buttermilk fried chicken. I'd wave bye to you from the front porch as my Pop-Pop took you out to hunt past the apple orchids on his land." She blinked away tears and tried to keep the pain of their loss from her voice. She missed them so much. She had learned to live with the loneliness after their death, until she found Fabiana. The sister she never had. Now even she was gone. All she had was the family they made together.

"I would have loved to meet them," he said in earnest.

She kissed his nose. "Take me to meet your mother."

"How about breakfast? Sophia put things in the cooler. I can cook for us." Giovanni grinned. He sat up. She was forced to do the same.

Mira frowned at his attempt to change the subject. Maybe it was painful for him to visit his mother's grave. She couldn't bring herself to visit her grandparents' grave.

"Don't dismiss what I'm asking of you, please. I think we should do the hard things together. It makes us stronger."

He glanced her way and then averted his gaze. "You should eat. Let me fix something. I'll think on it."

She loved him for offering breakfast but he was not a cook. And her keeping him from the stove averted the accidents in the kitchen. "We can shower and I can cook for you? How does that sound?" Mira offered.

"And then... my beautiful wife... I will take you to meet my mother."

Mira smiled. "Thank you."

"Because you are right, Bella. She's important to me, just as you are. And I want her to see how happy you've made me."

Mira grabbed his face. She kissed him. "Can we be like this always?"

"*Sì. Per sempre tua—forever yours.*"

* B *

Marietta yanked hard on the curtain and dragged it across the window. In an instant the room was flooded with the bright side of morning. Lorenzo shielded his face. "What the hell is going on?" he demanded. The sheet was tangled around his waist and thigh. The bed covers had all been kicked over to the floor.

"Wake up." Marietta folded her arms over her breasts and approached the bed. Their clothes were tossed everywhere. Carlo disappeared into the night. Lorenzo booked a room at a small hostel instead of returning her to their yacht. After the drinking and celebrating over his proposal neither of them could be trusted on the open sea. The rest of the evening was a blur. If she hadn't woke up stripped naked with the familiar aches in her lower back and pussy from sex with Lorenzo, she wouldn't have been able to piece together what happened last night.

"What is it, Marie? I'm tired," he groaned. "Damn. Close the fucking curtain."

He called her Marie from time to time. A pet name she liked. And therein lie the problem. She liked him—the good, the bad, the confusing. No. She loved him. She had to know the truth. It was killing her.

"You proposed," she said.

He froze. He lowered his arm and looked at her. She felt her heart sink. It was definitely the booze talking last night. And that hurt. She never wanted to be married. Never wanted a mobster boyfriend either. But with Lorenzo she wanted many things. Now he had gone and opened his big fat mouth. He reopened a wound on her heart she thought had long healed. The need to be loved, truly loved in return.

"Were you serious? When you asked me to marry you, Lo?"

Lorenzo sat up in the bed. "*Mi dispiace molto. So sorry, cara,*" he said.

Marietta closed her eyes and rubbed the tension from her brow. She bit so hard on her tongue she feared her teeth would sink through. She wanted to scream at his dirty ass for tricking her into believing he could be serious. She wanted to rage against her own stupidity for thinking their fling could ever mean more to him.

"*Sdraiati.*" He told her to lie down. He took her hand and pulled her closer to the bed. Despite her hurt she went into his arms and lay on top of him. "I should have never proposed to you that way," he admitted. "In a dirty discothèque after we'd been drinking."

"Forget it. I didn't want to marry you," she mumbled. "Never thought of you that way."

He chuckled. "You break my heart, *cara*. Was I serious? Yes."

She lifted her head and looked up into his face. "Yes what?" she asked with a tremulous voice.

"*Sposami o morirò*—marry me or I'll die," he said.

Her heart stopped beating. She had learned to tell when he was lying, to read his expression and tell when he was tricking her. She saw nothing but deep sincerity in his eyes and heard it in his voice. He flashed her that smile of his and she smiled back. "I want you to be my wife. The mother of my children—"

"I don't want children," she reminded him.

"*Basta!* The things you say woman. Of course you want children!" he stated. "And you will give me sons," he smacked her on the ass.

She dropped her head on his chest and hugged him tightly. The light of love he sparked in her heart melted her defiance. She wasn't making him any damned babies. But that was an argument for another time. At the moment she wanted something more. She wanted to be his.

"Today we get your ring. Do you have your passport and birth certificate?"

"Yes," she said. She tried to contain her excitement. "I don't want to get married in a church. Let's do it at sea! On the yacht, with the ocean around us."

"Whatever you say, *cara*. I will visit a friend of mine, one who can expedite things here in France. We will marry. As soon as possible."

"After you propose to me properly." She sat upright. Lorenzo winced. She moved so she didn't crush his legs. "I need a proposal with you on bended knee."

"Knee?" Lorenzo frowned. "You want me on my knees? *Che palle!*"

Marietta pushed up and stood on the mattress. She crossed her arms and glared down at him. "I want a proper proposal. I want to do it official. And then I will marry you and make you miserable for the rest of your life!"

Lorenzo laughed. He tackled her knees and she screamed. Lorenzo flipped her on the bed. It didn't hurt, but she was surprised by his swift maneuvers. He pinned her beneath him. He held her face. "I will propose on my knees, I will do it in front of the world. And then we buy you the most beautiful dress in France, today."

"Okay," she wrapped her arms around his neck. "I'm so happy."

"Why are you happy, beautiful? Tell me?" he asked.

"I came to Italy looking for something. I don't know. I wanted to belong, to something, to someone. And I found you." She kissed him shyly and opened her heart to him. "I love you, Lorenzo Battaglia."

He kissed her in return. *"Ti Amo, Marietta,"* he said before slipping inside of her again.

* B *

Mirabella watched her step. It was extremely bright out today. The sunlight buttered the trees, flowers, groves and landscape. Every color of the day from the flowers to the trees held such vibrance. Together they strolled along a path that scaled up a hill. The forest grew denser and the breeze felt much cooler. She wore Giovanni's shirt over the top of her summer dress. He walked at her side, his hand holding hers, in just his slacks and bare feet. She feared for his feet. Even in her thong sandals she found the grass prickly with rocks and rough patches that caused her to stumble a few times. But Giovanni kept a protective watch over her.

Between Villa Mare Blu and the sea there was a clearing, and on the emerald green land a safely guarded private garden of blue roses. For the first time since she arrived in Sicily she saw his mother's flower, her flower. Whoever cared for the roses nurtured their growth and they bloomed everywhere. No other flower was allowed to thrive within the same vicinity.

The crypt was four feet tall and three feet wide. It was made of grey Italian marble that glistened under the rays of the sun. To the left was a matching marble bench for those who came to visit. Mira took a step forward. She could read the scripture carved into the surface. It said Evelyn 'Eve' McHenry was a beloved daughter, mother, and wife in Italian. *Wife?* Clearly that was Giovanni's attempt to give her some dignity in death though he could not give her the Battaglia name.

She glanced to her husband. His dark hair was tussled from a whipping breeze with most of it in his eyes. He stared at the grave with not a trace of emotion on his face. His mother's image was preserved in a small cameo picture on the crypt. She was a striking woman with red hair and piercing blue eyes.

Mira removed her hand from his. She stepped to the rose bush, careful of the thorns when she plucked the prettiest bloom. She walked over and placed it on top of the crypt. "*Mi chiamo Mirabella. Giovanni's wife. Piacere.*"

The words felt heavy as they left her heart. Being so close to someone so loved brought forth emotions of her dearly departed mother. *What if her mother had lived?* What if she had been there for her when she found herself alone at sixteen? Would she and Giovanni have ever met? He says they were destined to meet, but love didn't happen through destiny. Look at Evelyn, stolen from her family so young. Forced into the role of mistress, and then mother. In love with a man who caused her so much pain. Did she consider herself destined for this life?

Giovanni's hands landed on her shoulders. Mira smiled. "We can go. I wanted to pay my respects," she said. "I have."

He kissed the back of her head and then embraced her. "She would have loved you, Mira. And our children. Madre wasn't like the rest of them. She had no prejudice, no envy or spiteful nature. No matter who a person was she loved and accepted them into her heart. That's why my father could never let her go. He told me once that he wanted that love all for himself. I guess I'm like him in that way."

"No, honey, you aren't that selfish."

Her husband sighed. She tried to look back at him but he buried his face in the crook of her neck.

"Are you okay?" she asked.

He lifted his face. "I can remember how happy my mother was when she was blessed with a girl. From the moment she brought Catalina home my mother was changed."

They stood there for a moment staring at Evelyn's crypt. If she listened hard enough she could hear the soft sounds of the ocean waves breaking across the shore.

"It's beautiful here. Peaceful. Did you do this for her?" Mira asked.

"I did. I told her when she took sick after Patri died that I would bring her body back to Ireland. I'd lay her to rest with her parents, and sisters. She refused. She wanted to be here. Close to Patri and us. She loved Mondello." He dropped his chin on Mira's shoulder and his hands held the lower swell of her belly. "My father's murder broke her. I knew she loved him despite everything. In the end I never understood why."

"They had a complicated love story," Mira said.

"Like us," Giovanni admitted.

"No, not like us. We are honest with each other. We respect each other. And I'm your wife." She brought his arms up to hug her tighter and she hugged him in return.

"I wanted to give her peace," he said.

"You have. One day I want us to go to America. I want to take you to where I grew up. To where my grandparents and mother are buried." She turned and looked up at him. "Would you want to go?"

He touched the side of her face. He stared at her for a long moment.

"Giovanni? Would you want to go?" she asked.

"Yes," he forced a smile. "*Andiamo.* There is more I wish to show you before Domi and Catalina arrive."

"Shouldn't they already be here?" Mira asked.

Giovanni drew her under his arm and they started to walk away from the crypt toward the path. "Dominic has a thing for the trains. They aren't very pleasant. But since he was a little boy he has loved to travel by train and ferry to Sicily. Especially with Catalina. They'll be here later this morning."

"Oh, okay. Dominic really is a younger brother to you? Isn't he?"

"I raised him to be a man," Giovanni said with pride.

"What about Lorenzo? Where is he? It's been months."

"You will see him soon. He has a new friend. You know how we Battaglia men are when we find that special lady."

Mira laughed. She eased her arm around his waist. "I suppose we'll be hearing wedding bells soon? Another woman married into the family."

"No," Giovanni said abruptly. "It's not that serious. And Lorenzo isn't the marrying type. He's having his fling and tending to business in Europe."

"Okay," Mira shrugged.

They continued on the path lined by roses. A breeze travelled with them and she loved the comfort of his body heat. The walk lasted longer. She moved slower. The boys were up doing the hokey-pokey in her belly. She struggled with masking her discomfort. If he thought she was tired or in need of rest he'd delay his plans for their excursion, and she needed the freedom to be out and about. It helped with her anxiety. They argued less. Mira felt another sharp pang of guilt over how she's treated him. He was such a good, attentive, caring husband. How did she ever get so lucky?

When they returned to the villa they were greeted with silence. She saw a few of his men but they barely spoke. And then she heard her daughter crying. Giovanni stopped and kissed her head. "I'll join you in a minute. Need to make a few calls."

"Okay. I'll see to Eve and then shower. What should I wear?" she called out to him as he walked off. He threw up his hand as if it didn't matter. She smiled and went in search of her baby.

Later –

Giovanni put his face in the palms of his hands. He calmed himself before he spoke.

"How much is gone?"

"I assure you, Gio, I have everything under control," Santo said through the speaker system on the phone.

Giovanni wiped his hand down his face. He sat back in his chair. "If you had it under control why did I hear this from someone other than you?"

"Domi—"

"It wasn't Domi!" Gio shouted. "There's nothing you do for this family that's beyond my knowing!" Giovanni believed forty percent of the truth was missing from Santo's tale. "The Mottolas have taken over Chiaiano," Giovanni said. "It happened under your watch. Now answer the fucking question. How much is gone?"

There was a brief pause before Santo cleared his throat. "The urbanization project. Francesco Mottola now says the region is his and so are the deals we've made. He has several villagers signing over their land to him. I had intended to meet with him to settle the matter, civilly. To challenge him will raise the brow of the other clans. The *Camorra* is the priority here."

"*Mannaggia!* Don't lecture me on the *Camorra*." Giovanni rocked back in his chair. "*Che disastro!* You had your chance and you fucked it over. You fucked me over."

"Gio, maybe I should come there. We can sit down and talk about this reasonably. Give me the opportunity to make this right with Mottola without your intervention. I can fix this."

Giovanni looked at Renaldo who stared back, waiting on an order.

Giovanni bit down on his lip. "No one takes from me. For now do nothing. Let Mottola make his move. I expect to see you in two days. Bring me Giuliani." Giovanni ended the call. The news came from an informant in the Mottola clan. The seizure of Chiaiano happened thirteen days ago and Santo hadn't said a word. Which either meant the work he thought they were putting in to settle disputes over the rival clans' thirst for drug trafficking had fallen through, or Santo had another agenda.

"Call in Marco. He's to shadow Santo from now on, and to make sure Giuliani comes to Sicily."

Renaldo stood and walked out. Giovanni checked his watch. He'd been distracted. He'd also been a fool to believe vultures like the Mottolas would not see his generosity as weakness. If he gutted Mottola then that meant he'd inherit his business, drugs and whores would fall under the name Battaglia. That pollution was the very last thing he wanted in his business. He picked up his pen thumping it against the note pad. Lorenzo's warnings against legitimizing the family echoed in the recesses of his mind. His father's hatred of heroin and how it divided the Mafia remained at the forefront of his mind.

"Hi?" Mira knocked on the door. She had changed into khaki brown shorts and a lemon yellow halter maternity top. She looked refreshed from her shower.

"I thought we were leaving?" she asked. "Eve's with Nico and Cecilia. They are taking her to the beach so we can sneak out and she won't see us."

"Yes. Yes." He rose from his desk. "Let's go."

5.

There was a homey sense of familiarity with Mondello. Sweet memories of their motorcycle ride through Chianti, Italy surfaced as she and Giovanni travelled off their land on a single lane highway. Still in two days *Sicilia* had not replaced Sorrento in her heart.

Mira adjusted the seatbelt. It fastened a bit snug over her middle. Giovanni didn't drive like a man transporting his pregnant wife. Every time he braked, cursed and made gestures at slow moving drivers with his hands, the seatbelt tightened. Several times she grabbed the handle of the car door as he passed a slow moving vehicle or rode the bumper of another.

"Can you slow down please?"

He glanced her way. She couldn't see his eyes because of the reflective lens of his sunglasses, but she noticed a sly tilt at the corner of his lips. That expression of his said: *I'm having fun, baby, don't question it.* So Mira held her tongue and endured his driving for the moment.

"First we visit Porticello near Palermo," he said.

"Really, is it like Mondello?" Mira asked. She stared at the sailboats. Several drifted on turquoise blue waters.

"It's a small fishing village, yes. Not as beautiful as Mondello."

The car veered off the steep cliff down to an open two-lane highway. For twenty minutes they travelled with the sea to their left and the rocky edge of the mountain to her right. And eventually Porticello crept up on them. She gaped at the approaching little market town. It looked like something from a picture book. The buildings were all stone structures of cream, lemon, melon and shades of pink. With plants and laundry hanging from the windows. Old men sat around card tables gawking at their shiny black sports car moving through their town. A few local men carrying fishing nets stopped to observe.

"I guess the tourists don't venture here huh?" she asked.

"They do. The villagers recognize my car," Giovanni said, and cast her another sly smile.

Mira should have known her husband's infamy would be felt here. She placed her hand to her belly. She swallowed down the hunger bug when she saw the quaint little eating spots and the open sidewalk produce market. Giovanni navigated the narrow cobblestone streets by taking one-lane alleys. Mira fiddled with a radio station until she found one with music that was pleasing. Of course it was in Italian.

"Do they have festivals here?" she asked.

"Mondello has a few. A windsailing festival that many people love."

"Windsailing?" Mira frowned. "Is it like sail boating?"

Giovanni cut his gaze over to her. "Something like that, but more personal. It's just a man, his sail, his board and the sea. You will let me teach you to swim?"

"First the gun, now swimming," Mira chuckled. "Yes, we'll try it after the babies are born."

"Speaking of, your gun is in your vanity drawer. I made sure Leo put it there for you. Keep it on you if you go out to the beaches."

"I'm not carrying a gun to the beach." Mira scoffed.

"Then you won't be going to the beach alone," he said in a matter-of-fact tone.

They drove around the market square of the town and travelled down a very steep hill into the countryside. She was almost ready to ask how much further when the car veered off to what looked like private property. Ahead of them was a wood and stone farmhouse situated upon a hill. Through dense foliage, the upper level of the cottage could be seen. From her limited view the place looked older than Villa Mare Blu.

"Does someone live here?"

It was a valid question. So many historical cathedrals and stone structured buildings were in Sicily.

"My father called this place *Acqualiquida Rosa* which translates to liquid water rose. In the spring all that you see surrounding here are beautiful pink roses. Nowhere else in the countryside do these roses bloom but here. My dad's sister was named Rosalie because she was born here instead of Bagheria. She was born outside of my grandfather's marriage."

Mira found it distasteful to hear that another Battaglia man had forsaken his vows. But she decided to not harp on it. "Your father was close to her?"

"He was, he raised her." Giovanni continued to drive slowly up to the cottage.

"Is there a reason why?" Mira asked.

"He considered her, Rosalie, his sister I suppose," Giovanni shrugged. "Family."

"No. I mean is there a reason why he was so big on roses?"

"You think he was big on roses?" Giovanni scoffed.

"They're everywhere in your life." Mira smiled. "Oh c'mon, baby," she reached over and touched his thigh. "Tell me? Why did the great fearless *Don* Tomosino Battaglia like pink, purple, and blue roses? And don't tell me that crap that you do it all for the pussy," she laughed.

Giovanni looked over the top of his sunglasses at her. She smiled and he smiled. "Roses represent love. I suppose love is the strength of the family. Love is what we Battaglia men need."

"Fair enough. A beautiful rose reminds me of love too." Mira gazed upon the cottage. A closer look changed her opinion. It definitely appeared to be lived in. There were clothes on a line flapping in the wind.

"Rosalie died at thirty-three. She died in childbirth. The place has been kept in the family," Giovanni said. "Funny I never met her child, never knew what it was. I believe her husband moved with the child to England some say America."

"Who lives here now?" Mira asked.

Giovanni parked. He turned in his seat. He put his arm around her headrest and looked at her again over the top of his sunglasses. "My father's wife is from Porticello. When they were married she loved the place so he gave it to her. They stayed between here and the family home in Bagheria. I'll take you there next. My uncle Vito, Rosetta's father, he and the rest of the family live there now."

"Okay?" Mira said returning her gaze to the cottage. The grass so tall it nearly swallowed the car. "But who lives here?"

"Esta asked me, after his death, permission to be allowed to live out her days here. I think it holds some fond memories of their time together."

"You have a relationship with her?" Mira asked in surprise. Giovanni nodded his head yes. "Does she stay here by herself?"

"Her younger sister who is in her late sixties stays here too. I make sure they are provided for. My father made no provision for her in his will."

"Why didn't he? Nothing against your mother, but why did he treat his wife Esta so horribly?"

"You know how this goes, Bella. Don't make me explain it again." He looked back to the cottage. She stared at it as well when he answered. "She considers me her son. I consider her nothing more than a burden. One of many my father left me." Giovanni sighed. "I intend to make this visit short." He removed his sunglasses and tucked them into the front pocket of his shirt. Mira reached over and grabbed his face with both of her hands. She kissed him, twice.

Giovanni gave her a slight smile and then threw open his car door. Mira emerged from her side of the car. Her gaze landed on the window to the front of the cottage just as the curtain fell back. "I think they know we're here."

"Of course they do," he said and took her hand into his.

Together they approached by walking across the unkempt lawn. At the door he knocked twice. Mira heard one lock, two, and then three disengage. The door slowly opened, but only an inch. A petite grey haired woman peeked out at them through the dingy lens of her eyeglasses. After a brief pause she opened the door wider.

"Benevenuti," the old woman said with a curt nod. She wore a white and blue floral housedress, and slippers with socked feet.

"Ciao, Fiona. Dove è Esta?" Giovanni greeted the old woman with a pleasant tone. Mira watched as he kissed her on both of her cheeks.

"Bene," Fiona stepped back to allow them to enter. Mira smiled before she stepped inside. There was a brown cloth sofa and loveseat in the living room with a coffee table in between. Newspaper was scattered and stacked with books and magazines on the floor and chairs. Across from the sofa was a TV on top of a piano. There was no rhyme or reason to the way the house was organized.

"Fiona, this is my wife Mirabella Battaglia," Giovanni said.

"Nice to meet you," Mira said. She extended her hand. Fiona looked at her hand for a second as if it weren't attached to Mira's body. The old woman reached for it, shook it briefly, and let it drop. Mira was surprised to see her wipe her hand against the side of her dress as if in disgust. "Esta is upstairs, you can go right up," she answered before she shuffled off to what Mira suspected was her kitchen. "We've already eaten so I can't offer you anything," Fiona said.

Giovanni led Mira by the hand to the stairwell. She felt a very personal sting of anger pierce her gut. The woman was unnaturally dismissive of her husband. She'd only seen people show Giovanni respect. And to Mira's surprise she had grown to expect the humility from others when they were in his presence.

"Are you sure you want to do this?" Mira whispered.

He winked. "Of course."

A sour stench greeted them as they entered the hall. There were only three doors upstairs. Esta's door was the first they arrived to. He knocked and then pushed the door open. He stepped in first and she followed. The room reeked of bleach. Putrid and unrelenting she bit back a wave of nausea. Mira instinctively put her hand to her mouth and nose to resist the urge to puke.

An old woman lay in her bed propped up by pillows. A crocheted blanket covered a patchwork quilt that was tucked around her. She was as still as a corpse.

"Esta?" Giovanni said.

The woman's sagging lids parted to reveal murky grey cataract eyes—a steely pair that fixed on Giovanni. Time had been unkind to her. She had to be well past the age of seventy. With very wrinkled skin dotted with moles, her hair was thick, silver, long. She wore it parted down the middle with two braids. Maybe in her hay day she was striking, but Mira saw no evidence of that beauty now. She reminded Mira of the witch that gave the poison apple to Snow White. And like the old woman, Esta's mouth twisted with displeasure over the sight of Giovanni's new American wife.

Mira gaze switched to the silver picture frame at the side of the woman's bed. The strikingly handsome man who looked like Giovanni had to be his father in a dark coat and fedora. He stood next to an expensive car. Beside Tomosino's picture was one of the Pope, and above the bed a wooden cross was tacked to the wall. No other furnishing besides a portable toilet and a dresser with a television propped on top was in the room.

"Giovanni? That you? I had hoped you would come." Esta's voice was very soft, almost meek. It surprised Mira. The woman extended her arthritic hand and welcomed Giovanni into a hug from her bed. He kissed her on both cheeks and said something to her that Mira couldn't hear. The woman actually managed a smile. And then those cool eyes fixed on Mira once more.

"Esta, meet my wife Mirabella. We have a daughter Eve and she's pregnant now with twins. Sons. I will be a father again soon. With sons," he said in a single breath.

Mira blinked at him confused by his hurried introduction. "Nice to meet you," Mira said.

"You're different," Esta replied in English. "But beauty and babies often make wives out of whores."

"Now Esta, I will only caution you once about your manners," Giovanni said in a tight voice.

Esta quickly added, "I meant no disrespect. You and your father have always had a thing for the exotic. I'm happy to meet you, Mirabella."

Giovanni spoke. "How's your health?"

"The same, the doctor treats me horribly. Fiona said you must be skipping payments on my bills. Why else would the doctor be so uncaring about my suffering?"

"Not true, Esta. You know me better than that." He picked up one pill bottle then the other, which Mira was sure he paid for. "How about we get you a private nurse?"

"No!" Esta snapped. "No nurse. I won't have strangers in my home." Esta's cold eyes switched to Mira. She caught Mira staring at the photo of Tomosino near her bed. "That is my husband, *Don* Tomosino Baldamenti. The family took on the name Battaglia when they left Sicily and started up with that godless *Camorra*. They all did. His brothers, everyone. But he is a Baldamenti! He was a great man. A powerful man," Esta boasted. "They have an entire village named after him."

Mira didn't know how to respond. So she kept quiet.

"Will you stay for dinner, Gio? You haven't spent time with me in awhile," Esta said in a voice wavering with emotion.

"Maybe we should go. Let her rest," Mira blurted. The last thing she could stomach was dinner with these ladies. And she didn't like the odd relationship Giovanni had with this woman. Something about it felt unnatural. The truth of his devotion soon unraveled before Mira's eyes. He wasn't caring for Esta in the way the old woman needed. He forced her into this isolation with this meager existence to torment her. Mira was almost certain of it.

"You go. I want to speak with Gio alone." Esta answered in a sharp, brisk tone.

"Esta! *Basta!* One more word of disrespect to my wife and I will leave. I came to check in on you. To make sure you were okay but I won't put up with it."

"But I'm so lonely Giovanni. No one comes to visit Fiona and me. I'm not trying to be disrespectful. I didn't get an invitation to your wedding," she whined.

"You weren't well." Giovanni reminded her.

"The doctors said I was. I sent word that we could come. I was told—"

Giovanni put up a hand and Esta silenced. The wrinkles in her face creased deeper with anger. Mira cringed at the hatred she saw boiling in the old woman's glare. It made her even more uncomfortable that her husband enjoyed it.

"Whatever you need, you will have." Giovanni kissed her forehead. "Mira's right. It's time we leave. Be well." Before he was fully righted Mira started for the door. She couldn't take another moment of this scene. She didn't bother to look back. She heard Esta protest and Giovanni respond. Mira had enough. She went on without him and down the stairs, headed for the door. Fiona watched with a cup and saucer in her hand.

"You know he is evil. Don't you?" Fiona asked to her in Italian. Mira glanced over to the old woman. "To his rotten core," Fiona grinned.

Mira could hear Giovanni coming down the stairs behind her. The witch shuffled away to not to be seen talking to her.

"Ready, Bella?" Giovanni smiled.

"I think I'm going to be sick," she replied.

Once outside near the car she could breathe again. Giovanni reached to open the car door and she stopped him. She couldn't hold it any longer. "Why do you keep her here this way?" she asked, her voice trembled with emotion. He opened the door for her instead of answering. She was helped inside and then he went around the car and joined her.

"They were awful. The both of them," Mira said. "But you keep them out here isolated in misery on purpose. Don't you?"

"She's had a hard life, Mira," Giovanni said. "That's not my fault."

"So it's your burden? Or is it something else that makes you keep them locked away here?"

How should he answer? The truth was something he rarely admitted to himself. This was Esta's exile. Instead of his Bella seeing the façade, she saw the prison he put the bitch in. The woman who tormented his mother relentlessly would rot in this hell kept locked away from her family and friends. He paid Fiona to make sure it remained that way. He turned over the engine and sped backward down the drive.

"Fine. You don't have to answer. But I'm your wife," Mira said.

"This I know," he replied.

"As your wife I've decided I don't want you to see those two women ever again."

"You've decided?" Giovanni asked.

"I'll see to their needs. The bills and the doctors, whatever it is you take care of for them. I'll do it."

Giovanni stopped the car just before turning on the main road. "I see to Esta. No one else."

She spoke while staring out of her window. "It's not healthy for you."

"I will handle it as I do all unhealthy things," Giovanni replied.

"I'm saying that this isn't your burden alone." She looked him in the eyes and he felt his resolve weaken. "You have enough to deal with. I want you to stay away from your stepmother. I'll take care of Esta and Fiona."

He chuckled. "I don't think you understand—"

"I'm serious. This is non-negotiable," Mira said. "Either I handle the family affairs or I don't? Which is it?"

"And you think handling the family affairs means dictating to me what should and can be done?" Giovanni asked and kept a smile from his lips when she answered him.

"I sure do. I won't have anyone hurting you. And more importantly I won't sit back and watch you hurt others in this family." Mira touched his hand. He took her hand into his and pressed a kiss to her knuckles. "She's your family whether you like it or not. Forgiveness, Giovanni. Sometimes it takes a stronger person to give it freely."

"Have I told you how sexy you are when you protect me?" Giovanni chuckled. He leaned over and kissed her nose. "I will have to get used to having a life partner."

She smiled in return. "Yes you will."

* B *

"We're here!"

Catalina strutted in through open double doors in four-inch stilettos. She had a hard time getting cleaned up for her arrival on the train. But she managed it. She spun with her arms outstretched. She was so excited to be home.

"I said we're here!" she shouted.

No one came forward to greet her. Catalina figured they were upstairs or in the gardens. She walked through the open foyer toward the back of Villa Mare Blu where the stairs were. Her heels clicked across the tile floors. It had been over three years since she last visited her mother's favorite home, and it was with Franco of all people.

The trip into Sicily was grueling. She had suffered the train ride and drive into Mondello like a good girlfriend. Now she needed food, a shower, and sleep, in that order. Catalina stopped. She put her hand to her hips. "Where's everybody?"

"They're probably at the beach," Dominic said. He walked up behind her with luggage in hand. She had so many bags he'd need to make at least three trips to bring them all in. Catalina checked her watch. "It's too early, Domi. It's not even noon yet."

"Nippy!" Eve sang from the top of the stairs.

Catalina glanced up at the call of her name. Cecilia walked down the stairs holding tight to Eve. The little girl bounced and grinned excitedly in a yellow and green sundress. Eve stretched her hands out to her aunt. Catalina and Mira were often amazed over how Eve could laugh, sing, and talk with her pacifier tucked to the side of her mouth. And Eve spoke clearly. "Nippy! Nippy! Nippy!"

Love surged through every chamber of Catalina's heart over the sight of her blue-eyed, brown baby girl. Her usually wild and free locks were brushed into a single ponytail to the top of her head. Her blondish brown curls were longer than when she last saw her. Catalina hurried up the steps and met them half way. She brought Eve into her arms and the toddler spat out her pacifier and kissed Catalina on the lips.

Dominic chuckled behind her.

"Look at you! How big you've gotten."

Eve smelled like powder and lilac. Catalina inhaled her and kissed her face. "*Ciao, bambina,* I have missed you."

"*Ciao!*" Eve said.

Dominic started up the stairs so Catalina had to step to the side. She held Eve to her heart and smiled at Cecilia. "How are you? I didn't know you had come with the family."

"I'm good thank you. I take care of Eve. The *Donna* and *Don* have left to visit Bagheria."

"Where's Rosetta?" Catalina turned on the step and started down. The name hadn't fully left her mouth when she saw Rosetta approaching. And her cousin looked really beautiful in a dark blue summer dress with thin straps. She wore her hair styled like Catalina's with bangs and long wispy curls. Catalina frowned at how much Rosetta favored her.

"*Boungiorno, Catalina.* You made it."

Things had changed between Catalina and Rosetta. They would never be close, but the hostility between them was tolerable. "*Sì,* why haven't you returned to Palermo to see your father and mother?" Catalina asked. She shifted the weight of her niece in her arms. Eve now rested her head on her shoulder.

"I intend to. I have a project I'm working on for the *Donna*," Rosetta smiled. "In fact this is one of them, you like?" Rosetta turned for her to get a good look at the blue dress. Catalina opened her mouth to respond but Rosetta's attention was averted to the stairs. A girlish smile and blush rose in her cousin's cheeks. Catalina glanced back to see Dominic coming down from the rooms. He didn't look at either of them. He appeared deep in thought. Catalina's gaze swiveled to her cousin and she couldn't help but feel anger clench in her gut.

"*Ciao, Domi!* Welcome home," Rosetta said.

"*Ciao,*" Dominic grumbled. He walked over to Catalina. Eve's head popped up. Dominic took her from Catalina's arms and held her up above his head to get a good look at her. Eve grinned down at him. Dominic kissed both of Eve's cheeks before handing her back to Catalina. "I need to pay a visit to a few people. I'll be home this afternoon. Thanks for the talk, the time on the train," he winked.

"*Prego, ciao,*" Catalina said and kissed him goodbye. Dominic turned and headed for the door but Rosetta stepped in his way. Catalina believed her cousin did so on purpose. Dominic blinked in surprise. He greeted Rosetta with a kiss to both cheeks and then left. Rosetta's head turned to watch him go.

"I saw that," Catalina seethed.

"Saw what?" Rosetta asked with a touch of sweetness in her voice.

Catalina narrowed her eyes on her cousin. "Don't even dare cross that line. I'll cut your fucking throat."

Rosetta batted her long lashes. Her forced innocence infuriated Catalina. But mindful of Eve in her arms she resisted striking out. And then Rosetta took a step toward Catalina never breaking the stare off between them. "I was happy to see him as I am you. He's a brother to me. Like he once was to you. I don't cross those lines, Catalina. It would be obscene. Family fucking *famiglia*, tsk, tsk, so unnatural."

Catalina took a step toward Rosetta. Cecilia reached and touched her arm. "*Signorita Catalina?* Eve hasn't had lunch. Sophia's here. She's prepared one for us. Care to join us?"

Catalina bit down hard on her bottom lip until it pulsed. She glared at Rosetta who didn't blink. She wasn't going to take the bait. Rosetta was just a jealous rat. Why waste the energy? She heaved Eve in her arms and looked over to Cecilia. "Where's Carmella? I'll want some adult conversation at lunch."

Rosetta chuckled and crossed her arms.

Catalina glared at Rosetta. "I haven't seen Carmella since the wedding."

"She left," Cecilia answered.

"Huh? Why?"

"The *Donna* sent her away. She was jealous. She took one look at Carmella and knew Giovanni would be tempted since she is now fat and pregnant." Rosetta called back over her shoulder as she headed up the stairs.

"Not true!" Cecilia interjected. "The *Donna* didn't send her away. *Don* Giovanni did. I heard him tell her to leave. He preferred that I stay and help Sophia."

Both explanations for Carmella's absence seemed odd. Carmella loved Giovanni when they were kids, obsessed over him when they were adults. But Catalina had never seen the two of them even close to intimate in all these years. It wasn't like Mira to be jealous of anyone. And lord knows she had good reason. The way the women glared at her and refused to talk to her unless spoken to at the wedding had left Catalina's teeth on edge.

"Lunch?" Cecilia reminded her.

Catalina's stomach growled. "Sure, let's have lunch."

★ B ★

St. Tropez, France—

"Sign here, *mademoiselle*. And here." The clerk with a nasal voice and disapproving smirk instructed in French.

"She wants you to sign your name," Lorenzo said, interpreting the lady's instruction.

The pen slipped and Marietta fumbled to pick it up. She tried again to sign but her fingers were weak from the nervous tremors in her hand. She peeked up at the woman who tapped the line she was to sign with a pointy half polished nail. The clerk's face was austere, her manner haughty. Their eyes met. Cool brown eyes observed her from above a pointed nose.

"Mademoiselle?"

A hundred butterflies swarmed in her gut. If she signed the document then it was official. *Am I ready?* The touch of Lorenzo's hand, a slow caress of her spine, broke through her reserve. She signed her name next to his on a contract written entirely in French.

Apparently Lorenzo had more influence with these people than she initially believed. She didn't know French law, but she figured a marriage contract would take weeks if not months to get pushed through for two non-French citizens. However, they were a day away from getting married.

"*Mercì,*" The woman said with a nod of her head.

Another woman began to explain the process and Lorenzo listened attentively. He spoke fluent French. Marietta didn't. So instead of paying attention she inspected her diamond ring. The gem flashed, sparkled and caused beams of color to dance before her eyes.

"We're done, *cara*. Tomorrow you will be my wife. Tell me you're excited." Lorenzo hugged her in front of everyone.

Marietta smiled. "Very much so. I really am!"

Carlo entered the office and a bell chimed over the door. He didn't approach. Again he had that remote, cool… intense manner of his that drew her attention. He'd been absent most of the day. The way his lips thinned into a firm, straight line indicated he disapproved. Why that hurt Marietta's feelings she wasn't sure. *Fuck him.* She kissed Lorenzo in front of Carlo, but peeked at Carlo to see if he watched.

"*Bonjour, Lorenzo!*" A man's deep voice bellowed. The man walked out from around the counter. He greeted Lorenzo as if they were old friends. The two embraced. Marietta glanced to Carlo. He leaned against the door and his gaze never left her.

"Come here, Marie," Lorenzo said. He extended his hand. "I want you to meet the man that will make it all happen for us."

She stepped forward and took Lorenzo's hand. The stranger arched a brow with approval. "*Enchantè mademoiselle Marietta,*" he took her hand and kissed it. Marietta nodded her hello but removed her hand from his. "She's lovely, Lorenzo. I'd expect nothing less," he said but kept staring at Marietta's breasts. He raked her from head to toe with his leer. She knew that look. Lorenzo gave the man a shove to the shoulder and the stare off was broken. He said something in French that had the man both laughing and apologizing. Together they started to walk off. Marietta figured the meeting between the two would be the part of the deal where money exchanged hands.

"I won't be long, *cara*." Lorenzo called back over his shoulder. "Carlo, keep an eye on her and make sure she doesn't try to escape," he winked and entered the door to the office of the man. It closed.

Marietta gazed down at her ring. It was the most beautiful and valuable piece of jewelry she'd ever owned. She thought of her adoptive mother and the talks they would have about her being a wife and mother when she was a little girl. She felt a pang of regret for how things were left between them. Though her adoptive mother never spared her the wrath of her abusive father, there was love between them. And she wished they weren't so far apart now. What family did she have to share something this special with?

"Nice."

Marietta jumped. Carlo peered over her shoulder at her ring. She turned and found herself closer to him than appropriate. Marietta took a step away. "It's better than nice, it's beautiful," she said. She extended her hand so he could get a full view.

"I see you made him bend down to his knees to put it on your finger," Carlo said.

"Oh you saw that? Yes. Lorenzo did it in front of everyone at the jewelry store. He's very happy to be mine," she smiled.

"Why are you doing this?" Carlo asked. "You don't know him. You sure as hell don't love him. So I have to wonder why do *you* want to marry him?"

"I don't owe you an explanation," Marietta said. The accusation cut her to the bone. She didn't understand the hostility. Carlo's gaze lowered and his dark eyes held a sinister challenge that made the hairs to the back of her nape stand on end. But she didn't blink. Lorenzo would kill him if he touched her. Of course he wouldn't have to because she'd rip his balls off first.

"I think you should go back to America. Take the ring and go. I'll give you money. Whatever you want. End it now," Carlo said.

Stunned, her mouth dropped open. She never thought she and Carlo were friends, but never enemies. She saw how Carlo stared at her. She caught desire in his eyes several times and deep down inside his cool hardness enticed her. They had formed a friendly enough bond around Lorenzo to mask hostility. There was nothing flirtatious in his manner now. Now he looked deadly serious. "I do love him." Her voice came across weak. She cleared her throat. "And I will marry him. And you know what else?"

Carlo's left brow winged up with amusement. *"Dica?"*

"The first thing I will do as his wife is break the bond between the two of you," she finger poked his chest.

A flash of predatory rage passed over Carlo's stony face. Marietta stepped forward to show her bravery. He was indeed dangerous, and something else. She couldn't put her finger on it but there was something off about Carlo. Still she held her ground. "For you to come at me like this behind his back proves you aren't his best friend. I won't have you doing anything to hurt my man. And trust and believe, Carlo, taking me out of his life will hurt him, and before I go I *will* end you!"

Carlo let go a mocking laugh until it lowered to a soft chuckle. The women in the office were staring. Marietta could sense it. She didn't dare break the stare off with him. He smiled and it was deceptive. "Trust and believe me, bella, I will be here for Lorenzo long after you are gone. And if I want to make you disappear I know many ways to do it."

Marietta crossed her arms. "We'll see, playboy."

"We're done!" Lorenzo announced behind her. But she and Carlo couldn't take their eyes off one another. Lorenzo swept her up from behind and spun her around then planted her on her feet.

"*Ti amo, bella.* You have made me the happiest man in the world by agreeing to be my wife."

"I love you too, Lorenzo. So much."

To her surprise he picked her up again with a manly growl. Marietta laughed as the others watched. He kissed her and she wrapped her arms around his neck and kissed him back. She was the happiest woman in the world. Lorenzo ended the kiss and she slid down his tall frame. Grinning up at him she couldn't look away from the man she loved. She loved him with all of her heart.

When given the chance she glared at Carlo.

Carlo winked and tipped his head to the challenge.

* B *

Armando Mancini strolled toward the front of his family home a bit curious. He was summoned. The men said Dominic Battaglia had come to pay a visit. Once he saw the Battaglia runt standing there alone, the anger in his gut tightened. The fool had arrived with no entourage to protect his scrawny neck.

This intrigued and tempted Armando.

"*Ciao, Dominic,*" Armando said.

Dominic nodded. Armando gave him the customary embrace and cheek kiss. "This is a surprise? *Come sta?*"

"*Molto bene, grazie.* I would have called first but I just arrived in Palermo and thought it would be okay to pay you a visit. Giovanni sends his hello."

Armando chuckled. "Of course he does."

He started off to his office. Dominic followed. Armando hadn't expected any Battaglias after the last unannounced visit. But even if they were brave enough to visit his home they certainly wouldn't do so alone. He glanced back at Dominic. He had always known this one had bigger balls than the others, considering the hellhole he escaped as a boy.

"How is Don Mancini?" Dominic asked of Armando's father when they entered the office. Armando went to his bar and reached for the crystal decanter of freshly poured wine. "He's doing quite well. He's in the garden. Is that why you came to visit? To see Papa?" Armando turned with glasses. He walked over and handed one to Dominic and then returned to his desk to take a seat. "Please sit. I'm curious about this visit."

Dominic sat. He let the wine swirl in the bottom of the glass but didn't take a sip. "As you know Giovanni has returned to Villa Mare Blu. He's brought his wife and baby daughter. It's a holiday for them."

"I've heard," Armando said. "I am disappointed that he didn't call to inform us of this holiday."

"That's why I'm here." Dominic grinned. "I came to let you know of our intention to stay, until the babies are born."

"Babies? Twins?" Armando asked.

"Yes. We are blessed. Twin boys."

Armando glared at Dominic from over the rim of his wine as he took a sip. "So you are *consigliere* again?" When Dominic didn't answer Armando chuckled. He knew that Dominic killed Catalina's husband Franco. They all did. He also knew that he was stripped of the title *consigliere* for the dastardly deed. Though it appeared the punishment was brief. Another weakness of Giovanni's was this dirt rat who they adopted into the family. Armando sat his glass down on the coaster. "Forgive me. I find it funny how you *Camorra* pretend at understanding *Cosa Nostra*. One day a *consigliere*, the next day an errand boy, the next day *consigliere* again," Armando chuckled.

"We are no pretenders, I assure you," Dominic replied. His unfazed manner set Armando's teeth on edge.

"Of course you are pretenders. The *Camorra* is the lap dog of the Mafia. We Sicilians own the traditions you play with in Italia."

Dominic sighed. "We are just as Sicilian as you. Our fathers took the same oath of *omertá*, instilled the same values. The *Camorra* is stronger because of our mutual Sicilian blood."

"Is that what Giovanni teaches you?" Armando asked, with a sardonic smile.

"I'm not here to debate you, Armando. We exist. And that will never change. I'm here to pay respect to your family and inform you that we will be in Sicily for some time. If that is a problem, you should tell me now."

Armando sat forward. "You've got some fucking nerve arriving here without my blessing. If I do have a problem you were foolish enough to make it easy for me to rectify it."

Dominic stood. He put the glass of wine down on the table without having a sip. Another insult. "But you won't, Armando. Will you? Until the old man dies you play at being the mafia *Don*. And my guess is Mancini doesn't want a Battaglia war, he never has."

Armando smiled. "You'd be surprised by what my Papa wants these days."

Dominic started for the door.

"Come sta Mirabellá?" Armando asked, slouching back in his large wing back chair.

Dominic stopped.

He turned his gaze back over his shoulder. Armando rocked back in his chair. The cold congested look of rage on Dominic's face was the first show of emotion since his arrival. Armando was pleased he had pushed the right button. "Tell her that my Papa sends his love and blessings for the twins."

Dominic gave a single nod of his head and then walked out. Armando stroked his chin. The Battaglias had a secret and it was the same secret his father carried. Armando guessed that if he uncovered why those bitches mattered he'd finally have the means to destroy Giovanni Battaglia. He smiled. That indeed would be gratifying.

"Dominic Battaglia?" Ignazio entered his office and spat the words with distaste. "What the fuck is Dominic Battaglia doing showing his face around here? Did you invite him?"

Ignazio was Armando's left hand. And when Armando took the crown from his father, Ignazio would be his *consigliere*. Armando picked up his wine and sipped it. Ignazio stood there with his hands in his pockets.

He lowered the glass of wine back to the table. "He came to say that Giovanni Battaglia will be staying in *Sicilia* for the next couple of months. He and his black wife."

"Let me deal with him, a nice little accident on his drive back to Mondello."

"No," Armando said. "The old man wouldn't like it. Besides, I have a better plan."

Ignazio's brows lowered with interest. Armando leaned forward on his desk. "Giovanni's wife. She's here to give birth to twins. That means they have a doctor in mind. Find out who it is. I'd like to meet him."

Ignazio nodded his head and walked out.

Armando smiled. Giovanni was home. It felt like old times.

* B *

Mira sat up on the exam table. She was helped down to her feet. Giovanni insisted on being the one to put on her underwear and then shorts. The gesture was so sweet but a little oppresive. Mira was still able to manage the effort, however, she knew allowing her husband the priveledge appeased him. They were always both so tense when making a doctors visit. And of course he took the liberty to touch her intimately. He pulled up her shorts and kissed her nose.

"I can't believe you had him come to Sicily." Mira smiled.

"I told you I would have the best doctors for you. Besides he's part of a team here in Palermo that will be seeing to you. I made sure they were the very best," Giovanni winked.

"You're a wonderful husband. Thank you, sweetie," Mira said.

The doctor knocked and returned. His name was Abdul Buhari and he was African. He was a tall handsome dark black man with a bright white smile that matched his cool bedside manner. At first Mira thought Giovanni would be uncomfortable with this doctor, unfazed by the man's natural charm. The doctor spoke fluent Italian, Spanish, French and English. She first met him weeks ago when she bled so heavily she thought she was miscarrying. He said that it was her cervix expanding and nothing to worry about. The bleeding stopped as suddenly as it started and she began to feel better.

"I'm happy to report everything looks well *Signora* Battaglia. *Molta brava!*"

"That's great. Will I be able to carry them full term? You were worried about my blood pressure. And look at my feet."

The doctor and Giovanni glanced down to her swollen ankles and feet. After walking around today they were so puffy she feared if a needle poked them they'd explode.

"Can I suggest that you remain off your feet? Relax. I'll be doing home visits for you three times a week until delivery day. I've already worked it out with your husband."

Mira looked to Giovanni who nodded that he and the doctor had met. "Then I'm confident that it will be fine. I will do whatever is necessary, Doctor," Mira said.

The doctor glanced to Giovanni. "*Signor* Battaglia? Can we speak?" The doctor asked. Mira tried to mask her frustration. She hated when the doctors always pulled him aside to discuss her. But she knew it was a matter of respect for Giovanni. She watched the men go. Alone in the exam room she stepped over to the mirror above the sink. She turned sideways. Her stomach had a nice round swell to it. She would be seven months in a few days. A mother again in a few weeks. She couldn't wait to hold her sons, love them, and build their family. But she also wanted to talk to Giovanni about future kids. Three children was a blessing, more than either of them hoped for. After having these two she wanted to go on birth control. Zia told her it was against their faith. Mira shook her head with a smile. Faith or not she was not a baby-making machine.

"What is wrong?" Giovanni asked once they were behind the doctor's office door.

"As I explained to you before, her situation is delicate. The low-lying placenta hasn't covered her cervical opening. But it hasn't moved up as we hoped."

"Go on," Giovanni said.

"And her pressure was dangerously elevated when she got here. It does give me concern. I want to suggest you cut back on her activities. I, ah, it's hard for me to say this."

The doctor looked nervous. His brow was damp and he kept avoiding looking him in the eye. He didn't like that manner. A man should always look another man in the eye. Giovanni had heard from Dr. Ricci that Buhari was the best in his field. Still something about the doctor struck him odd.

"What is it?" Giovanni demanded. "And look me in the eye when you say it damn it!"

Shock flashed over the doctor's face. He forced a smile. "Of course. My recommendation is that you cut back on her physical activities. Recreation. We need to get her to the eighth month."

"You said that already." Giovanni frowned.

"Also sexual activities need to cease. Uh, as well, I uh, suggest," he stammered.

"Oh?" Giovanni said. "I understand. Have I caused this?"

"No. No this is the natural course of things with a woman in her condition." The man flipped open a folder and shuffled through the documents. Again he avoided Giovanni's eyes. "How is her depression, mood swings, anxiety?" the doctor asked.

"She's the same. She has her good days and bad days,"

Giovanni said.

"And the bleeding?"

"It's stopped, none for a week. I ask her every day."

"Good. Good. I won't recommend bed rest yet. If her next ultrasound shows no improvement then of course that is the decided course of action. Let's give it another week."

"Okay. Grazie, *dottore*." Giovanni stood and extended his hand. The man shook it. He turned and walked out. *No sex?* He chuckled. That would prove to be a challenge

* B *

St Tropez, France –

Under the instruction of her seamstress Marietta held her arms out at her sides. The seamstress then carefully placed pins where needed. Marietta's head tilted left and she looked her dress over. She loved everything about it. Not the typical fashion style for a wedding dress.

The garment was overlaid in antique white lace and fit like a sleeve when pinned down to her dimensions. The front was a heart shaped bodice. The waist was so slimming thanks to the corseted fit that laced up the back. And the hemline stopped considerably high on her thigh. But it was the overlay that made the dress. The lace had pearls and tiny white crystals woven in.

"This is a Mirabella original?" Marietta asked.

"*Oui*, it is. Since Mirabella has risen from the dead her dresses are in high demand. This dress, *mademoiselle,* is from her 1989 collection. She designed it personally before her accident. A vintage piece that we only recently received."

Marietta didn't think the snooty black Barbie could design something so damned sexy and edgy to walk down the aisle in. She might have to rethink her opinion of her.

"Do you approve?" the woman asked. She stepped back and Marietta ran her hands down her figure.

"I do. Yes. I like it. I hated the other ones but this was made just for me."

"*Oui!* I believe it was. You will be beautiful." The woman celebrated with a clap.

Marietta grinned. "I feel beautiful."

Lorenzo sat on the circular sofa with his arms stretched out over the top of the plush furniture. He watched Carlo pace in front of him. The shop girls were quite attractive. Leggy blondes with nice asses. Not one of them turned the head of his friend. He was in no mood for Carlo's paranoia.

"Would you sit the fuck down? You're giving me a headache," Lorenzo sighed.

Carlo stopped. He pointed at him. "Do you know what you're doing? Marrying her!" Carlo seethed. "Giovanni will lose his fucking mind! This will undo all your progress with him. He will punish us both. He'll fucking cut our balls, Lo."

"He can suck my dick," Lorenzo grabbed his groin and gestured obscenely.

"I'm serious!" Carlo said.

"Fuck Gio!" Lorenzo shouted. He leaned forward and glared up at his friend. "I don't exist to be his puppet, to suck his prick for the rest of my life. I'm my own man. And she's my woman. My woman!" Lorenzo pointed at Carlo. "He has no fucking say in this. And I'll tell him to his face. I'll fucking marry her, and go back home and tell him to his face. It's done."

Carlo shook his head. "You're doing this to gain leverage over Gio aren't you? You're using her. You telling me you're over Fabiana? She's the one you want."

The accusation cut open a wound that had barely healed. Yes he wept in his heart for Fabiana. But Marietta was different. She made him strong. The woman knew his deepest and darkest secrets. "Say that to me again, Carlo, and I will forget we're brothers. Say it to her and I'll cut your fucking throat."

After a deep sigh Carlo wiped a hand down his face. "I'm telling you what you need to hear."

"Why? If Gio can see Mirabella from across the room and fall in love with her why the fuck can't I do the same with Marietta?"

"Because that one in there is trouble! She isn't Mirabella. She's you in a fucking skirt!" Carlo shouted.

Lorenzo laughed.

Carlo shook his head smiling.

His friend plopped down on the other sofa and dropped his head. Lorenzo couldn't stop smiling. "She's a handful. Yes she is. I can't explain it. Maybe it's what Gio sees in Mirabella, maybe it isn't. She understands me. She accepts me. And she has this way of controlling me the way I need." Lorenzo's smile faded. He spoke with quiet emphasis on his words. "I want to go home, Carlo. The only way I can bring her through the doors of Villa Mare Blu is as my wife. You and I both know it. This plan will work. Giovanni will have to deal with us. He will have to deal with me."

"But do you want a wife?"

"No. I want Marietta, and fucking her on a boat is only going to get me so far. I can't risk her going back to America. Leaving for another mission to find her identity. I can't risk her learning from someone else that I knew who she was and that I never told her. I want her. And this is how I can keep her."

"Do you love her?" Carlo asked.

Lorenzo nodded his head. "I love her."

"I pray you know what you are doing," Carlo shrugged.

Lorenzo shrugged. "Has that ever stopped me before?"

Careful of the pins attached to the seams Marietta handed the dress over to the sales clerk. When she arrived it was her idea to ask for Mirabella Originals. If she were to be Lorenzo's wife then it would mean she was a Battaglia. She would have to deal with the Queen Bitch and cranky *Don*.

However, when Marietta saw the beautiful dresses she felt an overwhelming sense of pride. There weren't many black American women with the power and talent in the fashion world as Mirabella. It made her intrigued by the Queen B's success.

Her selection would be the perfect dress to show Lorenzo how much she loved him and wanted to be part of his family. Her life had changed overnight because of their love.

"We will see to it, and have the changes altered immediately."

"I need it delivered to me tonight. I get married in the morning," Marietta said.

"*Oui*, it will be done." The salesclerk affirmed.

She walked out and found Lorenzo and Carlo laughing. She was still pissed at Carlo over the argument they had earlier. But when he looked at her she didn't see the disapproval from earlier. He actually smiled at her. Marietta rolled her eyes at him and went to Lorenzo.

"The dress?" he asked, pulling her down to his lap.

"She's making a few adjustments. They will deliver it to us tonight. It's so beautiful. And guess what?"

"What?" He lifted her chin.

"It's a Mirabella Original," she said.

The smile dimmed a bit on Lorenzo's face. He glanced over at Carlo who shook his head while wearing a deep scowl.

"What? What's wrong with you two? I thought you'd want me to wear a dress by her!" Marietta exclaimed.

"I do." Lorenzo quickly added. "Surprised you wanted to... I'm just surprised."

Marietta scanned his face to see if he was lying. All she saw was his love for her. She hugged him around the neck tightly. "We have to celebrate. It's our last night before we become man and wife," she said.

Lorenzo kissed the top of her head. "A private celebration. Me and you." he whispered in her ear. "I want you to dance for me."

Marietta giggled. "Oh baby, you haven't seen the dance moves I got planned for you."

"And then tomorrow you're mine," he said.

"I already am!" she exclaimed.

6.

Discomfort in her back sharpened. Painful spasms knifed its way up her spine. Mira breathed through her nose and arched a bit underneath the seatbelt. She was exhausted. The last stop they made was to visit family in Bagheria. At Giovanni's side she walked through the huge estate and greeted each family member personally. In doing so she found that Esta was right, the Baldamentis/Battaglias were a huge family. And they had the respect of the people who lived in the village. A quarter of the countryside was named for the family. And the house where Giovanni's family dwelled had been rebuilt and expanded over the years—extending it from every angle. The family members who lived there numbered twenty-three. She met so many, aunts, cousins, and distant relatives that her head spun.

"They loved you, Bella." Giovanni glanced over to her instead of focusing on the road. Mira exhaled and resolved herself to the discomfort. She glanced over to her husband who looked like he wanted her to respond.

"I remember many of them from the wedding," Mira said. "Your family is so huge. It's really something. I don't understand why we are Battaglia and not Baldamenti?"

"Many of them are Battaglia. Some Baldamenti. All of us are family."

"But why?"

"My father's mother is a Baldamenti, she married a man under the Battaglia name. But the Baldamenti family has been here for close to four hundred years. Even with my father taking on Battaglia, his father's name, he is a Baldamenti. A lot of his siblings feel this way. He and Rocco didn't. They wanted to strike out on their own. Battaglia is how they formed such a strong alliance with the *Camorra*," he answered. "Are you okay? You look like you're in pain?" Giovanni asked.

"It's my back again," Mira said.

"Rest. I'll carry you into Villa Mare Blu if I have to."

She reached over and touched his thigh. "I'm okay. Do you want to tell me what the doctor said?"

He kept driving.

"Giovanni? I don't like secrets, and you won't let me keep any. Remember? So what is it? Am I and the babies okay?"

"Yes, love. You are okay, but your cervix has opened. It's nothing to worry over. The doctor wants you to take it easy."

"Bed rest?" she asked. Terrible regrets assailed her. What if her working on her collection had caused this? Had she pushed herself too hard like before? The last thing she wanted was to be confined to a bed for the remainder of her pregnancy. What could she do to prevent pre-term labor? And then there was the blood. She never heard of a woman having the spotting and blood in urine that she has and being able to have a healthy pregnancy. God help her but she buried her head in the sand on this because she was so afraid.

"Bella? Calm down. No bed rest yet. But..." He pulled up to Villa Mare Blu and parked. He gazed at her with a bland half smile and Mira braced for the ne. "No sex," he said.

"Excuse me? Sex?" Mira laughed. "Sex? Are you kidding?"

"I'm not kidding. He said we have to stop having sex until you deliver my sons," Giovanni said.

"So what?" Mira shrugged.

"What does that mean? So what?" Giovanni asked. "You saying sex with me doesn't matter?"

"Giovanni? At some point we were going to have to. I'm carrying twins. Yes, we've found other positions but my body... sometimes I'm tired and it hurts."

"Hurts? I hurt you?" Giovanni frowned.

"You know what I mean," she sighed. "Your dick is too big, and you get rough."

Giovanni laughed. He shook his head smiling. "I don't understand. Are you saying I force my dick on you? I thought—"

"Oh good grief, baby! I want sex, all the time. My hormones are off the charts. My coochie aches though, sometimes." She shrugged. "That's all I'm saying." He didn't smile so she tried a different approach. "Physically it's becoming uncomfortable. The babies react by tensing up into knots under my ribs or kicking me hard. It can be too much."

Giovanni wheezed out a deep sigh and looked straight ahead. "You should have told me. I had no idea I was harming you, Bella."

"I do tell you, and you say relax!"

Giovanni frowned. "I… ah…"

"Oh stop. It's not that bad. Besides it's only a few weeks. Our marriage can survive a few weeks with no vaginal sex," Mira reasoned.

"We have sex every day," he grumbled. "Wait, what do you mean vaginal sex?"

Mira laughed. "True. Wow. That is true. Except for my menstrual cycle you and I have a lot of sex. I don't think Kei and I did it as much—" she stopped herself. She looked over and he glanced over to her. She saw the spark of jealous anger in his eyes. She chuckled and cut her gaze away. "Never mind."

"Do you think of sex with Kei?" he asked.

"NO! Let it go, Giovanni," she sighed.

"What do you mean vaginal sex Bella?" Giovanni asked.

She chuckled and reached over to massage his groin. "Do you think I will let my husband lay next to me and not touch it, suck it? Whatever I want?"

He laughed. "I can give you massages. Make you feel how much I love you," he said trying to change the subject. He removed her hand from his erection and forced images of bunny rabbits into his head.

"I can let you push this into my ass, make you feel like my man," she teased and reached over to touch his groin again.

He dropped his head shaking it with a smile. "You need to talk to me like this more. I like it," he said.

"I think I can handle that," Mira said. "I've gotten a potty mouth since I married you."

Giovanni leaned in and brushed his lips over hers. She closed her eyes and reveled in the tingling of her nipples when the tiny hairs of his mustache brushed her lips. "What have I ever done right in life to deserve a woman like you? *Ti voglio bene*," he said.

He often said *ti amo* to express his feelings for her, but when Giovanni said *ti voglio bene* it was indeed the deepest meaning of love. Sweet as honey, the sweetest expression of the unbreakable love between them. That is how she cherished the translation. No man had ever made her feel more desired and appreciated.

"I love you too," she said.

It was close to five in the afternoon. She knew Catalina and Dominic had to have arrived. Mira couldn't wait to see her. He opened his car door and she opened hers without waiting for assistance. She could hear him curse inside the car. Mira was able to exit. She held onto the top of the car door to steady herself. "See, baby? I can still handle myself quite well."

"Yes, Bella, you can. I wish you would allow me to do it."

"I do, sometimes, but I gotta pee. And I want to see Catalina. Now move," Mira said and pushed his hands away. She hurried. Giovanni closed the car door and caught up with her. He insisted on holding her hand. She allowed it, even though in her mind she walked fast, her legs didn't quite follow through. It took a full three minutes to reach the door. But as soon as she drew near the door flew open and Catalina let go a piercing scream.

"Mira!"

Catalina rushed Mira and hugged her. Eve raced out the front doors behind her aunt with Cecilia in pursuit. She too went for Mira. She wrapped her arms around her mother's legs. Mira laughed out loud.

"Venga qui, Evie," Giovanni said, and lifted their daughter up into his arms.

Catalina kissed Mira on the lips and tears bordered her eyes. She spoke with tight repressed emotion. It choked her voice. "I've missed you so much."

"What has it been? Almost a month?" Mira grinned and hugged Catalina tightly.

"Inside, ladies," Giovanni ordered. They couldn't break from their embrace. When Giovanni gave Mira a gentle shove Catalina let go of her first and pulled her inside the door by the hand. She placed her free hand to Mira's belly and rubbed it.

"Oh wow, they are growing huh? How much longer do we have?" Catalina asked.

"Eight weeks. I can't wait. These boys weigh a ton. Got a big head like their daddy."

Giovanni winked. He put Eve down and immediately she went to Mira with arms stretched to be picked up.

"Where's Domi?" he asked.

"Oh he had business, or someone to see." Catalina walked over to her brother and grabbed his face. She kissed him on the lips and patted his cheek. "You miss me, Gio?"

He shook his head no.

Catalina laughed. "Liar! You see him, Mira?"

"I see him. He complains all the time about you not being here," Mira said.

Catalina hugged her brother tightly and he hugged her back, kissing the top of her head. "Domi will be here soon," she said before letting him go.

"I'll wait in my office. Send him to me when he arrives."

They watched him go. A crying Eve ran after her father and he stopped to pick her up and carry her with him. Mira headed toward the parlor, which opened to a garden terrace. The day was nice and the breeze had a pleasant cool temperature. "So I want to hear all about it," Mira said.

"First you have to tell me what you and Rosetta are up to? She showed me what you are working on for *Fabiana's*. It's so fresh. I like it a lot," said Catalina.

"Do you? I was hoping so. Came to me last month in a dream. All I can think of is the color red for *Fabiana's*. She was such a fireball. I'm thinking the color scheme will span the gentlest shades of pink to blood red. From daywear to evening I want to do the entire collection with her signature flare. Even a shoe line with red bottoms."

"Mira? What are you saying? Carole Montague is working on her collection for *Fabiana's*. We agreed she'd design the collection for the first year until you had the boys and then we'd talk to Giovanni to let me use your designs for the next year," Catalina said.

"Nope. I don't want to wait. Giovanni knows I've been sketching my ideas and teaching Rosetta to be my sewing needle." Mira laughed. "Once he came in the sewing room and found me on my knees. He raised hell so bad the poor girl was scared to come out of her room for two days." Mira shook her head. "He's a handful but I can control my husband. And—" Mira continued.

"Hey. Slow down. I'm only saying that we pace ourselves. There's no hurry. Right? Besides we can do whatever you want. *Fabiana's* is your house. You tell us what you want and it's done."

Mira looked at Catalina and felt such a surge of love. In a matter of months she had matured, changed, become her Fabiana. She was so proud of her. "What about Teddy? Did you convince him to come to Milano? Is he there?"

"Teddy has no desire to return to Italy."

"Wait? Return? When did he come?" Mira asked.

Catalina bit her tongue. She only accidentally stumbled on the discussion. It was for the grand opening of *Fabiana's*. Teddy came a few days before. Giovanni forbade him from seeing Mira and Catalina never spoke of a return visit again.

Milano, March –

"Signorina Catalina, your brother is here."

Catalina stopped in her tracks. She had to pick up Teddy from the airport in half an hour. They had a plan to surprise Mira on the day of Fabiana's opening. Giovanni wasn't expected to bring Mira for three days.

"Here? Where?" Catalina asked her assistant. The place was a noise factory with drills and hammers pounding the last fixtures in the walls before they brought in the clothes and set up the displays.

The young assistant she hired was American. She would be at Catalina's side for the next few months to help her launch Fabiana's. They called her a Project Manager. The woman pushed her glasses up her nose. "They are upstairs with Mr. Tate. They arrived only a few minutes before you."

"They? Tate? Teddy is here?"

"Yes ma'am, I thought you knew. I believe they went up to Mirabella's office." The woman said. Catalina hurried away. She walked fast for the elevator doors, and finger punched the button. The doors opened and she couldn't stop her heart from slamming a rapid beat in her chest. The elevator took forever to climb three floors. She was out the door and hurrying through the halls.

And then she stopped.

In Mira's office Theodore Tate sat in a chair. There was no furniture, just him and a chair. Above on the wall hung the large portrait of Mira and Fabiana back to back. Before Theodore stood a displeased Giovanni. He wore a dark suit, and a dark cashmere trench coat over it. He glared down at the man with glacier blue eyes.

The scene would have been normal if Catalina hadn't seen Dominic. He stood over Theodore with a large silver gun pressed to the side of the lawyer's head. Catalina put her hand to her mouth. She didn't utter a word. But her brother's gaze lifted. His stare impaled her from across the room. Without a word Catalina turned and walked back toward the elevators.

Later Dominic informed Catalina that Teddy would be returning to America. He would not be allowed to surprise or meet with Mira. She didn't question him. She knew Giovanni was a jealous man, but to threaten Teddy with a gun seemed extreme even for her brother. She also knew not to mention it to Mira. There had to be another reason he and Dominic treated Mira's lifelong friend so horribly.

When Catalina spoke with Teddy he pretended nothing happened. He claimed he had so much to do in America that he could barely keep things straight. And it was true. *Mirabella's* was thriving. Still Catalina knew differently.

"Uh, he's been to Italy remember? You were the one who told me he and Fabiana scouted out Milano before you came."

"Oh?" Mira said. "I thought maybe you meant he came recently. Damn him. He has an excuse every time we speak. I'll call and invite him to Sicily." Mira said. "I'm dying to see him."

Catalina forced a smile. "Yes, you do that. Things are going so well. I'm thinking I will have to travel to America soon," Catalina said. "Carole is going to be part of a feature spread in this year's Metropolitan Museum Gala. She's working on that collection for *Mirabella's*. I have to be included. She can be... you know, how she is," Catalina said.

"I want her gone." Mira exhaled. She placed her hand to her belly. One of the babies kicked her so hard she nearly peed herself. "I want her out of my fashion house. Why do I have to keep explaining this to you all? It's my damn company!"

"Mira—"

"Why aren't we interviewing more designers? There's a talented designer over at Fendi that would be perfect for us. He just did a national interview saying he would love to work under me since I've 'risen from the dead'," she said with air quotes. "Damn it!"

"Giovanni said no, Mira," Catalina sighed. "It's a family business. After Carole it will be you and me. No other designers."

"He doesn't know what he's saying no to! I want the bitch gone!" Mira shouted.

Catalina's brows shot up with surprise. Mira had to laugh at her expression. She rarely cursed. She shook her head smiling.

"Well okay. I think I get it now. Don't go into labor over it," Catalina smiled.

Mira closed her eyes and rubbed her belly to settle the babies. "My temper is getting the best of me lately. I'm sorry. I understand why Giovanni wants us to wait. We're taking on a lot with *Fabiana's*. We have to make sure there isn't too much of a shakeup in our company. Chaos could affect my brand. But I'm not going to sit here and let my work, my fashion house, the one Fabiana and I built from scratch become Carole Montague's. I'm not going to do it!"

"What do you want me to do?" Catalina asked.

"You said you have been working on your own collection? Right?" Mira asked.

"Yes. I brought my sketches—"

"*Perfetto!* I have an idea," Mira grinned. "You've seen Rosetta today haven't you? I've taught her to sew and all she wears are clothes she's made. Beautiful dresses. I think she's wearing the blue one today."

"I saw her," Catalina said with a flippant cut of her eyes away.

"She's a good seamstress. Quick learner. And she's helped me with this collection I've been working on. We'll call it The Scarlet Letter, it'll be FWS&S."

"I don't understand?" Catalina frowned.

"We'll release the first line in Fall under the scarlet letter F. Remember the collection is different shades of red. And then we'll do winter and have a line under the letter W with muted shades of dark red, and then we'll launch Spring and Summer with resort and bikini wear, a line under the letters S&S with bright exciting shades of red. It'll be huge. It'll be *Fabiana's,* and you will be the head designer. With my designs of course."

Catalina's eyes stretched. "And mine? Can I have some of my designs included?"

"We'll see," Mira smiled.

"I love it! But it's lying to Giovanni. If he learns that you are designing while pregnant for me he'll be pissed."

"That's the beauty of it. I'm really not. I will give it over to you and Rosetta for final approval. And I will let you manage the launch of the line. I'm really going to stand you up as a designer. And when you emerge using my work you will blow their socks off. It gets Carole Montague out of my company, keeps my husband happy, and protects my babies from me overworking myself. And finally I can out some of these ideas I have in my head while I sit around and wait for my babies to be born."

"So we tell Giovanni?" Catalina asked.

"Let me worry how it is explained to your brother. He's sensitive, hard-headed, but reasonable when I put it to him the right way," Mira smiled.

"One thing, Mira. I want to use some of my work. *Per favore.* I want to be a *true* designer. I know I'm not fully ready, but if you are using me as the face of the fashion house, then it's going to be my talent too. I can't be just a mask for you," Catalina said.

Mira hadn't considered Catalina's ambition in her plans. It would be wrong to use her this way and not let her have real creative input. "I'll draw from your ideas if they align with the overall vision. Go get your work. And find Rosetta. Let's put my designs and yours together and see what we come up with."

"Oh my! Oh my goodness! I'm so excited." Catalina put her hands to her mouth. "This is going to be wonderful." Catalina clapped.

"Help me up. I got to pee." Mira tried to push up from the sofa. Catalina helped her rise to her feet. Mira felt so much better with her new idea. It would only be a matter of time before she could get Carole Montague out of her company for good.

* B *

"*Lucciola*, put it down," Giovanni ordered. He looked up from his desk when he heard the first bang of glass on a wood surface. Eve turned, sucking her cherry red pacifier. In her hand she held an ashtray made of crystal. She blinked at him and then looked at the ashtray as if trying to decide.

"Put it down," he said in a stern tone.

Eve shoved the pacifier to her cheek with her tongue. "Mine," she said. She plopped down on her butt and put the ashtray between her legs to play with it. Giovanni reached for the phone and dialed Santo again when there was a knock at the door.

"Come in."

Catalina stuck her head inside. She smiled at him. "I came for Eve?"

"Take her. She doesn't listen to Papa," Giovanni said.

"Giovanni! You can't let her play with this!" Catalina rushed over to take the ashtray from her. Eve protested. "I also want to talk to you," Catalina said. She put the toddler on her hip.

"Is that so?" he glanced up at her. "Everything okay? How are things at Fabiana's?" he asked. Catalina looked different. Mature. He wasn't sure he liked the change. The more independent his sister became the more he worried. Maybe allowing Dominic and her to marry would settle them both and bring them back into the family? He'd been considering his disgust over their relationship and their future.

Catalina laughed. "As if you don't know how I am. I know you have your men keeping an eye on me. I can't go to the bathroom and they aren't at the door."

"That's not me. Thank Domi for the surveillance." Giovanni corrected her. Though he had to smile at the truth in the statement. He got regular updates on who Catalina kept time with, her schedule, and her bathroom breaks. He wasn't a fool. Milano was 'Ndrangheta territory. The friendly binds between them and his clan was fragile since he acquired more territory in the triangle.

Rosetta strolled through the hall. She headed for the stairs, which meant she'd have to pass Giovanni's office. She had hopes to run into Dominic. If she innocently inquired after him maybe Giovanni would tell her when he was expected. She slowed her steps when she heard Catalina's laughter. Maybe Dominic had returned and they were all gathered in Giovanni's office? She would stick her head in and say hi to him. So he could see how much she had changed. When she stopped outside of Giovanni's office she found the door half open. From where she stood she could see in but they couldn't see her.

Before Giovanni stood Catalina with a fussy Eve on her hip. Rosetta turned to leave when she heard Catalina's request. It gave her reason to pause.

"That's my sweetie. He's always been my protector," Catalina chuckled. "But he worries to much. You both are too overprotective."

"You're my baby sister. I'm allowed to be overprotective," Giovanni replied.

"True." Catalina said. She looked to Eve and gave her a kiss. "I wanted to talk to you. I have a request. You're my Godfather right?"

Giovanni rocked back in his chair and frowned. "What are you up to?"

"Oh wow, so I want to talk to my brother and I'm up to something?"

"You asked to speak to your Godfather, so you don't want to talk to you brother." Giovanni arched his left brow.

Catalina purposefully pouted.

He waved her off. She took a step forward. "It's about Domi, Gio. We need to talk about him and me."

Her brother's gaze lifted from the page he was reading. "Continue."

"He's... well... he really wants to marry me. Dominic wants me to be his wife." She sat in the chair before him and put Eve on her lap.

"I told you both that you will have to wait a year," Giovanni groaned. He dropped his head back and closed his eyes.

"I know. And I agree. We should wait. I, uh," she lowered her eyes and tone. Unable to look at her brother as she explained, she used Eve as a distraction by allowing the toddler free play with her bracelets. "Dominic's going to ask you to let us marry sooner. I have to be honest. I love him, Gio. I want to be his wife, but... I'm not ready. I have so much to learn about Mira's company. So many exciting opportunities. I can't get him to understand, to let me have a little freedom to do this. I thought, well I thought maybe you could talk to him. No. My request is that you help him see that we should wait, a year or two."

"A year... or two?" Giovanni sat back dumbfounded.

The look on her brother's face sent her into panic. She was taking a huge risk appealing to him this way. And behind Dominic's back. It could put Dominic in danger. She knew Giovanni, and those stupid oaths these men took.

"Let me explain." Catalina said.

"Yes," Giovanni smiled, but the sinister way in which he did so made the blood in her veins cool. He leaned forward on the desk. "Explain it to me, *piccoletta*," he said. "Explain how you go from one day not being able to breathe if you don't have Dominic to the next day wanting to be free of him?"

"Have you seen what I've done with *Fabiana's*?" she asked.

Giovanni did not respond.

Eve fought to get down out of Catalina's lap. She struggled to hold on to the toddler and find the words. "I want to marry him, Gio. I do love him."

"Then why are you sitting here trying to make sure that doesn't happen?" Giovanni asked.

"I'm asking for your help. Look at what happened with Franco and me. Look at all that Dominic did to protect and hide our love. He put his life at risk, his brotherhood with you and Lorenzo at risk. I don't want to mess this up with him, Gio. He's my heart. But you know him. He's like you. He doesn't want a wife that's a fashion designer, he wants a wife, and a mother of his children."

Giovanni snorted.

"I am not saying I won't be ready to marry him next year. Hell maybe even six months. I just want the chance to see what being Mirabella is all about."

"What does Bella have to do with this?" Giovanni asked.

"I envy her. Not your wife. The fashion designer and business woman she is. She was so different than us. Her and Fabiana were both so different. Mira was the first woman I knew personally that was her own person. Mama never was, Zia never was. Name anyone else who is like Mira?" Catalina could see him processing her explanation. So she continued. "You're the leader of this family. Dominic worships you. He'd do anything for you. Loving me is something he did for him. And he's never done anything selfish in all of his life. Right, Gio? Help us. We're struggling here. Help us have what you and Mira have."

"Sure, Catalina." Giovanni's cold hard look was softened by his smile. "I'll help you."

"Don't tell him that I asked you to step in. Please? Just make him see that we aren't ready to marry. Not yet. Okay?"

Giovanni gave her a single nod. She tried to read the look in his twilight blue eyes. Was he agreeing to help her because he believed in them? Or had she made a big mistake by sharing with him her hesitation? "Gio, I love him. I swear it. I just… well you understand. You and Mira figured it out. Right? I do want to be his wife. Just not right now."

Giovanni didn't answer.

Eve said something to her father in her baby voice. He cut his eyes to his daughter and the smile on his face looked genuine. He sang a chorus of her firefly lullaby. And Eve kicked her feet laughing.

"Blow Papa a kiss. Like I taught you!" Catalina said. She made the gesture. Eve blew him a kiss.

Giovanni chuckled. Catalina relaxed. Her brother understood.

Rosetta backed away from the door. She turned and nearly collided with Cecilia in the hall. The young girl stared at her frozen. Rosetta knew she was caught. She glared at Cecilia and prepared to ring her neck if she said a word to alert Giovanni to her snooping.

"The *Donna* sent me to collect Eve. She sent Catalina but—well she needs me to collect her now."

"Oh who cares," Rosetta said. She pushed past Cecilia and started off. "Watch where you're going next time."

Rosetta had no worries that Cecilia would tell of her eavesdropping. If the stupid wench did she'd do far worse than push her down a flight of stairs. Rosetta smiled over the information she'd learned. Just as she suspected, Catalina didn't appreciate Dominic. She wondered what Dominic would think of this news?

* B *

"Something smells good?"

Marietta glanced back over her shoulder to the man who spoke. "Oh it's you," she said and rolled her eyes. Carlo stood at the entrance of the cramped kitchen on the ship. He wore swim shorts and no shirt. The sun had baked his skin to a deep olive tan. The man had more muscles, scars and tattoos on his chest than Lorenzo. The whole sordid story of his life could probably be told by the mean cuts and slashes she saw on his chest and side. Carlo stared at the frying pan with a wolfish grin to his face.

Earlier she told them both if they cleaned and gutted the fish she'd fry them up southern style. Lorenzo loved her fried fish. It was hard as hell to find anything equivalent to fishfry on the boat so she made her own batter, which turned out to be a good compromise.

"It'll be done soon," she said under her breath and wished he'd leave.

"It does smell good. Can I help?" he asked. From behind her she could feel him move in closer.

"Hell no." She turned and stopped his advance with a glare. "In fact why don't you go back up on deck and smoke your cigars or scratch your balls while *my* man keeps catching the fish for you to eat," Marietta snickered. She turned down the heat on the simmering oil and then used the spatula to pick up the fish and drop it on a napkined plate with four others.

"I wanted to apologize, beautiful," Carlo said. "I was a mean bastard earlier."

"Don't want, or need your apology, honey. We understand each other perfectly," she answered.

"I don't think we do." Carlo touched her shoulder. She flinched and he dropped his hand. She glanced back at him. He was as tall as Lorenzo but even more muscular in the shoulders and arms. She didn't like him standing so close. It made her feel funny. A strange mix of arousal and apprehension often overcame her. And his attention when they were alone, be it threatening or seductive, was unhealthy for her and Lorenzo. This she felt in her core.

"I was wrong to insult you," he said in Italian. "To tell you that you shouldn't marry him. He does love you. We've been friends since kids. He's a brother to me."

Marietta picked up the frying pan and moved it off the gas flame. "Alright that's enough!" she turned and faced off with him. "I don't give a *fuck* about your brotherhood. Lorenzo is *my* man. Mine! You have no say in what goes down between us. You got that?"

Carlo smiled. "I got it, *bambina.*"

"Then go away. Leave us alone. Go back to wherever it is you came from. And don't ever touch me again or I'll kick you in the nuts."

"Cara," Carlo chuckled. He leaned in and his face was close. "Lorenzo didn't tell you?"

"Tell me what?"

"I'll never go away. You marry Lorenzo, you marry me," he kissed her forehead and she slapped him. Carlo chuckled. Marietta didn't know what else to do. Her instinct said to hit him again, because the other instinctive nature in her, the one that was much more reckless said to do something else. He winked and then walked out. She exhaled deeply. After a few minutes she smiled. Carlo was a bastard. He was just messing with her head. No harm done. She shook her head and went to the fridge to make a salad. Carlo wasn't a threat. And he wasn't as smart as he thought he was. Marietta knew the secret that could blow Lorenzo and Carlo's friendship apart.

"You'll go away if I say so," she said with a smile.

* B *

"Gio?"

Dominic found him. He was in the zen garden, sitting and smoking his cigar. It looked like he waited for someone. The sun had nearly set and Dominic made it just before dinner. He walked straight in.

"Sorry I'm late. Had a few stops to make," Dominic said.

"Where?" Giovanni exhaled a thick stream of smoke.

"Mancini's for one. I met with Armando." Dominic took a seat. "He's the same arrogant bastard."

Giovanni nodded. "And what did the brat Mancini have to say?"

"He's delusional. I informed him of our stay. He wasn't pleased that you didn't call him personally."

"So?" Giovanni asked.

"He mentioned Mirabella."

Giovanni looked over. "Did he? What did he say about my wife?"

"You do know bringing her here was a risk. I've advised against it. This isn't our territory. The Mancinis could pose a problem."

"What did he say about my Bella?" Giovanni asked.

"He asked if she was well. I don't think he knows their connection. The inquiry was possibly to push my buttons."

"He's of no threat to her or us. Not even in Sicily. To be sure of it call in a favor with the Casalesi clan, I hear they have unresolved issues with Armando. The distraction should keep Mancini busy while my Bella relaxes and delivers our children." Giovanni pushed up in the chair and stood. "I wanted to see you. We have real problems. Chiaiano is gone—the entire territory is now under Mottola's control. Santo's fuck up."

"Mottola would never claim that region. I don't believe it." Dominic said.

"It's true. Giuliani informed me by phone. I've summoned him to Italy with Santo. It appears Mottola believes I have gone soft. That our attempt to legitimize Battaglia makes us weak." Giovanni looked at him. "And maybe he has a point."

"A point?" Dominic stood. "What you are doing is more than making a point. You're changing—"

"I'm losing sight of who we are. I've gone too far to forget what our legacy in the *Camorra* means."

"You have not, Gio. No one has ever betrayed you in our clan. You've taken the Neapolitan clans further than any other leader. You've brought in the discipline of the *Mafioso*. The rest of the clans are animals, tearing at each other's throats. You're a leader." Dominic began to pace. "Since Tomosino died we have acquired 1200 properties in the *Campania*, 23 companies in Italy excluding *Mirabella's*, and over 200 bank accounts."

Giovanni exhaled. "That's not the point."

"Listen to reason. We shouldn't go backwards. We can't go on as just the *Camorra*. We are bigger than that now." Dominic pleaded. "*La Polizi di Stato* has started investigating us ever since the Kei Hyogo and Fabiana incidents. I'm hearing that they have a new inspector who has an agenda. He works with the Americans. The next few years we need to remain above reproach." Dominic stepped closer and lowered his voice. "We deal with Mottola. Yes. Swift and decisively we put him down. But we don't stop moving toward legitimization of our assets. We don't become the dogs of society because we fear walking upright on two legs. Your actions make you a different leader from Patri."

Giovanni grabbed Dominic by the back of the neck and pulled him close. He patted his cheek. "You have always been a smart boy, like a son to me. But don't tell me what to do. I don't need a lecture."

"I'm a man now, Giovanni. I'm your *consigliere*. And I will never let them bring you down. Trust me. Let me do my job."

After a pause Dominic wasn't sure what Giovanni would decide. He then pulled him into a fraternal hug. Maybe the time of dissention between them was over. They let each other go. The hug was only brief and the words between them thoughtful, Dominic paused waiting for Giovanni's decision.

Giovanni had come close to acting on his impulses. Dominic was a good voice of reason. And to think he had every intention of ending the life of his brother over loyalty. Who in his life had ever been more loyal than Dominic? His Bella knew this, and saved them both from the curse of their fathers. And now Giovanni understood why compassion and forgiveness is needed in their family. He released Dominic who rubbed the soreness form his neck.

"We do it your way, Domi. Let Francesco continue his exploits. Send word to Carlo and bring him back from France. We will decide how we remind the clans that I have not softened. So we can continue to be the dogs who walk on two legs!" Giovanni roared with laughter.

"Hi!" Mira said

Giovanni and Dominic both looked back to the door. His Bella stood there grinning at them both. In Sorrento they conducted business at *Villa Rosso* and never worried over an unannounced interruption.

He would have to be careful.

"Ciao, Donna." Dominic walked over to Mira and kissed her.

"We've been waiting for you to come home. It's time to eat. You too, baby," Mira said. "Domi, can you come with me. I want a word."

Giovanni nodded and she turned and walked out. Dominic followed her. Giovanni stepped into the garden. Everything was manageable. And if it wasn't, he knew how to make it so.

* B *

Dominic found Mira in the billiard room down the hall. She stood there with her arms crossed waiting for him. He approached her and greeted her properly with a cheek kiss. "How are you?"

"I'm good." Mira sighed. "And don't worry I don't want to hammer you with questions about the company."

He chuckled. There was a chair close to her. He insisted she sit in it. He drew a chair over and sat before her. "Tell me what it is you want to talk to me about?"

Mira stared at him for a moment. She looked worried and that gave him pause. Did she learn the truth about her condition? A truth he told Giovanni he'd eventually have to share.

"He took me to see Esta and Fiona today," she said.

"Oh?" Dominic sat back.

"I saw how they're living. What Giovanni is doing to them. He pretends he's honoring Esta's wishes by locking her away in that village but I saw their meager existence. And... and the look in his eyes Dominic. He's torturing those women. Esta is sick. She should have round the clock care."

Dominic sat back with a deep sigh. He could give a shit about Esta. He remembered how cruel that bitch was to his madre Eve. But he masked his hatred for the sake of the conversation. "Esta is well cared for. You misread what you saw. She's a stubborn old woman. She doesn't want for anything."

"Bullshit, Domi," Mira chuckled. "I'm new to running a family like this but I'm not crazy. My fear is that this is unhealthy for him and you to treat her like this. My main goal is to protect my husband, even from himself if I have to."

"Don't worry about Esta, I'll handle it," Dominic made to rise.

"No." Mira stopped him. "I'll handle it. I want her moved to Bagheria. Where she has family, a better place for her. I want a nurse to tend to her round the clock. I want..."

"I have to advise against this, Mira," Dominic warned. He glanced back over his shoulder and lowered his voice. "You need to discuss the matter with Gio. He would not be happy if you stepped in and did things this way."

"Why?" Mira asked. "If what you say is true and he wants the best for Esta why would he care if I make sure that happens?"

Dominic slouched in his seat. He was tired. He had a lot to contend with, especially now that they had issues with the Mottolas. The last thing he needed was Mira's crusade of justice. So he decided to give it to her straight. He sat upright. "Esta suffers because of the last insult she did to our mother. Do you know Eve is buried here?"

"Yes, I know." Mira nodded.

"Well Esta could have shown kindness and allowed her to enter the family plot. The church would have granted it if Esta permitted it. But she refused. Giovanni also believes she convinced many people to stay away from our mother's funeral. It hurt him deeply."

Mira looked away. "He has to move on."

"Does he? Giovanni has endured scorn and ridicule all his life. It's part of him now. Those that took pleasure in the suffering of his mother earn no kindness in return."

"It bothers me. Worries me. I saw the look in his eyes, and it scared me. I don't want him to be a man that could torture an old woman no matter what her sins were," she reasoned.

"But he is that man, Mira," Dominic reminded her.

Her gaze returned to him.

"And you should realize that now." Dominic warned. He then smiled. "How about a compromise?"

"I'm listening," Mira said.

"I'll hire a nurse to tend to her, to make sure her medicine is administered correctly. The nurse will give you regular updates on her health. But she stays where she is."

Mira looked relieved. "Thank you, Domi."

He winked. "*No problemo*. Let's keep this between us. For now."

She grinned. "I agree."

* B *

Giovanni had to smile at the way his wife fussed with Eve who protested being locked in a high chair. To settle the dispute Giovanni moved the baby chair closer to his seat. They ate and listened to the updates on *Fabiana's* in Milano from Catalina. A few times Giovanni observed how Dominic looked uncomfortable when Catalina talked about her future projects in the company. *He knew that feeling.* He was glad arguing with Mira over her desire to work was over.

"We have something to propose, honey," Mira said, and silence fell over the table.

"We?" Giovanni looked up from his food, chewing. Apparently Mira wanted the family to hear her idea, or she would save the proposal for pillow talk.

"Yes me, Catalina, and Rosetta," Mira announced.

Giovanni's gaze cut away to the other two and both were

unable to look him in the eye. Bella didn't have that problem. In fact she glowed with excitement. All of it spelled trouble. "Let me hear it?"

"Catalina showed me her designs. She has a great concept for *Fabiana's*. I'm so proud of her. Sooooo...."

Giovanni looked from Mira and Catalina. Mira did a drumroll with her fingers on the table and Eve laughed.

"I think Catalina should be the head designer for *Fabiana's*." Mira announced.

Giovanni swallowed. "What?"

Mira laughed. No one at the table did. Either his wife didn't care or was too pumped on her idea to notice. "She's ready for it."

"No she isn't," Giovanni frowned.

"She is. And we have to strike now. Rosetta and Catalina will go back to Milano and get to work right away. Everyone is raving about the boutique and the project releases they've done so far. Carole Montague has so many commitments in New York. It's perfect."

"Let's not discuss it now." Giovanni waved it off. He glanced over to Dominic whose face was red as a tomato. However, Catalina couldn't be happier. Giovanni shook his head. Those two were headed for trouble. Mira opened her mouth to say more and he gave her a look that his request was not to be challenged. His wife dropped it. Not before giving him a serious scowl over being silenced.

Giovanni winked at her and continued to eat. Talk of designing dresses ruined his appetite.

* B *

The night ended and Dominic retreated. He couldn't get out of there soon enough. It took every fiber in his being to keep his cool through dinner. Catalina and Mira blindsided him with their talk of *Fabiana's* and his girlfriend's future. Not once did Catalina mention their plans to marry. And when Mira talked to him about Esta she didn't mention it either. He had to wonder if Giovanni's warning was true. And that realization made him feel like an ass. He couldn't be the man to hold her back from her dreams. But was he the man to let her dreams override his own?

Dominic decided to take one of the smaller villas on their land, one close enough to the beach to give him some perspective. Once inside he polished off a bottle of wine before he calmed himself enough to let go of his anger. The darkness of the evening had filled the inside of the villa and he didn't bother to turn on a light. Instead he closed his eyes and reclined his head on the chair. Sleep and some space was all he needed.

Several minutes had passed before that tranquility was disturbed. A knock at the door at first faint grew stronger. Dominic squinted in the dark not sure if he was fully awake.

"Domi? Are you here?" Catalina asked. "Domi? Open up!"

"Yes," he groaned. He sat upright and his rational thoughts swirled in his head. He forced himself to stand tall and walk on steady feet to the door. It took effort. How much had he drunk? Catalina stood on the bottom step with a red and yellow shawl around her shoulders. She wore a strawberry red strapless dress that billowed by the wind around her thighs. And her long dark hair was blown in her face. Dominic looked out to the sea. In the distance he could see a high tide rolling in over the shore. Possibly rain was coming.

"I thought you were out here. Can I come in? It's cold!"

"Not a good idea. Giovanni. Rules. Talk to you tomorrow." He tried to close the door.

Catalina threw up her hand and stopped him. "They've gone to bed. We need to talk, Domi. Please? Can we?"

"For fuck's sake! Do I have a choice?"

Before she answered he turned and walked off.

Catalina stepped inside the dark villa. There were several on their land and one that was actually on the beach. The men who worked for her family used most of these smaller cottages. Dominic rarely spent the night out here. She could sense his disappointment at dinner. The last thing she expected was to find him sulking in a dark villa that reeked of wine.

She closed the door and reached for the light switch. Dominic's hand went up to his eyes immediately. He dropped in the chair behind him.

"Were you out here drinking alone?" she asked. She could see he was. The empty wine bottles were sprawled over the floor. "Domi? Why do this? Why not talk to me? It's so childish."

"Do you want to get married, Catalina?" Dominic asked.

"Of course I do." Catalina answered.

"Then what was that bullshit at dinner? You going back to Milano and then heading off to America? You didn't discuss any of it with me. You knew I was going to ask Gio to let us marry. You humiliated me."

"I'm sorry. I am. Mira blindsided me with the news. After she saw my designs she came up with the idea of me launching my own line under *Fabiana's*. How could I say no? It's my dream."

"Since when do you dream of making clothes?" he asked.

"Since I grew up and lived a little from under your shadow." She fired back. "I don't see how any of this threatens us, or you." Catalina walked over to him. She got on her knees before him. "Domi, look at me. You know me. Am I running away from you or just becoming my own person? You have always supported me. What's changed? Tell me," she pleaded.

"You think I don't know when you're lying? This was your idea. You changed. I've been too distracted to see it," Dominic said.

"How do you make that leap? You haven't proposed. Giovanni hasn't given his consent. I don't even have a ring." She touched his knee. "You can ask Giovanni for us to marry. And if he says yes, then I'm yours."

She waited a pause for her words to sink in. Dominic closed his eyes and slouched deeper in the chair. Catalina continued, " If he says yes or no I can still be a designer. I can still be a wife. And I will always be your Catalina."

Dominic laughed. "Is this how you fooled Franco? With empty promises?"

The accusation stabbed her in the heart. She recoiled a bit inside and swallowed her hurt. *Damn him.* He was just like her brother. When they hurt they hit hard. "I'm going to ignore that comment because I don't want to fight with you, not over something as important as how we respect each other, how we love each other."

Dominic's eyes opened. He leaned forward and stared directly into her eyes. She couldn't look away from the soft love in his brown eyes. He grabbed her face with both hands. "Giovanni said this day would come. Are we here already, *piccoletta*? Tell me now and I swear I'll learn to live with it. I swear it. But don't play games with me, *cara*. If in your heart you need something different then tell me. You were so young—"

"Stop it!" she tried to break away but his hold on her face was tight as a vice.

"It's true. You were young and I—I don't know why I couldn't help myself. I love you with everything in my heart. I always have." Dominic confessed.

"He's wrong about us, Domi. They all are. There's nothing

impure about our love. I swear it. I want you, and this life we have. Different from the life my mother had with my father. Do you understand?" She kissed him. She wrapped her arms around his neck and held on to him while surrendering within their kiss. "I love you, Dominic Esposito Battaglia," she repeated after several kisses. "I'll give you a family, our own family. Trust me. I will marry you when the time is right. I will never leave you. And I'll never let you leave me."

Dominic relaxed. He was surprised, because he hadn't realized how much of his long buried fears of rejection had turned in on him. Self-hatred and loathing was beat into him by fists and vicious words before he learned to crawl. His biological father was a cruel sadistic bastard that even in death visited his nightmares. But never when his sweet Catalina protected him with her love. She was his shield against the word of doubt.

He lifted her by her arms and she came willingly to his lap. The soft round cushion of her ass snuggled his groin. His heart pounded. His dick went rigid when she settled in his arms. Deep down he had to admit that her defiance, independence, free will, pleased him on a primitive level. Every man loved the chase. Why else would Giovanni work so hard to make a woman like Mirabella his mafia wife?

Catalina shrugged off her shawl. In doing so she revealed her slender shoulders. He moved her dark locks away with the brush of his hand so he could see the lovely contour of the shoulders that extended up her neck. She was gentle, serenely wise, and beautiful. She was his salvation. Dominic rubbed the tip of his nose against hers. She blinked once but maintained his gaze. Her soft hands touched the side of his face and slowly stroked down his jaw. "Love me, Domi, it's okay," she whispered as her lips brushed his brow. "I won't let you down."

Dominic closed his eyes and titled his chin upward as Catalina's petal soft lips met his and he opened his mouth, allowing her to sweep him up in her gentle kiss. Her lush breasts mashed against his chest as he held her tightly. Catalina was the sweetest kisser. Her tongue touched his, retreated, and then swept over and over. Even more satisfying was the fact that no other man had ever tasted what was his and lived to tell the tale.

Her fingernails scraped his scalp as she gathered his hair. She pulled his head back and released him from her kiss. Dominic opened his eyes and blinked as she opened her dress and she then drew his head down to give him her rosy perked nipple. To feel her nipple scrape his tongue was wildly erotic. His tongue circled the circumference and then he sucked on each thick morsel hard and strong. Catalina's eyelids fluttered. Her hand glided from his scalp to his neck and she held it She exhaled deeply.

Why did he feel like he was seducing an innocent each time he slipped into their passion? Dominic forced the doubts from his mind and claimed her as his woman. His hands went around her small waist to her back. He released the nipple to ravish the other with his tongue and mouth. The sucking became urgent and intense. She allowed him the freedom. Dominic let go. He dragged his tongue up her collarbone, neck, across her cheek and halted at her ear to whisper: "I will fuck you tonight. I love you. I want you. So bad."

"I believe—" Catalina sighed. He slipped his hand between her thighs and she parted them. Her head dropped back in a silent gasp. "Yes."

Dominic eased aside her panty and rubbed his two fingers over her wet slit.

Catalina saw it constantly. Saw her father and mother work to protect Dominic from his feelings of inadequacy. She watched Giovanni and Lorenzo protect and rough him up to make him stronger. Dominic had abandonment issues. Yes he was smart and loyal, but he was also vulnerable and wounded. Only she could save them. She believed it with everything in her. As his fingers slid into her she gripped his arm and her pelvis seized, she made a silent vow to be careful with his heart. He removed his hand.

She clutched his shoulders when he lifted her up in his arms. She wrapped her legs around his waist and rubbed her cheek against his scruffy jaw. Dominic carried her into the dark. He was on her the moment they hit the bed. Taking off his clothes and her dress, and underwear, he did away with them so fast she barely had time to catch her breath.

And he was inside her driving hard, long strokes of his dick, thrust after thrust. The lovely weight of his virile body pressed her down into the mattress. He leaned his forehead against hers and they stared into each other's eyes.

"*Tu queria*," he said thickly. "I must have you, *cara*. I must."

She heard him catch his breath when she moved up against his driving thrusts. He eased his hands under her buttocks to lift them so her tightness could fully encase him. His smile widened. Catalina held to his shoulders and moved beneath him, she rode the wave of pleasure. He rolled his hips with each thrust and fucked her deep. He withdrew to the ring of his cock and then plunged in once more. Catalina sighed. He took her left leg and pushed it down over to her right side and positioned himself on his knees to fuck her. And he did so well. Dominic turned her. She got on her knees and hands. She tossed her long locks and looked back at him as he steadied his strike.

A single thrust and he was fucking her again. She looked back at him to see the pleasure contorting his flushed face with sweat breaking over his upper lip and brow. Catalina dug her fingernails into the bed sheets and mattress. Deep long dick strokes beat at her pussy causing lovely friction that heated her inner walls, melting her core. She liked how controlled he was in his delivery. Catalina collapsed on the mattress, weak, unable to keep up. Dominic lay across her, fucking her. She turned her head to the side. He pressed his cheek to hers. His ass lifted and fell and his dick went in and out of her repeating the rhythmic dance until her toes curled.

"*Sei incredibilie. Sei bellisima. Sei uno dono*—you are a gift. *Amore mia*—my love."

Dominic gripped her by both hips and raised her a bit so he could hit spots beyond her belief. Strong pelvic spasms rippled currents of the sweetest pleasure through her. He dropped his head on the back of hers and they climaxed together.

And then they crashed. Dominic dropped on top of her. Catalina squeezed her eyes shut and forced the tears back. She hated hurting him. All she ever wanted since she was a little girl was her Dominic—and she intended to have him, to have it all.

7.

"*Buongiorno*," Marietta said. She rubbed the sensitive peaks of her nipples over his chest and planted a gentle kiss to his lips. Her arms were raised, her hands pressed flat to the wall above his head and pillows. She straddled him and the spry pubic hairs that grew wildly over his lower pelvis tickled her pussy. "Nice," she said as she shivered from the pleasurable contact.

"*Mia moglie*," he groaned. His hand reached and stroked the side of her thigh.

"I'm not your wife yet. Today is your wedding day silly." She removed a hand from the wall and traced her finger across his bottom lip. Lorenzo's lashes parted a fraction. She could barely see the color of his eyes they were so heavily lidded. "You ready to be mine, bad boy?" she asked.

"I'm ready," he rolled her over to her back. "*Sei tutto ciò che voglio*—you're everything I want." Lorenzo kissed her lips, her chin, under her neck, her collarbone. No words spoken in Italian or English had ever affected Marietta so deeply.

Marietta giggled. He parted her legs and positioned his body between. He settled on top of her with his hands firmly gripping her ass. He squeezed. His kisses began the sweet wet trail from the peaks of her nipples to her navel. Marietta swallowed and relaxed a little more knowing he'd keep going. She tingled with anticipation. She drew her knees up and rested the bottoms of her feet on his shoulders as his head lowered to her pussy. Lorenzo opened the outer lips of her pussy with his tongue and plunged it in to swipe up sweetly. His hot breath fanned her distended clit and she shivered. His tongue licked the sensitive skin at the entrance of her pussy and then dipped inside. Marietta tilted her head back and her jaw clenched to suppress a moan, her thighs clamped shut on his head.

And then his lips sealed over her clit and he sucked hard and strong. She lost control. She yelled his name and a slew of curses as she gripped his hair, and thrust her pelvis up to keep his face buried deep. Marietta was lost in pleasure.

Carlo usually smoked his marijuana to unwind. Alcohol tended to make him aggressive, even violent. Tonight neither alcohol nor marijuana could settle his mood. He dropped his head back and listened as Marietta cried out again in pleasure. Lorenzo fucked her good. Envy and guilt warred within him. The sound of her pleasure would haunt him the rest of the night. He should leave the cabin and go top deck. He should turn on the music box in his room or the television. He should do anything but listen to his best friend fuck his woman.

Carlo did neither. He took a long drag of his marijuana and listened.

To his left the satellite phone rang. Carlo exhaled the potent smoke in his lungs and dropped the joint in his ashtray.

"Pronto?" he answered the line.

"It's me."

Carlo sat up. The cabin walls were made of paper. Lorenzo and Marietta's sex play grew louder and louder. She laughed. He growled. Carlo heard what sounded like her running in the room and Lorenzo's hard foot falls chasing her down before he dragged her back to the bed to punish her. Carlo grimaced and tried to focus. He never coveted another man's woman and if he did that woman would be his.

The entire matter had him questioning his sanity.

He had called Melanzana and left the number to the boat for Dominic to call him back. He waited all night. He left another message at Villa Mare Blu. Finally the phone rang.

"I called you hours ago," Carlo said.

"So?" Dominic answered.

Carlo's jaw went tight but he kept the anger and impatience from his voice. "I'm with Lo. Your orders."

"Gio's orders," Dominic corrected him. "How is he?"

"The same. He—" Carlo paused. He could betray his friend and tell Dominic of Lorenzo's plan to marry Marietta or he could trust Lorenzo and play the dangerous game of disappointing his *Don.* Either choice left him fucked and hosed with the stench of betrayal. He was no fucking snitch, he was no fucking coward, but after spending a day with Lorenzo and the brown temptress named Marietta he wanted to be both.

"Carlo? What is it?" Dominic asked.

"Nothing. Nothing. Like I said I'm out here on this fucking boat with him. Wondering when we can come back?"

"We?" Dominic asked.

"Yes we. He's our brother. Why can't you remind Gio of that fact?"

"Gio needs no lessons on brotherhood," Dominic replied.

"Agreed. I'm not questioning Gio. The problem is, Lorenzo thought I came here to bring him in," Carlo said. "He wants to come home."

Dominic went silent.

Another burst of laughter from the couple echoed out of the wall. He heard Lorenzo curse loudly and Marietta squeal with girlish delight. He shook his head and clenched his fist. "So when can we come back?" he nearly shouted into the phone.

"That's why I'm calling. Gio wants *you* back. We have some opportunities to settle disputes in the *Campania*. Namely we can resolve problems with the Mottola clan. Need you on it," Dominic said. "I'm considering pairing you with Nico for the job."

No one was better at enforcing the might of the Battaglia clan than Carlo and Lorenzo. Nico was fearless, but a robot. He only followed orders. Not a thinker. And with his menacing height and build he didn't need to. As soon as Nico entered a room every other motherfucker bowed his head in respect. Carlo liked running with Nico. He liked being primitive in his hunt. But the administrators of Battaglia justice should be he and Lorenzo.

Either way he'd go with the flow. No more of the political shit that Santo and Dominic preached. Fuck a motherfucker up, gut him for retribution; step in his blood and tears on your way out. He had a bloodlust now to work off his frustration.

"How bad is it?" Carlo asked now on edge with excitement.

"Best explained in person. How long before you can travel back? We're in Sicily, Villa Mare Blu."

Carlo mulled the question over. The giggling, fucking, chasing ruckus had ceased in the other room. He could think clearly, breathe easily. He smirked at the idea of crushing a Mottola with his bare hands. "Tomorrow. I can be there tomorrow night or Monday morning at the latest."

"Good. See you then."

The phone line disconnected. Carlo dropped his head in his hand. He closed his eyes and thought it over. "Fuck this shit." He tossed the covers aside and found his pants. He put them on and left the cabin. He pounded on Lorenzo's door. "Need to talk to you!"

A few seconds passed and Lorenzo was at the door in his boxers, he looked sweaty, disheveled. The bastard still had an erection. Carlo rolled his eyes as Lorenzo pulled on his dick. "What is it?" Lorenzo emerged with a lopsided grin to his face.

"Home. We got trouble. I need to head back. We're done."

"Wait!" Lorenzo stepped fully out of the room he closed the door. "What kind of trouble?"

"Mottola. I think Santo has fucked up. Who knows? Gio wants me home to discuss it."

"When?" Lorenzo asked.

"Huh?"

"When does he expect you?" Lorenzo panted.

"Tomorrow night." Carlo started back to his door.

"Good. Slow down." Lorenzo walked up behind him. "We're coming."

"We?" Carlo asked.

"Me and Marietta. Today we get married and tonight we leave for Sicily."

"No. Fuck no, man. Gio wouldn't—"

Lorenzo pushed him back into his room and he had to shuffle his feet to keep from tripping over them. Lorenzo closed the door so Marietta couldn't hear them. Carlo guessed he wasn't aware of how thin the walls were on the boat.

"It's a perfect idea, Carlo. She's my wife as soon as the sun rises and we get the priest on the boat. Think on it. Gio needs me too. When I show up with her he'll have to settle things, accept Marietta. Tell the women the truth so I can leave this fucking exile."

"Or he'll cut your throat and mine for disobeying him!" Carlo said.

Lorenzo chuckled. "Trust me. I know what I'm doing. Gio's weakness is Mirabella. This plan will work. If he wanted Marietta dead he would have ordered it. He's trying to buy himself time. Well time has run out. We're coming home."

Carlo slapped his head. "Fuck, Lo, you're playing with our lives and hers!"

Lorenzo glared. "I know what I'm doing! Are you in with me or not?"

* B *

Giovanni walked outside in bare feet across the ebonized hardwoods of the belvedere that extended from their bedroom. Here the beach could be seen and felt. A sweet ocean breeze cooled him as the sun boiled in the sky at such an early hour. Mira was always most beautiful in the morning with their daughter. And it was a tradition that they dined on the terraces or on the balconies of their vacation spots. Her hair puffed about her head like a lion's mane. When she wore little makeup and didn't work tirelessly to straighten her hair, her beauty was personified.

While he slept she had their daughter's highchair brought inside the room. Mira sat at a white linen clothed table with Eve on her left. She fed their daughter what looked to be warm cereal.

"Morning," Mira said. "You okay? You were tossing and turning last night. You said *Chiaiano* in your sleep. What is that?" She squinted at him and used her hand to protect her eyes from the bright rays of the sun illuminating her face. Bathed in sunlight her brown skin glistened with a golden tan.

"Chiaiano? I said that?" he plucked a strawberry and tossed it in his mouth.

"Yes. You did. What does it mean?"

"It's a village in the *Campania*. Nothing to worry over." He kissed her forehead. He took a seat next to her at the table. A fruit tray and a fresh pot of coffee waited for him. "You know I dream of you when I sleep, Bella."

"Papa's lying, Eve." Mira fed her daughter another scoop and Eve hit her hand on the tray with an approving grin over the taste.

Giovanni eased his feet out from under the table and felt a sharp sting. "Fuck!" he yelled. Mira and Eve both glanced over. He lifted his foot and brought it to his lap. "Damn splinter."

"You need to wear shoes. You are constantly walking around here barefoot," Mira said.

"I don't need shoes," he scoffed. He concentrated on lifting the tiny sliver of wood from his toe.

"Well do it for me. You rub those calloused feet of yours over mine and I swear I have scratches in the morning."

"What are you talking about, woman?" he glanced up.

"Your feet. Put on some shoes, rub some lotion on them when you get out of the shower," she said.

"Or my wife could take care of my feet. Make me feel like her man."

"Me? Take care of your feet?" Mira frowned. "You mean wash your feet?"

Giovanni chuckled. "Jesus did so for his apostles."

"So I'm Jesus?"

156

He winked. "As close to God as I've been in a long time."

Mira shook her head smiling.

The moment passed between them with shared laughter. And then she saw a scowl deepen the crease between his brows. Mira's head turned and she looked in the direction he stared. Dominic and Catalina walked along the beach, hand in hand. They were headed back from some place. They laughed and talked together looking more in love.

"Did they spend the night in our beach house?" Mira asked.

"No." Giovanni answered in a tight voice. "One of the other beach villas I'm sure. After I specifically forbade it—"

"You talking about the rule at Melanzana? Oh stop," Mira said. "Look at them. They're happy. Let them be happy."

The request fell upon deaf ears. The look in her husband's eye said he would not be tolerant or forgiving of this infraction. Giovanni then dismissed the lovebirds. "I have business today. So I'll be tied up. What will you do?" Giovanni asked as he took a sip of his coffee.

"Spend time with the girls. Speaking of, what about my proposal yesterday? You said you would think about it. I know you're busy but I need an answer."

"You disappoint me, Bella," Giovanni answered.

"What? Why?"

"You think I'm an idiot?" he asked. His crystal gaze leveled on her for an honest answer.

"What does that mean? Of course not." She gave a nervous laugh. That critical stare of his always made things tense when she just wanted to talk to him. He lowered his gaze and continued to eat. She exhaled a breath and spoke to him in her reasonable voice. "We made a proposal that works for the family. We came to you first, out of respect."

"Catalina did not come up with a bunch of dresses and fancy skirts to sell at *Fabiana's*. You and Rosetta have worked day and night on your special project, I've seen the drawings." His gaze flipped up to her and she was frozen in the reflective blues watching her reaction. "Catalina can barely sew on a button unless you hold the needle."

"That's not true—"

"And now you want her to represent your fashion business? Give me more credit than this, Bella. The plan of yours, it's your way to get back in the business. No? Am I wrong?"

"More… gim-me!" Eve hit her tray to emphasize her request. Mira fed her some more cereal.

"Okay. You're right. It's ours. She has designs of her own, but I've sketched out a line and a project plan for *Fabiana's*. I'm not asking to do the work—"

"So you thought you needed to manipulate me?" Giovanni frowned. "After we discussed this? After everything?"

"It's just you've been really intense about this pregnancy. And I've put up with your need to control everything since we had the miscarriage scare. For Christ's sake I'm watched like a hawk. If you thought I was stressing over this project we'd argue and I didn't want to fight about this. It's hard for me to not do what's in my nature."

Giovanni dropped back in his chair. He stared at her until he stopped chewing and swallowed. "So you thought you should manipulate me to keep from fighting?" he asked.

Mira looked over to her daughter who drank from her baby cup. "Yes. I am trying to manipulate you. I'm sorry. I should have been honest. Honesty is our vow. And I respect you, Giovanni. I do. Forgive me."

He smiled.

His smile did not mean he approved. It only validated his point in the argument. Mira waited for his decision. After several long torturous minutes he gave it. "I have no problem with you, Catalina, and Rosetta doing what you dream up for *Fabiana's*. What I do have a problem with is you keeping secrets, scheming or manipulating me. I won't put up with it. I accept your apology but the answer is no." He pushed from the table and walked out. Mira shook her head. She pushed up from the table and walked to the edge of the door to their room. He was at the dresser snatching out clothes.

"You expect honesty from me when you live a life of secrets?" she shouted at him.

He paused.

She had his attention. Mira stepped inside and lowered her voice. "Don't you stand there and pretend you've never tried to manipulate me. Remember I was a woman that ran a multi-million dollar company before I became some shut in, knocked up wife. I'm not stupid, Giovanni. I'm a lot of things but I'm never stupid! And you're not in as much of control of me as you think you are."

Once the accusation was made plain between them she refused to retract it. Giovanni often told her half-truths. She accepted it because she loved him—desperately. He had to stop treating her like a possession or she'd suffocate in their marriage. Hell she was suffocating a little every day.

Instead of his typical reaction of anger or bitter accusations he stared at her with genuine hurt. Mira wavered in her anger. Those blue eyes of his could convince her of anything. She could never bear hurting his feelings. But what about hers?

"Don't be upset with me," Mira tried to approach him. He blinked out of his stunned tableau. Her husband grabbed his things and went into the bathroom to shower. The conversation was over.

"Mama!" Eve yelled.

She turned away also. "Okay, Eve. Okay. Mama's coming."

* B *

"Aww, *ti desidero*. Come inside, Domi. No one will know." Catalina pulled on his hand to bring him across the threshold of her bedroom door.

Dominic kissed her nose. "Don't tempt me."

"I intend to," she said.

"No, baby," Dominic said and drew away from her. "I need to shower and meet with Giovanni. We've already crossed the line. Let's not push it. Eh?"

"Mmm, do you know what the best part of fighting with you is, Domi?" she ran her hand down his chest. His beautiful, brown, heavy lidded eyes made her want to kiss him. Go to her knees and take him in her mouth. Dominic could seduce submission from a nun if he set his mind to it.

"Tell me?" he asked, and his voice had a thick texture to it. She knew he was tempted to be bad. And lord help her but she loved it when Dominic was bad.

"Making up, silly. Last night our fight felt like a release." She kissed his lips and squeezed his groin. "I released." She ran her tongue over the seam of his tightly pressed lips. "And then you released." She bit his chin. "And then I released again. Remember? It was... so good. I love you so much."

Dominic removed her hand from his dick. Catalina pouted. She brushed the tip of her finger over the tiny silver St. William medallion hanging from the chain around his neck. Dominic never took it off. She enticed his tongue into her mouth and her nipples brushed his chest. Soon he'd break and she'd have him in her shower, between her thighs.

He grabbed her chin. Her mouth torn from the promise of paradise she looked up at him with pleading eyes. "I can't wait for us to marry. Tonight, meet me back at the beach house," he said with a smile. He kissed her and then turned left. She had to force herself to close the door. Catalina grinned. It was possible that she could truly have it all. Her career, Domi, and lots of babies! She was determined to see it happen.

"You two look happy."

Catalina turned and found Rosetta in her room. Her cousin walked out of the bathroom. Again how much Rosetta transformed her look and style to look like her struck Catalina. Same hair color and style, same body shape, even the same tan.

"What the hell are you doing in here? Is that my dress?" Catalina asked.

"I was looking for you. The *Donna* wants to meet with us this morning. She told me to come find you. I guess she has Giovanni's answer."

"Are you fucking kidding me? Is that my dress?" Catalina shouted.

"You don't mind do you? Versace? It's beautiful. I saw it in your closet and tried it on. I waited for you last night to ask if I could borrow it but you were gone." Rosetta smiled sweetly. "All night. Where were you?"

"Take it off! And get the fuck out you psycho!" Catalina marched to her suitcase and opened it for the things she hadn't had time to unpack. She'd hung up her favorite designer summer dresses so they wouldn't wrinkle.

"I said I want to talk to you," Rosetta stepped closer. "A lot has changed since you've been gone."

Catalina looked over at her cousin. "Really? Doesn't look like much has changed. You're still imitating me. Wanting to be me. It's getting to be a bit creepy. Pathetic."

"I'm not trying to be you, I'm better than you," Rosetta tossed back.

"Oh brother." Catalina sighed.

"I've grown," Rosetta said with an air of confidence. She walked around the room and sat on the chaise near the window. "While you were off being a business woman I was learning from the *Donna*. I can sew now. I can make things, and I also have had a lot of ideas for this new clothing line that the *Donna* is creating under your name."

"Ha!" Catalina smiled. "So you're a designer now? After what, four months?"

"You're a business woman after four months. What's the difference?" Rosetta tossed back.

"The difference is I'm out there. I've been to America," Catalina said with pride. "I work in the industry and I know how to make things happen. You've been sitting at a sewing machine stitching together the *Donna's* design ideas not your own. So don't come in here trying to pretend you're special. While wearing my dress! You are pathetic!"

Rosetta shot to her feet. "That's your fucking problem, Catalina. You think you're the only special girl in the family. You always have!" Rosetta sneered. "*La piccoletta,* the little one in the family of the big bad men. Well things have changed. The *Donna* loves me too. And she is going to give me a place in her company. Don't you dare try to get in my way!"

She marched toward the door. Catalina watched her with a raised brow. "You will never have what I have, Rosetta, unless you steal or copy it." Catalina smiled. "But be my guest and try."

Rosetta cast her a sly smile. "We shall see, *piccoletta.* We shall see."

Catalina rolled her eyes. She'd been dealing with her cousin's jealousy for years. She could care less. With a dismissive shrug she walked over to her closet to decide what she would wear for the day. She decided to never touch the Versace dress again.

* B *

Marietta faced the mirror—eye to eye with her reflection. She had worked tirelessly on her makeup and hair. Not in a gaudy fashion. Her lashes were extended and dark liner was evenly smoothed over her lids, which gave her smoldering appeal. She covered her lids with bronze shadow to add a natural look. She curled her hair with her curling irons and picked it out with her fingers. Her roots were frizzy and wavy thanks to life at sea, and it added to her natural curl pattern. She used a white rose plucked from the bouquet the dress shop sent her to pin up one side of her thick locks.

Pierced in her earlobes were the three carat solitaire diamonds Lorenzo bought her in Nice, France. When she turned her head left and right the sparkle was almost as bright as the one dazzling on her ring finger. And lastly she dabbed her lips with pink lipstick and overlaid it with a shimmering gloss. Marietta puckered, shook her locks, and pulled them out with her fingertips. She felt beautiful.

A dash of Shalimar behind her ears and between her breasts was her perfume of choice. She reached in her jewelry box and found her necklace. For a moment she paused and stared down at the gold engraving. This charm, which was once a baby's bracelet, was the only thing she had from her mother. Wearing it today would make her feel like her real mother was there. Marietta put it around her neck and fastened it with a prideful smile.

"We're ready," Carlo beat his fist against the bathroom door. "*Andiamo!*"

She rolled her eyes. "Go away! I'm getting dressed."

"We can't wait all day," Carlo said. "What's the issue?"

"Oh shut up and go away!" she shouted back at him.

She heard him march off. Marietta would not be rushed. This was her day and for her this was the most important day of her life. She exhaled tension and fear of unworthiness from her lungs. A man like Lorenzo Battaglia didn't marry just any woman. Hell he was rich, charismatic, and dangerous, therefore his choices had to be calculated and wise. And she knew from the sideways glances he received from women wherever they travelled he could have any woman he wanted. Lorenzo had chosen her for the same reasons she chosen him—love. For the first time in her life she truly felt loved.

Marietta thought of Gemma. If she hadn't lost touch with Gemma, her godmother could have stood as her bridesmaid today. Though she doubted Gemma would be pleased to see her marrying a Battaglia.

"All done!" Marietta smiled. She sucked in another deep breath and exhaled slowly. Marietta opened the door and sashayed down the narrow hall of the lower deck. They would be married on his yacht. She didn't care for exchanging her vows at church, and Lorenzo, although Catholic didn't object. He had set sail a mile away from shore and anchored the boat for the ceremony. The women at the boutique delivered the Mirabella original with flowers she'd chosen for her bouquet and hair. She was all set. But her legs shook with each step she took. And she had to keep her breathing steady when she climbed the steps out to the back starboard of the yacht. Lorenzo wore a tux. Her sweetie looked so handsome. His brows lifted when he saw her. Marietta's gaze volleyed over to Carlo who was dressed equally handsome. He stared at her in the way he always did. The only person who appeared to have a look of concern was the priest. Her dress had a low bust line and high hemline, which prompted the reaction.

She grinned.

Lorenzo stroked his chin. Mancini's daughter had bloomed. Marietta was undeniably the most beautiful and complicated woman he's ever loved. He loved the hard edge to her that didn't lessen her femininity, but often distracted others from it. Exquisite and fragile she was special. Wispy curls fell around her lovely face, and spiral locks blew about in the wind. The rose in her puffy hair, the dress, and the soft smile on her lush pink lips made him humble, appreciative, and grateful. And the dress she wore was bold and daring just like her. *His Marietta.* She had branded his heart. No other woman except Fabiana could occupy it now.

"*Bellisima!* You take my breath away. *Sei tutto per me*—you are everything to me." He approached. He lifted her chin. She looked up at him from under her long lashes. "*Sposami*—say you will marry me," he whispered.

"I will marry you," she said. "*Sei il grande amore della mia vita*—you are the love of my life," she said to him.

The happiness in her teary eyes made him a believer. In that moment he knew that his mother was wrong. He too could have a destiny, one different than being second best. He understood what Giovanni found in Mira. Why Dominic risked his life to be with Catalina. She was indeed worth everything they faced in the future. He was marrying a Mancini. And he didn't give a shit. Marietta was the most special woman he'd ever met.

"Ahem," said Father Christian.

Lorenzo chuckled. Marietta smiled brighter. He took her by the hand and walked her the few steps over to the priest. The sea was calm and the boat steady. The wind however whipped up around them. Carlo found the priest for the occasion. A generous donation to his church enticed him to perform the ceremony. The man spoke no English, but luckily he did speak Italian. So they went through their ceremonial exchange of vows fully understanding what their commitment would mean. And he added a last one in English for her understanding.

"Marietta, you are mine now. Always. I will gut any man who tries to step between us."

She nodded and grinned.

"Lorenzo, you are mine now. Forever. I will cut your balls if you ever try to cheat on me."

He roared with laughter. Carlo chuckled. The priest stared at them confused. He forced them back into continuing their vows. It was an exchange of solemn promises to each other. Only death would part them now. When Marietta said I do, he couldn't keep his hands

163

off her. Marietta squealed. She jumped at him and he spun her around on the deck, almost dropping her.

"I'm fucking married!" Marietta screamed out to the universe. She threw her bouquet into the sea. The Priest excused himself when the kissing and groping between the newlyweds became amorous. She wrapped her legs around his waist and her dress went so high the cheeks of her ass were uncovered. He cradled both butt cheeks in his hands. She locked her arms around his neck and kissed him deeply.

"We need to leave. Now." Carlo grumbled and walked off.

Marietta released his tongue but she kissed his face. Smearing her pink lipstick all over it.

"*Cara*, stop, listen to me." He grabbed her face, but held her. "We're leaving for Sicily. You need to pack. We will take a flight later this evening."

"Huh? Sicily? You want to honeymoon there?" she asked. She looked disappointed. Her legs dropped from around his waist and he let her ease down to her feet. Marietta tugged down the raised hem of her dress. The churn of the anchor being raised on the boat could be heard and he knew Carlo had set course for their return to shore.

"You're my wife now. I want the family to know it," Lorenzo explained.

"But I thought they were in Sorrento?" Marietta asked.

"No, *cara*, they are in Sicily, Mondello Beach. I can't wait to introduce you as my wife." His hand eased to her neck and his eyes fell upon the necklace. It was fine for her to wear it when they sailed through Europe, but she couldn't walk through the doors of Villa Mare Blu with that necklace on.

"I thought the clasp was broken?" he asked. He touched the necklace.

Marietta looked down. "I had it fixed when we were in Paris. Remember? And don't change the subject. I want a honeymoon, Lo. I mean it. Send Carlo away and let it be just you and me. Please?"

"*Senta*," he pinched her chin. "Don't nag me. I've spent months giving you the honeymoon. Haven't I? Haven't I?"

She frowned. Her brows lowered and her gaze darkened with anger. Lorenzo smiled. "Have you ever seen Mondello Beach? They have grottos that mermaids use to sunbathe in. We can fuck on the sand."

"I don't want to fuck on the sand!" she protested.

"Marie! We can eat the best food you've ever tasted in your life. We're family now. And that means you belong to the Battaglia clan."

She rolled her eyes. "I only belong to you. To hell with the rest of them."

Lorenzo shook his head. "That is not how it works, Marie. I've explained your life to you. Haven't I?"

"Yes," she pouted.

"Paradise is where I'm taking you, sweetheart. I will give you the best honeymoon of your life. I promise."

"You better!" she hit his chest playfully."

"Do me a favor? Wear this dress all day." He bit her cheek. "Beautiful."

Marietta eased her arms around his waist and then dropped her head on his chest. The boat surged forward and they swayed. They started to sail.

"I will make you happy, Marie, I swear it."

"I know, Lo. I already am happy. The happiest bride on the planet."

Lorenzo stared out at the sea, keeping her in his arms. He risked her life by taking her back to Sicily. He risked his reputation by marrying her. A Mancini? How the hell did he end up in love with a Mancini? Life was all about risks, and Marietta was one worth taking.

* B *

Catalina laughed. She dropped her head back and chuckled until tears formed behind her tightly shut eyelids and her cheeks and throat hurt. Eve shot past Catalina bottomless and ran for the terrace.

"Can you please bring her back?" Mira wheezed. Never in Catalina's life had she seen a little girl so stubborn. Mira walked over to the edge of the bed and lowered to it. Catalina saw how tired her sister in-law looked and felt a pang of pity. She went for Eve. She scooped her up in her arms and carried the screaming toddler back into the room. The baby had the strength of Hercules. It was no wonder that Mira could barely keep up.

"Where is Cecilia?"

"She asked to go visit her family in Palermo. I gave her the day off. Nico volunteered to drive her."

Catalina tossed Eve to the bed. Eve rolled over and giggled. Mira grabbed her daughter by the ankle and dragged her closer. Eve gripped the sheets pulling them with her.

"She has a little rash on her bum again," Mira said. Catalina stepped over to see the red patches of raw skin. "That's probably why she keeps stripping off her training panties," Mira said.

"I thought she was trained to go to the *toilette*?" Catalina asked.

"We've had several accidents in the night. I've asked Cecilia to keep her on the diaper in the evenings. Can you go over to my cosmetic bag and get the Desitin?"

"Sure." Catalina walked over to the luggage Mira had tucked in the corner. It looked like she hadn't fully unpacked their things. She glanced back and saw Mira rubbing Eve's little bottom as Eve lay still on the bed sucking her pacifier. Her niece was a heartbreaker and a master manipulator. As soon as Mira believed Eve was settled Catalina had no doubt Eve would run for her escape again.

"Mira? I spoke to Rosetta. She says you've been training her to be more than a seamstress. That you've groomed her to be a designer," Catalina asked. She picked up a small black velvet jewelry box. Underneath she found the tiny tube of Desitin.

"Rosetta's a good student, like you," Mira said. She rubbed the raw spot on her little one's butt cheek. "That feels better baby? Mama so sorry she didn't know your bum hurt. I'll make it all better I promise."

Catalina brought over the Desitin. Mira opened the tube, put a dollop of the white cream on her fingertip and then smoothed it over Eve's little bottom. Catalina walked away. She needed to be careful of her words. She didn't want to sound petty or childish. Mira respected her. "I don't think she's ready for Milano."

"Who?" Mira asked, clearly distracted.

"Rosetta. It's so busy at *Fabiana's*. I won't have time to tutor her."

"Of course you don't have to tutor her. Did anyone have to tutor you?" Mira asked. She turned Eve over and started to pull on her training panties. "The best way to learn is to dive in. And she's really excited about learning."

"I bet she is," Catalina mumbled. She walked back over to the vanity case. Again her attention was drawn to the velvet jewelry box. She picked it up. "I just think that the launch of *Fabiana's* is going to be so difficult to manage the first few months, we need to be focused."

"And we will be. Catalina, you and Rosetta are family, my family. And this is a family business. What she doesn't know she'll learn. If she makes mistakes you'll help her fix it. I want you two to get along."

Catalina sighed.

Mira continued, "The only way this works if we stick together. You have no idea how hard it is to force my husband to stand down."

Catalina opened the jewelry box and stared at the beautiful gold child's bracelet. In raised lettering it said Mirabella. "This is so cute."

Mira helped Eve down from the bed. Her daughter backed away sucking on her pacifier. She blinked at her mother and began to once again pull down her training pants.

"No, Eve!" Mira said in a stern voice.

Eve pulled them all the way down and stepped out of them. She then headed back for the outside terrace. Catalina held the bracelet up. "Where did you get it, Mira?"

"Catch Eve!" Mira said.

Catalina sighed. She went after the toddler and dragged her back in. She slid the door shut to the terrace to keep her inside. "Where did you get the bracelet, Mira?"

"My mother gave it to me when I was a baby. The only thing I have from her," Mira said. "Eve, pick up your training pants and bring them to mommy. Now!"

Eve walked over and did as she was told. She burst into tears as she returned to Mira to have her once again force them on. Catalina ignored them. She turned the bracelet over. She looked down in disbelief. A Del Stavio insignia could be clearly seen on the back of the gold plate.

"What is it?" Mira asked. "You look pale as a ghost."

"Del Stavio? I think this is his work. No. It can't be. Yes. Yes, I think it is," Catalina said.

"Del who?" Mira walked over. Catalina showed Mira the insignia. "I think that's his stamp. He put this insignia on all of his custom pieces."

"Who is he?" Mira asked.

"A jeweler. Del Stavio was the jeweler to the Five Dons of Sicily. He made them family heirlooms. Children were given gifts at birth from him. Dominic told me about his work."

Mira laughed. "Well then it's not his stamp. My mother lived and died far from Sicily." Mira took the bracelet and sighed. "I love and loathe this thing. Do you know it's how your brother and I fell in love?"

"Really?" Catalina asked.

Mira smiled as if drifting on the memory. "When I arrived in Napoli my purse was snatched. I had this bracelet in it. I cried my eyes out for days over it. And when I met your brother I told him about the incident. In a matter of 24 hours he had the purse and bracelet returned to me."

Catalina laughed. "Sounds like Gio was putting the moves on you."

"Oh he put moves on me alright." Mira grinned. She rubbed her belly to emphasize the point. They both shared a laugh.

"I don't understand. Why do you loathe the bracelet?" Catalina asked.

"Because it's a reminder of all that I never had with my mother. If she had this made for me she did it out of love. But I can barely remember her. Just her shadow sometimes when I close my eyes or dream. I can barely look at the bracelet without missing her. I think it's time for me to let that emptiness go." Mira wiped at her tears. She laughed and cried. Catalina hugged her. When she released her she nodded she was okay. "Every little girl needs her mother. I was so afraid of being a bad mother I kept my distance from kids. And then I met your brother and look at me," Mira chuckled.

"You are a wonderful mother," Catalina said. "Look at you."

Mira nodded as if she agreed but Catalina could see she remained unconvinced. Mira stared at the bracelet. "I can't explain where the bracelet came from. For all I know she could have met this Del Stavio and had him make it."

"No, that's not possible. He's a Sicilian jeweler. He wouldn't make a bracelet like this for an American child. No matter who your mother was. Hell he only made a necklace for Dominic because of my father's relationship with Mancini."

Mira paused. "Who?"

"Mancini," Catalina repeated.

"I know him." Mira said.

"You know Mancini?" Catalina stepped back.

"Not personally." Mira laughed. "He was an investor. He helped us lease a building in Napoli and obtain our work visas. Your brother was pissed. That's how we met. Giovanni expected me to pay him to be in Mancini's building. Claimed the building was his. Can you believe him? I told him to kiss my ass." Mira whispered so Eve didn't hear. "He took me up on my invitation." She winked at Catalina.

"Wait a minute." Catalina frowned, dismissing the joke. "How did you meet Mancini?"

"I didn't. Teddy did. He came to Sicily for vacation. When he returned he was so excited. He called a meeting with Fabiana and me to pitch an idea. It was an idea that changed our lives forever. Strange, huh?"

Catalina didn't believe in coincidences. And the history between her family and the Mancinis made the bracelet even more confusing. "Did Giovanni see the bracelet, Mira? The stamp on the back?"

Mira nodded. "Should I ask him about it."

"No!" Catalina smiled. "No, it's probably a coincidence. Let's forget about it."

"Come here, baby," Mira said to a crying Eve.

Her daughter walked over with a crown of curly locks all over her head. Mira put the bracelet on Eve's wrist and the little girl stopped crying to observe her mother curiously. *"Perfetto!"* Mira exclaimed. "Your grandmother Melissa gave this to me and now I will give it to you. Because Mommy loves you and Grandma loves you too."

Maybe it was all a coincidence. If Giovanni saw the bracelet then certainly it meant nothing. Still the fact that Mira had any connection to Mancini puzzled her. In their life it was really hard to believe or trust coincidences. She would have to ask Dominic about it.

"Now, let's get dressed and meet down in the garden. I want to put all the designs out for us to go over. Giovanni said we can proceed after I convinced him he didn't want to fight me on this. Isn't that exciting?" Mira grinned.

"Yeah, exciting," Catalina mumbled. She watched Eve walk off with the gold bracelet glistening on her wrist. She looked at Mira again and wondered.

* B *

"Carlo will be here tonight or by the morning," Dominic said.

"Santo will bring Giuliani in." Giovanni rubbed his brow as word through the *Campania* spread of his losing Chiaiano. He dreamt of revenge every night. But he wouldn't act on impulse like he did with the Calderones. When he struck against his enemies it would be a decisive blow.

"You still trust Santo?" Dominic asked.

"I know Carlo and Lorenzo don't. But they haven't since we were kids. I've known Santo for many years. He's spent time in jail for the family. Bled for this family. He has earned the benefit of the doubt."

"Not every sacrifice is a testament to a man's loyalty, Giovanni. I think we need to hear the facts from someone other than Santo," Dominic advised.

"We know the facts! Mottola wants to be *capo di tutti capi* and he thinks I'm weak enough to hand him the crown. The fucking bastard has no idea what he has done by dividing the clans this way." He wiped his hand down his face and reclined in his chair. "Santo isn't the problem. I am. Lorenzo was right. I've made mistakes."

"Gio—"

He put up his hand. "Let me finish. I can't lead this family from my wife's bedside. I need to be as strong as my words. I need to remind the clans of who we are."

Dominic stared at him for a moment before he spoke. "Then we will do it. Together."

Giovanni exhaled. Dominic was missing the point.

"I want to talk to you about Catalina," Dominic said.

"I'm listening," Giovanni replied. He welcomed a change in topic.

"You heard the idea from the women, about *Fabiana's*. What Mira wants to do with launching a clothing line with Catalina as the head designer is a ruse the women cooked up. You know this right?"

"Bella and I discussed it this morning," Giovanni answered. "She plays these games with me. I am in no mood to fight with her. As long as she isn't on her knees sewing clothes for other people I can give a shit. Let Catalina be the designer."

Dominic sat forward. He put his face in his hands. He then lifted his head and looked at Giovanni. "I want to ask you to allow us to marry, Gio. Catalina is ambitious but she's naïve. I can't be heard if I'm not her husband. I know you said a year. But—"

"You agreed to a year of waiting to have this discussion, Dominic. Not because of its impropriety—you can give a shit about how nasty it looks that you want to bed your sister." Dominic flinched. Giovanni didn't give a shit. He continued. "You agreed because you took a man's life without my permission. You corrupted her and yourself by your actions. Why do you think she is so impulsive now?" Giovanni sat forward. "A year's penance is very light for your sins."

"It is not, Giovanni." Dominic replied.

"I try every day to see the boy I raised with the values of our *famiglia*. I have to remind myself that I love you like a brother to keep from putting a bullet in your skull. I do this for us both. Both you and Lorenzo test my patience, my love for you. How far to the edge do you really want to push me on this?"

A red flush darkened Dominic's face. "We want to be together, Gio," he said through clenched teeth. "You are right. I did the unthinkable, and I'm sorry. But what's done is done. Waiting a year is not going to change my mistakes. It's not going to make you accept us. Do you want to lose Catalina to that freaky world of fashion designers and indulgence? You won't even let Mira return to that world. You toy with her and pretend she has control, but she has none. We both know it. The only reason why we have your wife's company is to wash the blood off our money. What about Catalina? As my wife I can protect her." Dominic reasoned.

Giovanni laughed. He shook his head smiling. "You have a gift with words, Domi. I swear you can talk Satan into the gates of heaven. You always know what to say, how to reason away a man's actions including your own. Don't you?"

Dominic stood. He paced away. "I will never make the mistake of betraying you and our brotherhood again. I've proven myself since then, Gio. And Catalina has proven herself. Look at all she's accomplished. She's old enough to make the choice."

"Yes, Domi, she is. And you want to take those choices from her?" Giovanni asked.

"No! No damn it. I want to love her, to be respectable. To do it in front of the eyes of God and I want you to bless me."

"Doesn't look to me like marriage is the choice she wants to make with you, Domi," Giovanni said.

"It is. I assure you. Talk to her. She'll tell you. We want to get married and start a family. Give us your blessing."

Giovanni sighed. "You two aren't ready. You need to stop thinking of what you want and listen to her. She doesn't want the same thing, Domi. She never has."

"Hypocrite!" Dominic shouted.

The accusation hit him like a brick. Giovanni froze. Dominic glared and stood his ground. He shook with rage. "Look at you and Mira. You keep her from her sister. You keep her from the truth. You do all of this for *you* not her. And then you tell me to not be selfish with my heart. Why do you think I want to control Catalina? Why! Because I learned how to love her from you!" Dominic stormed out.

Giovanni didn't call after him or rise. He dropped the side of his face between his finger and thumb and stared at the open door. He always thought Catalina needed to grow up. But maybe it's Dominic who needed to mature and learn to let go.

* B *

Rosetta looked up in time to see Dominic walk in a brisk manner past the door to the room. Mira and Catalina were busy marking and going over sketches and spreadsheets. "Excuse me," Rosetta said. Mira glanced up but Catalina didn't. In fact she pretty much found ways to ignore her the entire time.

"Be right back," Rosetta smiled. "Need a break."

Mira nodded and Rosetta quickly left the room. As soon as she entered the hall she took a guess as to which direction Dominic would have went. He must have headed from Giovanni's office, and he wasn't walking in the direction of the cars. So she ventured to the back entertainment room that had a large television set. When she turned the corner she could hear him cussing under his breath. Rosetta peeked in at him. It was as she suspected, Dominic would be cast aside for Catalina's pride and ego.

In an excited hurry she fixed her hair and unbuttoned the top of her blouse before she walked inside. Dominic glanced up and his gaze locked in on her.

"Hi, Domi," she said in the sweetest voice she could muster.

He paced the floor as if she hadn't spoken. Like a wounded lion he paced. He grumbled under his breath and shook with repressed fury. He then turned to the bar and began to pour his drink.

"Have you seen Catalina? I was looking for her," Rosetta lied.

"Leave me," Dominic answered. He took down a swig of something she couldn't see. Rosetta braved a step closer.

"I'm sorry. I didn't mean to disturb you. I know things are tough now that you and Catalina have decided you don't want to marry," she said and then pretended to turn to leave.

"What did you say?" Dominic glanced back. He glared at her. Rosetta flashed the most innocent look. "What the hell did you say, Rosetta?"

"Oh, I didn't mean anything. I'm sorry," Rosetta said.

"Where did you hear Catalina and I won't marry? Were you listening to me and Giovanni earlier?"

"No. No, Domi. I swear it." She walked over to him. "I heard Catalina. She went to Giovanni yesterday and told him that she didn't want to get married. I accidentally overheard them talking about it. I thought you both agreed or something."

Dominic's nostrils flared.

Rosetta kept talking. "She and the *Donna* are making big plans for *Fabiana's*. I was looking for them. We're meeting now to discuss it. Catalina told me this morning that she's going back to America. Didn't you know?" Rosetta put her hand up to her mouth. "Oh my God. I'm sorry. I don't want to get in any trouble, Domi. Me and my big mouth."

He looked away from her. He shook his head.

"Domi? You okay?" she touched his back. He didn't resist her touch. Rosetta smiled and rubbed his back. "Are you okay?"

Dominic walked out without a word. Rosetta crossed her arms and smiled.

8.

The flight was late—which put their arrival in Palermo close to midnight. As soon as the plane lifted to the clouds Marietta reclined her seat and drifted to sleep. She still wore her wedding dress for him, and he couldn't help smiling at how she turned heads as she walked through the city, and airport with him. He stared at her under the dim lamplight from above. Across from them Carlo slept. Lorenzo could not.

Before he looked away from his wife a spark of light gleamed from Marietta's necklace. He'd forgotten she wore the damn thing still. Lorenzo reached over and touched the shiny nameplate. The raised letters scraped his finger. His wife sighed from his touch and dropped her head over to the right. Thankfully in doing so she revealed the tiny clasp that kept the necklace attached. He gently ran his finger over it. Marietta didn't stir. Careful and with ease he worked open the clasp with his middle finger and thumb. The chain and charm dropped to the crease of her breasts.

Lorenzo reached in and lifted the chain. He held it out in front of him aware of what its discovery could cost his wife. He reasoned he'd put it somewhere safe, until the time came when she could wear it again. Lorenzo tucked it into his pocket. He returned his gaze to the dark sky outside of his window. His plan had better work.

* B *

Catalina knocked. When she heard no answer she opened the door. Dominic was in his room, not the villa they shared. She waited for hours before finally giving up. And to find him in bed reading documents by lamplight tore at her heart.

"What are you doing in here?" she asked with a curious smile.

"Need something?" he anwered in an unusually dry clipped

manner. He continued to read the contract before him. The dismissal threw her. Dominic never dismissed her.

"Need something? Look who has an attitude," Catalina chuckled. "You were supposed to meet me down at the beach house. I can't very well sleep in here with you now can I?"

Dominic didn't respond. Catalina pulled her bottom lip between her two teeth and looked around. She didn't understand his mood. But her guy had a tough job. He was entitled to it. "You missed dinner, Domi. I waited for you. I can warm something up for you and bring it in here? What's wrong? Do you feel okay?"

He sighed. He snatched off his spectacles and pressed the bridge of his nose with two fingers. "I'm tired. Get out."

"What did you say to me?" Catalina asked.

"I said. I'm tired. *Vattene!*" Dominic shouted.

"Why are you acting like this?" she asked.

"Why?" he answered.

"Yes! Why?" Catalina demanded.

"I talked to Giovanni, asked him to let us marry." Dominic stared her in the eye when he spoke. "What do you think he said?"

A deep sigh escaped her lips. He wasn't angry with her. He was mad with her brother. For a minute she felt the uncertain panic that she had done something to hurt him. "He said no?"

Dominic smiled. "And you know why."

"I told you Gio wouldn't let us get married. You can't get mad at me for any of this. I'm just as upset about his attitude as you are."

"Are you? Because I think it's pretty fucking scary to see how easy it is for you to lie to my face!" He tossed aside the covers and sat upright to the side of the bed.

"Wait. Wait, I'm missing something? You're mad at me for predicting how Gio would react? Or are you mad at me for something else? Stop talking around it and tell me what has you behaving like this!"

Dominic let go a bitter chuckle.

"Domi, I'm serious!"

"After everything we've been through, you go to Gio and tell him that you don't want to marry me?"

"No! No I did not. Gio is twisting things. I only asked him to talk to you. To help you see that marrying right now isn't right for us. I never said I didn't want to marry you. Never!" The pain and hurt deep in his eyes stopped her heart. "Let me explain, Domi."

"Fuck your explanation!" he seethed. "I never wanted to be your fucking crush, your plaything. I wanted something... fuck what I want.

It's over. Do you hear me?" He pointed his finger at her. "Giovanni has won. You've won. I know my place."

"No, stop this, stop talking to me like this!" she began to cry.

"We're over. Go be a designer, whatever it is you want. I give up on this bullshit."

"Why?" she shouted now reduced to tears. "Why is it all or nothing with you? I don't want to get married right away and that means I don't love you? I want a career and that threatens you?"

Dominic stared at her unmoved.

"Answer me you coward!" she shouted and sobbed.

"You play too many fucking games to be the woman I need. Always pulling my fucking strings. Going behind my back to Gio makes me look weak. And you knew that! But you did it for you, not us. I'm done!"

Catalina wiped away her tears. "You're so full of shit, Dominic. I never forced you to do anything. Ever! You're just scared. I don't know what of. But just like you I don't need a fucking boy. I need a man. And it evidently isn't you!"

She turned and walked out. Just as the door closed she heard something crash inside the room. Catalina sobbed and fled to her room.

* B *

Giovanni closed the door to his bedroom softly. He had to take a call that kept him away from his bedtime story duties. Mira and Eve slept in soundless bliss together. The summer moon bathed the room with a silvery natural light and he could see them both clearly. He approached the bed with his hands shoved down in his pockets. Eve slept on her stomach. The little cherry plug she loved so much was stuck in her mouth.

When would his firefly ever let the thing go? He wondered.

His gaze switched to Mira's form. It had been a strange day. The argument with Dominic left things unsettled between them. The disturbance in the *Campania* kept his thoughts muddled with worry. Tonight he needed his wife. He wanted to feel her against his heart and hold her until sleep claimed him. Giovanni lifted his daughter from the bed. She didn't wake. He carried her to the crib they had placed in the room. When he laid her down her little hand fell over and he saw the golden bracelet on her wrist.

He paused and stared at the jewelry unsure of its origin. He then lifted her wrist and inspected it. Mira had taken the Mancini bracelet and put it on his daughter. *His daughter!* His first inclination was to snatch it off. The sight of it against Eve's skin made the hairs to the back of his nape rise and his stomach sour. But if he removed the bracelet he would have to explain his reason. He glanced back to the bed. Mira slept on her side, with her back toward him. She had hurled some very truthful accusations at him earlier. He did feel guilty over his decisions regarding her Mancini blood, and the sister she didn't know existed. Yet he tolerated no manipulations on her part. The hypocrisy of their life wouldn't change as long as he felt justified in his actions. And keeping her from Mancini was for her wellbeing, and their daughter's.

He picked up the blanket and covered his *bambina*. He stared at her for a long moment. He imagined what type of woman she'd grow up to be. Strong, confident, intelligent, she'd have the life she deserved.

Afterwards he dragged himself to bed. He eased under the covers having stripped off his clothes. Mirabella wore a nightdress that had risen up to her expanded waist. He lifted the covers and stared at her thighs. Even swollen with child she had a remarkable body.

Giovanni eased in closer to her. He ran his hand over her thigh to touch her and ignored the rising in his erection.

"Mmm, I'm horny," Mira scooted in close to him. Her belly pressed up against his chest. He caressed her spine, squeezed her ass.

"So am I." he said.

Her eyes flashed open. "Are you, baby?" she touched his face. "Awe, my poor husband." He stared into her eyes liking the way she touched his face. He had to nod and admit that he wished he could have more than a kiss good night.

"Then let me take care of that," she lifted.

"No, we can't—" he started to say. Her hand slipped under the covers. She carefully untucked his cock from the front of his boxers and pumped her fist up and down his shaft. Giovanni's breath stilled in his chest as her petal soft lips brushed his chest and her tongue flicked at his nipple.

"Mira," he exhaled.

"Shhh… baby, let me take care of my man. You deserve it."

Her mouth went instantly dry, unlike her pussy, which ached with desire for him. Night after night her body needed him. She worked his erection with her hand strokes. And Giovanni's head sank back deeper into his pillow, causing his jaw to go rigid, tight with muscle strain. Mira sucked in a deep breath of restraint to keep from climbing on him and riding his dick.

Mira yanked back the covers and Giovanni's eyes opened. He panted and looked down at her with concern. She got to her knees and went between his. Mira remembered to breathe when she opened her mouth and wrapped her lips around her teeth taking him in.

Giovanni hissed. He gripped both sides of her head as he stroked his dick up into her mouth to the back of her throat with his slow hip movements.

"Yes, *bambina,* that's it. Suck it harder. Fuck me, your mouth feels so good," he said.

The praise spurred her on. She withdrew, held the root of his shaft, and swirled her tongue over the broad cap of his cock. She licked the pre-cum in the dimple at the top and then curled it around the cock when she swallowed several inches of his shaft. Her husband's scent was musky and earthy. She missed the smell of his dick and it had only been twenty-four hours.

"Ugh!" he cried out as she suctioned harder. He thrust a little faster and tapped the back of her throat. "Loosen your jaw, baby, let me get, yeah, like that," he breathed.

The graveled texture of his voice turned her on. Mira gave a whimper but opened her jaw wider and relaxed her tongue to receive him, allowing his dick to tunnel deeper. She could barely see his face when he arched his back. But she knew he was coming.

"Swallow it! Swallow!" he said holding her head not wanting to let her go.

Scalding, salty spurts both tangy and thick filled her mouth. Her jaw burned and she had to swallow to keep from choking.

"Fuck!" he let go of her and pounded his fist into the bed.

"Hey! Don't wake the baby!" Mira whispered.

"Oh? I'm sorry, baby, yeah, you're right. Sorry," he panted.

Mira chuckled. She scooted back off of him and the mattress. She headed for the bathroom. A quick gargle and wipe of her mouth and she was good. She felt better. Which surprised her because she didn't have sex. And when she looked out of the bathroom door she realized why. She had done her duty well. Her man was completely satisfied. He groaned in the bed, holding his dick. She smiled. She loved him so much.

Mira flipped off the light switch. She walked over to the crib and peered down at Eve. She had flipped to her back with her arms flung open and legs too. She touched her cheek.

"Come to bed, Bella," he asked hoarsely.

She looked back. He was staring at her while he lay on his side. Those violet blue eyes of his were as clear as moonlight blue. They shined with so much love for her she was filled with gratitude. "I'm sorry about earlier, the things I said to you. How can I keep your respect when I don't give you any."

"Bella—"

"Let me finish. I want to do my project. But I want your approval and support even more. If you say now is not the time then I accept it." She walked over to the bed. He reached and helped her return to him. She laid on her side and he spooned her.

"Now is not the time. But soon, okay?" he asked.

"Okay," she said.

"Go back to sleep," he whispered.

"As long as you stay with me I will," she smiled. He touched her cheek and kissed her forehead. He had no intention of ever leaving.

Giovanni closed his eyes and joined her.

An hour later he was awakened with some unsettling news.

* B *

The drive to Mondello was only visible by moonlight. With Carlo behind the wheel she and Lorenzo relaxed in the back seat. Her legs were crossed over his lap. Lorenzo held her with one arm as she rested her head on him. And for what seemed like an eternity they travelled along steep two lane roads with the ocean waves breaking across the shore in the distance.

"Are we here?" she yawned. The car ride smoothed out and their speed slowed to a crawl.

"Yes we're here," Lorenzo patted her thigh. Marietta moved off him and stretched her eyes to wake. The car stopped. A person with a flashlight approached. The beam was so bright she had to look away. The moment the person recognized Carlo the man began to speak to him excitedly in Sicilian, welcoming them home. They were allowed to drive further up the road. If there were other men out patrolling they were just shadows in the dark woodsy area that surrounded the villa. The car's high beams sliced through the darkness and guided the way. And then Carlo braked to a stop.

She dropped her head back and sighed. At last the journey was over. Marietta was exhausted. It was close to one in the morning. The dress felt so tight and restricting she began to feel her skin itch. And her feet hurt from the high heels she wore all day. Her wedding day had been spent being shuffled from one destination to the next. Lorenzo got out of his side of the car and came around to her door. He reached in to help her step out.

Marietta purposefully held back, waiting for him to do so. He'd taught her many things these past months. One of which was to always allow him to treat her like a lady. He opened doors for her everywhere they went. Escorted her in and out of every store or restaurant they visited.

She placed her hand in his hand and let him guide her from the car.

"Benvenuta in Mondello, cara," he kissed her brow.

"Grazie, Lorenzo," she replied.

Two men appeared out of the darkness. Both were armed with large mean looking guns. They exchanged looks and then swept her appearance with hard eyes. Lorenzo took her hand and they walked toward the villa. In the dark she could see the purple flowers blooming under moonlight that paved the way. The place wasn't as grand as the one she visited in Sorrento or as exquisite as the villa he took her to in Bellagio. But still it had a majestic appeal to it. They entered a dark quiet house. Lorenzo cast his gaze to Carlo. And they exchanged a nod that she figured had meaning. Carlo turned and walked back out of the front door. A man from Lorenzo's crew followed them down the hall to a room. It was a large room. A sheer curtain circled the bed. Once the luggage was brought in Lorenzo closed the door and watched her. She walked around admiring everything.

"I love the bed," she ran her hand over the sheer drape. "This is sexy."

"So are you," Lorenzo said. He eased off his suit jacket and dropped it on the chair. There was a knock to the door. He opened it to allow additional luggage to be hauled in. Marietta drew back the drape on one side of the bed to give them easy access. She felt giddy with excitement over her wedding night. She then went to the large window and stared out at the sea in the distance. Her hand covered her throat. She froze. "No! No." she spun around looking on the floor. "Oh God please no!"

"What is it?" Lorenzo asked with evident alarm.

"My necklace. It's gone. Oh God no. It can't be. It's gone, Lo."

"Where did you last see it?" Lorenzo asked before she bolted for the door. He caught her and blocked her escape.

"I don't remember," she said with tears dropping, she sobbed hard, barely able to formulate words. "Let me go, I have to check the car. I have to find it!"

"Marie? Slow down. You stay here and I'll go look for it? Okay? Just calm down, sweetheart."

She put both hands to her mouth. He kissed her brow. Let me check the car and tell the boys to look for it. We'll find it. Why don't you get changed for me?" he asked with a sly smile. She couldn't bring herself to smile back. Her heart was seizing in her chest. If she lost her necklace she didn't know what she'd do.

"Please find it, Lo. It... it means a lot to me."

He winked and walked out. Marietta closed her eyes and put her hand to her heart. It beat so fast in her chest she feared it would go into cardiac arrest. "He'll find it. I know he will." She calmed herself. "Please God it's all I have. Please let him find it."

★ B ★

Armando walked the halls of his family home prepared to retire for the evening. A light from his office was on and the door was half ajar. The hour had extended well after midnight. No one should be in his office. He stopped before it and eased the door open slowly with his hand. His father was inside going through his papers, opening and slamming doors, in desperate search of something.

He had wanted to confront the old man, but decided to wait and formulate a plan to get the answers he needed. Ignazio delivered some disturbing news earlier. Armando worried that the hunt for his surrogate sister Isabella, and the mission to track the American women with the Battaglias was all tied to something his father wanted to keep hidden.

Don Mancini glanced up and saw him watching.

"*Avanti.* Come in," his father commanded.

"Why are you up at this late hour?" Armando asked. He scanned the disarray to his desk.

"Where is it?" Mancini wheezed. "Where?"

"What are you talking about?" Armando frowned. "Where is what?"

"My gun. Where the fuck is it? You had it removed from my room. I can't find it!" Mancini slammed his hand down on the desk.

Two days ago Ignazio said his father fired the gun in the house

181

when he was gone. He had the gun removed from his room for safety reasons. There were times when his father had rage issues over his feeble state and confinement. Those times were often the most unmanageable.

"We discussed this, Papa. The gun..."

"Give it back to me." Mancini sneered. "Now!"

Armando walked over to the wall cabinet and unlocked it. He brought out the gun. He turned with it in his hand and he could see the anger softening on his father's face at the sight of it. "I have a question," Armando said before he returned it.

Mancini nodded.

"Dr. Buhari? You had a meeting with him two days ago. A meeting I was not invited to attend."

"I meet with doctors all the time," Mancini replied.

"But he's not a doctor for you. He's a doctor for a woman. A pregnant woman."

Mancini didn't respond.

Armando continued. "I'm told he gives you updates on Giovanni Battaglia's wife. That he now works for us? In secret."

Mancini stared at the gun.

"What are you up to, Papa? If you want Giovanni dead or his bride, just say so." Armando said.

"And you will handle it? Is that so?" Mancini asked. "Like you've handled the Isabella situation? That *puttana* makes a fool of us each day she lives. And still you are no closer to killing the bitch!"

"We are looking for her. She slipped away from us in China. I have no idea why she went there in the first place. Or why she is our enemy now. But we will find her I assure you." Armando walked toward him. He kept the gun at his side. "Now, what of Giovanni's wife. Why do you care to know about her pregnancy?"

Mancini scoffed. "It's none of your concern."

"It is, Papa! All of it is my concern!" Armando shouted at him. Mancini leveled a lethal gaze on him and Armando swiped his hair back from his face. He tried to calm himself.

"You are never to touch Mirabella." Mancini seethed. "The business I have with her doctor is none of your concern." Mancini stood upright. He reached for his cane. He was absent his oxygen mask or tank. His breathing was harsh. He walked around the desk with slow measured steps. He held out his arthritic hand to his son. Armando passed his father his gun.

"I can't run this family on secrets, Papa. First you want Isabella dead. And then you want me to track down Lorenzo and his bride. Now—"

"Bride!" Mancini doubled back on his cane. "What is this bride shit?"

Armando heard it in his father's voice: shock, hurt, confusion. He found it even more confusing. He rarely saw weakness in his father.

"Answer me, boy!" Mancini roared. "Who's a bride?"

With a sly smile Armando delivered the news. "Yes, Papa. Yesterday Lorenzo married the black whore—"

Mancini struck Armando with the butt of the gun. The blow to the side of his face knocked him to the floor and blood sprayed from his mouth. Darkness descended on his mind and threatened to extinguish all conscious thought. The pain was so searing he lay there unable to speak. His father stood over him. "You let him marry her? You did this to spite me! You let him steal her from me!"

At first Armando just moaned. It took a long a moment for him to recover. As he lay dazed on the floor his father shouted English obscenities at him. Whenever his father was enraged he stopped speaking in Italian and cursed like an Americn mad man. Armando's hearing dulled. There was a slight ringing in his ear. He stretched his eyes and focused. He had to get up, recover. His father was sick, his mind all but rotten and gone. He had no idea how far the old man would go if allowed to continue in this state. He struggled and managed to speak. "You're fucking crazy, Papa. You told me to just keep an eye on them, to keep my distance. Why would I give a shit if they married? Why do you?"

He looked up and his father had the gun aimed down at him. Armando stared into the barrel of the gun. And the hard rage in his father's eyes felt like the icy betrayal he's felt over Mancini's callous treatment of him and his mother through the years. It was then he had to question his father's true motives. Maybe it wasn't revenge against the Battaglias his father sought. Maybe the mission of his to kill Isabella and learn more of these American women was all a product of his diseased mind.

Mancini lowered the gun. He dropped his head. "I can take no more of this. I want you to take her. Bring her to me. I want them both. Before I am dead. Before—"

"Who?" Armando asked. He held the side of his face and tried to sit up. But his vision blurred and a wave of dizziness overcame him. He kept swallowing blood in his mouth and he felt it dripping from his nose.

"Marietta. Bring her to me. She will be told the truth. And after Mirabella has the babies and is well enough we will storm the doors of the Battaglia's home and take her. They are mine. They belong to me!" His father slammed his chest. "We will tell them both the truth," Mancini said.

"What is the truth? Why don't you start by telling me?" Armando asked.

Mancini looked at him with tears bordering his eyes. The question aged him. His father looked as if he would top over. Although Armando bled from his mouth and nose he struggled and succeeded in rising. Violence was part of his relationship with his father. He held no grudge for his father's actions. He helped him to a chair in the office. "Do you need your oxygen?"

"No." Mancini waved him off. "Sit."

Armando went to the desk and grabbed the Kleenex and put it to his nose to stop the bleeding. He sat with the swelling on the side of his face rising with heat and pain. "What's the truth, Papa? Why are you so determined to help these Americans? Is it because of their mother? The one you left Mama for?"

Mancini looked up surprised. He cast his gaze back down in shame.

"Let me tell you a story, Papa. When I was a little boy I found Madre crying. I couldn't console her, Isabella had to. She then shared the story of your life in America. She said you had a whor—woman in America. A black one. That you were going to leave us for her."

"Her name was Melissa," Mancini said. "And she was special to me. Your mother forgave me for my weaknesses. I hurt your mother. But what became of Melissa was far worse. I couldn't have them both. I couldn't save them both, from me," he repeated and shook his head. "So I made the only choice I could. I chose your mother and *la Cosa Nostra*."

Armando didn't think it a choice. *Don* Marsuvio Mancini could never marry or be with a black American woman here or in America and carry on the Mancini name. First their faith would never grant him the divorce. Second his grandfather would have put a bullet in him for the insult. But the choice explained his father's attitude. Possibly this was guilt for leaving the American. He wanted penance for her daughters. But why did he want Isabella dead? "Where is the woman, Melissa?" Armando asked.

"Dead. She died when they were babies. She was murdered because of Tomosino Battaglia. Slain in the gutter because of what she was to me, what she will always be to me," Mancini confessed. "I buried what was left of her with her family and then I left America for good."

Surprised Armando sat forward. This was the piece of the puzzle he needed. It explained the Battaglia connection. "So we need revenge on Giovanni. For what Tomosino has done?"

"You don't understand boy. Revenge is the very least of it. We need much more than revenge. Isabella is blackmailing me. That is why I put the contract out on her life. For the insult," his father spat. "She learned the truth, a secret buried so deep I would have never known if she didn't come here to toss it in my face. A secret her real father Flavio taught her." Mancini glanced up and shared the rest of the tale while looking Armando in the eye. "Flavio convinced Tomosino to hire Capriccio and the dirty bastard killed her. Tomosino convinced my father her death would bring me back to the *Mafioso*, bring me back to my son and wife. And it worked. I am here now. I have been ever since."

"Why not tell me this?" Armando's voice choked on emotion. There were so many emotions in him at that moment he couldn't settle on one. Thankfully the pain to the side of his face was a persistent distraction.

"For the reasons you and I both know. If my love for Melissa was revealed I would risk dishonor to the family and put all that we have built in jeopardy. *Omertá* brought me back."

"There is more to it. Isn't there?" Armando cringed. "Why would Tomosino involve himself in the affairs of the *Mafioso*? What did he gain?"

Mancini shook his head.

"You must tell me, Papa. You're weak now and so am I because of your lies! Tell me."

Mancini shot him a withering glare. Armando held firm. "You live on borrowed time, Papa. If you die and leave me blind to what my enemies know what chance do I have to save our family name?"

"It was different times. Men like me, like us, were being hauled into jails, and the Five Dons had lost all influence in government. Every police agency wanted to end the *Mafioso*, *Camorra*, *'Ndrangheta*, all of us. We needed to stand together. Especially here in Sicily, we had to take a stand. Tomosino fled to Italy to be his own man in the *Camorra*. But our downfall would be his and he knew it. He made a promise to your grandfather after exposing my affair with Melissa to him. In exchange for the alliance we have had for over three decades between our families, I would recommit to my vows and fight to restore the integrity to the Mafia. To help us overtake the enemies who wanted to wipe us out. I was the offer he presented to the *Dons*."

"What else, Papa?" Armando demanded.

Mancini wiped his hand over his mouth. "Mirabella and Marietta are my daughters. They are your sisters. I named them. I held them when they came into the world. Had them christened under my name. And I lost them both."

Armando sat back. In all of his pondering over the trouble with his father and his fixation with the Americans he never guessed this. His mind wouldn't allow it. They took vows as men. What made the Mafia pure was his vow of family—it was the first vow instilled in each man that took the oath of *omertá*. The men of the mafia put tradition and Sicilians first. It was disgusting to take another woman, especially one who wasn't Sicilian and give her your seed, taint your legacy. It was why he had not decided on a bride. It was why Giovanni was laughable to him with his Irish blood and his Negro wife.

He didn't understand his father at all.

"It's not true." Armando rejected the thought. "We do not have niggers in our family," Armando said.

"It is true boy. They are you sisters, twins. They don't know each other exist. Giovanni keeps them separated. And I can't protect them from my grave. They need to know the truth before I die." Mancini lifted the gun and put it on his lap. "I may be old, and feeble minded, but I'm still in here and I am still the *Don* of this family. You will help me bring them home. Or I'll bury your dreams of inheriting my legacy first."

Armando stood with the aid of the back of the sofa and glared at his father. "If you want this then I want something in return, the end of the Battaglia truce. I want Giovanni dead. Give me this and I'll give you your bastards."

Mancini nodded his head. "You have my blessing."

* B *

Lorenzo knocked. After a brief pause the door opened. Carlo walked back into the room. "Giovanni rises at five. I think I should see him first."

"He knows you're here. You know the men have told him." Carlo paced.

Lorenzo saw his friend was on edge. He understood his anxiety. Giovanni would punish them both. "I can handle Gio. I saw Renaldo. He told me Santo arrives in the morning. There is a sit down with Giuliani Mottola. Gio has a lot on his plate. Hell he needs me. I can't even believe Giovanni returned to Sicily with all that he knows. He can't trust the Mancinis. I'll help him see that."

"You married her, Lo. That's a game changer and you know it. We have no way of knowing how Giovanni will deal with this, us, her! The one thing we do know is he is a madman when it comes to protecting his wife. If he sees Marietta as a threat he could hurt her, Lo."

"Let me worry about my wife, I'll protect her. You stick to the plan. We meet with him at five. Agreed?"

Carlo wiped his hand down his face. He scratched his brow. Lorenzo understood there would be no convincing his friend. Whatever the consequences of their return he'd face them and make sure Carlo didn't. Carlo had suffered enough heartache because of Lorenzo's mistakes. He wouldn't add to it. "See you in the morning."

When he left the room and started toward his own his thoughts returned to his wife. He reached in the pocket of his trousers and fingered the necklace. If he gave it back to her she'd wear it. And that could spell disaster. If he told her it was lost she'd be broken hearted, and he hated the idea of hurting her. Lorenzo opened the door to their room. Marietta stood and wiped the tears from her eyes. She hadn't changed into one of those sexy camisoles she wore for him. It looked like she'd been crying and pacing the entire time he was gone. "Did you find it, Lo?" she asked with meek quivers in her voice.

"No, sweetheart. I'm sorry I didn't," he replied.

"Oh no," Marietta put a hand to her mouth. He closed the door and went to her. She hugged him and cried against his chest. He stroked her back and tried to soothe her. But she was inconsolable. Lorenzo scooped her up in his arms and carried her to bed. He joined her. He held her.

"Why does it mean so much to you? It's just a necklace," Lorenzo reasoned.

"It was all I had. The only thing from my mother," she wept.

He lifted her face. "Let it go, Marietta. You have me. We're family now. That will never change. You have my ring."

She nodded, and rested her face next to his. She held him and continued to cry and tremble in his arms. It was not how he wanted to spend his wedding night. But he accepted his role as her husband willingly. After all he was the cause of her suffering.

9.

Cold steel pressed in against his temple. There was only one source or reason. Lorenzo's lids parted. He looked up into Dominic's glaring eyes. The gun aimed at his head was steady with its lethal intent. Lorenzo nodded that he understood Giovanni's wishes.

Dominic lowered the gun and stepped back in the darkness. Lorenzo lifted on his elbows to watch Dominic walk out the room as silent as he arrived. He sat up in the bed. Marietta wrapped herself tighter around him. At some time during the night, despite her grief, he had to have her. Lorenzo stripped Marietta of her wedding dress and made love to her until she climaxed and professed her love to him. Now she lay close to him, her beautiful body only partially covered by the sheets.

"Shit," he said, and checked his wristwatch. It was three in the morning.

He tossed aside the covers. He found his pants and pulled them on minus his boxer shorts. He picked up a wrinkled white shirt and slipped it, on misaligning the buttons in his hurry. He had no time for shoes. When he opened the door Dominic stood in the dark with the silver gun clasped before him in his hands. Nico and Renaldo leaned against the wall. The three men stared. All of them were ready to escort him to the boss.

Defying Giovanni would often send a welcome party. Though he considered these men brothers they would not hesitate to deliver his punishment.

"Let's get this over with," Lorenzo said.

Giovanni drummed his fingers on his desk. Like a power surge when all the needles swung over to the red he felt his anger mounting to a nuclear event. His gaze never left the door. The minutes ticked on and his patience ebbed with each. When he pushed back in his chair Dominic entered.

"Where is he?" Giovanni asked through clenched teeth.

Dominic gave a nod and Lorenzo walked in. His cousin looked at him with a sly smile. "Gio? *Come sta?* Miss me?" Lorenzo said with open arms.

Nico delivered the first blow. It was a sledgehammer punch of his massive right fist to Lorenzo's kidneys. His cousin dropped immediately. In deadly earnest Nico and Renaldo began kicking and pounding on Lorenzo with their fists. The eruption of violence turned and Lorenzo fought back. Furniture was broken as he overpowered Renaldo. Dominic and Giovanni watched. Renaldo suffered Lorenzo's wrath until Nico brought his strong arm around Lorenzo's neck and his cousin went near limp from the stranglehold. His face turned red. It was smeared with blood from his nose and mouth. Giovanni sneered and enjoyed the suffering.

"*Basta!* Stop it, Gio. Give Nico the order," Dominic warned. "Before he kills him!"

Lorenzo's eyes rolled in his head.

"Gio!" Dominic said in a panic. Nico looked at Giovanni with pleading eyes, not wanting to be the man to take down their brother.

Giovanni slowly nodded for it to end.

Lorenzo was released. He dropped forward hacking. Eventually the desperate gasps and drags of breath turned to laughter. *Lorenzo laughed.* He cursed in a hoarse choking voice as he struggled to rise off the floor.

"What the fuck is so funny?" Dominic asked. Giovanni just stared on. Lorenzo looked up with blood shot eyes and a goofy grin. He held up his left hand. Giovanni zeroed in on the ring finger. It was a gold wedding band.

"*Che cosa?*" Giovanni asked.

Lorenzo sat back on his haunches. He wiped the blood on his face off with his white sleeve. He wheezed his response. "Congratulate me, Gio," he said. "I'm married. Marietta is my wife."

* B *

A monstrous bolt of pain hammered his skull. His vision blurred. Every breath Armando breathed, every throb of his pulse increased his suffering. Blinded by his misery he reached in the darkness for the pain pills. Carmella woke. She turned on the lamplight next to her side of the bed.

"Are you okay? Do you need more ice for your face?"

"No." Armando swallowed three pills, dry.

Carmella sat up. "Let me see." She touched him and he knocked her hand away. "We need to call the doctor. You could have a concussion."

"Wait." He grabbed her arm. He let her go and she reached for her robe to cover herself. Armando studied her beauty with his good eye. After all these years she remained the most beautiful girl in Palermo. "Do you continue to have feelings for Giovanni?" he asked.

"Why would you ask me that? No," Carmella answered. "I feel nothing for him, nothing romantic."

"You're lying." The alarm in her eyes was the only answer he needed. Of course she denied it.

"How am I lying? It's been over fifteen years since... you know. We were kids, Armando. And you won that battle. I'm yours. I always have been," she said with not a hint of satisfaction in her voice. He had once loved her, but the fight for her love as kids turned his stomach on her loyalty when later he saw whom she truly longed for. He'd never marry her. Hell there was a rumor once that Giovanni would. Armando knew the truth on that score.

"Let me get you more ice, at least. I really wish you'd allow me to call the doctor."

"Sit. I want to know some things," Armando said.

Carmella sat.

"Giovanni sent you away from Mondello, because his wife didn't like you?" Armando asked.

Carmella sighed. "I told you this already. Madre and Anthony stayed behind. I'm not needed."

Armando chuckled. He immediately stopped and winced. It hurt to laugh. "Sounds more like you're not welcome."

"Whatever. It doesn't matter. I don't want to return."

"And she carries twins?" Armando asked.

"Yes. She does."

Armando sighed. "You will return." He cast the sheets aside. "I want you to find a way to get close to the family, namely her. I need to know the movements of his wife. Her routines. Everything."

"Why? You and the Battaglias have a truce. Right?" Carmella asked.

Armando smiled. "Of course. But truces are made to be broken. How do you feel about twins? Giovanni having sons from that woman?"

"It's none of my business." Carmella replied.

"But how do you feel?" Armando asked.

Carmella looked away. "What is it you want me to say? He married her. Giovanni hasn't touched me since we were fifteen. What does it matter how I feel?"

"It matters, *cara*," he touched her chin. He turned her face to look at him. "If he is widowed who will he turn to?"

Her eyes stretched. Armando forced a smile, one he used to calm her. "I'm willing to let you go. I'm willing to help you have what you always wanted, Giovanni. But you have to help me."

"By doing what?" Carmella asked.

"I have a contact who says that Lorenzo has bought a ticket to Sicily. He's on his way home, with an American black woman he has married."

Carmella frowned.

Armando laughed. "Why look surprised? Lorenzo has copied Giovanni all his life. This is no different."

"I don't understand any of it," Carmella said with evident disgust.

Armando shrugged. "The two American women with the Battaglias are trouble. They don't fit our world, neither do Giovanni's bastards."

"Again I have to ask you what do you want from me? I won't spy on the Battaglias, they're my family," Carmella said.

"Was he your family when he tossed you to me and my boys to play with when we were kids?"

"He didn't do that. It was you and Lorenzo that set it all in motion. Don't rewrite history."

Armando chuckled.

"My mother, my brother, their lives will be in jeopardy if I'm caught conspiring with you," Carmella pleaded.

"You will do whatever the fuck I tell you." Armando eased back and closed his eyes. He would try again to rest. The room was filled with silence. Still he sensed her distress.

"What am I to you, Armando? A plaything? A companion? A friend?" Carmella asked. "No matter how many years are between us you still hate him more than you can ever love me."

"He deserves every bit of my hatred." Armando opened his eyes. "Trust me. No one will suspect. I'm not at war with the Battaglias. I'm at war with those two bitches they've married."

"Why?"

"Stop asking me why!" he shouted.

The women were a threat. If his father did anything to include them in his will he'd lose everything. If their children were born they could lay claim to his fortune as well. He wanted them gone. And Mirabella's difficulty with her pregnancy as explained to him by her doctor was the key. If she dies because of those complications it will weaken Giovanni. He'd seen proof of it with the Calderones. Armando's father would never suspect him. It was a perfect plan to destroy Giovanni and the Battaglias once and for all. He cast his gaze to a stunned Carmella. "You will help me. What's left of Giovanni when I am done with him will be all yours."

She looked away. "What is it you want me to do?"

* B *

"You married her?" Dominic asked.

"Nico. Renaldo. *Vattene!*" Giovanni said. Nico and Renaldo left. They closed the door behind them. It was do or die. Lorenzo spat a blood clot on the floor.

"Did you marry her?" Dominic repeated.

Lorenzo didn't look to Dominic. He fixed his gaze on his cousin who met his stare with an unwavering intensity. Deep down he felt a sense of triumph at finally having the upper hand on Gio. But for the sake of his new bride and his return to the family he had to reach a common ground.

"Yes, Domi I married her. I love her. Like Gio, I followed my heart and married American."

"Does she know?" Dominic asked.

Pain covered his limbs. He couldn't summon the strength to stand. He swallowed blood and pushed at the loose tooth to the back of his mouth with his tongue. "She does not," he answered. "She has no idea who she really is or how she is related to the *Donna*. She's just a woman who fell in love with me."

"Madonna Santa!" Dominic slapped his forehead.

"I can't let her go." Lorenzo quickly added. "Marrying her was the only way to make sure she stayed. You gave me no choice, Gio. What if I turned her lose and Mancini got to her? I didn't expect to fall in love with her. But she's a passionate woman. I spent every day of the past four months seducing her to be mine. What did you expect would happen?"

Giovanni wiped his hand down his face. He turned away. He faced his desk and leaned forward with his hands spread apart and arms straight and rigid. "I've pretended at being a man of patience," Giovanni began. "I do this because of what I am. But you, Lorenzo, you test me, at every turn. You tempt me." Giovanni dropped his head. "You will be the death of me, or I of you. Either way you tempt me."

Lorenzo stared at his cousin's back. He wore a dark black silk robe tied over black silk pajama pants. Giovanni grabbed the edge of desk and it lifted on two legs an inch from the ground before he slammed it back down. "I told you what was at stake. My fucking wife! The birth of my sons. I told you why I needed you to keep that woman away from us."

Lorenzo grabbed his side. He forced himself to stand. "Marietta is harmless. The sisters' knowing each other can't hurt Mirabella."

"Mira has been diagnosed with Placenta Previa," Dominic said. "Giovanni has not told her. She also suffers from anxiety attacks. She's had many episodes in Sorrento but none since we've arrived in Mondello. Keeping her calm and safe is not only for the life of his sons but Mira's life as well." Dominic informed Lorenzo. "That is why Giovanni is here with her instead of in the *Campania*."

"No one told me! Gio, I didn't know," Lorenzo said.

Giovanni didn't respond.

"There's something you both need to know. Something I just picked up on," Lorenzo winced as he staggered forward. "Mancini tracked us. He had his people tailing us in France. Carlo confirmed it. Marietta was his target. Gio, I think he wants to tell her the truth."

"We are done, Lorenzo. Leave. Get out," Dominic warned.

"Gio? I am trying to tell you the truth!" Lorenzo pleaded.

"Out! Out! Out now!" Giovanni flipped the desk sending it crashing with a thunderous boom. Lorenzo looked over to Dominic. The *consigliere* nodded that he should go. Lorenzo turned and held his side as he managed to walk out of the room without assistance.

Before Dominic could say a word Giovanni put his face in his hands and spoke. "You go too. Get the fuck out."

Dominic walked over to the desk. He heaved it up from its side and set it right. He then went to the bar. He needed a drink. Not only had his sweet love with Catalina ended because of jealous rage. But now he had a new war in the family to contend with. No matter what transpired Giovanni would not admit defeat. But he was certain that his *Don* knew in this situation he was defeated. He'd have to tell his wife the truth.

"There is a benefit to this, Gio," Dominic began. "If we think on it."

Dominic drank the brandy and exhaled as the bitter and the

sweet coated his tongue. "She's his wife. She's one of us now. You can turn this around. Take the credit for uniting the sisters. Tell Mirabella you didn't know who she was until he brought Marietta here to Sicily. Let the sisters get to know each other under your supervision."

"Or I could go with option two," Giovanni said.

Dominic stopped sipping his brandy, the glass was frozen to his lips. Giovanni cut his gaze over to Dominic. He leaned forward and braced the side of the desk once more. "I could cut her throat and his. Be done with them both. Show Mancini that nothing, not even Bella's sister can come between me and my wife."

"Gio? You won't do that. You harm her, and we go to war with the Mancinis. The world knows who Mira is and she becomes a pawn to use against you. Mira learns the truth from anyone other than you and you lose her. Think about it, Gio, I beg you."

Giovanni looked away. "Do you know what I fear, Domi?"

"What?" he asked.

"This. The day I become him." Giovanni said.

"Who?"

"Patri," Gio confessed. "I swore to my mother that I would never. But when Nico had his arm wrapped around Lorenzo's throat I came close. So close to giving in."

"But you stopped it." Dominic said.

"Did I, Domi?" he looked over again at Dominic. "Or did you?"

Dominic put the brandy glass down. "What if Lorenzo is telling the truth. She's Mira's twin. Can you blame him for falling in love with her? Look at what you will do to keep Mira. Lorenzo is no different than you, Gio. And neither of you are Tomosino. You are changing this family for the better. Legitimizing us."

Giovanni closed his eyes, his profile revealed his torment. "She and my children are the only ones that keep me... from... giving in. I learned that lesson with the Calderones. Madness has a taste. It's sweet, decadent, intoxicating. If she finds out how I betrayed her... I can't risk what Tomosino did to her mother ever coming out. I know my woman. There are limits. She'll close part of her heart off from me."

"Then tell her your version of the truth and bring her sister into the family. Stand Lorenzo up. Unite us. Don't be like Patri and rule with your prejudices and pride."

"I need to be alone." Giovanni said.

At first Dominic hesitated, but like himself Giovanni proved there was no reasoning away a man's fears. He understood Giovanni in ways many didn't. From the moment Giovanni learned that his father had fault in how Mira's mother died he knew Giovanni walked in fear. Dominic suffered the same affliction. And tonight he had driven Catalina away. Lost the only person in the world that kept him sane.

Yes. He understood Giovanni in ways no else did.

"Mira is strong, Gio. And she loves you. Trust her," Dominic warned.

He turned and walked out.

Emotion shamed him. Here he was fearless among killers, men that lived beneath the belly of society, and suddenly he was weak with self-pity. Giovanni sucked down deep slow breaths to stay away an anxiety attack unlike anything he felt since he put his mother in the ground. He was trapped. Boxed in between lies and deception. Lorenzo had done the unthinkable and he had to accept it. If he struck out at either of them and lost control of the situation it would most certainly destroy his marriage. If he confessed, he'd lose her faith and trust in him. If he did nothing his enemies in and outside of this family would find the moment to slit his throat and take it all.

Grief swept through him like a black oppressive wave of defeat. Giovanni dropped to his knees. He never let them see him afraid— never let them see him fall. Not even Mira knew his deepest darkest fear. The one of dying alone, unloved, unworthy. He pressed his face to the cool wood surface of the desk and tried to regulate his breathing. And then the terror tremors squeezing his gut and lungs ceased. He exhaled, turned, and put his back to his desk. He sat on the floor staring at the blood glistening over the marble floor.

The damage was done. His actions would have consequences. He would sit there the entire night until he figured out how to do away with those consequences.

* B *

Marietta smiled as the warmth of the sun warmed her face. She felt wonderful. Stretching she turned and opened her eyes to look for her husband. At first her vision blurred but she blinked twice and her vision cleared.

Her heart stopped.

A startled cry of horror escaped her. Marietta shot upright in bed. Dried blood was on Lorenzo's pillow and face. He had a busted lip and red swelling to his cheek and both eyes. She moved the blanket and looked underneath to find his body peppered with bruises. Lorenzo let out a snore and flipped over to throw his arm around her waist.

"Baby? Baby wake up!"

Lorenzo grunted and peeked with one eye up at her. "Huh?" he said.

She kept her tears at bay and tried to find her voice. "Waa-wha-what happened to you?" she stammered. "Who hurt you like this?"

With a frown of confusion he lifted his head. "I'm fine. Come here, beautiful."

"No!" She fought to stay upright but he pulled her down under the covers and rolled on top of her. Marietta pushed at both of his shoulders and moved her hips left and then right to keep him from parting her legs. He won the battle forcing her thighs apart with his muscled thighs and pressing his erection hard against her pussy.

Instead of resisting him she took hold of his face and cradled it in her hands. "What happened?"

"I fell on my way to the bathroom last night," he smiled.

She opened her mouth to call bullshit on his explanation and he kissed her brow while feeding her pussy an inch of his dick. Marietta let go of his face and gipped his shoulders. Lorenzo hissed in pain.

"Oops! I'm sorry, stop. You aren't well. Stop it, Lo."

"Bullshit. *Ti desidero.*" Lorenzo dropped his face into the space between her shoulder and neck. He grabbed her hard by the hip and ass to pin her down. From over his shoulder she watched his ass rise and fall as he thrust inch by inch into her. Marietta's lids fluttered shut and her eyes rolled beneath. The sexual assault lasted longer than she expected and she clung to him as he climaxed his release. She achieved none. How could she when her heart raced with worry the way it did.

Marietta sighed.

Lorenzo lay on her, buried inside her. She rubbed his back gently to give him some relief. *When did he leave their bed and return? Who could have beaten him so horribly here?* And more importantly, why?

She felt a surge of protective rage with the ferocity of a lightening bolt. She'd be damn if she let anybody hurt her baby. Ever. Marietta dropped her face over to the side of his head and held on to him, closing her eyes. Lorenzo lifted his ass to withdraw his cock and turned to his side bringing her with him. She clung to him. She drifted back to sleep.

* B *

Giovanni sat on the edge of the bed. He gazed down at Mira. He brushed the back of his hand across her cheek. Mira's eyes opened.

"Giovanni? What is it?"

"Something I need to tell you," he said. The words lodged in his throat. He pressed his lips together searching for a way to begin. Dominic said if he owned the situation he controlled the outcome. But to have Lorenzo drive him to this act made his pride swell and crush his bravery.

"Okay, sweetheart. Tell me." Mira lifted on her elbows. He remembered when he found her, after thinking she was dead. He remembered how close he came to losing her. But things were different now. She was his wife. Even if she wanted to punish him she would never leave him. He'd make sure of it.

"I've done something," he began. "I don't know how to explain."

"Oh, Giovanni." Mira tried to sit up fully and he helped her. He positioned pillows to her back. "I've always told you, no matter what it is, you can talk to me."

She touched his face.

He closed his eyes.

"I make tough decisions for us all the time, Bella. I'm selfish because I have to be. I have to think of what we need first. There are so many things you don't know, so much I can never tell you to explain why I do what I do."

"It's okay," Mira said. Giovanni looked up into her eyes. She smiled sweetly at him. "What I said yesterday, about you manipulating me. Is this what it's all about?"

He nodded.

"You're not perfect. I know who you have to be for them, but for me you don't. Talk to me. I can handle whatever it is, if you trust me."

The tortured malady of his heart froze his tongue. No matter how he looked at it, explained or reasoned the past, his actions were inexcusable. And he just couldn't bring himself to compound the deception with another lie. He glanced up at her. Mira smiled. He leaned in and kissed her. "You were right, I did keep Zia and Rocco away from you on purpose. I told them they weren't needed. I wanted to keep the family in the dark about your pregnancy."

"What about my pregnancy?" Mira asked.

"You have what the doctors call Placenta Previa. The doctors have concerns that the placenta has moved to cover part of your cervix. Remember the bleeding and the cramping. It's a symptom. And they... they say it will get worse."

"And the babies? What about them? They need the placenta right? For oxygen and food. Right? What happens to my babies?"

"The babies are fine, Bella. Healthy and fine I assure you. But the doctor thinks you might go into pre-term labor. That's the reason I brought you here, to relax you. Buhari has a good prenatal facility in Palermo."

"They already said I have high blood pressure. Now this? Why did you keep this from me!" she asked. He could hear the anger and disappointment in her voice. "You had the doctors lie to me and tell me the bleeding was normal! I trusted you."

He nodded under the weight of his guilt. "You were having panic attacks, Mira. Nothing I could do or say calmed you. I thought the less you knew the better. But I was wrong. I'm sorry."

Mira sighed. She reached and touched his face. "Good grief. I can't believe you sometimes. The lengths you will go to. What do we do now? Do I stay in bed? What?"

"The doctor said its okay for you to move around. He'll check you later this week. Have you had any cramping? Any bleeding?"

"A little bleeding not a lot. No cramping."

Giovanni forced a smile. "Then we're okay."

"Don't do that again. Don't lie to me about something this important. About my life, my health. I trust you babe. You put us at risk when you keep secrets this important from me."

"I understand."

"Come here... you look tired. Let's get some more sleep. We don't have to start the morning just yet."

He rose and removed his robe, pajama pants. He stripped nude before he climbed across the bed and got in with her.

"Do you forgive me?" he asked, and kissed her face, then her belly. Mira stroked the back of his head as he listened to his sons.

"Nothing you do could ever make me stop loving you, Giovanni. Nothing."

Giovanni closed his eyes. He had to wait to tell her the truth another day. One confession was all he could stand.

Morning –

Mira's head lifted from her pillow. Eve stood in her crib. She sucked her pacifier and observed her parents. When their eyes met Eve blinked at her mother while dancing on one foot and then the other to be released. Giovanni slept with his arm around her waist and his thigh thrown over her leg. His face was buried in her hair and his breath warmed her nape. She could only sleep comfortably on her side and no matter how many times she explained to him that his holding her in the night made her uncomfortable she constantly found herself in this position.

Eve began to cry.

Mira sighed. She pushed out of his embrace and sat up. The babies jostled for space in her belly and she felt a sharp cramp in her side. Several more weeks of this and she was done. After learning the truth about her pregnancy last night she prayed to see her babies to be born healthy.

She pushed up to her feet from the bed and walked over to her daughter. Eve immediately lifted her arms to be rescued.

"Morning, baby," Mira said. She balanced her daughter's weight in her arms with her against her belly. "You hungry?"

Eve rested her head against Mira's shoulder.

"You shouldn't lift her, Bella. Let me next time," Giovanni yawned.

"You heard her. You didn't move." Mira put Eve in the bed between them. Eve immediately crawled over to her father and he sat up to stretch the toddler out against his chest. Mira lowered to the bed, turned her legs and put them on top.

"Her diaper bag is over there. Can you change her for me?" Mira yawned.

She looked over and saw the frown on her husband's face.

"I thought she went to the pink plastic toilet?" he asked.

"Giovanni? She can't very well climb out of the crib and go. She wears disposable training pants to bed. They're in the diaper bag by the door."

He grumbled but got out of the bed with Eve in his arms. Mira watched him bring the bag over. She was too sleepy to argue. But sitting up against the pillows instead of being trapped in his arms did help with comfort.

"Why did you put the bracelet on Eve's wrist?" he asked.

Mira glanced at Eve's wrist. Her daughter seemed oblivious to it now. Earlier Eve was fascinated with the jewelry and touched it constantly. "It fits. So cute."

Sienna Mynx

"It's a family heirloom. You should put it up don't you think?
Let Eve wear it on special occasions," Giovanni said. He worked the
training pamper off Eve and Mira grabbed the baby bag to hand him
the wipes.

"You're right. That reminds me, Catalina saw the bracelet."

"And?" Giovanni asked. Eve flipped over and he turned her
again to finish changing her.

"She said it looked like a copy of a man named Del Stavio."

Giovanni froze. He looked over at her. "She said what?"

"Give her to me, Gio. You've got to secure the sides, baby,"
Mira sighed. Giovanni let Eve go and she went to her mother and lay
out across her lap.

"What exactly did Catalina say?" Giovanni asked.

"You're getting to be a big girl aren't you, baby?" Mira cooed
at Eve. "Soon we have to buy you your own bed."

Eve laughed and started playing with her bracelet.

"What did she say, Bella?"

"Huh? Oh, remember the man? The one that got the visas for
Fabiana and me? I think his name was Manchichis?"

"Mancini?" Giovanni corrected her.

"Him. Yes. She said the jeweler was his. And some other Dons
here in Sicily. That the jeweler only made custom pieces for the
mafia families. So I figured..." Mira lifted Eve and let her hug her
belly. "My mother must have met some Sicilians in America.
Someone made a counterfeit bracelet. Isn't that strange?"

Giovanni didn't answer.

"Not surprising," Mira continued. "If I hadn't had it tested to
prove it was real gold I would have thought it was fake. My mother
was a strange woman."

"Take the bracelet off Eve. I couldn't get the clasp open last
night." Giovanni demanded.

Mira looked over to her husband. He looked pale. "What's
wrong? You feel sick?"

"Take it off, Bella. Now!"

She removed the bracelet from Eve's wrist. She turned it over
and looked at the insignia. "See? Here it is? This is the one that
looks like it belonged to Del Stavio."

Giovanni took the bracelet and never looked at it. He got up from
the bed and went to retrieve her bag. Mira found it odd that he knew
exactly where to put it. "It's destiny isn't it, honey?"

He glanced back at her.

"That bracelet is how I knew you were a man of your word. I

200

swear when you found it for me that was the sexiest thing." Mira smiled. "Remember? When I ran from your room and you came after me. Remember what you told me? I think the next day we made Eve."

Giovanni smiled. "Yea, I remember."

"If my purse wasn't snatched... if Mancini never leased that building to us... if you weren't Lorenzo's cousin and met me in Bellagio... we'd never have Eve. Our family, and our life together may have never happened. *Destino*." Mira blew him a kiss.

Giovanni returned to bed. He took Eve from her and pulled her over to sit closer. She liked the quiet moments between them. Eve seemed to settle down when her father held her.

"I was thinking that I would take Eve down to Mondello's beaches. Catalina said there are some great shops there she wants to show me. Will it be okay? I mean I'm scared of this placenta thing," Mira said.

"No. You shouldn't go for long walks in the shopping market. A walk over to Serenity, our villa, would be okay but nothing more strenuous."

"Wanna come? We can let Eve build sand castles," Mira joked.

"Can you delay it? There's something else you should know," Giovanni sighed.

"Okay?" Mira asked.

"Lorenzo has returned." Giovanni answered.

Mira felt a surge of relief to hear that Lorenzo had returned. It had been months. Although Lorenzo wasn't her favorite person she had begun to worry about him. It just didn't seem like Lorenzo to stay away for so long.

"He came in last night? Really? Where has he been?"

"Off getting married," Giovanni answered.

Mira froze. "Say that again?"

"Lorenzo married an American black woman named Marietta. You met her at the wedding. She came to Eve's birthday party also."

"My God. He did?" Mira put a hand to her chest. "I had no idea they were that serious."

Giovanni shrugged. He looked away as if uncomfortable with the conversation. "They will be staying here for now," he said. "Lorenzo and I... we have business. So I think you should make her feel at home. But... keep your distance. I want to look into her past. Learn more about who she is and where she is from."

"That makes no sense. How am I to make her feel comfortable if I keep my distance?" Mira asked.

"We don't know her, Bella. Bringing someone new into the family has to be done with caution. I think we keep it polite but not delve into anything personal. Let things develop."

Mira nodded. She understood the rules of their life. Trust no one. But still she couldn't help but be curious. She met Marietta at Eve's birthday party after the wedding and the woman was kind of standoffish. Lorenzo choosing a black woman for his wife felt odd too. She knew of the scorn her husband received for his choice. Mira suspected he received some from Lorenzo too, but never heard or saw any proof of it.

"I guess he's over Fabiana," Mira said. "Well I need to get up and get dressed. I want to meet with Sophia and prepare a great dinner to celebrate."

"Why?" Giovanni asked, bouncing Eve on his lap.

"We didn't get invited to the wedding. Let's make it a celebration for them. To show we're happy for them both," she eased out of bed smiling. She looked back over and discovered Giovanni watched her. "Take her to Cecilia's room. Then come join me in the shower. I want a back rub."

He smiled and nodded. "Will do."

* B *

"I don't want to get out of bed. Can we lay here all day?" Marietta asked.

They were wrapped in each other's arms on a mattress that felt as soft as clouds. The curtain around their bed was drawn. She felt like royalty. And with the doors to the balcony in their room open she could hear the sea.

"We can stay here for as long as you like. But I think we should get dressed and see the family. They really want to meet you."

"Bullshit," Marietta chuckled.

"Why do you say bullshit?" Lorenzo asked. He smacked her playfully on the ass.

"For starters look at you. What happened to you last night? Did King B freak out because we arrived unannounced? I'm not stupid, Lo. Your homecoming was not welcomed with roses. Right?"

"My cousin has a different way of showing love. Trust me everything is fine." He took her chin and forced her face up to look into her eyes. "Enough of this shit with King B and Queen B. You will address him as *Don* Giovanni for now, and Gio when you two

202

are more familiar. You will address Mirabella as *Donna*. Always, unless she tells you different. Do you understand?"

"I understand. But in private she's Queen Black Barbie and he's King Barbarian. Okay?"

Lorenzo chuckled. He shook his head and laughed until he winced in pain. "Let's shower together. I wash your back you suck my dick—"

She elbowed him hard and he howled in pain. Marietta shot up. She rubbed his side as he turned over in agony. "I'm sorry, baby. I forgot. My God how hurt are you?" He remained balled tight. Panic went through her. "Lo? Lo? Talk to me. How bad is it? I'm so sorry." She pulled on his shoulder. "Lo?"

Like the release of a tightly wound spring he seized her. Marietta squealed. He kissed her face and tickled her. She kicked under him and tried to push him off. Lorenzo bit her neck hard. Marietta laughed and shook her head.

"I want a morning kiss," he said.

She lifted her arms around his neck. "Come here and I'll give you one."

"A proper kiss," Lorenzo dropped over to his back and pulled her with him. He then lifted her by her hips. Marietta braced her hands to the headboard. Lorenzo cupped her ass with both hands and lifted her as if she weighed nothing. He brought her pussy down on his bruised face.

"Lo... Wait!" she gasped.

He groaned and swept his tongue up from her pussy to the swollen nub of her clit. Shock held her immobile for a moment. She bumped her head on the headboard as her eyes fluttered shut. His mouth nibbled her and then he proceeded to tickle her clit with his tongue and started foreplay that sent spasms of pleasure through her pelvis. Marietta worked her hips as her pussy was rubbed back and forth over his open mouth. His tongue teased the entrance of her pussy. And the involuntary clenching of her inner walls left him gasping, wheezing. The climax he drove through her had her beating her head against the hard wood and digging her nails into the grain.

Lorenzo lapped up her sweet juices and she trembled and wept with joy. He brought her down his chest and opened his legs to force her to lie back between them. Her knees were spread. Her feet rested on either side of his hips, on the bed. The glistening pink walls of her pussy were on display. He thumbed her and her breath gusted from her. The sight of her beautiful body, the thin gold chain she wore around her waist that connected to the diamond piercing in her navel, and her bushy curly hair splayed wildly around her face excited him. Something akin to raw, primitive love inside of Lorenzo sharpened the hardcore edge of lust making his cock pulse for domination.

Her large eyes glittered. "What you waiting for, baby?" she asked.

"No one will ever touch you again, Marie. I'll kill any man that does. Do you understand me?"

She reached down and touched herself for him. "Of course not. I'm your wife. Forever."

Lorenzo groaned. He watched her fingers play with her sweet pussy. He wanted her to feel him. The stretch of his cock, the heat of his dick as he owned her. He put a hand to hers to stop her and she moved her hand away. He angled his cock at her opening and she stretched her arms above her head. He was sitting up. She laid flat to her back. She wrapped her legs around his waist as soon as he entered her. He had dragged her a bit closer and his dick tunneled deeper. His gaze fastened on her nipples. The dark almond brown peaks tightened as her breasts quivered with each measured thrust. She arched her hips to angle his strike better.

He lifted her to bring her to his chest, in the upright position, but he slipped out of her. "Come on, baby, slide that juicy pussy over my dick," he chuckled.

Marietta centered her sex and eased back down on him. Lorenzo wielded a steady stare of dominance neither could break. He now had her by the hips and controlled her rise and fall on his dick with ferocious intensity. Through gritted teeth she breathed in and out of flared nostrils. When their bodies joined this way she felt desperately in love with him. It explained why they'd fuck three to four times a day on the yacht. There was never enough sex for either of them.

And she loved to watch him too. The muscle alongside his jaw flexed and she cupped the side of his face in her hand, while holding on to him with her other arm around his neck. Marietta knew he was no closer to a climax than she. Which meant he'd be fucking her all morning. She clung to him, shuddered against him and gave in to his passion.

This is what it felt like to be married...

204

* B *

Mira nodded that she agreed with everything on the menu for the family brunch she intended to serve. Most had already started gathering on the outside terrace for coffee and pastries. "Looks very delicious, Sophia."

"*Donna*, I have a request," Sophia said in a voice so soft she barely heard her.

"Okay?" Mira asked.

"My sister is ill. She lives in Bagheria. I need to see to her." Sophia turned and looked to the floor instead of Mira as she shared the story of her sister's chronic illness. Mira felt her heart break with sympathy. "I hate to do this with you and the family here but I have to leave this afternoon. I would like Carmella to come and see to the cooking and household needs. She needs the work, *Donna*, and she is a good girl. I swear she would not do anything—"

"It's okay," Mira smiled. Carmella's return meant so little in the grand scheme of things. It was silly for her to be jealous of the woman. "She can come back and work here. Do you need anything? Anything?"

"No." Sophia said with tears in her eyes. She walked over and hugged Mira. The gesture was so tight Mira felt another pang of sympathy. "Forgive me, *Donna*, I have no choice."

"Of course you don't." Mira rubbed her back. "No worries, Sophia. Anthony has been a great help and Carmella will be too. Thank you for taking care of my family."

"*Grazie, Donna. Tante grazie.*"

Mira let her go. She picked up a tray of meat and cheeses and so did Sophia. They brought the food to the family. Everyone was gathered except for the newlyweds. However, they were the talk of the conversation.

"But who is she, Gio? This woman he married. I barely remember her from the wedding," Catalina said.

"She came to Eve's birthday party," Rosetta chimed in. "But of course you arrived too late to meet her."

"Oh shut up," Catalina tossed back.

"It doesn't matter who she is, Catalina. Make her feel welcome. Okay?" Mira said. She noticed Dominic's chair was empty. She hoped that he would arrive before Lorenzo and his wife did so they could toast the couple together.

"*Donna*," Carlo stood from his seat and Mira walked over and greeted him.

"How are you, Carlo?" Mira asked.

"*Bennisima.* Good to see you." He kissed her on the left and then the right cheek.

"If only Zia and Rocco were here. We'd have all the family," she said. She returned to the head of the table where Giovanni sat. She saw his plate was empty and picked it up. He and Eve would starve themselves rather than eat from the plate fixed by anyone other than her. Mira didn't mind. Which would probably have Fabiana turning over in her grave. Neither of them were the type of women to be found barefoot, pregnant and in the kitchen. Mira smiled to herself and stacked the plate with everything she knew her hubby and baby liked.

Once done with her mommy and wifely duties she returned the plates to them and gave her daughter a sweet kiss. Silence fell over the family. Mira lifted her head and her gaze. Lorenzo entered the room holding hands with the woman she'd seen before.

Marietta was quite lovely. She wore a turquoise maxi dress with a very high split up her right thigh. The low scoop neckline revealed a respectable hint of cleavage. And her figure rivaled every woman's in the room. She was a bit fairer skin than Mira but with her hair drawn back from her face in a curly puff her features were similar to Mira's. Strikingly similar.

Which explained why the family stared at her and then glanced back at Mira with evident shock. Or it could be Lorenzo's appearance. He wore a white long sleeve shirt un-tucked from his dark trousers and opened at the collar to reveal his muscular chest. He had a gold chain around his neck. He would be devilishly handsome if it weren't for the fresh bruises to his face and the line around his neck as if he'd been strangled. *Why was it each time she saw Lorenzo he had bruises to his face?* Mira shook her head and smiled.

"*Benvenuti!* Welcome!" Mira exclaimed. She hurried down the table to them both. Her legs didn't move as fast as she liked. "Congratulations to you both! Giovanni told me the news this morning. I'm so happy, so very happy for you."

Lorenzo kissed Mira's cheek and she embraced him. She then turned to his wife. "You're Marietta right?" Mira asked.

Marietta glanced to all the others staring at her. Besides the black Barbie before her there wasn't a friendly smile in the room. She instantly felt unwanted.

Before her now was the woman the media constantly speculated about. Mirabella was strikingly beautiful as a pregnant woman. She wore an all white-layered dress that flattered her expanding curves. And though her skin was several shades darker than Marietta's she could see passion marks on her neck. *What the hell? Who walked around with hickies on their neck?* Face to face with Madame Mafia, Marietta recognized the resemblance they shared. It made her uncomfortable. Lorenzo squeezed Marietta's hand and she opened her mouth to speak.

"Yes I am Marietta. Pleased to meet you, *Donna*," Marietta said.

"*Donna?*" Mirabella laughed. "Call me Mira."

Marietta nodded and removed her hand from the woman's.

Mira pointed to two chairs reserved for them. "Have a seat. I know you must be hungry. Sophia prepared everything. If you want fish we have some on the table over there with some fresh pasta salads."

Lorenzo escorted Marietta to the table. She waited for him to pull out her chair and then eased in like a lady. He sat next to her. The family was a lot to take in. The men at the table leered at her with hard relentless stares. Carlo wore an amused smile over her discomfort.

The women at the table were equally hostile in their silent staring. And when she looked down the table to the man who sat at the head of the family, *Don* Giovanni Battaglia, she found it hard to hold his stare. The *Don* was as intimidating as his reputation. And like any other kingpin he remained stoic and observant of her. What Marietta found unique was his striking violet blue eyes. They were cold as ice. She didn't understand how he fit with a woman like Mirabella, who gushed and ran her mouth while everyone else sat silent.

"We have to celebrate. I'm so happy for you both. We're going to have a big dinner and party for you. Giovanni insists." Mira nodded her head. "Right, sweetheart?"

Don Giovanni continued to stare at Marietta, he didn't answer. And the blue-eyed little brown toddler in his lap ate her food as if Marietta hadn't joined the table.

Mira continued. "Today I want to invite you to join me and the girls on the beach. Unfortunately I can't go out sightseeing, but the private beach we have is beautiful. We can have a picnic, take some of the things from brunch with us. How does that sound? I would love to get to know you better. Oh look at me. I'm talking your head off. Please, help yourself. I can't believe Lorenzo got married," Mira chuckled. She waddled like a duck back down to her husband and daughter. Marietta nearly laughed at how ridiculous she moved. She rolled her eyes to her and her fake offer of friendship. She had no intention of spending a day with her. Maybe she and Lorenzo could go visit the grotto he told her about. As she reached for the food she felt the cold stare of someone else at the table. Marietta looked up into the eyes of a woman with dark raven hair and piercing eyes. The woman glared back. Someone addressed her as Catalina. *Whoever the bitch is, she better watch her step.*

Everyone returned their attention to their meal. Mira rejoined Giovanni at the end of the table. He was feeding Eve from his plate. "Baby, maybe you should say something. Congratulate them in front of the family," Mira whispered.

"You already did. That's enough, Bella." Giovanni answered. The sharp tone he used with her stung. Mira looked down the table and realized she might have made a fool of herself by being overly friendly. But she was sincere. She really did hope to make this a way to mend her relationship with Lorenzo. And besides she felt a little lonely for a friend. A black American woman joining their clan felt like a big deal. They were the same age, could talk about home. Mira sighed. The woman looked up at her and Mira smiled. Marietta ignored her smile and started a conversation with Lorenzo. Mira gave up.

Catalina caught the rude dismissive look Marietta gave Mira. *Who the hell did the puttana think she was?* And to further insult her brother Lorenzo had picked a woman who looked like Mira. The resemblance between the two of them made her sick. It mocked Giovanni's marriage, and Mira.

From the moment she saw them appear she thought they were a disaster. Lorenzo looked like a train wreck and his trophy looked cheap in her clingy dress. The harlot was unworthy to be his wife.

"So how did you two meet?" Catalina asked.

Marietta stopped smiling over what Lorenzo whispered in her ear. She locked eyes with her. Lorenzo kissed her cheek and spoke. "In Milano. We had a mutual friend."

"Really? That's funny, you met Fabiana in Milano." Catalina smiled. "Guess that's where you meet all your girlfriends."

"I'm not his girlfriend, I'm his wife." Marietta replied.

Catalina smiled. "Ah yes, well in our family men like Lorenzo keep both."

"That's enough, Catalina." Lorenzo warned.

Catalina leaned forward and steadied her stare with Marietta. "Fabiana and Lo were going to get married. That's before she blew up in front of—"

"Enough!" Lorenzo slammed his fist on the table.

Giovanni and Mira both looked down at them. Catalina glared at Lorenzo. She was still hurt over the way Dominic dumped her. And now this bitch shows up. "Who the hell is she, Lo? You bring her here... force her on us!"

"Stop it, Catalina!" Mira said. "Excuse yourself from the table if you can't be civil."

"Fine with me. I lost my appetite." Catalina sneered at Marietta who only smiled in return. Catalina stormed out holding back her tears.

"I'm so sorry—" Mira began.

Marietta saw the *Don* grab his wife's hand to silence her. Mira nodded to her husband. "Please forgive the rudeness."

Marietta shrugged and continued to eat. She'd been treated worse. Catalina's response to her felt genuine. Marietta respected that much. It was the fake platitudes by Queen B on the other hand that set her teeth on edge. Lorenzo shook his head chuckling. "No harm done. Wouldn't be breakfast if someone didn't storm out in a bitch fit."

A few others at the table laughed.

"I like your ring," Another young woman said. Marietta looked up and recognized her. It was the woman she'd seen months ago when a young girl was pushed down the stairs at Gio and Mira's wedding. Now they sat side by side as if nothing happened.

"My name is Rosetta," she said. Marietta noticed she looked strikingly similar to Catalina. "Can I see it?"

Marietta held out her hand and the girl leaned forward to inspect it.

"It's beautiful," Rosetta said.

"Thank you."

Marietta tried to finish her breakfast. The sooner it was over the better. She had made up her mind. She and Lorenzo would not stay here for long. She couldn't stomach these people.

* B *

Dominic waited. A sleek white two-seater car sped directly toward Villa Mare Blu. He checked his watch. They were on time.

The car rolled to a stop a few inches in front of him. Santo opened the door to the driver side and stepped out first. Giuliani was who Dominic expected to see. And he emerged from the car next. Giuliani wore dark sunglasses over his eyes and a dark suit. He wasn't a tall man but he was known for being flashy and argumentative to be recognized.

Santo approached.

He embraced Dominic and kissed both cheeks.

"Giuliani, we thank you for coming." Dominic greeted the top earner of the Mottola clan with a cheek kiss.

"I risked a lot by coming. I can't stay long. Can we do this now?" Giuliani popped his collar and dusted invisible lint from his suit. Dominic looked to Santo who gave him the same look of irritation. Appeasing this one wasn't appealing to either of them. No matter how he was viewed by the Mottola clan, to Dominic and Santo he was no more than a bug beneath their shoe.

"Welcome to Villa Mare Blu. We have food and wine for you. You are in good hands."

"I thought I might see Giovanni, speak to him alone," Santo interjected.

Dominic shook his head no. "For now can you just see to our guest?"

"Follow me," Santo said to Giuliani.

* B *

"Bella?"

"Mmm?" Mira said as she wiped Eve's mouth. Her daughter tried to push her mother's hands from her face. Eve reached again for the pastry on her father's plate and brought the sticky dough to her mouth. Eve had been eating and drinking since she sat at the table. A healthy habit taught to her by Zia. Which meant plenty of poopy pampers or accidents today if Mira wasn't careful of her potty schedule.

"I like your idea. Take a walk today, a short one to the beach with Eve. Leo will accompany you."

Mira sat back. "It would be good for me huh? I think so too." She looked down the table at Marietta. "I'd really like to try to get to know Marietta better. I'm so embarrassed over Catalina's outburst. It was awful."

"She's not interested, Bella. Why force it? Just you and Eve

210

should go. Tonight if I finish early I might take you into the village for dinner. There are more things we need to discuss."

"We're having a celebration dinner tonight? Remember?" Mira reminded him.

Giovanni sighed. "Right. I forgot."

Eve blinked at her mother. She chewed and rested against her father's chest. Giovanni and several others looked up when Dominic walked into the room. He stood with his hands clasped in front of him. Giovanni pushed back from his chair. He lifted Eve in his arms and kissed her. He then handed a disappointed Eve to Mira and put her on Mira's knee

"No, Papa!" Eve shouted. The tears were immediate.

Marietta looked down at the screaming kid.

"Cara?" Lorenzo whispered in her ear. "Make a friend. Go talk with the *Donna*."

"What? No. Where are you going?"

He kissed her lips. "Business. I've been gone for months. I will be gone most of the day."

"What about the grotto? I thought we would spend time together?" Marietta asked.

"We will. Please. For me. Be nice to the *Donna*. She really is a sweet lady. Make me proud."

"Shit," Marietta said under her breath. Lorenzo and Carlo both rose from their seats. The men walked out without explanation. The other men at the table, hired to protect the family, stood and took their drinks or whatever was left unfinished on their plates and walked off too. It left only Mira, Marietta, and Rosetta.

Mira cleared her throat. "While the boys go play why don't we go for that walk?"

"I'm not feeling well," Rosetta said.

"What? Are you okay?" Mira asked.

Rosetta pushed back from her seat. "Headache, I will take something and lie down." Before Mira could object the young girl walked out. Mira watched Rosetta go. Eve stopped crying and hugged her mother's belly. Mira stroked her daughter's back, and Cecilia finally arrived. She had returned from her trip to visit her family in time to be a godsend. Eve was harder to manage for Mira now.

"Marietta. I hate to keep harping but the beach is nice and well, I need the exercise. Will you join me?" Mira asked.

Marietta gave a thin lip smile. "Sure. I'd like too."

Mira exhaled in relief. The woman was a hard one to impress upon. "Awesome." She set Eve down. Mira pushed up from the seat and Cecilia was at her side. "I will go change her and meet you down at the beach."

"Yes, and get her little play bucket. We can let her have some fun in the sand."

"*Sí, Donna,*" Cecilia said.

Leo walked in. He was often her shadow. She preferred him to carrying her gun. She still couldn't bring herself to warm up to the weapon even after learning how to use it. Mira started out of the terrace down the steps. Marietta was right behind her. With Mira's slow walk her guest caught up quickly.

"So where are you from?" Mira asked.

"Chicago."

"I love Chicago," Mira said. "Very yummy city. Some of the best food on the planet."

"I agree. Where are you from?" Marietta asked.

"Virginia. Left home when I was a seventeen. Enrolled in Parsons in New York and that became my home, until I arrived in Naples," Mira said.

"The press has some wild stories about your life, girlfriend," Marietta shook her head. "I read you were kidnapped. That your husband murdered your friend Fabiana and you killed an assistant of yours to run away from him. Then he forced you to marry him and—"

"None of that is true," Mira said softly. She stared down at her belly as they walked. She smoothed her hands down the swell. "My story with Giovanni is complicated. I admit that. But I never killed anyone and my husband did not kidnap me."

"But he is a killer? Right?" Marietta asked.

Mira glanced over her. "As much as your husband is," she answered.

Marietta laughed. "Good one. You got me there."

Mira smiled. "Is there a reason why you don't like me?" she asked.

Marietta stopped. Mira turned and looked at her. The wind blew her hair and dress forward.

"Why do you say I don't like you?" Marietta asked.

"Because I got that impression the day I met you. And today, I can tell. I'm curious. What makes you dislike me?" Mira asked.

Marietta shrugged. "Nothing personal. Girls like you and I never got along."

"Like me?" Mira asked.

"Uppity, snooty, pampered, like you," Marietta gestured toward her.

"I'm none of those things." Mira started walking away again. Marietta joined her. "I grew up on a farm, an apple farm. We were so poor every day there was something on the table made out of apples. Even our chickens tasted like apples."

Marietta laughed. "Damn that is poor. I hate the country," she shivered. "I'm a city girl all the way."

Mira shrugged. "I like the city too. My grandparents were both dead by my senior year. I had nothing, no family. A guy I dated was pretty abusive in high school so I had to get away."

"Physical abuse?" Marietta paused.

Mira glanced up at her, she then averted her gaze. "I don't talk or think about him. There are many ways to be abused. Trust me."

"Wow. You don't strike me as the kind who would take any shit from anybody like that," Marietta said.

"I have my weaknesses, trust me." Mira forced a smile. "But I'm strong too. I remember the day I sat in the library and filled out an application to Parsons. I was shocked when I got a scholarship. The rest is history."

"Well, I was a whore and a stripper in Chicago," Marietta said.

It was Mira's turn to pause. She looked over at Marietta and frowned. "You were?"

Marietta laughed. "According to my adoptive-mother a stripper had to be a whore. It is written in the Bible somewhere I think."

Mira smiled. "Interesting career choice. You don't strike me as a stripper."

"I love to dance. Really dance." Marietta nodded. "But I never had sex for money or nothing crazy. I just like to be free, and dancing does that for me."

They arrived at the beach. There were three steps to take down to the sand. Leo hurried closer to help. "Here, let me help you." Marietta volunteered and Leo stepped back.

"Thank you," Mira smiled. "Boy it's a nice day today."

"It is," Marietta agreed. "I can't wait to see more of Sicily."

"Is it your first time here?" Mira asked. She had to grab on to Marietta's arm to steady herself as she walked out across the lumpy sand.

"Yeah it is. But I think I'm going to like my new life in Europe." Marietta smiled. "Here take my hand, I can help you."

Mira smiled. "Thank you."

Mira noticed how pretty she was when she smiled. She wanted to know more about Marietta.

Giovanni watched the sister's step out on the sand from the balcony. Lorenzo walked up behind him. He stepped to his side and observed. "Strange seeing them hand in hand. Strange and beautiful," Lorenzo said.

"I could kill you for bringing that woman here," Giovanni replied.

"Look at them, Gio, twins. What if something happened to you and Mira? Would you want your sons separated the way they were?"

He did look at them, and they were beautiful. He refused to see it in Marietta. Hated her on sight for having a bond to his Bella. But Mira had lost so much when Fabiana died. What kind of cruel bastard was he to deny her this?

"When will you tell Mira the truth?" Lorenzo asked. "I only ask because I will have to then tell Marietta."

"Soon. Let them spend time together, bond. Then we will sit them down and explain. My way."

"Of course, Gio. I won't interfere any further. We go at your pace," Lorenzo nodded. "I hear Giuliani and Santo have arrived. Trouble with Mottolas?"

"Yes," Giovanni said in a terse voice.

"Then it's good I came home." Lorenzo dropped his hand on Giovanni's shoulder. "No one believes in protecting this family as strongly as I do. You need me, cousin, let me help."

Giovanni cast a sideways look to Lorenzo. He had missed him, and like men the grudges between them were easily settled with an apology. He embraced Lorenzo, who hugged him back. "You will help me reunite the women. We do it together and Mirabella never knows that I came between them. Agreed?" Giovanni asked.

"Yes, cousin. Agreed." Lorenzo patted his back with a sly smile.

Giovanni let him go. Lorenzo threw his arm around his shoulder and they walked back to join the other men. "Now let's talk business."

"Does that beach house belong to the Battaglias?" Marietta pointed to Serenity.

"It sure does." Mira smiled. "The only villa directly on the shore. Guess that's why it's raised for the tide. We call it Serenity."

Mira glanced back. Cecilia carried Eve on her hip and a beach blanket, toy bucket and shovel in her arms. Eve waved at her mother. She wore a yellow swimsuit. Mira blew her daughter a kiss.

"Do you want kids?" Mira asked Marietta.

"Can't stand the little fuckers." Marietta answered. She glanced back at Eve and realized her comment was crass. "Sorry. No offense."

"None taken. I never wanted kids either. Then woke one day and found out I was pregnant. Now I can't stop making babies." Mira laughed. Marietta smiled.

"Mommy!" Eve hurried toward her in the sand. She fell to her hands and knees. Mira walked over to her and helped her stand while Cecilia and Leo spread out the blanket over the sand.

"Once they are your babies, your attitude toward them will change," Mira said. Marietta observed as Mira guided Eve to the edge of the blanket. The toddler dropped on her chubby knees and started immediately to shovel sand into the bucket. It took Leo and Cecilia both to lower Mira to the blanket. Marietta looked up at the sun boiling hotly in the sky above. If it weren't for the breeze they'd bake. Still she burned easily and she considered the fact that she needed to return to get some sun block for her skin.

"C'mon, join us." Mira waved her over.

Marietta glanced toward the villa. From the beach she could see the upper levels. Lorenzo was nowhere in sight. Maybe she was wrong about the black Barbie. She did seem nice. However, a sit and talk session on the beach with her and her kid would bore her silly. But she made a promise to Lorenzo. It was possible the sacrifice would prove to him that she could be a supportive wife. Marietta walked over and found a spot to plop down. Though they were on the blanket she felt sticky grains of sand over her arms and legs. She pulled her maxi dress up to wipe off.

"Tell me about you? Any brothers or sisters?" Mira asked.

"None. I was adopted," Marietta said.

"Oh. That's nice," Mira replied.

"Actually it wasn't. And not to be rude I don't want to discuss my personal life."

Mira nodded. "Making conversation. I understand."

"I do have a question," Marietta had only one. And when that snotty bitch Catalina threw her jab earlier it made the question burn like a hot coal in her gut.

"Go ahead. Ask?" Mira said. She managed to help Eve turn over the sand in the pail. Without water the sand did little to stick. Cecilia came over and took Eve by the hand and grabbed the bucket.

She walked the baby to the sea.

"Fabiana was your business partner?" Marietta asked.

"Yes. She was like a sister to me. I loved her very much." Mira answered.

"Lorenzo mentioned her. He said she died. He blames himself."

Mira didn't immediately answer. She covered her brow with her hand and watched her daughter. Marietta believed it to be a stall tactic. After all she was chatty Kathy just a minute earlier. Marietta tried a different approach. "How close were she and Lorenzo to marrying?"

Mira lowered her hands to her belly. She turned her gaze to Marietta. "Fabiana loved Lorenzo. But my friend had a habit of always loving complicated men. Guess she and I are the same on that score. Personally I never thought he loved her as deeply."

Though it was insensitive of her Marietta smiled. She didn't like the idea of her husband carrying a torch for some dead woman.

"You're smiling?" Mira said. And for the first time Marietta saw Queen B flash anger toward her.

"Oh I'm sorry. I wasn't smiling because your friend's dead it's just—"

"Let me be clear on something, Marietta. I never thought Lorenzo loved anyone more than he loves himself. He's the most selfish man of them all. And he is the reason my friend is dead. He's no catch, honey!"

"The explosion was an accident," Marietta tossed back.

"It was a hit. A contract hit on his life. There are no accidents in this life," Mira said.

"You blame Lorenzo? How does that make sense when he serves your husband? Like he's some king or something."

"It makes sense because Lorenzo plays games, he lies, he—" Mira stopped herself. "Fabiana's death was the most devastating event in my life, and trust me I've had a few. I saw my best friend die. She was blown to pieces in front of my face," Mira's voice faltered with emotion. "I can't get the image out of my mind. I've never seen a person die before. And I never want to again."

"Hey? You okay?" Marietta asked.

"I have a pain… a cramp." Mira grabbed her side.

Marietta got to her knees. She touched Mira's arm. The man who watched them was at their side in an instant. "Maybe we should get you back to the house."

"Help me stand," Mira wheezed.

Marietta stood. She and Leo helped. As soon as Mira was on her feet a blood spot could be seen to the back of her all white summer dress. "You're bleeding. Oh my God!" Marietta gasped.

Mira nodded. "Don't panic. It's okay. Get Cecilia and Eve. I'll be fine."

"Fine? You're bleeding. We need to—" Marietta stopped as Leo half walked, half carried Mira back across the sand. She wasn't sure but the woman looked to be in the last stage of her pregnancy. Blood could not be good. She turned and saw Cecilia running up the sand. "We need to get back to the house. Something is wrong with Mira—er the *Donna*."

"Sí, andiamo!" Cecilia said. Marietta snatched up the blanket and Cecilia hurried up the sand with Eve in her arms. Marietta was close behind.

10.

Giovanni wiped his hand down his face and exhaled to quell some of his anger. He was tired of the discussion. He let his gaze sweep the faces of the men gathered. His inner circle stared back. "If we cut off the head of the snake it still lives. We will need another to reign in and organize what is left of the Mottola clan."

"And you think Giuliani Mottola is the man for this job?" Dominic asked.

"If I put him in power he's mine." Giovanni drummed his fingers on the desk surface. "But is he strong enough to control the Mottolas? That is the real question."

"What about Santo?" Lorenzo interjected.

"At the very least Santo shouldn't be over the triangle any longer," Carlo added.

Giovanni looked over to Dominic who shook his head no. He returned his gaze to Lorenzo and then Carlo before he answered. "Santo is another matter. I need to see him. Then I will decide on the triangle."

"They wait for you. I made sure Giuliani was well received." Dominic said.

"Boss?" Renaldo charged inside. "It's the *Donna*, she's not well."

Giovanni was up and around his desk in seconds. He and the others walked down the hall to the stairs and up. He met Catalina on the step.

"How is she?" he asked.

"She's had some bleeding. I've already called the doctor that she told me. He said he'd be here within the hour. I think we should take her to the *ospedale*, Giovanni. Blood? What the hell is going on?"

"Is she cramping?" he asked as he rushed with hurried steps to her room.

"I don't think so, not anymore." Catalina glanced back at Dominic and then looked at her brother. "Why aren't you listening to me? We need to get her to the *ospedale*."

Giovanni rushed inside the room. At her bedside was Marietta. He paused a second at the sight of the woman comforting his wife. Marietta stepped aside and he went to Mira who was upright and resting against a stack of pillows.

"I'm fine. The doctor will be here and he can decide if I go in. The cramps stopped," she said with tears in her eyes. "This is normal right? I mean it's part of it right? Nothing is wrong right?"

Giovanni wasn't sure. Was this like before or something worse? Did he rush to the hospital or wait and ride it out? How was he to know for certain?

"We need to get her help. A doctor's home visit isn't right," Catalina said, and he could hear the fear in his sister's voice.

"Everyone leave. Bring the doctor when he arrives. Get out." Giovanni told them. Lorenzo led Marietta out the door. Dominic touched Catalina who snatched her hand away and marched out. He closed the door behind them.

Giovanni put his hand to his wife's belly. He bowed his head. "Let's take you to the hospital. We can't take any chances. It'll take us thirty minutes to get to Palermo. What if… we need to take you there now."

"Giovanni, look at me." She lifted his chin. "I'm fine. You told me today what this meant. The bleeding has stopped. The cramping has stopped. I'm fine."

He stood. He stood and paced. He checked his watch over and over until finally he relaxed as Mira did. He sat back on the edge of the bed and held her hand. "No cramps? No blood?"

"None." She smiled. "I'm fine."

She pulled his shirt and drew him over to kiss him. There came a knock at the door and she let him go. The doctor was escorted in. The wait had been too long. Giovanni shook his hand and silently vowed the next incident they'd take her in if he had to drive her to Palermo himself.

"How are you *Signora* Mirabella?" he put his bag down and approached the bed.

"Better. The cramping and bleeding has stopped," she said. The doctor removed his equipment to check her pressure. Giovanni was the only other person in the room. He asked Mira a few questions and did a very quick exam and feel of her. "I suggest we take you in to have another ultrasound, we should run some additional tests.

Your pressure is elevated."

"I feel fine!" Mira said.

"Is something wrong doctor?" Giovanni asked.

"Not from what I can tell. There's a hospital in Mondello. I've already called ahead. We can get her there and do a thorough exam. I'm sure she's okay. But with her condition," he lowered his voice.

"Speak up," Mira said. "Giovanni told me about my condition. I want to hear it."

"Of course. Well you are carrying twins. The pressure on your cervix presents a problem. Were you doing anything strenuous when the cramps began."

"No. Just walking on the beach."

"Let's take you in be safe." The doctor said.

"Okay. I agree." Mira wiped at her tears. "Giovanni, can you help me change? Get ready?"

"We'll meet you there, Doctor."

The doctor walked out. Giovanni went to Mira's side and helped her stand. She seemed to weaken and sadden over the news. "I guess I thought if I denied it the babies would be okay. They aren't ready to be born, Giovanni. It's too soon."

"They're okay, Bella," Giovanni reassured her.

"I should have stayed in bed. I don't want to do anything to make this worse for our children."

"Hey, look at me. The babies are fine. And so are you. Let's get you changed into something and then go to the *ospedale*. Okay?"

"Okay."

* B *

"Stop pacing." Rosetta said.

"Shut up!" Catalina hissed.

Marietta observed them both. She said nothing. Though she barely knew Mira the thought of her miscarrying brought her inexplicable anxiety. No woman should have to suffer that amount of pain. The door opened. A man entered and Catalina rushed into his arms. Marietta watched.

"How is she, Domi? Is she okay?"

"They will take her to the *ospedale*. Gio is going with her. She's okay. It's just to make sure nothing is wrong with the babies." Dominic turned his gaze to Marietta. "Thank you for helping her on the beach."

"She didn't do anything." Catalina walked away. Marietta smiled at the diss. She nodded to Dominic that he was welcome.

"As soon as Gio knows more he will call us and let us know," Dominic announced.

Marietta stood. "Where's Lo? Is he going to the hospital too?"

"No. He and Carlo had a meeting. He told me to tell you he will join you for dinner." Dominic cast his gaze to Catalina once more. They exchanged a look and then he left. As soon as he was gone Catalina began her worry routine again.

"Would you stop pacing?" Rosetta said. "You're making my headache worse."

"Shut your fucking mouth," Catalina hissed.

Marietta decided she'd had enough of the drama and started for the door.

"Where do you think you're going?" Catalina asked.

Marietta paused. She looked around the room to be sure she heard her right. "Are you speaking to me?"

"I saw how you treated my sister in-law at brunch. What happened on the beach? She was fine a few hours ago."

Marietta stepped to Catalina. "You accusing me of something?"

"Should I be?" Catalina dropped her hands to her hips.

Marietta looked her over. "Bitch please. I suggest you be careful of your step around me. I'm not a fan, a friend, or a person on your staff. Bite and I bite back."

Catalina frowned. "What the hell does that mean? Is that supposed to make sense to me?"

"I wouldn't suggest you push me is what it means. I'm not your enemy, Catalina. I did nothing to your precious *Donna*. But if you get in my face it'll cost you your ass."

Catalina laughed. "*Beh!* I can give a damn about your tough girl act. This is my family. You're a stranger. Be careful where you step, Marietta." She took a step toward her. "Because if you get in my way or do anything to hurt Mirabella it's you and me." Catalina looked her over and then marched out of the room.

"She's a royal bitch," Rosetta said.

Marietta cast her gaze over to the other one. "And you're not?"

Rosetta's smile faded.

Marietta shook her head. "You're all crazy."

* B *

Mira had to show a brave face. The more her husband became agitated the more he paced the floor and barked at whoever entered. Two tests had turned into six different tests the doctors needed to run. And now two different doctors were consulting on her case. The small *ospedale* had a polite staff who showed respect toward Giovanni. But even she had to wonder if they needed to leave this one and head to the bigger *ospedale* in Palermo.

"Are you okay, Bella?" Giovanni's head turned when she let out an exhausted sigh.

"I'm okay. What do you think is taking so long?"

Giovanni wiped his hand down his face. "I'm not sure, possibly the lab work. That would take a while in this place, don't you think?" he looked around at the minimum equipment and rudimentary tools.

"Can you stop pacing please? It makes me nervous," she smiled.

"Yes, of course, Bella. I wish, the doctor would tell us something." Giovanni stared at the door. "Maybe I should find him. Get some answers."

"No! C'mere, Giovanni." She extended her hand to him. "Come."

He walked over and she took his hand, kissing his ring. "You need to relax. I have no cramping, no bleeding. The worst is over for now. Let them do their job." She put his hand to her belly and he spread his fingers as he held the swell. She pushed at the side of her belly to cause the babies to wake. One gave a powerful kick to his daddy's hand. Giovanni laughed. "He's a strong boy."

"A soccer player," Mira chuckled.

Giovanni leaned in and kissed her belly. The door opened and the doctors entered. Dr. Buhari was the first to speak. "How do we feel *Signora* Battaglia?"

"Better. I haven't felt a single cramp since we arrived."

"Good. Very good." Buhari looked to Giovanni.

"Go ahead, Doctor. My wife can hear her diagnosis," Giovanni said.

"This is Doctor Pallario. He has joined me to make sure I've missed nothing. We are still dealing with a partial Placenta Previa. Which is good. If we had complete Placenta Previa we would need to take the babies." Mira squeezed Giovanni's hand and listened intently. "However, because of the size of your uterus and the bleeding, we suggest full bed rest for the remainder of your pregnancy."

"Really?" Mira asked alarmed.

"And…" The other doctor spoke again. "An ultrasound must be done weekly. Must."

Mira nodded.

"What are the risks?" Giovanni asked. "What does this mean, will she have the babies naturally or will you have to operate when it is time?"

"I have to be honest with you both, her pressure is increasingly high. If the bleeding becomes worse and the placenta shifts lower we risk her hemorrhaging. Worst case scenario is death, best case scenario would be a full hysterectomy to stop the bleeding. Keeping her calm and in bed is important. It is the most important thing for the health of the babies as well."

"Oh my God." Mira said. "You're telling me that besides losing my children, my life, if I survive this I might not be able to have anymore children?"

"It's a risk we intend to avoid. We have the best specialists in Palermo. You will be in capable hands."

She glanced over to Giovanni and he paled. Sick. He squeezed her hand and tried to reassure her with a smile. Mira nodded to her husband that she was okay.

"The good news is the twins have strong heartbeats, they are growing adequately. You should be able to carry them for a few more weeks if we are careful."

"I want Zia. Can you send for her, Giovanni? I want her to come as soon as she can." Mira said through her tears.

He kissed her. "Of course. I'll send for her immediately." He walked over and shook the doctors' hands. "Grazie to you both. I will bring her to the appointments myself. Personally."

Mira began to cry after the doctor's left. Giovanni returned to her side and held her. "No worries, Bella. We will get through this. We will do as the doctors ask."

"I'm so scared."

"Shhh, with me you should never be. I will protect you and our children. Always."

"Yes, Giovanni. But some things even you can't prevent."

* B *

Giuliani smoked a cigar. Santo sat in a chair across from him, watching him as if bored. The Mottola rat glanced up in surprise when Lorenzo walked in. "Where is Gio? I demand to see him now! I came here as a courtesy and you've kept me here for four hours!" He pushed up in his chair. "What the hell is going on?" Giuliani demanded.

Behind Lorenzo entered Carlo, Dominic, and Nico. Santo slowly stood. He parted his suit jacket and eased his hands into his pockets.

"Is Giovanni ready for him now," Santo asked. Shock registered on his face at the sight of Lorenzo.

"Gio has been called away. I'm here." Lorenzo smiled. Santo looked him over. Giuliani's gaze volleyed between the men. "I have a few questions for you, Giuliani."

"I've told Dominic all I know." Giuliani answered.

"I'm not Domi or Gio. Ask Santo," Lorenzo said. "Domi's a man of reason. I'm a man of instinct. And what I think is that you told Domi all that you wanted him to know. All that a rat like you could say to protect and serve your own personal interests. Now sit your ass down you Mottola runt. We shall go over the details of Chiaiano, my way."

The man did as he was told. Lorenzo chose a chair. None of the other men did. Santo looked on. Lorenzo hoped he'd say or do something for him to take his balls as well. But he held his tongue. So he focused on Giuliani.

"Why Chiaiano?" Lorenzo began.

Giuliani looked around. "I don't understand?"

"We are dividing a lot of Battaglia territory for the clans in the *Campania*. Mottola is the strongest clan next to ours in the *Camorra*. He can have top pick. Instead he goes for the region clearly under-developed. Why?" Lorenzo asked.

"He is a madman. There has not been a *capo di tutti capi* in the *Camorra* in over sixty years. Giovanni has too much power and it worries the other clan bosses. When Giovanni took down the Calderone family and moved into the triangle it made my cousin nervous. They don't believe he is cleansing his business."

"What do they believe about Gio?" Lorenzo asked. "Look at me when you speak, Giuliani. Santo won't help you."

The man sweated profusely. He wiped his hand down his face and wiped the wet stain onto his pants. "Ah, er... I... they think he is undeserving of the title. That he wishes to change the *Camorra* to the traditions of the *Mafioso*, like the Sicilians. They believe he is partnering with the 'Ndrangheta to seize more control over the clans. It's what Mottola is telling the other bosses."

Lorenzo cut Santo a look. "And you have heard none of this?"

Santo stared at Lorenzo with a stoic face. Lorenzo's gaze then shifted over to Dominic. "We need to pay a visit to Mottola. A sit down. A personal one."

Dominic nodded. "Giovanni said you can decide on this one. Take Carlo and Nico."

"Wait!" Giuliani spoke up. "He's not there. He has travelled to a place just outside of Turkey to meet with the Armenians. He won't return for another week or so. That is why I was able to come here for this visit."

Lorenzo sat back and considered the news. He then leaned forward when he spoke to Giuliani, keeping him locked in his sight. "This business with the Armenians, are we talking an alliance with Yeremian?"

Giuliani's voice was shaky, his gaze shifted from one man to the next when he spoke. "I don't know who he meets with."

"This means Mottola doesn't want just Giovanni's territories he wants his friends as well." Lorenzo glanced to Dominic. "This is good news if we act now. We can pay a visit to Yeremian and see if he is aware that his interests are now being divided within the *Campania*."

Santo cleared his throat. "I want to be heard in front of Giovanni before we act on any information."

Lorenzo laughed. "I'm home, Santo. You will be heard in front of me and Gio," he smiled. Santo did not. He returned his gaze to Giuliani. "Giovanni will meet with you tonight." He turned and left.

* B *

Marietta returned to her room hopeful. But when she found it empty her heart dropped. It had been over five hours. Dinner would be served soon. Lorenzo had better be back by then. She was sick of wandering these halls in search of him. The sideways glances of the women, the snarky attitude of one in particular was wearing her down. And she was growing a bit anxious over the news of Mirabella. Since the incident on the beach she's felt a reoccurring soreness in her pelvis, possibly sympathy pains.

If Marietta were honest with herself she'd have to admit she liked Mirabella. Especially when Mira showed her bitchy side in defense of her dead friend Fabiana. There was a quiet strength to Mirabella that Marietta would have never guessed from her surface beauty and poise. This she could respect.

Around the room were castaway clothes. Marietta had asked that no one clean their room. She didn't want strangers going through her things. And she didn't quite trust the Battaglias not to snoop. Besides she was Lorenzo's wife and this was their domain. She would keep it tidy.

The Battaglias didn't trust her. Lorenzo warned her they might not. In his life it was wise to be leery of strangers. The family and staff seemed to watch her as if she was some thieving whore Lorenzo brought home off the streets. Marietta walked around the room picking up his clothes. Her hubby was the biggest slob. Marietta stooped and picked up his trouser pants. A gold chain dropped out of the pocket.

She stared at it for a moment. When she bent to retrieve the necklace she touched the charm and her hand froze. Marietta picked up her precious jewelry and inspected the necklace with such relief tears clouded her vision. But slowly her smile began to fade. Lorenzo told her he didn't know where it was. *Why was it in the pocket of his pants? Why lie about it?"*

She tossed the clothes to the bed. She checked to see if the clasp had broken once again. It was intact. What did that mean? Marietta clenched it in her fist and looked around his and her things. No matter how she tried to understand his deception it made no sense.

Lorenzo had plenty of explaining to do.

* B *

Catalina waited in the hall. When she saw Dominic approach she walked up to him. "I want to talk to you."

He glanced at her and then passed her without a word. She caught up with his steps. "Now, Domi. I'm serious. I want to talk to you now."

He walked into the room he occupied when staying at Villa Mare Blu. She followed him and closed the door.

"Are we over?" she asked.

"I said we were," he answered.

"And you mean it?" she asked.

"I meant it, Catalina. We're done."

"How could you say that to me? After everything we've been through. How?" she demanded.

Dominic sighed. "It's because of everything we've been

through. I need a break. You need a break. If we don't take one we will lose each other for good."

"We already have. You called off our engagement!" she shouted at him.

"I did not!" he said through clenched teeth. "You did when you went to Gio behind my back."

"I'm sorry, Domi. Forgive me. It was a mistake. I make them sometimes. Don't punish me like this. I can't take it," she choked down her emotion and tried hard not to cry. "I'm not going back to Milan. Not until Mira has the babies. That's two and half months away. We can work on us. Together."

Catalina couldn't breathe. Each time she tried her chest went tight and her lungs became restricted. She approached him. "Please, I'm begging you."

"Stop it, sweetheart," he forced her hands down from his face. "We're done."

"Please." She touched him again. He grabbed her by both her arms and yanked her forward. There was such raw hurt in his eyes she believed he suffered too. "Please," she brought her trembling lips close to his. They brushed over but he drew back from her kiss. "I love you, Domi, I'll do anything. I swear it." He loosened his hold on her. She broke free to wrap her arms around his neck and claim the kiss. She felt his resistance soften. Dominic forced her back up against the wall causing the picture to their left to fall off the hook and the glass to shatter when it hit the floor. Catalina gasped as he forced her up the wall, his hand stroking her between her thighs as he licked and sucked her neck.

She smiled through her tears. She laughed. "Yes, baby, yes, Domi! Yes!"

The door opened to his room and he released her before undoing the zipper to his pants. Dominic looked back and Catalina quickly fixed her dress and brought it down.

"Oh my God! I'm so sorry. Forgive me. The *Donna*'s here. Giovanni needs your help, Domi. I knocked."

"The hell you did!" Catalina hissed at Rosetta.

Dominic walked out of the door. Catalina's heart raced. She still had tears on her face. And Rosetta's smug smile made her boil with fury. "What the hell do you think you're doing? I know you did this on purpose."

"Oh please. Everyone knows that you and Domi are not to fool around in Giovanni's house. How was I to guess you were in here begging for sex?"

"That's a lie!" Catalina shouted at her. She charged at Rosetta to strike her.

"It's the truth." Rosetta stepped back. "And here's something else, Catalina. Dominic deserves better. You're going to lose him. Not because of me, but because of you." Rosetta smiled and walked out. Catalina double blinked. She sat down because her legs felt weak. What happened between her and Dominic wasn't the forgiveness she sought. It was lust. Feeling desperate and lost she closed her eyes. Maybe he was right. Maybe she did need time to live outside of his protective shadow. But how could she when loving him was all she's ever desired until now? Could she ever let Domi go?

* B *

"Too much fuss over me. I'm fine!" Mira said at the bottom of the stairs. The family had her boxed in. Before she could ask Giovanni to confirm it, he swept her up in his arms. "No. Giovanni, put me down! I'm too heavy. Don't!"

Her protest didn't matter. Giovanni carried her effortlessly up the stairs and a troop of his men followed him close in case he wavered. Mira smiled at the determination on his face that made his jaw thrust forward and his lips tightly pressed. She knew she weighed a ton but he'd never let any of them see his struggle. And he did as he intended, he carried her directly to bed. So many people gathered in their bedroom she felt claustrophobic.

"Are you okay, *Donna?*" Nico asked.

"Do you need anything?" Renaldo asked.

"Should we move her downstairs to make things better?" Dominic asked Giovanni.

"What did the doctor say?" Leo asked.

Question after question was tossed her way. She exchanged a look with Giovanni and he nodded that he would handle it. "That's enough!" he shouted. The room silenced. "She's fine. I will tell the family what is going on in a minute. Right now everyone out! Out!"

Those gathered started to walk out. Giovanni stopped Dominic last. "Lorenzo and the others?"

"We have more information. Lorenzo was pretty good at getting it for you." Dominic said.

"Really? Give me an hour and bring Santo in. I want to speak with him personally."

Dominic nodded. He walked out.

"Where is Eve? Is she with Cecilia?" Mira asked, she scooted back into her pillows.

"I believe so. I'll bring her to you in a moment. First we need to talk about what the doctor said. What it means." He sat on the edge of the bed. "I should have taken you to Rome. The best *ospedales* are in Rome. I should have never insisted that we come here."

"I think our doctors have it under control," she reasoned.

"What if I move you to Palermo? Bring Zia here and get us a place close to the *ospedale*. The closer we get to the due date. What about that?"

"I like that idea," Mira said. She tried to keep the fear from her voice.

"Hey, come here, baby," she said.

Giovanni went to her and she put his face to her breasts. He was careful not to put any pressure on the babies. She felt calmer when she relaxed him. And she knew he was afraid. The entire family was afraid. "I intend to stay in bed. No designing, no nothing. Can you bring the television in here?"

"I can do that, Bella."

"Good. And I can rest. If you promise me a foot and back rub every night I'll be extra relaxed. Think you can do that for me?" she chuckled.

He lifted his head and his eyes glistened with tears. "I promise."

"We will be just fine, sweetheart. I promise you," she reassured him.

"I love you," he said.

"I love you too. With all my heart." She smiled.

* B *

"Well? What is it?" Mancini asked.

"She had an attack of some kind. Dr. Buhari has put her on bed rest." Armando informed him. He stood and walked around his desk "The doctor says if it gets worse she could hemorrhage and die."

"Her mother had the same problem," Mancini said. "By the time I found her she was near dead. The doctors had to deliver the twins early."

Mancini remembered the blood, and how badly Melissa suffered through the birth of their daughters. He feared her death more than the loss of life to his little girls. Ironic that she was the one lost to him eventually.

"Interesting that they share the same issue," Armando said.

"Lisa was out of it for days. The doctors weren't sure she'd recover. I wasn't sure. When she did come through it I trusted the wrong people to care for her. I shouldn't have abandoned her."

"So she died after giving birth?" Armando asked.

"No. She died two years later," Mancini said.

"You left her? You returned to Madre and left America. For good?" Armando said instead of asked.

Mancini nodded his head slowly. "I left her."

"Then why was she killed by Tomosino? You were gone…"

"That I don't know. All I know is Isabella's version of things. She said Flavio told her of the contract and that Capriccio carried it out. I had thought my leaving gave her a chance at a life without the burdens I gave her. I provided for her. I thought I had. It confuses me still, what became of her." Mancini released a burdened sigh. "She was murdered. End of story." He looked up into his son's eyes. "Mirabella has to know the truth. She doesn't know how much danger she is in with this pregnancy."

"The doctors know, Papa. You have given them all the information," Armando said.

Mancini clenched his fist. "Giovanni is a selfish bastard. He should have taken her to Rome. Not brought her here. I had to tell Ricci to recommend Buhari in the first place!"

"Yes but when I spoke to Buhari he said that Giovanni and Mira were both made aware of the dangers. The babies could come early, and possibly will. They are going to do weekly doctor visits. I'm told that Giovanni is inquiring about renting a place in Palermo. To be closer to the *ospedale*."

Mancini looked up.

Armando smiled. "If we take them out of Mondello Giovanni has less control. And I have good news. Francesco Mottola is looking to expand his operations within the *Camorra*. He's moving in on Giovanni's territory. I'm sure Gio will strike predictably soon, which will further distract him and Lorenzo. I should be able to get to the women—"

"Yes. But Isabella is out there," Mancini said. "And she has been plotting against me for years. I don't want to risk the chaos with Mirabella in so much physical danger. No. No. We are to be cautious until after the babies are born. I will be there for the delivery of my grandchildren," Mancini smiled.

"And then afterwards I can deal with Giovanni. We can blame it on the Mottola clan. Make the *Camorra* turn in on itself. Our hands will be clean," Armando said.

Mancini waved off the comment. "This childhood feud between you and Giovanni keeps you distracted. The greater goal is yours sisters. Giovanni is necessary as an ally."

"How?" Armando snapped.

"The truce keeps the Mafia and the *Camorra* separate. The truce keeps business clean on both sides. Who in the *Camorra* do you trust to adhere to our blood oaths? Open your eyes boy and see the big picture!" Mancini said. He shook his head. "This is why you aren't ready. Why I fear dying. You have to think ahead, strategy is what you lack! That and proper motivation." Mancini coughed.

Armando held his tongue.

Mancini reclined with a sardonic smile tipping the corner of his mouth. "It's time you know another truth. My intention to motivate you properly."

"How do you intend to do that?" Armando asked.

"The will has been changed," Mancini said.

Armando sat forward. He narrowed his eyes on his father. Mancini coughed, hacked up phlegm and spat it in a napkin before he spoke again. "If something happens to your sisters or their children. If they walk away from the family and disavow their tie to Mancini then you too will lose it all. Everything is bequeathed to Georgio."

"Georgio! That runt can't wipe his own ass without written instructions. Are you fucking kidding me?" Armando shot to his feet. Mancini agreed with his son. Georgio was only made in the Mafia because of blood. His sister's son was a buffoon, dimwitted, and spoiled. He would shit away their fortune in a year. But he needed to motivate his son and this proved to be his only option. "It's done," Mancini said. "I will unite you three. Do what I was a coward to do so many years ago. They are your sisters, and you will protect them if you want to protect the family legacy. If Mirabella loses the babies or stumps her toe it comes out of your hide. Do you understand?"

"This is fucking bullshit! Why would you think I'd do this! Are you insane?"

"I know you, son. You're full of ego and the prejudices I've beat into you since you were a child. I know you as I know myself. This is the only way I can ensure you try to know your sisters and that this family becomes stronger with the three of you." Mancini began to hack and cough. "Don't bother with contesting the will. Don't make claims that I was of feeble mind. I set this in motion three years ago when I brought her to Italy."

Armando fell silent. He stared at his father in disbelief.

Mancini coughed again. "If you kill Giovanni, you will have to kill Lorenzo. And my girls will be widows. Your sisters will blame you. And if they turn from you, you lose everything. Bring them in and make them family. Teach them our ways. Be a better man than me."

"I will not. Never! They will never be part of this family!" Armando said.

"Then there will be no family." Mancini started for the door. He paused. He had never been a good role model, but he did love his son. He glanced back toward him. The ugly discoloration of his attack on him the night prior was on his face. Mancini hadn't even realized he attacked his child until he returned to his senses and found himself standing over Armando holding the gun. His mind was going, along with his health. What he did now was desperate, and he knew this. But what choice did he have?

"Forgive me," Mancini said.

Armando said nothing.

Mancini shook his head and walked out.

* B *

The door opened. Marietta lifted her head from the pillow and looked out past the gauzy sheer veil of the curtain that surrounded her bed. She had fallen asleep in her maxi dress and sandy feet. Tears had streaked her mascara. Her hair had frizzed to the point of a lion's mane.

"Lo?" she asked. She squinted at the shadowy figure approaching.

"Why are you in here? Everyone is downstairs for dinner." He drew the curtain to their bed open. He stared down at her with the concern. "What's the matt—" His voice faltered when he saw what she held out in her hand. He looked at the necklace and then at her with guilt-ridden eyes.

"You told me that you couldn't find it. You held me all night while I cried over losing my necklace. Do you know where I found it? I found it in your pants pocket. Why did you lie to me?" Marietta asked.

He blinked at her.

The silence between them lengthened. Marietta's heart raced with panic. Had he intentionally deceived her? *Why would he?* The bruising to his face didn't look as severe as it did that morning, but it made his features hard and un-shifting. "Answer me, Lorenzo. Why would you want to deceive me about something so important?"

"I-I-I didn't," he stammered.

"Liar! You told me you didn't find it!" Marietta shouted back.

"Wait, sweetheart." Lorenzo put his hands up. "I didn't find it when I told you that. I hadn't found it, is what I mean. But remember I left the room later that night. You see my face. You know I wasn't in bed with you all night."

Marietta frowned. "So you found it later and got beat up?"

He chuckled. "The other way around. I got into a disagreement last night with some of the boys. On my way back to the room I found it. I was going to surprise you, but this morning you surprised me. And today has been crazy—it slipped my mind. Of course I wouldn't hide your necklace. For what purpose? You ruined my surprise."

Marietta wiped at her tears. "Sorry. I'm sorry for accusing you. I don't know what came over me. I don't like being lied to. When I thought you lied I just... I'm sorry, Lo."

"No one likes a liar," Lorenzo said.

Marietta crawled across the bed to him. She got up on her knees and stretched her arms up around his neck. "Forgive me."

"Forgive? There's no need." He squeezed her ass. "It was a silly misunderstanding. But it taught me something," he said.

"It did? What?" she smiled.

"How important this necklace is to you." He took it from her hand.

She stared at it and was filled with relief. The thought of losing it had uncovered all her fears and feelings of abandonment. "It's funny."

"What is?" Lo asked, while he inspected the charm.

"The clasp." She pointed to it with the tip of her nail. "See there. It isn't broke so I don't know why it came off."

"That is odd." Lorenzo agreed. "Why don't we put it up somewhere safe? I know a jeweler. We can take it to him, and he can replace the clasp to make it secure. Okay?"

"Good idea," she nodded. "Thank you, baby." She kissed him trying to bring him down on the bed with her. "Mmm, I've missed you, baby, come to bed."

"I can't, sweetheart. We need to talk." He pulled her over to straddle his lap. Of course Marietta loved the position. She wrapped her legs around him.

Lorenzo chuckled. He took her chin. "I need to leave for a day or two. A few days and then I'll return. Promises."

"No! Hell no!" she tried to get up but he held her to him, bringing her arm behind her back and pinning it there so she wouldn't escape him.

"It can't be helped, sweetheart." Lorenzo looked her in the eye. His voice was firm and tight.

"The hell it can't. We just got married. I know you have a lot on your plate but leaving me? Here? I'm not staying here! Where you go I go. Period."

"Yes you are." He grabbed her chin a bit forcefully. Marietta glared at him. *How could he do this?* She felt such raw betrayal her voiced objections were choked down with emotion. He turned and maneuvered her to pin her down to the bed. He let her arm go only to bring both wrists up above her head.

"I'm sorry, *cara*. I have some serious business to attend to. I need your help."

She blinked away her tears. "How can I help if you're leaving me behind?"

"The *Donna* isn't well. I was thinking maybe you could look out for her?"

"She has her husband. She has a legion of people to look out for her. Why me?"

He smiled. "She can't handle stress. Make friends with her. Spend time with her. Keep her relaxed."

"I'm not a fucking babysitter. I don't even know her." Marietta pouted.

"No, Marie, you don't. But you're family now, we all are. I want you to start acting like it. Do you understand? I will be gone no more than forty-eight hours and then I'm yours. We'll see *Sicilia*. Do whatever you want. Visit the grottos I told you about."

"I can sunbathe like a mermaid?" she smiled.

He bit her chin.

She laughed and her tears sparkled like diamonds in her eyes. She smiled for him again. He kissed her soft. "I am sorry to disappoint my lady. I don't want to leave you."

"This is hard, Lo. Being around these people. But I can try. For you," she said.

"For us?" he said.

"For us," she repeated.

He wanted his honeymoon as well. If he hadn't strong concerns about the safety and security of the family he'd pass on this mission.

But with the Armenians involved it required his immediate attention. He reached and pulled down her panties with his free hand. He kept her arms pinned above her head with his other hand.

"What are you doing?" she asked.

"You know what I'm doing." He held her stare. Marietta closed her eyes and scooted up a bit so he could angle her sex for the right strike. Penetration was swift. His dick longed for this reunion all day. She gritted her teeth as her sex stretched and accommodated him. Then came that lovely rhythm that made his heart race. Lorenzo pulled down the front of her dress with his teeth and sucked her nipple into his mouth sucking her hard. He wrapped an arm around her left leg and forced it back with the hook of his arm. He opened her up to him and fucked her hard. He loved it. She buckled under him and enjoyed the ride.

* B *

Giovanni glanced up from his conversation with Dominic when Santo entered the room. He approached Giovanni and kissed his ring. "I've been wanting to meet with you all day. They told me about the *Donna*. How is she?"

"Better. Have a drink with me," Giovanni said.

Dominic left his chair and offered the seat to Santo. Giovanni watched Santo's every move. His appearance was sweaty, disheveled, not at all like the confidence Santo had shown in the past. In fact nothing he admired in Santo could be seen now in the wake of his failure.

"I spoke to Lorenzo. He gave me insight I wish you had."

"The Armenians." Santo wiped the sweat down his face with his hand. Dominic passed him a drink. Santo looked relieved to have it. "I admit to managing things with blinders on. I knew that there was some dissention between the clans. But I never thought anyone would dare stand against you. When I found out what Mottola was up to I had plans to bring him under control."

Giovanni picked up his cigar. He hadn't had one in two days. He fired it and took a drag allowing the tobacco to fill his lungs. "How?"

"He has a weakness, sons and a nephew that he thinks he's grooming for leadership. He even has two of them managing affairs in Chiaiano. I was going to send a message. One Mottola would understand."

Giovanni exhaled and stared at Santo. "Is that all? Wouldn't that bring me more grief from the other clan bosses? Killing innocent people is a stigma I've been unable to shake since Calderone."

"I wasn't going to kill them. I just—" Santo inhaled deeply and exhaled slow. "I needed his attention. It's an effective method."

"I guess I should get up from this chair. Let you have a seat." Giovanni chuckled. He took another drag of his cigar with a smile. Santo glanced over to Dominic who wore the same sinister smile.

"No. Everything I do, I do for the family. I wasn't acting alone on this. I have an ally. There's a woman who wants to help us. Her name is Isabella. She's travelling now but she—"

"A woman?" Giovanni chuckled. "You hear this, Domi? Now we have a woman telling us what to do."

"I'm getting ahead of myself. Forget I mentioned her. What I'm saying to you is that I have a lot of things in the works for the family. I'm strengthening our hold on the *Campania* and I always include Dominic in the planning as it develops."

"All I hear you doing is talking. Talk. Talk. Talk," Giovanni said. He stared at Santo for a long silent moment. "I thought the sacrifice you gave for the family meant you were courageous. Now I know that I need more than courage to keep this thing we do together." Giovanni sat forward. "You will stand down. Are we clear?"

"Yes," Santo said, through clenched teeth. Santo sat back. "Have I ever betrayed you, Gio? Ever?"

"A wise man once told me that loyalty is not a test of friendship, a man's actions once proven are. That man was my father. He died after enemies pumped six bullets into his chest. And no friendship he forged in the forty years he ran the *Camorra* could prevent that fate."

"Can I have in on the Mottola visit?" Santo asked. "Giuliani is a personal friend of mine. The Armenian connection is a surprise to me as well. I might be of use in seeing this to a peaceful resolution. I'm not assured that Lorenzo and Carlo will do that for you."

Giovanni dragged on his cigar. He didn't bother to answer. Far as he was concerned Giuliani was a dead man when he turned on his own blood to help Giovanni. Nothing worse than a rat, and Santo damn well knew it.

"Grazie, Giovanni." Santo stood. He walked over and took Giovanni's hand. He kissed his ring. *"Grazie."*

After a single nod of his head Santo was dismissed. Giovanni watched him go. The timing for all of this couldn't be worse. Now he had to trust Lorenzo to bring them through it. He had to trust Dominic to keep them on course. And he had to believe that his enemies would not learn how weakened and vulnerable they were. And he had to find a way to tell his wife that she had a sister he's kept from her for months. He had little faith in his ability to do any of it.

* B *

Mira groaned. She turned over to her side. Rosetta brought dinner to her room. But she barely ate. Eve had been in a whiney and clingy mood so she sent her away. Now she felt discomfort all through her pelvis. The babies were wrestling with each other all morning in her uterus. Nothing she did, drinking cold water or massaging her stomach, could soothe them.

"*Donna*? Are you okay?" a gentle voice spoke with concern.

Mira opened her eyes. At first she didn't recognize the face hovering above hers. "Who?"

"It's me Carmella? Ma-ma told me to come. To help. I brought you some tea." She put the cup down. "Do you need anything?"

"No," Mira said weakly. "I'm a little uncomfortable. It'll pass."

"I heard about what happened earlier. I'm so glad the babies are okay," Carmella said.

Mira slipped her a look. Though Carmella didn't appear to be mocking Mira something in her tone made her feel as if she were. And the anxiety she thought wouldn't return did with Carmella hovering over her while she was in such a vulnerable state. "Where is Catalina? Rosetta?"

"Last I saw everyone was gathered downstairs. Why don't you try this tea? I insist." Carmella pushed the mug toward her.

"No thanks. I want you to leave," Mira said.

"But I can—"

"Leave. Please. I'm fine," Mira said.

When Carmella stepped away she took the cup of tea with her. Mira immediately felt better as she watched her go. Catalina walked in just as Carmella reached the door. She paused. "I didn't know you were here?" Catalina said.

Carmella smiled and gave Catalina a brief hug. "I came back to help while Ma-ma sees to her sister. I told Antonio to take some time off. He needs to be around his friends at his age. Not working. I can handle things."

"Oh good," Catalina smiled.

"I was just checking on the *Donna*. Do you need anything?"

"Some of that tea would be good." Catalina reached for the pot.

"No. Not this tea. I need to make some more. I'll bring you a fresh cup. Excuse me."

Catalina closed the door behind Carmella. Mira put a hand to her forehead. "I can't wait for Zia to get here," Mira sighed.

"How do you feel?" Catalina asked. She climbed in bed with Mira. She put her hand to Mira's belly and gave it a kiss.

"I was a little uncomfortable but I'm getting better," Mira smiled.

"It's been a crazy day," Catalina said. "Nothing is making sense. First Lorenzo and his mail order bride, then you and the babies, and now Domi."

"What about Domi?" Mira asked.

"He broke up with me." Catalina rested her head on Mira's shoulder. Before she knew it she started to cry. "And it's all my fault. I lied to him. He can't forgive me."

"Oh, sweetheart. It can't be that bad. Domi loves you. We all know it," Mira reassured her.

"I took his pride. He's trying so hard to get Gio to respect him and I went behind his back and told Gio that I don't want to be married," Catalina confessed.

"You did?" Mira asked. "I didn't know that you changed your mind on getting married."

"Me either. It's like the past four months I've been seeing things differently. Not my love for Domi, but myself. Domi and I had our life all planned out when Franco died. My life was to be about our love. And kids. But I don't want to be a wife and mother right now. I want to be a designer. Like you."

Mira opened her arm to Catalina. She tried her best to bring her in closer and comfort her. Catalina rested her head against Mira's breast. "That's to be expected. You're so young. Giovanni and I have talked about this. How important it is for you to have a chance to strike out on your own. And look at you. You make me so proud."

"Fabiana would be proud too." Catalina said and wiped her tears away from her cheeks. "She used to whisper to me when you were making my dress and I was getting ready to marry Franco that whatever happens on my wedding night, make sure it ends with me on top. You know, riding Franco when he lost control and had an orgasm."

"That doesn't surprise me, "Mira chuckled. "Sounds like advice she'd give."

"I never understood before now why she said it. I guess she wanted me to be in control. She never got a chance to explain," Catalina said.

Mira stroked Catalina's arm. "It could have been her way to tell you to not give up all of your independence. Fabiana believed in love, marriage, and family. She told me constantly that a woman should have it all. She taught me to believe in family too," Mira said.

"So I shouldn't fear getting married? I should do it all?" Catalina asked.

"You need to listen to your heart, what it tells you. I can't make that decision for you. And Giovanni and Dominic shouldn't either. You have to ask yourself, Catalina, what it is you truly want." She lifted Catalina's chin to look into her eyes. "And then be brave enough to go after it. Even if it means letting Domi go."

"But Domi is special, Mira. I don't want to lose him. He deserves a family of his own. He loves kids, Mira. You've seen him with Eve. He had a really bad childhood until he came to live with us."

"What happened to him?" Mira asked.

"Abused, beaten, tortured. His father forced him to sleep on the floor and play in a shed with the animals. In the winter fed him frozen food, in the summer fed him rotten food. Treated him worse than a dog," Catalina said.

"That's awful," Mira said.

"He used to have these nightmares, wake up with night terrors. Giovanni made him sleep with him until he was eight years old. And Gio took care of him. He protected Domi. That's why Domi was so overprotective of me. That's the way it works. It's why Giovanni has a hard time seeing us as lovers. He sees us as his children I guess," Catalina said.

"I understand now," Mira said.

Catalina sighed. "You're lucky. You don't have a big brother to rule your life."

Mira laughed. "Yes but I have your brother."

Catalina laughed. "Oh yes! You aren't so lucky after all."

They held each other for a moment. And then Catalina spoke again. "What do you think of her? Marietta?"

"I like her," Mira said. "She's different. Straight forward."

"She's sneaky," Catalina said.

"Catalina!"

"I just feel it. Like she's turning her nose up to us. Like she thinks she's better than you. She needs to show you respect," Catalina said.

"Oh stop. No she doesn't. Respect is something we earn. Giovanni has earned it with me. I had to earn it with you. Didn't I?"

"I guess," Catalina answered.

"Okay, give her time. Coming into this family can be difficult," Mira chuckled. "Besides she's married to Lorenzo. The girl has her hands full."

"She sure does!" Catalina reached up and kissed Mira on the cheek. "You know you are prettier pregnant? Your cheeks are fat, your hair is bushy, and you have huge breasts."

"That makes me prettier?" Mira chuckled.

"Earthy. Mother Earth! I like the change. It inspires me. Maybe we can think of doing a maternity line for the retailers in America who want your affordable daywear clothes. What do you think?"

Mira smiled. "I think you should work on the idea a bit more." Mira grinned.

"Me too," Catalina sighed.

Mira closed her eyes. The discomfort she felt earlier eased. She felt safe and loved hugging Catalina. She loved her family.

Later -

Giovanni opened the door to the bedroom. He had just left Eve. She would sleep with Cecilia for the night. So he could take care of Mira. In a few days Rocco and Zia would return. He agreed with Mira, they needed them both.

The room was dark. The windows and doors to the belvedere were drawn shut with the shutters closed. Catalina slept next to Mira. Both women were on their side facing away from him. Giovanni tapped Catalina on the shoulder. She turned over and looked at him.

"Mmm, *ciao*?"

"Go to bed," Giovanni said.

"Is Domi still here?" Catalina asked sitting up.

"To your own bed," Giovanni said sternly.

Catalina gave him a sly smile. She kissed his cheek and started out of the room. She stopped at the door. "She had a little discomfort earlier, but she said she felt better before she slipped to sleep. I'm not going to Milano until after the boys are born, Gio. I'll help her."

"*Grazie,*" Giovanni said.

Catalina winked and left.

Giovanni shed his clothes. He tossed them to the floor and eased in bed with her. He drew the covers up over them. Mira didn't stir. He adjusted her body and pillows. She looked to be comfortable. When he was satisfied that she was, he lay behind her. He turned over to his back and stared at the ceiling. He'd spend the rest of the night watching over her.

* B *

Ignazio knocked before he entered the room. He took one look at Armando and froze. "What happened to your face?"

"Me and the old man had a disagreement. Any news on Isabella?" he asked.

"She's not back in Rome. And our contact in China is full of shit. Another dead end. Again she disappears." Ignazio spoke with his hands.

"Why do you think our contact is full of shit?" Armando asked.

"Because he says she's under the protection of the Triad." Ignazio laughed. "Those mean son-of-a-bitches are worse than the Armenians. They'd never do business with Isabella. What reason would they have to do so? It's all a dead end. Personally I'd rather focus on what I heard about the *Campania*. Chiaiano is under Mottola's control now. Were you aware?"

Armando waved off the news. "I know. Mottola makes Gio his bitch. And all Gio does is hide out in Mondello under his wife's skirt. It's old news."

"Maybe. But it's an opportunity. Giovanni is spreading himself thin with his business deals in Milano, Turin, Genoa. The Bonaduces are still looking for a way to get revenge. How long before the deals he's making unravel? We should reach out to the `Ndrangheta,"* Ignazio advised.

"No." Armando said. "Things have changed." The news his father gave him on his legacy had him seething with rage. To make matters worse he's been unable to reach Carmella and call off the hit on Mirabella. If she dies or her brats die his father would surely believe it to be him.

Armando groaned. Even in death the old man threatened to have control. He had to be smart about this. Turn it around to his favor. He just didn't know how.

"What has changed?" Ignazio asked.

"I can't say right now. We need to appease the old man. He wants Isabella dead and right now I don't give a shit if she lives. Find her. Put more money into the search. Do you understand?" Armando asked.

"I don't understand any of this," Ignazio sighed. "But I trust you, Armando. Whatever it is between you and your father you will figure it out."

"I will." Armando nodded in agreement. "I'll figure it out."

Mancini stepped back from his son's office door. He had heard enough. On his cane he started slowly back up the hall. He had little time to rethink his decisions. And he carried no guilt over it. After learning that Mirabella suffered the way Melissa did when she carried twins he knew his actions were justified. Before he died he had to reunite his children. Make this family the way it should have been all along. He failed Melissa. But he would keep his promise to protect their daughters. And maybe the saints will grant him a pardon and let him into heaven to see his darling Melissa once more.

Philadelphia –

"You fucking piece of shit, I will fucking rip off your head and shit down your neck!" Mancini growled with spittle spraying through his mouth and his hands clenching tighter than a vice around Capriccio's neck. He slammed Capriccio's head down on the concrete floor. Her refused to let go of his stranglehold. Capriccio spit up blood and thrashed about. Mancini choked him. He put all his might into choking him. Several of the Gallucci men acted. It took three of them to save Capriccios life. The hospital nurse entered the room just as they dragged Mancini cursing and shouting death threats to them all as he was dragged out of the door. Capriccio lay as still as a corpse as the nurse rushed to aid him. He had better be dead or Mancini vowed to make sure of it.

"Calm yourself, Sicilian," Gallucci said. "Calmare!"

"Che due palle!" Mancini spat. He shook off the men holding him back.

Donato Gallucci was short and plump in the waist. His arms and legs however belonged to a skinny man. Making his suit jacket difficult to button. "You are in America you crazy fuck! This shit will not fly here. You nearly killed him." Galluci looked around. Mancini never took his eyes off the door they dragged him through. If he had his gun he'd shoot every motherfucker in his path to put the kill bullet in Capriccio. When Gallucci looked at him again he let go a deep sigh. "The people will call the police and haul you out of here. Do you understand?"

242

Donato looked to one of his men and signaled for him to go find the nurse and make sure she didn't report what she'd seen. Mancini wiped his hand down his face and saw his bloody bruised knuckles. The Don stepped close. "We found the negro woman. We found her in time. The babies were born and she lives. This hospital doesn't let coloreds in. I pulled some strings for you. Show some gratitude. Eh?"

Humility was not in Mancini's DNA. The blood. There was so much blood when they found Melissa in that roach infested apartment. She was near death. The fact that she lived and the children did too was a miracle. And all of the blame should be laid at Capriccio's feet.

The Don patted his arm. "Be reasonable. Capriccio's death solves nothing," he said. "I won't wack a capo over your nigger goumada. It's not done. You know this."

Mancini switched his glare to the old Don. "Fuck your laws. He is dead." Mancini drew a line across his throat to signify the slicing of Capriccio's throat.

The Don closed the distance between them. His eyes went dark as a serpent's. His voice was as hard as steel. "You lay a hand on him and your father won't be able to save you. Mi capisci adesso?"

Mancini glowered.

"Answer me!" The Don shouted.

"Si, capisco," Mancini nodded that he understood. He couldn't speak further. The bloodlust within him was too great.

"Boss?" Another of the Gallucci men entered. "The nurse is handled. The doctors want to meet with you and him."

The Don removed a handkerchief from his pocket. He passed it to Mancini to wipe the blood from his knuckles. "I don't understand your obsession with the nigger. But I respect it, Manny. Now you respect my reputation and authority here. We go out and speak to these doctors and you keep your temper cool and your mouth shut. You listen to them. And then we decide what is best. Capice?"

Mancini nodded.

Together they walked out. With every step Mancini took, his vision continued to narrow. As if he were in a dark tunnel with light and sight at the end. He blinked through his fear, his heartache, his panicked state because she needed him. His sweet Lisa could be dying at that very moment. He had to get it together.

"Donato!" The doctor greeted Gallucci with a handshake and then kisses to both cheeks. "Please if you both can come in here we can have privacy."

The doctor ushered them to a room and closed the door. Gallucci sat but Mancini chose to remain standing. The doctor looked at Mancini's blood stained shirt and then averted his gaze. "She's in a coma." The doctor said. "She had a stroke during the delivery."

Mancini felt his gut clench.

"It's not uncommon considering the condition she arrived in. It's a miracle. I have to say so. You saved her life, and the twins. She's lost a lot of blood. We had to perform a hysterectomy. She won't be able to have any more children."

"The babies?" Mancini asked in a strained voice. "Are they still alive?"

"Yes, they are. And the odds are in their favor. Premature babies have it tough but the best success rate in healthy preemies is in favor of those of colored girls. We aren't sure medically why, but it's good news. Already they show signs of breathing on their own."

"I want to see her. Lisa. I want to see her and my... and those babies," Mancini said.

"Gentlemen. This is a private hospital. We can't keep them here... it's causing some upset with the nurses, the other patients."

"You will keep them here." Mancini took a threatening step forward.

The Don put up his hand to silence him. Again Mancini had to summon strength beyond his ability, and he did so. The Don smiled at the doctor when he spoke. "What my friend means to say is let's work out the best way to accommodate them and keep them separate from the other patients. I'm willing to compensate the hospital for the trouble."

The doctor met Mancini's glare and dropped his eyes away immediately. "Okay. Yes. We can do that." The doctor exhaled. "Right now it's a waiting game. We have to see if she wakes. As for the babies, they are in the neonatal ward. We are doing what we can."

"I want to see her," Mancini said to both men. "Now!"

"Of course." The doctor pushed up from his desk. He walked out and Mancini followed. He glanced back to see the Don and two of his men watching him in the hall. He was taken to another wing and then showed a door.

"We must keep the visit short, please." The doctor asked humbly. Mancini ignored him and entered. The curtain was drawn around Melissa's bed, maybe to keep her identity from shocking others who might stumble in. He snatched it back nearly yanking half of the curtain off its rings. Melissa lay still with a breathing apparatus in her mouth. Mancini felt his knees go weak. Why did she run? If what Capriccio said was true she left the apartment he paid for and ran from him. If he had found her an hour later than he did she would be dead. Why did she do that? What was she afraid of?

"Cara, bella mia, what has become of you?" he asked taking a seat at the side of her bed. He took her hand into his and kissed it. "We have daughters. Our daughters. I'm here now. But they need a mother. They need you, sweetheart."

She didn't stir, she didn't move. He sat at her side searching for the words. He had none. This was his fault. He remembered her, who she was before he laid a hand on her. How lovely and full of innocence she once was. Now she was a junkie, a mistress, a mother to illegitimate twins. This is what he had turned her life into.

When a nurse entered he asked to be taken to his daughters. In order to visit them they put a gown over his clothes and a cloth mask on the lower part of his face. But he was granted the privilege. In his pocket he carried gifts. Two bracelets made by Del Stavio for his angels. He had envisioned his reunion with Lisa differently. He had hoped for much more for his girls.

Mancini walked closer. There was tape over their eyes. Each baby was small enough to fit in his hand. He could see their little chests move with each draw of breath. One was ghostly white and the other just a few shades darker towards brown. And for the first time Mancini believed in miracles. He said a prayer taught to him in Sicilian by his madre.

Three Weeks Later

Mancini looked at the flowers in his hands and then to the door. After taking in a deep breath he pushed the door open to the hospital room. Melissa looked up as soon as he entered. "Buongiorno bella mia," he said with a smile.

She cast her gaze away, back toward the windows. In the room were several vases with flowers in bloom. He put the one he carried down on the desk near the wall. "Today is a good day. The doctors say we can leave."

"Manny, please," Melissa began and he could hear the quiver in her voice. "Please let me go. Let me take my babies and return to Virginia. I think I can convince my mother to talk to my father to let me return home. They wouldn't turn away their granddaughters."

Mancini could not believe his ears. He nearly lost them all, and she thought he'd let her and his daughters go now? He cast his gaze toward her. "The little ones need care. You were in a coma for several days. We've discussed this. I've forgiven you, Lisa, for running away from me. I've forgiven you for putting my daughters' lives at risk. And none of that was easy for me."

"Manny—"

"Madonne!" he shouted. She flinched. He sucked down a slow breath to calm his anger. "Why can't you forgive and trust me?" he asked.

"Because you are death," she said in a detached tone. "And if I stay with you, I'll die. I know it. I believe it. I even accept it, Manny. What am I now but your whore? If I am anything I'm a mother. And I have to protect my babies."

"Never my whore. I will protect you. I swear it. And our daughters." Mancini reasoned.

"Then take us to Sicily with you. Don't leave us here," Melissa begged.

He walked over to the bed. "I have something to show you. A surprise I wanted to keep for the day we take them home. He reached in his pocket and withdrew both small velvet boxes. "I've chosen their names."

Melissa accepted the jewelry boxes and opened each. "Mirabella. She is the one that we almost lost, the brown baby. I talked to her every day when you were in the coma. Told her to fight, and she did. Mirabella means my beautiful Mary, a blessing from God. A blessed name. I want her christened under this name." He pointed to the other bracelet. "And this is for Marietta. She is the fighter. She is strong. She weighed more. She will keep them both strong."

"They're beautiful," Melissa said.

"I am taking you to New York. Gemma will go with you. We'll get an apartment, a nurse, and I will stay this time. I promise. Gemma will help you with the babies. And I swear when I return…"

"Wait? You're leaving me again?" Melissa asked in disbelief.

He pinched her chin. "It is the final time we will be separated. I will return for you. I have to tend to my… there are family matters that require my attention. But you will be okay. Trust and believe me this time."

Melissa nodded. "I love the names. Our daughters. They are all I have."

"Not true, Bella, you have me. I swear it on my life. You have *me." He turned her chin up and kissed her. She softened and returned his kiss. He felt stronger if she believed him. Once more. All he asked is for her to trust him once more.*

Mancini entered his room. He closed the door with a heavy sigh. What if he had let her go? What if she left that day and returned to Virginia with his daughters? Would she have lived? He dragged himself to the bed and sat on the edge of it. Reaching for his oxygen mask with his arthritic hand he saw the tremors of his grief in it. He closed his hand into a fist. The simple act of breathing had now become a chore. Each day that passed he grew weaker and weaker. Time was gaining on him.

He could not change the past. The abandonment of his beloved that cost her life is his burden. But he would not go to his grave before he held his daughters.

He would not.

11.

Every man had a weakness. For a long time Lorenzo believed his weakness to be his pride. No longer. Lorenzo was stunned over the depth of his feelings for Marietta. He had showered with his cock buried deep in her, made love to her again against the sink, and then the bed before his heart could release enough of his passion to let her go. The silent admission of these feelings in his head was dredged from a place in him beyond logic and reason. For her safety and his sanity, love should have never been on the menu. In his life he had enjoyed women. Even lowered his guard to develop feelings for them. But Marietta, and what he felt for her, was far different.

In a hurried pace back and forth beyond the bathroom door she packed and unpacked his things. He watched her reflection in the bathroom mirror while he dressed. He studied her beauty, her curves in the cut off t-shirt that barely covered her breasts and a pair of his boxer shorts she had pulled on. He put every inch of her body to his memory. It should sustain him before he dealt with what awaited with the Armenians.

She packed a small duffle bag for him to ensure his early return. And she asked questions on whether he would be in danger and where he would travel to. None of the questions deserved an answer. What he did in this life, for *la famiglia*, would *never* be something they would *ever* discuss. Though he hated the idea of leaving her so soon. But he felt charged over the responsibility of being a husband. Giovanni was coming around. Santo had been put in his place—a step behind Lorenzo. The plan had worked. And if he got with the Armenians and stopped Mottola then all would be resolved between he and his cousin.

It would surely follow with the reward to be able to stand up as his own man again. And he'd shower Marietta with all the privileges she deserved. Lorenzo smiled. He had played a bad hand and came up aces.

He couldn't be happier.

"Why are you smiling? I'm about to freak out." She put her hands on his back. "Will you call me when you get there?" Marietta asked. She had come into the bathroom. She peeked around him as he slapped his face with aftershave. There were scrapes and scratches on his face and he hissed because of the after burn. Marietta wrapped her arms around his waist and rested her face against the middle of his spine. "Call me every hour until you can come home to me. So I know you are okay."

He chuckled.

"And bring me something. Diamonds. Bring me diamonds," she grinned bouncing on her feet making her nipples brush up and down his back.

"I'll try. It's a quick trip, Marie."

"Make time," she demanded. "I want something to show that you were thinking of me," she said. And he could hear the plea in her voice. A vulnerable pitch he rarely heard. It sounded like fear. He turned and she stepped back. Lorenzo leaned against the sink and drew her closer to him by her hips.

"*Tutto va bene.* Why are you upset?"

"I got this feeling, Lo. A very bad feeling. I get it sometimes. When I was sixteen the first boy I loved was killed after school in some random gang violence. I had that feeling like something would happen all day. And I got it now. I got it the moment you brought me here."

He lifted her chin. "It's a false feeling. I'm in no danger."

"That's not true. My stomach hurts. It feels like a weight is on my chest," she said.

"Marie—"

"I don't want you to go. I've never had good luck with this... men... love. Stay. Send someone else. Please."

"Nothing bad will happen," he said.

"Stop saying that! Bad stuff happens to good people all the time. And we aren't good people."

Lorenzo chuckled. "Maybe not. Still, I control my destiny and now yours. Bad stuff only happens when I make it happen." He brushed his lips over her brow. "I'll return before you miss me. *Tutto a posto?*"

She nodded yes.

"This is what you do. Today you take money and go to Carini. I'll have one of the boys drive you. Spend my money. How does that sound?"

She rolled her eyes. "I'm not a child. I took care of myself just fine before I met you. Without your money!"

"You're my wife. I want you protected. Relax, *cara*. Life is falling into place—yours and mine. We are going to have it all, you and me. *Va bene*."

She nodded that she would do as he wished. He cupped her face in his hands. "Keep it warm and sexy for me?" he said, softly.

"You know it." She kissed him. She wrapped her arms around his neck and locked him in for her deep tongue kiss. Lorenzo chuckled and lifted her the way she liked. Immediately she crossed her legs around his waist. He felt like he could conquer the world with her by his side.

* B *

"Ugh," Mira gasped.

She gripped her side again. The baby had kicked her hard. A monstrous bolt of pain slammed up against her right side. Her vision began to swim and she squeezed her eyes tightly shut. Relief never came easily, only measures of it when she practiced her breathing and massaged her side. She rubbed the sore spot. The noise from his shower could be heard through the closed bathroom door. Giovanni took his showers alone since she could barely stand for long periods of time.

At some point in the night he returned to bed. And of course he rose early. She pushed back against her pillows and breathed slow and easy out of her mouth. How does one spend days, weeks, confined to a bed and not go crazy? Already she felt restrained.

There was a knock at the door.

"Come in."

The door opened. Carmella appeared with a tray of her breakfast food. The young Sicilian beauty wore jean shorts and a grey t-shirt tied into a knot under her breasts. Her long legs were shapely and evenly tanned. Her breasts perked and bounced with each step and her nipples peaked. *Of course this hefa would go braless.* Her tiny waist made Mira lower her gaze and look away with envy.

"*Buongiorno.* I thought you might be ready for breakfast, *Donna.* Ma-ma left me your dietary needs," she said with a smile. "She made sure to tell me you were allergic to mushrooms. And that you didn't like melons of any kind."

Mira didn't answer. She watched as Carmella placed the tray of fruit and poached eggs with some shaved ham on the table next to her. *"Come sta, Donna?"*

"Not hungry," Mira answered.

"Maybe some tea then. I made you a fresh pot. I can pour some."

"No thank you," Mira said. "I'll fix it myself."

The door opened and Giovanni walked out with a towel tied around his waist and another in his hand drying his hair. He paused when he saw Carmella. The look of disapproval hardened his features. "What the hell are you doing in here?" he asked.

"Buongiorno, Gio," Carmella replied.

Mira looked into the woman's face and saw the flush of desire redden her cheeks. Mira then looked to Giovanni's muscular form, beaded with moisture from the steamy shower. Even after weeks of staying by her side his body was packed tight with muscles. Mira rolled her eyes. They both made her sick.

"Allora... Madre had to see to her sister in Bagheria. She asked me to come and fulfill her duties. The *Donna* approved."

Giovanni's gaze switched to Mira. She didn't answer. She felt like an idiot for bringing the woman back into her home. But what choice did she have? She could barely bathe herself. They would need the help.

"Se ne vada Carmella!" he ordered.

Carmella turned and picked up the teapot and the mug to take with her. Mirabella thought that odd since she was trying to push the tea on her just minutes earlier. More surprising was the nasty way in which Giovanni dismissed Carmella. Still Mira didn't care. She wanted her gone. She watched as the woman left and Giovanni closed the door. He turned on her with angry eyes. "Why did you bring her back here? If she upsets you, why would you okay her return? Do you want to be stressed?"

Mirabella burst into tears. Giovanni threw the towel in frustration. When she wept harder he walked around the bed and went to her. He pulled her upright into his arms and she cried out her frustration. "I'm sorry. I don't mean to cry. But I'm so damn frustrated."

"Because of Carmella?" he asked.

"No. No of course not. I don't care about her, not really. I agreed for her to come because... Cecilia is busy with Eve and I know you and your men won't live off of sandwiches. What else was I to do?" she sighed. "I don't know. I feel so miserable. I'm trying but some days it's hard. Some days I feel fat and miserable, and trapped in a body I can't control. I'm a terrible mother."

Although she considered her twins to be the final round of pregnancy for her the idea that she couldn't conceive after this pregnancy tore at her heart. "I know you want more children, Giovanni. Don't lie to me."

"I want you, Bella. I always have. Always. And nothing within my power will ever take you from me. Not even the birth of our *bambinis*. Do you understand?"

Mira stared into his eyes and read the truth there. He meant every word. She nodded that she understood.

"I'm here. I'm not going anywhere. We'll get through this together. I'll find a place for us in a few days and we will leave Mondello. We'll stay in Palermo next to the *ospedale*. I've called Zia. She's returning to Sicily to be of help to you. Anything you want, Bella. Name it."

"*Ti amo, Giovanni*," she said through a smile.

He kissed her lids, her face, and her mouth. He kissed her cheeks. She felt better.

"Hungry?" he asked after letting her go.

"I am," she replied.

He picked up her plate and a fork. Mira settled back against her pillows and wiped her tears. She opened her mouth and he fed her. She studied him as he did so. "So many people don't know the real you. Not the way I do."

"Of course they don't. No one other than my wife has that privilege."

"You came to Sicily at a great risk to your business didn't you?"

Giovanni stopped feeding her. "Why do you say that?"

"I hear the calls, I see the whispers. We could have stayed in Sorrento but you love *Sicilia*. You brought us here and even from this bed I see why. This is where family is. Isn't it?"

"Yes, Bella. This is where family begins and ends for us. Sicily." He winked and for the moment everything felt right in the world. So she ignored the dreaded feeling of doom she woke with. It was just her anxiety. There was nothing to fear. Nothing bad could happen with them now.

* B *

Marietta waved bye to Lorenzo and Carlo as they backed out of the drive. The car turned and sped away from Villa Mare Blu, and then was gone.

Alone so soon? A cynical inner voice cut through her courage.

"He'll be back," she said softly to herself.

Marietta's gaze lifted to the sky. The entire eastern arc of the horizon just beyond the mountainous cliffs was bright and vivid with sunlight. Not a cloud to be seen. Thankfully the moisture in the air from the sea tempered the morning heat. She felt like a swim, or some time to lie and relax in the sun. Even though she was a black woman her skin was fair enough to bring her ethnicity into question. Often she purposefully tanned to a deep shade of brown if she stayed in the sun. She preferred her darker skin tone.

Alone again? Her inner voice whispered.

With the cross of her arms she ignored her anxiety. She turned and walked back inside determined to start the day free of her insecurities. Where should she begin? She loved to cook. Over the past few months Marietta had gotten in the habit of feeding Lorenzo her special recipes. Maybe she could cook herself a nice omelet before she ventured out to the beach to go for a swim. She used to have a terrifying fear of water. But an ex-boyfriend helped her get over it. She never drowned or anything, but she could recall dreams as a little girl of drowning that left her screaming in the night.

When Marietta turned the corner she heard a woman weeping. She paused. The woman spoke in a hushed tone on the phone to someone in Italian.

Armando, per favore, I couldn't do it. She wouldn't even drink the tea. Yes. Yes. I understand, but... really? Oh God bless. Thank you so much for changing your mind. If I had gone through with it I wouldn't have been able to live with myself. I trust you, I do, but I can no longer be your weapon, your spy. Of course. I will call you everyday with an update on her condition. Thank you.

Marietta peeked inside. The woman hung up the phone. She wore jean shorts and a grey shirt. She had a short haircut with thick brown curls, and looked to be in her mid-twenties or a bit older. Marietta observed her as she dumped a powdery substance in the sink and ran water to wash it away. She then poured out the tea she had in a teapot.

Who was she? A spy? That shit can't be good. What was it she couldn't do? Did it have anything to do with Mirabella? The woman turned and saw her. Marietta stepped inside to make sure she understood she was heard and seen.

"*Madonna! Dio mia.*" The woman put her hand to her heart. "You surprised me. *Ciao. Buongiorno. Mi chiamo Carmella,*" the woman said as she quickly wiped away her tears.

Marietta looked her over. "What were you pouring into the sink?"

"Sorry? I don't understand?" Carmella said.

"The sink. You dumped something in it," Marietta pointed.

"Oh, the tea went bad. I make it from fresh herbs for the *Donna*. I wanted to make a new pot. Are you hungry? I can fix you something to eat." The woman said and began to tidy up. Marietta glanced at the clear baggie that was left on the counter. It still had a white residue in it. Apparently the woman noticed what drew Marietta's attention and immediately picked up the baggie and crumbled it in her hand.

"Who are you spying on?" Marietta asked. She stepped closer.

Carmella laughed. "No one! I work for the Battaglias. My mother and I keep this place in order."

"Who were you talking to?" Marietta took another step closer.

"*Mi scusi?* That was a private conversation."

Marietta smirked. "Really? So I'll go tell King B what I heard... what was the person's name you spoke to? Oh, Armando?"

"*Aspettare!* Forgive me. *Non importa.* It was my boyfriend. He wanted me to quit and come home. I told him I couldn't go through with it. He wanted me to spy on one of the men here, Leonardo. He owes him money and he... he wanted to know if he had his car tuned, if he was being flashy so he could catch him in a lie about the debt." She stepped forward wringing the dishrag nervously. "I am no spy. And I could not abandon *la famiglia* in their time of need. I couldn't live with myself. We worked it out. Please don't say anything. I don't want to disappoint the *Don* or *Donna*."

The explanation would have worked if she hadn't heard the conversation and seen the dumping the evidence.

Carmella smiled. "*Permesso,*" she said as she passed. "If you need anything let me know."

"Like a cup of tea?" Marietta gripped her arm and kept her from escaping. "You can run that bullshit on the people here but I saw you. If I find out you are doing anything to hurt Mirabella or that you have lied to me, I will share with the *Don* what I overheard. We clear?"

"*Sí, arrivederci.*" The woman hurried out of the kitchen taking the plastic baggie with her.

Marietta shook her head. "People in this place are shady as hell," she said with disgust.

"Mira? Are you up?" Catalina asked. She peeked inside.

"Yes." Mira said, as she turned the page on the book she read for Eve. Her daughter pointed at a picture of a bear. Mira read to her some more. Catalina closed the door.

"Cecilia said you wanted to see me." Catalina walked in.

"Did Lorenzo leave? I heard Giovanni on the phone saying they were leaving today. Is he gone?" Mira asked. Eve took the book from her mother's hands and pretended at reading it to her.

"Yeah, they've left. Dominic and Gio are locked up in the office. But everyone else is gone." Catalina took a deep unsteady breath and tried to sound casual about it. The truth was she wanted to talk to Dominic again. She had lingered for a long time outside of her brother's office before eventually giving up. She stood motionless until she felt Mira and Eve's curious stares. Catalina didn't want to worry her sister in-law. She walked around the room. "I came to hang out with you," she said in a cheerful voice. And then she decided to open the door to the belvedere to allow in some fresh air. "It's such a pretty day outside. I hate you are locked away in here."

"Oh, me too. That's why I wanted to see you. And thanks for opening up the room for me." Mira smiled. Eve began to scoot away from her mother and down the bed. She hurried toward her aunt but ran past her to go outside. Catalina laughed and so did Mira.

"I'm going to tell Cecelia to take her to the beach again. She loves the beach," said Mira.

"She's growing so fast." Catalina glanced back at Mira. "What is it you want to see me about?"

"Marietta. If Lorenzo's gone she must feel a little isolated. I was wondering if you could take her into the town and do some sightseeing, maybe a bit of shopping with her?" Mira asked.

"Are you kidding me? Why me?" Catalina whined. "We can't stand each other."

"That's not true. You don't know each other. I want her to get to know us. And because you were rude to her yesterday I think it would be nice if you offered." Mira said. Her sister in-law threw her hands up in the air in dramatic fashion and turned away. "Catalina? You're better than this. She has done nothing wrong," Mira said.

"Oh good grief. Send Rosetta with her. I can't be bothered," Catalina said. "Besides I have some boutiques to visit in Palermo today for *Fabiana's*."

"Listen to yourself," Mira said. "Please do this. She's Lorenzo's wife."

Catalina sighed. "He marries a stranger and I have to make nice?"

Mira smiled. "I'd do it but I can't now can I?" Mira gestured to the bed. "I'm only allowed out to go to the bathroom or do some light standing. It'll make me feel better if I know she's with you learning about our family. And maybe you can learn a little about her. She has me curious." Mira admitted.

"Fine. But you owe me." Catalina pointed a finger at her. "I want six dresses made just for me after you have the babies."

Mira grinned. "I always pay my debts!"

* B *

Marietta had found a fashion magazine. It looked to be a year old but she fingered the pages with mild interest while eating her omelet. She put everything in it but mushrooms. She was deathly allergic to mushrooms.

"I said *buongiorno*." Catalina repeated herself.

Marietta stopped chewing. She glanced up and blinked at the raven-haired beauty staring down at her. She chewed and swallowed. "Morning," Marietta said.

"I think we got off on the wrong foot." Catalina drew out the chair to the table and took a seat without invitation. "I was uh," her voice faltered.

"Don't worry about it. I'm okay with you." Marietta ate more hoping that was the end of the visit. But when she looked up she saw Catalina staring again. "Need something else?"

"Yes. I had intended to do a bit of shopping in Palermo today. I wanted to know if you'd like to come. We can ride through Mondello, stop at the Charleston for gelato or sweets."

Marietta listened.

"I have a few dress shops to visit," Catalina prattled on. "I have some order requests to pick up. I can show you the city."

"Why?" Marietta asked after a deep swallow of tolerance. She tossed her fork to her plate and crossed her arms.

"Excuse me?"

"Why do you want me to go with you?" asked Marietta.

"Truth?" Catalina smiled.

Marietta nodded. "Yes. I want the truth."

"It's the *Donna*'s idea. She wants me to make the effort. Personally your attitude gets under my skin. But I understand it I suppose. We are unfamiliar. I tend to be suspicious of people I don't know."

Marietta chuckled. "So Queen B is giving me charity?"

Catalina leaned forward and her tone lowered with a lethal intensity. "Don't do that. Don't disrespect her—ever. I'm only going to tell you once."

"Oh please! I meant nothing by it." Marietta laughed. "And you know what? Why not? I want to get out of here today. So yes. I'll go. I'll need to change first." Marietta pushed back from the table and stood. She saw the look of surprise on Catalina's face. If she was stuck for two days with these women she might as well find a way to get along with them. It would make Lorenzo happy if she tried.

* B *

"Is that everything?" Giovanni signed the last document before him.

"It is," Dominic said. He folded the docs and tucked them back inside the leather sleeve of his satchel. "I'll be leaving soon. Taking the train out of Palermo back to Rome."

"Today? I thought you'd stay until Lorenzo and Carlo returned?" Giovanni asked.

"No. The 'Ndrangheta is a problem. It's best Santo and I make sure things haven't gotten worse with the clan bosses. I need to be assured Bonaduce hasn't been stirring up trouble as well." Dominic advised. His manner was cool and abrupt. Giovanni had detected a change in attitude from him all morning, but didn't speak on it. Dominic turned to leave and stopped. He looked back at Giovanni. He set the satchel in the chair and braced his stance by gripping the back of the chair. "I think you should know that Catalina and I have ended our relationship."

"Is that so?" Giovanni asked. "So soon?"

"You were right, Gio. We don't work. I think we both see that now."

Giovanni suppressed a smile. He loved Dominic. A blind man could see his brother was in pain. Dominic lowered his head. The silver medallion Giovanni put around his neck when he was only a boy swung out of his shirt and caught the light. "I know you have issues with me still, Gio. My betrayal of your trust may never be forgiven. Do what you wish. Letting go of Catalina is the hardest thing I've ever endured in this life. And I don't do it because of my fear of you." He looked up at Giovanni. "I let her go for her. She's growing up. She's a woman now and she deserves this opportunity Mira is giving her."

"I understand," Giovanni said. And for the first time he had the insight to see it from Dominic's point of view. He too walked with a shadow of doubt and uncertainty over his actions with the woman he loved. He wished things could have been different for Dominic and Catalina but he felt a larger measure of relief that they would end their relationship. They are blood, whether they share the same bloodline or not. Brother and sister is all they were ever destined to be. "I respect your decision. Travel safe," Giovanni said.

Dominic gave him a respectful nod of his head. He picked up the satchel with a weary sigh. "You'll hear from me soon."

He turned and walked out. Giovanni rocked back in his chair. "What's done is done," he smiled. "Never to be undone."

* B *

To her delight he approached. She was quick to duck behind the corner and avoided being seen. He could only be headed to his room from this end of the hall. Rosetta carefully peeked out at Dominic. The man wore handsome effortlessly. He wasn't as tall as the others in the family but the dark suit and open shirt he wore screamed masculinity. And those eyes were to die for. Though they were downcast Rosetta loved when he focused them her way. He stopped halfway down the hall and went inside his room. She could walk away. In fact she knew it might be best with tensions so high now in the family. But her chances with Dominic were always so few. She approached his room and knocked.

"Come in."

"Domi?" she said. She peeked inside to see him running the zipper along his luggage shut. "Are you leaving?"

"I am. What do you need, Rosie?"

"I was hoping to talk to you. I wanted to know if you would... well it's hard to say."

Dominic glanced up at her. Rosetta forced herself to continue. "I wanted to know if you would speak to Gio about renting me an apartment in Milano. One near *Fabiana's*."

"That won't happen. Gio won't have you living in the city

alone," Dominic said. He picked up his suitcase and started toward the door. Rosetta stepped in front of him.

"After the babies are born the *Donna* is sending me and Catalina to Milano. We don't get along Domi. You know this. I can't live with her. I need my own place. So I can be you know, on my own two feet." She stepped closer. "You come to Milano a lot. You could always check in on me. Make sure I'm okay."

He stared down at her. Those eyes! Brown swirls reminded her of warm honey. They were always cast low and dreamy under dark lashes. She loved his eyes. And he smelled nice too. Catalina was a fool. If she had a chance at being with Dominic, and secretly she prayed she would someday, Rosetta would be sure to drag him to the priest. Make him hers immediately. You didn't let a man like Dominic slip away.

"You and Catalina will stay together in Milano. You'll just have to learn to get along," he smiled. "I think you can manage it."

Rosetta acted. She couldn't help herself. And her actions were quick, giving Dominic no room to respond. She hugged him. A *famiglia* hug. She wrapped her arms around his waist soft enough to be feminine but strong enough to secure him to her. In doing so her breasts, that were slightly larger than Catalina's, grazed up his chest. Dominic didn't drop his luggage or return the embrace. But he didn't tell her to let him go either. And God help her he felt so good.

Eventually the hug felt inappropriate. She looked up into his eyes and was slow to let him go. "How long before you come back?"

"Soon. You help the family take care of the *Donna*," he said.

"I will," she stepped aside. Dominic stared at her for a brief moment then shook his head and walked out. Rosetta followed him to the hall and watched him go. She couldn't contain herself, she was so happy.

* B *

The day would be an interesting one. Marietta had changed three times before she decided to wear a fitted low waist army green pencil skirt that nicely defined her hips and ass. Lorenzo loved her in skirts instead of pants. She chose a midriff white halter-top. Her belly piercing and chain was revealed. Not the typical attire of a Mafia socialite she supposed but it gave her such a sultry feel and she couldn't help but grin at her reflection. She took the time to smooth her bushy curls into a French braid to the back of her head.

She pinned the long plait. And soon the time forced her to hurry from the room. When she arrived to the front of the villa she could see Catalina was impressed with her transformation. Catalina wore a lime green summer dress that belled out around her hips and stopped a few inches above her knees. She wore matching strappy sandals.

"Sorry to make you wait. I'm ready," Marietta said.

"*Benissima! Andiamo.*" Catalina's voice faltered and the light in her smile dimmed. Her gaze now focused on someone behind Marietta. The stark change in Catalina's demeanor caused Marietta's head and gaze to turn. The man Lorenzo referred to as Dominic approached with his luggage. He was a handsome guy. He looked younger than the other men and less intense.

"You're leaving?" Catalina asked.

He nodded his head in response.

"You weren't going to tell me?" Catalina shouted.

"Did I need to?" he asked in an aloof manner.

"So nothing has changed?" Catalina asked. She took a step away from the door to the man. "Answer me, Domi? Nothing has changed for you?"

He didn't bother to answer.

"*Che palle!* Fine, Domi. Go. I won't stop you." Catalina opened the door for him. He walked out without missing a beat. "We're over!" she shouted to his retreating back. *Vattene! Vai via!*" Catalina continued to shout after him until tears sprung to her eyes. She slammed the door. She paced and cursed in Italian. Marietta watched her a bit amused. She liked her fire. Catalina put her face in her hands and Marietta's smile faded.

"Do you want to call it off? Our trip into Palermo?" Marietta asked with a hint of frustration in her voice. Catalina looked up and realized Marietta waited on her still.

"Hell no. Let's go," Catalina said with the toss of her hair. She opened the door and marched out of it. Marietta shook her head and followed. She had to pause as Catalina began to yell at the men who worked for her brother to bring the damned car around for them. Marietta rolled her eyes at the temper tantrum. Maybe she should be the one to call it off. Her gaze switched back to the door to the villa as she tried to decide and then lifted up to the windows. There before the glass stood Mirabella. She wore a long white night gown. Her baby daughter was at her side. The toddler pressed her hands and face to the window glass with a playful grin. Marietta's and Mira's eyes met. Queen B smiled at her and Marietta couldn't help but smile in return. She felt a deep pang of sadness looking at her that way. As if the *Donna* of the Battaglia family had been locked away from the world—stripped of her identity. And then the moment passed. Mira turned away from the window and the brown, blue-eyed toddler raced after her mother.

"You coming?" Catalina shouted from the inside of the car. The door to the car was open. Marietta felt like she should stay. Go upstairs and sit with Mira. The incident with Carmella still gnawed at her gut. But she wasn't sure what she'd be protecting the mafia queen from.

Marietta walked over to the car and with the help of their driver eased inside. It was of no surprise that Catalina openly wept. A tantrum of any kind usually ended in tears. Marietta looked away. She was so uncomfortable. Not sure what to say.

The driver pulled away from the Battaglia estates and they drove out around the side of Monte Gallo. Catalina sniffed a few times and then exhaled. Marietta's gaze switched over to her. "Are you okay?"

"I will be," Catalina replied.

"Is he, your husband?" Marietta asked.

Catalina gave a snort of disgust. "Hardly. He's the man I gave my heart to when I was barely able to walk. The man who crushed it to dust because he has no spine. The *bastardo*. He's a coward. A *bugiardo*! And I hate him!"

"No you don't," Marietta chuckled.

Catalina laughed through a veil of tears and she grinned as she made obscene gestures with her fist and arms. They laughed together.

"Maybe not. But I'd cut his balls off if he was here right now," Catalina confessed.

Marietta nodded as if she understood. And she did. "Men can be disappointments."

"He's my ex-boyfriend-fiance, oh hell he's just my ex. And he will be sorry for dumping me."

"I thought at one time you two were related? But Lorenzo said no?" Marietta asked. She remembered that Lorenzo referred to Dominic as a brother. And Catalina was his cousin. But he then referenced them as a couple. And then suddenly he said they were both his cousins. It didn't make sense.

"No. Not relatives the way you think. My father adopted him when he was five or six. He and I fell in love, now it's… it's done," Catalina said. "I'm sure Gio is somewhere smoking his cigar laughing at us." Catalina's bottom lip quivered and her eyes glistened with repressed tears. Marietta opened her purse. She had a travel pack of tissues and removed some to hand over to Catalina. She hated to see anyone cry.

"Why would the *Don* laugh at your misery? He is your brother."

"Ha!" Catalina said bitterly. "More like my dictator. He rules all of our lives and yours too!"

"No I don't think so—"

"Yes! The day you married into our family you married into our family." Catalina said with quiet emphases. "Gio turned Dominic against me. He hates our love. He could never give his blessing. I went to him for help and he told Domi that I didn't want to marry."

"Why?" Marietta pressed.

"Because that is what Gio does. He's a traditionalist, a chauvinist, a tyrant when it comes to the rules of this family. He has to be because of who he is I suppose. He never approved. He thought our relationship was incestuous. We fought hard to be together, and now my mistake is our undoing. I should have never trusted Gio," Catalina said softly.

They continued to ride in silence until the cover of trees cleared and the citrus orange sun blazing over the turquoise waters of the beaches glared inside each window. Marietta had to put on her sunglasses to withstand the cheery day.

"Give it some time. Maybe you two will work it out," Marietta said with disinterest.

Catalina sighed. "Maybe." She cut her gaze over to Marietta. "So you and Lorenzo are married? I find it hard to believe."

"Me too," Marietta said. She glanced down at her ring. She resisted the urge to kiss the diamond. She cherished the damn thing. No man had ever put a ring on her finger. No man had ever asked her to be his wife. And no man had ever made her feel more cherished.

"How did he propose?" Catalina asked.

"In a nightclub, over some drinks while smoking his cigar." Marietta grinned. When Catalina didn't she shrugged. She loved her first and second proposal, her wedding, every single minute of it. "He made up for it when he took me to buy my ring. We got married at sea."

"You didn't get married in a church?" Catalina gasped.

"Is that a problem?" Marietta frowned.

"Um, yeeesssss. Lorenzo is Catholic. Mirabella had to switch faiths to marry into our family. Are you Catholic?" Catalina asked.

"I was raised Catholic by my adoptive parents. They are Italian. But I don't believe in God or Catholicism. Never seen any proof of him. The devil exists though. Met a few of his disciples a couple of times."

Catalina made the sign of the cross over her and side-eyed Marietta as if she had spiders in her hair. Marietta had to laugh. "No disrespect, Catalina. Seriously you have to get over yourself. The whole world isn't Catholic."

"Then I feel sorry for the souls of the lost," Catalina said. "Because they are all going to hell."

"Are you serious?" Marietta asked.

"My faith is nothing to joke about," Catalina answered.

"Oh brother. Does it make it better that we had a Catholic priest marry us?" Marietta asked.

"But the church…?"

"The priest came from a church and went back to one after the ceremony!" Marietta shouted. "Oh please. We're married, on our terms. It's fine with me. Don't need your approval." Marietta then ceremoniously kissed her ring.

Catalina shook her head. She returned her gaze to the window. They soon arrived in the fishing village that was connected to Mondello. The streets were cramped and narrow.

"Parking is limited," Catalina said. "Leonardo will have to drive around if we decide to get out. But over there is the best gelati in *Sicilia*. Do you want to get a cone?"

"No, I'll pass. Maybe on the way back," Marietta said.

Catalina leaned forward. She spoke in Italian to the driver and told him to take them to Palermo. After a drive through the village they were back on the main road headed to Palermo.

"So what did you do in America?" Catalina asked. "I've been to New York. I run Mira's business now."

"Good for you," Marietta said.

Catalina chuckled. "Your mouth. It takes some getting used to. Kind of reminds me of the way Fabiana spoke."

Her gaze returned to Catalina who held her stare. She didn't want to show any emotion, but it was hard. It irked her when Fabiana's name was tossed at her. "I'm nothing like Fabiana," Marietta said.

"Of course you aren't. Fabiana is one of a kind. She could never be replaced." Catalina smiled.

"You think that threatens me? A dead white woman who barely knew Lorenzo as I do is my competition? Honey, please. You can stop tossing her name at me. Cause I can give a shit."

"Fabiana was more than a dead white woman. She was Lorenzo's true love. I've known many women in Lorenzo's life. I also saw how hard her death was on him. She may be gone, but she will always be the woman he blames himself for losing," Catalina said.

Marietta clapped. "*Brava*! There we have it. Fabiana the ghost lurks to take away my husband. I'm so scared! Happy?"

"Forget it," Catalina sighed.

"I'm not trying to fight with you, Catalina. I'm pretending to be nice just like you are. Lorenzo is my husband whether you like it or not. I'm the one he chose. But even more important *signorina*, I chose him. And he tells me every day how grateful he is that I did. Maybe if you learned to make better choices you wouldn't waste tears on a man who can easily walk away from you."

Catalina's mouth fell open. She blinked in shock. Crossing her arms she looked away. Satisfied that the small talk between them had ceased Marietta relaxed and enjoyed the scenic route.

* B *

"*Bella?*"

Mira looked up from her book. She removed her headphones from her ears. She was one of those rare people who liked to read and listen to music at the same time. Giovanni walked in. With his hands shoved down the deepest reach of his pockets he walked closer to the bed. "What are you reading?" he asked.

"A romance book I found in the drawer downstairs the other day. It's by this new author Sienna Mynx. She's pretty good. You done with your business?" she set the book on her round tummy.

"I am. Where's Eve?" Giovanni asked.

"Nico and Cecilia took her to the beach. I told Cecilia to take the camera and get some pictures of her today for me. I can see her play in the sand."

Giovanni stepped toward the open doors of the belvedere. "I've asked Carmella to bring up lunch. So we can eat together."

"That was nice of you." Mira observed her husband. "Is there something on your mind, Giovanni?" She got the impression he wanted to talk. But every time he broached whatever weighed on his heart he found a way to retreat from the discussion. "Is it the babies? Something else I don't know?"

He looked over to her. "Not with the babies. I've told you everything. There is something that I've recently learned. I want to explain it to you."

"Okay," Mira nodded.

"But it's hard news to share. Can I ask you to give me the next few weeks? To work through it and when my sons are born and you're all are out of danger we'll have a long talk. Really talk," he said without taking a breath.

"If you need the time to work through it then I am concerned. There is nothing you can't talk to me about here and now, Giovanni," she replied.

"I don't want you stressed," he said.

"Yes, I understand. Stress is off the menu. Believe me I know how hard it is to talk about your business. I just want you to know I'm your wife and you can tell me anything. Especially now with me stuck up here in bed. I'd welcome the conversation."

He walked around the bed. She moved her legs a bit for him to sit down. "Who says you have to stay up here in bed? Huh?" he asked, giving her a kiss on her nose. "What if I carry you downstairs to the television room. We watch a movie together? Have lunch in front of the television?" he teased.

"Can I pick the movie?" she grinned.

"Anything you want, Bella," he touched her belly. "I'll do anything to make this better for you, Bella."

"Then let's do it." She cheered. "Let's get the pregnant lady out of the room!"

* B *

It was the fourth dress shop they visited. Immediately when she entered the doors she suffered a bought of claustrophobia. Standers occupied all available space in the boutique. Once she and Catalina moved past them, deeper into the boutique, she understood the wait. A showroom with designer rack rejects was packed tight with anxious shoppers while many waited their turn. There were so many people stuffed inside yanking on clothes and then tossing them to the store sales clerks to find the right fit it was hard to see the clothes. Madness.

"Where the hell are we?" Marietta shouted over the noisy chorus of yelling shoppers.

"Down in *viale della Libertà* at *Francesca's*! You Americans call this place 'free spirit' " Catalina yelled back as she elbowed through.

"Never heard of it!" Marietta yelled back. She remained close. It was apparent Catalina knew where to go, but if they didn't reach their destination soon she'd scream.

"Of course not!" Catalina yelled back with a laugh. "Follow me!"

A tall lean woman with blue black hair that had blunt bangs over deep set brown eyes shouted in Italian at Catalina. Marietta looked up to see the woman waving them through. Catalina reached back and clasped Marietta's hand and she soon knew why. They were pulled hard through the crowd nearly knocking over several women. It was crazy. After reaching the woman they were ushered into a room and the door closed.

Marietta could at last catch her breath. The women embraced and spoke fast in Sicilian. Marietta could only catch a few words. Turns out from what she could tell Catalina and the lady were related, or considered each other family. Marietta looked around the office. All around were swaths of fabric and sewing material.

"Francesca," Catalina turned and grinned at Marietta. *"Posso presentarle la signora Marietta Battaglia!"*

The woman couldn't mask her confusion. Catalina had just introduced her as a Battaglia.

"Non capisco?" Francesca replied that she didn't understand.

Marietta extended her hand and told the woman in Italian that she was Lorenzo's wife. They had just married. The woman's eyes stretched. Her mouth gaped. Marietta braced for an insult but the lady released such a gust of laughter that Marietta smiled. She then charged Marietta and hugged her neck.

"Congratulazioni!" The woman cheered.

"Grazie! Millie grazie!" Marietta said overwhelmed by the sincerity.

"Francesca isn't like the rest of them. She's married to an African!" Catalina grinned. Marietta's brows lifted. She knew Catalina meant nothing by it. Francesca grinned in agreement with Catalina.

"I. Speak. English," she said pointing to herself. "I. Am. Coooo-zin to Giovanni and Lorenzo!"

Marietta nodded.

The woman hugged her again and Marietta shook her head smiling. Francesca informed them that the day had been crazy since she announced the shipment of *Mirabella's* clothes to the community. The women were lined up to get their hands on the designer originals. She thanked Catalina for giving her the business and went behind the desk to get a small gift wrapped in pretty pink paper. "For the *bambina* and *Donna*," Francesca nodded.

"*Prego.* I'll give it to her." Catalina kissed Francesca.

The women went around the desk to discuss the next delivery and Francesca whispered some additional wishes and concerns to Catalina. Marietta felt a bit charged. She never considered the sense of self-confidence she felt when visiting these dressmakers as a Battaglia woman. At first they'd ignore her or cast her a dismissive look. And always Catalina would introduce her as Lorenzo's wife. Immediately the attitude would change. It was an air of importance she never truly had in her prior life.

The business between the women concluded. Marietta loathed making her way back out of the door.

"*Piacere di fare la sua conoscenza,*" Francesca said she was glad to meet her and hurried over to Marietta. Before she could respond the woman hugged her again. "*Mia Dio!*" Francesca took Marietta's face in her hands. "She looks like the *Donna*," Francesca glanced back at Catalina. "Do you see it?" she asked.

Marietta wasn't sure what to say. Catalina just stared at Marietta and didn't respond. Francesca laughed. "*Lei mi è molto simpatico!*" she kissed Marietta on both cheeks and told her she liked her very much.

"*Ciao,*" Marietta said looking to be released from the uncomfortable assessment.

"*A più tardi,*" Catalina said as she kissed Francesca on both sides of her cheeks. Together Marietta and Catalina braved the crowds to elbow their way out of the store. Leonardo smoked a hand rolled cigarette outside on the street. He looked up when they emerged from the front doors of the boutique. Behind the dark lens of his sunglasses his stare remained fixed on them. He tracked their every move in and out of the stores. Smoking a cigarette was the first time she saw him take a break. It felt weird to have a shadow for the simple task of shopping. However, Catalina prattled on as if Leonardo didn't exist.

"How about we eat? I know a great place. *Benissima!*" Catalina emphasized her point by kissing her pinched fingers and gesturing to the sky. "On my life, they have the best food in Palermo. The cook is a family friend."

"I suppose." Marietta agreed. Though she tired of being a tag-a-long she knew the alternative was the mundane existence at Villa

Mare Blu. They started up the smoothly worn cobblestone street together. The shade of the joined three story buildings with medieval architecture along the narrow alley veered obliquely left casting her in the sparse sunlight. She looked down at herself and how she was dressed. Maybe she should have reconsidered her attire.

"It's just around the corner," Catalina pointed.

"Okay," Marietta said. She noticed a few people, men mostly, step out of their stores to stare at her and Catalina as they walked up the street. At first she ignored the stares but soon it became hard to. "Did I miss something? Why are people staring at us like this?"

Catalina chuckled. "You are in Mancini territory. They are really staring at me."

"Why?" Marietta asked.

"Let's talk about it over a glass of wine," Catalina smiled. She gestured for her to go to the restaurant with sidewalk seating to the left. Marietta was the first to step inside. It was quaint and noisy but the smell from the kitchen had a smell and heat to it that made her stomach muscles clench with spasms of hunger.

"Catalina!" A woman said. Startled Marietta stepped aside as a short round-bellied woman pushed through the diners and rushed over to greet them. The woman kissed and hugged Catalina to the point of squeezing her too tight.

"Prego!" the woman then said to Marietta.

Marietta smiled her response.

The woman then solely focused on Catalina. *"Come sta la sua famiglia?"* she asked.

"The family is good, Belina. Thank you for asking. We are all very good. And Giovanni sends his love," Catalina smiled.

"I hear we have twins coming? *Bambinos!"* Belina exclaimed.

"We do." Catalina winked.

"Ah! Saints be praised!" The woman clapped. She stared at Marietta curiously. Catalina again made the same introduction she had done earlier. Belina's eyes stretched. She laughed. "Lorenzo! He is just like Giovanni, no?" she said.

Marietta didn't get the comparison but Catalina chuckled.

"Come." The short lady started for the back of the restaurant. She pulled Catalina by the hand. Marietta and their bodyguard-chauffeur followed. Together they climbed a narrow stairwell barely wide enough for one person. At the top of the stairs they entered another dining area. This one wasn't as crowded. The few diners were all men. Several gave respectful nods to Catalina and others leered from their tables. A few watched them with scowls to their faces and said nothing.

"Here... have a seat. I have something special for you both from my oven." Belina announced. A young boy arrived with a wooden cantor and wine glasses. He poured dark wine into their glasses and filled them to the rim. Leonardo took a seat at the table next to them. He sat facing the men who kept cutting him deadly looks. He seemed unfazed by the tension. Marietta felt more jumpy than she ever had.

"Are we safe?" she whispered to Catalina.

"Huh? Oh them," Catalina laughed. "Trust me they know better."

"Where are we?" Marietta asked.

"I told you Mancini territory. This place is friendly to my brother, not the people, but the owners. That was Belina. She was a friend to my mother. And Ma-Ma didn't have many friends," Catalina said softly. Marietta looked over to the men staring at them. One of them with the darkest eyes lifted his glass and sneered at them. Catalina dismissed him and returned her gaze to Marietta. "Those men staring at us, they all work for Armando Mancini. He hates my brother."

"I thought the *Don*'s name was Marsuvio?" Marietta asked.

Catalina's eyes stretched. "You've heard of him?"

The slip was unintentional. Over and over Lorenzo warned her to not speak, but to listen and observe. Today her curiosity got the best of her. What she knew of the *Don* and Capriccio was very little but intriguing. It hurt deeply that there was nothing she could find to tie the man to her mother. "I heard Lorenzo mention him," she answered.

"Oh," Catalina said. "Well Armando Mancini is his son. He runs the family. I believe his father is ill. Either way, he and my brother have a truce. They've had it for years. Those assholes won't harm us."

Marietta let her gaze sweep the men. A few met her stare. One winked. All of them had the same dangerous aura that drew her to Lorenzo. She sipped her wine, cleared her throat and spoke. "So you were going to explain why people stared at us on the walk over? If there is a truce between the Battaglias and Mancinis why do I get the feeling that we aren't wanted?"

Catalina chuckled. "You will have to learn to live with that feeling. Whether we are here or in Sorrento you will get stares, and a few scowls. It comes with the life."

"Mafia?" Marietta asked.

"What do you know about our family?" Catalina asked.

"That you're in the mafia. That your brother is the *Don* and my husband is one of his hired guns I think."

"The *Don* huh?" Catalina grinned. "Is that what you think he is?"

"Of course. Isn't he?" Marietta glanced around. Where was the joke in all of this? It was evident the man wasn't the leader of the boy scouts.

Catalina leaned forward. "The *Mafioso* is birthed from Sicilians. My father is Sicilian. My mother is Irish. That makes me and Giovanni mix-breeds."

"Mix breeds? Are you kidding?" Marietta laughed.

"I'm serious. He could never be a *Don* of the *Mafioso*. But he can be boss of all bosses of the *Camorra*. And trust me the *Camorra* makes the *Mafioso* look like toddlers." Catalina sipped her vino. "My brother is the first *capo di tutti capi* in the *Camorra* in sixty years. Not even my father had as long of a reach as Gio."

"So he is the *Don* and boss, right?" Marietta asked.

"Yes. Think of him as both and the two aren't the same." Catalina nodded.

"They sound the same." Marietta replied.

"No. The *Don* of the *Mafioso* runs a single family, a region, and his reign is rarely challenged by the men in his *famiglia*. Traditionally his sons are the future, and their sons. If the family dies, then another family may take years to establish the respect he has gained. The *Camorra* isn't just one family. It consists of family clans. In the *Camorra* you have a boss and he is respected but replaceable. No clan boss is higher than another. And if he is the *boss of all bosses* he must be the fiercest, most ruthless of them all. Giovanni has earned the right to be both. And that is why they stare at us. They stare because I 'the half-breed' and you 'the black American woman' are from a *famiglia* able to command respect where we go only because of the blood my brother has shed," She tossed her chin a little higher. "We are Battaglia. We are the alpha and the omega."

"You say all of this with so much pride," Marietta said without judgment. "How does your faith fit in with this?"

Catalina smiled. "Everyone is given a path in life. God chose mine at birth. I have no problem with my faith or my lifestyle. To me one can't exist without the other."

"Well that doesn't make me feel better. In fact it only confirms that we are in danger in here," Marietta whispered.

Catalina laughed. "Possibly. There is always danger. But we

don't live our lives according to it. I've made this trip many times with no trouble. We're safe. Trust me."

For some reason Marietta doubted Princess' confidence. It seemed like she purposefully walked into the lion's den. Possibly to make sure her Prince learned of her actions and would react with concern. Hell Marietta has played those games before with men she wanted to tame. She knew how to piss a man off, or at the very least get a reaction. Maybe staying at Villa Mare Blu was the best.

Food arrived. Marietta's mouth watered.

"*Focaccia* is the very best here. Belina makes it so it melts in your mouth." Catalina pointed at the hot bread roll filled with meat, cheese and onions. "Because it's close to summer she's given us a taste of *alfresco* too. Yummy!"

Marietta chuckled. After three glasses of wine all flavors exploded on her tongue. She ate voraciously. Stopping to comment on one thing then another. Swallowing and stuffing her face some more.

"Hungry?" Catalina asked amused.

"It's good," she said with an embarrassed smile.

Catalina nodded her head in agreement. "I told you!"

Marietta learned a lot from Catalina about the young girl's life in the family of men. She also learned about Lorenzo's likes and dislikes. Especially when it came to cooking. For instance Marietta never knew that he hated fruity dishes. She hadn't made any and couldn't recall him ever eating any fruit when around her.

"I'm allergic to mushrooms," Marietta volunteered.

"Really!" Catalina exclaimed. "So is the *Donna*. They make her ill. She told me once she got really sick as a child when she ate a pizza with them on it."

"Oh my God! I gag as soon as they come in my mouth." Marietta shivered. "Guess she and I have more in common than I thought." Marietta smiled. She downed the last of the wine. "Where's the bathroom?"

"Downstairs, to the back of the restaurant. And dn't be alarmed but Leonardo will go with you." Catalina shrugged. "You get used to him after a while."

"What about you, up here alone? With them?" Marietta looked over to a few men now drinking and laughing.

Catalina smiled. "Trust me. I'm *la picolletta*." She tossed a challenging look toward a table of men. "They wouldn't dare."

Marietta liked her style. Catalina had an edge to her that reminded her of some of the hard chicks she used to run the streets of the south side of Chicago with before she ran away for good. She pushed back her chair and stood. When she did, so did the tall brooding bodyguard that shadowed them. Marietta picked up her purse and started to walk toward the exit. A man to the left said her pussy smelled like chocolate. He thought because he said it in his native tongue she wouldn't understand.

She leveled her glare. "Your breath reminds me of shit!" She shot back in Italian.

The others at his table roared with laughter. The man's stare darkened and his face flushed pink with rage. When Marietta looked back Catalina raised her glass in a mock toast. Marietta descended the stairs and headed to the back of the restaurant with a bit more confidence. Hell Lorenzo was her man. She had nothing to be afraid of.

She found the bathroom to be more than just a private one. There were several stalls and a separate room for changing. Odd to see such a layout in such a quaint place. She wasted no time locating an empty stall to go in and relieve herself. She wiped and flushed. The manic urge to release had now passed. When she left the stall she found herself alone in the bathroom. So she took the time to adjust her skirt and her halter-top. She then washed her hands.

The door opened behind her.

Marietta turned off the tap and lifted her eyes to the mirror. "Gemma? What the hell are you doing here?"

Gemma grabbed her by the hand and dragged her to the closest stall. She forced her inside and closed the door. She looked frazzled, her cinnamon hair loose about her face, perspiration dotting the top of her brow and lip. She wore a green dress and sweater which didn't really suit the warm summer weather.

"We don't have much time," Gemma said, or rather panted.

"What's wrong—" Marietta was silenced when Gemma's hand went up abruptly over her mouth. Startled her eyes stretched. Gemma leaned in close to whisper her words.

"You married him. How could you? After I told you not to trust him."

Marietta forced her hand off her mouth. "How did you know I was here? What are you doing in Sicily?" she demanded.

"I can't believe you married him!" Gemma said in a hushed angry tone.

"I wanted to call you. I couldn't find you. I love Lorenzo. You're wrong about him." Marietta hugged her neck.

"Listen to me." She brought down Marietta's arms. Her eyes

bordered with tears, her nose was red as if she had indeed been crying. "You're in danger. This is my fault. Forgive me," Gemma wept.

"Okay you're scaring me," Marietta said.

"It's time you know the truth about the Battaglias," Gemma said.

"What is the truth?" Marietta asked.

"Lorenzo lies to you. He knows who your father is and what happened to your mother. All the lies are connected to Giovanni's wife."

"His wife?" Marietta couldn't digest the information. "Mirabella?"

"Yes! Mirabella. She's your sister!"

Marietta double blinked. She wasn't sure she heard her right. "Are you insane?"

"Dammit, Marietta! Damn it! I can't explain it to you here." Gemma opened her purse. She forced a letter into Marietta's hand. "Take this. Read this. It has everything in it. My number is in there. Promise you will call me tonight? So I can help you get out of there."

"I don't believe you," Marietta said. She pushed the letter hard on Gemma.

"Take the letter damn it! Have I ever lied to you? Ever?" Gemma asked.

"Yes you have. By saying Capriccio was my father when it's evident you knew more! And I've met Giovanni Battaglia's wife. She's not my sister. It's not possible." Marietta said. She found it hard to breathe and speak at the same time. And then the deepening despair deadened all of her faculties. She couldn't speak, move, or do anything to defend the attack on her heart. She stood there like stone as Gemma berated her.

"Yes. She. Is." Gemma said again, slow and precisely. "You two are twins. You were separated and then kept apart by a conspiracy that traces all the way back to here. Sicily. The letter explains it. And the proof of what I'm telling you is at Villa Mare Blu. Mirabella should have it. Read the damn letter." Once again the letter was placed in Marietta's hand. She didn't reject it this time. How could she? Gemma left her like that in the bathroom. Staring at the letter she felt a strange almost melancholy type of emotion and then an ineffable sense of sadness descended on her. Marietta walked out of the bathroom stall in a trance. She forced the letter into her purse with shaky hands.

The walk back to Catalina was the hardest of her life. With every step she processed the truth from the fiction that had been her life. Marietta was never one for restraint or discipline. She had to employ both to keep from bolting out of the restaurant doors to run down Gemma and demand a reason for the hurtful lies. Lorenzo betrayed her? *Bullshit!* Mirabella Battaglia is her long lost twin? *Bullshit! Bullshit! Bullshit!* What was Gemma's angle with all of this?

"You okay? I thought you had fell in?" Catalina asked.

"I'm fine." Marietta sat. She hoped her smile was convincing. It was hard to maintain it with bile rising in her throat. Marietta tried to steady her breathing. "On second thought I don't feel well. Do you mind if we leave? Besides Lo is supposed to call me to tell me he arrived."

"Aww... and I was just having some fun with you," Catalina said. She winked. "I'm kidding." She scooted from the table and rose. Marietta did the same. She barely saw or heard anything on their way out. Catalina stopped a few times to speak to people as if she were a celebrity. Marietta kept her hand on her purse and her eyes on the door.

Outside of the restaurant she took down deep breaths to fill her lungs with air. Still she felt like she couldn't breathe. She bit hard on her lip to keep her tears of doubt at bay.

Marietta had known Gemma since she was a baby. A family friend who always helped her endure the smothering love of her adoptive mother and physical and verbal abuse of her adoptive father. Gemma was family. When Marietta was a teen Gemma shared that she met her mother, only briefly. She gave her the baby bracelet and told her of Capriccio. Gemma had been the true constant in her life. She wouldn't lie to her. But she had to be. Because what she said made no sense.

"You're quiet," Catalina said, as they drove out of Palermo.

"Am I?" Marietta tossed back with casual ease. The truth was her body was tensed all over to read the letter inside her purse. It was a physical pain.

"You sure you okay?" Catalina asked.

"I am. I have a question. Ah, is Mir, uh, the *Donna*, is she adopted?" Marietta asked.

"Adopted? No. She was raised by her grandparents."

"Really?" Marietta's voice cracked with emotion. Repressed tears kept clouding her vision. She put on her sunglasses to cover them. "Where is her mother, her father?"

274

Catalina dropped her head back and her brow furrowed as if she were thinking it over. "Her father? Hmm? I never heard her speak of him. I think Gio said he was dead. I think. But she told me her mother died when she was a baby. Her mother was a drug addict."

"What?" Marietta's fist clenched. "Dead? Drugs? You sure?"

"Yes." Catalina nodded. "She doesn't talk of them. But she has this bracelet. A really sweet baby bracelet that her mother gave her and it has her name on it."

"No. That's not true." Marietta said. "It's not!"

"Huh?" Catalina frowned. "What's not true?"

"Nothing. Sorry, my head hurts." Marietta put her forehead in her palm with her elbow resting on the door. "Tell me about this bracelet? What did she say about it?"

"She didn't say anything about it. I was the one that told her about the weirdness."

"What's weird?" Marietta asked.

"It has a stamp of Del Stavio's signature on the clasp. But it couldn't be his insignia." Catalina waved it off.

"Why is that?" Marietta mumbled with concealed restraint.

"Oh, just because. Remember what I told you about the *Mafioso*? How each *Don* has *famiglia* rule? Well there were five *dons* of *Sicilia*. They pretty much lorded over this island from coast to coast. Like a five-point-star. Mancini is one of them. Del Stavio was the jeweler to the *Dons*. He would not have made the bracelet for an American child. A non-Sicilian. And Mira says America is known for counterfeits."

It was the last straw. The innocent truth stripped her raw. Marietta broke down in tears. Alarmed Catalina reached out and touched her. "Are you well?"

"Get your fucking hands off me!" she shouted at Catalina. "Don't fucking touch me!"

Shocked Catalina obliged. Marietta slammed the side of her fist against the door. *She had to keep it together. She had to. There was an explanation. A reasonable one. There had to be.* She wiped at her tears. Biting her lip to control her sob she managed to gain a sliver of control over her heartache, enough to speak. "I'm sorry. Please forgive me. I'm so sorry. I... when I..." she couldn't find the words to explain any of her conflict.

Catalina braved another touch. She grabbed Marietta's hand. This time Marietta held hers in return. She squeezed it. Even if they wore the same bracelet, or were both American, they weren't sisters let alone twins. If she had a twin she would have known it. Felt it.

Wouldn't she? After a long scenic drive they returned to Villa Mare Blu. The women travelled the entire trip in silence while holding hands.

"Are you sure you will be okay? If you aren't—"

"I'm good," Marietta said. She glanced over to Catalina and squeezed her hand. She was thankful for the friendship. Surprised by it. And heartsick over what she struggled to accept as truth. "I had a bit of anxiety. I have it sometimes."

"So does the *Donna*. Another thing you two have in common," Catalina smiled.

Marietta shook her head, unable to stand it much longer. She flung the car door open and grabbed her bags to hurry away. She had to get to her room. Calm down. Think it through. Find out what was truth and what was coincidence. She fast walked through the front of the house and was surprised that Catalina caught up. They turned the corner and started down the hall. Marietta wasn't sure if Catalina followed her or not. All she knew was that she had to escape.

When they passed the entertainment room Marietta slowed her steps to look inside. Mirabella looked up. She sat on a L-shaped red leather sofa with her feet stretched out over her husband's lap. She waved and smiled. "Hey you two! Did you have fun? Come tell me about it!"

Marietta stared at her. For the first time she truly saw Mirabella. A face though several shades darker than hers mirrored her. And eyes of the same color stared back at her. Marietta's gaze swiveled over to the *Don* who met her stare. The cold hard look he gave her was like a tumble of ice cubes down her spine. His shirt was unbuttoned at the top. He massaged his wife's feet. His violet blue eyes didn't shift or leave her. Maybe women found his unique eye color attractive. In that moment they looked like the eyes of the devil. She tried to swallow the lump that lingered in her throat. Her instinct was to attack them both with her knowledge, or flee.

Fight or run. Fight or run. Fight or run.

"Marietta? Are you okay?" Mirabella asked with serious concern.

Her emotional conflict both jagged and painful made her act. She fled.

Catalina watched Marietta storm off. "That one is strange."

"What happened?" Mira asked. "She looked like she'd been crying."

"She has!" Catalina walked in. She dropped her bags by the

sofa. She looked to the television. "Who is playing?"

"Wait!" Mira dismissed the soccer game. "What is wrong with Marietta?"

"Calm down, Bella. It's not your business," Giovanni said.

"Catalina?" Mira insisted. "What's wrong with her?"

"Sick. Said her stomach hurts or something. She then started crying about it in the car. Like a baby." Catalina shrugged her shoulders.

"Go get Carmella, have her fix her something. Make sure she is okay," Mira said as if she were going to rise. Giovanni stopped her. Catalina rolled her eyes. She was not about to chase down Carmella. She was exhausted. Besides she had resisted the urge all day to keep from crying herself. "She's fine, Mira. She wanted to lie down. I'll have Carmella check on her in a minute." Catalina yawned.

Her reply settled Mira. The Argentinians scored and Giovanni cursed loudly.

Catalina plopped down on the sofa. "What's the score?"

* B *

Marietta shut the door to her room. She braced her back against the door and dragged down deep gulps of air. Her eyes brimmed with tears of frustration. Her lips clamped down on the sob that shook her entire body. Marietta closed her eyes shaking her head no.

"Marietta?"

Frightened to paralysis, her only option was to hug her knees and pray to disappear. She kept her face buried and eyes tightly squeezed shut. Her butt hurt and the back of her thighs stung with heat and pain from her spanking. She was only four. The beating her father gave her was the meanest she could recall.

"Marietta it's me, come out please." A soft voice whispered close enough for her to know her hiding spot had been found. She lifted her eyes above her knees. The closet was her punishment. She was sometimes locked away for hours in it. But her father had forgot to lock her in this time. She escaped and hid in the toy chest in her room. For her mother to come for her so soon had to be because her father was gone or asleep from too much drinking.

"Mama?" Marietta asked.

"Yes, sweetheart." The lid to the chest lifted. "Come out. Come..." her mother reached in for her.

Marietta raised her arms and was lifted out of her safety zone.

277

She had soiled herself. Surely if her father knew he'd punish her again. He was so angry that she knocked over his chess pieces when she bumped the table while chasing her puppy. Her mother swept her into her arms and brought her to her breasts. "Chiedo scusa. Sono molto dispiaciuta. I'm so sorry I can't protect you," she wept.

Marietta clung to the only mother she'd ever known. "Why does Daddy hate me?"

"It's your mother's fault. Your real mother," Teresa Leone said. Marietta could not process the news that she had another mother who cursed her with brown skin and the rage of her father. Her face lifted from her mother's breast. "Your other mother was an evil woman. He thinks you have that evilness inside of you. Let's pray, Marietta. Pray that you don't. Pray that your father can forgive."

"I want to pray so he won't hurt me any more," she said through her tears.

Teresa kissed her brow and lifted her to her arms. They would go to her mother's room and get on their knees and pray. And maybe this time things would be better. Maybe her father would love her.

"No. No. No. No." Marietta said through tears. "She's not dead. Please God. All I ever asked you for was my mother. My mother!" she wept. "She's not dead!" Marietta, blinded by grief, raced over to the bed and yanked so hard on the sheer drape that surrounded it she ripped half of drape off the rings. She yanked on the covers on the bed, knocked a lamp off the nightstand. Turned over a chair. Like a madwoman she trashed the room until she dropped to her knees crying.

"Gemma!" Marietta ran to the front of the house. She leapt at Gemma grinning. And her godmother nearly caught her. "I've missed you so much!" Marietta said, she hugged her neck tight.

"Look at you. Ten years old?"

Marietta nodded. "My birthday was last week."

Gemma smiled. "And I have a present for you."

Before Marietta could claim it Gemma greeted Teresa and embraced the woman. Marietta waited impatiently as they addressed her father. Anyone who came to visit them had to address Octavio first. Gemma traveled in from Italy, so of course the conversation would take forever. Marietta lingered by the adults until her mother gave her a warning look to stay away. She sighed and returned to her room. The last thing she wanted was to anger her father. He'd been in a good mood for over a week because of a bonus. But his drinking could backfire on the family happiness.

Marietta picked up her favorite doll and sat on the bed. She looked around the room at her toys and dolls. Many girls her age had moved on from playing with them. Not her. She loved to play make believe. The dolls were her friends, someone she could tell her secrets to. She wished she had a sister or a friend to play with, but her adoptive mother couldn't have children and her father wouldn't allow people in the house. She wished she could run away and find her real mother. She knew her mother couldn't return because of her father. She wondered if her mother knew she was forced to live here with the mean bastard. Her imagination left her pondering many things.

"Knock knock!" Gemma said, after knocking she came inside. "Ciao, cara mia!"

"Gemma," Marietta grinned.

"What are you doing in here alone? Hiding from me, eh?"

"Just thinking. Tell me what you brought me for my birthday?" Marietta asked.

Gemma came over and sat next to her on the bed. Marietta's heart raced with excitement. "I've kept something for you. Something special. I think it's time you have it."

"Really? What?"

"I never really knew your birth mother, Marietta, I only met her a few times. But I can tell you she did love you," Gemma said and stroked the side of her face. "So much, Marietta. More than any little girl can be loved."

"She did?" Marietta asked.

"Sí, cara, she did. And she asked that I give you something." Gemma opened her purse. She removed a black pouch. "Now, no one can ever see this. Keep it hidden. Promise me."

"I promise, Gemma."

Gemma dumped the gold bracelet into her palm. Marietta lifted it up and saw the engraving. "It's beautiful. But it's for a child."

"It comes from Sicilia. From a special jeweler."

"Really," Marietta repeated.

"See here, this is his stamp," Gemma showed her. "He only made something this special for special little ones. Like you. Do you know what Marietta means in Italian?"

"No? What does it mean?" Marietta asked.

"The bitter one," Gemma smiled.

Marietta frowned. "But bitter means bad?"

Gemma lifted her chin. *"Sweetheart, bitter does not have that meaning when given to a child from God. A sweet little baby that was desperately desired carries your name. Bitter means that the young girl will grow to be courageous and determined with an iron will and spirit. It means there is a duality that lives in you, Marietta. Lives here."* She pointed at her heart.

"Duality?" Marietta blinked. *"What does that word mean?"*

"You will grow up to be two women not one. It means that part of you will be adventurous, altruistic, and extremely sensitive to the needs of those you love."

"And the other part of me? The other woman that lives in me, what will she be?" Marietta asked.

"Life will teach you to be secretive, cautious and careful with others. You will learn after growing up here with the Leones how to protect yourself by appreciating solitude with a critical mind." Gemma tapped her head for emphasis. *"That is your duality and you will persevere—bitterly. Your name shows your spirit for rebellion. Your mother believed you would be the fighter of the two."*

"Two? What two?" Marietta asked.

"Did I say two?" Gemma gave her a nervous laugh. *"I meant you would be the strongest of us all."*

"But why would my mother give me an Italian name?" Marietta stood. *"Isn't she black? That's what they all say. My mother was a black whore who had an affair with Octavio. Why would she give me an Italian name when they talk about her so badly?"*

Gemma looked away. *"Your father. You know this."*

"Octavio Leone is not my father!" Marietta said. She glared at Gemma. *"I can never believe he is. I dream that someone else is, all the time. He hates me. And I hate him!"*

"Shhh," Gemma put her finger to her lips. *"Stop it now. Of course he's your father. He's a mean bastard but he takes care of you and this family. He protects you, Marietta. There are men in this world far meaner than Octavio. Trust me!"* Gemma said.

Marietta smiled down at the bracelet. She kissed it. Some day she'd find her mother. Some day they'd be reunited again.

Marietta paced the floor. The truth she sought all her life threatened to crush in on her from every direction she turned. She didn't believe her mother was some street junkie that died. She refused to believe that the woman who named her to be courageous, a warrior, had been nothing but a whore and slave to her own weakness. Mirabella wasn't her sister. And more importantly her man, the love of her life, her husband, had known all along and lied to her. *Bullshit!* Another strong jolt of pain seized her heart when she thought of Lorenzo. She couldn't know. She walked over to the phone that was now on the floor. She dropped to her knees and found the dial tone. She dialed Lorenzo's pager and put in the code he gave her. A code she was only to use in case of extreme emergency.

She needed him.

She needed him desperately.

12.

Yerevan City, Armenia

Lorenzo's pager buzzed in his pocket. He tossed his luggage in the back of the car and reached in his trouser pocket to retrieve it. The code '888' was Marietta's. Eight was a sexy number, full of curves, that's why he gave it to his lady. The page was an emergency flare from his bride. One he told her to never use unless it was damn important. And she would use it just five hours after he last saw her? He shook his head with mild amusement. "Damn woman. I miss her too."

"Cosa c'è?" Carlo asked. He slammed down the trunk and walked around the car.

"Marietta. She wants me to call home." Lorenzo grinned.

Carlo snickered. "And so it begins. Will you be able to piss without asking for permission to hold your own dick?" he asked before climbing inside behind the wheel.

Lorenzo laughed and got in on the passenger side. He could give a shit about Carlo's taunts. He missed his wife too. They were newlyweds. She made it almost impossible for him to leave her bed. Lorenzo could still smell the sweet fragrance of Shalimar. He should have packed a bottle to take with him.

He had no time to find a phone to ring her back. The sooner they met with Alik Yeremian the better. "Drive into the city. Domi said Yeremian's men will meet us in front of the Katoghike church," Lorenzo instructed. He dropped the passenger seat back and slouched a bit to get comfortable for the drive. Immediately they encountered a traffic jam of honking motorists. Lorenzo removed his pager and stared at the number again. He knew Marietta was strong. He knew she was safe. But still to see the emergency number did give him pause.

Carlo glanced over and he could feel his stare. "You worried about her? Do you want me to find a phone?"

"She's there with Giovanni. He wouldn't do anything to harm her," Lorenzo said.

"He won't do anything to make her feel welcome either," Carlo said.

Lorenzo exhaled. "Have I put her in danger. Am I a fool, Carlo?"

"Truth?"

"Yes," Lorenzo said.

"You love her. And love makes any man a fool. I respect Gio but I'm with you on this, Lo. He needs to step aside and let the sisters know each other. I lost a brother. If I had done things differently with Carmine he'd be alive. I have to live with that. What you do for the *Donna* and Marietta is just."

The truth was very sobering. Lorenzo churned on it. "I regret what happened with Carmine. You do know that. Don't you?"

Carlo didn't answer. The pain for him must still be too raw. Lorenzo relaxed. The page from Marietta could only mean she was bored. He'd make it up to her later. "After we conclude our business we find the first thing out of this country." Lorenzo said.

"Strange, you and her. Never seen you like this." Carlo shrugged.

"Like you said, she's my heart. I won't fuck this up. Not her. Not this time. I learned my lesson with Fabiana. No one will hurt Marietta."

"She's different," Carlo said. "Different in a good way. I think she's perfect...uh, for you."

Lorenzo looked over to his friend. "You do?"

Carlo forced a half-smile. "Not easy to find a woman who can stand at your side. You and Gio are lucky to have these sisters. That's what I think."

Lorenzo laughed. "Since when do you have a soft spot for women?"

"I'm not a monster," Carlo grumbled.

"Says who? I know your ass. You've been a monster since you crawled out of your mother's snatch!" Lorenzo teased. When Carlo didn't laugh in response he stopped smiling. They were boys, only fifteen when a girl in the village accused Carlo of raping her. Lorenzo knew his friend didn't do it. Yes they loved their dicks but they never forced any girl into sex. No one believed Carlo. Not even Patri Tomosino. The girl only made the accusation because she was caught, and losing her virginity to a village boy like Carlo was blasphemous. She was a distant cousin of the Mancinis. Because of the accusation Mancini made sure Carlo was sent to a juvenile center until he was eighteen. Locked away for three years. When he came out he had changed, particularly his attitude toward women. Lorenzo saw the anger he flashed the other sex in an instant and ignored it. He watched over the years the trail of tears after Carlo seduced, romanced and quickly discarded girlfriends. It became an unstated rule amongst the men to never leave their woman alone with Carlo. That might be unfair, but behind every lie there is a little bit of truth. Besides Carlo's mother, sister and the women in the Battaglia family, Carlo showed no person of the opposite sex respect. It was the way it was.

"I'm kidding. You aren't a monster." Lorenzo said.

"Yeah, fuck you," Carlo mumbled making the lane change. Lorenzo relaxed. He'd deal with his Marietta later. They had business to conclude.

* B *

Marietta wept. She paced. She waited for the phone to ring. Lorenzo swore to her if she were ever in trouble she could page him. No matter the distance between them he made the sacred vow to protect her even from herself. And she vowed to do the same. Until death do they part.

After thirty minutes of waiting, pacing and waiting she was in a state of sheer panic. She needed to hear his voice. Tell him of the letter. Let him convince her not to read it. Trust him again. *But he hadn't called!* And the letter taunted her. Called her name.

To silence the doubts Marietta put her hands to her ears. "Stop!" she begged. But nothing stopped the voices in her head. The lies of Teresa Leone, Gemma, the nasty predictions from her so-called father that she'd be nothing but a whore like her mother. She shook her head hard to stop the voices.

"Please call me, Lo. Please." she wept.

Marietta dropped to her knees. He would call. He had to. He was all she had. And she sat there for thirty more minutes believing in him. After the last of her tears fell she knew a different truth. He would not save her, no one could. Marietta glanced to the letter on the bed. She stared at it. If she didn't read the letter she would be running again. If she did read it she could prove it was lies.

There was something else to consider. If the letter had been given to her by anyone other than Gemma she'd have tossed it in the trash. What was Gemma's angle? The bitch had more than enough opportunities to share this truth with her. Why confess it all to her now?

She sniffed, wiped her tears with a shaky hand. Catalina said Mirabella owned a bracelet like the one she's cherished. *Proof.* Gemma said that Mirabella possessed the evidence.

"No. No it's a lie." She shook her head hard. She felt her sanity slip. It was as if the darkness in her life was slowly winning. "Not true. It's not true," she said.

Someone knocked at the door. Marietta nearly jumped out of her skin. She wiped at her smeared mascara and managed to get to her feet. "Yes?" she answered.

"*Ciao!* The *Donna* asked that I check on you. Do you need anything?" a voice inquired.

"Go away!" Marietta shouted.

Whoever it was walked off. Marietta's gaze returned to the envelope. She looked away. "Call me, Lorenzo. Please, my love. Please," she said trying to hold on to some hope. She forced herself to wait.

* B *

Carlo stood outside of the car. Lorenzo remained inside. He watched the few pedestrians strolling along the sidewalk in front of the church. They'd been waiting for close to an hour. Yeremian was a friend of the family, but in their world the definition of friend was always shifting. With Mottola now trying to cut deals with the 'Ndrangheta and the Armenians, Lorenzo had to wonder if Alik was in on it. The meeting he'd asked for could be his last if Yeremian had decided so.

He opened his car door to tell Carlo his suspicions when two passenger vans arrived. They boxed him and Carlo in. A dark window with tinted glass rolled down. "Get in!" a man said.

Lorenzo and Carlo entered the vehicle without a word passing between them. The van sped off. Neither the man behind the wheel, nor the one on the passenger side spoke. Lorenzo glanced back to see the van following could have up to six or eight along for the ride. He glanced to Carlo. They exchanged a look to be ready no matter what was to come next.

There were brutal men and crime families across the globe and they've dealt with many. But the Armenians were different. They lived by a code unmatched by any other. Like the *Camorra* they had clans and clan bosses who ruled by regions. They were known as the 'Akhperutyuns'. Most of the clan bosses learned and organized the rules of their brotherhood in Russian and Turkish prison camps. Each clan could be recognized for their ruthless and often sadistic forms of torture. Having the Akhperutyuns as allies after Mottola's betrayal was a must. Having them as an enemy would be an entirely different matter.

They drove out of the city toward the mountains. Lorenzo reflected on his last visit and how many times he had put his life on the line for the family. Now he did care to live. He had someone to live for. It gave him a perspective he rarely accepted in his life. The silent buzz of his beeper in his pocket vibrated once more. He removed the pager to see it was Marietta.

He frowned with concern.

* B *

"Damn you!" Marietta yanked the phone from the wall and threw it across the room. "Damn you, Lorenzo-Asshole-Battaglia! Damn you to hell!" she yelled.

Marietta didn't care who heard her. The truth sank like a steel blade into her heart. Never had a betrayal of anyone in her life hurt so badly. Desperate for relief she marched over to the bed and threw herself on it. She rolled away and her eyes fastened to the letter. Marietta squeezed her eyes shut. To read it would only make her suffering worse. To ignore it would only prolong the inevitable. She sat up and snatched letter. Through a veil of tears she opened it.

Marietta,

When I learned you had arrived in Sicily I came. I've been in Milano for months waiting to hear from you. In my heart I knew this is where I would find you. I write this letter in haste to get the news to you. My prayer is you will believe and forgive me for all that I have kept from you.

I've closely guarded the secret of who you are for years. Not to hurt you, or deny you, but to protect you. I had hoped that what Capriccio and I did would keep you far away from the people who harmed your mother.

It has gone beyond that now.

First, I must confess who your mother is. Her name was Melissa Ellison. We called her Lisa. And yes, I lied to you, I knew her well before she died. The question I must answer for you is why I kept her identity a secret. Lisa was a sweet generous girl when I knew her. She hated and feared a man named Marsuvio Mancini. He was and still is an evil Sicilian monster who went by the name Manny Cigars. He terrorized many people in Philadelphia, black or white, it didn't matter. He stole your mother from her family and kept her with him for years. He put her on drugs. He raped and brutalized her until she had nothing in her life to hope for.

I first met your mother at a club Manny owned. She was a very shy, very nice girl. She had the voice of an angel. She used to sing, and sew costumes for us girls who did other things for Manny Cigars and his men. Until she gave birth to you and everything changed.

I'm sorry to tell you that she's dead. This is important for you to understand, Marietta. Your mother was murdered. A contract was put out on her life, yours, and your twin sister Mirabella Ellison. I'm sorry to have kept this from you. I was the one that helped hide Lisa from the Sicilians. I was the one that kept your identity secret along with your birth father. Capriccio and I only wanted to make sure that the Battaglias and Mancinis never knew you lived. Mirabella was given to her grandparents. She does not know she has a twin sister. She never knew her mother's story.

I know this is confusing. There is so much more to this story to tell. But for now you have to get out of Sicilia. You have to get away from these people. Don Giovanni knows who you are. Lorenzo Battaglia only married you to control you. He will kill you, Marietta. Please heed my warning.

If you doubt what I am saying then seek proof. Mirabella owned a bracelet. A childs' bracelet. I don't know if she keeps it still but she owned it at one time. Show her your necklace. Ask her the name of her mother. And then give her this letter. But leave.

Call me. I will help you Marietta. I swear it on my life.

Forgive me,
Gemma

Marietta turned the letter over and read the number scribbled on the back. There had been so many lies. All her life she had been lied to. And Gemma was now the queen of lies. How many times had she wept against her breast after suffering so much physical and mental

abuse from her adoptive father? How many times had she begged
Gemma to help her find her mother? What about the trip to Milano?
What about the hunt for a father by the name of Capriccio? What
about the fake birth certificate that sent her on a wild goose chase? A
lie. All orchestrated by Gemma way before she met Lorenzo.

She could trust no one.

Except Mirabella. Her sister was being deceived. Marietta
dropped over to the bed and closed her eyes. She clutched the letter
to her chest and wept.

* B *

Mountainous hamlets were accessible out of the city of Yerevan
through long winding unpaved roads. Most of the journey was a
bumping, jostling ride. Lorenzo swallowed his lunch and suppressed
the nausea of carsickness. They passed pastures of cows, and bulls
with horns herded by farmers. The remote location, decrepit living
shacks and thinning herds was a product of the villagers' descent
into poverty after the end of Soviet rule.

Men like Alik Yeremian lived in the impoverished terrain, such
as, Khoznavar like Kings while those around them suffered. Alik's
legitimate business doled out machinery and farm animals to the
villagers to produce milk, cheese, and sour cream to be sold and
profited upon by him solely. The villagers' were only able to scrape
by with feeding their families.

The stone houses that peppered the landscape were small and
unassuming. When they arrived at the tall gates of Yeremian's
private territory men with guns flagged them in. They drove in to
progress on a newly paved circular drive. A prosperous three-story
mansion greeted them. The gates to the old brick fort, which guarded
such a lascivious monument to wealth was once again sealed.

"Alik has done well for himself," Carlo whispered.

Lorenzo nodded with worry. He wondered if Giovanni realized
the extent of Alik's prosperity. "I'll do the talking," Lorenzo said in
a voice barely above a whisper.

Carlo shrugged. He was a man of few words. In an engagement
such as this it was always Lorenzo's wits over Carlo's brawn.

Lorenzo opened his car door and left the vehicle. Two armed
men greeted him, their guns leveled. He put up his hands as a third
approached. He was searched for a gun or weapon. They found
none. He and Carlo could not arm themselves properly on this

impromptu trip. If they entered Turkey or Armenia with a weapon and were caught the consequences would be grave. So he allowed the search without complaint.

The man grunted in his native tongue for Lorenzo to follow. He did. Carlo was held back. This did give Lorenzo pause. He didn't want to be separated.

"Parev Lorenzo! Intcbess es?" A voice boomed above. Alik stood at the top of the grey marble stairwell with his arms open in greeting. Alik Yeremian was at least five to six years older than Lorenzo. He was plainly dressed in green pleated baggy trousers a grey button down shirt and sneakers. "When Giovanni called and requested this visit I had hoped that he would accompany you." Alik bounded down the steps with his hands shoved down into his trouser pant pockets.

"Giovanni sends his regrets," Lorenzo said. He embraced Alik and smiled. "What is with the welcome party?" Lorenzo half-chuckled at the others flanking him with guns. "Are the Battaglias no longer welcome in Armenia?"

"Trouble." Alik replied. "I have to be careful these days. Come. Let's talk." Alik dropped his arm around his shoulder. They walked off toward the left wing of the estate. The room they entered had all kinds of military monitoring equipment, and weaponry as if it were a command post for a small army. Lorenzo frowned.

"Now you have me curious, Alik. What trouble are you facing?"

"The same trouble at your door. A group of rebels who follow a man named Varo. He has started his own clan in the Akhperutyun in an attempt to overthrow me. He has ties now to the *Camorra* I'm told. This I learned after Giovanni informed me about his concerns over Mottola. So you see my concern."

Lorenzo exhaled. "Let me guess? Mottola wants to arm Varo in his fight against you."

"Ayo. And I hear he's already done so. Men of mine have fallen thanks to the *Camorra*." Alik walked away. "How does any of this happen on Giovanni's watch?"

Lorenzo's gut clenched. Behind him a shadow drew closer. Lorenzo felt rather than saw the approaching danger. A man, possibly with a gun, drew closer. If the word was given a bullet would be launched into the back of Lorenzo's skull. Alik's friendly smile had been replaced with a malevolent glare. There were only seconds left to turning the conversation around. Lorenzo's jaw went rigid tight, which made his voice stiff and unrepentant. "It has not gone unnoticed by Giovanni I assure you. Which is why I'm here. Mottola is one of the few clan bosses in the Neapolitan with an ego bigger than his might. Can you name a Battaglia who has helped him?"

Alik shook his head slowly no.

"I intend to get to the bottom of it."

Alik didn't appear convinced. The hard glare in his coal black irises made the hairs on Lorenzo's nape stand on end. He couldn't trust the situation further. If the Battaglias were tied to arming a rebel faction in the Akhperutyun, Alik had a right to be leery of them.

"How shall we prove it?"

"Prove it?" Alik smirked. "Why prove anything if you are not guilty?"

"The guns are Giovanni's. They come from his bay. We intend to rectify this matter. Prove our allegiance. Regain your trust. Stop Varo so we can bag our common enemy, Mottola. All I need to know is where to find this man?"

Alik laughed. He gave a look to the assassin behind Lorenzo and the person drew away. Lorenzo resisted the urge to glance back over his shoulder to be sure the threat was gone. Alik began to pace with his hands clasped behind his back. "We haven't been able to find the hole he scurries to. He and his men are constantly on the move near the mountains. The desert rat hides beyond my reach."

Lorenzo smiled. "Because he knows you search for him. If he is working with *Camorra* wouldn't he be willing to let us in the door that is closed to you?"

Alik stopped his pacing. A light of understanding flashed in his eyes. "It is dangerous to play this game here, Lorenzo. The republic is on the hunt for the Akhperutyuns. I cannot protect you. Nor am I inclined to risk the lives of my men."

"I assume all risk," Lorenzo stated.

"Yes. You will. Because if you fail we shall have another discussion. Are we clear?"

"We are." Lorenzo agreed.

Alik's gaze swept him. "What do you propose?"

"To take his head. We only ask for a way out of this country when the job is done."

Alik stroked his beard. "We have been friends for many years. I will extend the trust to the Battaglias once more. I owe it to Giovanni. But let me be clear I won't lift a finger to help you. And I want his head. Fail me? And I may be inclined to take yours if you survive the night."

Lorenzo nodded that he understood. "It's a deal I want to make."

He didn't know how he intended to pull it off. But he was certain of one thing, if he and Carlo wanted to leave the country alive they would have to.

* B *

"Thank you, baby," Mira smiled. "I wanted her to sleep with us."

Mira fixed the sheet around Eve. Her daughter spit her pacifier out. She seized the moment to take it from Eve and placed it on her dresser. Eve's lips puckered as if she still sucked it. She couldn't get over how adorable her daughter was when she slept. Giovanni yawned before joining them. She reached over and ran her hand over his bare chest. It felt good to touch him again. She had half a mind to ask that he put Eve in her crib so she could lay with his arms around her.

"You okay?" Mira asked, running her hand up and down his chest. His gaze lowered to her touch. Giovanni insisted on carrying her around the house. She thought it was cute. But she had to worry for his back. She weighed close to 190 pounds now.

"I'm okay. It's been a long day, Bella," he replied. The look he gave her made her smile. He too felt it. The loneliness in their bed since sex was now off the menu. He didn't mention it but every morning he woke with a hard-on.

"This is nice, Giovanni," Mira said. She caressed lower. Her fingers inched toward his groin. He caught her wrist and stopped her. Mira gave him a pout.

"Don't tease me, Bella," he said with not a hint of humor in his eyes.

She removed her hand. "Sorry."

He closed his eyes. Mira chewed on the inside of her jaw. She stared at her husband, and then her daughter. Her heart felt heavy with the burden she put upon them. Eve was crankier because she couldn't hold her or tend to her needs personally. Giovanni constantly watched over her, neglecting his responsibilities. And they had close to two more months of this.

"Giovanni?" she whispered.

"Mmm?"

"It feels nice to be here with you and Eve like this. I might get used to all the attention," she said. "I feel a bit guilty over it though. Monopolizing you the way I have."

He opened his eyes. His gaze dropped left and the cool violet beauty of his eyes made her heart skip a beat. She loved him so much. Giovanni turned on his side. He kissed Eve's fat jaw and then leaned over. Mira leaned over and kissed him. "Nothing is more important than giving you attention, Bella."

"You've been away from your business. That's important. I know you are missed. I hate you have to sacrifice this way."

"As you sacrifice your business and dreams to bring my children into the world?" he asked.

She grinned. "Yeah, I guess we both sacrifice."

"It's what marriage is about. Compromise, sacrifice," he said.

"And love, don't forget love," Mira said.

"How can I? When the love of my life reminds me of love every day," he said.

"I'm okay, though. Really. If you need to be away for a day or two I can handle it."

He gave her a silencing look. Mira settled down to a smile. "Did you find a place for us in Palermo yet?" she asked.

"I have two I'm considering. Waiting to hear if they are available."

Mira yawned and reached over to turn off the lamp. Giovanni placed Eve on his chest so he could ease closer to her. Mira turned on her side. She slept comfortably this way. She scooted back into him and rested her face against his shoulder and the inside cushion of his under arm. He rubbed her belly and folded his arm around her midriff to keep her close. This was what love felt like.

"Night, sweetheart," she said.

"Good night, Bella," he said.

Mira drifted to sleep. She thought of Marietta. She wondered if their houseguest had eaten dinner. Mira made a mental note to check in on her personally in the morning.

* B *

Marietta's eyelids parted. At some point in the night she fell asleep. The room was a shroud of darkness. She clutched in her hand the letter that had shattered her world. What should she do? Run? Confront the Battaglias? Confront and kill the man who made her believe he loved her? What?

She closed her eyes once more. She had no options that would cure her of the pain. And that truth hurt most of all. Deep in her heart she truly did love Lorenzo. Now what was she left to do? She had never felt more alone.

* B *

"Are you going to sit there and watch the phone?" Isabella chuckled. Her voice split Gemma's thoughts like fingernails on a chalkboard. When Gemma dared to lift her gaze to her nemesis she stared into the cold empty eyes of a ruthless bitch. One who had made her life a nightmare since the day it all began. She wondered how much of a strike she could deliver if she swiped the knife to the side of her plate across the evil bitch's throat. She weighed her options as she spoke.

"What you've done to Marietta is beyond cruel."

"Really? Telling her the truth is cruel? What about the lies you've told, Gemma?"

With a burdened sigh Gemma averted her gaze back to the cold dinner plate before her. She fed herself with mechanical motions, barely tasting the food as she chewed. Isabella chuckled. She sipped her blood red wine and licked her glossy lips.

"How do you sleep at night?" Gemma asked.

"Like a baby." Isabella leaned forward. "For years Marsuvio has pondered who turned his precious black whore into a heroin addict. The Sicilians didn't deal in drugs at that time. It divided them. Cast their sons to the wind. Yadda, yadda, yadda," Isabella laughed.

"Can I eat in silence?" Gemma asked

Isabella continued. "My father, Flavio, could not be bothered to solve that mystery and neither did Marsuvio the fucking hypocrite." Isabella smiled. "But I did."

She grabbed Gemma's arm. Gemma flinched. She was yanked forward with the top of her forearm exposed. Isabella drew up Gemma's sleeve and uncovered faded needle track marks across broken veins. "It was you, wasn't it, Gemma? The junkie Italian whore who spread her legs for any mobster on the scene. You made the whore an addict. Didn't you?"

"Stop it!" Gemma wept. She pulled hard against Isabella's grip and eventually snatched her arm away.

"Did you fuck Marsuvio? Were you jealous of his black bitch? Is that why you turned her into a junkie?"

"You have no idea what you're talking about!"

"Really?" Isabella laughed.

"Life was hard for all of us. Lisa was snatched from her boyfriend when she was just a kid. Marsuvio took her. He raped her. Made her think she had to suffer his desires to free the man she loved from prison. And then he lied to her and told her James was dead. The grief she suffered. The pain she suffered. I wanted to help her. Because I knew Marsuvio would never let her go. She needed to feel dead, disappear the way we all did. So yes. I gave her something to make it easier. And it did."

"Liar!" Isabella laughed. She threw her head back and laughed like a maniac. For Isabella to be so beautiful she had a cruel edge that made her features monstrous. Her bright red lips, coal black eyes and almost too perfect polished smile gave Gemma shivers.

Yes she lied. But how the hell would Isabella know her deepest shame?

Gemma resisted the urge to cover her ears. When Isabella regained control of her laughter she spoke with a wild grin on her face. "You wanted her hopeless because she took your place. That's the truth. Isn't it?"

"No," Gemma said. "I loved Lisa."

"Like a junkie loves her needle?" Isabella teased. "I doubt it."

"I was her friend!"

Isabella's smile faded. She tilted her head left and stared at Gemma. "I still don't know how you kept Marsuvio from discovering this? Who did he think put his whore on heroin?"

"Shut up," Gemma wept, she removed her rosary from her sweater pocket and kissed it. Silently she prayed. Not from Isabella's taunts but from the flood of guilt she drowned in. Her sins were too numerous to count.

"Women like you turn my stomach. Weak. Pathetic. Sniveling whores who think that the only option left to them in life is servitude. Men aren't the strong ones. We are. But whores like you make us real women look bad. The justice I bring to the Battaglias will be the cancer that will wipe them out for generations."

"You're not strong," Gemma spat. "You're just as much of a junkie to your hatred as I was to heroin. You don't want to help Marsuvio's daughters. You want to destroy them."

Isabella laughed. "Me? It's my fault?" She put a manicured hand to her breast. "So now I'm the one that lured Mirabella to Italy? I'm the one that forced her to marry the man whose father put a kill order out on her mother? I'm the one that gave two babies away, and left one vulnerable kid with a sadist like Octavio Leone? These are my crimes?"

"No, Isabella. You did none of those things," Gemma conceded. "You're the coward that plays these games with their lives. And how do you know... wait. It was Octavio who told you about me and Capriccio? He was the one that told you about my relationship with Lisa?"

Isabella smirked. "You would be surprised at how cheap that information came from the drunk. As soon as I told him who I was and what I wanted to do to his adopted daughter he sang like a canary."

Gemma shook her head sadly. She cursed Marietta, and her reasons were as vile as the woman sitting across from her. "It's revenge you want, nothing more," Gemma said sadly.

"And it's revenge I will have. Everything Giovanni loves will crumble. His family, his business, and his sanity. I want his sanity most of all. He will suffer a thousand times worse than Flavio. I will devote years of my life to seeing it happen. This is only the beginning, Gemma." Isabella pushed her chair back and stood. She sashayed out of the room with the bottom of her midnight blue silk dress swirling around her shapely hips. "Keep watching the phone," she tossed over her shoulder to Gemma. "Let me know if it rings." Isabella laughed.

Gemma stared at the phone once more. Why hadn't Marietta called her? If she did she'd tell her everything. Help her run from this nightmare. And maybe God would have pity on her soul for her crimes against Lisa.

* B *

"How the fuck is this going to work?" Carlo asked.

Lorenzo sat in the car with him drumming his fingers on the dashboard. The odds that they could play this caper as smoothly as they've done in the past were slim. Varo had a small army around him. Even at this local bar each man was checked at the door by three of the toughest he'd seen. They couldn't walk right in and slit his throat. They couldn't cross the street without being gunned down according to Alik. He had lost many men trying.

Instead they sat in the car and weighed their options.

"If we don't deliver Alik won't let us leave the country alive. And even if we escape we won't be able to avoid a war with the Akhperutyuns. Mottola has tied our hands. We have to be smart." Lorenzo said.

"Fuck being smart. It's suicide. One of us has to make the sacrifice but both of us can't make it out alive," Carlo said.

Lorenzo scanned the street. He didn't speak Armenian but he did know a little Russian. It was hard to say if the men he'd have to get past to see Varo did as well. Lorenzo watched as three men stumbled out of the front of the pub to smoke cigarettes. They laughed with the man standing guard, evidently familiar. And then they started to walk off.

"There!" Lorenzo pointed. *"Andiamo."*

"Wait!" Carlo yelped, but Lorenzo was out the door. He was ruled by instinct not fear, nor caution. Time was short. He wanted to get the fuck out of Armenia. Something was wrong with Marietta. The emergency pages had stopped. He tried to call her back. The private line to their bedroom was now busy as if the phone had been taken off the hook. He felt it in his gut, she needed him. And he sure as hell couldn't return home empty handed. They would have to get the job done and get it done quickly.

Together the best friends slipped into the night. They walked fast. They ran. Lorenzo led the way. They raced ahead of Varo's men who strolled south away from the nightlife on the streets. Lorenzo and Carlo ran far enough to be in their path if they continued their course.

There was a single street lamp lighting an isolated area of the street. "Let's do it." Lorenzo cracked his knuckles. Carlo nodded and began to pace around him. Lorenzo landed the first punch, hard. Carlo staggered. He showed no mercy in his response. A sledgehammer slam of his fist to Lorenzo's face and gut with the accuracy of a prizefighter. So ferocious was the beating the darkness threatened to collapse inward and drop Lorenzo to his knees. A sober Carlo was a killing machine. Lorenzo had to be quick on his feet and get his arm around his throat to get the better end of the fight. But the closer he got to Carlo the fiercer the beating. And they fought hard. Men rushed toward them. It took all four of the men to pull Carlo and Lorenzo apart.

Lorenzo shouted at Carlo in Russian, blamed him for getting them lost. Swore when he got to Italy he would tell Mottola it was Carlo's fault they failed to meet with Varo. The men at first didn't react. Carlo began to hurl insults. One after another they exchanged barbs and the blame.

One of the men shoved Lorenzo back. He pinned him to the wall. To Lorenzo's relief he did speak Russian. He demanded to know what business he had with Varo.

"Who the fuck are you?" Lorenzo replied in Russian.

The man removed a large knife from his belt and put it to Lorenzo's throat. He asked the question again.

"I will only tell Varo. I'm sent here by Mottola to deliver a message. So fuck you!" Lorenzo answered.

The man glanced back to his comrades. The others who kept Carlo restrained spoke to him in Armenian. This was it. The moment he'd hoped for. Lorenzo's heart thundered in his chest. His eyes connected with Carlo and they both knew the plan. They'd either waste these fuckers in the street with their own weapons or gain the access they wanted.

The man with a knife to this throat released him. He stepped back. He said he would see if a meeting was acceptable. Lorenzo pretended to doubt the man. To say he would find Varo on his own. But the angry bastard drew down on him. Pointed a gun to his back and told him to walk. He and Carlo were marched through the dark streets back to the bar that Varo supposedly frequented. At the door a few words were said before he and Carlo were pushed in. One of the men stayed with them. The other two walked toward the back of the musky establishment. Men crowded every table and corner. He didn't see a woman in the place. What he thought to be a bar was something far more sinister.

With silent restraint Lorenzo clenched his fists. To survive the night would be nothing short of a miracle.

* B *

Marietta woke.

She rolled over to her back under the crushing weight of a headache. It had to be late. The room was darker, the house silent. She had cried until she exhausted herself. And still she woke with more tears. The sadness centered in her chest, heavy and suffocating. It allowed no room for release. She sat up. Wanting desperately to breathe again. She wanted to feel anything but the numbing disillusionment. She set her feet down on the side of the bed and put her face in her hands. Lorenzo hadn't called her back. And she didn't care anymore if he did. When she looked up she saw the phone tossed to the other side of the room. She had yanked it from the wall. It was a private line to this room, so if he called he would have gotten no answer. Still she doubted he kept to his promise. The man was a liar, a conniving bastard. Her rage towards him had extinguished the light of love she carried in her heart.

Marietta's gaze lowered to her hand. The ring Lorenzo slipped on her finger when he made his vows glistened even in the dark. She turned it as if to pull it off and stopped herself, she couldn't bring herself to part with it.

"That's the one. That's the one I want." Marietta grinned. She put both hands to her mouth to hide her excitement.

"It's a wise choice, mademoiselle," the jeweler said. "Monsieur, in your hand you hold eight carats of clarity and perfection."

"Eight, huh?" Lorenzo lifted the ring to the light. The diamond sent bands of colors down across everyone. Marietta's hand slipped from her mouth to her throat. The gem was spectacular. "It's flawless, like my Marietta," he winked at her.

Marietta nodded. God she loved this man. The look of love in his eyes held her still, breathless.

"Is this the one you want, Marie? Are you sure?" Lorenzo asked.

She nodded her head and smiled. The ring cost more money than she'd ever fathomed for a piece of jewelry. She felt a bit strange asking for something so extravagant. But the moment she saw it in the display case she knew it was hers.

The jewelry store was a bit busy for the early hour. She and Lorenzo were to the back where the most precious of gems were sold. Marietta expected him to buy the ring and hand it over. She should have known he'd do much more than that.

When Lorenzo lowered to his knees every woman's head in the store turned and each gaze swiveled their way. Marietta placed her shaky hands at first to her mouth then to her heart until he gave her the look to hold her left hand out for him. She did so glancing around at the gawkers. Lorenzo kissed her knuckles. He then eased the diamond ring on her finger. "Ho un debole per te. Sposami, Marietta."

"I am weak for you too, Lorenzo. And yes I will marry you," she answered.

The shoppers and store clerks all applauded. He stood and lifted her into his arms and she hugged his neck with all her might.

"Until death do us part, cara," he said with a serious look.

She nodded her head. "Yes! Forever. Me and you forever, Lo! I swear it!"

With a deep sigh for strength she mentally released herself from the memory that chained her heart to the wedding ring. Marietta pushed up from the bed and stumbled through the dark. She stepped over broken glass and all other evidence of the destructive rage that had consumed her earlier. She flipped on the light. The fluorescent bulb buzzed and in a flash bright light flooded the room. The glare blinded her temporarily.

She squeezed her eyes shut and gripped the sink. After a second the dizzy feeling lessened. She lifted her head. She faced the woman staring back at her in the mirror. Who was she? The braid Marietta wore all day pinned neatly to the back of her head had unraveled and the natural curl pattern to her hair had left loose curls to drift around her face. Her eyes were puffy with grey half circles of fatigue in the pockets beneath. Her nose was red and felt raw to the touch. Her lips had a bruised purplish swollen pout to it. She stepped closer to the sink unable to look away.

She had a twin sister.

A dead mother.

A liar for a husband.

And a Sicilian father who wanted her dead.

"*La famiglia,*" she chuckled, drunk on grief.

The truth had finally come. There was nothing left to do but accept it. Gemma had the nerve to think she'd call her. Come running like some trained dog to be petted and controlled. *Fuck her.* Gemma was no better than any of them. In fact if she ever saw Gemma face to face again she'd put her fist into her throat. Lorenzo would not get off easily. Of course she could grab her things and leave, but not before she looked him in the face and told him what his lies and breaking her heart meant.

So what was left?

Mirabella.

The only thing Marietta truly believed was that Mirabella didn't know the truth. Her sister was a victim of the Battaglias just as she was. Marietta would fix that. She would blow the whole house of lies up before she left this place for good. A sinister smile crept over her mouth and she found a measure of relief. Revenge and hate felt much more comforting than love. She should have never forgotten that truth.

* B *

Smoke filled Lorenzo's lungs when after twenty minutes he and Carlo were shoved inside. They counted seventeen men out front. Maybe more. Killing Varo was not going to be easy. And then they met the man himself. Varo squatted in the back of a room with two of his men. There was a map on the floor he pointed to. Upon Lorenzo and Carlo's arrival he stood, walked over to a table and sat with an imposed air of importance. His posturing did not lessen the peril Lorenzo knew he and his friend were in. A coward pretending at being a leader was more dangerous than a true leader himself. Varo reeked of cowardice. Which would explain why he hid in the mountains instead of faced his enemy.

Lorenzo studied his opponent. Varo had black vacant eyes on an unshaven face with bushy brows. A dirty man who probably slept with the light on. Lorenzo decided to speak to Varo in Italian.

"Mi chiamo Lorenzo Battaglia," Lorenzo introduced himself. Varo put his gun on his table.

"Battaglia? You're a Battaglia?" Varo asked.

The tension in his voice changed the atmosphere in the room. A grumbling spread between the men gathered. Apparently each man standing knew of the Battaglias.

"I am. My cousin is *Don* Giovanni Battaglia," Lorenzo admitted.

"I've heard of him. Not you," Varo answered. "Why are you here? And why lie to my men and say you are a friend of Mottola?"

"Because you're the man to see. I want the deal Mottola has. No. I want a better one," Lorenzo said. He nodded to the chair. "May I?"

"Please," Varo said with an amused chuckle.

The men both rose from the table. One faced Carlo with his finger on the trigger of an assault rifle and the other kept his attention focused on Lorenzo.

Lorenzo took a seat. Unaffected by the deadly intent of the others he focused on Varo. "I know that Mottola is helping you arm your men. I know the guns are from my family. And I also know when Giovanni learns of this you will lose this war. He has a much further reach within the *Camorra, Mafioso,* and *'Ndrangheta* than Mottola."

Varo reclined. He blinked. The moment he did everything Lorenzo suspected of the coward was proven true. The man was no Yeremian. He was a scavenger. If he didn't hide so well this meeting would have never been necessary. Lorenzo would feel no remorse when he took his head.

"You have my attention, Battaglia," Varo said. "Continue."

"My cousin has kept me in his shadow for many years. He has now stripped me of everything, except one thing, the most important thing. My birthright. I can get you the guns, and the means to win this war with Yeremian. I can get you at the table with the men who will finance your pursuit to liberate your people. It is what you want, what all of this is about. No?"

"The Russians and Turks stripped us of our identity, our pride. Now we are stronger but men like Yeremian see nothing but greed. Yes I fight for liberation. And it is an honor to meet you Lorenzo Battaglia if you can help me obtain it."

Varo extended his hand. Lorenzo smiled. He reached across the table and shook it.

"Let's talk business. But not here." Varo cleared his throat. Lorenzo frowned. He glanced over his shoulder to Carlo who stood stone faced.

"Please come with me."

"My companion. He goes where I go." Lorenzo said.

Varo shrugged. "Of course."

Lorenzo and Carlo were led out.

* B *

Marietta felt better after the shower. Her hair was wet, slick, she combed it back over her head into a wavy curl pattern from her face. A bit freer from despair she left her room. The dark hall greeted her. At night men under the Battaglia's payroll patrolled the halls, the land, and the beaches. How many she wasn't sure. And in the dark she could feel the sense of being watched. Several times she stopped to glance back over her shoulder and found no one behind her. Lorenzo once joked that the eyes of Giovanni were always on her when she was in his home. Therefore, she remained alert.

Her thoughts drifted to her sister and her dead mother. She wanted to know more about her mother. She wanted to know everything. Marietta arrived at the end of the hall. She turned the corner and immediately doubled back.

Mirabella was in the kitchen.

Her twin stood in the open door of the refrigerator stuffing her mouth. Marietta watched her from the darkness. When Mirabella turned sideways her large belly protrusion was seen clearly through her long white nightgown because of the interior light in the fridge.

And she chomped, chewed, and stuffed her fat cheeks with food. It was so comical.

Marietta watched her eat, swallow and then grab at more food and eat. Before Marietta realized it she was smiling. From the moment she met Mirabella the fashion designer had been nothing but smiles and pleasantries. At first Marietta thought it was phoniness. But it wasn't. Mirabella was her other half, her better half. The one who grew up loved by their maternal grandparents. The one who didn't have the scars to jade her view of the world. Who would Marietta have become if she grew up on a farm and had love as a kid? Maybe she'd be confident, rich and famous like Mirabella. Maybe her sacrifice of blood and tears as a kid was so Mirabella could be the best of them. As she watched Mirabella she suffered a gamut of emotions most akin to love. A connection and bond she wanted to explore.

Marietta opened her mouth to say Mira's name when the *Don* appeared.

"Bella! What the hell are you doing down here?" Giovanni barked at her.

Mirabella whirled around with her eyes stretched. She swallowed. "I-I-I got hungry."

"Then why didn't you wake me?" he shouted at her. "I woke up and found you gone. You came down the stairs all by yourself!" he continued to yell. Marietta narrowed her eyes on the *Don* and clenched her fist. *How dare he speak to Mirabella that way? And why on earth would she stand there and take it?* Instead of her sister putting his ass in his place she grinned.

Mirabella set the bowl of pasta down on the counter. She stepped to her husband and touched his face, forced him to kiss her. She spoke to him softly and her husband turned his face away. Mirabella took his face in both hands and made him look at her. She spoke again to him in such a low tone Marietta could not hear her. But she could see the affect her words had on the evil bastard. Giovanni actually smiled. Marietta had never seen the man smile since she met him.

"You will be the death of me!" he laughed.

Mirabella hugged him. The *Don* kissed the top of her head. He held her in his arms and rubbed her back. And then the couple began to kiss. It turned Marietta's stomach. She drew away. She returned to her room determined as ever to get justice. She would tell her sister the truth about the bastard she had married. As soon as possible.

* B *

302

Cowardice lived in every man. Some fear love, others rejection, many fear failure. Varo was a man who feared everything and trusted no one. Everywhere Lorenzo and Carlo went men with guns accompanied them. The bastard had to stop to pee and three men went with him to watch his back. Lorenzo shot Carlo a look and he shook his head in disgust.

As Lorenzo considered his options lady luck took pity on his ass. They were brought to a remote location. Both he and Carlo piled into a jeep with Varo and he drove off with them alone. Lorenzo glanced back at Carlo. He too wore a surprised look. Could Varo the cowardly bunny actually have grown some balls?

"I can not let my men see me negotiate with you. It is a matter of respect and strength. We will need privacy to discuss my terms." Varo glanced over to Lorenzo. "But please understand me. My men are everywhere. You have seen them. No? You will not leave the countryside alive if anything happens to me."

"We're not here to make an enemy. Your interests are mine. I am curious though, how does Mottola service you? We have tight control over the Neapolitan clans. Nothing exports from the bay of Naples without my cousin's knowledge."

Varo chuckled. "Well those times have changed. Haven't they? Giovanni Battaglia allows the `Ndrangheta to move in and out of the bay. Mottola works through them and a cruise ship company. The problem is my shipments are small and all of them must come through the Turks."

"Ah that can be problematic." Lorenzo conceded.

"It's timely," Varo said, shifting gears and picking up speed as the jeep raced onward.

"What does Mottola gain from this?"

"Pledged assistance with his desires to take control of the clans in the *Camorra*," Varo smirked. "The Russians are looking for revenge against Giovanni. Many of his Russian enemies are my comrades in this war with Yeremian."

"But I thought you were liberating your people from tyranny of Soviet influence? Now you're partners with them?" Lorenzo asked.

Varo laughed. "Yes, I am. During occupation many Armenians were dragged off to Russian prison camps. The men I call brother hate the Soviets, just as I do. They don't know I deal with them. Your arrival reaffirms their belief we only deal with the *Camorra*."

And thus Lorenzo finally understood the depths of Varo's cowardice. Mottola was a shield. He remained strong and fearless if his men believed that he armed them without selling his soul to the

Turks, or Russians. All of it was bullshit. Lorenzo kept his face blank. Inside he fumed. He knew this pursuit of Dominic's and Giovanni's to legitimize the family made them weak. And now he had proof. But the war with the Russians was Lorenzo's fault. He misled Giovanni into believing that the Russians killed Tomosino. This disaster truthfully should be laid at his feet. "What about Santo? Does he assist you?"

"Santo? Never heard of him. Mottola is very secretive. He trusts no one in the *Camorra*. It's wise for him. No?"

Lorenzo found it hard to believe that Santo was totally blameless. He knew somewhere in this the bastard had to be dirty. But that was a mystery to solve for another day. He settled in his seat and let Varo fill him in on his operation. The night was blinding. He had no idea how Varo travelled through the blackness with the aid of his headlights only. Soon they arrived in front of a stone cottage that looked abandoned. Varo parked.

"Here is what I want you to see." Varo hopped out of the jeep, taking his assault rifle with him. "Come."

Lorenzo and Carlo followed him inside. And what they found stopped them both cold. Varo lit lanterns and revealed more. "All of this came to you through Mottola and the *'Ndrangheta*?"

"Not all, a lot. Some of it we stole. None of it can give me victory. I want a decisive strike. I need something to bring Yeremian to his knees. And this is what Mottola struggles to find for me." Varo set the lantern down. He cleared off a crate and removed a paper from his back pocket. He spread it out flat to show Lorenzo what he desired. As Lorenzo stepped to his side he glanced to Carlo who understood it was time for them to act.

"See here," Varo began. "The missile launchers, the kind with a scope. It is what the Americans give to Afghanis. I need to be able to do long distance strikes." Varo said, his voice alive with excitement.

Carlo eased out a short rubber tube from his deep pocket. The only weapon they brought. Lorenzo moved closer.

"We have these." Lorenzo's finger pointed at the image. "We send them down the coast to Africa. I can get my hands on them easily. For a price."

"Name it!" Varo said.

"Your life," Lorenzo smiled.

Varo frowned. Carlo attacked. He wrapped the black tube around Varo's neck with each end tightly gripped in his hands. He clenched his fist and crossed his wrist to apply bone-crushing pressure. Varo dropped to his knees. Lorenzo stared down at Varo and watched his eyes and tongue protrude. The scoundrel clawed at his neck, desperate for a breath. Carlo denied him the privilege.

Most believe it is quick and clean to administer death by strangling a person. Not true. It took close to ten minutes for the grimy bastard to die.

Once done Carlo released Varo and he dropped over, face first, dead. Carlo heaved down deep breaths, his eyes wild with excitement, his face covered in sweat. He stuck the band back into his pocket and spit on Varo's lifeless body. "I thought he'd never shut the fuck up."

"Do you see all of this?" Lorenzo looked around. "Now we're in the business of arming a civil war!"

"We trade guns. What the fuck do you think these people do with them?" Carlo tossed back. "We've always armed slugs like this. It's none of our business."

"That's not what I mean. I can give a shit what is done with the guns I give a shit that we are connected this way. Mottola has drug us into the middle of this shit with the Russians. Everything is at risk. What if the Soviet or Armenian police forces trace these guns to us? Do you understand what I'm saying?"

Carlo pulled back his sleeve. "We got ten maybe fifteen minutes before his clan breaks down that door. So what do we do now?"

"His head." Lorenzo kicked the box of guns next to him. He knocked over a few other boxes and read the writing scribbled on top. "We can't carry him out of here. We need to bring Alik evidence. Find something to take off his head."

"Fuck you," Carlo said. "I killed him you take his head."

"Find me something!" Lorenzo shouted. The quick search revealed a case of knives and saws. Why Varo needed them Lorenzo didn't care. "Get us a few guns, and wait outside. I'll be out soon."

Carlo walked out. Lorenzo had never dismembered a body. They usually tied weights to their ankles and dropped them in the sea. He was surprised at how easily Varo's head was dispatched from his shoulders. He shoved the bloody prize in a burlap bag. The disgusting smell of blood and excrement singed his noise and burned his throat. He staggered out of the front door of the cottage hacking for air with bloody hands.

"Carlo?" he wheezed and looked up. Lorenzo froze. Carlo stood with a small army of men holding a gun on him.

"Shit," Lorenzo said.

13.

Catalina groaned awake. The knocking on the door persisted. She felt hung over with the need for sleep. "Okay! What is it?"

"*Buongiorno, telefono,*" Carmella said. She brought in the newspaper she told her to fetch for her before retiring for the evening.

"Oh, okay. *Grazie,*" Catalina took the paper and tossed it the side of her. She reached for the phone while rubbing her eyes. She hadn't heard it ring.

"*Pronto?*" she answered.

"You went to Belina yesterday!" Dominic shouted from the receiver.

Catalina shot straight up in bed. "Domi?" she gasped.

"*Christo!*" he shouted. "Are you fucking insane? *Ammazza!*"

"Stop yelling at me," Catalina said, with a nervous chuckle.

"You think this is funny?" Dominic asked.

"No. No, of course not," she quickly added.

"Leonardo said you took Lorenzo's wife to Belina and dined up in the private rooms with Armando Mancini's men. Is that true? Is it?"

"Let me ask you a question? What business is it of yours? You don't want anything to do with me remember? I can go where I please." The answering silence in the phone made Catalina rethink her words. She knew Leonardo would tell Dominic before Giovanni. To tell Giovanni would bring her brother's wrath down on her, and Leonardo. She wanted Dominic's attention and now she had it. Catalina settled back into her pillow mildly satisfied.

"Calm down, sweetheart. I only had lunch there. The men looked at me, a few of them tried to flirt with me, but none of them dare approached. Besides Belina is a friend of Ma-Ma's she wouldn't let anything happen to me. Gio doesn't even have to know," Catalina said with a smile.

"You are not to leave Villa Mare Blu again until I return. Do you hear me?" Dominic said.

"You going to punish me if I do?" she teased.

"Che palle! Non comportarti da baggiana! Maledizione!" Dominic shouted back.

"Stop cursing at me! Calm down!" Catalina said.

"Don't you leave the fucking villa again!" he continued.

"You lost that right when you dumped me! You can't tell me what to do!" Catalina said.

"Do you hear me? Say it! Say the words, Catalina," he said in a voice as sharp as the edge of a blade. "Or I swear to Christ I'll come back and—"

She rolled her eyes. "I won't go back to Palermo until you return. When is that, Domi? When will you be—"

The phone line disconnected.

"Love you too." Catalina kissed the phone and smiled. He'd be home soon. Her rebellion would eat at him until he returned to her. This time she'd make him beg her for forgiveness. One thing she could always count on was Dominic's devotion to her. She hung up and reached for the paper. When she read the front-page byline she squealed. She jumped from bed and grinned happily, turning in circles and dancing around the room.

* B *

The night had been a hard one on her. No matter how Mira slept she ached. And the spotting returned. She had to change herself twice. She woke Giovanni and told him the news. He called the doctor. Now she lay in bed waiting. She didn't know if she'd be able to bear the next few weeks trapped this way.

"Buongiorno, Donna."

The greeting caught her by surprise. Mira's gaze flipped up. Marietta smiled at her. It was the warmest, friendliest smile she'd ever received from Marietta. A bit confused Mira smiled in return.

"Hi there, please come in," Mira said.

Mira tried to fix the covers around her. She knew she looked a hot mess. Her hair hadn't been combed from the root in two days. The tangles couldn't be brushed into a ponytail. It was hopeless. So she wore it mostly under a scarf to keep it from her face.

Marietta however looked beautiful. She wore a cream summer dress with spaghetti straps. Her curvy figure was perfectly outlined

307

in the thin material and the hem stopped mid thigh, inching higher when she walked. To be so petite she had curves like a dancer. She had thick thighs, a round shapely ass, flat stomach, and perfectly pert tits. She wondered if Marietta worked out.

"Am I disturbing you?" Marietta asked.

"No. I'm waiting on the doctor. Sit. Please. Talk with me," Mira said.

For a minute it looked as if Marietta wouldn't accept her invite. But that moment passed. She walked to the edge of the bed and sat on it. "You look funny," Marietta said.

"Funny?" Mira asked. She touched her face. "Funny how?"

"Tired. Under the eyes," Marietta said. "Did you get any sleep?"

"Not much. I am tired. But I guess that comes with the territory." Mira smiled. "How are you feeling? Catalina said you were sick after you had lunch together?"

Marietta waved off the concern. "She and I got off to a bad start. That's my fault. I've never been good at making friends." Marietta peeked up at her from under her dark lashes. "I didn't have many friends when I grew up. I feel really bad about how I've treated you. Especially with your hospitality and everything. You really have been nice. I was hoping we could start over."

"Oh, forget about that. I knew you'd like me eventually," Mira winked. Marietta frowned and looked away. *Did she say something wrong*, Mira wondered? An awkward silence settled between them. Mira tried again. "So, did you have fun yesterday when you went to Paler—"

"Do you know much about your mother?" Marietta blurted.

Taken aback Mira couldn't respond. Marietta was quick to explain her question. "I'm sorry. Forgive me. I'm curious. Yesterday when I was with Catalina I told her I was adopted and didn't know my birth mother. She said your mother died when you were young. Is that true?"

"Yes, it is. She died I think when I was two," Mira said.

"You think? Why don't you know for sure?" Marietta asked.

Mira felt her smile waver, and a deep pang of regret stab her chest. "My mother had a complicated life. She ran off from home, returned with me as a baby, and then left me behind when I was only a toddler. All for... she died shortly after. She was... she was a drug addict."

Marietta stood. She walked around the bed and began to pace. "Did she die from the drugs? Are you sure?"

Am I sure? It was a very uncomfortable topic. *Who the hell does she think she is?* Mira watched her pace, uncertain of the point for the line of questioning. Part of her wanted to tell Marietta to mind her own damn business and stay out of hers. The other half of her truly did want to be friends with Lorenzo's wife. Maybe the story of her mother would help Marietta cope with whatever seemed to have her agitated. Marietta stopped pacing and looked at her as if she expected a response.

"I believe so. It's what my grandparents told me when I was old enough to understand her death. I never pressed for details."

"But what was she like? Did they tell you that? Do you have any memories of her at all? A picture?" Marietta's eyes stretched. "Do you have her picture?"

"I beg your pardon?" Mira frowned.

"Oh fuck this shit! You need to know the truth," Marietta pointed an accusatory finger at Mira. "You walk around here clueless! You don't know shit about her. About who I am. Who we are."

Alarmed Mira pushed back into her pillows. Something wild and angry was now in Marietta's eyes. She didn't trust her. Not at that moment. The door opened and Giovanni walked in with her tall dark African doctor. Both men stopped at the sight of Marietta. The look she gave Giovanni was as lethal as the one she aimed at Mira. And without a word she stormed out of the room.

"What the hell was she doing in here?" Giovanni demanded.

"Oh stop it, Giovanni. We were just talking. She was upset," Mira said. She then looked to the doctor. *"Ciao, dottore* Buhari. Good to see you."

"I hear last night was uncomfortable?" the doctor asked.

"She left the bed. She went downstairs by herself," Giovanni said with evident disapproval.

"I was fine. I got hungry and couldn't sleep. The boys have been really active," Mira reasoned.

"Let's check your pressure. Do a quick pelvic exam and decide if we need to do more?" the doctor advised.

Mira nodded. She winked at her brooding husband as the doctor got out his equipment. And though her attention was focused on the condition of her pregnancy, she couldn't help but wonder about the curious visit from Marietta.

* B *

"Morning!" Catalina sang.

Marietta buried her face in her hands.

"I said morning!" Catalina chirped.

Marietta looked up at the perky Catalina who breezed into the room in a bright pink summer dress that was strapless. Her thick brown hair cascading about her shoulders made her even more beautiful. The spoiled princess sat at the table with a cup of cappuccino and tossed her bangs from her eyes. She stared at Marietta with an arched brow for a response.

"What has you so happy?" Marietta asked.

"Let me show you!" Catalina rose from her chair and walked down the table. She put the newspaper in front of Marietta. She tapped her magenta red nail on the article. The headline in Italian announced the successful fashion show for Mirabella's company *Fabiana's*. Marietta stared down at the image of the models posed in a store window. Each garment they wore was more stunning than the other.

"That, my dear is me! I did this. See right there. My name is mentioned. As soon as the doctor finishes with the *Donna* I will deliver the good news," Catalina said.

"What good news?" Rosetta entered the room and paused.

"None of your business," Catalina answered.

Marietta ignored them both. The article talked of Mirabella's accomplishments. Her sister was fierce to have done so much at a young age. Marietta once had dreams of turning her furniture business into something grand and profitable. But she could never focus long enough to make those dreams a reality. And her management of funds was always off. She ended up owing too much money in taxes and went bankrupt.

"Buongiorno," Cecilia walked in with little Eve. Marietta's gaze shifted from the article to the little girl. It was as if she were seeing people with a new perspective. The little brown toddler with blue eyes sucked on a red pacifier. She walked on bowed legs toward the table. The baby looked up at Marietta and blinked. She never liked kids. And kids never liked her. But if she were to have a little girl Marietta had to wonder if the child would be as beautiful as baby Eve.

The baby must have been a mind reader. She snatched her hand free of Cecilia and walked over to Marietta. She stopped at her chair and raised her arms as if demanding to be picked up.

"Look at Eve, she never goes to anybody," Rosetta said, who had been at the table eating silently. Catalina glanced up. Everyone looked to Marietta expecting her to respond. Eve sucked her pacifier and waited. Marietta gave an awkward smile and reached to lift the kid. Eve was placed on her lap. She rested against her breast and sucked her pacifier in a way she'd seen the toddler do with Mira. Marietta stroked her arm. "She's a special little girl," said Marietta.

"She likes you. That must mean you're part of the family now," Catalina chuckled. "Little Evie is a hard one to impress."

The other women agreed. Holding Eve in her arms felt natural. Being an auntie felt natural, she could really get into it. Marietta smiled. She needed to talk to Mirabella. Tell her everything. Her first attempt had been a disaster. Mira must think she's nuts.

Marietta needed to learn more about the family she never knew existed. Maybe see an image of her dead mother. But to do so meant she had to reveal the truth to Mira and she had no way of knowing what the truth would mean for all of them. Whatever she decided she must do so quick. Lorenzo would return soon, and she didn't trust herself with him.

Carmella, the servant girl, carried in a tray of food and a few men came in and sat at the table. Marietta was given a plate for Eve. The toddler spat out her pacifier and started to reach into the plate to grab the fruit she liked. Marietta laughed. She helped Eve and felt a little of the weight of sadness lift from her heart.

* B *

"How is she, Doctor?" Giovanni paced. The way he glared at the man and watched him closely had to have made the doctor nervous. Mira wished Giovanni would relax and trust the doctor to do his job.

"Her pressure is still elevated," Dr. Buhari said.

"It is?" Mira gasped. "But I have been doing everything you said."

"No you haven't! You got out of bed, Bella," Giovanni pointed an accusatory finger at her. "You got out of bed after I explicitly told you not to."

"Oh stop saying that. You're my husband not my jailor. I walked around a little bit. Not a lot." She looked from Giovanni's frustrated face to the doctor's concerned one. Mira felt such guilt her voice cracked with emotion. "Is he right, Doctor? Am I the cause?"

"I doubt a trip downstairs last night helped matters. But I have to tell you, we are going to have to take you in soon. After your last

311

test results I had my concerns. We have to be cautious. I will call the *ospedale* and have them ready a room for you."

"My babies? Will I have to deliver them? It's too soon." Mira said.

"We'll make that decision later. Can you return to Palermo in the morning?" Dr. Buhari asked.

"No. No, Giovanni, tell him. We aren't ready. It's too soon!" Mira exclaimed.

"Bella, calm down, sweetheart." He stepped to the doctor. "Should we take her in now? To be safe?"

"No. No more excitement today. Tomorrow is fine. We will take it from there. Trust me we won't take the babies unless absolutely necessary." He patted her hand. "Now rest. I will see you in the morning."

"Grazie," Mira said.

Giovanni stepped in front of the doctor. "I think you should stay."

"Well I have to be back at the *ospedale*. I need to make arrangements for her." Dr. Buhari said.

"You can use a phone here to make those arrangements. Bella may need you. Stay." Giovanni said.

"Don Battaglia, I am sorry but I have to decline," the doctor said.

Giovanni smiled. "I insist."

Flabbergasted the man looked to Mira for help. What could she say? She wanted him to stay as well. She felt her husband's nervousness and quietly agreed with him. Giovanni opened the door and Leo stepped inside. "Take the doctor to his room and make sure he has everything he needs."

The doctor looked again to Mira for help. She felt awful, but Giovanni could not be refused by either of them. The man nodded. He walked out.

"Was that necessary, Giovanni?" Mira asked.

"If it protects you and my sons then yes it was," Giovanni replied. "Besides it's not a prison. Many would like to spend the night here. They'll make sure he's accommodated."

"I agree. I have to be honest, I feel better now that you asked him to stay." Mira moved her legs over the bed and placed her feet on the ground. She put her hand to her side. The babies were unnaturally still. It wasn't surprising considering the fact that they kept her up all night. Mira reached for a pastry just as Giovanni returned to her side.

"Sit back, Bella," he ordered.

She did as she was told. He stacked the pillows behind her to ensure she was comfortable.

"I'm okay." Mira tried to reassure him.

"No stress today. None. Don't talk about that company, or do anything with it. Do you understand?" Giovanni said in a stern voice.

"I understand." She nodded her head like a good girl. She munched on the cream filled pastry he passed her. Lately her hunger was like that of a truck driver. Who knew sitting on your ass made you crave food?

"I had a meeting later today in Bagheria. I won't be going. I have to deal with Lorenzo and Carlo." He started toward the door.

"Something wrong?" Mira asked with a mouthful.

"Nothing to worry about. They've arrived a few minutes ago. Just got word."

* B *

Marietta passed a crying Eve over to Cecilia. She may be her aunt but she knew nothing about how to settle a tantrum. She did suffer a pang of embarrassment over the much-needed rescue. When she checked her watch she found the morning had slipped away. The doctor's visit had to have concluded.

She intended to see Mira. And it dawned on her how to approach the subject with her sister. Something that Gemma said in her letter. A true test to prove they were sisters. She would show her the necklace. When she pushed back from the table Carlo and Lorenzo walked in. Marietta froze. They looked haggard and sleep deprived in their appearance. They wore the clothes they left in. Her man's eyes were so heavy with exhaustion she wasn't sure he was looking at her or through her. Lorenzo smiled. He had kept his promise and returned sooner than forty-eight hours.

"Cara." He walked toward her and grabbed her up into an embrace. She shoved him off. There was such a ruckus on the terrace with everyone's excitement over their surprise return no one barely noticed her rejection of him.

"I want to talk to you! Now!" she seethed. "Now!"

"No. I have to see Giovanni. Give me an hour and meet me in our room." He kissed her cheek and squeezed her ass. "In our bed," he said. No matter how hard she tried to push out of his embrace he had a tight grip on her. He bit her cheek. "Be nice. I've missed you," he said.

When he released her she tried to slap him but he caught her wrist. He leaned in and his tone held a clear threat. "Don't ever do that in front of the family. I said we'd talk later."

She snatched her arm away.

"You asshole. I hate you." She turned and stormed away. When she looked back he wasn't even staring after her. He was busy hugging and laughing with the others. Blinded by her tears and hurt beyond her own comprehension she went to her room. Once inside she found her purse. She found her necklace.

"Fuck you, Lorenzo. Fuck you," she said. She fast walked out of her room. Just as she turned the corner she saw Giovanni descend the stairs. She stayed out of sight. When he was gone she raced up the stairs and hurried to Mira's room.

* B *

Giovanni sought his cousin with his eyes. The wild tale he was told at four in the morning had left him reeling. Mottola had taken betrayal to a whole new level. The offenses were beyond any of Giovanni's original understanding.

Eve raced for her father crying for his attention. He picked her up and kissed her. The affection calmed her immediately. She grinned and leaned in to kiss him once more.

"Gio!" Lorenzo walked over. "We have to talk. Now."

"I know." He glanced to Carlo who ate, chewed, and swallowed in a hurried manner. He nodded for him to come as well. Carrying Eve in his arms, his *bambina* waved at Lorenzo from his over his shoulder.

* B *

Marietta pushed the door open. Mira glanced up when she walked in. Marietta closed the door behind her to ensure they would have privacy. "Hi there? I hear Lorenzo is back. You must be happy," Mira said.

Around Marietta's neck she wore her necklace. Mira stared at her with a smile. There was no hint of recognition in her face. Maybe Marietta stood too far from the bed for Mira to see the charm. So she stepped closer.

"Are you okay?" Marietta asked with genuine concern. "Do you feel okay for a visit?"

"Oh I'm fine. Don't let my grumpy husband fool you. I'm more than capable of having a conversation without going into labor," she chuckled.

Marietta sat on the edge of the bed. Mira blinked at her. She showed no reaction to the necklace Marietta wore. So Marietta touched it to draw her eyes to it. "Do you recognize this, Mira?"

Mira sat forward. She squinted at the necklace and then looked up into Marietta's face. "It's beau—" Mira studied it again and looked up into Marietta's eyes.

At last Marietta saw the light of awareness in Mira's eyes. She reached behind her neck and released the clasp to take the necklace off. She then handed it over to Mira. "It was given to me as a child, by a mother I never met. You have one like it don't you?"

Mira stared at the necklace. She turned it over. Marietta watched as Mira ran her finger over the insignia to the back of the clasp. "That right there is the stamp of the jeweler. His name was Del Stavio," Marietta said.

"What is this about?" Mira frowned.

"Me and you. Our connection. One we've had since birth," Marietta replied.

"Is this some kind of joke?" Mira asked.

"No. Or maybe it's the biggest joke of our lives. Before I made this charm into a necklace it was a baby's bracelet. I have a twin sister who has one identical to it."

"Okay I've heard enough. Stop," Mira demanded.

"Your husband has been lying to you from day one. So has mine. We're sisters, and those bastards knew it and conspired together to keep us apart."

"That's not possible. I don't have a twin sister. Here take it!"

"No! Look at it dammit. It is possible!" Marietta said. "Our mother dated a man named Marsuvio Mancini. He's a Sicilian mobster who lived in Philadelphia. He didn't want us. She separated us to keep us safe from him. I think. I know this sounds crazy but look at the necklace. We're twins. Giovanni and Lorenzo have been trying to keep us apart because his father Tomosino Battaglia is the man who ordered the hit on our mother. His father killed our mother."

"Get out!" Mira said. She tossed the necklace back at Marietta. "Out of my damn room!" she shouted.

Marietta flinched. "Haven't you heard what I said to you?" she asked. "Yesterday when I was in Palermo with Catalina a woman who I knew since I was a little girl gave me this letter." Marietta handed it over. "I didn't believe it either at first. Until I read this letter. When I came to Italy I did so to find my father. I was always told my mother was a whore who slept with my adoptive father and left me on the doorstep. A lie. I knew that evil bastard who raised me wasn't my blood. So Gemma told me a man named Capriccio was. Another lie. So many damn lies I can't keep up. And all of them were told to keep you and I from knowing the truth." She forced the letter on Mira. "Read it. Giovanni knows the truth. He sent me away with Lorenzo to keep the truth from you. That's why we were gone for months. Read the damn letter!"

Mira's hands shook. Tears bordered her wide stretched eyes. She accepted the letter and opened it slowly.

* B *

"You two look and smell like shit!" Giovanni chuckled. He sat down and put Eve on his lap. For some reason she was very clingy. She refused to sit forward. Instead she turned and clung to his neck, resting her face on his shoulder.

"We barely got out of Armenia with our lives," Lorenzo said.

Carlo sat down next. "It was pretty intense, Gio," Carlo agreed.

"So tell me about Varo. Is what you said true? He's been buying my guns through the `Ndrangheta and Mottola?"

"You need to bring Dominic back in. Santo too. No one is safe. The fool led us to his arsenal. I had to take off his head," Lorenzo chuckled. "Then I walk out to a small army with nothing but guns facing us. Turns out it was Yeremian's men. They were tracking us. Using us to bring them into Varo's compound. While we were killing Varo the crazy bastards nearly wiped out all of his men. That's why they had to put us on a plane. To get us out of there before the authorities discovered what we'd done. We haven't slept."

"Or showered," Carlo said.

Giovanni rocked back in his chair. "And Santo? Did Varo name him?"

"No," Carlo said. "But do you really think he's clean in this?"

The news was a lot to digest. How many enemies were in his midst now?

The door flew open.

Mira and Marietta arrived together. The men shot to their feet. Giovanni couldn't stand fast enough. Mira charged straight at his desk.

"The truth! I want the truth!" Mira seethed.

Eve was startled. Giovanni could feel her tiny heart beat rapidly in her chest. He too was stunned beyond speech. Mira's face was wet with tears. Her eyes stretched wide with horror and he was her sole focus. She slammed down jewelry on the desk. Her bracelet and another item that looked just like it. "Did you know this?" she asked pointing a finger at him. "Any of it!"

"Carlo!" Giovanni said. Carlo reached for Eve who fought to stay with her father. He walked out of the room. Lorenzo grabbed Marietta who immediately started to shout and fight back for control or at the very least a voice in the confrontation. He picked her up by the waist and carried her out of the room. None of it mattered. Giovanni could only hear and focus on his wife. He walked around the desk aware of how dire the situation had become. The doctor had just told them only minutes ago she was to remain calm. "We'll talk about what I knew later. First you have to go back to bed."

"Don't touch me!" she screeched. She backed away from him. Her hand protectively covered her tummy. She kept the other one out to make sure he didn't come closer. "You did this. I didn't believe it. Not a word. Until I looked into your eyes. Until now. You did it!"

Giovanni grabbed her wrist and she snatched back creating a tugging back and forth. "Let me go!"

She touched her side as if she felt a pain. Panic and fear sliced like an ice spear through his gut and he had to summon all of his strength to not drag her ass back upstairs by force. What was more important the truth or her life?

"How could you do this to me? To us! Sweet Jesus! How could it be true? Any of it? I don't understand why you would hurt me like this."

He let her go. She backed away from him with both her hands to her mouth, and tears streaming. She stood there with eyes stretched wide and in visible pain. She couldn't speak. He feared she wasn't even breathing. What could he say? Another lie? Now? Her eyes warned him against it. It was her eyes that hurt him the most. So much pain and disbelief there it made him desperate.

"I'm sorry, sweetheart. So sorry," he pleaded.

"Oh God what have I done? What have you done?" she shouted at him doubling over. "My mother was murdered by your father? I have a twin sister and you knew! You bastard. Did you have Fabiana killed too?" Mira wept. She wiped her tears and snot from her face with the back of her hand.

Violent spasms seized her pelvis. She felt like the air was

squeezed from her lungs. She gasped. Mira knew instantly something was wrong. Through the discovery of her sister and her husband's undeniable lies she had forgotten the most important thing. Her babies. "Gio—something, it hurts," she went to her knees.

Giovanni caught her by the elbows to make sure she landed softly.

"What is it?"

"Pain," Mira wheezed. She clung to him. "I can't breathe," She gasped, and tried to catch her breath. "Help me," she begged.

"I got you." He brought her up into his arms. "Get the doctor! Help me!" he yelled to his men who Mira saw had gathered in the hall. She squeezed her eyes tightly shut as another monstrous bolt of pain speared her pelvis. And that was when she felt her water break.

"Giovanni, my…"

He looked at her with horror as he laid her on the sofa outside of the hall. At first she wasn't sure why until she looked down and saw the blood stain at the bottom of her dress. "Noooo! No God please!!"

He caught her face. "Calm down, Bella. Look at me. We're going to take you to the hospital. The only thing you concentrate on is being calm. Do you understand?"

She panted breaths and contractions came again severely swift. She nodded and worked on her breathing. Giovanni looked around with tears in his eyes. "Bring him. We're going to the hospital. Now!"

He picked her up again. When she looked back she saw the bloodstain she left on the sofa and felt weak. She closed her eyes and forced herself to concentrate on breathing. She was put in a car with Giovanni. In his arms she pretended he was still her sweet caring husband who would never destroy her heart the way the lies have. She had to. It was the only way she could find some peace.

He kissed her face and whispered in her ear that he'd protect her. She nodded that she believed and clung to him. Too afraid to speak or argue. She'd never argue with him again if God would spare her babies and her life.

Mira began to cry. "I'm so scared," she wept.

Giovanni clung to her. "Me too, Bella. I need you to breathe. For our sons, breathe, Bella."

Mira nodded her head and practiced on her breathing.

* B *

"Put me down!" Marietta screamed.

Lorenzo threw her into the library. "What the hell have you done? Are you fucking insane!" he shouted at her. He put his hands to his head and began to pace. "What the fuck has happened? How did you find out? Fuck! Holy Fuck!" Before she could answer Lorenzo swung and put his fist into the wood of the door. "Damn it, Marietta!"

"Yu-yu-you… you lied." Marietta backed away. "You tricked me. You used me. You lying dog!"

He dropped his hands to the door and lowered his head trying to calm down. "What you've done could cost Mirabella her life, Marietta! Do you understand!" he glanced back at her. "Do you?"

"Nooooo." Marietta shook her head hard. "I just told her the truth."

"They're taking her to the fucking *ospedale*!" Lorenzo turned on her. He was so full of rage that for the first time since that violent fight they had months ago in her hotel room she feared him.

"I didn't mean for her to flip out like that. I swear. I just wanted to talk to her. She started screaming and crying. She went to her dresser and got the bracelet. I couldn't stop her! Things got of control."

"Things? Things! You should have never said any fucking *thing* to her!" he shouted with a finger leveled at Marietta. "You should have come to me!" he slapped his chest.

"How? How can I come to you when I can't even trust you!" Marietta yelled back at him. She wouldn't stand for him blaming her when all of it was his fault. He advanced on her. The look in his eye, the panic in her heart, the tension coiled tighter between them and her instinct was to escape. She'd seen this rage before. She'd seen it every time Octavio came after her. Every time he'd punish her. "Stay away from me! Stay back!" she said shaking all over.

"Enough of this shit, Marie. Come here…"

"Stay away!" she screamed and started throwing things at him from the desk behind her. Whatever her hand landed on she threw it. "Stay back!"

"Marietta, stop acting fucking crazy! Stop it dammit! What the hell is wrong with you?" He lunged for her. Marietta grabbed something round and hard from behind her. She was barely aware of her surroundings when her hand connected with it. When Lorenzo grabbed her arm and his nails bit into her skin she swung and hit him hard to the side of his face. Lorenzo dropped to an unconscious state.

Breathing hard with her hand gripping the weapon she stared

down at him. Her tunnel vision cleared and her thoughts became muddled with confusion. She looked at the weapon in her hand and at Lorenzo who lay sprawled out on the ground. *How did he get there?*

"Lorenzo? Lorenzo, are you okay, baby?" She dropped the large globe paperweight. It hit the ground with a thud and then rolled away. She went to her knees. There was blood in his hair. She touched his face. *Did she kill him? Was he dead?* "Lorenzo, please wake up." She shook him. She looked down to the blood now on her fingers and struggled to breath. "Lorenzoooo? Wake up! I'm sorry. Wake up. Please. I'm sorry."

He lay still as a corpse. She had killed him. She had murdered him. "I didn't do it. I didn't." She scrambled to her feet and fled the room. The house was in a state of chaos. Men were shouting. Catalina, Rosetta, Cecilia, Eve, all of them were crying. Blinded by tears she raced out of the villa and tried two different cars before she found one with the keys inside. She turned over the engine and sped away.

* B *

Lorenzo groaned.

He touched the side of his head in response to the pain.

"Merda!" he spat. Not sure of what happened he tried to rise from the floor but was brought back down by a wave of dizziness. *"Che palle!"*

"What the fuck happened to you?" Carlo walked in. He reached down and brought his friend to his feet. "Who hit you?"

"Marietta, she's gone fucking crazy," he groaned. His vision was blurred and the pain made it hard for him to open his eyes. "Where... where is she?" Lorenzo staggered toward the door. Carlo kept him from dropping again.

"Maybe you should sit down," Carlo said.

"Fuck no!" Lorenzo shoved Carlo off. He had to drop a hand to the wall to keep standing.

"I thought you had her in here? What the hell happened?" Carlo asked.

"Find her... we got to. Now!" Lorenzo stretched his eyes to regain sight. "Motherfucker! What the fuck did she hit me with?" Lorenzo groaned.

"This." Carlo picked up a marble paperweight. "She could have killed you," he chuckled.

320

"None of this shit is funny!" Lorenzo turned on him. "She's having one of her fits. We have to find her."

"What kind of fit?" Carlo asked.

"Rage. You know the fucking kind. When she's backed in a corner she gets like this. She fights. It's complicated." Lorenzo dragged down a breath. He dropped a hand to the side of the door to steady himself. "How did she and Mirabella find out the truth?"

"I don't know. Gio has left. They are driving the *Donna* to the *ospedale*. She bleeds. It must be the babies," Carlo said.

"Damn it. This is bullshit. What the fuck has Marietta done?" Lorenzo groaned.

"Is this Marietta's fault or yours?" Carlo asked.

"What did you say to me?" Lorenzo asked.

Carlo stepped closer. "You lied to her, brother. She's special and you fucked it up."

Lorenzo shoved him. "Special? She's my fucking wife. I'm the man that knows how special she is. *Capice?*" He took a step toward Carlo. "Unless you have eyes on my woman? Do you—*brother?*"

Carlo glared but backed off with his hands up. "Of course not. I only want to help you."

It took a moment for Lorenzo to calm himself. He trusted Carlo with his life, but not with Marietta. He trusted no man with Marietta. He closed his eyes and breathed through his nose slowly. "We have to find her before Giovanni does. You want to help, then help me find her." Lorenzo marched out of the room. In the hall he ran directly into Cecilia who carried a screaming and hollering Eve in her arms.

"Where is Marietta?" he asked her.

"I don't know," Cecilia said and hurried off.

Lorenzo and Carlo split up. He went straight for the bedroom and Carlo went in search of her on the lower level. No one understood Marietta the way he did. To her his lies were proof of something inconceivable to him, that their love was false. And he couldn't let her go another minute believing that. When he entered the room he froze. He couldn't believe the destruction wielded by his lady. She trashed everything she could lift or throw. Marietta wasn't fragile. She'd take a man's balls if he turned his back on her. And that made her even more dangerous.

Carlo rushed inside. His eyes stretched at the destruction. He shook his head. "Spoke to the boys, she took Leonardo's car. He had just stepped out of it and left the keys inside. He said when he saw her speed out of the drive he couldn't catch her."

"Where the fuck could she go?" Lorenzo demanded

"How the fuck would I know? She's your wife. Remember?" Carlo replied.

Lorenzo paced. "How did she find this out? What the fuck happened here? What am I missing?" Lorenzo put his hands to his head. "You head toward Carini. I'm going towards Palermo. Page me if you find her," he said.

"Wait." Carlo stopped him. "I can't bring her back here, Lo. You saw the scene with Gio. He'll be out for blood for what she's done. If I find her I'll take her to my mother's in Capaci. You go there as well. I'll call ahead to make sure the house is empty for you two."

"Thanks." Lorenzo panted. "About what I said earlier. I didn't mean to say..."

"Forget it. I understand," Carlo said.

"*Grazie.* She means a lot to me. She's my life," he said.

"You can trust me, Lo. I... I like Marietta," Carlo said.

"*Andiamo.*"

★ B ★

There was so much pain she feared for her life. The lower half of her body felt as if it were twisted into a pretzel knot. Mira opened her eyes. Beyond the blur of tears shadows hovered. Men? She heard voices. She was being pushed. No. She was being wheeled fast down a hall. Fast.

Mira closed her eyes. "Giovanni," she wept. None of it made sense to her heart. He was her soul mate. No matter what flaws she saw in him she believed in him. Swore her life to their family and their love. Until now that faith had been unshakeable.

Who was he now?

The doors swung open with a loud swoosh. Mira was lifted by the aid of the sheets beneath her. She felt people transfer her to another bed. She could feel the blood sticky between her thighs. And worse of all she didn't feel her babies any more.

"Something's wrong!" she cried out.

A nurse cut her clothes and underwear from her body. In her heart she knew that the worst had happened. There was no more shouting between the doctors. Those with her had a controlled patience in their tone.

"Help me please! Something's wrong. I can't feel my babies!" Mira said.

322

"*Signora*, relax. We have you." A person replied before a plastic mask covered her nose and mouth. Mira's lids fluttered she blinked twice into a blinding light and then slipped into darkness.

"Giovanni... what have we done?" she whimpered and fell silent.

* B *

Giovanni brought both of his hands to his face oblivious of the blood on them. One day his life was what he knew it to be. The next everything he'd done to protect his family collapsed.

"Bella, I'm so sorry. Please forgive me," he cradled her in his arms. Renaldo drove dangerously fast around mountainous curves on the two lane highway. He prayed for speed. He prayed for her forgiveness. And he most importantly prayed for her life and the life of his sons.

"Gino and Gianni," she said, to him. The tears had stopped. She moaned in pain but said very little about his betrayal. She clung to him as his wife, deeply in need of rescue.

"I don't understand," Giovanni asked. He brought his ear close to her mouth. "What did you say?"

Mira opened her eyes. She looked at him with a glazed look of despair. "I want you to name them Gino and Gianni. Promise me."

"You are going to be okay, Bella. We will name them together. Soon." Giovanni smiled and blinked away his tears.

"Promise me!" she said in a stern voice.

"I promise. I will name them Gino and Gianni."

She closed her eyes and relaxed. He kept kissing her face and she managed a smile. That smile strengthened him. The guilt over her suffering became too much for him to bear. "I confess, Bella. I kept the secret. Not because I wanted to harm you. I did it to protect you, us, our family. I failed you. I will make it up to you I swear." He cradled her in his arms.

Mira began to sob again.

"Faster, Renaldo! Drive faster!" he shouted.

"Boss?" Renaldo said.

Giovanni's face lifted from his palms. Renaldo stepped back.

Something in his eyes made the fearless enforcer keep his distance. It scared Giovanni as well. Was it the madness that Flavio told him was his father's curse? He'd suffered some really hard losses; his mother's death being the worse before he knew Mira. This was something far different from the others. He had no defense to hide his weakness.

Giovanni lowered his gaze to the floor to conceal his despair. In his life weakness, even seen before the most loyal of soldiers, was a costly mistake.

"The doctors say they will come for you soon, Boss," Renaldo said.

Giovanni mumbled a thanks for the update. He replayed the events of the day. Mira woke up happy. The doctor came and said she was to stay in the bed. The next thing he knew Mira was in his office hysterical with Marietta.

The recollection rocked him. He sat upright. Marietta? Mira had the necklace and bracelet. Mira knew the truth of his deception because her sister told her. His gaze lifted to Renaldo. "Where is Lorenzo's wife?"

"I'm not sure. I believe Villa Mare Blu."

Who told Marietta the truth? The women were kept guarded at all times. He owned the truth. He was the dispenser of justice or injustice. And some snake had slithered past him. Yes Marietta was at fault. So was Lorenzo for bringing her to *Sicilia*. There was, however, another player.

"Mancini." Giovanni pounded his fist into his palm. Somehow Mancini had gotten inside his camp. And the old bastard had gotten to his wife. "I want you to find a phone. Call Dominic and tell him to return. Make sure he knows that I need him here now."

Renaldo nodded and walked off. If she died, if he lost his children, he'd put a bullet in Mancini himself. He'd burn everything in Palermo to the ground.

The doctor approached from the left and at first Giovanni didn't see or hear him. "We must speak, *signor*. Please come with me." Dr. Buhari said as he passed. Giovanni was up to his feet and following. They went through doors to another hall and then down to a waiting room that was conveniently empty.

"What is going on with my wife? Is she okay?"

"No she isn't. She's got preeclampsia," the doctor said.

Giovanni refused to believe the news. "She's fine. She stopped crying when we got here. She said the pain had eased up. Give her something to calm her and—"

"I'm sorry, *signor*. We are past that option now. We have to take the babies, to save their lives and hers. Your wife's organs are shutting down. And her blood pressure is giving us the most concern."

"Okay?" Giovanni said. He wiped both hands down his face. "Okay. Let's do it. Get the fuck back in there and do whatever it takes!"

"Let me finish." The doctor put up both hands that were trembling with nervousness. A nurse walked in with hospital garments for him to change into. "You have ten minutes. You need to get changed into those," Dr. Buhari said. "Baby A's head is crowning. If he's too far down the birth canal we have to deliver vaginally. The ultrasound shows that Baby B hasn't turned fully. We will massage her belly some more after the delivery of Baby A. We had to sedate her. To relax her, we needed to do this."

"How can you deliver the babies if she is sedated, naturally?" Giovanni frowned.

"We can do it." The doctor reassured him.

Giovanni grabbed the doctor by the throat. His sudden act of violence caught him and the doctor by surprise. But he felt trapped by his fears and the glaring reality of his wife's plight. He couldn't stop himself. "You save them both you motherfucker. Do you fucking hear me?" The man gripped Giovanni's wrist in fright. Giovanni tightened his hold on his throat. "You save my sons and my wife or I swear to God I will come for you!"

"Of course, of course. I will." The doctor wheezed.

Giovanni threw the doctor aside and began to change. He kept his gaze trained on the man as he left the room. He shouldn't have attacked him. He shouldn't have put fear in the man who was the only one capable to save his family. But everything he did and said was primal now. Without Dominic and Mira to reign him in he could barely get control of his rage.

"*Signor*, they are ready?" the nurse stuck her head inside.

He pulled on the hospital jacket and belted it. Giovanni was then ushered inside. He paused. Not much of her face was seen. A breathing mask covered the lower half of her mouth. A bonnet covered her hair. With legs stiff as boards he approached Mira. She looked as if she were sleeping. He found her hand and caressed the top of it. The doctors talked in hurried voices. He knew the urgency. He understood the risk. But he focused on how much he loved her and the babies. It was love that kept him standing.

"*Signor?*" the doctor said.

His gaze lifted in time to see the first of his boys pulled from between his wife's legs. Apparently they had to take the baby naturally. Giovanni left her side to be witness to the tiniest living human being he'd ever seen. The baby made no noise. The cord was cut and the little one was hurried away.

"Is he-e-e-e okay?" Giovanni stammered.

The doctors began to work frantically. When Giovanni glanced over he saw Bella had been cut surgically. With clamps opening the incision the doctor removed a bloody baby who did let out a startled cry. So small and fragile was he that Giovanni could barely speak. He'd seen a lot in his life including the death of his own father. But nothing made him weak with humility the way the sight of his boys entering the world did.

The specialist that shadowed the doctor left his side and Buhari glanced up to Giovanni. In his eyes he recognized the truth. Something was wrong.

"She's hemorrhaging," he heard the doctor say. "We will try to save her uterus. But I make no promises. The damage is..."

"Save her first. That is your priority," Giovanni said. He'd give up the future of any other kids to have his wife.

The nurse touched his hand. "*Signor,* you must go with the boys. Go, let the doctors help her."

He was torn as to what to do. He glanced back and saw the babies pushed out in separate clear boxes. He didn't want to leave Mira. With her in the state she was in. But he had to see his sons. The choice split him in half. The nurse helped him decide by gently pushing him out the door. They weren't taken far. He walked into the next room to seem them both being tubed. He could see their little feet and hands move. He stood at a respectable space.

"Their names?" the nurse asked.

"He is Gianni, and the one who cried. He... he's Gino," Giovanni said. The nurse patted his back.

"*Congratulazioni*, they're beautiful," she said.

Giovanni pulled down his mask from his mouth. "They are."

14.

Carini was a very old village with buildings made of stone architecture and tall cathedral doors that dated as far back as to Spanish occupation. Carlo drove through the village square. He decided to continue his search along the narrowed single-lane alleys that led in, around, and out of the heart of the city in search of Leonardo's car.

Leonardo drove a black two-seater with a red stripe that went from the boot over the roof and down the front hood of the car. It would be hard to miss. And though he was thorough in his search he wasn't hopeful that he'd find her. She was probably in Palermo headed for the train or airport to get the fuck out of Sicily. It's what Carlo would have done if he were a woman running from men like him and Lorenzo.

After a thirty-minute drive through every road open to him he considered abandoning the search. That was until he travelled down *via delle Scuole*. Parked curbside of a building was Leonardo's car. Carlo braked. He reversed and checked the car out. It was definitely Leonardo's. He swerved into the vacant spot ahead of it. The location felt odd. Where would she go?

Two men full of spirits stumbled from the doors of the pub. They roared with laughter, and slapped each other on the back. They stopped several others and pointed at the bar and encouraged them to go inside. Curious over the excitement Carlo exited his car. He hit the sidewalk walking fast to the pub. And was stunned at what he discovered inside.

On the bar danced a seductive Marietta Battaglia. She turned up a jug of wine and drank it dry before hurling it across the bar nearly hitting a patron. Many of the men laughed and cheered. She rolled her hips and began to pull the short hem of her mini dress up to reveal her beauty for the men. Carlo smiled and enjoyed the show for a moment, before the jeering of the men pushed him to act. The few women in the bar looked on horrified.

Once he approached several of the men recognized him. The ones that didn't got shoved to the ground or thrown out of his way while the wise quickly retreated to avoid him.

"That's enough, sweetheart. Get down!" he shouted at her. When Marietta saw him she started to run. She kicked over customers' drinks and nearly had a fatal slip on the spillage. He lunged for her and caught her by the legs. Marietta could have fought back, but to do so would have sent her sprawling over the bar to the floor. He forced the screaming woman over his shoulder. Her bare ass was up for all to see. Carlo made sure to smack her hard on it to calm her down. Marietta bit hard into his back and he grunted but kept going. Angered from the spanking she screamed like a wild cat and started hitting and bucking to be free of his hold. When he reached the door he saw a man with her thong panty on his head. He glared at the man and the guy quickly handed them over. Without missing a beat he kicked the door to the bar open and stormed out into the street.

People stopped in shock as Marietta cursed and shouted in Italian that she was being kidnapped. She yelled at those watching the scene for someone to call the *polizia*. Carlo laughed. He patted her bare ass again, unable to deny the opportunity to touch her once more.

"Let me go!" she wept.

He opened the door to the back of the car and put her inside. She scooted away from him but didn't try to flee out of the other door. Something in the way he stared at her must have communicated he was tired of the chase. Carlo threw her panties in after her and closed the door. He got behind the wheel and sped away.

"Leeeeeeeet me oooooooooooout!" she screamed and kicked the back of his seat.

Carlo turned up the radio. Marietta tried to open her car door and he cut the wheel of the car to the left almost throwing her out. His erratic driving forced her to close the door. "You are such an asshole. You're a fucking perverted asshole! You let me out now!"

"Can't do that, love. Your husband wants you," Carlo reached in the glove compartment and got out his cigarettes. He put one between his lips as he eyed her from the rearview mirror.

"Lorenzo? He's alive?" she asked, wiping at her tears. Relief flooded her heart. She saw Lorenzo on the floor, bleeding. She left him there. Carlo stared at her in the rearview mirror and their eyes

328

met. She wouldn't let the bastard see her broken. None of them would ever break her. Marietta let go a bitter laugh. "Of course he's alive. You can't kill the devil. No matter what," she said to disguise her hurt.

"What's with the whore show I walked in on? You put every man in that bar at risk. Do you know that? Lorenzo will kill anyone that mentions seeing your lady parts."

"My what? Oh you mean pussy? The one you were staring at?" Marietta tossed back. Carlo laughed. Marietta crossed her arms. "I don't care! Tell him what you saw. I don't give a shit about none of you!" she shouted.

"Oh you care. You did that to piss him off. Bad move," Carlo chuckled. He cut the wheel again and she was thrown hard into the door. Marietta suffered a strong bought of carsickness. She drank too much wine. But she didn't say another word. She couldn't. She was relieved that Lorenzo wasn't dead. Relieved that he didn't find her in the bar humiliating herself that way. But she remained too disillusioned by her hatred to say thank you to Carlo for saving her from herself.

Carlo glanced up to the rearview mirror again. He couldn't help himself. A woman's tears never got to him. But hers did. He couldn't summon the words to comfort her. But he understood her misplaced rage. And he also remembered a time when he felt his lowest and how she fed and cared for him. He took the country roads to his mother's villa. They arrived in twenty minutes. When he stopped she finally lifted her head and he could see her looking around in a panicked state.

"Don't take me back," she pleaded in a soft voice full or remorse.

"What are you talking about?" he asked.

"I can't. Let me go, please. You said you'd give me money to leave him. To disappear? I'll take it. I'll go away and I'll never come back. Help me," Marietta said.

"I thought you loved him?" Carlo asked.

"If I stay we'll just keep hurting each other," she said.

Carlo got out of the car. Marietta bolted from the door to the other side of the vehicle.

"Fuck!" he grunted and ran her down. She fought him but he got a good hold on her and half carried, half dragged her to his mother's cottage. "You fucking bastard! Get your hands off me!"

"Damn it, woman! Enough of this bullshit!" he shouted as he

forced her into his sister's room. She literally tripped over her own feet and fell back on the bed. He reached in his pocket and threw her panties at her that she dropped when she ran out of the car. "I'll page Lo and tell him to collect you."

"You're such a fucking idiot!" she shouted at him as he walked to the door. He threw up his hand as if to blow the comment off. "You think Lorenzo gives a shit about you? Huh? He killed your brother you stupid fuck."

Carlo paused.

"Che cazzo dici?" he asked.

Marietta glanced around the room. There was nothing to use as a weapon. She was trapped. And from what Lorenzo told her of Carlo to be trapped with him alone would never be a good thing. But she refused to back down. Not even when her mind screamed she should. She flipped off the bed and backed up until there was good distance between them. "I said he killed Carmine!" she challenged him. "Set up, used him and killed him dead."

Carlo approached her. Marietta swallowed hard. He was before her now. So close he could touch her if he wanted. Marietta dared him with her unwavering stare to do so. She may be petite compared to his huge frame but she was quick and she knew how to hurt a man if needed. Her adoptive father had forced her to learn how to defend herself after years of his abuse.

"Che cazzo dici?" he repeated. He slammed his fist into the wall next to her head. "Say it to my face," he said and the words came over barely above a whisper but chillingly clear. A knot of cold terror formed in her gut. Marietta never looked away from his eyes. Those piercing eyes that were now void of his sardonic humor. His face was close. He bared his teeth in a sly smile and it reminded her of the smile like that of a mad dog. His nostrils flared and his face flushed with contemptuous black-layered rage in his eyes.

Marietta cleared her throat. "Say what?"

"Say it!" he shouted.

"What are you going to do if I don't? Punish me? You get off on beating women. Is that it? Lorenzo told me you were a psycho-freak!"

He dropped his other fist on the wall. Now both fists were pressed to the wall and she was caught between his arms. He brought his face closer. She bumped her head back against the wall to avoid their lips brushing. Fear wasn't what she felt when she looked into his eyes. Primal urges surfaced.

"It's a lie," Carlo said. "You're a lying bitch."

"And you're a punk, a worthless thug who can't think for himself. A bastard. Nothing but a—"

"*Bugiarda!*" he yelled.

Marietta shrugged refusing to deny the truth. He brought his face so close his forehead rested against hers. "Don't push me. Don't…"

There was no escape. She had effectively taken her anger and frustration and made it his. And why had she done so? To torment him? To force his hand? Why was it so easy for her to hurt people when she knew how badly it felt?

"I lied," she said. "I said it to piss you off." She shoved at his chest. "Now get off me!"

His gaze lifted under his lowered brow. Marietta's hands never lifted from his chest. He felt hot under her palms. Was his skin always feverish, or only when he was pissed? She ran her hand smoothly down raw muscle. His dark gaze remained locked on her and hers on him.

"I shouldn't have said it, Carlo. But you called me a bitch! You shouldn't have said that," she breathed. "Right?"

Why hadn't he moved? His stance, the way he looked at her, she felt trapped. *He needs to move away from me.* Marietta ran both her hands back up his chest slowly until she reached his neck. She cupped the back of his neck and pulled herself from the wall closer to his mouth. He had mean lips because of the vile things he'd say and the sly smiles he gave. But at the moment they were the most kissable lips, a deep unrelenting temptation. Maybe it was the alcohol. Maybe it was the look of pain in his eyes when she told him Lorenzo killed his brother. She didn't bother to further rationalize the meaning. She acted on impulse. Before he could escape, before she could rethink her actions she brought her lips to his. Carlo turned his head away and she kissed the corner of his mouth.

"Carlo," she breathed against his ear. "Kiss me."

His gaze returned to her. His left fist left the wall and his hand went down her hip. Her lips were a mere centimeter from his. "You know you want to."

His forehead pressed to hers as his hand went beneath her skirt to caress up her thigh. He grabbed her right butt cheek and squeezed. He brushed his lips against hers. Marietta's eyelids fluttered as his tongue gently grazed the seam of her lips and she parted her lips for the sweep. Her fingers and toes curled as if an electric current went through her pussy.

Marietta opened her mouth fully for the kiss. She shook with the effort to remain standing. Carlo was slow to bring the kiss to closure. She could kiss him for the rest of her days. She dragged his breath into her lungs as she accepted his invading tongue. Carlo crushed her to the wall and ravished her. His large hands gripped her waist to keep her pinned to him as the steel groin between his legs pressed hard up against her sex. She wrapped her arms around his neck and kissed him deeply. Marietta struggled for control beneath the ravishment of his kiss and with the powerful push of his body frame pinning her to the wall. She was soon his. Carlo lifted her and she brought her legs around his waist. He kissed her face and neck. Together they went down on the bed.

"The things I want to do to you," Carlo breathed deeply. He brought down the front of her dress and lifted his head from her neck. He gazed down at her breasts. He dragged the garment lower. He stared at the piercing in her navel. His gaze flickered up to hers. She said nothing.

We should stop. We need to stop. Stop. Stop. Stop. Her inner voice shouted in response to the voice screaming *yes, yes, yes* in her head. Carlo lowered his face, flickered his tongue at her navel piercing while twisting her left nipple until the pleasure was tight and unrelenting. She squeezed her eyes shut. She wanted to disappear. She wanted to punish Lorenzo. She hadn't realized she was crying until Carlo stopped.

She opened her eyes and he stared at her.

"I want it. I do…"

"Sei una donna bugiarda," he wheezed hard. He withdrew. *"Bugiarda!"*

"I'm not lying…" She tried to bring him back to her but he knocked her hands away and stormed out of the room slamming the door. Stunned. Marietta screamed and rolled over to beat her fist against the bed. She broke down sobbing.

★ B ★

Lorenzo received the page half way through Palermo. Carlo had her. He'd drove around with no sighting. The longer he couldn't find her the more desperate he became. It took Lorenzo thirty minutes to make it to Carlo's mother's house. And he arrived to find his friend sitting outside smoking a hand rolled cigarillo possibly laced with marijuana.

"She inside?" he asked as soon as he was out of the car.

Carlo glared at him. The way his friend looked at him slowed his approach. He knew an angry Carlo and what greeted him was fury.

"Is she inside?"

"Look me in the eye and tell me you didn't kill my brother," Carlo said.

"What the fuck are you talking about? Where's Marietta?" Lorenzo shouted.

Carlo flicked his cigarillo. He exhaled a long stream of smoke. "Carmine. How did it go down?"

"We've been through this, Carlo. You know how it went down. Fuck! You want to do this now?" Lorenzo seethed. Carlo looked him over and stepped back. He wasn't sure if his best friend would take a swing or walk away. The look in Carlo's eyes said he was on the edge.

"Do you have her?" Lorenzo asked again clearly.

Carlo smirked. "Yeah. I had her."

"Had? What the fuck does that mean—had?" Lorenzo stepped in his face. Carlo didn't back away. "Where is she?"

"She's inside. She's upset. That's what happened. We're brothers right?" Carlo asked.

Lorenzo stepped even closer. His face so close their noses nearly touched. "Just so we're clear. You ever lay a hand on her I'll kill you, brother."

Carlo smiled. "Right... because a brother should never betray another." He strolled off to his car. Got behind the wheel and sped away.

Marietta observed the men from the window. When Carlo drove off Lorenzo's gaze switched to the window and she let the drape go. She found her underwear and pulled them on. To her surprise the front of her dress did have a tear. Panicked she tried to fix it. Nothing she did compensated for the rip. So she smoothed her hands back over her curly hair and wiped away her tears, preparing for her husband.

Lorenzo threw open the door.

Her stomach cramped at the sight of him. It wasn't the reaction she expected. She was still furious with him. But one look at him and her courage drained from her bones. The side of his face was bruised with dried blood from a scratch just above his brow. How many times has she seen him hurt by her hand or another? Too many to count and yet he always remained standing. Like an unchangeable force forged in a world set against him. That is not what she wanted for them. He was her partner. They were a team. Until now.

Marietta had to avert her gaze. Lorenzo closed the door behind him. She crossed her arms to the front of her breasts and kept her eyes trained to the floor. "I'm not going anywhere with you. Do you hear me? I don't want you anywhere near me. In fact we're done. I want a divorce."

"It won't happen," Lorenzo said in a flat tone.

Neither of them spoke for what felt like an eternity. Lorenzo's gaze swept her appearance and she could not mask her shame. He didn't approach her. He gave her the space she needed to breathe. She was grateful for that much.

"I'm sorry, sweetheart," he began. "I lied to you. I never wanted to. The day I found out who you were I wanted to tell you. I swear that on my life. I brought you back to Sicily because I intended for you to know the truth. No matter what it cost me."

"Then why lie? Why hide my necklace, make me think I'm crazy. Why all of it?" she shouted at him. Her mask crumbled. She couldn't prevent the tears from slipping. No matter how fucked up she was, Lorenzo was the man she loved. Even now she hurt just looking at him knowing what he'd done.

"You know why," Lorenzo answered.

"I don't! You're my husband! Or are we even married and that was a lie too!" she shouted back.

He chuckled. He shook his head. His gaze leveled on her once more. "There are rules in my life. Our life. Rules in the family I follow without question," Lorenzo said.

"Not always," she said with a snide smile. "Did you follow them when your uncle was murdered? When Carmine was murdered?"

"Fuck, woman! The shit that comes out of your mouth!" Lorenzo put his hands up to his head. He winced but chuckled. His gaze shifted to Marietta once more. "No. I didn't follow them. And where has that gotten me?" He took a step toward her and he made sure it wasn't threatening. "You have no idea what I've been through the past forty-eight hours. What I do for this family and what I've done for you. I risked my life, and everything else to bring you here. For you to know your sister."

Marietta went to him. He opened his arms to accept her. "I'm sorry, baby," Marietta said. "I'm so sorry. I shouldn't have hit you. I didn't know what to do. I called you and…"

He lifted her chin. He stared down at her. "Are you okay?"

"No. I think I'm crazy," she confessed. "I keep doing things, Lorenzo."

He kissed her. "You're special not crazy. And if you're crazy I don't give a fuck. You're mine."

"Don't make jokes. Not now," she said sadly.

His brow lifted as if to say he wasn't joking.

She relaxed and held on tightly to him with her head pressed to his chest.

"Your sister is in trouble. Do you want to stand here and fight me, or do you want to see her?" he asked. "I'm the only one that can get you in the door."

"The babies?" Marietta asked. "Did they survive?"

"I don't know. She needs you now. Let me take you to her," Lorenzo said. "Tonight I will tell you everything. You have my word."

Marietta felt foolish. She reeked of alcohol. And her actions had her filled with shame. What was wrong with her? Why did she fuck up everything in her life that was important? Did Lorenzo know how lost she was and used it to his advantage? Even if he did, he was all she had at the moment to keep her grounded. Alone and free without the family she wanted she feared her next move. "Yes. I want to see her."

"I married you because I wanted you, Marie, no one but you. Every lie I told, every secret I kept, I kept them to protect you. Look me in the eye. Am I lying now?"

"I can't tell anymore," she said softly. "All of it is more than I imagined when I came to Italy to find my father. I hate you for lying to me, and as crazy as it sounds I love you for lying to me, for protecting me from this truth."

He cupped her face in his hands. "I'll win your trust back. We are all we have, Marie. You must stop this. I'm never going to be your enemy. Never."

"I didn't mean for this to happen. Everything I love turns to shit," she said.

He kissed her brow. "Not true. This isn't your fault. None of it. And it's not Mira's. She needs you."

"I can't go to the hospital like this. I've been… I've, uh, been drinking. I can't see her like this."

"There's no time to change. I'll be with you."

She nodded. She let him go. She started toward the door and pulled his hand but he didn't move.

"Marietta?" Lorenzo said.

She stopped and glanced back. "Yes?"

"What happened with Carlo?" he asked.

The question though innocent in the delivery felt like an accusation. Marietta was careful to keep any reaction in her face absent and her tone casual. "Nothing, baby," she said. "The asshole kidnapped me from the streets of Carini and then locked me up in here. I was pissed."

Lorenzo stared at her.

"Let's go. I want to see my sister," she left the room. She held her breath praying he followed and didn't ask any more questions.

He did.

* B *

"Gio!" Catalina went straight to her brother. He stood and she was in his arms. "How is she? How are the babies? *Mio Dio,* please tell me they're both okay."

"The boys were taken to special doctors who can help. They have problems I think," Giovanni held his sister's face gingerly while he shared what he knew. He was ashamed to admit it but he couldn't bear to face the news of his sons. The only crisis his heart could manage was with his wife. Before Catalina arrived he paced outside of the doors to the operating room for news and turned anyone away who wanted to discuss anything else with him.

"And Mira? What about Mira?" Catalina asked.

"She's still in surgery," Giovanni glanced back down the hall. He half expected her to walk out of the doors grinning that the whole thing was some huge joke and she was fine. "They've had her in there for over two hours," he said.

"*Che cosa?* What is going on? What happened, Gio? How did this happen?"

The 'how' and 'why' was not something he dared ponder. If he did his rage would send him on a futile mission of revenge. For now the 'how' and 'why' would have to wait. He kissed Catalina's brow. "We have faith."

"I want to see the *bambini.* Who is with them?" Catalina asked.

"Leo, take her." Giovanni released his sister from his embrace.

"Gio, you look so tired." Catalina touched his face and he turned his head away. He didn't want to be consoled. He didn't deserve it. All of the blame for this disaster was his. Catalina must have sensed his conflict. Her voice softened, as did her touch.

"You're right, she'll recover. But you need to see your sons. Come with me. We'll go see your sons together."

They were both given cloth masks to loop over their ears and cover their mouths. They eased on cloth robes over their clothes that tied to their backs before they went inside with the twins.

"*Signor,* I was just coming to see you," the Neonatal Specialist said. He was a tall lean man with a mustache that curled on the ends. He didn't wear a mask like the others in the room and that did give Giovanni pause. He vaguely remembered him from Mira's last visit. But his mind was so filled with mournful thoughts he couldn't recall his name.

"How are they?" Catalina blurted.

"Can we speak?" the doctor asked in a hushed voice which reminded them they should keep their voices low as well. Giovanni looked to his boys and then the doctor. He dreaded the news, but with Catalina at his side he forced himself to accept whatever came next. He nodded his response. His heart had permanently lodged in his throat. He kept his arm around Catalina. Together they walked into an adjoining room to where the twins were kept. She sat. Giovanni insisted on standing.

"Baby A, I believe you named him Gianni. He's three pounds and twelve ounces. Baby B, who I believe is named Gino is two pounds nine ounces," The doctor said.

"*Mio Dio,*" Catalina made the sign of the cross before her and put her hand to her mouth. Giovanni knew one was smaller than the other. He saw the boys come into the world and was humbled by the event.

The doctor smiled at Catalina and then returned his gaze to Giovanni. "Our concern right at this moment is desaturation."

"What does desaturation mean?" Catalina asked.

"It means there was too little oxygen in the bloodstream at the time of birth. The babies were in distress, one already in the birth canal, the other had to be removed through a cesarean. Dr. Buhari did an excellent job. Your wife is strong, and so are the *bambini.*"

"What do we do, to help them through this saturation thing?" Giovanni asked. Whatever held him immobile had passed. He found his voice once again.

"Gino is the one to watch. We are treating him with higher dosages of oxygen through his breathing tube. He's responding well. But I have to be honest, his lungs are not fully developed and his vitals register weak."

Catalina stood. She put her arm around her brother's waist.

"Can you develop his lungs outside of the mother's belly? Is that what the incubators are for? Are they ovens, like healing ovens?"

The doctor frowned at Catalina. Despite it all Giovanni smiled. His sister's innocence reminded him of why he cherished her. Catalina continued with her questions. "Or will you have to operate? What does it mean when the babies' lungs aren't developed?"

"Operating is a last resort. We can give them both something to help them develop their lungs naturally, but it will take time. It means they will need assisted breathing for now. It could change in a matter of days. We are optimistic," the doctor said.

"Is it okay if I touch them?" Giovanni asked. "Hold them?"

Catalina and the doctor both looked at him surprised. Giovanni cleared his throat of any weakness. "I want to hold them," he said again.

"Not today, *signor*. Not yet. But you can see them and talk to them. It helps."

They followed the doctor out. The nurses left the care for the little boys and Giovanni was allowed his visit. One of the nurses placed nametags on each cube. He couldn't help but smile at Gino. The baby kicked his feet and moved his tiny hands. His son had a warrior's heart. He looked over to Gianni who slept peacefully. At least he hoped so. Both babies had tubing taped to their noses and their stomachs. Their lids were taped shut. They wore tiny diapers and little cloth caps on their heads. He wondered if Eve came into the world fragile and cherished.

"Look at your boys, Gio. Your sons. They're beautiful," Catalina rubbed his back.

He put his arm around her shoulder. "Gino and Gianni is what we call them. Those are the names Bella wanted. She never told me until they took her from my arms. I had decided on different names, ones from the family. Gino and Gianni are perfect for our boys but I'm not sure why Bella chose the names."

"She's naming them after you, silly," Catalina grinned.

Giovanni's brows lifted and his eyes stretched. He hadn't made the connection. How could he have missed it? He smiled behind the mask covering his mouth. "Yes, I think she was. Even now she gives me what my heart wants." He glanced back to the door. "And what have I given her?"

"A family, Gio. Our family. She's told me more than once she always wanted one again after she lost Fabiana and her grandparents. You gave her a family." Catalina said. "Mira is so proud to be your wife."

"I need to see if she's out of surgery," Giovanni said.

"Go. I'll stay with the *bambini*. They will know we're here for them."

Giovanni kissed the top of his sister's head. "*Grazie, cara mia,* I will come again as soon as I know Mira is out of danger."

"Go." Catalina waved him off. She stepped to the incubator. She touched the top of it smiling down at the baby inside. "I can handle it, Gio. Isn't that right Gianni? *Sei incredibile.* Zia Catalina is here for you little one. *Per sempre.*"

He turned and walked out.

* B *

"How did you learn the truth?" Lorenzo asked. He tapped his fingers on the steering wheel and stared straight ahead. Lorenzo always wore leather driving gloves when he drove a car and his dark lenses on his sunglasses concealed his eyes. But she sensed the hard way in which he stared.

"I tried to call you. The moment I found out I sent you a page. Two pages," Marietta said. She looked over at him. "You told me that you'd always call back. You didn't."

"I want to know, Marie. Tell me the truth. How did you find out?" Lorenzo asked again.

"Why? What difference does it make? You of all people shouldn't demand the truth," Marietta answered. If he learned that Gemma was the one to deliver the news her lifelong friend and surrogate mother would be dead. She was certain of it. And right now no matter how badly she hurt over Gemma's lies she wouldn't put her at risk.

"You will tell me, Marie. Sooner or later." Lorenzo started the car. She cut her gaze away and stared out of the window. She glanced back to the cottage where she and Carlo nearly committed the most unforgivable sin. She was grateful he stopped her. But how could she ever look him in the eye again?

* B *

There was a war raging. An eternal battle of personal restraint against crippling grief, it controlled his emotions. Giovanni concealed the inner conflict like that of a man born to live on the edge of death and consequence. He was a master at this game. However, each time a nurse or doctor appeared in the hall his façade chipped, weakened. If God took her from him he could not predict his future or be held responsible for the consequences. And there would be consequences.

The doctor approached. Giovanni held his breath.

"We're taking her to recovery," Dr. Buhari said. The man looked exhausted.

"Then she's okay?"

"We've stopped the hemorrhaging. Her uterus is in tact. She's lost a lot of blood. We're concerned about her... her heart. *Signor* Giovanni, we've induced a coma for her. It's a waiting game now."

"Waiting game? I don't understand. You took the babies. What else is wrong? You're keeping something from me." Giovanni slowly stood. He could smell the cowardice on the doctor. He could read the deception in the chosen words the doctor selectively used. The man said heart. Why would his Bella have a problem with her heart? "Tell me what is wrong with my wife?"

"I'm sorry, *signor*." The doctor put both hands up as if to back Giovanni away. "I'm sorry to be the one to tell you this."

"TELL ME!" he shouted and he felt the veins in his neck and forehead bulge.

"Your wife had a stroke." The doctor said.

Giovanni shook off the news. "No! She didn't."

The doctor blinked in puzzlement. He glanced to Giovanni's men and then back to him. "*Signor*, she did. We aren't sure how bad things are, but we got her heart started again," the doctor said in a tremulous voice.

"How the hell did she have a stroke?" Giovanni grabbed the man by the collar. He shook him. "How?"

"It's rare but it happens. Your wife arrived with a severe case of hypertension. We are lucky we brought her here in time. I don't know what caused it. I had just examined her and her blood pressure wasn't nearly as high."

Giovanni let the man go and shoved him so hard he was cast several feet away. The doctor stumbled and nearly tripped over his feet. He rubbed his temples and processed the news. A stroke? He imagined a lot of things, but a stroke was never one of them. He glared at the doctor. "Don't hold back information. I want to know everything."

For an African man his face was flushed and red. "*Signor*, your method, your threats, it's not helping. I'm her doctor and it is my duty to do the best that I can. You told me if she died so would I. Trust me I am doing everything in my power to make sure that does not happen. But she must not have stress, or chaos now. Do we understand each other?"

The doctor's gaze swung left. The man's eyes stretched with recognition. Giovanni's head turned and he sought what had the doctor so caught off guard. And suddenly it all made sense. Armando wheeled his father *Don* Mancini down the hospital hall. The old man had dressed for the occasion in a suit and tie, with a dark fedora on his head. He would look as imposing as his son if it weren't for the oxygen tubing out of his nose and hooked around his ears. And behind the father and son were eight of Mancini's men.

"What are they doing here?" Giovanni said under a stilted breath. He approached the troupe. Two of Giovanni's men were right on his heels. The Battaglias met the Mancinis halfway in the hall. "Leave," Giovanni said.

"You are in my home, Giovanni. Everyone and everything here belongs to me." The old man said and then coughed. "I will not go anywhere until I know how Mirabella is."

Giovanni glanced over to Armando and caught the gleam of smug defiance in his eyes. It was true that he had chosen Mancinis territory to have his children. Any conflict with the Mancinis now in the hospital would put his family in jeopardy. Again he had calculated things wrong. He wasn't sure how Mira and Marietta learned the truth but one look at Armando and he sensed the son-of-a-bitch knew that Mira and Marietta were his sisters. He couldn't risk his men finding out this way. He was certain Mancini wanted the same.

"You and I will talk, and then you will go old man. I can give a shit about territory. I can give a shit about your authority." Giovanni said.

Don Mancini's head tilted back. Steely dark eyes glared up at Giovanni from under the shadow of his fedora. "We shall see what is important to you, Giovanni. Yes. Let's talk."

Armando wheeled his father toward the waiting rooms. Giovanni wiped his hand down his face and calmed himself. He had no choice but to follow.

15.

"I can't go in there, Lo," Marietta said. "I thought I could, but I can't."

Lorenzo sat with her in the car. He stared at those arriving and leaving the *ospedale*. Marietta's fear was understandable. He wouldn't, however, let her be ruled by it. He hadn't lied when he said he wanted to unite her with her sister. He truly wanted to heal what was broken in his wife. Maybe if he did so he'd find a way to heal what was broken in him?

"Did you hear me? I said I can't go in there," Marietta said.

"You can. We'll sit here until you accept it." Lorenzo's gaze slipped over to her. "What are you afraid of?"

"Well for one your evil cousin. He'll blame me for what happened," Marietta said.

Lorenzo smiled. "You aren't afraid of him. You should be," Lorenzo chuckled. "But you're too damned stubborn to realize it. Now, tell me who you are really afraid of."

Marietta combed her fingers back through her thick bushy locks. She sucked down a deep breath. She spoke with her head down. "Mirabella. I'm afraid for her, my sister. What if something happens to the babies? She won't forgive me for telling her the truth. She's all I've got and I've been a bitch to her from the day I met her." Marietta lowered her hands. "I'm not good at this. I don't know how to make things right with people. Look at us. I should be wearing your balls as earrings after the way you deceived me."

Lorenzo lifted her chin with his finger. "It's not for you to make right. She's your blood. She's your family. What happened to you happened to her. Go in there and help your sister. You need this, Marie, and she does too," he chuckled. "As for my balls, I'd rather them in your mouth than on your ears."

Marietta smacked him playfully. He reached over and hugged her. She kissed him. "How come I can't stay mad at you?" she asked.

"Because you and I don't deal in bullshit. We are who we are, and we accept it." Lorenzo teased with a sly smile. "Besides, I think we should fight more later. It's good for us."

Marietta let him go. She looked to the hospital. "Can we stay in the car for a little longer? I think I need a little longer," she said.

Lorenzo turned on the car and put the a/c on full blast. "Take all the time you need."

* B *

Giovanni paced. It was just he and Mancini. Not even Armando was allowed in for their closed-door meeting. The old man watched him from his chair. He showed no fear or concern for his safety. Men like him never did. Mancini had crushed so many others' lives that he now had little respect for his own. Giovanni had to force down the urge to not snatch him from his wheelchair and body slam him into the wall.

"How is my daughter?" the old man asked.

"Don't fucking call her that!" Giovanni seethed.

Mancini arched a brow. *"Perchè?* She's mine, Gio. I made her." He sneered. "She has my blood in her veins." The last of his comment stripped Giovanni of his restraint but Mancini continued and his pursuit stopped him cold. "You have a daughter. What is the child's name? Eve? Ah, yes you named her after your mother. Would you let any man stand between you and Eve?"

"You fool, no one old man. You can give a shit about the twin daughters you left in America. Who she is has nothing, absolutely nothing to do with why you are here now!"

"Then enlighten me. Why am I here now?" Mancini choked down a cough that broke his question midway through.

"To test me. To find my weakness. To destroy my marriage!" Giovanni shouted.

"Son," Mancini smiled, and to Giovanni he seemed more confident than he should. "I've told you. I want Mirabella, not you. Only her."

"Bomba!" Giovanni shouted. "She wants nothing to do with you."

"Then tell her who I am," Mancini replied with the upward toss of his chin. "Let her tell me to my face."

"How did you know we were here? How?" Giovanni demanded.

Mancini wheezed. He inhaled a deep dose of oxygen before he spoke. "Her mother, that's how I knew, that's why I came."

"Her mother's dead," Giovanni said.

"Yes. But they are connected on this day in ways you don't know. Lisa, Mirabella's mother, almost died when she delivered my girls." Mancini did a deliberate pause and Giovanni held his breath for the rest of the news. The old man took his sweet time in sharing it. After several seconds of him dragging air from his tank he spoke. "She had a stroke when giving birth. It was bad. She could no longer have children. She sat in a coma for days."

The news twisted and turned his gut. He never considered the medical information Mancini may have on his Bella's mother. Mancini's defiance and entitlement did not overshadow the hurt and longing that lay naked in his eyes. "Is it true? Did Mira deliver my grandsons early?"

"She did." Giovanni turned away. He closed his eyes and struggled for his own breath. He felt as if his heart had been squeezed by a vice in his chest.

"And how is she?" Mancini asked He nearly pleaded with a tremor in his voice.

Giovanni didn't answer.

"How is she?" Mancini barked.

"Her heart stopped." Giovanni confessed in a voice heavy with anguish.

"This is your fault, Gio. Yours. Bringing her here. Feeding your ego to have all things Sicilian when you're not."

"I'm as much Sicilian as you." Giovanni answered.

Mancini chuckled, "No, but thanks to my daughter your sons are more Sicilian than you."

Giovanni cut his gaze back over his shoulder. Mancini smiled as he spoke, a sadistic turn of his lips that had no humor present. "Ignoring the doctor's warnings. Keeping her locked away from me. All of it put her in jeopardy."

"My wife, my kids, my *famiglia* old man. Mine!" he shouted. "I brought her here because I am Sicilian and so is she—we belonged here. You were never a fucking factor!"

Mancini sucked down more oxygen.

Giovanni leaned in. "She knows about you, Marsuvio. I told her the truth."

Mancini gaped.

Giovanni nodded that he was telling the truth.

"She knows?" Mancini asked.

"Yes. And it didn't matter to her. You were not even a consideration for her."

"Does she know what Tomosino had done?" Mancini replied. "Did that matter?"

"She's a Battaglia, it ends there. She's Catholic now, married me before God. My father's sins and yours can never change the fact that she is my wife. Never. You can go." Giovanni turned for the door.

"Gio!"

He stopped.

"You don't want to go to war with me, son. Not over this. I have nothing to lose. Death is the only thing waiting for me now. I'll take you with me to have five minutes with my daughters."

He glanced back. "And Armando? Does he want to know his little sisters?"

Mancini picked his hat up from his knees and rested the fedora on the top of his head. "My son puts family first in all things. Like you."

"Bullshit! Your late need to be a father makes my wife and her sister a target in your son's eyes, you and I both know it. Your men learn that you have a daughter who is my wife what does that do for you, for him? Huh?" Giovanni expelled a deep sigh. "I'll tell you what happens next. We go to war. Because there is no way the Mancinis and the Battaglias can be family. And for the first time since we were fifteen Armando and I agree on something."

"I've put Mira in my will. I've put Marietta in my will." Mancini wheezed. "When I die they inherit everything with their brother. If anything happens to them he loses his fortune. I have planned this for years, Gio. Have you done the same?"

Giovanni shoved the door open and stormed out. He wouldn't hear another word. Armando glanced up when he walked out into the hall. Their eyes connected and locked.

Marietta walked a step behind Lorenzo. He held her hand. When they arrived in the wing of the hospital where Mira was her courage had all but evaporated. Just as they turned the corner she saw Giovanni step out of a door. He glared at a strikingly handsome Sicilian who leaned against the wall in a tailored suit.

Lorenzo stopped. So Marietta had to as well.

"What is it, Lo?" Marietta asked.

Another man wheeled out of the room Giovanni exited. He was older. He had an oxygen tank fastened to the back of his chair. At first none of the men saw them. It was Giovanni who looked left and his eyes connected with hers.

"Who is it, Lo?" Marietta asked.

The old man in the wheelchair's gaze turned her way. He stared at her.

"It's your father, sweetheart," Lorenzo said.

"My fa-ther?" Marietta asked. Surprise stabbed her heart. "That's him? Marsuvio?"

"Now is not a good time, Marietta. Do you understand?" Lorenzo said through his teeth. "We are here for Mira. Only Mira."

The suffocating feeling of restraint tightened her throat. She couldn't reply. She stared into the eyes of the man and felt so many things at once. He looked powerful. Even in his chair he looked intimidating. The fedora on his head didn't give her a clear look at his dark penetrating eyes. But she could tell at one time he'd been strikingly handsome. His broad shoulders and long legs in the chair made him over six foot tall at the very least. The inner torment over the confrontation she's wanted to have with this man since she learned Octavio Leone was not her birth father tore at her heart.

The bastard wanted her dead. It's what Gemma told her. And he was a rapist. It's what Gemma said of him. He was the man who destroyed her mother—made her a junkie and left her for his enemies. She wished she had a gun to unload on him. Lorenzo began to walk. Marietta knew she matched his pace but somehow she felt as if he dragged her along. She went numb all over. Her eyes never left the old man. He may have been feeble in the chair he sat in but his eyes were alarmingly focused.

"Gio? How is Mirabella?" Lorenzo asked.

Giovanni's stare never wavered. Marietta sensed she shouldn't look away and she didn't. But she ached to look to her father who watched her.

"I want to see her," Marietta said.

Giovanni frowned. He glanced up at Lorenzo. Neither spoke but Marietta sensed they communicated. The men in the hall stared on in silence. Her father stared on in silence. Giovanni turned and started off. Lorenzo's gaze lowered to Marietta. "Go with him."

"What?" Marietta asked alarmed. "Without you?"

"Go. I need to deal with our guests." Lorenzo glanced over to Marsuvio. She dared look at the man. He said nothing. She felt nothing for him. Without another word of objection she did what she was asked. She glanced back twice to Mancini. The old man never took his eyes off her.

When she caught up to Giovanni around the corner, he stood there waiting for her. "I will let you see her, because I owe it to her and maybe you. But let's be clear, I have not forgotten your role in this. I will not have you or anyone say or do anything to harm her."

"I understand," Marietta said. "I have not forgotten your role in this also."

Giovanni's left brow arched. He looked her over. "You're nothing like my Bella," he said with disgust and walked off. Marietta shot her middle finger at him when his back was turned. She followed him. He stopped and spoke to a nurse. She said a few things and then pointed.

He addressed Marietta without a glance backward. "Stay out here until I send for you."

"Wait! You said I could see her," Marietta said.

Giovanni didn't respond and walked inside the room. Marietta crossed her arms and dropped back on the wall to wait. She'd wait all night if she had to. The hall, rooms, staff, everyone was extra quiet. She assumed they were in the ICU wing of the hospital, but didn't ask.

* B *

Mira lay tucked under a thin blanket with a breathing tube down her throat. Like her sons she needed the oxygen fed to her. Her hair was thick and untamed, her body still and quiet. Giovanni stepped to the foot of her bed. The endless day of waiting had finally grayed into this despondent dawn. A new anguish seared his heart. Giovanni wondered if she suffered. He gripped the railing at the foot of the bed and dropped his head.

Did she suffer because of me?

For the first time since he thought she had died because of his negligence, he wept. Not since the nightmare started did he allow himself a single tear. But alone with her in that moment he couldn't hold his anguish back any longer. Terrible regrets assailed him. Smothering his sob, his fingers curled and his fists tightened as he gripped the cool steel of the footboard. The release freed him. It took several long minutes before he could regain control of himself. He did.

He walked around the bed to the other side. He grabbed a chair and pulled it close and sat in it. With extreme care Giovanni took her listless hand into his. It felt warm to the touch. A smile formed on his lips. Often when they slept he'd feel her touch in their bed either to his

347

chest or his face. He'd open his eyes to find she'd reached for him in her sleep. Giovanni pressed his lips to her knuckles and closed his eyes.

"Bella," Giovanni cleared his throat. "You did it," he paused only because he found it hard to breathe at the moment. He pressed on past his anxiety and smiled to keep back the tears. "Our sons are alive, they are beautiful little ones. Gianni is three pounds. Gino is two. He had the toughest time. But he's strong, like you. He will survive. We are survivors, you and me."

There wasn't any sign that she heard or understood him. Giovanni pressed her hand to the side of his tear soaked face. "No more secrets. They've hurt us too much, mine and yours. I understand that now. I've learned a lesson... I have. I swear it." He kissed her hand.

Giovanni set her hand down gingerly. He dropped back in his seat with a deep exhale. He stared at his wife and considered all they faced. He would have to do today the things necessary to make forgiveness between them possible.

"Someone wants to see you," he said. He chewed on his bottom lip and struggled with the rest of his news. "I won't lie to you... I want to be selfish. I want to keep them all away. But I know you need me to be stronger than my pride." His gaze switched to the door to the room. "But I swear to you, Bella, none of them will come between us. Ever." After a long moment he forced himself to stand. He leaned over and smoothed her hair from her brow. He kissed her on the forehead twice. *"Sei la mia blu rosa. Vita mia,"* he whispered that she was his blue rose, his life.

Giovanni walked into the bathroom in her room and cleaned his face to ensure his face was cleared of any evidence of tears. Once done, he collected himself before he opened the door. Marietta looked up at him. She had eyes like his wife. It was damn hard to look into her eyes. Unable to speak he simply nodded for her to come inside and held the door open wide for her to pass through. Before he didn't see the resemblance between the sisters, now each time he looked at Marietta all he saw was his wife. She was hesitant in her steps at first. He observed her as she passed under the threshold. Marietta paused just inside of the door. "What is wrong with her?" Marietta asked softly.

"Her heart stopped during delivery. Thanks to you," Giovanni said. He regretted the comment the moment it parted his lips.

Marietta's head sharply turned. She looked up at him with defiance. "You mean thanks to us. Me and you," she replied.

Giovanni had to smile. "Yes, because of us," he agreed.

Marietta returned her gaze to Mira. "Will she wake soon?" she asked.

"They put her in a coma. The doctors say we can only do short visits. You have ten minutes." Giovanni left the room. He sucked down a deep breath in the hall and stood guard at the door.

Marietta found a chair had been brought close to the side of the bed. She wanted to sit but she didn't know if it was appropriate considering what happened between them. She approached the foot of the bed. "Mirabella, it's me. Marietta," she said. She cleared her throat. "I... I'm so sorry, about everything. Forgive me. I knew you were on bed rest and I..." Marietta stopped herself. Nothing she said could change the events of the day. "You have to wake up. I never had a sister. I've always wanted one." She wiped her tears. The admission was dredged from a deep place of longing.

"Your boys and little girl need you." Marietta sucked down a deep breath for bravery and continued. "So many people need you."

Mira didn't stir. Not a hint of understanding was evident. Marietta walked around the bed and sat by the side of it. "Weird, huh? You and me? When I think on it I always felt I had... someone like me in the world. I hated my adoptive father he was a... very cruel man. He used to lock me in a closet when I was little. He would hit us for anything he thought we did wrong. I... uh, I would hide in my room and pretend I was somewhere else. Like with another family, ya know? I knew I had one. I felt you." Marietta wiped her tears from her cheeks. "That's why I came to Italy. Because of this feeling that I belonged somewhere, to someone. I thought it was my real father or mother, but it was you. Wasn't it?"

Marietta closed her eyes. "I'm rambling. I know. I'm not good with words. I just say whatever's in my head. There's so much I want to know about you, about my real family. Our grandparents. The farm? Is it still there?" Marietta sighed, deeply. She cleared her throat and tried to be more eloquent. "I want to tell you about me. I owned a store, a business. I make things, like you. I was a decorator. Or I tried to be..." her voice trailed off.

Marietta's eyes fell on Mira's hand. Her sister's diamond wedding ring glistened on her finger. She lifted her own hand and reached to touch Mira's but her courage failed her. She couldn't. She lowered her hand back to her lap. "You don't know me. You don't have to know me if you don't want to. But you have that little girl, and your twins. Do you want your children to grow up without you?" Marietta asked. "Please don't give up!"

"You heard her." A voice said. "You aren't a quitter are you?"

Mira's gaze volleyed from left to right. The atmosphere was thick like smoke. It smelled and tasted of nothing but the fogged air made visibility impossible. When she turned in search of an exit the person who spoke walked out of a cloud of nothingness. Fabiana. Her friend looked unchanged. Her thick scarlet hair hung in graceful curves around her shoulders and was as radiant as her blue eyes. She wore the yellow dress Mira loathed and shook her hips as a reminder that she loved to tease Mira.

"Well? Do I get a hello?" Fabiana grinned.

Mira went to her friend. Fabiana opened her arms to her. She hugged her. She wept.

"How could he do this to us?" Mira sniffed. "How could I be so wrong about Giovanni?"

Fabiana hugged her tighter and Mira clung to Fabiana with all her might. "I'm sure he had his reasons, Mira. Men. They always have their reasons. And a man like Giovanni Battaglia has the most complicated of reasons. Right? You do realize that now?"

Mira let her go. "Everything has fallen apart. My children, I don't know if they will make it. And Giovanni..."

"What about Giovanni?" Fabiana asked in a voice that sounded eerily similar to her conscience.

"I know what he is. But with me... he was supposed to be different. I thought trust was something unbreakable between us after our past mistakes. He's not the man I thought he was."

Fabiana touched her face. "Isn't he?"

Mira closed her eyes to the question. Giovanni was many things, but with her he was supposed to be different. Now she knew he wasn't.

"You have a sister?"

Mira nodded and tried to hide her smile. How could joy and anger exist in her at one time? It made no sense. "I think so."

"A twin? How the hell did that happen?" Fabiana laughed.

"I have no idea. All of it is so strange to me." Mira lifted her gaze to Fabiana's. "I can't do this. I don't want to see Giovanni, hear his excuses. I don't know what I feel right now about his lies. And her... Marietta. Who is she? Really? I don't know how to wake up one day and find out you have a long lost twin. How does a person deal with that?"

"Giovanni first. Deal with him. He's your husband."

"Don't remind me," Mira sighed.

"I have a question?"

"Go ahead," Mira said.

"Is it possible you feel how he did?" Fabiana asked. Mira walked away from her. She stared out into the emptiness. Fabiana was close. She could feel her even in the haze of her mind. "When you took Eve from him, how did he feel the day he learned you kept his daughter a secret?"

"So that's why he did this? Revenge? To punish me?" Mira asked.

"Possibly, or maybe he did it for the same reasons you did back then." Fabiana touched her shoulder. "Maybe he did it out of fear. Love can make you do some of the craziest things. Look at me."

"Look at you. None of this is real. You're gone. Forever. And some days I can pretend it doesn't hurt. But there are other days. Hard days. I can barely get out of bed because I miss you so much."

Fabiana's smile dimmed, her blue eyes glistened with tears. "I'm in your heart. Whenever you need me I'm here. Always. Forever." Fabiana said.

Mira nodded. "Did you know, Fabiana? When you met Mancini, did you know he was my father?"

Fabiana didn't answer.

Mira put her hands to her head. "Teddy had to have known. He set us up." Mira remembered the days of Teddy selling her on the idea of moving to Italy. How relentless he was. "The letter Marietta gave me. It said... Giovanni's father put a contract on my mother. That can't be possible. Can it?"

"I don't know, sweetheart," Fabiana answered.

"Did Giovanni know?" Mira touched her heart. "When he met us, when he found my bracelet? Did he know? Were we set up by him? Why? Is my entire life with him a lie?"

"Ask him, Mira. None of the answers are here with me. I wish I had them for you. I wish for so many things. You have to stop running from what you fear. The only thing that can heal your family now is your love for them. Your strength."

Mira sighed. "You said something was coming. This?"

Fabiana walked towards her. "You are Donna Mirabella Battaglia. That means so many different things to so many different people, including your husband. You're going to have to decide what it means to you. Something is coming, a big change, and that something is you," Fabiana said.

"Will you stay with me?" Mira asked.

Fabiana laughed. That musical laughter of hers was the same. "Where else would I go? I'll stay, sweetheart, for as long as you want me to."

The door opened. Marietta lifted her head and Giovanni walked back inside. She glanced to Mira. Her sister continued to breathe through the tube. Not even a flicker of movement under her eyelids. "Can I stay? I want to," Marietta said.

He nodded his head. She watched him go to the other side of the bed and bring another chair with him. He sat to Mira's right. They faced each other with Mira between. Giovanni's cool violet blue eyes were hard and his stare unrelenting. She held his stare with equal accusation and dislike until she could no longer stand it. She returned her attention to her sister. This time she reached for her hand and touched it. She caressed the top of it. No matter what happened she would not leave her side. No matter what comes next.

* B *

Lorenzo watched from the parking lot. Armando helped Mancini into their car. Lorenzo made sure to escort them out of the hospital without incident. His effort did little to quell the tension between them. Mancini glared at Lorenzo from the inside of the car. The raw anger he saw in the old man was an open threat they would have to deal with. And soon. Before Armando got behind the wheel he smirked at Lorenzo and gave him a simple nod. Lorenzo nodded his head in response to the challenge.

The Mancinis drove out of the lot with their men following.

"Lo?" Renaldo said.

"How many men here?" Lorenzo glanced back at Renaldo.

"Six."

"I need ten more. Every floor and entrance of this *ospedale* needs to be covered. Understand?"

"That means I can only keep three at Villa Mare Blu," Renaldo said.

"Do it."

Renaldo nodded. "I have been unable to reach Domi. I've left several messages and contacted Santo. He will locate Domi and deliver the news."

"How is Gio? How has he been?"

"Not well, Boss. But Catalina's here and she helps. She's with the *bambini*. I heard one of the nurses say they don't expect one of the *bambinos* to make it. He's really sick."

Lorenzo glanced up at Renaldo. "Call Bagheria. Speak to Vito. Tell him the news. He'll bring in the family—my aunts and cousins.

352

If we lose one of the babies we need the family here."

Renaldo turned to leave and Lorenzo stopped him. "Call *Cardinal Callori di Vignale* and inform him of the birth of the twins." Renaldo nodded and walked off. Lorenzo wiped his hand down his face. He could kill Giovanni for this. He warned him. They all did. His cousin was blinded by his selfish almost arrogant devotion to his wife. He could never see clearly when it came to Mirabella. History between those two predicted this outcome.

The only option left to Lorenzo was to bring Giovanni through his anger and fears. Lorenzo looked up to the sky. He felt the weight of his wife and cousin's suffering on his shoulders. Both would blame themselves if the baby died. Mira had to survive this. The boys had to survive this. If they didn't he'd lose Gio to insanity and Marietta as well. He turned and walked back inside.

* B *

Giovanni's gaze switched from his wife to the door when Lorenzo walked inside. He watched his cousin approach Marietta. He squeezed and massaged her shoulders before leaning over and brushing a kiss across her cheek. Lorenzo whispered something to Marietta that made her nod her head with obedience. *Where was this obedience when she was with his wife telling her all of his secrets?*

Lorenzo's gaze lifted and locked on Giovanni. Without a word between them Giovanni stood and walked out. He could sense Lorenzo followed. The conversation they needed to have couldn't be had in the hall. They searched two rooms before they found an empty one. He threw the door opened and walked inside. Lorenzo closed the door.

"How bad is it?" Lorenzo asked.

"Her heart stopped. A stroke is what they said. The doctor put her in the coma. They were worried about organ failure," Giovanni said. He sat on the edge of the bed. "She's been through hell but she's alive."

"And Mancini?" Lorenzo asked.

"He said Mira has the same issue her mother had."

"Issue? What issue?" Lorenzo asked.

"Her mother almost died delivering twins—our wives. He said he came to warn me. Bullshit. He came to beat his chest. To show me he had more control over my wife's fate than me."

"To be her father?" Lorenzo asked.

Giovanni glanced up. "How did Marietta find out the truth? Who told her?"

"Working on figuring it out. The entire situation is a mess. I just found her an hour ago," Lorenzo said.

"Found her?" Giovanni frowned.

"She ran from Villa Mare Blu. Carlo found her in Carini. I had to bring her back." Lorenzo wiped his hand down his mouth and chin. "I warned you, Gio. We all did."

"What the fuck does that matter now?" Giovanni stood. He paced around the bed. "I did what was necessary and you know it. Mira would be fine, my sons would be fine if your wife hadn't gone to her and filled her head with lies!"

"Lies?" Lorenzo arched a brow.

Giovanni put his hands to his head. "I had it under control. I had it all under control."

"No, Gio. You never did. Those two women are blood. What have we always said about blood? About family?" Lorenzo asked. "Nothing either of us could do would have prevented this day. We should have been the men to make it happen. Now we have to deal with it." Lorenzo stepped further into the room. "I want your word that you won't take any of this out on Marietta. She's a victim. Mancini's victim, your victim, mine too. She never asked for any of this."

"I would never harm your wife, Bella's sister. But you keep her in line," he leveled a finger on Lorenzo. "This isn't about me wanting to drive them apart. You saw Armando and how he looked at her."

"I did." Lorenzo said through clenched teeth.

"Good. Then you know what's at stake. Armando will not divide his family legacy for our wives—for us. He is not going to sit back and accept this."

"They're married to us, why the fuck does he care? We have no intention of advertising the blood tie." Lorenzo scoffed.

"The old man has put your wife in his will. Mira is in his will. The Mancini fortune is to now be cut three ways."

"Really?" Lorenzo's brows lifted.

"Now do you understand the threat?"

"So what now?" Lorenzo asked.

"I'm beginning to think the old bastard really does want to reunite with Bella and Marietta. That makes him weak enough to give me a choice."

"Then give him the reunion," Lorenzo said. "We have the Mancini fortune at our fingertips."

Giovanni waved off Lorenzo's advice. "I don't give a fuck what happens, he will never come near her! Never! But if Mira and Marietta are both willing to sign over their inheritance to Armando we can have a different truce after the old fucker is dead."

"Why take that course, Gio? You are talking about millions at stake."

"I don't want his fucking empire by default. I won't use my wife that way!" Giovanni snapped.

Lorenzo nodded. "Of course. We need to get the women out of Sicily. I can't control much here. This is Mancini's territory. You know how this goes."

"Yes, I know," Giovanni said. "What was I thinking bringing her here? How could I have been so blind? I wanted the boys born here. Now my sons barely cling to life. And she... she's not well."

Lorenzo walked over to his cousin. He gripped his shoulders and squeezed. "You are going to have to tell the men. Tell the family who Mira and Marietta are to each other. And then tell the Neapolitan clans that we both have married Mancini's bastard daughters. We can't let any of this go beyond us. We need to unite."

Giovanni nodded. "Agreed. But I won't leave here. Not until Mira and the boys are well."

"I'll think of something." Lorenzo assured him. He patted Giovanni's cheek and turned for the door.

"Lo?" Gio said.

His cousin stopped.

"I should have listened to you. Trusted you." Giovanni admitted. "I won't make that mistake again."

Lorenzo smiled "Good to see you coming to your senses," he said and left.

* B *

Marietta continued with her vigil. The nurse arrived. She used a syringe to insert something into the drip bag that ran a line of fluid to Mira's veins. The doctor visited next and read her chart. The man checked Mira's vitals and left. No one gave her an update. If she spoke they acted as if she wasn't in the room. She found that odd. But typical of the behavior of the staff that bowed whenever her sister's husband entered the room.

God never answered Marietta's prayers when she was younger. It was only now with the discovery of the family she never had she began to believe in his existence. She closed her eyes and said a silent prayer for a healing.

The door behind her opened. Someone watched her. She could sense the presence of the other but didn't open her eyes to confirm. And then the person's soft foot approach grew closer. A hand rested on her shoulder. *"Andiamo,"* he said in a deep voice that filled her with warmth.

"I'm not leaving her," she replied. "She needs me."

"You need to change clothes, eat. Your dress is ripped." Lorenzo whispered.

Marietta glanced down at the front of her dress and immediately fixed the tear.

"I'll bring you back," Lorenzo reasoned.

Marietta glanced up at her husband. The nasty mark to the side of his face was still there. Each time she looked at it she was reminded of the pain and deception between them. Still she loved him. And she feared that even his disappointing her could never change that. What would life as his wife mean if she had to learn to live with disappointments?

Lorenzo brushed the back of his hand across her cheek. *"Mi manchi,* I was in hell for almost two days, *cara.* All I could think of was you, returning home to you. Come with me. I need you."

"Don't, Lorenzo," she turned her face away. He captured her chin and turned her face back upward to gaze into her eyes.

"Let's go home. Fight. Talk it out. Make love. *Per favore,"* he whispered. "My head hurts. Look at what you did to my face. I need you to take care of me too."

"I can't. I don't have the energy," she turned her face away and he released her chin. Her heart still burned with guilt over how close she came to seducing Carlo. And she didn't want to leave Mira. Not now.

"I insist," Lorenzo said.

Marietta wished to be alone with her thoughts and guilt. With Lorenzo it was either an ignored or unreasonable request. She looked up at him once more. Lorenzo arched a single dark silky brow to whatever he read in her eyes. Defeated she stood and he helped her. She touched Mira's hand. "Will they call me if something changes? Will you bring me back as soon as she is awake?"

"You have my word, Marie," he said, rubbing her hip and then ass.

"Your word means shit," she knocked away his groping hands.

He chuckled. "True. But it's all I can give you right now."

Marietta leaned over and kissed Mira's brow. She felt such a sharp pang of love for her sister. *How was that possible?* They barely knew each other and it felt as if she had known her all her life. "I read somewhere that twins feel each other's pain, that we know when the other is in trouble. I wonder if over the years we did—feel each other."

"It's possible. What do you feel now?" Lorenzo asked.

"Sadness. Deep sadness," Marietta said. "The birth of her sons should be a happy time for her but all I feel is sadness, like this open wound in my chest."

Lorenzo eased his arm around her waist and held her. He kissed the top of her head. "She'll come out of it. She's like you, *cara*, a warrior."

Mira shook her head unable to stop her tears. She couldn't believe how much she cried. "Do you cry in dreams?" she asked Fabiana.

"It's your dream remember?" Fabiana chuckled. "Guess I suck at cheering you up. Huh?"

Mira wiped her tears and laughed. But soon her laughter hollowed out. "Why am I dreaming? Am I dying?" she asked aloud. When Fabiana didn't answer she turned and looked to her friend. The smile had faded from her best friend's lips. "I don't want to die."

"Death isn't all bad," Fabiana shrugged.

"Don't make jokes. Not about death," Mira said.

"Alright, girl, stop being so damn sensitive. I'm the one dead, remember?"

Mira sighed. "Maybe when you die you move on and it's not bad. But for the people you leave behind it's a never ending feeling of loss." When she spoke her voice echoed from every direction. She could see no walls, ceiling or floor. She just existed in the depths of her mind. "I lost my mother and I always felt empty because of it. Like half of me was incomplete. Turns out it was. I had a sister and never knew it."

"What will you do?" Fabiana asked. Suddenly she was standing off to her left instead of her right. "What will you do about Giovanni and your sister?"

"I don't know. Should I punish him for being what's in his nature for him to be? Should I punish myself for being so weak? I can't believe I have a sister." Mira smiled. "And Marietta of all people. We have so much time to make up for."

"What is she like?" Fabiana asked.

"Bold, sassy, full of courage. She has this sexy confidence about her. You know she could be my muse. Since I lost you," Mira smiled at Fabiana "She has this thing about her I never had," Mira said. "I kind of envy her free spirit."

"I wish I could know her," Fabiana chuckled. "We could've been the three musketeers!"

Mira glanced to her friend. "She married Lorenzo."

Fabiana laughed. "Now that there is irony. The man sure does like his women hot."

"They make some pair." Mira agreed.

"What about Giovanni?" Fabiana asked. "Every time I ask you about him you change the subject."

Mira closed her eyes. "I'm so angry, so hurt. I'm afraid for him, for me."

"Afraid of what, Mira?" Fabiana asked.

"That something is broken with us. Something I can't fix. I'm afraid I can't forgive him." When Mira opened her eyes she was alone. She didn't call for Fabiana. She didn't need to. Fabiana was dead. In this she would remain alone with her sadness.

The day had all but slipped away. When Giovanni entered his wife's room twilight had cast shadows about. After concluding another visit with his sons he passed Lorenzo and Marietta in the hall as they were leaving. Marietta said there was no change.

The doctor passed word to one of the nurses that he would meet with him once he finished his rounds. He had hope in his heart that maybe some news of improvement was forthcoming. But Mancini's warnings kept surfacing to the front of his mind. Why hadn't he considered the fact that her mother gave birth to twins? The medical history alone could have helped the doctors understand the care his Bella needed, or at the very least the risks.

"Bella, I've visited the boys," he said. He sat next to her bed and took her hand into both of his. He held it with gentle loving care. "They rest. They are doing well. Gianni and Gino, your sons."

She didn't move. He brought her hand up to his mouth. He kissed her hand. The answering silence was the worst. Fatigue weighted his shoulders, his lids. He closed them and held her hand. "I won't leave you, sweetheart. I'm here. Right here."

"Catalina?" a soft voice whispered.

Catalina lifted her head from her hand. She had dozed off in the chair. Rosetta appeared in a green dress she recognized. She glared at her cousin. Once again she had raided her closet without asking. "What are you doing here?" Catalina stretched her arms up from her seat. She chose to ignore Rosetta's actions. The dire situation of the twins and Mira was more important than another theft of one of her dresses.

"Lorenzo came home. He told me to come and sit with the babies. So you could go home. Eat something, shower."

"I'm fine, you can go." Catalina stood. She walked over to Gino's incubator. She stared down at his little chest that rose and fell with each breath he took. Rosetta ignored her order to leave.

"He's so small. I've never seen a baby this small."

"He's premature you idiot," Catalina hissed.

"Don't call me an idiot!" Rosetta snapped.

"Shhh!" The nurse admonished them both. Catalina threw her hands up in defeat. She was tired. She'd been at the hospital for six hours. When she checked the time she found it was close to seven in the evening. She needed the reprieve. Maybe she could go and return before she was missed.

"I'll be back. Just need to shower and take a nap then I'm coming back."

Rosetta moved on to the other baby. She tapped the top of the incubator. "What're their names?"

"Don't do that!" Catalina hissed. The nurse looked up with a disapproving scowl. Rosetta smiled down at the baby.

"But they're so cute. Like little dolls. Are they well? Why are their eyes taped shut?"

Catalina stepped closer to Gino's incubator and looked at him. "He's the smallest. His name is Gino. He has a problem with his lungs. They both do. That baby is Gianni. They are giving them something, baking them in these ovens so they can grow I guess."

"Oh wow," Rosetta said. She glanced over. "Did you hear?"

"Hear what?" Catalina rubbed the top of Gino's incubator.

"What made the *Donna* go crazy? Why she was brought here to have the babies?" Rosetta asked. Before Catalina could respond she continued. "Leo said he heard them before they left the room. That he tried to stop the *Donna* from going to Gio. But she was crying and upset."

"Heard what?" Catalina asked. "Heard who?"

"They're sisters!" Rosetta whispered.

"Who?"

"Lorenzo's wife and the *Donna.*"

Catalina laughed. "Bullshit!"

"It's true. Leo said that Lorenzo's wife showed up in the *Donna's* room and told her that they were sisters and that Gio and Lo knew. That's why the *Donna* flipped out. She didn't believe her. So she went to Gio and he admitted it. That's when all hell broke out."

The news made no sense. But Catalina believed something happened, something so terrible that Mira would leave her bed and risk her health. Rosetta walked away from the babies and took a seat. Unable to say or do anything contrary Catalina stood there in complete disbelief.

* B *

Giovanni had no concept of time. For all he knew night could have passed with him sleeping by resting his head in his arms to the side of the bed.

"*Signor.*"

Giovanni managed to stand. He ignored the ache to his back. "She hasn't wakened yet. Is she still in this forced sleep? The coma?"

"Yes. We'll bring her out of it after we run more tests. At that point it is up to her." The doctor said.

"But she had a stroke?" Giovanni asked.

"She could very well come out of it. Depends on which part of the brain was most affected."

"And the worst case scenario?" Giovanni asked.

The doctor's gaze returned to his patient. "Worst case she doesn't wake at all. Best case scenario will be impairment of her motor skills. Eating, dressing, and walking could all be affected. She would need rehabilitation. Since she has a family history of hypertension we have been really careful to avoid this outcome, *signor*, I assure you. I believe—"

"What do you mean her family history? I never told you her family had a history of hypertension."

The doctor cleared his throat. "Ah, your wife did, *signor.*"

Giovanni narrowed his line of vision on the doctor. He weighed the response for truth and it came up weak. The man went silent. He sweated profusely. "There's more to her family history. Her mother had a stroke when she gave birth. It took her four days to recover."

The doctor nodded. "As I said, we've done everything we can. We have to run more tests and then we may learn more."

Giovanni leaned over Mira and kissed her brow. "Be strong, sweetheart. I need you to be strong."

★ B ★

Marietta stepped under the pour and the warm pellets of water splashed, soothed, and relaxed her weary body. She felt drained, hollow, and lifeless. She didn't care if she drowned under the tide. There was so much of the day she wished to rinse down the drain.

The image of her sister's agony as she left her bed and tore through her room looking for the baby bracelet that matched Marietta's necklace seared her mind. The sobs from Mira when Marietta put the jewelry side by side for Mira to inspect should have stopped her. *Why hadn't she stopped?* Marietta stepped under the shower and turned her face up to the spray. Water filled her nostrils, pooled over her closed lids and rained down her face.

"Beautiful," Lorenzo said.

Her head whipped right and she opened her eyes in time to see Lorenzo step inside naked. She turned on him, surprised by his arrival. They had agreed she needed space. "Not now. I want to be alone. Get out, Lo," she pointed to the door.

He ignored her protest. "I want to be with you," he touched her face. She crossed her arms over her breasts as his gaze raked lower over her body. She was not going to have sex with him. She refused to even consider it after all that he had done.

"Do I have to go?" Lorenzo pouted. "You're my wife. We need to comfort each other."

She laughed. "You're so selfish, Lorenzo."

"When it comes to you, I am selfish," he said with quiet emphasis. "I will never let anyone come between us, take you from me. Ever."

Deep down inside Marietta was glad he insisted. She needed someone to show that they cared. She needed him. She was afraid of her guilt. What her self loathing would make her do next.

Lorenzo reached for the soap. "Turn," he said.

She obeyed and closed her eyes. He lathered his hands with the bar of soap. The touch of his calloused palms as they rubbed down her back was better than any loofah sponge she could use. Marietta slowly lowered her arms. She then lifted her hands and pressed them to the wall. She leaned forward to rinse the soap from her skin.

He touched her. Lorenzo pressed his finger against the dimple in her lower back just above her ass. He ran his hands around and then up her stomach to her breasts. He pinched each nipple and pressed his rigid, stiff cock between her buttocks. Marietta's lids fluttered upon contact. She opened her mouth to deny him the privilege but nothing escaped. Lorenzo brushed his lips over her shoulder and the head of his cock nudged deeper. Her eyelids slipped down. He said something to her in Italian. Her mind was too weak to formulate the translation.

"I control your pleasure," he said in English. "And your pain."

Marietta exhaled as he thrust into her. Her nails scraped the damp tiles of the shower. The spray soaked them both. She bit down on her bottom lip to keep from crying out. He lifted his chest off her back and withdrew before slamming into her. He fucked her hard and her body shook with the thrusts. "Sweet pussy," he wheezed. "You're mine," he repeated. She'd ponder the reason for the proclamation. Did he suspect what she had done with Carlo? Did he know how divided her heart was now? If it weren't for the pleasure she'd focus on the pain and uncover the answer.

Her world narrowed down to sensations and not just emotion. His cock twitched, expanded, slammed in and out of her cunt with a rhythmic urgency that sent hot currents of undiluted pleasure through her pussy. Her vision blurred and she closed her eyes once more. Wave after wave of pleasure went from the tips of her fingers to the bottoms of her feet. He continued to pound her sex but this time his free hand tickled her clit.

Marietta screamed.

All of her frustration and suffering released in her screams. She hollered until her voice went hoarse. She shook with the effort to stay upright, braced against the shower wall with her hands flat as he pumped his hips and she worked hers.

A soft groan fell from his lips. He came over her once more, with his arm circling her waist. He licked the center of her spine. She believed he would truly fuck her into unconsciousness because his cock kept tunneling. The gyrations became harder and he thankfully shot his seed deep into her womb.

Marietta gasped. She weakened to the point of collapse and wept. But he kept her up, stayed inside of her. *"I have you."*

She surrendered and the world felt right again. He released her, lathered her and himself while she did nothing but cry. He dried her, dressed her in nothing but a thin lace camisole after he ate her pussy while she was pinned up against the sink with her right foot resting on his shoulder. She wept. She smiled. She sobbed hard. When they left the bathroom she was stunned at how quickly he had cleaned the room to the best of his ability when she left him alone to shower. He'd even hung the sheer drape around the bed after she tore it off the rings. And under the covers he refused to stop holding her. Eventually she allowed herself to give him enough forgiveness to embrace him back. She rested on his chest. Lorenzo fired up his cigar and smoked. He blew smoke rings as he sat up against the headboard.

"So he was my father?" she asked and wiped away the last of her tears.

"He's your father," Lorenzo answered.

Marietta stared into the darkness of her room. The burn of tobacco tickled her nose. She poked a finger through a ring of smoke Lorenzo puffed and it broke away into a curvy wave. "He looks sick," she said. "Not what I… he isn't what I expected."

"He's dying," Lorenzo answered.

Marietta closed her eyes to the news. Of course he would be dying. Why she cared for the bastard who could give a shit about her or Mira was beyond her understanding. "He didn't say a word to me. Not a word," Marietta said.

"He's an evil man, Marietta." Lorenzo said.

"You all are," she turned from his embrace.

Lorenzo set his cigar aside. He eased on top of her. He pinned her wrists down and forced himself between her thighs. Out of instinct she wrapped her thighs around his and crossed her ankles over the back of his legs. "Yes, we are the tyranny of men. But I love you. I won't let him or anyone hurt you. Ever."

"You already have, Lo. Don't you understand that?" Marietta answered.

"I'll fix that," he grinned.

"Maybe. But something else will happen and we'll be right here again. Hurting each other."

"No. No. We will get this right. You need to think about giving me a son. I want one," he said. "And a little girl like Evie who sucks a red pacifier and sits with me in my meetings," Lorenzo grinned.

She stared up at him. He couldn't possibly be serious. If she could have her ovaries removed she would. She just might. Kids were the last thing she wanted. She'd be a shitty mother. She'd never bring a child into this world to suffer the way she had.

Lorenzo kissed her. Marietta turned her face away from the kiss. "Who was the man with him? The man that leaned on the wall?" she asked.

Lorenzo peppered kisses along the column of her neck. "He's your brother. His name is Armando." Lorenzo groaned as he began to grind his pelvis against hers and stir life into his flaccid cock.

"Lo, stop, listen to me." She broke free of his hold on her wrist and pushed at his shoulders. "The maid. She works for him."

Her husband froze. He lifted and his gaze banished all traces of the desire it once carried. "What do you mean she works for him?"

"I think she was trying to give Mira something to make her sick. I found her in the kitchen pouring out tea. She had a powdery substance in a baggie."

"Carmella? That's bullshit," Lorenzo moved off her.

"I'm serious! I heard her on the phone. She was speaking in Italian. Talking to a man named Armando. She said she couldn't go through with it. She was telling him stuff about Mira. I wasn't sure at first. I shouldn't have dismissed it. She could have hurt my sister and I said nothing. I'm so fucked up."

"Hey," he caught her chin. "If what you say is true you did do something." He pulled her back into his arms and she rested on his chest. "I'll get to the bottom of it. Don't worry."

* B *

"Gio?" Catalina pushed the door open. She found her brother alone in Mira's room. He looked up at her and forced a smile. "Where's Mira, Gio?"

"They've taken her for more tests. We should know something soon."

Catalina entered and was careful to close the door behind her. "Rosetta's here. She will sit with the babies until I return."

"How are they?" he asked.

"Alive. Getting stronger. You missed the feeding. They fed them through tubes, and the little ones ate up. So cute, so sad, Gio."

He nodded. "They will be stronger when Bella wakes." Giovanni wiped his hand down his face. "She'll feed them from her breast. We talked about it. She said it's best for the babies."

Catalina stepped closer to her brother. She stroked the top of his head. "Gio?"

364

"Yes," he said refusing to look at her.

"Is Lorenzo's wife Mira's sister?" Catalina asked.

Giovanni closed his eyes. He didn't respond.

"Is she? Did you know? Did you keep it from Mira?" Catalina pressed.

"Let's not do this now," Giovanni answered.

"How could you do this to Mira?" Catalina asked.

"I said not NOW!" He looked at her with such raw anger she knew it was the truth. For the life of her she couldn't imagine her brother being that selfish, especially with Mira. He did everything in his power to constantly prove his love for her. Instead of questioning him she knelt before him on her knees.

"Gio? Mira will forgive you. No matter what has happened she will forgive you. But you have to atone." She reached up and touched her brother's face. "We all make mistakes, we aren't defined by them. That's what you would tell me when I was a kid."

"I'm not a kid," Giovanni chuckled bitterly.

"No, but you are lost. When she wakes we do whatever it is to make it right." Catalina rose from her kneel and hugged him. Her brother hugged her back from his chair. She felt his sadness when she held him to her heart. She wished their mother were alive. The only other woman who could help Gio see the good from the bad was her mother. But Madre was dead. So she would have to do the job. And she vowed to do just that.

"Before I go I wanted to give you this." She reached into her pocket and removed a pearl rosary. "It's Mama's. I brought it with me because I heard the twins were born too soon. I want you to pray. Do you hear me? Keep it with you and pray."

He took their mother's rosary and kissed the cross. Catalina stroked the side of his face. She kissed his brow. *"Nel nome del Padre, e del Figlio, e dello Spirito Santo. Amen."*

"Amen," Giovanni said.

* B *

"Avanti," Mancini said.

Armando opened the door to his father's private reading room. He blinked in surprise to see Marsuvio drink his scotch and walk upright to the desk for another pour. The old man poured more than a swallow in his whiskey glass and turned with it raised. *"Salute!"* Marsuvio tossed back the scotch.

It was as if the man had received a jolt of youth after their visit. The energy and drink was risky if not suicidal behavior considering the medication his father was on. "Who gave you that?" Armando demanded.

"Shut the door." Mancini replied with a broad smile.

He did as he was told. His father set the whiskey glass over to the desk and then walked slow and steady to the reading chair in the room. "I just got off the phone with Buhari. They are running more tests. I was right! She did have a stroke like her mother. I was right all along!"

"And this makes you happy?" Armando frowned.

"No! It makes me right. I knew Gio was wrong for her. That he'd harm her. And this is proof." Mancini's smile broadened. "My daughter can see firsthand how dangerous and inept he is."

Armando sighed and held his tongue.

Mancini's smile faded. "But I'm at fault too. I should have done more to prevent this."

"How could you, father? You gave the doctors the information. You even hired a specialist to work with their doctor. You did all of this behind Giovanni's back. What else could you have done?" Armando reasoned.

"Plenty. Instead of warring with Gio I could have told him the truth. But with Isabella out there, my hands are tied. It doesn't matter now. The damage is done." Mancini leveled his gaze on his son. "You saw your sister today."

Armando rolled his gaze away. "She's not my sister. She's your bastard."

Mancini chuckled. "A feisty bastard isn't she? Her name is Marietta. I knew it the day she was put in my arms that she was the stronger of the two. A father knows these things!" Mancini wiggled a finger at him. "Just as I know you are weak."

"I'm not going to listen to this." Armando turned to leave.

"Did you see her? She knew who I was." Mancini slapped his chest with pride. "I could see it in her eyes. They've told the women. That means we need to act. I want to see my daughters. I must have access to them now. I want you to meet with Giovanni and Lorenzo to arrange it. Do you understand?"

"They threw us out of the *ospedale*. Neither one of them are open to it. I could force the issue. If you like," Armando said.

"I can't have the girls come to me by force. Damn him. No. No. No. Let Mirabella recover. Buhari says she should wake soon. He thinks in two weeks the babies will be well. He predicts it. As soon as she is recovered you meet with Gio and barter a deal. Promise whatever is necessary to make the meeting with my daughters happen."

"But?"

Mancini put up his hand. "Don't worry. I won't hold you to any of it. Giovanni's life is still on the table—after your sisters have come to me. Until this happens you don't strike at Giovanni or Lorenzo."

"And my inheritnce?" Armando asked.

"There will be only one family standing. Mancini," he said. "Tomosino's legacy will be crushed. Every Battaglia man owes me his life, for what was done to Lisa," Mancini smiled. "Giovanni will pay. I promise you this."

"My inheritance, Papa. We need to talk about the will. It can't stay this way," Armando said.

Mancini's gaze lifted. "What about Isabella?" he asked.

"We believe Isabella is in *Sicilia*." Armando said.

Mancini paused. "She's here? Why are you just telling me this now?"

"I just learned it. She was seen just this morning. I have someone on it. I'll have her soon."

"Good. Finish the job I asked of you and we will discuss your inheritance." Mancini grinned. *"Cin-cin!"* he said and tossed back another drink. "Have some, it's time to celebrate!"

∗ B ∗

The doors opened and Mira was wheeled into the room. Giovanni watched as they transferred her to the bed. The doctor stepped inside. He waited until the nurses finished with the doctor before he asked. "How is she?"

"Her body is stabilizing. We see no lesions or brain damage." The doctor looked back to the bed and Giovanni's gaze returned to Mira as well. "The rest is on her. She's recovering. We must wait."

"You saved her life. You knew how to respond, how to help her. You saved her life." The doctor smiled. The man expelled a deep breath of relief. Giovanni turned and looked him over. "That's because you knew about her mother. Didn't you doctor?"

"I don't understand?" Dr. Buhari said.

"Mancini has been one step ahead of me this entire time. He knew Mira was here. He knew her condition before I told him."

367

"I don't know a Mancini." Buhari vehemently denied the accusation.

Giovanni smiled. "Now you insult me by lying to my face." Giovanni continued. "Mancini said something to me today that I only just now considered. Do you know what that was?"

The doctor's gaze lifted. He'd seen fear on a man many times in his life. Even from a small child as his father ruled over his men and brothers with an iron fist, he'd seen others cower. Today the doctor didn't look afraid. He looked petrified. "Mancini said to me that he owns this *ospedale* and everyone in it." Giovanni stepped closer. His face was barely a breath away. "Are you *his*?" he asked.

Buhari swallowed. He didn't dare make a move.

"Rispondetemi," Giovanni said.

"*Don* Mancini contacted my office. He gave me her mother's medical history. I've only given him basic updates. The information helped us treat your wife."

Giovanni patted the side of the doctor's face hard. He grabbed the man by the throat. "You saved her life so you have yours. If you want to keep it you will stop all communication about my wife and her condition with Mancini."

"Understood. Understood, *signor.*"

A nurse entered and quickly made a hasty exit. Giovanni shoved the doctor away. The man left the room without delay. Giovanni returned to Mira's bedside. He dragged a chair close. He pulled the rosary from his shirt pocket and wrapped the pearl strand around his fist. He had to breathe in and out several times, very slowly to calm down. He lowered his head. *"Nel nome del Padre, e del Figlio, e dello Spirito Santo. Amen,"* he began, and the door opened. He turned and saw Father Chris enter. The timing was uncanny. He hadn't seen the father since his wedding.

"Gio," the priest said. He walked over and they embraced. *"Cardinal Callori di Vignale* called me. Why didn't you, son?"

"I haven't had a chance to think," Giovanni said.

The priest smiled. He glanced to Mira. "How is she?"

"Not well," Giovanni sighed.

"I want to christen the twins, here, now. And we will bless her."

Giovanni was so grateful. He wished it to be a different occasion but even he couldn't deny that his wife and children needed the father's blessing as did he.

"Come, son, we will get through this together."

16.

Sleep stole away his mission to never take his eyes off his wife. He blinked and discovered he slept with his head buried between his folded arms on the bed. The touch on his shoulder jostled him. He lifted his head and glanced back over his shoulder. Dominic stood there. He wore a grey tailored suit and a sad smile. Giovanni had to blink again to be sure. He saw Rocco in his overalls and plaid shirt standing at his side. Zia was on the other side of the bed. She wept, kissing Mira's face, fixing her sheets, begging her to wake up in Italian.

Giovanni had never felt so relieved to see everyone. He stood with the help of Dominic, weak from lack of sleep and eating. Dominic patted him on the back. "So things fall apart when I leave huh?" Dominic chuckled

The two embraced. "How is she?" Dominic asked.

"She should wake soon. They brought her out of the induced coma. We have to wait and see." Giovanni's gaze swiveled back to the bed.

"The rest of the family is here. Zia wants a prayer circle. Let them take care of her and *la bambini*. You and I should go for a drive." Dominic grabbed Giovanni's face. "You haven't eaten, Gio. Have you?"

"I'm not leaving her," he said emphatically. He broke from Dominic. He reached over and brushed Mira's brow with the back of his hand. He had to compete with Zia's touch. She was kissing and stroking Mira's face, whispering to her. Giovanni again realized how wrong he was to keep her from Zia. "I have to be here when she wakes."

He didn't care what anyone said. He wasn't leaving anything to chance. Mira had to open her eyes and see him first. See he was there, and he loved her.

Dominic stepped close. He kept his voice low so Gio only heard it. "*Per favore.* You need to step outside and have a conversation with me. It's important, Gio," Dominic said.

Rocco came over and Giovanni smiled at his uncle. He hugged him. "Go with Domi, Gio. We are here now."

The door opened and the women in his family entered. His aunts and cousins, older and very spiritual had all come. Zia began giving orders to them. He'd seen them do this before. As his mother lingered near death they prayed for her. She lived for weeks instead of days because of the sheer will of the family not to let her go. And now they would pray for Mira. It should help.

"Now, Gio," Dominic insisted.

With reluctant acceptance Giovanni walked out of the room. He reeked from lack of sleep and tears. He could smell himself. A shower would do him some good. There had to be a place in the hospital to take one. He stopped and signaled for Renaldo. "Go back to Mondello, have Catalina pack me a fresh suit, all my things to shower and change."

"Yes, Boss." Renaldo turned and left.

"They gave me this room. I didn't sleep in it. We can talk here." Giovanni walked a bit stiffly. Sitting up all night as he watched over his wife had wrecked his back. "I want Eve brought here. She should be close. So when Bella wakes she can see her. Bring her."

"It might frighten the child to see her mother this way, Gio. I would advise against it."

His head hurt. His thoughts muddled. "Right. Yes, you are right. I guess I need to clear my head. I'm not thinking straight."

"You haven't slept since this began," Dominic said. "I got the call from Santo and came immediately. Things are not good, Gio. The `Ndrangheta has pulled out of our agreement. They are aligned with Bonaduce yet they still think we are we blind to it. I've left Santo in the *Campania*. We now have the *Polizia di Stato* in our yard. The Prime Minister has not returned my call. My contact says that they have the bay under surveillance. They are building a case for trafficking and tracking what we have allowed the `Ndrangheta to export. So we must stop all shipments immediately."

Giovanni flinched. The last thing he needed was the Mafia Criminal Investigation Unit digging into his affairs. Dominic continued, "Mottola is gaining support in the *Camorra*. Everyone is on edge. The clan bosses blame us for this division, the investigations, the `Ndrangheta, all of it. You were right to bring everyone to *Sicilia*. Home isn't safe anymore."

"Bullshit. No one chases me out of the *Campania*. Mottola will pay for this. I'll take the life of every man who stands with him." Giovanni sat down on the edge of the bed.

Dominic said nothing. They both knew that war was just what the authorities hoped for. The best way to infiltrate his organization would be the chaos.

"The women know the truth, Domi. My Bella knows I lied to her. She knows Patri ordered her mother's death. She knows everything." Giovanni lifted his gaze. "That's why she refuses to wake. I think she's given up on me, on us."

"Gio—"

"Marietta told her. I have no idea how Marietta found out, but she told her," Giovanni said.

"I might have an idea." Dominic said.

"How?"

"Catalina took Marietta to Belina. They sat up in the private rooms and dined with Mancini's men."

"She did what?" Giovanni asked. "Who drove her to Belina?"

"Doesn't matter, Gio. The damage is done," Dominic said.

"It does fucking matter!" Giovanni stood. "Which of my men drove them to Belina? Leonardo? Right? He was the one that took them to Palermo. I want him brought to me."

Dominic shook his head. "Gio, it's happening."

"What's happening?" he asked.

"You. Look at yourself. Who gives a fuck if it was Leonardo? Who gives a fuck? He only did what he was told. Mancini got to her, because we didn't tell them the truth," Dominic said.

Giovanni rubbed his brow. "I don't need you reminding me of my mistakes, Domi."

"You need to be thinking clearly!" Dominic shouted. He paced like a caged lion. "You need to keep us from repeating the mistake we made with the Calderones."

The rare occasions when Dominic was bold enough to shout at him always got Giovanni's attention. "So now I'm insane? You motherfuckers keep throwing Calderone in my face!" he kicked the chair next to him. He picked it up and threw it into the wall. He turned on Dominic. "I regret nothing I did to the Calderones. Nothing!" Giovanni pounded his fist into his hand. "I will get a handle on things. I just need Bella... I need her... to be okay. And then..." He paused. He cut Dominic a glare. "Give me a couple of days, a week. And then I'll deal with the *Camorra*."

Dominic nodded his head in respect. Giovanni knew Dominic was right. He knew the state of things with the *Camorra* would weaken him if he didn't act. But nothing, not even his own fucking empire, could take him away from Mirabella. Not until he was certain she and his *bambini* were okay.

"The clan bosses have been told of Mira's delivery. Everyone is giving you respect, Gio. But we will have to settle this matter with Mottola, swiftly. Let's discuss it after Mira wakes," Dominic conceded.

Giovanni glanced back at him. "Meet with Lorenzo and Carlo. They have some information on the Armenians. Yeremian is pleased with how we helped him solve his problem in Armenia. He can be an ally against Bonaduce and `*Ndrangheta.*"

"I'll speak with him. I heard that Mancini paid you a visit. Here? I'm sure that didn't go over well," Dominic said.

"He thinks I don't know his game. He wants Bella to recognize him as her father. The minute she does he'll try to end me, separate us. He has no intention of letting his daughters remain married to Battaglia men. As if he has a fucking say in the matter. What I don't understand is the timing of everything." Giovanni sat on the bed.

Dominic eased his hands into the pockets of his trousers. "It could be his death. The man doesn't have much time left."

Giovanni shook his head. "If Mancini was the one to tell Marietta the truth then he wouldn't unleash her on Mirabella knowing her medical history. I could see it on his face when he laid eyes on Marietta. He hasn't had contact with her."

"You think Armando is undermining him? Trying to stir chaos between our families so he can keep control of his father?" Dominic asked.

"Possibly. But in my gut I feel we are missing something. Question Marietta. Find out exactly how she learned the truth and who told her. There's something we don't know, Domi. I feel it."

"I think you should rest, Gio."

Giovanni tried to rise. Dominic gently pushed him back. "Lie down. Twenty minutes on your back will do you good. When Renaldo returns with your clothes you can shower. Zia Josefina has brought in food for you. I'll have it brought here."

Giovanni wanted to protest. The moment he reclined in the hospital bed the battle was lost. His lids slipped lower and lower. "If any thing happens? If she stirs have them wake me. Immediately," he yawned.

Dominic patted his shoulder. "Rest, brother. I'm here. I'll take care of everything."

"Christo!" Carmella exclaimed. She turned directly into Lorenzo. "You scared me Lorenzo."

Lorenzo dropped his hand on the stove and trapped her near the counter. "Fixing breakfast are we?" he asked. He stared into her eyes. The exchange was brief. She immediately looked away. Lorenzo lifted her chin and brought her gaze back upward. "Well? Are you?"

"Huh? Yes. I thought everyone needed to eat, especially little Eve. She was so upset yesterday. Pardon," Carmella said and she tried once more to escape. Lorenzo touched her hip and prevented her from leaving. He kept his hand there. She looked down at his touch and back up into his eyes.

"You and I haven't had time to catch up. I hear you still fuck Armando Mancini?"

"That's a lie!" she said. She pushed her way out from under him and moved over toward the block of knives near the sink. Lorenzo smirked. He watched her with semi-amusement. The other half of him was prepared to snap her neck if what Marietta said about her proved true.

"Is it? A lie? So you deny it?" Lorenzo asked.

"Our families are close. I work for Gio and I work for Armando. I have for years. And there have been rumors that I fucked them both. For years." Carmella tossed back.

"At one time you did," Lorenzo said.

"We were kids. What you and Armando conspired to do against Gio forever ruined any chance of my having him. You think I don't know what you did? What you are? Gio may not see through your fake loyalty but I do! I know you have been jealous of him for years, and have constantly undermined him."

"So says the whore," Lorenzo plucked an apple from the fruit bowl and bit into it. Lorenzo stepped toward her. "The past is the past. Giovanni never gave a shit about you."

"That's not true! I was his girlfriend!"

"You were his first piece of ass!" Lorenzo chuckled. "As I recall you played a dangerous game between the boys."

"Your fault!" she shot back.

"Me? I didn't spread your legs. You did. Or have you forgotten?" Lorenzo chuckled.

There was no quick comeback. Carmella cast her gaze down.

Lorenzo recalled the debt Giovanni had to pay for having Del Stavio make Dominic his little charm necklace. Armando wanted his girlfriend. Giovanni refused to give her up, fought Armando in the street to keep her. Made all the boys fight Armando's boys every day after school. That was until Lorenzo met with Armando secretly behind his cousin's back and made another deal. He wouldn't war with them over pussy. Giovanni was too soft on girls, and love. Together Armando and Lorenzo set Giovanni up to see Carmella for the whore they knew she'd eventually become. Carmella gave her soul to Armando. That was her choice. He could give a shit that she could never live with it. Lorenzo bit into the apple as he glared at her.

"What do you want?" Carmella asked.

"I've heard you've been quite the little helper for the *Donna*. Fixing her tea?"

Carmella paled. She opened her mouth to deny it. Nothing escaped. Lorenzo slowed down his chewing and watched her. He took a threatening step toward her. "Are you spying on us for Mancini?"

"No," she said.

"What was in the tea?" he asked.

"Nothing," she answered.

"That's a lie, Carmella. You know Battaglia men don't like to be lied to," he smirked.

"I don't know what your wife saw but it was nothing!" Carmella protested.

"I never said my wife saw anything," Lorenzo replied. Before she could bolt he grabbed her by the throat. He threw the apple into the sink hard enough for it to split. Carmella gasped. Her eyes stretched with horror. "What was in the tea, bitch?"

"I didn't do it. I swear it. I couldn't do it. Armando threatened my mother and brother. He left me no choice. Please, Lorenzo. Please don't tell Gio. He'll never forgive me."

"You shouldn't fear Gio," Lorenzo tightened his hold on her throat. "You should fear me."

Carmella wept. "I didn't tell him anything. I knew nothing. Just how she was. That's it. I don't know anything. I'm so sorry."

"You will be, *cara*, of this I promise you."

"Let her go." A voice spoke behind him. Lorenzo looked back to see Dominic watching them. "Let her go. Now."

Lorenzo let Carmella's throat go. She dropped to her knees gasping for air. She crawled away. Dominic calmly stepped around the kitchen to cut off her escape. He extended his hand. Carmella looked up

374

at him. Dominic nodded that she should accept his offer. She reached with a shaky hand and grasped his. He brought her to her feet.

"Dominic, *per favore,* I swear to you that I didn't do anything. I swear," she whimpered.

"It's okay. I just want to know everything Armando asked of you. What you two discussed. Don't be afraid. Sit, Carmella." He drew out a chair.

"Are you fucking kidding me?" Lorenzo snarled. "You think Gio wants to let this one go?"

"Giovanni wants me to handle things right now in his place. Not you. Leave us," Dominic replied.

Lorenzo nearly took a swing at him for talking to him in such a dismissive tone. The rotten bitch could have killed Mira or the babies. He knew how Giovanni would want this handled.

"Call Carlo and bring him in. We have a few things to take care. There is much I need to update you both on," Dominic said.

The request was indeed reasonable, but still his fury at Carmella made it hard for him to comply. He glared after her. When she looked at him terrified he made sure to wink in return. To let her know they weren't done. Lorenzo threw up his hand in a dismissive gesture toward Dominic. He walked out.

"He'll kill me. And if he doesn't Gio will," Carmella said.

Dominic pulled a chair closer. "Giovanni does not give orders on the death of women."

"Bullshit!" Carmella said. She wiped her tears. "I heard about what he did to the Calderones. I'm not stupid!"

"You are stupid. Very," Dominic said. "To betray a family that has been good to yours before your birth. That makes you stupid and reckless."

"No. Domi, let me explain. I was here. Mira saw me when she arrived and didn't like me on sight. She told Giovanni to send me away. I needed the work. So I went to Mancini. The old man is ill. Armando is never there. You know I do domestics both here and there. It was approved by Gio and Armando years ago. Your families have a truce."

"Not anymore. Am I right?" Dominic searched her face. "Armando no longer believes in the truce between our fathers."

"How would I know?" Carmella wept. She dropped her face and cried.

Dominic lifted her chin. "I need to hear the truth. You know I can tell the difference."

"Armando and his father had a fight one night. The *Don* hit him with something that bruised his face really bad. Afterwards I was tending to Armando's wound when he asked me about Gio, about his wife. What she was like, stuff like that."

"And then what happened?" Dominic asked.

"He was upset. Said his father wouldn't destroy the family. He said the children couldn't be born. That he wanted nothing to do with her or the kids. Then he threatened me. He wanted me to make it look like an accident, so his father wouldn't suspect. I begged him not to ask it of me but he forced me. So I called Mama and told her that I needed the work and that her sister had taken a turn for the worst. All of it true. She agreed to let me come back. But she didn't know anything about this. So I come. And that's it. I couldn't do it."

"The tea?" Dominic asked.

"The *Donna* never took a sip," Carmella said.

"What was in the tea?" Dominic asked.

"Arsenic."

Dominic sat back. After a moment of contemplating the deception an idea formed. "I have plans for you, Carmella. A way you can make this up to the family."

"I'll do anything." Carmella wiped her tears.

"Yes," Dominic agreed. "You will."

"Does Gio have to know, Domi?" Carmella asked.

"Gio will be told. His mercy will depend on how you help us," Dominic said. "Pack your things, you're returning to the Mancinis."

* B *

"I'm okay to go back to the hospital without you." Marietta put her earring in. Lorenzo paced behind her. She watched him from the mirror. "Why are you so agitated?"

"*Non imoporta!* I will come as soon as I finish business with Dominic. Nico will drive you in personally. You and Catalina."

"Yes, Lo. I know. You told me already." She turned. "Did someone call? Is it Mira? The babies? Are they worse?"

"No. But they aren't better." Lorenzo paused. He looked at her as if it were the first time he had. "You look beautiful."

Marietta smoothed down the sides of her dress. It was white, and so were her heels. All white. She felt that it would be better than bright cheery colors or a muted dark color. But then she thought of the attire of those that worked for the hospital and frowned. "Do I

376

look like a nurse? Maybe I should wear the pink dress?"

He took her hand and pulled her to him. "Am I forgiven?"

"Yes," she said sincerely. "I know you did what you thought was right at the time. But you get one pass at lying to me, Lo. Never do that again," she said.

He kissed and silenced the rest of her speech. She lifted her arms around his neck. She had to admit it was nice to make up with him. All morning they'd been making up. She ached all over from the workout.

"Mmmm," she let him go. "Catalina is waiting on me, Lo. Stop." She peeled his hands off her ass. "Seriously. I have to go. I got a good feeling Mira will wake up today."

"Me too," Lorenzo said.

Marietta grabbed her purse and started for the door.

"Sweetheart?" Lorenzo said.

She looked back at him. "Yes?"

"I need to know who told you the truth about Mira. How did you find out?"

Marietta's heart stopped. She truly thought they were past it now. He hadn't mentioned it again since they left Carlo's mother's house. She sighed. "It doesn't matter."

"It matters," he said in that serious tone.

"Can we talk about it tonight? When I come back? Please?"

"Why? Why not just tell me. Is it someone you know? Someone I know?" Lorenzo asked.

"I don't want any drama. What about the maid? Did you take care of her? The one I told you about who was spying on everyone?"

Lorenzo stared at her. He was unmoved by her attempt to dodge his question. She smiled sweetly. "Tonight. We'll talk." She blew him a kiss and hurried out the door. Her heart raced so fast she was damn near running in her heels to get down the hall. She glanced back twice expecting to see Lorenzo in pursuit of her to demand an answer. Without warning she ran directly into Carlo.

Startled Marietta nearly fell. Her purse dropped from her hand. Carlo caught her by the arm and kept her steady on her feet. Marietta looked up into his calm eyes. He stared down at her for a moment, and then knelt and picked up her purse. Marietta stepped back wanting a little distance between them.

"You dropped this," he said.

"Ah, uh, thanks," she said and walked around him.

Carlo couldn't believe how beautiful she was today. What had changed? She wore a snug fitting white mini dress. Her thick hair had sprung curls that brushed her shoulders with an exotic flare. He felt those curls, how different the texture was from his own hair. He'd felt the trim fuzz over her pussy too and wanted to touch her again. Even the feel of her skin was burned into his brain.

One look at her and it all came back. He'd spent the night trying to get her out of his head. Drinking until his mind went numb and the ache in his loins soothed. She was his best friend's wife and he was a dumb fuck to have fallen in love.

Marietta stepped back from him. She mumbled some kind of thanks and walked around him. He waited, his breath held. Once he asked her the fragrance she wore. She said it was called Shalimar. He'd buy a truckload of it just to own the scent.

He hoped she hesitated. Looked back at him as if she was undecided. But she kept going. The sway of her hips and slender shapely legs in perched by white heels caught his attention. He wiped his hand down his mouth and forced the image away. He turned and continued on.

Marietta didn't dare look back. She didn't have to. She felt his eyes on her. The heat banked in his stare made her cheeks warm with shame. He'd seen her body. Kissed her. Touched her. She couldn't undo the intimacy they now shared. And even if it didn't go as far as it could have she knew she betrayed her husband.

"You ready? What took you so long?" Catalina huffed.

"Sorry. Lo kept me. Let's go," Marietta said. She walked to the door and stole a glance back. Carlo wasn't in the hall any longer. He had moved on. So would she. They went to the car and eased inside. As soon as the door closed Marietta felt the tightness in her chest cease.

"Are you okay?" Catalina asked.

"Am I what?" Marietta answered, realizing she panted for breath. "Yeah, I'm nervous. I mean. I'm worried about Mira."

"Because she's your sister?" Catalina asked.

Marietta's gaze slowly turned to Catalina. There was no denying the truth. Soon everyone would know. "I guess."

Catalina stared at her.

Marietta rolled her eyes. "What? Why are you staring at me like that?"

"You're nothing like her. I mean you look like her a little, but you two are so different. Mira is... she's different than you," Catalina said.

"That doesn't matter. We grew up apart. We aren't identical twins."

"Forgive me," Catalina's voice was soft and sincere. "I just don't understand any of this. How is it possible that you both marry Lorenzo and Giovanni? How?"

"No one told you?" Marietta asked.

"Told me what?" Catalina answered.

"Marsuvio Mancini is our father." Marietta said.

Catalina began to laugh. She laughed so hard she started choking. Marietta patted her on the back. Catalina waved off her assistance but tears leaked from her eyes. "You are funny."

"I'm serious. Catalina, I wouldn't joke about it. That's what the fight was about that made Mira go into early labor. Your brother and my husband conspired to keep us apart. To keep us from knowing that Mancini is our father."

"That is utter bullshit! No way."

Marietta shrugged. "Believe what you want."

"Wait. Who told you this? What proof do you have?" Catalina demanded.

"The bracelet you said Mira has. The Del Stavio bracelet, remember?" Marietta opened her purse and dug out hers and Mira's. When she returned she found them on the floor of the *Don's* office, where Mira had thrown them. "See for yourself."

Catalina accepted the necklace and the bracelet. "See mine? I had it made into a necklace. They were given to us when we were babies. From our father. He gave them to us before he left our mother and returned to Sicily."

"Incredible." Catalina handed the necklace and bracelet back. "I'm sorry you found out like this, but my brother—"

"Had no right to keep this secret. Don't defend him to me," Marietta said.

"I wasn't." Catalina shot back. "I was going to say my brother has a very complicated relationship with the Mancinis and whatever he did, he did it to protect Mira. Not to keep you two apart. Family comes first with Gio. Always."

"Well I'm her family. And keeping us apart didn't turn out so well, for *his* family now did it?" Marietta cut her eyes.

"I suggest you drop the attitude," Catalina replied.

"Why?" Marietta challenged.

"I know you were wronged in this situation, but this is about Mira. And trust me she loves my brother. She doesn't know you," Catalina said.

Marietta looked over at Catalina and could not counter the argument. The truth was she gave Mira no reason to want to know her. And she'd seen the Queen B and her King. They had a relationship that she didn't understand.

"Well she's my blood. And I intend to get to know her, to support her. No matter what. So let's just leave it at that."

* B *

Giovanni buttoned his shirt. He stared out of the window of the hospital room. Mira's condition was unchanged. He slept hard for three hours. She never woke. He ate and showered, and she never woke. The doctor had said she should have come out of it by now. He couldn't stop worrying that she may never.

There came a knock. Giovanni's head turned to see his uncle enter the room. "Is she awake?" he asked with alarm.

"No. No, Gio. I came to say I will go with Vito to Villa Mare Blu. The women refused to leave."

The news didn't surprise Giovanni. They prayed hard over Mira. Some sat in chairs rocking and crying. Others read from their Bibles or held their rosaries, chanting. It was quite comforting and disturbing to see eight of his aunts and cousins surround Mira in this vigil. But faith worked. He believed it with all his being. "Rocco? Wait. I want to apologize, to speak with you."

Rocco moved slowly to the chair in the room. He sat. Giovanni turned from the window. He walked over to his shoes and stepped into them. "You warned me about bringing her here. Keeping the secret. I guess I live my life so much without fear I've forgotten caution. I should have listened."

The arthritic hand of Rocco's went up in a silent wave to silence Giovanni. Rocco shook his head slowly. "Do not apologize. You did what you needed to do to keep Mira protected. No one could have foreseen this outcome."

"Oh someone did. Mancini," Giovanni replied. "Bella's mother suffered a stroke when she gave birth. She had the same affliction with her blood pressure that Bella has. Mancini interfered. Got to Bella's doctors and gave them her history behind my back."

"I'm told that he showed up here?" Rocco asked.

Giovanni nodded.

"And so it begins," Rocco sighed. "Tomosino and Mancini created this nightmare. You and Mira shouldn't have to suffer because of either of them. What is your plan, Gio?"

"Lorenzo has married the woman, Mira's sister. You've met her."

Rocco blinked. Giovanni sat on the edge of the hospital bed. "Mira and Marietta both know the truth. All of it. And they didn't hear it from us. The truth is out so I can only shape it to my benefit. Try to protect the family from war with the Sicilians. Just as we go to war with Mottola and the `Ndrangheta."

"War? Mancini wouldn't go to war over those two girls. His men would never follow that disastrous path."

"Because they're black? You think that still matters to him now? The man is dying, uncle." Giovanni shook his head. "Armando will not share his dynasty with my wife or her sister. And we can't co-exist. Armando and I never could. One of us has to stand down. And I have no intention of doing so. Besides these are delicate times with us and the *Camorra*."

"Then what is your plan, Gio?" Rocco asked again.

"There you go. You, Domi, Lorenzo, all need to know my plans. Council me which choice to make, when it is my choice to make!" Giovanni seethed.

"We support you," Rocco said.

"Maybe. Or maybe since you witnessed my madness and the Calderone slaughter none of you trust me."

This time Rocco didn't blink.

Giovanni nodded that he understood. "My wife and *bambini* need to be well before I strike. I have to see her through this. Get the babies out of this hospital to some place safe. Then we return to Sorrento and settle things."

"That doesn't sound like a plan." Rocco said with concern.

"She comes first. Period." Giovanni didn't waste another minute on the conversation. He left the room and started toward Mira's but stopped himself. First he'd check on his sons and then he'd see to his wife.

17.

"What eats you?" Dominic asked.

Carlo poured himself another drink. They waited for Lorenzo. Dominic could always tell when trouble brewed between the two best friends. Carlo was tense, solemn, fewer words than customary were spoken when he arrived. He wore a black suit, shirt and tie. He had a fresh shave and trimmed mustache. On the outside he looked well put together. But his eyes were red-rimmed and heavy lidded. He had to have suffered through a night of drinking.

Carlo turned from the bar and sipped his whiskey before Lorenzo strolled in.

"Started early huh?" Lorenzo asked Carlo.

The answering silence was all the confirmation Dominic needed. There was definitely something brewing between them. "We don't have much time," Dominic said. "I know a lot went down in Armenia, and I want to hear all about it. But first you need to know what we face."

"Where is Santo?" Lorenzo asked.

"Home. Holding back the *Camorra* off our asses," Dominic said.

"You shouldn't trust him. I believe he helps Mottola. I can't prove it but I believe it."

"Well until you can prove it I can't act. Can I? Besides. We need him now. However we choose to use him." Dominic stepped forward. "Gio is not himself with Mira and his sons in danger. He can't focus on these matters. Not like we can."

"Send me to Sorrento," Carlo said.

"What?" Lorenzo glanced over to him.

"I'll go and work with Santo. Hold things down until Gio is ready to deal with it." Carlo set his drink on the bar. "I can leave tonight."

"The fuck you can! I need you here with me," Lorenzo said.

"Mancini is ready to kick in our door. We can't get out of Sicily without some serious bloody shit. I need my ace," Lorenzo argued.

"I'm not your fucking trained dog. Find another ace," Carlo hissed.

Lorenzo's brows drew down in concern. Dominic observed the stoic posture of Carlo. He glanced to Lorenzo. He started to understand a bit more about them both in that moment. "Nico is here and Renaldo. I think we should send Carlo back to Sorrento. The sooner the better," Dominic said.

Lorenzo threw up his hands in defeat. Carlo pushed up from the bar. "I can pay Mottola a visit," Carlo said.

"No." Dominic replied. "It's Gio's call and for now he's not ready to make it, but soon. You go and keep an eye on Santo. Report back on the situation with the `Ndrangheta."

"Carlo, this is bullshit. We're a team." Lorenzo reasoned.

"Fuck you, Lo. Be a team with someone else," Carlo said. He then walked out of the meeting. Dominic's brows lifted. Lorenzo watched Carlo go with a face flushed with anger.

"What's between you two now?" Dominic asked. "Evidently something is."

"We'll work it out." Lorenzo waved it off. "Maybe you're right. He's good for Sorrento now. But I want some action done about the Sicilians. Fuck Mottola. Mira and Marietta are in danger. I can feel it."

Dominic nodded in agreement. "Maybe I should pay Mancini a visit?"

"No. I don't think it's safe for you to do that alone." Lorenzo advised.

"We need to know how Marietta found out," Dominic said.

"Mancini," Lorenzo replied.

Dominic shook his head in response. "Couldn't be. Mancini wouldn't let this one go so sloppy. Someone else told her. What has she said to you?"

"Nothing yet. I'll get it out of her tonight." Lorenzo went to the bar. "What about the whore? You planning on keeping Mirabella's hired assassin as the family cook?"

Dominic chuckled. "She's on her way back to Mancini."

Lorenzo glanced over his shoulder.

"She's going to get some answers for me. Let us know Armando's movements. First call will come tonight. I think it's a better plan than ending her life. What about you?"

"I guess." Lorenzo shrugged.

"Sit, Lo. We have to talk about Bonaduce, the clan bosses, and I want to know about the Armenians."

"Shouldn't Carlo be a part of this discussion?" Lorenzo looked to the door with a furrowed brow.

"You update him before he leaves. Time is short. I need to get back to the *ospedale*." Dominic unbuttoned his suit jacket. He chose the closest chair to sit in. He rested the side of his face in his hand. He hadn't seen Catalina yet. He wasn't sure what he'd say when he did. All he knew was that right now he needed her comfort desperately. There would be many dark days coming their way.

* B *

"Gino had a rough night, *signor*. He has a fever. We're treating him now. In his fragile state it's not good," The neonatal specialist said.

"And Gianni?"

"He's gained a pound already. He's at four pounds. You can hold him today."

The news rocked him to his core. He looked from the doctor to the baby. Holding his son was more than he had hoped for. "I would like that."

The nurse took him by the elbow and led him over to the chair. Giovanni sat with a bubble of excitement expanding in his chest. The other nurse brought over a tightly wrapped bundle. Giovanni positioned his arm as instructed and his son was placed in his care. He stared down at the little face. The boy's eyes were closed. But he breathed on his own, which was remarkable for two days. "*Ciao, Gianni. Sono Papa,*" Giovanni said with a smile. "Papa's here *piccoletto.*"

He rocked with Gianni in his arms for ten minutes before the short visit was terminated. Giovanni then returned to Gino. His son didn't kick or move his hands as before. He lay still and his breathing appeared a bit labored in his tiny chest. He could see how the fight to exist exhausted him with every breath. "You must stay strong, Gino. Fight for life. Mama will be up soon and she will want to meet you." He pressed a kiss to his fingers and then to the top of the incubator.

Giovanni removed his mask and the hospital gown before he left the room. He found many people in the halls. Many of those gathered were members of the family of men who worked for him. Some brought gifts. The Battaglias had taken over the *ospedale*. Though the threat of Mancini loomed, he felt certain his wife and children were safe with so many friendly faces to encourage them on. When he reached Mira's room he half hoped to find her sitting upright and talking from her bed. His heart sank to see her as he left her. Zia stood and set aside her bible. Giovanni never took his eyes off his wife.

"She hasn't responded to the doctors. They are worried, Gio. I can tell by the way they keep coming in here."

Giovanni put his arm around her shoulders. "She's strong. She will wake. Give her time."

"The boys?" Zia asked.

"Gino isn't well. He struggles. Can you go see him? Take Josefina. Pray for him." Giovanni kissed Zia's brow.

"Of course. I can't wait to see him. They wouldn't let me in earlier." Zia turned and signaled for his aunt and she stood. Josefina and Zia could be twins, and both were only related through marriage. His aunt wrapped her shawl around her shoulders tightly and the two of them kissed Giovanni on both cheeks before they left. The others sat in separate corners of the room watching and praying. Giovanni ignored everyone but Mira. He brought the chair to her bedside and sat in it. He took her hand in his.

"Sweetheart, it's been two days. The doctors think you should have woken by now. I know you're tired, but we need you, Mira. Can you hear me, my love?" He kissed her knuckles. He got no response, not even a flicker beneath her eyelids. "I held Gianni today. In my arms, Bella!" he said with tears of joy. "He's four pounds now. That's good. Soon he will need his mother. Your breast. Remember, we talked about how to juggle two babies on your breasts?" he chuckled. The joke echoed to silence. Giovanni closed his eyes. "Gino is sick. He's fighting for his life, Bella. He needs you, needs to hear your voice. See you. He needs his mother. Please. Please, for them if not for me. Please wake up."

Giovanni opened his eyes.

No sign of her understanding him could be seen.

He closed his eyes again and vowed to wait.

* B *

Catalina shared with Marietta that she wanted to visit the babies. Marietta sensed Catalina feared Mira's prognosis. They all did. So she didn't question Catalina's decision. She continued on to

Mira's room. When she entered, the small gathering of little old ladies with their bibles surprised her. Giovanni sat next to the bed staring at his wife. He didn't bother to look around or acknowledge them. And Mira's condition seemed unchanged. The longer she slept Marietta had to wonder what the medical implications would mean.

"No change?" Marietta asked.

"None," he answered.

"What do the doctors say?" Marietta pressed.

"They've run their tests on her brain mostly. They said everything looks good, but they won't know for sure until she wakes," he replied.

"How long, Giovanni? How long before wakes? A day, a week? What?"

"As long as it takes!" Giovanni's gaze lifted to Marietta. "You aren't needed here. I will make sure to call when we know more."

Marietta sighed. "She's my sister. Of course I'm needed here. I won't be separated from her again."

Giovanni looked away. Marietta didn't want to fight with him. Lorenzo warned her against it. Yes she knew who he was, but he didn't seem as intimidating as everyone claimed him to be now. He was a broken man, torn apart by his fears and guilt. She understood his warring emotions. They both knew if Mira didn't wake soon it had to mean something was terribly wrong with her.

After an uncomfortable silence settled between her and the *Don* her gaze swept the others. Two ladies rocked in their chairs with their eyes closed. They seemed to be in prayer or some kind of meditation. Another stared directly back at her with a scowl of disapproval. And yet another read from her bible softly, aloud. It felt a bit too chaotic. Her sister should have peace and quiet. But she knew she shouldn't raise the objection.

Instead she found a chair and brought it around the bed. She sat in it and focused on Mira. She and Giovanni both stared at her and waited.

* B *

Rosetta approached the kitchen with Eve on her hip. The little girl had been fussy with her parents gone so she and Cecilia took turns at entertaining her. To her surprise Rocco and Dominic were both at the kitchen table eating. Rocco looked up. Dominic did not. She heaved Eve higher on her hip and walked in.

"*Ciao,*" she said. She went to Rocco and kissed him on the cheek. He immediately reached for Eve who went to him with a bit of reluctance. Dominic continued to eat.

"*Ciao, Dominic,*" Rosetta said again.

He glanced up and winked.

She smiled. "I didn't know you were here." She took a seat at the table. Neither Rocco nor Dominic turned her away. Eve had removed her pacifier and started to nibble from Rocco's fork. "How's the *Donna*? Does anyone know? I had to come home to see after Eve. Catalina and I took turns with the babies. They are so cute. Have you seen them, Domi?"

"Not yet. I intend to go back soon," Dominic replied.

"Can I go?" Rosetta chirped.

Dominic smiled.

Rosetta could barely stand it when he smiled in return. He was so devilishly handsome. How any woman controlled their desires around Dominic was a mystery. "I want to see the *Donna* and the babies. I want to make sure they're okay."

"They will be fine!" Rocco declared. "Won't they, Eve? Just fine."

Dominic wiped his mouth with his napkin and then tossed it to his plate. "Stay with Eve. I'll call if there is any change," he walked over and leaned in to kiss Eve. The toddler turned her face upward to kiss Dominic on the lips. He smiled. Rosetta observed with envy. Maybe someday soon he'd do the same for her. She reached and touched Dominic's hand. He paused.

"Call me if there is any change. Promise?"

He kissed Rosetta on the top of her head and squeezed her hand. "I promise."

She reluctantly had to let his hand go. She watched him leave until he disappeared out of the kitchen. When she looked back to Rocco she saw him staring directly at her with disapproval.

"What? What is it?"

Rocco didn't answer.

Rosetta sighed. "I know better than to cross any lines with Dominic."

"Good," Rocco said.

Rosetta rolled her eyes.

* B *

Lorenzo found Carlo on the outside terrace. His friend smoked a cigar and stared out across the land to the sea. He walked over and joined him. Carlo made no attempt to acknowledge him.

"I never got to thank you. For Marietta," Lorenzo began.

Carlo dropped his head back and exhaled a thick wave of smoke.

"What is it? What has you pissed?" Lorenzo asked.

"I need a break. I'm sick of this shit," Carlo said. "I need to get back home. See my woman, gamble, cut throats, what the fuck ever... I need to go," Carlo sighed.

"I'm talking about me and you brother. Something is between us. I feel it."

Carlo sat forward. He cut Lorenzo down with an angry glare. "I'm your friend. Not your brother. I had a brother. He's dead now. Remember?"

"You blame for me that?" Lorenzo asked.

"Should I?" Carlo asked.

Lorenzo shook his head. "What the fuck did Marietta say to you? Did she tell you I killed your brother? That I lied to you?"

Carlo stared at him.

"The woman runs her mouth when she's pissed. She'll go for your balls. She knew how badly you were hurt after Carmine's death. You can't see what that was?"

"It's not about that. Not really." Carlo stood. "I need a fucking break from you and your problems. I have my own shit to deal with."

"Got it. But you're wrong. We are brothers. We have always been brothers," Lorenzo said.

Carlo glanced back. "How is she? Marietta?"

"You know how she is. Difficult. Complicated. She's scared for Mira. We all are."

"Any news?" Carlo asked.

"Not yet. One of the babies is sick. They say he may not make it."

"Gio will take the loss of his son hard." Carlo said.

"True. We should talk about Santo. How you will handle things. We need to contain this thing in the *Camorra* until we can get the family under control."

"There may not be enough time for that," Carlo said.

"Agreed. You'll let us know? If time is up?" Lorenzo asked.

"Don't I always?" Carlo started down the steps of the terrace and walked away. Lorenzo observed him. He didn't like the way things felt between them. He had to wonder what the true cause was. Later –

Marietta woke. She saw several women hugging Giovanni and saying their goodbyes. She looked to her sister. Mira lie as she had all day, still and silent. Marietta stood and fixed the sheet around her. The day had passed without event. She only left the room twice to eat. Giovanni had been in and out. Now it was late.

"Nico will drive you back," he said.

"What time is it?" Marietta asked, straining in the dark shadowy room to see the minute and hour wand on her watch move. Giovanni turned on the lamp by Mira's bed. "Eight. Nico's waiting."

Marietta had no choice but to stand. It was evident the *Don* wanted her gone. He appeared as tired as she felt. If there was only one thing Marietta knew to be true about her sister it was that she loved this man. If Marietta were able to set aside her anger for Giovanni maybe it would make things easier for them all. At this point she'd do anything to make things more peaceful for her sister. She cleared her throat. He glanced up at her. "Maybe you should get some rest. Tomorrow might be the day she wakes."

He nodded. The exchange felt genuine. Marietta smiled. No. She didn't care for the man, but she had to respect how much he loved her sister. She gave him a small smile and left.

Giovanni rested the side of his face in his hand. The door closed and a soft swoosh echoed behind him. He stared at his wife. They were alone now. All day he'd seen visitors and met with Dominic and the doctors to discuss her wellbeing. They agreed that if she didn't wake tomorrow they would consider some additional treatment options. He didn't want to go this direction. But what options did he have? He felt totally powerless.

"Bella?" he said, leaning forward. "The doctors say you should be awake by now. Please, Bella. It's time," Giovanni pleaded. He dropped his head. Soon his grief and exhaustion got the better of him. He rested his face on the side of the bed and drifted. In his dreams he could rewind time. Do it all over. He dreamed back to the day Renaldo handed him the purse that belonged to the American fashion designer with her precious bracelet inside. If he had opened that purse, that day, and saw the bracelet what would have happened? Would they be here now? Would he have gotten the chance to fall in love with her? Maybe the price for their love was his lies.

The soft touch of her hand over his head soothed him. Fingers raked back through his hair and combed his scalp. She often stroked the top of his head when he needed her comfort. In his dreams she delivered the hope he needed.

But this wasn't a dream?

Giovanni opened his eyes. He blinked. The breath in his lungs seized. Slowly he lifted his head and looked into the eyes of his wife. "Bella? Bella!" he stood *"Mio Dio, Bella mia,"* he cupped her face in his hands delicately to be sure. "You're awake?"

She nodded. Her bottom lip quivered and her eyes glistened with guarded tears. She didn't speak. She didn't have to. Giovanni knocked over the chair as he hurried out of the room into the hall. He saw Leo first. "Get the doctor, tell the nurses. She's awake! Get them now!"

Giovanni returned. She was still awake and aware. The adrenaline rush had come too quick and potent to his weakened state. "You're okay. You're going to be fine."

She nodded.

She understood him. Mira lifted her hand weakly and dropped it. He took her hand and kissed it. "The babies are here. We have sons. They need you. We all have been so worried."

The doors opened and two doctors entered. Buhari wasn't one of them. Giovanni had to step aside to allow them to examine her. Giovanni kept a hand to his brow in anticipation. Then he heard her speak. She did so with single word answers. But he heard her. The doctor asked her a couple more questions and used his light pen to look into her eyes. The wait was torture. The exam extended. She was fine. Couldn't they see what he saw?

"Signor, we need to take her for a few tests." One doctor said to him.

"Is she okay? She's awake? She's okay then?" Giovanni asked.

"Yes. It looks good. Let us examine her, please. It won't be long."

He glanced to Mira and smiled. She didn't smile in return. She stared at him. "I won't be far, Bella. Okay? I'll be right here."

She didn't respond. He walked out feeling as if the weight of the world had been lifted from his shoulders. Dominic had left hours ago. Giovanni nearly ran to the hall where the nurses were.

"Telefono?" he asked.

She handed it over.

* B *

"Bring her to me," Mancini said. He set aside his book. He

removed his reading glasses. When he looked up again a young beautiful woman walked in. He had known her most of her young and adult life.

Carmella seemed shy and hesitant. She kept glancing back to Armando for reassurance. Over the years he'd seen her with his son. Armando had a wandering eye. And this woman did their domestics as well as shared his son's bed. "Why have you returned?" Mancini asked.

"The _Donna_ was taken to the _ospedale_. Dominic Battaglia returned to Villa Mare Blu with family. He said my services were no longer needed," Carmella answered.

Mancini's gaze switched to his son. Armando nodded in agreement with the news.

"Have a seat," Mancini gestured. "Tell me. What had happened? How did Mira-ah-Giovanni's wife have an attack that made her deliver the babies early?"

"I'm not sure. She and Giovanni argued behind closed doors. The next thing I heard was the men shouting for the doctor and the car. They carried her out. I had to help with the baby, Eve. I saw nothing more."

Mancini figured it happened this way. Giovanni was a reckless idiot. He glanced to his son. "Any news on Isabella?"

"We are searching Carini for her. The monastery there could be where she's gone. We should find her soon, Papa. I promise you."

If they found Isabella and silenced her no one else could counter his objective to be reunited with his daughters. Mancini felt a cooling sense of satisfaction.

"_Don_ Mancini, I wanted to know if it were okay that I continue to work here for the next few weeks?" Carmella asked.

He waved her question off. "Of course, now go."

"_Grazie! Grazie tanto,_" she said.

"_Prego,_" the _Don_ nodded.

Armando opened the door and Carmella walked out of it. He closed the door. He stared at his father for a moment. "We need to decide on what's truly a priority."

"Kill Isabella. That is your priority." The _Don_ reached for his spectacles and then his book. "I expect a call from Buhari when Mirabella's condition improves. As soon she wakes we make our move. Go."

His son left without a word of objection.

The _Don_ ran his hand smoothly over the book. The title was To Kill a Mockingbird. It was Lisa's. Her favorite. On his long journey home she gave him the book to take with him. It spoke of racial intolerance; it spoke of the human spirit. He often read it over the years. He'd trace his fingers over the passages underlined by her with a red pen. Words that leapt off the pages, felt real. Each highlighted sentence seemed spoken from Lisa.

He smiled.

The doctors had already informed him he existed on borrowed time. And when he met Lisa on the other side he'd have the forgiveness from their girls to bring to her.

Mancini kissed the weathered binding of the book and opened it to read.

* B *

Relaxed with contracts strewn about him as he lay in bed propped by pillows Dominic struggled to focus on the fine print. He couldn't sleep. He had done well to avoid Catalina all day. But in the night he found it hard not to think of her. He wasn't sure if she knew he had returned. He had lost the privilege to see her. Right now he just existed.

The phone rang.

"Pronto?" he answered.

"She's awake!" Giovanni said.

Dominic sat up. He removed his glasses. "When?"

"A minute ago!" He could hear the elation in Giovanni's voice. "She woke up and touched my head. The doctors have her now. She's awake and she spoke. Bella is fine."

"I'm on my way!" Dominic pulled back the sheets.

"No. Come tomorrow. I want to be alone with her. Tell the family and come tomorrow," Giovanni said.

"I will. I'm so relieved, Gio. I'll tell everyone."

"Ciao," Giovanni hung up the call. Dominic got out from under the covers and found his robe. He eased his feet into his slippers and walked out of his room. The first door he visited was Lorenzo. After two knocks Lorenzo answered in his boxers.

"What is it?" he groaned.

"Mira's awake."

"She is?"

"Tell Marietta. Gio expects us to come in the morning."

"Bene. Grazie," Lorenzo said.

"Prego," Dominic replied.

Lorenzo closed the door.

"Mira?" Marietta asked. She held the sheet to her bare chest and stared at him with fear in her eyes. When Marietta returned home to him late in the evening she was so emotionally exhausted he made love to her and put her to bed without questioning her about the events of the day. It felt good to be the one to deliver the news.

"Your sister is awake. She'll want to see you first thing in the morning."

"Oh my goodness." Marietta covered her mouth. "Thank you God!" she got of bed, and ran to him naked. Lorenzo brought her up into his arms and hugged her. "Thank you God! Thank you!" Marietta cheered and kissed his face repeatedly.

* B *

Catalina heard a gentle knocking at the door. If she had been sleeping the visitor wouldn't have woken her. But how could she sleep? She heard from Rosetta that Dominic had returned. He'd travelled between the villa and the hospital yet she never saw him and he made no effort to see her.

The knocking came again.

Catalina turned on the lamp at her bedside. She didn't bother to put her robe on. She went to the door in her nightshirt and panties. "Who is it?"

"Domi."

Catalina fixed her hair and wiped the sleep from her eyes. She sucked down a deep breath and exhaled before she opened the door. "What are you doing here?" she asked. "I thought you were avoiding me?"

"I came to tell you that Mira's awake," Dominic said.

"Really?"

"Gio called. The doctors are with her now," Dominic smiled.

"Come in." Catalina further extended the invitation by opening the door wider. He looked tempted. She could see by the way his gaze climbed her body and lingered at her nipples or dropped to her bare thighs.

"It's late. Get some rest. We'll leave early in the morning," he said and turned.

"Domi!"

He paused.

"Is that all? Really? Is that all you have to say to me?" Catalina asked.

He glanced back at her. She waited. She hoped. But he nodded

393

yes before he walked away.

"Domi!" she called after him as he kept going. *"Vaffanculo!"* she slammed the door. His rejection after delivering such good news cut her deep. Catalina fumed.

* B *

The doctors kept with their exams for over an hour. The waiting was torture. Eventually the door opened and the nurses wheeled her bed back inside the room. Mira sat up against her pillows, alert.

"Signor, Dr. Buhari has been called. The doctors will meet with you when he arrives."

"Grazie," Giovanni said.

"Babies?" Mira rasped.

Giovanni looked to his wife. She had tears in her eyes. Her hand went to her heart. "My babies?" she asked again while patting her heart. "Where?" she asked.

"Yes. They're in the neonatal unit. They're premature remember? Small. But they've been waiting on you." Giovanni smiled.

"Take. Me." Mira moved the sheet aside. Giovanni hurried over.

"Bella, let's wait for the doctor. And then I'll take you, sweetheart," he took her hand and tried to kiss it but she snatched it away. Mira glared at him.

"I'm not keeping you from them. You had a complicated delivery. Your heart stopped."

She frowned.

"It's true. The doctors said your recovery is miraculous. It'll take a minute. Okay?"

"Liar," she said.

"I'm not lying to you, Bella," Giovanni said.

"Not. This!" she said, and struggled to capture her thoughts. "Liar," she said and her eyes welled with tears. It dawned on him what she truly meant. The lies he told about her sister, and father. The omission of truth had caused the premature birth of his sons and her suffering.

"Let's not do this now," he reasoned.

"Go!" she said pointing to the door.

Stunned he froze.

"GO!" she shouted and pointed to the door.

"I won't *go* dammit. I've been here every day, every minute. I've been worried. I was here when the babies were born. I was here when you... when we almost lost you. I *will* be here."

"GO!" she shouted again.

Giovanni rubbed his temples. "Stop this, Bella. You know me. I'm not going anywhere."

She turned away from him and slumped down on her pillows. The rebuff cut him to his core. He wasn't sure what to say next. But he knew he had to say something.

"You want to do it now? Let's do it now." He brought the chair back to the bed. "I lied to you. I learned who Marietta was and who your father was after the wedding. I didn't believe it at first. How could I believe something so incredible? And when I did believe it, I couldn't face it. The idea that our fathers were connected this way, Bella. How could I have handled it any different? It's my job as your husband to spare you the ugliness—"

"Stop!" she said.

She looked back at him. "Go, please. Beg you. Go."

Giovanni sighed. The look in her eyes left no room for negotiations. She didn't deserve the stress of his presence. He understood that. It took considerable effort to stand but he did so. Mira turned back over to her side and looked away. He hesitated. He searched his brain for a reason to delay his leaving her bedside. He wished he could force her to look at him. But nothing came to him. Defeated, Giovanni left. He kept walking. He walked until he arrived at where the hospital kept his sons.

Inside he found only one nurse present. She smiled at him with her eyes. Giovanni put on the breathing mask and hospital robe. He walked over to Gino and stared at his son. The boy moved his hand. He kicked his foot. "You know don't you, Gino? Mama's awake."

The baby breathed slow and easy. It had to be a sign of improvement. Giovanni's racing heart calmed. It dawned on him that his Bella could be mad now, but when she saw their boys everything would certainly change. It had to.

"*Signor,* the doctors are with your wife. They want you to come."

He backed away from Gino, removing his mask and his robe. He handed it over to the nurse and hurried to meet with them. He arrived to find all three doctors present. Though the late hour the men looked alert and excited.

"Your wife is doing well. We're all surprised."

Mira stared at him. She wore no expression. But Giovanni

smiled at her. "She can't speak. Not fully," he said without judgment.

"Her speech may be impaired a bit. If she requires physical therapy we can arrange it. But she seems to be recovering well."

"Babies?" Mira said to the men.

"Can I take her to the boys?" Giovanni asked.

The doctors exchanged a look. "Of course. I'll have chair brought in."

The other doctor excused himself as well. Giovanni extended his hand to Buhari. The man looked surprised. He extended his hand and shook Giovanni's. They exchanged a nod and the doctor left. Mira continued to stare at him She didn't bother to say what she felt. And there were too many words for him to express his feelings. So they stared in awkward silence. Before long a nurse brought in a wheelchair. Giovanni walked over to the bed. She looked up at him as if she wanted to reject him but he knew she could not. He scooped her up in his arms. Her arm eased around his neck. To hold her again felt right. He carried her to the chair and put her down in it gently. Mira let go of him as soon as she was seated. Giovanni wheeled her out.

"I did as you asked, Bella. We named them Gino and Gianni. Gianni was born vaginally. He came out at over three pounds. Gino struggled. They had to remove him by cesarean. He was two pounds. They had problems with their lungs." Giovanni told her everything he could without taking a breath. He wheeled her slowly, wanting to delay their arrival so he could prepare her. Mira didn't speak. If she spoke to him maybe he'd better understand her disappointment in him. The silence was the worst punishment she could give.

He had to open the door and ask for assistance before he was able to push her through. He wheeled her to Gino first.

"This is Gino," he said.

"Beautiful," Mira whispered. She put her hand on the glass. Giovanni watched her. She stared and cried tears of what he hoped were joy. He could see the smile on her face as she looked at Gino. "Wrong? What?" she asked. She looked up at him for an explanation.

"Right now his lungs. But look at him, Bella. He's moving his feet. He hears you," Giovanni said.

"Mama. I. Here," Mira said. "Mama. Here," she said again.

"Do you want to hold Gianni?" Giovanni asked.

She looked back at him surprised. She nodded yes. He could kiss her in that moment. But he didn't dare try. "Nurse?"

Giovanni wheeled her into position and put down the break on the chair. The nurse brought the baby over as she had done before. Mira needed more help getting into position. She was weak. He could tell without her saying so. When he put their son in her arms he saw such love and happiness restored to her. He stroked her hair and knelt beside them. "Gianni. He's our champion. He was in a hurry to come into the world. The doctors said he was down in the birth canal pushing his way out."

"Love. Him," Mira said.

"I love you both." Giovanni said.

Mira's gaze slipped over to him. His heart fluttered in his chest. The moment was brief. Her attention returned to their boy. "Small," she said.

"He's tiny, but growing. He's four pounds today. The doctors said when they are both five pounds we can take them home."

"Good." Mira nodded. "Love. You," she kissed their son's tiny forehead. Giovanni observed, he couldn't leave her side. The time she had with him felt short. He could see the anguish on her face when they took Gianni away. She pointed back to Gino.

"He's too weak now, Bella. You can't hold him yet. But soon."

She nodded that she understood, and wiped at her tears.

"Are you ready? To go?"

She shook her head no. "Stay. Me. Please me stay?" she asked.

Giovanni released the brake. He wheeled her over to the incubator and parked her chair there. Mira was given a glove and she then was able to slip her hand into the sleeve of the chamber. It was the only way she could touch Gino. He and the others never did. They feared how weak and small he was. But Giovanni knew Mira needed to feel their child and he sensed Gino needed her touch.

"Baby. My. Baby," she said softly. She swallowed and tried to say more but her words didn't form. He stepped back and gave her, her moment. Everything was right with the world again.

18.

In the darkness Mira blinked. She was awake. After what felt like the deepest sleep of her life she was alert and aware. She blinked and stared at the ceiling before her gaze lowered to her surroundings. At some point after visiting the kids she drifted. Giovanni must have put her to bed. She turned her head to the right slightly. Her husband was there. He slept slumped in an uncomfortable hospital chair. Though her mind processed slowly, the events of the evening came back with rapid clarity. She and he had exhausted themselves by staying so close to their sons all night. By the time they returned to her room she was half asleep. He put her in bed and she allowed it. She didn't have the strength to deny him.

Her heart hurt. Mira pressed her lips together to keep from crying. Giovanni slept with his head dropped back, and his mouth open. Had he taken to sleeping in the chair since this nightmare began? Careful not to dwell on his torment she cast her gaze away from him. Mira closed her eyes. She wanted out of the bed. She wanted her children. She needed to be with the boys. And what about Eve? Her poor baby girl had never been separated from her. Not even on their honeymoon. Eve had to be terrified.

She shifted in the bed. Her body felt stiff, almost frozen. The movement of her head exhausted her. So she vowed to gather her strength. She had no idea what she would say to Giovanni. How they could possibly go forward. But his betrayal and her lack of faith in him had taken them too far from each other.

"Morning," she heard him groan.

She looked over and realized he was awake. Or had she woken him with her soft grunts to find comfort on the hospital bed?

"How did you sleep, Bella?" he asked with a deep yawn.

She nodded her head to indicate she felt fine. And she did. Other than the rigid stiffness to her joints she felt better.

"Hungry? I'm sure you are. I'll call Zia and tell her to bring you something good to eat," he said.

"Zia?" she asked. A surge of hope pierced her heart. If Zia were near then she'd finally have the support she wanted.

He smiled at her. "Everyone is here. Zia prayed over you for two days."

Mira had no idea how long she'd been out of it. She vaguely recalled hearing their voices, and responding to the pleas to wake from her deep sleep in her head. But her thoughts faded and cleared irregularly. She could trust nothing. Part of her thought Fabiana would walk through the door.

Giovanni dialed a number. He spoke to someone in Italian and laughed. He looked over at her and smiled. Mira managed to smile back at him. She loved her husband. Even now. The door opened and Catalina and Marietta rushed inside. She was shocked to see them so early, so soon.

"You're awake!" Catalina exclaimed. "I could barely sleep. I was out the door as soon as the sun came up." She kissed Mira on both cheeks. "How do you feel?"

Mira nodded to her.

Marietta stepped closer to the bed. "Hi," she said.

What was Mira to do? How was she to go from no family to having a sister, a twin? She glanced to Giovanni who stared at her with so much love it was impossible to reconcile the facts. How could he think she wouldn't want to know her sister? It infuriated her even more. Mira extended her hand to Marietta. And her sister accepted.

"Hi," Mira managed to say.

The immediate connection between the women hurt him deeply. Not because of jealousy or envy. It was because the sisters were denied this bond due to his insecurities. Giovanni glanced to Lorenzo who noticed the way the sisters held hands and smiled at each other. Lorenzo looked up at him and gave him an encouraging nod.

"It's good to see you two together," Giovanni said.

His reply was sincere but felt awkward in the moment. Both Mira and Marietta looked at him with distrust. Zia and Rocco arrived and his Bella lifted on her elbows with a wide grin. Tears coursed down her cheeks. There was such a flurry of excitement he had the urge to shut the reunion down and chase them all from the room. Mira needed her rest. She needed him, the inner beast whispered darkly in his ear. *Trust no one with her. Keep her to yourself* it said.

"Love you," Mira said, and pointed to Giovanni. She then put her hand to her heart to express herself. "I... love you. Gio."

Giovanni felt relieved. Everyone went quiet because the tears in Mira's eyes showed how much she suffered when she tried to communicate. "Alone." Mira said to Giovanni. "Me. Them." She pointed at Mira, Catalina, and Zia. "Alone. You, go," Mira said. She looked at him directly. "Please, Gio."

"We'll be out in the hall." Giovanni agreed. "Come let's give them a minute." He put on a brave face as if the request was his idea. It hurt that she dismissed him in front of the family. But her saying she loved him did soothe a bit of the sting. He reasoned she didn't single him out. She wanted to see her sister and the other ladies. It made sense. There were too many in the room at once.

He and the men left. Giovanni paused at the door. He glanced back to see Mira being hugged again by Zia. Their eyes met. She blinked and her gaze shifted elsewhere. With a sad smile he closed the door.

"I was so worried. So scared!" Zia said with tears in her eyes.

"I... good." Mira managed to speak. Her words formed easier when she took her time and felt less agitated. As soon as Giovanni left the room the crushing weight on her heart lifted. "I feel... happy," she smiled. She looked to Marietta and then to Catalina. "Do every... one... do you... know?" she asked.

"Know what?" Zia asked. She looked across the bed at Catalina and Marietta. "What is it?"

Mira smiled. She reached for Marietta's hand again and squeezed it. "Sister. Mine. She is mine."

Zia straightened from her lean. She looked at Marietta and then back to Mira. "Sister? You two are related?" she asked.

"Yes. Found out," Mira sighed. She closed her eyes and tried to speak slow and precisely. "Giovanni knew. Kept it from us. Lied."

"Mira, he only meant—" Catalina interjected.

"He knew. Lied," Mira said with emphasis that silenced her sister in law. "No matter reason... wrong." Mira swallowed and continued. "All knew," she looked to Zia. "Rocco. Lorenzo. Domi. All knew. Because that's... how it works... with the men. They know. We don't. Their terms only," Mira said.

Zia put her hands to her mouth. She blinked at Marietta and for a long moment she stared at their hands. Understanding settled in and Zia lowered her hands to cover Mira's and Marietta's. "You're upset with Gio?"

Mira laughed. Tears welled up in her eyes. "Upset? No. Angry!"

"Mira, please understand why he did what he did," Catalina pleaded. "Please try to."

Mira shook her head. "He wrong."

"Mira?" Catalina pleaded.

"Wrong! Wrong! He... is why... I'm in this bed right now."

"That's not fair," Catalina shouted. "Gio has been here every second, Mira. He's been at your side. He's been sick with worry for you and the babies. And let's not forget it was you who got out of the bed and confronted him. You knew the risk and you did that. You put the babies at risk, not my brother!"

Shocked Mira and everyone else fell silent. The accusation hit too close to her heart. It was true. She could have handled things differently. But the shock and pain over the truth made her react irresponsibly. In doing so she put her children's lives in jeopardy. And the worst part of it was she never even considered her role in any of it until Catalina said so.

"I... to blame. Me." Mira wiped at her tears. She dropped her head. "Babies. My babies. I hurt babies."

Zia hugged her. "Hush now. They are okay. Let's not focus on who is to blame. Let's focus on healing our family. That's what is important." Zia kissed her face. "Gio loves you. Don't punish him. He's punishing himself already."

She didn't want to hear the defense of her husband. There was no defense for what he'd done. One minute she loved him with all her heart, but the next she wanted out. She wanted to break from the obsessive love that had now controlled her life and made them both into people she didn't like. "I need help," she said. She had to collect her thoughts to articulate in a clear precise manner. "Across the hall from my room. It is where I want. Babies. Babies' room."

"We've already decorated the nursery, Mira," Catalina said, with a sad smile. "I'm sorry for my harsh tone earlier. I'm sorry. It's just that I've been so worried about you and Gio. I didn't mean..."

Mira shook her head and put up her hand. "Listen. Babies' room. My room too!" Mira pointed at herself. She glanced up at Zia, then let her gaze connect with Catalina, and finally Marietta. "Room for me. Me and Babies. I want it. No Giovanni. Don't tell Giovanni. Just do it."

"Mirabella," Zia said. "I know this is a shock for you. I am so sorry that you were denied your sister. But the more important matter is your wellbeing and the health of the babies. No?"

Mira nodded in agreement.

Zia stroked the back of her head and smoothed her hair. "Don't be ruled by your anger at your husband. It does him and you no good. Please. Let us focus on the blessing God has given us."

"I can't. I don't want to fight him. Hurt him. Need space. Help me." Mira wept.

Zia pulled her to her breast and Mira sobbed against it. The girls were silent before Marietta cleared her throat. "I'll help you, Mira," she said.

Mira's head lifted from Zia's breast.

"If you want me to. I'll help. I can prepare the room for you and the children," Marietta said.

"It's none of your business!" Catalina shouted. She went to Mira. "If you do this it will break Gio's heart. He loves you, Mira. He loves you so much. Please. Forgive him. Talk to him. I know he will do whatever you want to make it right again. I know he will. Please."

Mira sniffed. She weighed Catalina's words against Marietta's offer to help. The only way she could gather the strength to understand Giovanni and forgive him was if he gave her space. She loved him too deeply to even try when he was close to her. She'd forgive him of anything. And if she did, what would become of them? She was tired of being controlled. She couldn't take another minute of his insufferable hold on her heart. "Space. Focus... on my children." Mira touched Catalina's face. "Babies need me. Not Gio."

"Can I say something?" Marietta asked.

Mira glanced to her. "Yes."

"You have to stay here for awhile. You will need help. We all see that you aren't fully yourself. Why don't you let us take on some of the burden." Marietta glanced to the other women. She tried to speak in a reasonable tone. "We take turns ladies. Like shifts. We can help Mira dress. We can get her to the babies, whenever she needs to nurse them. That way you can have some space from your husband. And maybe when the babies come home you won't need this space as badly?" Marietta smiled at her sister. "Don't do anything rash. Trust me I'm the queen of overreacting. And I have a husband I'm upset with too. Focus on getting well. Let us help you do that."

"We are not going to stand here and conspire to break up my brother's marriage!" Catalina said. "Focus on your family. That includes Gio. Space only divides you. Talk it out. Work it out. But don't banish him from the hospital or his home. It's not right!"

"Oh calm down." Marietta said to Catalina. "My sister just came out of a coma. Her world has been turned upside down. If she wants our help to get things right again we will do it."

"Your sister?" Catalina frowned. "You couldn't stand her a week ago. So don't stand here and pretend like you two are so much in love."

"Enough, Catalina!" Zia shouted over a loud clap of her hands. "That is enough! No more fighting! I won't have it!" Zia lifted Mira's face in her hands. "Marriage is hard. It's private. We will help you in any way you want. But you will have to speak with Gio and prepare him for your wishes. Out of respect."

"Agreed." Mira glanced to the others. Catalina walked off with her arms crossed. But Marietta stood at the foot of the bed smiling. "Thank you. All. I know it... hard. We've been through so much. We'll get through this." Mira said with clarity. "Together."

The woman all nodded in agreement. They'd do it together.

* B *

"Congrats!" Lorenzo hugged Giovanni. He grabbed his cousin by the shoulders. "See! You see! It will all work out!"

Giovanni grinned. He'd never been happier. He felt like he could breathe again. He hugged Lorenzo and then Dominic. He hugged Rocco. Nico, Renaldo, Leo and Carlo patted him on the back all in congratulations. More than twenty of his most loyal men had gathered in the small waiting area with their boss. Their support overwhelmed yet strengthened him. "The doctors say it's a miracle." Giovanni grinned. "A Battaglia miracle!"

The men cheered. Giovanni laughed.

"When can we take them home? Get them out of here?" Lorenzo asked over the roar of celebrating.

"I'm not sure. The babies have to be stronger with their lungs fully developed. Gianni is almost there. Gino struggles. But he's getting better. I know he is. I'm sure Bella won't leave without them. So I'll be staying here." He glanced over at Carlo. "I thought you'd left for Sorrento?"

"Not yet. One more person I need to see. No worries, Gio. I've called Santo. He expects me. He sends his congratulations," Carlo said.

It had all come to fruition. The healing first, the forgiveness next, all of it would make his family stronger. Giovanni felt alive again. His head was clear. It was time to settle things. "Mottola is the priority. Bonaduce and the 'Ndrangheta won't move into the Campania without him. I want you and Santo to visit Chiaiano and report if we have any allies left. Visit Father Andrew at St. Yves Parish. He will help you navigate those who want our protection." Giovanni looked to his men. "There is only one way we will deal with Mottola and send a message to the 'Ndrangheta. We grind him to dust."

Dominic cleared his throat. "The meeting with the clan bosses. I think we should take the lead and schedule it."

"A week. We bring Bella home I'm sure within a week. Schedule it at Melanzana. I'll fly in."

Everyone agreed.

"There's something else." Giovanni said, he scanned the faces of his men. "Something I want you to hear from me." He glanced to Dominic and then Lorenzo. They both gave him the nod. He intended to say what was needed. Of course the decision was his, but he hesitated. His wife and her issues with family were a private matter. Still the men gathered were closer to him than any relative.

"Bella, Mirabella, my wife, your Donna, she... we have learned that she has a sister. Lorenzo's wife, Marietta." Giovanni glanced to his cousin. "They were separated as children. They never knew of each other." The silence was complete in the room. It lengthened while he struggled with the news. Giovanni scratched his brow. "The reason they were kept apart was because of who their father is. He's... Marsuvio Mancini."

More than a few of the men exchanged glances. A soft rumble of voices rose.

"It is shocking. Neither of them knew Mancini or what this blood tie means. But as men of my clan each of you do. And so do I." Giovanni stared any man who looked him in the eye down. "With everything going on now, including the polizia di stato investigating us, this news is not good. I understand that. Mancini is going to make an issue of our connection. He wants to infiltrate the family. He thinks he can divide my wife and me. It's why I've been so protective of her safety. Now we must prepare for what comes next."

* B *

Marietta had wanted the moment alone with Mira. But she didn't dare ask for it. When Zia insisted on helping Mira shower and change clothes the others did little tasks like tidying her things and helping Mira from one side of the room to the next. After her sister showered she truly did seem happier.

"Let's go," Zia said to Catalina.

"What? Why?" Catalina objected.

"Give the sisters a moment," Zia winked at Marietta. She ushered Catalina to the door.

"Zia likes... you. Good," Mira said. She buttoned the front of her shirt.

"It's all a bit overwhelming. Catalina is right. Just a week ago I didn't want to know any of you. And now. I can't stop thinking of us being sisters. Being separated."

"Sit." Mira pointed to the bed.

Marietta found a spot near the foot of the bed and she sat. "Do you want me to fix your hair? It's kind of wrecked," Marietta said with a smile.

Mira touched her hair. It had drawn into knotty tangles. "Yes. Vistors come. I feel messy."

Marietta rose and found her purse. She located a comb and brush. She could feel Mira watching over her. She tried not to appear nervous. "About what happened. How I told you... all of it. I'm so sorry." She glanced up at Mira. "I never wanted any of this to happen. You having your babies so soon or any of it."

"Understood," Mira said. "Gio's fault and mine."

Marietta froze. She looked up at Mira. The look on her face and the tone in her voice felt odd. Before any of this began, Mirabella the black Barbie doll married to the mean ole *Don,* was happily in love. Marietta could sense the change and it didn't feel right. "He only did what he thought was right I suppose."

"No. He did.... the thing that serves him. Man he is."

Marietta walked over with the comb and brush. She looked over Mira's hair. The tangles were all the way to the root. "Do you relax your hair?" she asked.

"Press it," Mira said.

"What if I put it in two braids?" Marietta asked.

Mira nodded. "Nice. Like that."

"Our mother. What's her story?" Marietta asked.

"Runaway. Sixteen. Boy from her hometown. An older boy. Name is James. Ended up in Philadelphia."

"That must be where she met Marsuvio Mancini?" Marietta concluded.

"Maybe," Mira said softly.

"And the drugs? How did that happen?" Marietta asked.

"Don't know. Grandparents never explained. Never. Don't want to know," Mira said.

"I understand," Marietta said. "I think your husband knows."

Mira looked up at her. "Why?"

"Lorenzo said he only knows part of the story but your husband knows the rest. I hate to ask this but…"

"Giovanni to tell me? He won't." Mira half-joked.

"You're upset with him. I understand it. I was mad as hell at Lo," Marietta chuckled.

"Was? Forgiven him?" Mira asked her with a deep frown.

"Of course I've forgiven him. He's my man," Marietta shrugged.

"Lie and manipulate you? He did," Mira said.

"Honey I love that man. The good and bad in him. That's what forgiveness is. Love. Lo puts it down, he takes care of business and me. I ain't going to throw that out of the window because he made a mistake."

"Mistake? More than a mistake," Mira said.

"True. But it's our first mistake together. He did things and I've done things. Now I want to wipe the slate clean. I don't care for your husband but even a blind man could see how much he loves and cherishes you. Catalina was right when she said he was here every minute. He wouldn't leave your side. He didn't even eat. I was here. I saw it."

Marietta completed the part down the center of her sister's head. She began to braid down the left side. She did so in silence. When she finished she walked around the bed to do the other side.

"I'll ask him," Mira said.

"Don't you want to know?" Marietta asked.

"Part of me. Yes. Part of me afraid."

Marietta paused. "Gonna give it to you straight about your man. He's a mafia *Don*. You're a mafia *Don*'s wife. Lies and manipulation are in the wedding contact. Don't sit here and say you never knew this would be your life," Marietta said. "You're my sister and a part of me. We're married to two of the meanest damned men this side of the world. We got to be strong."

"No fantasy," Mira said sadly in agreement. "I know… now. There's just this."

* B *

Catalina waited. Dominic entered the hall. She left Rosetta and Zia. She walked straight for him. He looked up at her once she drew closer. "We need to talk."

"Not now, Catalina," he said.

"It's about Mira and Gio!" Catalina insisted. She tried to keep up.

He looked back over his shoulder. Giovanni was laughing with Carlo and Lorenzo in the hall. He hadn't seen him look happier. He nodded to Catalina and they went inside a patient room. He wasn't fully inside before she turned on him with tears in her eyes. "Things are bad, Domi. Really bad!"

"What are you talking about?" Dominic asked.

"Mira," she wiped her tears. "She blames Gio for everything. I've never seen her like this. She wants to separate from him, possibly end their marriage."

Dominic ran his hand back through his hair. "No, she knows that won't happen. She's just upset."

"No! She wants us to set up a room for her and the babies. Separate from Gio. She wants us to take shifts at the hospital to keep Gio away. You didn't see the way she spoke of him. She blames him, Domi! I think she hates him."

"Okay. I'll take care of it." Dominic said. "Calm down."

"You can't take care of it! That's the point. You should have prevented this! Gio lied to her, he broke her heart. And I know what this feels like," Catalina said. "So do you!" Catalina put her hands to her eyes. "I don't want my family to fall apart. But how can we help them if we can't keep it together? Huh? I love you, Domi. I love you and that doesn't matter anymore to you. Does it?"

He pulled her into his arms. Catalina's body was up against his. His lips brushed her cheek. At last, her lips parted and he was able to taste her again. That sweet almost sad note of surrender escaped her throat. His hand went to her hip questing, keeping her pinned to him. She kissed him deeply. Passion pushed them back up against the wall. And when her slender leg lifted and circled his waist, he could press the ache in his dick hard into her sex. He bore down on her wet heat. "Fuck me, Domi," she whispered into his ear and gripped his ass.

The door opened to the bathroom. A patient who resided in the room gasped in a loud startled voice.

"Domi, stop! Stop!" Catalina brought her leg down and Dominic's head lifted from her neck.

The female patient covered her mouth.

Catalina fixed herself and so did Dominic. They couldn't contain their laughter. Somehow they had forced themselves into an occupied room.

"*Scusi!* Sorry!" Catalina said.

They left the room laughing, and laughter felt good. She couldn't stop. He didn't try. Dominic swept her in his arms and turned her around. He held to her. She wrapped her arms around his neck. "Let's get married. Let's do it!" she said.

"Are you proposing to me?" Dominic smiled.

"Can you handle that?" she grinned.

"Yes. Let's do it!"

She squealed and kicked her feet as she hugged him tightly.

Dominic had to calm her. "First we need to help Gio and Mira. Agreed?"

"Agreed," she grinned and held to him.

* B *

Giovanni opened the door to the celebratory sounds of laughter. He found Mira and Marietta sharing something intimate and personal. Marietta looked up at him and flashed him a welcoming smile. Mira never looked his way. His wife's hair was combed down neatly into two braids. She had changed into a pair of jeans and a button down shirt. Maybe it was too soon for her not to be in her hospital gown.

"Sorry to interrupt. Bella, the nurses want to know if you would like to try to feed Gianni. They said he's up."

"Really?" Marietta asked. "That's great news. Isn't it, Mira?"

Mira turned her gaze in his direction. "Talk. Alone."

"Okay." Marietta hugged her. She kissed her cheek. He couldn't help but feel a pang of envy. Mira hadn't hugged him once since she woke. Marietta approached. She stopped before him. Giovanni wasn't sure why. Marietta glanced back at Mira and then to Giovanni. She reached and hugged him. Surprised he embraced her. It was brief, but it felt genuine. She winked at him.

"Hang in there," Marietta smiled and left.

Alone with his wife he pressed his lips together and shoved his hands in his pockets. Mira stared at him. She waited for him to speak first? He cleared his throat. "So what do you think? Are you up for feeding our boy today?" Giovanni asked.

Mira looked down at her hands. "Yes."

Giovanni approached her bed but kept his distance. "You're still mad at me? Aren't you?"

"Mad?" Mira chewed on her bottom lip.

"Yes. Are you still mad?" he asked, hopeful she'd give him a good tongue lashing and move past it. Marietta had done so. Couldn't she? Mira seemed to weigh her options on which emotion to choose. Giovanni had to hope she'd go with love and forgiveness. It's what they both needed. "I wish I were mad." She stopped and slowly breathed in and out of her nose. "Not mad at you," she said clearly. He almost applauded to hear her speech improving.

"Talk to me, Bella? Tell me what I can do? How I can make our nightmare better?"

"You'd like that. Huh? Wipe it all clean," she asked.

"Yes. I'd like to put the past seventy-two hours behind us and to never look back," he said.

"Past four months? Wipe clean? Should we... never... look back?" she asked.

"What do you want me to say, Bella?"

She sighed.

"Sweetheart," Giovanni said. "It's me. I love you more today than I did yesterday. You're everything to me. I made a mistake. I'm sorry."

"I believe," she said and nodded her head that she believed him. Giovanni expelled a sigh of relief prematurely. "Sorry caught. Keep me from learning... what you've done."

"That's bullshit! I told you there was something I wanted to share, something deeply personal. I told you to give me time because I was worried. Well this is what I was worried about. Ending up here, with you and the kids in jeopardy. That was my fear."

She looked away. To his dismay she wiped at a tear that slipped to her cheek. "Want." She sucked down a deep breath. He watched her exhale and control her emotions. She spoke in a business manner that unnerved him. "Space" she said. "You and me. Space."

The request made no sense. Giovanni struggled to process how she'd even suggest exile as his punishment. But for the life of him he couldn't. Mira continued. "Asked Zia and... the girls for help. Be here, for me, until I get out. You see the babies. Space me and you." She exhaled. It must have drained her to articulate the hurtful request. She then added, "For now."

"You're my wife!" Giovanni reminded her. "You don't get to change that fact."

"Love you!" she shouted with her bottom lip trembling. Tears brimmed in her eyes. "Love you much! Wife? Yes. Property? No!" she shouted. "I'm not a thing you own!"

"I didn't mean it that way, Bella, you're twisting things." Giovanni said.

"Which part? Explain lies? Okay. Explain secrets? Okay? Explain being a hypocrite? Don't! Don't explain. No more talk. Love you. I do. Hurts me. But need it. Space."

He shook his head in defeat. Mira continued. "Known for months. My mother. My sister. My father. You've known. For months you... you... said nothing!" she said as she sobbed with tears streaming down her cheeks. "Hurt." Mira put a hand to her heart. "Hurt so bad, Gio," she said her speech slurred.

"It was never my intention," he shook his head.

"But you did it! What plan? Explain it to me, Gio? Was I ever to know? Marietta? Or your father... kill my... kill my mother? Huh?" she asked.

"Don't!" he pointed a finger at her. He clenched it into his fist. "There is a lot about this you don't know. But know this. I only did what I had to to protect you, our children and our marriage—in that order."

"You're a coward," she said. "Coward!"

"Maybe. That's what they don't know about me, Bella. I'm a coward. I can't think of anything in my life more important than you. My fucking business is in shambles because for the first time in my life I put someone before me, before this family. And that someone was you." He put his hands to his head. "I confess it. I was afraid of you finding out. Especially after I learned what Patri had done. You're my life. How can I share something so horrible? How?" He shook his head sadly. "It happened by accident. I swear it on my life. I was in your makeup bag one night looking for some oil to give you a massage. I found your bracelet. And I saw the Del Stavio stamp. I didn't know what it meant. But I knew it meant something." He paced. "So I sent Domi and Catalina to America to find out the meaning, to learn the truth about your mother."

Mira stared at him with such grief in her eyes he had to look away. "I lied to you, about the purpose of that trip. Dominic visited the man you said ran away with your mother. He's in prison for the rest of his life for a crime he didn't commit." Giovanni pushed his hands down into his pockets to keep from wringing them. "James is his name. He was put there by Marsuvio. Back then they called him Manny Cigars. James worked for him, your mother is who Manny wanted. So he separated them to have her. And he destroyed her,

Bella. Put her on drugs, took her from your family. That's the truth. And when Dominic told me it made me sick."

"Your father?" Mira asked.

"My father didn't know your mother. He wanted control and your mother was keeping Mancini from returning to *Sicilia*. So he put a contract on her life. Yes. He did this. But the story wasn't something I could easily share."

"And my sister?" Mira asked.

"We didn't know about Marietta," Giovanni continued. "We knew there were two babies born to your mother but we didn't know the truth about her."

"Forgive me... if... can't believe you," Mira said.

Giovanni laughed. "Forgive me that I can't make you believe me, Bella." He looked back at her. "Marsuvio sent for you, brought you to Italy through that man you call Teddy. He set you and Fabiana up. And I believe he brought Marietta here too. When I found out that you were sisters and he was your father you had already suffered a miscarriage scare. The doctors were talking to me about your blood pressure, warning me to be careful."

"I remember, when you found out," Mira pointed at him.

Giovanni frowned. "I don't understand?"

"The cellar, boxing. That day. Told me that you weren't a good man. Said one day I'd see it. I'd leave you. Blamed myself. For Eve. You let me."

"You should have blamed yourself!" Giovanni seethed. "You took my child. You hid for two years. I found you with another man. What you did should have cost you your life!" he shouted. "But I didn't let any of it keep me from letting you back into my heart. Because I know that love and fear make people do unforgivable things!" Giovanni said.

"The real you... *Don* Giovanni Battaglia." She gestured at him.

"It's who I am. Who you married. And you knew from day one!" he said.

"Go!" she pointed to the door.

"Like you said, I'm *Don* Giovanni and I'll come and go as I damn well please." He stormed out and made sure to slam the door. In the hall the family had gathered. They looked at him. He could see it on their faces. They knew. He turned and went in the other direction.

Mira flinched. She dropped back on her pillows and tried to catch her breath. The door opened and a nurse arrived, followed by Zia.

"Are you ready, *Signora*?" the nurse asked.

"Yes," she wiped away her tears. "Let's go."

Zia and the nurse came around the bed. They both helped her stand. Instantly she felt strength in her legs. She didn't need their aid much. When she sat in the chair she released the breath she held and allowed the nurse to wheel her out.

She would deal with Giovanni later. Right now her focus had to be their sons.

* B *

Someone grabbed her hand. Marietta had little time to respond before she was yanked into a room and the door shut. Even in the dark she could see his face. "Carlo?"

He kissed her. Hard and passionate he kissed her. She was crushed under the warmth, the overpowering strength of his body. And the kiss was more persuasive than she had the will to reject. Her tongue darted in and out of his mouth with eager pursuit. No girl in her right mind could turn from a kisser like Carlo. His lips seared a path from her mouth down her neck and his hands travelled the length of her body. *What the hell were they doing?* She pushed back and slapped him. Hard. Shoved at his chest to force him further away from her.

"Are you crazy?" she hissed. She wiped the kiss from her lips. "Don't ever touch me again! Ever!"

He touched his lips and stared at her. Marietta trembled with fear, shock, shame. What if Lorenzo had seen them enter the room? Or one of his men?

"Don't ever do that again, Carlo. Never!"

"I'm leaving," he said.

"So? Go!"

It was ridiculous. They hated each other. That was until she was foolish enough to cross the line. She put her hands to her head. "Oh God. What have I done? Oh God." Marietta felt weak with guilt and fear. She couldn't decide on one ruling emotion. "We can't do this. Do you understand? Lorenzo will kill you. He'll put a bullet in the both of us. And he's my husband. I love him. I love him! I could never hurt him like this."

"And me? What is it you feel for me, Marietta?" Carlo asked. "Because that kiss——"

"Nothing!" she shook her head. She stepped back. "I feel

412

nothing for you! We hate each other remember?"

Carlo laughed. "No. We've never hated each other."

"We did, we do. We aren't anything," she insisted.

"That's a lie and you know it!" he shouted at her.

Marietta jumped. She looked to the door. What if someone in the hall heard him shouting and tried to walk in. She had to get a handle on things and quickly. "What happened at your mother's villa was wrong. I had been drinking. I was upset. It would have *never* happened if I was sober. And we didn't go through with it. We stopped ourselves. There is time to fix this," she pleaded.

"I have feelings for you," Carlo stated. "Maybe it's love?"

"No. No. No." She put her hands to her ears. "I'm not listening to this. No you're not."

"I fucking know my heart!" he shouted her down. "I've got feelings for my best friend's wife." He walked toward her. "And I'm crazy, because I can swear you feel it too."

"Don't touch me." Marietta screeched.

He took her by the face. She knocked his hands away. He reached for her again, she fought him off. "You're crazy, man. I'm not in love with you. I love Lorenzo. He's my man."

Carlo pressed his head to hers and held both her arms at her side so she would be still, and be his.

"I don't want this, Carlo. I don't!" she pleaded.

"I know," he said in defeat. "I won't do anything to hurt you, Marietta. Never. That's why I'm leaving. I'll stay away from you. I just... I needed to say... something." He kissed her. She closed her eyes, turned her face up and returned his kiss. A gentle press of their lips she refused to deny. He let her go.

"I'll stay away. I promise," he said with a small smile.

"I'm sorry. For everything." Marietta said. "I never hated you. But I love Lorenzo. He's my life. He just is. I mess up a lot of things in my life, but not him. He's the one I want. Period."

"I understand." Carlo left.

She closed her eyes to fight back the panic stunting her breath. She felt such shame for coming between them, for even entertaining the sexual tension she had with Carlo. She didn't love him. But she cared about him, and what she'd done had hurt him and Lorenzo beyond her intention.

Marietta wiped her eyes. She dried her face the best she could with her shirtsleeve and left the room. Lorenzo was the first person she saw. She wanted to turn and hide, get herself together but he approached her fast.

"Where have you been? I just saw Carlo and he said he hadn't seen you." Lorenzo looked her over suspiciously.

"Huh? I don't... I just needed a moment. A moment... went to the bathroom. I, ah, with this thing with Mira."

Lorenzo took her hand and led her back into the room she had just escaped. Marietta sucked a deep breath down. She could still smell Carlo's aftershave inside the room. Did Lorenzo?

"I know what you did," Lorenzo said.

"What?" Marietta gasped.

"Marie, don't play games with me. I wasn't going to speak on it. But now it's between me and Carlo. So I have to. How could you do it?" Lorenzo demanded.

"I-I-I don't know. I'm so sorry. Forgive me, Lo. I swear I'm sorry," Marietta confessed.

He grabbed her shoulders. He looked her in the eye. "When I tell you something in confidence it's because you are my wife. I trust you with my life. To tell Carlo about Carmine is unforgiveable. He's my brother, my best friend. I never meant to hurt him or bring my mistake between us as brothers. I can't change my actions. But you can't use my weakness against me when you are hurt. Do you understand?"

She nodded. Shocked that the confession was for a sin no greater than the one he didn't know. He pulled her into his arms. He hugged her. "It's a dangerous game, Marie. Take your anger out on me. But don't push Carlo on me. Don't ever get between us. It won't end well for either of us."

She hugged him and squeezed her eyes shut. "I won't do it again, never again. I swear.

* B *

Dominic sent Catalina in search of Mira. He would locate Giovanni. It was best if he were the one to prepare him for Mira's attitude. He sought him out in all the usual places and couldn't find him. He eventually located a nurse who told him that Mira had gone to feed the babies and Giovanni had gone to the outside annex where people went to smoke. It was a bad sign. He found Giovanni sitting on a bench staring out at nothing.

"I hear Mira is breastfeeding Gianni. Why aren't you upstairs with her?" Dominic sat next to him on the stone bench. Giovanni stared out at the pond. "Give her time, Gio. A lot has happened. A lot of trauma."

"I was right. She does hate me. After everything I couldn't prevent the outcome," Giovanni said. He sat forward and leaned with his elbows resting on his parted knees. "Never seen her like this. I can't even get close to her. Hold her. Be her hero. I can't get her to look at me without tears."

"She doesn't hate you. She's angry. It might be the first time she's been hurt, angry, and scared since Fabiana's death. She woke from a coma just several hours ago. You have to give her time," Dominic reasoned.

Giovanni turned red, angry eyes on Dominic. "She's my wife. Whether she wants to acknowledge that fact or not, it won't change. She can take the time but she doesn't get to push me away! From her or my children! Ever."

"Gio?" Dominic sighed.

"Get the hell away from me!" he said. He put his face in his hands. Dominic would normally obey the request. Today he chose not to. He sat in silence next to Giovanni and waited, for whatever was to come next.

* B *

"There, there... there you go. Sweetie," Mira said. "Oh goodness. Look." She gasped in surpise. "He does it," she laughed.

Zia clasped her hands together. "Yes. Yes. I see," she chuckled. "He knows mama."

"He has an appetite like his father," Catalina said with a wide grin.

"So beautiful," Mira answered. "And yes. Does look like Giovanni. Doesn't he? When a babe? Does he Zia?" Mira asked.

Catalina gave a nudge to Zia. Zia nodded that she agreed. "When Gio was born he was so tiny. Just like Gianni. And yes, he does look like him. They both do."

Mira brushed her finger over Gianni's cheek as he nursed. "Mama happy. Sweetheart. So happy my baby."

"Mira?" Catalina said.

"Mmm," she answered.

"Maybe we should find Gio? So he could see his son nurse. See that Gianni is getting stronger."

"He doesn't care," Mira said.

Catalina looked to Zia. Zia stepped closer. "Of course he cares, Mira. He loves you both. Don't deny him this."

"He can come. If he wants." Mira shrugged.

Zia nodded for Catalina to go find them. Catalina hurried out of the room. She found Renaldo in the hall first. "Do you know where Gio is?"

"Downstairs I think," Renaldo said.

"Can you go get him? Please. Tell him Mira said she needs him to come quick. It's Gianni," Catalina said.

Renaldo walked off to do as she ordered. Catalina went back inside. Mira hummed a nursery rhyme to Gianni, it sounded so sweet. She glanced up to Zia who met her stare. They nodded that they were going to help Mira to the best of their ability. When the song ended Gianni stopped suckling. He opened his eyes.

"Hi, sweetheart. See me? You see me don't you?" Mira looked up and smiled. "Come quick! Eyes like Eve. Like Giovanni."

"Are they blue?" Catalina came close. "Oh my, they are blue. He is truly Gio's son," Catalina chuckled.

The door opened and Giovanni walked in. He looked at Mira holding his son and stopped his approach. Catalina walked over and hooked her arm around her brother's. "His eyes are open. Mira wanted us to go get you. Your wife and son need you. Come on, don't be shy."

Giovanni nodded. He went to Mira and got down on his knees. She covered her breast and leaned forward for Giovanni to get a good look at his son. Gianni looked at his father and then shut his eyes. Mira chuckled. Giovanni smiled. Giovanni kissed Mira on the lips. Catalina was relieved that Mira kissed him back. Mira was careful to hold him in her arms and gently soothe his back to help him burp. Everyone cheered when Gianni did so.

"Want to hold him?" Mira asked her husband.

Dominic brought a chair closer for Giovanni to sit in. Mira nodded encouragingly to Giovanni who opened his arms and Mira gently passed the baby over to him. The family hovered as Gianni opened his eyes and looked up at his father. "He sees me!" Giovanni said.

The others laughed. Catalina could see the love bloom again between Mira and her brother over their son. Mira even joked that Gianni better not have Giovanni's appetite because she only had two breasts. She watched them and silently prayed that the worst for her family was past them.

Dominic's hand slipped into hers. She squeezed it. He gave her a look that melted her heart. Catalina dropped her head on his shoulder. When she glanced across the room she caught the look of envy on Rosetta's face. Catalina paused. Rosetta looked away. She hadn't realized that Rosetta had come to the hospital. But more importantly, she hadn't paid much attention to Rosetta's fixation with Dominic. It felt strange.

* B *

"*Signor, Signora*, I'd like to speak with you about Gino." Dr. Buhari came in amongst the family celebrating. He glanced around at how many were in the neonatal room at once. "I'm sorry but we can't have this many people in here. Please, only two to three people at a time."

Giovanni stood and put Gianni in Mira's arms. She accepted her son. She was careful. She glanced up to see Giovanni escort the others out the door. She hadn't seen her husband smile as much since their wedding. Mira glanced over to Gino. While the family had cause to celebrate with Gianni, Gino's progress was more of a concern. Her heart ached to hold him and feed him from her breast as well.

"What is it with Gino? Is he improving?" Giovanni asked.

"Yes. He is." Dr. Buhari glanced over at Mira. "We see much improvement and he's put on a little weight for his weigh in. He's three pounds and six ounces. His lungs are developing. I'm very optimistic."

Mira expelled a deep sigh of relief. "Thank you. So much. For everything. You've done.."

"You mustn't tire yourself. Remember you are recovering as well. Take your time. The doctor admonished. "Your speech will correct itself soon. But you need to be careful not to over stress yourself."

"I will. I want… pump breast milk for Gino. Okay?" she asked.

"Certainly it will be good for him." Buhari smiled. "But your body may not be fully ready. You need to slow down the pace, *signora*."

The doctor nodded respectfully to Giovanni and left. Mira's gaze lowered again to a sleeping Gianni who had now settled against her breast.

"Things are good, Bella. *Va bene*."

Mira didn't want to hurt or punish Giovanni. She kissed him because it was expected in front of the family, but she felt no need in private to reassure him. She just couldn't look at him without anger after what he said to her. Until she could she refused to try. But her husband was stubborn. He brought the chair closer to hers and sat in front of her. Mira had no choice but to look up at him.

"The food isn't great here. Josefina has brought some thing for you to eat. Marietta is going back with Catalina to collect some clothes and things you need. What else do you want? Maybe something to read?"

"I've told you. Question? You going to… give it to me?" Mira replied.

"How can you ask that of me?" He leaned forward and lowered his voice. "The happiest I've been in days is right here and right now with you and Gianni," he glanced back. "And Gino. Being here with you and our boys is what we both need, sweetheart. How can you ask me to go away when you know how much I love you?"

"Not from them. Never ask that," Mira said.

"Really? Because you didn't care when Eve was born now did you?"

"Stop it, Gio," Mira sighed.

"I want forgiveness!" he insisted.

"No!" she said in a hushed but firm tone.

"My loving you isn't about controlling you. My life has rules. And you know damn well why I do what I do," he answered.

Mira nodded. "I do. Joke's on me. See the boys. Wheel a bed in here. Sleep with them. Every night. But not me. No more talk. Space. My way."

"No," Giovanni said, his gaze narrowed and his voice was tight with restraint. She knew he wanted to shout his refusal to the top of his lungs. But he held back. "You won't keep me from—"

"Nurse!" Mira cut him off. Giovanni fumed but withdrew. When the nurse came closer he had no choice but to end their argument. She knew he wouldn't be seen arguing with her in front of others. "Please take Gianni. Need someone to wheel me to my room. *Zia* is out in the hall. Ask her to come."

"Sì, signora," the nurse took the baby.

Mira fixed her eyes on Giovanni. "Goodbye."

Giovanni wiped his hand down his face. "Fuck this," he said. He stood and walked away from his chair. He walked to the door and stopped. He looked back at the babies not her. Mira felt another deep pang of regret. But she didn't say anything. Giovanni left. Mira forced the tears in the corners of her eyes.

When Zia returned Mira had already made up her mind. She wasn't going to live by his rules any longer. She was done being the dutiful Mafia wife.

Later –

Catalina checked her appearance in the mirror. She looked ravishing and she knew it. From the scarlet red lipstick, to the plunging low cut negligee with just a strip of lace to cover her sex. To the way she teased and curled her black hair, she was beautiful.

And the room in the villa was lit with tall vanilla scented candles burning brightly from every corner and pedestal she could find.

Tonight her date with her Romeo would secure her future as his wife and in his life. Screw all other distractions. Catalina's dreams for a career could be put on hold for a while. The most important thing to her was Dominic. Period. And she'd prove it to him. The door opened somewhere in the beach villa. "I'm in here, Domi!" she called out.

He told her he had to meet with Carlo and Lorenzo before Carlo left for Sorrento. She told him to meet her down at their villa. She waited two hours for his arrival. Dominic stepped in the door. She didn't bother with a robe. And the choice was wise. His gaze raked over her body with the kind of heat that made her skin warm all over. And then his eyes connected with hers. A sly ease upward of the left corner of his mouth meant he approved. *"Che cosa è questa?"*

"What is this? Is that what you ask me? You know what this is, Domi. This is me and you. Only me and you," Catalina said. "Our private reunion, silly man."

Dominic shed his suit jacket. He smiled with approval. "I need you," he said.

Catalina helped him out of his jacket. She carefully draped it over a chair before he was pulling her to him. She turned into his arms. "Mmm… slow down, I want to seduce you," she said as he picked her up and carried her to bed.

"Later."

He came down with her. Arousal curled tighter in the pit of her stomach. Her pussy clenched when he palmed her sex. And with two fingers he tickled and then unsnapped the clasp. Dominic brought his two fingers to his mouth and sucked them before lowering and inserting them into her cunt. She hissed in a breath and her eyelashes fluttered shut. He surged his fingers deeper. She knew her soft sighs and moans rewarded him.

"My pussy, Catalina, say it."

"Your pussy," she said with a naughty smile. "Lick me, Domi," she pleaded.

He removed his fingers and trailed them up her slit and played with her clit until she wiggled her hips and gasped from pleasure.

"Benissima," he said as his face lowered to between her parted her thighs. He blew on her labia and then parted the lips of her sex with two fingers. The flick of the tip of his tongue to her clit caused her to shiver.

She tasted tangy and then sweet. The spicy edge of her essence compelled him further. He licked her pussy, toyed with the tiny nub of sensitivity until her ass bounced on the bed sheets. Dominic chuckled. He slowed the lap of her sex with soft strokes just as her hands sank into his hair and she pushed his face deeper between her thighs.

"Yes, Domi! Oh yes!" she cried out. *"Scopami! Scopami!"* She gyrated against his mouth, smashing her sex against his lips and invading tongue.

Dominic wanted her to come but not yet. The first time she released he had to be inside of her, deep inside of her.

With great reluctance he pulled away from her pussy. He rose up on his hands and knees then sat back on his haunches. Catalina let go a small cry of frustration. Her sex was on display to him, a pink dewy plump center he owned. His dick thickened and he stroked himself. Catalina's lids were half cast and her eyes held a dazed look of desire. She touched herself for him. Tweaked her nipple and fingered her pussy. Dominic smiled. The room smelled of her and the waxy burn of candles. It was intoxicating. Hunger washed over him like a wave of heat. He stroked his dick harder, to the point of eruption.

"Scopami!" she cried out. It was a desperate plea to be fucked by him. *La piccoletta*, his beautiful Italian princess. His heart's wish. Oh yes, he'd fuck her. He'd fuck her all night.

Now he was ready.

Without warning he knocked her hand away and came down on her hard and urgent. He thrust his hips forward and sank into her tight heat. Her inner walls contracted tight with a securing grip around his plunging dick. Dominic pulled out slow and thrust in hard, with repeated frequency. He rocked up and down against her body desperate to hold back his climax until she was ready.

"Faster! Faster! Fuck me harder!" she clawed at his back and rolled her pussy around his dick with each thrust. It was all he could do from coming right then and there. His mind and heart was swimming with emotion. She met every thrust and clung to him.

With a deep groan he gripped her by the buttocks and fucked her with unrelenting mercy until they both succumbed to their joyous reunion. And what sweet bliss it was.

* B *

Giovanni lifted his face from his hands. He checked his watch. It was close to midnight. The staff at the hospital gave him a room next to Mira's. But he hadn't gone inside. Instead he sat outside of her door. Waiting for the impossible, for his wife to send for him, welcome him back into her heart. The impossible never came.

After another indecisive moment passed he stood. He had grown accustomed to the body aches he's suffered the past few days. He walked toward Mira's door and stopped himself. She fed Gianni and pumped milk from her breasts for Gino. All of this was done with the aid of the nurses and Zia. He was updated on her actions both successes and stumbles, but not included. With Zia gone and the hospital staff off on other duties there was no one between them.

He pressed his palm to her door and turned the handle with the other. Slowly he eased it open. Darkness greeted him. He stuck his head inside. Mira lay on her side. She slept. Giovanni was careful to not disturb her as he entered. When he approached the bed he saw that she looked peaceful. He couldn't help but smile at her. He adjusted the blanket and made sure she was comfortable. He brushed his lips very lightly across her cheek. He then found his usual spot in the room and settled back into a chair to watch over her while she slept. He vowed to do so for only a few minutes until the anxiety in his chest lessened. That was his vow.

Mira turned in her sleep. She opened her eyes. Giovanni had posted up in the chair not far from her bed. The man refused to listen or respect her wishes. He was as stubborn as he was adorable when he slept. Mira flopped on her back with heavy sigh. She glanced over to him once more. It was cold in the hospital room. Possibly all hospitals kept the temperature low to ward off germs or freeze the patients into staying alive. She had to smile. Zia told her Giovanni slept in the chair all through her coma. What he needed was to be in bed with her, so she could comfort him. Put him against her breast as she did often when he returned from a hard day. But even if she could bring herself to let go of her disappointment in him to do so, her bed wasn't big enough.

She tossed her sheet back. She put her feet to the ground. She felt strength in her legs. When she stood she felt even more. She lifted the extra blanket folded at the foot of the bed and walked over to her husband with a sluggish yet straight posture. She shook out the blanket and covered him. Giovanni didn't stir. He was a light sleeper usually but she imagined that he was quite tired.

Standing over him she noticed everything about him. How undeniably handsome and overgrown he was for the tantrums he was throwing. She derived no pleasure out of his suffering. She wished she could do as Marietta had done with Lorenzo and just let this one go. But the trust between them was all she had in their stormy life. Without it she felt lost, deceived, and disillusioned. If they continued this way it could destroy their marriage. How else could she make him understand the consequences of his lies?

Mira reached to touch his face and stopped her hand with her fingers just centimeters from his cheek. She lowered her hand. Maybe tomorrow things would feel different? Maybe the anger will have gone? She prayed so.

She shuffled back to bed. Climbing under the covers she drew up the blankets and lay on her side. She watched over him from her bed until sleep stole her away.

* B *

With quiet reverence Lorenzo ran his fingers over his wife's body. He loved her body. Every inch of her was burned into his memory. There were times when he could just watch her, not touch her. And he'd often felt such raw intense passion for her he'd have to fix himself in his pants. It was lust, yes. But there was something else about his Marietta. Such a fiery undeniable love tie that he was certain of his fidelity and commitment to her unlike his past relationships with women.

Lorenzo's fingertips brushed her navel piercing and the belly chain glistened on top of her brown skin. He kissed the toffee colored peak of one nipple and then the other.

Marietta stroked the top of his head. "It was Gemma," she said. "She was the one who told me the truth."

His gaze lifted from her belly to her face. "Gemma? Where did you see Gemma?"

"I bumped into her at the restaurant called Belina's in Palermo. I told her about us being married and she told me about the secrets you and the Battaglias kept. Why I should fear you and not marry you."

Lorenzo eased up on the bed to lie on his side. He put a hand to the belly he hoped one day would carry his child. "I understand why you held back from telling me," he said.

She placed her hand over his and stared down at their fingers as they intertwined. "She was like a mother to me, Lo. She was the only person in my shit life to give me hope. I owe her so much." She glanced up at him. "I'm telling you because trust goes both ways. I broke your trust with Carlo. I can't take it back, just like you can't take back lying to me about my mother and father. But I want us to move forward. Can I trust you not to hurt Gemma?" she asked.

He kissed her brow. "How does Gemma know so much about your mother and Mira? Did you ever stop to think it over?"

"She said she met my mother. That she knew her before she died."

"And she has lied to you before. You choose to believe her now?" he asked.

He saw Marietta consider his words. He didn't like a loose cannon like Gemma running around and bad mouthing his family. Especially with knowledge no one outside of the family knew. Marietta turned over and wrapped her arm around his waist. He held her. They lay in silence for a long moment. "I won't hurt Gemma. But you have to promise me to stay away from her. If she contacts you again you tell me immediately where she says she is. I want to have a talk with her."

"I promise," Marietta yawned. "Let's go to sleep."

He closed his eyes and settled under the warmth of their blankets and her embrace. Soon his lids grew heavy and his thoughts narrowed to one: Gemma.

* B *

"Boss? Boss!"

A hand shook Armando awake. He sat up. "What the fuck is it?" he groaned. Carmella pulled the sheet up over her nudity and kept her back to them.

"A visitor at the gates. It's a woman."

Carmella's eyes opened. She listened. But she remained silent and still.

"What woman? Who the fuck is it?" Armando barked as he left the bed and looked for his robe.

"Gemma. She says she has an urgent message for your father," the man said.

"Well bring her in." Armando ordered. He turned and stormed out. Carmella looked back as soon as the door closed. She was quick to get out of bed. She found her nightgown to pull on and a robe. If Carmella considered the danger in what she set out to do she'd lose her courage. The last conversation with Dominic didn't go well. She had nothing to share other than the old *Don* celebrating a reunion with his daughter that Armando vowed would never happen.

Dominic made it plain. Either she gave him something he could use or he'd have no more use for her. And Carmella dreaded the meaning of his threat. She opened the door and peeked out into the hall. Careful to not be seen she crept from her room.

Armando stood in the foyer. After a moment Gemma Scafidi was brought into his home. He looked over the woman. He'd met her a few times. She knew his father from years ago. Gemma was quite attractive for her age. Her figure, sultry eyes and pouty lips reminded him of Marilyn Monroe or Sophia Lauren. Old glamour. She wore a raincoat over a blue dress that flattered her curvy figure. Her auburn hair was pinned up at the back of her head but limp loose curls fell about her oval shaped face.

"Thanks for seeing me," Gemma said.

"What do you want? My father doesn't receive visitors at this late hour," Armando replied.

"I came to see you. Can we speak alone?" Gemma asked.

Armando looked her over once more. He then glanced to his man to his left and decided with a nod. The man walked over and took Gemma's coat, purse, and umbrella from her. She shivered but looked relieved.

"Come with me." Armando walked off. He decided to take the meeting in the upstairs parlor for privacy. He climbed the stairs with Gemma closely behind him. When they entered she walked over to the leather chaise and sat on it. He observed her curiously. "Something to drink?"

"No thank you," she replied.

He took a seat in the chair across from her. "So? What is it you have to warn me about?"

"Not what, but who. Isabella. I came here because of Isabella," she said.

Interest piqued he sat upright and uncrossed his legs. "What about her?"

"First, you have to know who I am. I'm the daughter of Montague Scafidi. I own a sweet desert shop in Milano." She cleared her throat. "Years ago I worked in America. I was only nineteen at the time. I... worked for a man named Manny Cigars." Gemma held Armando's gaze. "Your father."

Armando shrugged.

She sighed, but continued. "I knew a young black girl in America. We called her Lisa, her real name was Melissa Ellison. I was her friend."

"So you know the story of my bastard twins?" Armando asked.

"I know more of the story than you, Armando. I also know your father is headed directly down the path that Isabella wants for him. She's dangerous, full of hate and revenge. Her goal is to plunge you and the Battaglias into war. She wants to destroy both of your families. And she's almost succeeded."

"Is that so?" Armando smiled.

"You have to believe me. I'm risking my life by coming here. I know I can't approach the Battaglias. You are my only hope." Gemma reasoned.

"And where is Isabella?"

Gemma pressed her lips together. "You can't get to her that way. She has friends in the *Mafioso*, in the *Camorra*, hell she's got friends everywhere. She's been planning this for a long time." Gemma sat forward. "I know where she will be in another week. She's coming to Palermo. I can give you the date and time. It'll be the only opportunity you will have to stop her. If you don't she intends to stop you."

"I have a question for you, Gemma. What's in this for you? Why help my family rid ourselves of Isabella?" Armando asked.

"Because Marietta Leone means a lot to me. I owe her and her sister Mirabella this. I owe their mother."

Armando smiled. He could give a shit about Isabella's goals for chaos. He didn't believe for one minute any of his father's allies in and out of the *Mafioso* would align themselves with Isabella. He could smell the set up. But if it got him closer to his goal of ridding himself of Isabella and Giovanni, so be it. "Tell me about her plans," he said.

Carmella drew back from the door. To stay another minute would surely put her in jeopardy. She stole away from the hall and raced to her room. It was the second time she heard the name Isabella evoked. She needed to find out who this woman was and warn the Battaglias. Inside the room she closed the door gently. She crept over to her bed and reached for the phone.

She had only one number to Dominic in Villa Mar Blu and she prayed he slept in the room in the villa instead of out on the beach with Catalina. The phone rang three times before it was answered.

"Yes?" Dominic groaned.

"It's me." Carmella whispered.

The line went silent.

"I don't have long. Gemma Scafidi. Do you know her? She's here. She's meeting with Armando. She says that she knew the *Donna's* mother and that she came to warn him that the woman Isabella is out for revenge against both your families. That she wants you to go to war."

"Is that all?" Dominic asked.

"Yes."

"How does she know the *Donna's* mother?" Dominic asked.

"America. She says she worked for *Don* Mancini when he was called Manny Cigars. She said that she met a woman named Lisa in America and she owes her. I have to go. I will call again later." Carmella hung up just as Armando walked into the room.

He paused. "What are you doing up?"

She looked back at him. "I had to use the bathroom," she smiled.

He stared at her. Carmella pushed up from the bed and turned around. She opened her robe and drew her nightgown over her head. She flashed Armando a sexy smile. "You coming back to bed?" she teased.

He smiled and shrugged off his robe. Carmella held back her temperament and put forth a seductive one as she had on many nights. And when he rolled on top of her she closed her eyes and pretended she was fifteen again and in love with a cute boy named Gio who would fish for her, and fight other boys in the street to defend her honor. It could be her who gave him children, who ruled the family at his side. It should have been her. Her heart seized.

It would never be.

19.

Ten days later –

    Tremors quaked through the center of his hand and spread through each finger. Giovanni clenched it, opened it, and clenched it again before he reached for his bottle. It didn't work. He brought his hand back and stared at it curiously. Typically his body responded with inexplicable spasms after binge drinking and a lack of sleep crashed in on him. However these quakes didn't feel typical. He glanced at the clock and realized it was six in the morning.
    When was the last time he slept?
    Giovanni pushed back and the wheels on his office chair squeaked as they rolled over the marble tiled floor. He used the edge of his desk to aid him in his attempt to stand. A feeling of buoyancy swept him and he swayed a bit. He grunted. He shook his head and got his bearings and then walked out of his office. Maybe a shower would help?
    On autopilot he returned to his room. The moment he crossed the threshold his gaze was drawn like a magnet to the empty bed. Another reason he preferred his office most days and nights. In his office he didn't have to think of that fucking empty bed. Instead he worked with his men and Yeremian to establish control of his territories. The carnage in their wake inspired a cruelty in him that had lain dormant for close to three years. Mottola was on the run. The clans were split evenly. Every man that stood against him would be dust in his wake.
    Dominic asked him for the end game. There was no end to his wrath in sight. Giovanni exhaled. His gaze shifted away from the bed and landed on the doors to the closet.
    The doors to Mirabella's closet were partially opened. It meant someone had come into his room to collect clothing for her. It was possibly Catalina. Giovanni walked over to the closet and flung open

the door. Immediately Mira's soft floral fragrance swept over him. He inhaled. He reached in and touched one silk summer dress and then another, and another. The fabric felt as soft as cream in his fingers. He yanked the dress down and brought it up to his nose and inhaled his wife. The memories her scent evoked soothed him.

When they first started dating she would wear sexy wrap around dresses for him. They tied at the waist and draped around her heart shaped hips so sexy. Each garment was a tribute to her curves and femininity. When she became pregnant she wore silk scarf summer dresses that swept around her ankles in layers and held her large bosom with easy to pull down thin straps. Giovanni smiled. He dropped the dress, and shuffled through to the next and the next to conjure the sweetest memories.

"Giovanni?" a voice spoke behind him. Caught he whirled with a dress in his hand and several at his feet.

Catalina observed him curiously. "What are you doing?" she asked.

He tossed the dress into the closet and shut the door. He kicked the dresses away from his feet and stepped on those in the way. "What do you want?"

"Have you been drinking all night again?" Catalina walked toward him. "Today isn't the day for this, Gio."

"What is it, Catalina?" he waved her off and went to his dresser.

"I came in here to see if you were ready. We're bringing them home. Or have you forgotten?" she asked.

Had he forgotten? He'd been on edge since the doctors told him it was a possibility. He counted the minutes on the clock until his eyes went cross and his mind numb. "How could I forget?" he said bitterly.

"Today is a good day, Gio. Please shave, clean up. I don't want Mira to see you like this." She walked closer and he cut her off with an angry glare. Catalina wouldn't be turned away. She ran her hand down his back to soothe him. "Get ready for Mira and your sons."

Giovanni let go a bitter laugh. "Why? My wife doesn't see me at all. How does a man get dressed for a wife who won't even look at him? Won't stop to talk to him? Can't stand to be in the room with him."

"Stop it!" Catalina begged. "She's upset. She's focused on the babies. She hasn't had time to digest everything that's happened to you and her."

"Bullshit. Bella knows her focus, and what she wants. She wants the family, she doesn't want me!" He tried to step away but staggered. Catalina caught him. Apparently he did drink too much. Surprisingly he remained thirsty for more.

He finished off the first bottle when he learned that the street fight in Napoli left three of his men dead and six in jail. The *polizia* were all over his clan. Lorenzo and Nico had left just yesterday.

"Gio? Please, listen to me. I know this is hard. I know you love her, that you're worried about her. But she has to see you want to make amends. She can't see you like this. None of them can. Your men need you."

"I'm fine, Catalina. Go. Bring her home. I'll stay away to make sure it's a happy occasion." Giovanni pushed her away. He walked upright without need of assistance to the bathroom. He'd piss and shower. He'd be fine after a few cups of cappuccino. He glanced back once at Catalina who watched him in silence. He winked. "I'll be fine, *piccoletta*. I can handle it," he said and closed the door.

* B *

"Did you see Gino? I can't pump enough breast milk for him. He's taking a bottle every two hours." Mira grinned. She turned to the silence. Zia stared at her. "Well? Did you see him?"

"It was good of them to let you stay in the *ospedale* with the boys. I saw him before I came to your room. He was awake. Eyes open," Zia nodded.

"Yes. They are both ready to go home." Mira couldn't contain her excitement. "How is Eve, did you tell her I was coming home?"

"She misses her mama. Giovanni has been seeing after her. I think it is good that you kept her out of the *ospedale*. Good for Gio to have Evie with him," Zia said.

"Yes, but it was hard," Mira sighed. "I did talk to her on the phone every night." Mira zipped her bag. She looked around the room filled with flowers. Everything was packed and ready to go. "What time does Giovanni get here?" she asked.

"Do you want him to come?" Zia asked.

Mira glanced back at her. "Of course, for the boys. They're his progeny," she half-joked. When Zia didn't smile she corrected her tone. "Of course he needs to come. We've both been so anxious for this day."

"Mira, when was the last time you saw Gio? Three or four days?" Zia asked.

"Six days," she replied, and went to the closet. She checked inside. "But I know he comes and visits the babies. Marietta tells me." She closed the closet. "Did they bring the car seats? We have to make sure they both have them before we leave."

Zia stepped to Mira. "Things have been hard for Gio."

"I won't discuss it, Zia," Mira turned away.

Zia pulled her hand. "You need to release Gio. Give him your forgiveness. He's not doing well. None of us are."

"I won't discuss it." Mira sighed.

"Stop!" Zia clapped her hands. Mira looked at her with surprise. Zia never raised her voice. "It stops now, Mira. I'm sorry but you are wrong in this. He is your husband you are behaving..." Zia sighed. "What you do now could damage your marriage permanently. Do you know what men in his lifestyle do with a disobedient wife?"

"Disobedient?" Mira frowned.

"That's right! Do you know?"

Mira shook her head.

"Why do you think Tomosino chose Eve? Why do you think Marsuvio left his wife and chose your mother? Rocco told me the story of what happened to your mother. These men are only as strong as we make them. And your marriage is only as solid as your role in this life. To know your place. To be as loyal to your husband as you expect him to be to you. You have compromised your marriage by shutting Gio out. What he does, he does with blind disregard for the values you want to teach him. And I fear you are too damn stubborn to see there is another way."

Mira regretted raising her voice. She also regretted the implications that her marriage was in jeopardy. But Zia's words hit home, and her insecurity deepened. "I know Giovanni and I have things to work through. It's been barely two weeks. He's a strong man. And this is my marriage. None of you have a say in how I treat my husband. Giovanni would not go take up a mistress just because we don't agree. He's not that kind of man."

"Maybe not. But he will self-destruct. He is that kind of man—"

"I'll deal with my husband. It's private, Zia. But thank you. For telling me your point of view. I won't let this get out of hand. Trust me. Okay?"

Zia nodded her head in respect. The door swung open and Marietta walked in with a widespread grin to her face. She wore a pair of jean shorts and a white tank top with bright pink sandals. She had wrapped a green and blue scarf around the front of her hairline causing her natural locks to puff out behind her head.

"Are we ready?" she asked while munching on gum.

"We're ready. Is Giovanni with you?" Mira asked. "He has to be excited to carry the boys out."

"He's not coming." Catalina walked in. "He's given up. He thinks it'll be a better occasion with him not here."

Mira shook her head. "Once again he makes everything about him. His sons need him and he wants to play this game with me?"

Everyone stared at her.

Mira tossed her chin higher with defiance. "Whatever. Let's collect my children. I'm ready to go."

* B *

"You wanted to see me?" Dominic closed the door.

Giovanni sat forward on the sofa. He had run out of liquor in his office. He found several bottles of scotch in the bar upstairs. "Sit. I just got off the phone with Lorenzo." He poured himself a tall glass. "It's time to kill Mottola."

"I've spoken to him. They believe they know where he is hiding in the countryside. The Armenians have been a big help in the triangle. The 'Ndrangheta are looking to barter a truce. It is possible to slit their throats if they believe we have one. They too fear the Armenians' presence."

"Good."

"But." Dominic cleared his throat. "We may not need to kill Mottola."

"He's dead," Giovanni said dryly. "And I want to be there when it happens. I want to be the one to put the knife in him," Giovanni said.

Dominic blinked. "You? Go to Chiaiano? With me?"

"Yes." Giovanni smiled. "Together. Make arrangements."

"Why not let Lorenzo and the men handle it. You need to stay away. The *polizia di stato* and the *carabinieri* both are looking to bring you in for questioning. Besides Mancini has been quiet since the bombing in Palermo."

Giovanni sipped his whiskey. A week ago Armando and several of his men were nearly killed in a public bombing. Carmella informed them that they were hunting a woman named Isabella. She'd escaped into a building and they followed. The bomb blew afterwards. And the interesting news was this Isabella was supposedly an enemy of Giovanni's as well. He had so many enemies he'd lost interest and count. His empire was crumbling while he sat on his ass and gave orders over the phone. No more.

"I'm going," he said.

"With Mira coming home it might not be good timing. She and the twins need you. I fear Mancini will strike now. I have information that—"

"Fuck Mancini. He won't dare. He has his own mess to clean up since the bombing. It's time I make a stand. Show the other bosses I'm still here. Mira can see to the babies, I see to this. We're going."

He picked up his breakfast of whiskey in a glass. He walked over to the bar with Dominic watching him. "Giovanni. I've kept some information from you. Because you have been distracted... with Mira and the twins. I can't any longer."

Giovanni stared at Dominic from over his glass as he sipped.

"Carmella continues to feed me information on the Mancinis."

"And? I already know this. You told me about Gemma, about Isabella, about the bullshit."

"I didn't tell you Carmella's reasons."

Giovanni paused.

Dominic exhaled slowly. "Carmella does the spying for us because Lorenzo caught her in a lie. Apparently she was sent into Villa Mare Blu to spy on you for Armando."

Giovanni lowered his glass, his eyes narrowed. "Spy on me?"

"She tried to poison Mira," Dominic said.

"Che cosa ha detto?" Giovanni asked again for clarification. When Dominic couldn't find the words to explain Giovanni hurled the glass to the wall and it exploded. "Say it again! She was in *my* home to poison *my* wife and *you* kept it from me?"

Dominic looked on grimly. "She was threatened by Armando. I sent her back to Mancini. And it was the right thing to do. Gemma was the one who told Marietta about Mira. And now we know that there is a feud with the Mancinis and this Isabella woman. This is the missing piece of information we needed," Dominic said.

Giovanni waved it off. "Fuck this Isabella bitch! Fuck some old whore of Mancini's named Gemma! Why am I just hearing this?" Giovanni demanded.

"You have not been yourself, Gio. Not in days. Weeks. Not since Mira went into the hospital. Don't you see that?"

Giovanni wiped his hand down his face. He tried to focus, but he felt sick. He swallowed and it tasted like shards of glass. Weak he staggered over to the sofa and sat down on it. Dominic was right. He drank so much lately he was barely conscious. Dominic kept his vice from the men, from everyone, and hid it well. But they all knew. He was weak. Unworthy of his title and his family.

"Now do you see? It's all connected, Gio. A woman's body was found in the explosion. They believe it was this Isabella. I did some digging. There was an adopted girl who lived with the Mancini's. Do you remember her? She was older than you and Armando."

Giovanni lifted his head. "I remember her. Vaguely. She was kept away in a monastery or something and then came to live with the Mancinis. I think Flavio mentioned her."

"Why did she want to put our families into war? Do you know? Could it have something to do with Flavio?"

Giovanni shook his head. "I've not seen or heard her name since I was a boy. I have no dealings with her. I don't know. What the fuck does it matter. She's dead right?"

Dominic sighed. "Yes. I believe so. But with all that we know we need you here to protect Mira, to protect the family. I'll go back to the *Campania*."

"No!" Giovanni said. "I need to be seen by the men, by all of them, to remind them of my strength. I-I-I can't stay here." He put his brow in his hand. "And like you said Mancini is preoccupied. I'll only be gone a day or two." Giovanni reclined. "As for Carmella, you should not have kept this a secret from me, Domi," he sighed. "I hate secrets."

"She's useful to us."

"And when she isn't, you know what I want," Giovanni said. He glanced to the window. The glare of the sunlight burned his eyes. "Are they here yet?"

"They should be here soon. Renaldo is bringing them in."

The pain in his heart repeatedly hit like a hard stabbing blow. He closed his eyes. Keeping any emotion from his voice he spoke. "Leave me alone. I'll be there soon."

"Gio…"

"It's decided, Domi. I need… I need to get away from her—I mean here. This is my mess. I'm the head of this family and I plan to remind every one in the *Campania* it is still so."

He heard Dominic walk out. He picked up his bottle and poured another drink.

* B *

Mira reached over and checked the blanket on Gino. He slept. Gianni's eyes were alert and wide with wonder. She smiled down at him. "You ready to see Daddy? He will be so happy to see you both." She kissed his forehead. She glanced to the window. Giovanni should have been at the hospital. The fact that he stayed away hurt her more than she cared to admit. It was what she wanted. So she said.

"Bella?" Giovanni whispered.

Mira looked up. Her nipple slipped from Gino's mouth and she returned it. Gino latched on to her nipple and began suckling again. She had cried all yesterday when he failed to take to her breast. Today was such an improvement she couldn't help but cling to her joy.

Giovanni walked in. "He's nursing?" he asked.

"Yes," she replied. "See?"

Giovanni stepped closer and peeked at his son. "That's good, Bella. Zia told me about yesterday. I'm sorry I wasn't here. Are you okay?"

"Why are you here now?" Mira asked him.

Giovanni blinked at her, as if the question caught him off guard. He'd honored her request and left two days ago. "I've been looking after our daughter. I wanted to bring her but I think you are right she should stay home. She misses you, Bella. We both do."

"I miss her too," Mira admitted. "The doctors said we'll be released maybe as soon as next week if Gino did well in his tests today."

Giovanni touched his boy's cheek. "I also came to see what you needed. Maybe we can talk again."

"No."

"Bella, I have so much to explain."

"Can't you see what is important? Our sons. That's all. I don't want to sit here and listen to your reasons for your lies. I'm sick of the discussion."

Giovanni stood upright. "I have a question. Do you still love me?"

Shocked by the question she frowned at him. From day one she said she loved him. She could carve it into her skin and he would still ask it of her. "Why do you always need that reassurance? Why can't I be angry with you and still love you?"

"Because I could never be angry for long with the woman I love," he said.

Shocked she couldn't counter the argument. He ranted, and

blew up, but once it was done, for Giovanni it was. He never stayed angry with her for long. Somehow she had wounded him. She saw the pain in his eyes. And it was cruel of her to not give her husband what he needed. Mira opened her mouth to take it back, to soothe him but the moment had passed. In a flash anger flared in his eyes. She stared up at him. He stared down at her. Without another word he turned and walked out.

Six days passed and he didn't return. He'd finally given her the space she so desperately needed. And the longer he stayed away, the easier it was for her to not think of how badly she wished she had handled that moment differently.

The drive up into Villa Mare Blu was a slow one. The unpaved road meant Renaldo would take care to not jostle the babies in their car seats by decreasing his speed. Mira glanced back to see the car following. Catalina, Zia, and Marietta were at her side every day. She smiled. In just under a week she felt closer to Marietta. She shared everything she knew of their family with her. Told her what Giovanni said regarding her mother's history with Mancini. They both agreed that Mancini was a man they didn't care to know.

The car stopped.

Mira looked over to her sons. Gianni now slept like his brother. "We're here," she cooed to them both. "We're home, babies."

The door opened and Mira stepped out. She glanced over the top of the car. On the step stood Dominic and Rocco. She searched for Giovanni. Within a minute he appeared. He stared at her. She felt a sigh of relief to see him. No matter their issues she wanted him at her side when they brought in their sons.

"*Donna*, let us take them," Leo volunteered.

She stepped aside. The boys were both unfastened from the back of the car and lifted off the seats in their carriers. Mira sucked down a deep breath and walked toward her husband. She had on a simple white blouse and jeans. She was surprised at how quick her stomach deflated but not enough to return her body to the state it was once in. Marietta told her of a diet, and workout plan that could have her in shape in 28 days. She intended to try it.

Giovanni made no move to approach them. Mira couldn't break from his stare if she wanted to. His gaze shifted to the babies. He then stepped out of the door. The men went around her with the boys. Giovanni accepted the first carrier and lifted it to peer inside. He leaned in and kissed who Mira thought was Gianni. He was then given Gino to do the same.

"Hey, sis," Marietta said. She hooked her arm around Mira's. "Ready to see your room?"

"You finished it?" Mira asked grateful for the distraction. She knew that Marietta took the lead on getting it ready for her homecoming. She went inside with her. Giovanni and his men were already climbing the stairs.

"Yea, your husband wasn't happy when he learned that we were putting a bed inside," Marietta whispered. "Catalina handled him. I think he was drunk. He's been drinking a lot."

"Has he?" Mira frowned.

"You might want to talk to him. Seriously. He spends all day locked in his office with Eve. Only Catalina can go for her." Marietta continued in a hushed voice. "He raised hell one day when Cecilia tried. Left the girl in tears. Lorenzo had to talk to him."

"I'll handle it."

"Mama!" Eve yelped her name. Mira stopped. She turned and her little girl ran straight for her. Mira knelt to receive her. Though a bit sore she managed to lift Eve into her arms with the help of Marietta. Eve began crying immediately. Mira kissed her face and tried to soothe her. But her daughter clung to her neck. Eve trembled as if frightened to let go. Her little body shook with deep sobs. "Mama is so sorry, baby. Hey, sweetie, it's okay. It is. I'm so sorry. I'm home. I'm here."

"She's missed you so much, *Donna*, welcome home," Cecilia said.

"I've missed you too, baby. Mama's so sorry. So very sorry." She hugged her tightly. They'd never been separated for such a long time. Eve settled down but continued to cry. She refused her pacifier. The guilt weighed heavy on Mira as she climbed the stairs with her. The women were all supporting her. Each walked either behind her, or to the side of her and to the front of her as she made her way to the nursery. The men at the door separated so she could enter.

Giovanni had placed the boys both in one crib. Mira put Eve down and her daughter wailed to be picked up once more. Zia thankfully took on the job. Mira walked over to Giovanni's side and looked down at her boys bundled up.

"Why weren't you at the hospital?" Mira asked.

He didn't answer.

He needed a shave. He smelled of whiskey. It was ten in the morning and he reeked of it. She reached in the crib to make sure they were comfortable. She looked back at the family. "Give her to her father." She told Zia.

Giovanni glanced over to Eve. He reached for his daughter and she eagerly went into his arms.

"Thank you, everybody, for all the support, for all the prayers. For taking care of Giovanni and me these past few days. I can't thank you enough. I need to be alone with my family now," Mira said. She hugged a few necks and ushered the crowd out of the nursery. She closed the door. When she looked back Giovanni had leaned a bit so Eve could look at her brothers.

"Lucciola," he said. "These are your brothers, Gianni and Gino."

Eve snatched her pacifier off her string clipped to her shirt. She put it in the crib close to her brother's mouth. Giovanni chuckled. "You will take care of them. Won't you?"

Mira clasped her hands in front of her. "I'll be staying here, Giovanni, for the time being. The boys have a very hard schedule to manage. I need to be with them."

He looked over at her. "To be close to the babies or away from me?"

"I can only focus on them now. They are my priority. Nothing has changed between us."

Giovanni lifted Eve up above his head. "Hear that, *lucciola*? Mama says nothing has changed. A lot has changed between Mama and I. Hasn't it?"

Eve grinned. Mira braced for the argument she knew would come.

"I'll be leaving tonight," he said and he put Eve down. Their daughter walked over to the crib and grabbed the bars to lift as if she could look up at her brothers.

"Leaving? Why?" Mira asked. "We just came home and you're leaving?"

"Does it matter? I'll be gone. It's what you want. Right? Sleep wherever you want."

"You need to shave. The drinking. Have you eaten?" Mira asked.

"None of it is your concern. If you aren't my wife don't pretend to care."

"Oh I'm your wife. You made it clear that doesn't change. The attitude isn't helping, Giovanni." Mira said.

"You won't discuss it with me!" Giovanni shot back. "You barely look at me now. And you think I need to change my attitude? I'm sick of it!"

"Don't raise your voice at me," Mira hissed. "I'm trying to talk to you."

"Bullshit!" he shouted at her. "We are done talking. No more words! No more apologies! No more of this bullshit!"

Mira blinked at him surprised. He stepped to her. "I'll fucking drink and do whatever I fucking want to. And you can stay in here and blame me for it. But you don't dictate anything to me. Two can play this game, Bella."

"Game? You think I'm playing games?" she stepped back. "Who are you right now?"

"Who am I?" he glared at her. "Right now I don't know. I think I need to go back to Sorrento to find out."

"You break my heart," Mira said. "Look at you, this is ridiculous!"

"Who cares? I'm a man with no heart. Remember?" He went for the door but she blocked his escape.

"We can't keep doing this. Not today and not in front of our children. Stay in here with me today for the children. Let's try. If you want to talk I'll listen to you tonight. But stop drinking, and stop punishing yourself. Deal with our issues like you deal with anything else in your life. Why is it different with me?"

"It just is!" He shoved her aside and stormed out. Mira looked to the door and almost went after him. She looked back to her daughter. Eve dropped her head and started to cry.

"Come here, baby," Mira knelt and Eve came running into her arms. "No, baby. It's okay. I promise. It's okay. Mama will fix it. Somehow. I promise." She held her daughter and tried to not cry as well.

* B *

"It's getting worse, Domi. We have to do something." Catalina paced. She chewed on her nail. "He drinks. He doesn't eat or sleep. He blames Mira now. He's angry with her. He's not reasonable."

Dominic sat at the table staring down in his tea. The fighting was bad enough but now Giovanni wanted to go into battle. With his mental state it could be disastrous. He took a sip from his tea.

"Do you hear me? Did you know they hadn't seen each other in six days? Six days, Domi!" Catalina threw her arms up. She crossed them in a huff. "Maybe today is different. She did say she wanted to be alone with him. That was good, huh? She said *her* family. Sounds like the old Mira, huh? Maybe? Being home can be good for them. But she had Marietta put a bed in the nursery. She intends to sleep there. I need to find a way to get them to sleep in the same bed. How long does a woman have to wait before she can have sex after giving birth? Huh? If they had sex things would be good, like it is with me and you," Catalina prattled on.

"Sit down, Catalina," Dominic took a sip from his mug.

He looked up as she pulled out a chair. "I will talk to her today. But I need to tell you something."

"What is it now?" Catalina sighed.

"Giovanni has closed the doors to *Fabiana's*." Dominic glanced up. "He dismissed the staff. He's stopped production in New York. He's shut everything in Mira's company down."

"What?" Catalina gasped. "Is he crazy? He can't do that! Legally we are obligated to so many... my God! What about Carole's show in Paris next month?"

Dominic nodded. "I've been on the phone all day yesterday. The projects that are in flight will continue. Theodore Tate is handling the New York division. No new orders. I have the attorneys going over our obligations. As for *Fabiana's*, I'm sorry, *cara*, it's done."

"What is he thinking? Mira finds this out and she will hate him for it," Catalina said.

Dominic wiped his hand down his face. "We leave tonight. He's returning to Sorrento. I can't prevent it. I need you to stay with Mira. Help her through her anger, whatever it is. But get her to see reason for when we return." He looked up. "And don't leave Villa Mare Blu. No matter what don't leave here."

"It's starting isn't it? He's starting again?" Catalina asked. "I read in the papers that there have been arrests and fighting in the streets of Napoli. Our family name is in the papers again."

"No. It's not starting again. Not like the Calderones. He won't go that far. I'll make sure of it. But he can't go on this way much longer. Mira has to be reasoned with. Unfortunately she has to make things right with him. Giovanni isn't in his right mind."

"Domi, she doesn't listen to me. She spends so much time with Marietta. She is the only person Mira wants to be around lately." Catalina didn't hide her jealousy. Dominic sat back and listened. "They whisper and giggle like school girls. And when I told Marietta she needs to talk to Mira about forgiving Gio do you know what she said?"

"What?" he asked.

"She said Gio made his bed so he must lie in it. What the fuck does that mean? Some American proverb bullshit!" Catalina spat.

"Is that so?" Dominic asked.

"Yes! That's so." Catalina stepped to the table. "I've been taking care of Gio. At night when he thinks no one else is around he watches the wedding video and drinks. Today I found him with Mira's dresses."

Dominic frowned.

"I think he was sniffing them." Catalina said in disgust. "He's losing his fucking mind. He's slipping, Domi, and that weakness is dangerous. The men have seen it."

"Then maybe we need to try a different approach," Dominic said.

"Huh?" Catalina said. "Different how? I've tried everything. They need to have sex! That's what I think."

Dominic chuckled. "Sex won't solve it Catalina." He pushed back his chair and went over to Catalina to kiss her. "You inspire me."

She kissed him back. "What did I do? What did I say? Sex?"

He winked and walked out.

* B *

Mira rocked in the chair with Eve resting against her breast. Her daughter had cried herself to sleep. She looked over to the babies. Gino had his hand on Gianni. She would have to get the camera and take a picture because it was so cute.

Soon her boys would be up for their first feeding. She needed to prepare the bottles. She managed to stand and walked over to the bed to place Eve down when the door to the room opened. She glanced back in time to see Zia step inside.

"I think it's time for a feeding," Zia said. "That's what the schedule says." Zia held a paper in her hand that she'd given to her and Cecilia with their feeding schedules.

"Yes. I was just putting Eve down." Mira looked over at her aunt with a smile. "Thanks for being so prompt."

"I know my babies," Zia smiled. "All of them. Where's Giovanni?"

Mira ignored the question. She walked over to the crib. Gino lay with his eyes open, he sucked Eve's pacifier. How it ended up in his mouth she didn't know or understand. The fact that Eve parted

440

with her pacifier was a shocker. "Look who's up. Hello there, Gino, it's Mama."

She reached inside and picked up her son. He was now five pounds. He gained weight every day.

"Mira?"

"Mmm?" she said, opening her blouse to remove her breast.

"Have you and Gio talked? Really talked? I know he is sorry for his actions. He tells Rocco all the time how sorry he is."

"Zia. Not now. Please. I want some peace. I did try with him, but he's upset with me. I'm thinking of a way to reach him. Just give me a moment okay?"

"Okay," she said.

"Can you check the bag and get out Gianni's bottle. Put the other bottles in the refrigerator please. He'll be up crying for it in a—" Before she could finish Gianni began to cry from his crib. Mira glanced back and laughed. "See?"

Zia went to the crib and tried to calm the boy. He wailed for his bottle. Mira wished she could nurse them both at the same time. But she and the boys would have to come up with their own manageable routine.

After a moment Zia had the bottle and was feeding Gianni. She sat on the edge of the bed. "It will be hard to do this alone. Cecilia will need to help you stay on schedule." Zia said. "Or Giovanni?"

Mira laughed. "You aren't going to let up are you?"

"No," Zia smiled. "Gio needs you and you need him. The entire family suffers with you."

Mira sighed. "You're right. Later I'll try again. It didn't go well earlier. He's so angry at me, which only makes me angrier at him. We're at an impasse."

"You'll get through it." Zia assured her.

Mira looked down at her son. "I pray we do."

★ B ★

Dominic found Marietta in her room folding clothes. The door was open. He knocked and entered. "I hope I'm not disturbing you."

She looked up at him and her pretty brow creased with worry. "Is it Lo? Something happen to him?" she asked. "I just spoke to Lorenzo an hour ago."

"No," Dominic put his hands up. "Nothing has happened to Lorenzo. I wanted to talk to you. If that is okay?"

"Oh! Me? Really? Cool," she said. "Come in." she waved him inside. "You're top guy around King B, right? You're Catalina's lover."

He wasn't sure he cared for her choice of words. "I'm family yes. I'm also the *consigliere*. That makes me Giovanni's relied upon council. But I'm also council for the family."

"I've seen Godfather. I know what you are." Marietta sat down. "Though Lorenzo says the Godfather is bullshit, but you guys seem to behave the same way. My husband is now his cousin's left hand and that makes him happy. A happy Lorenzo is a good Lorenzo," she smiled.

Dominic had to smile again. There was something refreshingly honest about her that he liked. He looked hard at her for a moment and could see the family resemblance between the twins. "I thought you and I should talk. Discuss things. I want to answer your questions."

"Questions? I don't have any questions." Marietta said.

"Of course you do," Dominic said. "This is all new to you. The family, the sister, the lifestyle."

Marietta stared at him for a moment then looked away. "Sort of, but I think most of it I can figure out as we go along."

"And your sister's husband?" Dominic asked.

She cut her gaze his way. "What about him?"

"What have you figured out about him and this situation with his wife?" Dominic asked.

"That he's a control freak. Guess it comes with his job description. He also loves tagging my husband to get his dirty work done. But he refuses to respect my man the way he deserves. And... he has royally fucked up his marriage to keep me and my sister apart."

It was Dominic's turn to be silent.

Marietta continued. "You have to understand. I wasn't just given to my grandparents like Mira. I was left with a family that hated me. No. Teresa Leone was a silent observer. The man who raised me was the evildoer, a sadist. He abused me. Things you never want to see happen to a kid happened to me. I came to Italy for a family because I knew I had to have one other than the Leones. Lorenzo would have helped me find my sister, and more about my mother if it weren't for your great high and mighty *Don*. How exactly am I expected to feel about that?"

"Do you want to know why he did these things or do you prefer to make up his reasonings on your own?" Dominic asked.

442

"How dare you!" Marietta said. "Hey, I know what this is. You're his watchdog. He still thinks my existence is the reason his wife won't look at him. Forgive him. Bullshit! He did this. Don't come in here and try to lay any of her attitude change on me. You have no idea what it's like to need a family as a child and only get a fist to your face instead. So don't sit here like you're counseling me!"

Dominic sat forward. He stared Marietta in her eyes. Slowly the motivations of Marietta became even clearer. Giovanni was wrong to cast this one aside. Marietta was strong enough to teach Mira how to be a true *Donna*. The women just needed a little help. He sat upright and reached behind his neck. She frowned as he unclasped his necklace and then passed it over to her.

"What is this?" Marietta asked.

"Patron Saint William. I've worn this necklace since I was five or six years old. We still aren't sure of my birthdate. There is no official true record of my birth. Only the one that the Battaglia's gave me."

He watched as Marietta held up the necklace and then saw her study the stamp of Del Stavio to the back. "Why don't you have a record of your birth?" she glanced to him.

"Because I too was born into hell. I needed a family and for many years as a boy all I got was a fist to my face. It's this necklace and that high and mighty *Don* who brought me out of it. Do you want me to tell you my story?"

"Do I have a choice?"

Fall 1972
Outside of Palermo - Sicily

The revving engines of cars approached and Dominic sensed he should hide. His papa didn't like for him to be seen. He crawled on his hands and knees across a muddy ground covered in bird shit, feathers and broken eggshells. The hens squawked and flapped their wings in panic. Feathers floated down from above like snowfall. The shack had been made of nailed planks of wood, which separated enough to give him a view if he remained on his hands and knees. The sulfuric stench of the coop nearly strangled him each time he took a breath, but he had grown used to it. He breathed through his nostrils instead of his mouth.

And it was as he suspected. Dominic stared through the opening and watched the man with the fedora hat and long cigar step out of a car. He had others with them. A few of the men ran into the villa ahead of the man to where his father slept. There was shouting. So much yelling Dominic got to his feet and covered his ears with his soiled hands. When the shouting came so did the pain. If the visit ended badly his papa would make him pay.

"No! No! No! No!" Dominic wept.

He squeezed his eyes tightly shut. "Noooooo," he whimpered.

The hens began to pick up on his anxiety. More than a few squawked and several pecked at his feet and ankles with relentless ferocity. They wanted to drive him out. Dominic cried. He tried to find a safe place from the attack. He didn't dare run out. He would be seen, and that would be bad. Very bad! The chicken coop was the only hiding place that spared him most nights when his father was drinking and on the hunt for him. What would spare him now?

The door to the hut was kicked open. Dominic ran for the corner. "No, Papa, no per favore!" he pleaded.

Hands reached in and grabbed him. Strong hands he couldn't shake off. He was dragged out into the light and he fought his fate with everything in him. "No, Papa! No!"

"It is okay picoletto. It is okay," a man said.

Dominic shook his head refusing to open his eyes. The man touched his face with care. "Look at me. Open your eyes."

With great reluctance he did. A man he'd never met before smiled at him. "I'm Rocco. You're safe." Confused by the kindness and dreading his father's wrath at being discovered he again tried to push away. "Bring the bastardo around here!" Rocco yelled to the others.

Dominic was lifted into the arms of the stranger as two men dragged his beaten father from around the front of the villa. And the man with the hat and long cigar walked behind him. He had mean dark eyes under the brim of his hat and the presence of authority.

His father wept.

"Is this what you do to your boy? Look at him!" Rocco said.

Dominic's father lifted his head. "He is my son. I do best by him! The best I can!" A stranger struck his father to the back of the head.

"Papa!" Dominic cried, stretching his arms to him. He'd never seen his father hurt, or weep. The sight of his father so wounded rocked him to his core. His limited understanding of the events only added to his terror. Who were these men? Why did they hurt his father?

The same stranger lifted his father's head. Blood and drool dripped from his mouth.

"Do you see, Tomosino?" Rocco said. "I was right. The pig bastard tortures the child. He plays liaison between you and Mancini like he's some kind of diplomat. Plays at being a man of principle. He's a baby beater!" Rocco spat on Dominic's father. A glob of spit hit his hair and the side of his face.

"Papa?" Dominic wept, "No, no, not Papa," he wept.

The man with the hat stepped into the scene. He glanced down at the scene of a broken man with a bruised and bloody body. His father blubbered for mercy and then the cold dark stare of the man with the fedora lifted to Dominic. He removed his cigar and smiled. "Ciao, picolleto. Come sta?"

Dominic could do nothing but nod.

"Mi chiamo Patri Tomosino."

The man reached and touched Dominic's cheek with affection. The other men stared. Dominic glanced from one to the other. Only his father wept and begged for mercy. He managed to smile for Tomosino. Tomosino chuckled. He addressed the one called Rocco. "You're right. Poor dirt rat is treated worse than a dog." Tomosino said. "I'll take him." The man strolled away as if the business they came for was concluded. Two others walked away with him.

Rocco heaved Dominic up in his arms. "Grazie, Tomosino!" he said.

Dominic was confused. Where would they take him? He glanced down to his father. "Papa? Perchè?"

"We do this for you, little one," Rocco said.

Not understanding the meaning of the statement Dominic held to Rocco's neck. He managed another smile for the men. Those who looked his way smiled at him. They were good men. Friends. Why was his father praying and weeping?

And then his father looked up at him and spoke with tears in his eyes. Did he understand his destiny? "I love you son—" he said and the front of his forehead exploded from the gunshot. Blood splattered over Dominic and he screamed.

"Jesus!" Marietta gasped. "That's awful."

"For years what I knew as life was nothing but torture. The man murdered my mother who tried to shield me from his drunken wrath when I was a baby. And Mancini covered it up because he was a high-ranking enforcer in the family. I could barely sleep without nightmares as a kid until Giovanni took care of me."

"But wasn't Giovanni a kid too?" Marietta asked.

"Fifteen. I was given to him at fifteen," Dominic said.

"Given to him?" Marietta repeated. "As... what? A pet?"

"A brother." Dominic clarified. "Giovanni made a deal with your brother Armando Mancini to have that necklace made. I've worn it every day since I received the gift. St. William protects me."

The story left her raw with emotion. Dominic told her of the days he spent with the Battaglias. How the family became his. She was riveted by his tale. "I can't believe you made it through any of this sane."

"Who says we're sane?" Dominic winked. "We're just family. And you're part of that family now. Giovanni isn't the black-hearted ruler you think he is. He's the leader of a family of flawed men with a united purpose. To ensure our children and our children's, children know their legacy. He had a father who made him witness and do things no child should suffer. It makes him hard and vulnerable. Do you understand? He loves his wife, she gives him purpose, keeps him balanced. Before her he lived and led us with the same cold evenhanded method that his father used. Since they met he has been a better man. You can help him and her by reminding your sister how badly things end when anyone is denied family," Dominic said. "Because you and I know as children what it is like to exist without a father's love." Dominic stood.

Marietta attempted to hand the necklace back to him.

"Why don't you hold on to it for now. When I return from Sorrento you can give it back to me." Dominic smiled.

"Thank you. For telling me your story," Marietta said.

Dominic cupped Marietta's chin and she stared up at him. He was handsome, and wise for such a young man. She couldn't help but be drawn in by his brown eyes. She felt a calm when looking into them. How could such a genuine human being exist after such a torturous existence as a child? Maybe there was hope for her to overcome her demons as Dominic once had.

"Talk to Mira. Help her past her grief and anger," Dominic said. "I'll try."

He leaned in and kissed Marietta's brow. Marietta closed her eyes as if the Pope himself had done so. She opened her eyes and watched Dominic leave. She stared down at the necklace and the charm. After hearing the story she knew it meant as much to Dominic as her necklace did to her. He was right. She did have questions. Lots of questions about the strange and complicated family she'd now inherited. Each day she learned more.

* B *

Mira wasn't prepared for the celebration. But she felt such a deep relief to see it when her heart had been so divided. She walked out onto the terrace and everyone cheered. She smiled. The decadent smells of Zia's recipes filled the air.

"Hungry, baby?" Mira asked. She waited until after the feeding of her sons to wake Eve to bring her downstairs. Cecilia sat with the boys and would come get Mira if she was needed. Eve laid her head on her mother's shoulder with a groggy yawn. Mira looked down the table to Giovanni who was eating. Rosetta brought him additional food. It stung to see Rosetta tend to her husband's needs. It had always been her role to fix his plate. And he wouldn't eat until she did. Zia said he'd first push her away, and then replace her. Deep down inside she felt a cold chill of fear that she could be denied his love—permanently.

Giovanni's gaze lifted to her and he dismissed her.

She tried to ignore how that dismissal unnerved her.

She walked in, a brave composed manner to his end of the table. Rosetta pulled the chair out next to him and she sat.

"Papa!" Eve said. Her daughter was absent of her pacifier. She hadn't asked for it since her nap. Eve opened her mouth. Giovanni's gaze cut over to his daughter and there wasn't much warmth there. It was as if he looked through Eve.

"Papa!" Eve demanded and hit the table. Mira frowned at Gio's cold dead stare. He seemed to come out of whatever fog impaired his judgment. He gave Eve a weak smile and fed her a helping from his fork.

"*Mio Dio!*" Rosetta exclaimed. She had returned to her seat at the other end of the table. Everyone looked to her. Rosetta looked down at Mira. "It's your doctor. He's on the front page of the paper!"

"What?" Catalina asked.

Dominic watched as did the others and everyone paused over the news. Giovanni was the only one to keep eating and feeding Eve as if Rosetta hadn't spoken.

"It says here his body was found on the beach. He'd been stabbed like over a hundred times."

"That's not possible." Mira said. "I saw him yesterday, just before he released me and the twins."

"Here." Rosetta pushed back in her chair and walked fast down the table. No one spoke. The men began to fix their plates as if the news wasn't shocking. Mira accepted the paper as Eve reached into her father's plate for what she wanted. A picture of Dr. Buhari was on the cover with a side shot of a covered body on Modello shores. The police were investigating. He was indeed murdered and his body washed up on the shore. Mira looked over at Giovanni.

"It's awful, Rosetta. Let's not discuss it now," she said. She folded the paper and slammed it down on the table. She glanced to her husband once more.

He looked up at her and the sly smirk to his lips chilled her.

"Excuse me," Mira said. She pushed back from the table. She handed Eve to her father and Giovanni took her without complaint. She needed air. She wasn't able to take a deep enough breath until she escaped them all. She walked through the villa and turned toward the zen gardens near the open terrace on the opposite side of the villa. She put her hands to her head and closed her eyes as her heart slammed rapidly in her chest. It beat faster than she knew it should. Was she having another stroke? She had to calm down. She went to the chair and lowered to it and fought back her tears.

"Mira?

She glanced up with tears blocking her vision. He stepped closer.

"Domi?"

"Are you okay?" Dominic asked.

"Yes, I am. I'm fine," she replied.

"You don't look fine," Dominic said. He stepped toward her and she had to look away to wipe at her tears.

"Did he do it? Did he kill Dr. Buhari?" Mira asked.

Dominic stared at her for a moment. "Why would Giovanni kill your doctor?"

"Why does he do any of the things he does!" she shouted back.

"May I?" he gestured to a seat.

Mira dropped back in her seat and shrugged. "Don't come in here and try to explain away his actions, Domi. I'm in no mood."

"I need to talk to you."

"Not now," she sighed.

"I'm afraid it has to be now," he insisted.

"What is it?" Mira asked.

"You're playing a very dangerous game with our lives, Mira, and his," Dominic said.

She sat up. "Me? I'm playing games?"

"You've seen him. How he is. You've heard of how he was

448

when he lost you before. And you continue to fight with him."

"This is my marriage!" she seethed. "Not some business deal for you to negotiate! I'll work it out with Giovanni, my way!"

"At what cost?" he asked.

"I can't believe you. My marriage is more than this family, it means more to me than your Mafia business."

"Is that so?" Dominic asked.

Mira scratched her brow. Dominic's voice was soft yet unyeilding. "Nothing he does or says to you will change the fact that he has lied and deceived you about your sister and mother. Nothing. He knows this, Mira. It's why he doesn't think he has an option to fix things with you."

"Stop, Domi," she sighed.

"The inevitable is that you will accept your role as the *Donna* to this family by force or even worse by giving up. Neither option helps you or Giovanni."

"No shit," Mira said sarcastically. "I'm trapped. I have three kids, and him… I'm trapped."

"I'm sorry you see it that way." Dominic withdrew.

"Wait. I'm sorry. I'm angry at him. But I love him. I just can't find a way to understand him right now."

Dominic nodded that he understood.

Mira put her face in her hands. "I'm scared, Domi. I'm scared for him and of him."

"So is he. That's fear not anger you see ruling his actions." Dominic said. "And if you don't accept your role as his wife, and find a way to make him accept your role as his partner it could very well cost more lives." Dominic tossed the newspaper article to her feet. Mira looked down at the paper then up to Dominic.

"So many men and women fear your husband. Even I do. It's because he has so much power over all our lives. It's ironic that you are the only person who has power over him, and you don't even know how to wield it. That is the reason Flavio put you on a plane and sent you away from Giovanni. The reason we all breathed a sigh of relief when you came back to him and agreed to marry and build a family with him. Don't abandon us now. Well all need you." Dominic smiled. He nodded respectfully to her and walked out. She reached down for the paper once more and looked at the picture of her slain doctor.

* B *

449

Armando paced. He had waited for this day but nothing prepared him for how deeply painful it would be. The man who ruled his life, taught him everything, was slipping away. The doctor looked up from his father and shook his head. Marsuvio Mancini had been confined to his bed. He shriveled. His skin was pasty pale, and his lips grey and chapped. He was on a constant supply of oxygen and too weak to bathe or feed himself.

"He was fine a week ago. Walking around and drinking." Armando reasoned.

"It's pneumonia. And his lungs are the worst of it. Too much fluid."

"How long does he have?" Armando asked.

"Days, we can't say. We've done all we can. You should consider bringing him into the *ospedale*. Let us treat him there."

"No!" Armando shook his head and blinked back his tears. "No *ospedales*! He doesn't want it. Leave us."

The man walked out. Armando went to his father's bedside. He took a seat and touched his hand. Mancini opened his eyes. "Papa? The doctors say…"

"I heard the doctors, Armando," Mancini chuckled. "They are fools. I'm not ready to die."

The old man began to cough with hard chest rattling rasps. Armando turned for the glass of water and the coughing stopped. He brought the water over and put the straw to his father's lips.

"Mirabella?" Mancini asked.

"She left the *ospedale* with the kids. Unfortunately it's all I know."

Though weak his father pushed back on his pillows. "Buhari?"

"We took care of him, Papa. His refusal to give you information on Mirabella and the *bambini* did not go unpunished. No worries. Rest. I have news," Armando smiled. "Isabella is dead. The body found after the explosion is hers. We are sure of it. She won't be a threat anymore."

"*Grazie*, son. Isabella was a threat to all we have. It had to end this way," Mancini said. "Now, I can go in peace."

"I called Dominic. Giovanni still refuses to arrange a visit for your daughters. There is nothing else I can do, Papa."

Mancini looked away. "Giovanni is right to deny me."

"What?" Armando said.

"I don't deserve the visit. This is just. What became of their mother was because of Manny Cigars. I don't want my girls to ever meet Manny Cigars," he said.

"Papa, the will. You have to give me control. Give me my birthright before you die."

Mancini stared at him from the bed. "You will run the family affairs, the clause in the will for your sisters is to make sure you do so without harming them. It stays. The percentage of the legitimate business deals should be split between you three. They are you blood," Mancini said weakly. "You're my son. I made you. I know this is... the only way... to be a family."

"It's too late for that kind of family, Papa. We are well past the time of being brother and sisters. All I am is what you leave to me. Giovanni will come for me and I intend to be ready. But I must have complete control. I swear no harm will ever come to your daughters. I swear it."

"Isabella is dead," Mancini panted. "The only threat... now... is you," he wheezed. "Try and understand."

Armando kissed his father's hand. "That is impossible for me to do."

* B *

"I want to talk to you!" Mira slammed the door to their bedroom. Giovanni zipped his travel bag. His back was to her. "Is it true that you have stopped all production at my company? That you have closed *Fabiana's*?"

He didn't turn or address her.

"Answer me!" Mira shouted.

He glanced back at her. The look in his eyes made fury boil the blood in her veins. "Is it true you now manage Esta's healthcare? You hired her a private nurse behind my back? Tried to move her back to Bagheria?" Giovanni asked.

"What?" Mira frowned. "I told you I would help Esta, because it's the right thing to do!"

"NO! You said you ran the family and I run the business. So run the family and leave your business to me!" Giovanni shouted.

"Stop this! It's not the same. That's my damn company. I built it! I own it."

"Not anymore." Giovanni tossed back. "It's my company now."

"You're doing this to punish me. It's so fucking childish, Giovanni! You're mad at me. I'm mad at you! We're fighting. So what! It happens in a marriage, damn it! It does. But you can't go off killing people and shutting down my business to get my attention. It makes you insane!"

Giovanni chuckled. He turned and faced her. "I can do whatever I want and you and I both know it. What makes me insane is constantly having to repeat that fact to you!" He put his hands in his pockets. "What makes me insane is a wife who can't face me so she runs and hides in another room! I own your business. I run this fucking family and I alone will make the decisions for it. That's not just the definition of insanity, that's the definition of your reality."

Mira put her hands to her head. "I can't believe you! Don't come back! I'd rather be locked away like your mother to raise your children than to spend another minute in this marriage with you!" she shouted through her tears. She turned and stormed out.

Giovanni watched the door long after she slammed out of it. Sleep deprived and heartsick he wiped his hand down his face to clear his head. He would have sat but he couldn't summon the energy to do so. Instead he pushed down the maddening urge to find his wife and drag her into this room and keep her locked here until she was his Bella again. The woman she was now he didn't care to know.

He glanced around the room for his things. He found his gun and put it to the front of his pants. He found her gun. He stared at it for a moment. He checked it to make sure it was loaded. He engaged the safety and placed the weapon on her pillow so she would remember to keep it close.

Giovanni picked up his travel bags and walked over to the door but stopped. A gleam of light caught his eye from the dresser. He looked over to see it was the sparkle of jewelry. He walked over and saw on top of the dresser was the charm bracelet he'd given Mira on Christmas. The tiny diamond pacifier sparkled. He had said he would add another charm for his sons. The sight of it reminded him of all the promises they made to each other when she told him he would be a father again. He lowered his bag and picked up the bracelet. He slipped it into his pocket and then picked up his things to leave the room. As he walked through the hall he noticed the door to the nursery was half open. He paused outside of the door and peered in. Cecilia tended to his sons. She changed the diaper on one of the boys.

Giovanni put down his things and went inside. The young girl looked up at his approach. *"Ciao, Gio,"* Cecelia smiled.

He smiled. "Gino?" he asked, hoping he guessed which son lay sprawled out on the changing table sucking his pacifier.

"Sí. Very good. This is Gino."

"May I?" Giovanni asked.

Cecilia looked confused. He would never ask her for permission to tend to his sons but he had. And Giovanni had never changed a diaper in front of any of them, although Mira made him change Eve's pampies regularly in their room. Cecilia nodded and stepped aside. Giovanni approached his son. He learned with Eve how to change a diaper with the elastic tape. But cloth diapers looked to be more complicated. He and Mira had said they would take turns in the night with the twins. And the crib would be in their room so their babies would never be far.

The tiny cloth diaper did cover Gino but he was at a loss on how to make it fasten.

Cecelia chuckled. "Let me help." Gino opened his little legs. His head was turned left and he sucked his pacifier with contentment. Cecilia brought up the middle of the cloth diaper to cover his tiny genitals. She then brought over the right side and the left side of the diaper to pin all three in the center. "See this here, you just pin it here. And there you have it," she said.

Gino's head turned, he blinked up at his father and Giovanni smiled. He leaned in and kissed the baby.

"He's not a crier, like Gianni. Very quiet this one," Cecilia said. "I have to check him to make sure he needs changing."

"He's a survivor. No need for tears," Giovanni said. "Tears never got a man anywhere."

"I have a bottle for him if you want to feed him," Cecilia offered.

"No. Take care of them. Help the *Donna*," Giovanni said.

"I will."

He turned to pick up his things and his eyes met with Mira's. She stood at the door. She glared at him. Fresh tears were glistening on her cheeks. He had hurt her deeply and sadly it was his intent. If she cried, it meant she cared. He picked up his luggage and avoided her eyes, ashamed of his actions. She stepped in front of him. She blocked his pass. She touched his chest. "I love you... so much, Giovanni," she said, and sobbed. "I don't want to fight anymore. Stay," she pleaded. "I can't go on like this."

On impulse he leaned in and kissed her. He expected her to push him away but she kissed him in return. "I don't want to stay," he said.

She stepped aside and he walked out.

Mira watched him go. She pressed her lips together and closed her eyes but the tears flowed. Wiping the tears away she sucked down a deep breath and returned to her sons. It was all she had left to do. "I'll take care of it from here, Cecilia. Go find Eve for me please? I think she's with Zia. I want my children with me."

"Yes, *Donna*." Cecilia walked over and gave her little Gino. He blinked at her. She removed the pacifier from his mouth.

"Maybe we should not start this habit huh, Gino? No matter what Evie thinks," Mira said and tried to sound normal.

The baby yawned and then fed his fist into his mouth, sucking. Mira laughed. She cried and laughed. If Fabiana were there she'd help. She felt so alone and so desperate. Gino's blue eyes sparkled like his father's. She kissed his brow. Her nipples ached and itched and the urge to nurse became greater. She went to the rocking chair and opened her shirt.

"Knock! Knock!" said Marietta. "Busy?"

Mira sniffed. "No. I was about to feed Gino. Come in."

"Ick!" Marietta smiled. "I could never let a baby lick my nipple. Creeps me out."

"Lick?" Mira frowned. "He's feeding. It's the best thing for your kids. You don't plan to breastfeed?"

"Don't plan to make babies," Marietta grinned. She dropped down on the bed. Mira didn't bother to disguise her tears. Her sister stared at her intensely before she spoke. "I saw King B and his crew roll out of here on a mission. Guess he'll be wherever the hell my husband is," Marietta said.

Gino's eyes closed as he nursed and she brushed his chubby cheek with her finger. Thankfully Gianni slept. She often chose to give her breast to Gino first because he was still underweight.

"Are you two upset with each other still?" Marietta asked.

"I think we're past being upset. We're in territory neither of us wants to be in. I don't know what to do," Mira said and she began to cry again.

"Awe, sis. Don't cry."

"I can't fix things with him. I don't know how. And it might be too late."

"Forgive him."

She glanced back at Marietta. "It's not that easy. I can forgive him. I've made mistakes too. Done things I regret. But he isn't sorry. He isn't the least bit remorseful. He's just consumed with having me kneel and agree to his orders. I can't do that. I need more in my marriage."

"You know what I think?" Marietta asked.

"What do you think?"

"I think you're just as stubborn as he is. You want him to kneel, to come to you on bended knee and beg for your forgiveness. Repent. So that you can put him in his place." Marietta laughed. "You married the wrong man for that, sister."

"I'm not trying to break him," Mira sighed.

"You could have fooled me. The man is a walking ball of fury now that you are home. And I'm telling you, honey, you didn't see how devoted he was to you when you were sick. How mean and nasty he was when you sent him away from the hospital. We all stayed out of his way. The poor guy is hurting."

Mira frowned. "Why are you defending him?"

"Listen to me. I know we are new at this sister thing. And I know we are trying to get to know each other. So please don't take this the wrong way. But I always hated women like you."

"Women like me?" Mira rolled her eyes. "Here we go."

"Let me finish. You married a mobster. You faked your death and left your career because of him. Yet you walk around here like you are above the shit in this family. It's ridiculous. Women like you who play both sides. Who fool themselves into believing the princess dreams and then freak out when things get tough. The man did wrong. Punish his ass. True. But get on and get over it."

"As much as you think you know me you don't! I want respect in my marriage. That's all. I won't sit here and pretend to think I have control over much else. I'm not sitting on the fence. Giovanni knew who I was the day he pursued me. And we made promises to each other that he should have kept!"

"Fine. All of that is fine, honey. But what did you do? You shut down. You locked the man out. You pushed him away. Tell me how that gets you respect? Ever hear that to have respect you have to give it? Shiiiiit, if I pushed Lo out of my bed he'd be kicking the door in. Your husband left the hospital and respected your wishes. What the hell else do you want him to do?" Marietta reclined back on her hands. "I'm sorry. I wasn't trying to offend you. I just don't get it. If I had the money, the fame, the sexy *Don*, the family, I wouldn't spend so much time at being miserable. Life is too short." Marietta sat upright and smiled. "I'm running my mouth and you're trying to feed your baby. I'll give you some privacy."

She stood and Mira frowned. "What is that on your neck? Is that Dominic's necklace?" Mira asked.

"Cool isn't it?" Marietta smiled. She walked over and showed the necklace to Mira. "Do you know who this is?"

"A Saint?" Mira said.

"It's the patron saint of lost children. Giovanni had it made for

Dominic when they were kids. Dominic said your husband protected him from a lot of pain. I guess there are some good sides to the mean ole *Don* after all," she said through a smile.

Mira smiled and watched her go. She rocked back in the chair and tried to focus on the positive. It was hard.

Later –

Mira stretched and heaved her weary body from the chair. She was exhausted. Before she put Eve to bed and laid the twins down for the night Zia showed her a really good way to wrap her newborn sons. She wrapped them so tightly that they slept for fours at a time instead of two. She needed to shower and eat something before the boys woke. She picked up the handheld baby monitor and made sure it was on and connected to the one attached to the crib.

Mira left her room. Leo wasn't posted outside of it and that was a first. With the men gone the others that remained spent more time outside guarding the perimeter of Villa Mar Blu than inside. She walked across the hall into her bedroom. The cool emptiness she found chilled her through her clothes. She glanced over at the bed neither had slept in since she discovered the truth. She smiled. How could she not look at the bed she shared with her husband and not smile?

Over the past few months of her pregnancy he had been there, day and night. She had gotten used to the constant. The separation between them now was unnatural.

Mira walked over to her dresser and set down the baby monitor. She returned to her bed. She picked up her gun Giovanni left for her on her pillow. She didn't fear the weapon any longer. She set it aside and stretched out over the sheets. She rolled over onto his pillow and took a deep intake. She could smell him. Forgive him? She could. She has. But what did she do with her anger?

Mira closed her eyes and her thoughts drifted to her mother. Soon she thought of Giovanni's mother. The comparison made her shoot upright on the bed. There was so much she still didn't know. Such as, why a man who abandoned her and her sister would wait nearly twenty-five years to rectify that mistake?

She needed answers. The truth. She needed to be free of all her anger and hurt by confronting the person who really put it there.

"Mancini," she said.

She scrambled off the bed. She grabbed the baby monitor and hurried out of her room, down the stairs and through the hall to

Marietta's room. She found her sister on the bed listening to music with a pair of headphones. Marietta painted her toenails. She glanced up.

"Hey?" she said. She removed her headphones.

Mira set the baby monitor down. "I know what we need to do."

"What?" Marietta frowned.

"We need to get answers. Real answers. Not from our husbands but from the man himself. We need to see our father."

20.

The flight ended shortly after take off. At least it was how he felt. Time and distance had no affect on him now. The strange dead feeling of blackness thickened in him. Giovanni blinked at the passing mountainous landscape of Naples from his window. From the moment he left Villa Mare Blu he reflected on his life, his past and current mistakes. He touched his lips. The brief kiss from Mira lingered there. The look in her eyes when they parted haunted him. Away from her, clarity returned. An image formed in his mind— Mira and him dancing at their wedding. How beautiful she was. How happy he felt. Such undiluted happiness it shocked and amazed him. No woman had ever made him feel such peace and torment.

He shouldn't have lashed out at her, or been cruel to her. He regretted so many things. Still he wouldn't change any of his actions. He was who he was. His wife had never accepted that fact. She'd never accept him. The plane taxied to a stop. A surge of energy returned to his bones. He harnessed it and resolved his purpose. There was a caravan of twenty-six cars waiting for his arrival. His top earners and enforcers had all come to welcome him.

Giovanni left his seat with his head bowed to avoid colliding with the plane's low ceiling. He stepped out of the plane as all his men exited their vehicles.

Santo approached first. He wore a tailored black suit. Carlo, Lorenzo, and Nico waited near a car reserved for Giovanni. Each man observed him. The mood of his men was tense, solemn. They'd lost territory and lives in their own clans the past few days. And the blood continued to flow through the *Campania*.

"*Ben tornato*." Santo kissed him on both cheeks. "Inspector Bonomo will meet with us. He waits for you at Melanzana. It's all been arranged thanks to my careful negotiations."

"Change of plans." Giovanni replied. "You and Nico are to head to Chiaiano tonight."

"I thought Lorenzo and Carlo would return and I could assist you in the—"

Giovanni walked toward the car waiting for him. Santo quickly caught up and matched his stride. "Boss? *Aspetti un momento.*"

"After I meet with Bonomo I will join you and the men in Chiaiano. End of discussion," Giovanni said.

Carlo opened the door for Giovanni and he slipped inside to the backseat. Dominic joined him from the other side of the car. Lorenzo got behind the wheel and when Carlo joined them Lorenzo drove them off the tarmac. The caravan of his men followed. Giovanni wiped his hand down his face and worked his neck from left to right. The lack of sleep had him numb all over.

"Are you sure you want to handle things this way?"

"It's already decided," Giovanni answered.

The tension in Dominic's tone coiled tighter when he spoke. "May I ask why? Why are we cutting Santo's throat? He has worked hard to get the inspector to agree to this meeting. What are your plans?"

Giovanni glanced up and Lorenzo looked up in the rearview mirror. Their eyes met. Lorenzo smiled. Giovanni looked away. "Santo will learn his fate soon enough," he replied.

* B *

"Wait? Let me get this straight. You want to go and see the man who is trying to kill us?" Marietta asked. She laughed. She laughed hard.

Mira didn't take well to being laughed at. She chewed on the inside of her jaw. Maybe she should try to explain herself another way. "This isn't a joke."

"Maybe not, but it's funny as hell," Marietta said with a dismissive flip of her wrist.

"I'm serious, Marietta. I want to confront the man who made us. The man who separated us. The man who destroyed our mother," Mira said.

"If he hadn't destroyed our mother we wouldn't exist," Marietta said. "Ever think of it that way? Besides it's in the past. I told Lorenzo I'd leave it there."

"I want answers. I need closure so Giovanni and I can move on. Don't you want that?"

"I have closure." Marietta shrugged. "I know what happened to my mother and I found you. That for me is closure."

"Not for me." Mira paced the floor. "For years I blamed her. Hated her for being so selfish and leaving me behind. I actually thought she deserved to be dead. I was afraid to be a mother because of my issues."

To this Marietta did look up. Mira recognize the look of confliction in her sister's eyes. So she continued. "The thing is it was all a lie. Our mother never abandoned us. She was taken. Murdered. And my husband is so torn up with guilt over what his father did he's put a wall between us in our marriage long before I knew it existed. I'm scared we'll tear each other apart if I don't get to the bottom of this."

"What does that have to do with finding Mancini?" Marietta frowned.

"There's more to the story of her death than either of us know. If we can't get the answers from that evil bastard then who can tell us?"

Marietta moved her feet off the bed careful to keep her toes raised and separated. "Remember this?" she asked. She opened the drawer in her nightstand and retrieved a folded piece of paper. Mira accepted the document and read it once more. It was the letter that was given to her the day she learned the truth.

"Gemma gave that to me, it's the letter I gave to you," Marietta said.

"Who is Gemma?" Mira asked.

"My godmother. That's the only way I can explain her. She says she knew our mother."

"How did they know each other?" Mira asked.

"Not sure. When I grew up Gemma was always there. At first I thought she was an aunt. But later I found out she was a family friend. She took me to have my ears pierced. She was the one who taught me how to use tampons. She came to America regularly to make sure I was okay. She said I was special and I was grateful for her."

There was so much Mira didn't know about her mother and her life her head swam. Each minute that passed she grew desperate to learn the full truth. "She never told you how she knew our mother?"

"She gave me my bracelet. Told me that she only knew my mother briefly. When I got proof of my original birth certificate, she later told me that my father was a man named Capriccio. So I came to Milan to confront him. Capriccio put me in his will to keep me from learning the truth. Mancini was my father. He and Gemma conspired together."

"Why? What is with all of the secrets?"

"Mira, we were supposed to be dead. I think Gemma and Capriccio kept us a secret to keep us alive. To help us."

"I don't know. I have a hard time believing something like this was done to protect two bastard babies. There's more to the story," Mira said.

"Maybe. But I guarantee you Mancini won't tell it. If you want answers, let's get them from Gemma."

Mira nodded in agreement.

"On the back is a number to call her. I think we should," Marietta said.

"I don't want to have this conversation over the phone," Mira said.

"We can't invite her over for tea now can we?" Marietta laughed.

"It's not funny." Mira sighed. "Giovanni and I are at a terrible place right now. I have to fix my marriage. If I get my answers I know I can find a way to fix my marriage."

"That's not what the truth does," Marietta said. "The truth chains you to facts about who you are and who our mother was. There is peace in ignorance, Mira."

"Not for me. I have to be able to look my husband in the eye. Face what is between us. And I can't trust him or myself to get past our hurt if I'm still clueless. I want you to call her." She handed over the paper. "Call her."

"And?" Marietta asked.

"Tell her we want to meet."

"Are you sure?" Marietta asked.

"Yes. We're going to go see her and get some answers."

"No. I should have never even brought her up." Marietta shook her head emphatically and began to fold the paper.

"Why?" Mira asked.

"There's an army guarding the door. There is no way we can get out of here."

Mira hadn't considered that obstacle. She chuckled. "Our grannie used to say to me when I was a little girl that where there is a will there is always a way," Mira said. "Call Gemma and ask her if she is willing to meet with us. See if she can do it soon. Let me worry about the how."

* B *

The phone rang.

Gemma's soul nearly jumped out of her skin. Her heart raced so fast she clutched her chest for fear of a stroke. She looked up over at the ringing phone on the night table as if it were some creature that had come to life and gave a death roar. Could it be Armando Mancini? He had been angered, and nearly killed by the explosion. She knew he hunted her. Isabella was dead. And that posed another problem. Who were Isabella's allies? Who helped her on her crusade for vengeance? And were they too looking for Gemma to avenge her death?

The phone continued to ring.

Gemma pushed up from the bed to reach over toward it. If she answered it would seal her fate. If she didn't, she'd never know where the threat was coming from. *"Pronto?"*

"Hi," a familiar voice greeted her.

Gemma's smiled with relief. *"Mio Dio!* Marietta? Is that you?"

"Yes. Did I catch you at a bad time?" Marietta asked.

"I can't believe you called and now of all times." Gemma put her hand to her heart. The very last call she expected to receive was from Marietta. *"Ciao, cara mia,* how are you?"

"I'm good. And you?"

Gemma ran her hand back through her hair. She looked around the small room and couldn't settle on an answer. The evening bus out of Carini into Palermo left in an hour. If she missed it she'd have to catch the next one tomorrow. If Armando hunted for her he'd certainly find her during the daytime travel crowds.

"Gemma?" Marietta called out.

"Yes. Yes, sweetheart. I'm here. You didn't catch me at a bad time," Gemma replied.

"I want to meet." Marietta said.

"You do?" Gemma asked.

"Yes. Tonight. Is that okay? I... My sister and I have questions. You said if we had them we could talk."

Gemma closed her eyes. "Your timing, kid, it couldn't be worse."

"Well that couldn't be helped. To be honest this is Mira's idea not mine. I... I'm angry with you."

Silence settled between them. Gemma put a hand to her forehead and tried to find the words to explain herself. Confession was good for the soul is what she was always taught. There were so many untruths that burdened her soul.

"I'm sorry," Marietta sighed and then continued. "If that hurts you. But you've lied to me so much. If you can't meet I understand."

"No. We have to meet. We should meet. You deserve to know the truth." Gemma said.

"Are you okay? You sound funny?" Marietta asked.

Gemma sniffed. "I'm fine!" she laughed. "Just homesick. In fact I was packing, heading back to Milano."

"Oh... okay well I will call you back in an hour to arrange the meeting spot. Thank you, Gemma. Thank you so much. I love you."

"I love you too, Marietta." Gemma hung up. She sat on the edge of the bed. The bus was the better option. To slip out of Carini before the Mancinis found her.

Gemma couldn't stay put. It was too risky. Agreeing to go to see Marietta could be another set up.

* B *

When he crossed the threshold of Melanzana the anxiety of the past few days slipped from his bones. Dominic walked at his side. Giovanni removed his suit jacket and passed it off to Ana who managed the staff.

"The inspector is here, *signor*," Ana said. "I've made him comfortable for your meeting in the parlor."

"*Grazie,* Ana," he gave her two cheek kisses.

"How's the *Donna*? The babies?" Ana gushed. Only on rare occasions did anyone see her smile.

"*Bennisima.* You'll meet them soon." Giovanni assured her. He walked through the foyer to the parlor. If Mira and the family were present he'd take the meeting in *Villa Rosso*. Thankfully he could have it here in his home without interruption.

"You have an hour and we need to be on the road to Chiaiano, before dark." Dominic advised. He glanced back. "Do you want Lorenzo in this meeting?"

"From now on Lorenzo is in every meeting," Giovanni said. He entered the parlor. "Inspector Bonomo, it's good to see you."

"Giovanni!" The inspector stood. He greeted Giovanni with an open arm hug. He kissed him on both cheeks. "I hear congratulations are in order?"

"Two sons. We've named them Gianni and Gino." Giovanni boasted. He snapped his fingers and Arturo came forward to freshen Bonomo's drink. "Please sit," Giovanni said.

"Two sons!" The inspector accepted his new drink. Giovanni

observed him. From what he knew of Bonomo he enjoyed a good merlot and a hot young boy to satisfy his appetites. The inspector watched Arturo with a wolfish grin.

Giovanni's gaze cut over to Lorenzo and his cousin picked up on it as well. He whispered to Arturo to leave and followed the boy out. He then drew the doors closed. The Battaglias have always counted on Bonomo in the past to help them navigate the legal traps set by authorities. Now the media and every political mouthpiece from within the parliament had something to say about the *Camorra*. Giovanni's marriage to Mira had kept the international press hot on his ass. The unwanted attention was made even worse by the election of a new inspector who promised to clean up southern Italy.

"I'm not going to lie, this is bad. Very bad. It has reached the desk of the Prime Minister. He's been accused of letting lawlessness rule the *Campania*."

"I understand. It troubles me that our progress in the parliament has devolved to this. And I take personal responsibility for it."

"I hear we have a new inspector?" Giovanni asked. "Who is he?"

Bonomo swallowed his merlot and avoided Giovanni's eyes. "His name is Donatello, and he's a fool if he thinks he alone can rid the *Campania* of the *Camorra*."

The words sounded sincere, but Bonomo's inability to look him in the eye when he spoke them gave Giovanni pause. He never trusted a man who could not look him in the eye.

"The true enemy to the good people of Italy is the `Ndrangheta* not the *Camorra*. They are raiders. Cockroaches!" Giovanni said.

"Bu-but..." the inspector stammered.

"Let me finish." Giovanni gestured for silence. "I know my hands in this aren't clean. I run the sanitation, I make sure nothing traffics in and out of my territories. However the `Ndrangheta* have arrived. And I hear they use the bay for their own purposes."

The inspector nodded. He removed his handkerchief and dabbed at his fat jaws and then forehead. "It's true. We have them under surveillance. And your men as well."

Giovanni smiled. At last he had gotten Bonomo to share something useful. "I'm sure Donatello is looking to make a big arrest, something to elevate his position. He does so, then what happens to you?"

Bonomo didn't reply.

Giovanni leaned forward. "All these years and you've never arrested a man in the *Camorra*. It must have harmed your reputation."

464

"I have been compensated." Bonomo said. He gave Lorenzo and Dominic a nervous smile before looking Giovanni in the eye. "I'm not complaining."

"Of course not. But I think it's time we elevate your position in the *Stato*. Eh?"

Bonomo looked around as if confused. "I don't understand?"

"What spoils go to the inspector who brings in a full confession from a clan boss in the *Camorra*."

Bonomo began to choke. He hacked and coughed while Giovanni and his men watched, offering no assistance. "Confession? You're going to confess to me? Publicly?" he asked in disbelief.

"Never forget who I am Bonomo. I will not bend or yield to you or anyone." Giovanni replied.

"Forgive me. Of course. But you must understand my confusion. We have never had a clan boss turn himself in. The *polizi di stato* have yet to level charges to indict any controlling leader in the *Camorra*. And you sit here and say it could happen?"

"It will happen, before sunrise." Giovanni said coolly.

Bonomo swallowed. He took a long drink from his glass as his face peppered with sweat. "May I ask, if not you, then who?"

Giovanni stood. The inspector was quick to do so as well. "You will bring the scoundrel in. Be in charge of his full confession of his crimes. I'm sure you will be elevated, promoted."

Bonomo nodded and smiled with gratitude. When the inspector shook Giovanni's hand Giovanni gripped the inspector's hand tightly. "You will remember this generosity. Donatello will no longer investigate my family or our business interests."

"I will. Of course I will." The inspector nodded. He kissed Giovanni's ring, bowed his head and was escorted out.

Dominic cleared his throat. He dusted his tie. "Well the line is cast, Gio. Care to tell me who you plan to pin this confession on for the Inspector?"

"Don't you know, Domi? You know everything else." Giovanni sat and picked up his cigar. Lorenzo returned after having handed the inspector off to one of their men to be escorted off the property. Dominic cast his gaze between Giovanni and Lorenzo in confusion.

"No I don't know," Dominic said. "But it's evident you and Lorenzo have discussed this without me."

"Mottola goes down. The *'Ndrangheta* goes down. And Santo... bows." Lorenzo grinned as he shared the news. "It's for the best, Gio. Santo can't be trusted. And I've proven it. This is how we show strength and own the territories."

Giovanni leveled an icy stare at Dominic.

"You have not proven it!" Dominic said glancing between the two men. "There is no evidence that Santo caused this breech. None." Dominic directed his comments to Lorenzo. "This war between you and Santo is petty, unfounded, and unproductive. While you sailed the Mediterranean, Santo has been loyal to Giovanni. He's done a lot of good." He then turned to Giovanni to plead his case. "Gio, you pull this trigger there is no going back. The fundamental rules of our brotherhood are broken. What's to make any man who works for you not believe you won't do the same to him?"

Giovanni took a drag of his cigar and blew a ring of smoke. "That's the fucking point, Domi. That's the fucking goal! My empire is crumbling, on your watch! Santo's watch! My watch! That can never happen again. I was distracted with my wife and her issues. She thinks it was to control her. Well she has her wish. I'm not distracted anymore. And I will make sure no one dares doubt me, including every man in this family. The message is clear." Giovanni stood. "Betray me and no matter who you are in this family you will bend." He cast Lorenzo a warning glare. He then looked back to Dominic. "No matter who you are."

He turned and walked out.

Dominic couldn't speak.

"Tsk, tsk, Domi," Lorenz stood, and chuckled. "I warned you of this when you stood silent as Gio replaced me with Santo."

Dominic cut his cousin a death glare. "Meaning?"

Lorenzo straightened his tie "Gio needs me. I'm his left hand. You can be his errand boy, and pretend at counseling him. I will keep him strong. This is the way it should always be. Santo is a pretender."

"Bullshit, Lo!" Dominic said. "You didn't do this for Gio. You did it for you. Now you will turn Santo against us. Hand him over to the authorities and he will want revenge. I had it under control!" Dominic shouted. "We are strong as a family of men. That is what *Omertá* means to us. Gio's full of rage and you stood back and let him loose. That is not how he should lead. That is his downfall."

Lorenzo chuckled. "The problem with you, Dominic, is you think you are his conscience. For Giovanni to be our leader he should have none." Lorenzo shook his head smiling and walked out.

Dominic lowered to his chair. He stared at the floor.

"*Signor* Domi, is there anything you need?" Arturo asked.

What he needed wasn't in a bottle. He rubbed his brow. No idea formed, just consequence. Before the night ended there would be a lot of consequence.

* B *

"She wants to meet with us. I told her I'd call her back," Marietta said as she entered the door. She paused and blinked at those gathered. Rosetta had been the one to deliver the news that Mira wanted to meet with them all in the nursery. Mira nursed one of the twins while Zia fed the other with a bottle. Catalina stood by the window. Her arms were crossed and her gaze trained to the setting sun out over the beach. Cecelia sat on the bed with Eve helping her turn the page on a book.

"We having some kind of family meeting?" Marietta asked.

"Close the door please," Mira said in a hushed tone, which reminded Marietta she should be conscious of the twins. Marietta did what she was told. "Have a seat," Mira smiled. "I know things have been really hard for the family the past few weeks. A lot has happened." Mira stopped rocking in her chair and stood with Gianni in her arms. She walked over to the crib and placed the sleeping baby inside. She fixed her blouse before turning and addressing them all. "I need your help. What I want to ask of you goes against everything we agreed upon with protecting this family and honoring Giovanni's wishes. I don't want you to think that I don't know this."

"What is it?" Catalina asked.

"It's the truth about Marsuvio Mancini and my mother. The affair they had. The reason for her death. Truths that Giovanni either can't or won't tell me. I need more answers."

Zia put Gino on her shoulder and tried to burp him. "Rocco told me some of it. Mancini and Tomosino were responsible for your mother's death."

"Patri? My Patri killed your mother?" Catalina asked. "That's ridiculous!"

"Yes. He put a contract on her life," Marietta confirmed.

The hurt of the accusation drained the color from Catalina's face. "He wouldn't do that. He would never put a hit on the life of a woman. Patri wouldn't!"

"He did it!" Marietta shot back.

"That's enough," Mira said. "Catalina, listen to me. We don't know the truth. Who killed my mother and why. I need to get to the

467

bottom of this."

"How?" Zia asked.

"Her name is Gemma, she's my godmother and she's here in Sicily. She knew my mother, our mother," Marietta clarified.

"We want to meet her. Tonight if possible," Mira added.

"No." Catalina said. "Absolutely not. Gio said we aren't to leave. We can't risk it with the men gone."

Mira smiled. "What do you suggest? I have to see her, Catalina. I can't bring her here. It's not safe."

"It's safer than you leaving to go and meet her," Zia said.

"She has a point," Marietta chimed in. "We really don't know what is going on now with our men and Mancini. Maybe we should try to bring Gemma here?"

Mira put her hand to her head. Each way she turned she hit a wall of uncertainty.

"What about the villa, the beach villa? We can get her there tonight," Catalina suggested. "It's a good compromise. The men don't go there. There's a road that I used to take as a girl to ride my bike. I can bring her in that way. With most of the men gone they'd never suspect."

"Much better plan." Zia agreed.

"What do you think?" Marietta asked Mira. "It could work."

"I think it could. But I don't want to sneak her in here. If she's discovered it will set the men off. It could put her in danger."

"So what are you suggesting? That we walk her in through the front door?" Rosetta asked.

Mira smiled. "I can't, but Zia, you can."

"Me?" Zia gasped.

Mira grinned. "She can drive up and say she came upon your request, for help in the kitchen. And then we put her out in the villa on the beach. This way the men won't be alarmed and..."

"Won't work." Catalina shook her head. "If anyone drives up here and steps on the property they need permission from Giovanni." Catalina reminded everyone. "None of the men will let a stranger in because Zia said so."

Zia walked over to the crib. She laid out a sleeping Gino. "Which men are here?" Zia asked.

"Leo, Leonardo, Antonio, David, Michael, Giulio," Cecelia offered.

"Renaldo is here." Rosetta reminded everyone. Renaldo was a very silent but strict enforcer of Giovanni's rules.

"Not at the moment," Catalina said. "I asked him to go into

Palermo to get some packages for me and Mira. He's not going to return from those pickups until tonight."

"Why would Renaldo run that kind of errand? Isn't he over these men?" Marietta asked. Mira had to agree. Renaldo was Giovanni's personal bodyguard. He'd take a bullet for the family. Giovanni would put him and Nico in front of the family at all times.

"Because of the bombing with the Mancinis," Catalina answered. "Everyone is on alert. Renaldo doesn't want the men out there or at risk. He'd rather be the only one to come and go from here."

"Why does any of this matter?" Mira asked Zia.

Zia smiled. "Because those men don't know my cousin Ines."

Mira loved the way Zia thought. She nodded understanding. She glanced at Marietta. "Call Gemma, tell her we can send a car for her. That she will be cousin Ines."

Catalina laughed. "That might work. If she's family and the men contact Gio, he'll approve. Perfect, Zia!" she kissed her cheek. "We can prove that my Patri did not kill your mother."

Mira winked at Catalina. "I hope we get to the bottom of many things tonight."

* B *

Giovanni bounded down the stairs. He was an hour behind. Dominic and Lorenzo waited for him at the bottom step. He had an early dinner minus the alcohol. He felt strong enough for all that would unfold in the evening.

"Are we ready?" he asked.

Lorenzo nodded.

Dominic stared at him. Giovanni ignored the concern in Dominic's eyes. He walked out and the men climbed inside his black van. It was a lot less conspicuous than the fancy cars he owned. Giovanni took a seat to the back.

"Home? How are the women?" Giovanni asked once Carlo slammed the door shut on the van and got inside.

"Got a call from Leo—he checks in regularly. Zia wants Ines to come and assist with the cooking. The twins are a handful."

Giovanni smiled. "They are. Bella is a good mother."

"Did you speak with her before we left?" Dominic asked.

He decided to ignore the question. The problems with his wife were private. He feared that the families' interference was one of the reasons Bella was so stubborn toward him. The other being that she could not forgive him for deceiving her. Once his affairs were settled he'd return and find a way to bring his wife to the understanding of his heart.

The ride out of the mountain of Sorrento toward Chiaiano was ahead of him. He settled back in his seat and closed his eyes.

Later –

"She's here!" Marietta said. She turned from the curtain. The women exchanged worried looks but Marietta was excited. Gemma was hard to convince to come to Villa Mare Blu. She sounded fearful. Marietta assured her Giovanni and Lorenzo were gone and not returning any time soon. She swore to her she was safe. And after a thirty-minute conversation of negotiations she feared that Gemma would decline. But she agreed.

Mira stood. "Let's greet her together."

Zia and Catalina sat on the sofa. Rosetta held Eve on her lap and sat across from them in a chair. Only Cecilia was missing, she watched over the babies in case either of them woke. Marietta and Mira walked out of the parlor as the doors opened to the front of the villa. Marietta held her breath for the meeting. She hadn't truly forgiven Gemma, but she did love her.

David held the door for her. Gemma walked in looking as regal and beautiful as ever. She wore a white and yellow striped dress with her hair down. Marietta went to her. Mira was hesitant but she followed.

"Ciao!" Marietta said.

Gemma hugged her in return.

"You can go, David," Mira said.

Marietta let Gemma go and she waited for David to walk out of the door. "Gemma this is…"

"I know who she is." Gemma extended her hand. Mira shook it. Gemma kissed Mira on both cheeks. "So nice to meet you, *Donna* Mirabella."

"A pleasure, come with me." Mira walked her into the parlor. The others were standing and waiting. Gemma nodded her head in respect at Zia. "Catalina and Zia, this is Gemma."

"Ciao," the women said in unison.

"Marietta will take you to a beach villa, to wait for me. The men won't question you but if by chance one does do you understand what you are to say?" Mira asked.

"Yes. Ines, from Bagheria. Zia Carlotta's cousin," Gemma said.

"Good. Let me check on my boys and I'll come." Mira said.

"*Grazie,* to all of you. I don't deserve your hospitality," Gemma said humbly.

Marietta squeezed Gemma's hand. With Catalina joining them they walked her out.

"She's not familiar to me, Mira," Zia said. "Are you sure we can trust her?"

Mira picked up Eve. Her daughter yawned in her face and dropped her head on her shoulder. It was close to eight in the evening. Well past her bedtime. "I'm not sure she can be trusted. But what choice do I have? She's the closest to the truth I can get."

"Dominic is going to be angry that we lied to him." Rosetta volunteered.

Mira frowned. She dismissed Rosetta's comments. "I need to lay Eve down and check on the babies. Rosetta stay here with Cecilia and help her if she needs any assistance with the twins. Zia, I want you to come with me to talk to this Gemma person. You can help me understand what she tells me. If she is telling me the truth."

Zia nodded. "I can try."

Rosetta did as she was instructed. As soon as Mira and Zia left the twins room she told Cecilia she had to go to the bathroom. Rosetta then dashed downstairs. She went straight for the front door and opened it. At first she saw no one. But when she stepped out David appeared from the left with a gun in his hand. He walked straight for her.

"Need something?" David asked.

"I have to speak with Domi. It's important."

David looked her over. "Why is it important?"

"I can only talk to him." Rosetta said.

David frowned. He glanced back to the cars parked out front. "Renaldo will be here later tonight. He's in Palermo still. I can page him."

"Yes. Call Renaldo and tell him I want to speak to Dominic. It's important. Something… something he needs to know from the *Donna* that he has to tell Gio. She only wants me to deliver the message."

"Why can't the *Donna* deliver the message herself?" David scoffed.

"They aren't talking stupid. She's mad at him remember? Get the message to Renaldo. Tell him I will be near the phone if he wants to talk to me. But I have to speak with Domi."

David stared at her for a moment. He then nodded and walked off. Rosetta breathed a sigh of relief. It was risky to betray Mira. Up until now everything she did to gain Domi's attention had failed. If this backfired she'd be sent back to Palermo and her chances of being anything would be squandered. But Dominic hadn't given her up the last time she told him of Catalina's actions. Maybe this time his gratitude would indeed prove her loyalty.

* B *

Yeremian grinned at Giovanni. "It's good to see you!"

Giovanni embraced his friend. "It has been some time. I can't thank you enough for coming."

Yeremian and his men arrived a week ago. They'd been working with Santo and Lorenzo to flush out and capture as many of the Mottolas as they could. The Armenians had a unique yet brutal way of dealing with enemies that Giovanni found exceptionally attractive given the depth of Mottola's betrayal.

He glanced to Dominic and Santo. They accompanied him to the back room. The stench of excrement, blood and sweat overwhelmed him. And soon he understood why. Three men were tied down to chairs and one hung from chains to the ceiling. As Giovanni entered the room he witnessed one man's suffering. The beaten brute hollered as a bucket of water was tossed over him. The Armenian stood next to a battery, which he wheeled over to the man, handcuffed to his chair. Giovanni guessed his age to be no more than twenty or so. The young man shook his head and slang water with his hair from his eyes.

"No! No! I beg you!"

Without mercy the Armenian flipped the switch on the battery and then stabbed the man with the end of the rod sending hot electricity through his body. The young man gurgled and jerked in the chair. He either passed out or died before them.

"That one is Mottola's oldest son. There hanging is his brother, and those two are nephews. We have his women in the room next door." Yeremian said as if it were the most common of things. Giovanni glanced over to Dominic who looked on with disgust.

"Do not harm the women," he said and smirked at Dominic. His

472

consigliere turned and walked out.

The door was kicked open from the back of the room. A sniveling man was dragged in. Giovanni recognized him. It was Giuliani. The man looked up at him with blackened and swollen eyes. "Giovanni! *Per favore!* I beg of you! I beg of you!"

Yeremian looked to Giovanni. "This one says he has a deal with you? True?"

"No." Giovanni replied.

The man holding Giuliani tossed him to the floor. He got up to his knees and made the sign of the cross before Yeremian gave his man a nod. A bullet to the back of Giuliani's head dropped him cold. "He had no further useful information. In fact he played you and Mottola at both ends."

It appeared to Giovanni he had misjudged many men and things in the past months.

"Like I said, we sent Mottola a gift this morning. He knows his family lives depend on his response." Yeremian said. "Of course we will honor your wishes and release the women without harm. But we haven't heard anything as of yet. I think he wants to call your bluff."

"He doesn't." Giovanni replied. Giovanni turned and looked around at the shit stain of a place. He saw a chair and Nico brought it over. He sat. "Then we wait," he said. "And enjoy the show."

Yeremian laughed and gave his men the signal to continue with the torture.

* B *

Marietta glanced over to Catalina. They both exchanged a look but neither of them spoke. Gemma ate as if she hadn't in days. When Gemma noticed the silence she looked up from her plate slowly chewing. "I've been... unable to have a good meal the past week."

"Why?" Marietta asked.

Gemma looked to Catalina and then back to Marietta. For some reason she held off from explaining. Instinctually Marietta felt Gemma wasn't to be trusted. And that instinctual feeling grew stronger. "Catalina can be trusted. What is going on, Gemma?"

"I came to *Sicilia* to find you," Gemma said.

"I know that," Marietta replied.

"I came to find you because someone forced me to, Marietta. She... she threatened you. I had no choice," Gemma said. "Maybe we should wait for your sister to return to allow me to explain."

473

"I'd like to hear it now. Was it all a lie?" Marietta asked. "The stories you shared when I was a kid. About how you briefly knew my mother. Was it a lie?"

Gemma sat back. For a moment Marietta feared she wouldn't answer. She glanced up to her and nodded slowly. "It was all a lie. Every thing I've ever told you including the fact that your father wants to kill you, has been a lie."

Stunned Marietta withdrew. The door opened, she glanced over to see Mira step through with Zia following. The sun had fallen. The beach villa's lamps became the sole source of luminance when the door closed. Marietta struggled to contain her hurt and rage. Lorenzo said she reacted too many times instead of thinking a situation through. She'd just learned that Gemma was a liar and the betrayal cut deep.

"Hi. Thank you for coming and meeting with us," Mira said.

"To be honest your call may have saved my life. It wasn't safe for me in Carini." Gemma admitted.

Mira walked over and occupied the chair across from Gemma. "Can I ask why?"

"I would like to speak to you and Marietta alone," Gemma said.

"That's not going to happen. We're a family. The four of us," Mira glanced back to Zia and Catalina then returned her gaze to Gemma. "You speak to all of us."

Marietta pushed back from the table and stood. She paced. "How can you sit here, and play at being so innocent, when you have lied to me all my life!" she said.

Gemma shook her head sadly. "There's a lot you don't know, Marietta. I want to fix it. That's the only reason why I came." She looked up and met Marietta's heated glare with an apologetic one. "I've wanted to fix so many mistakes I've made since your mother died. But I couldn't. One lie turned into many. I'm sorry"

"Can someone clue me in please? What lie is she telling?" Mira asked.

"Oh pick one!" Marietta threw her hands up. "We can start with our father not putting a contract on our lives. Or the fact that she knew our mother when she was alive but for years pretended otherwise. And she's known all these years how she died. Haven't you!"

Gemma's gaze bounced between them both. "I have been trying to protect you. Let me explain."

"Explain!" Marietta shouted at her.

"Marietta, calm down," Mira said. "Sit, please. Let's hear her out."

474

Marietta breathed through her nose. Her chest felt heavy and her eyes teared. Despite her desire to throw the chair she pulled it away from the table and sat down.

"I met your mother at a club owned by Manny Cigars. She first came in because of her boyfriend. A young man named James. When Manny saw her he gave her a job. Singing for an underage poor girl like Lisa in a club like Manny's was a big deal. She jumped at the chance. James knew it was a mistake. One look at Manny when he watched her sing and you could tell his real reason for offering her the job."

"And she couldn't see this?" Mira asked.

"No. For a long time Lisa couldn't see the evil in people. She didn't learn those lessons until years later." Gemma sighed. "Manny was older, meaner, and used to having whomever he wanted," Gemma said. "He set her boyfriend up. I remember what she told me the day they came for her. The night Manny took her."

"What happened the night he took her?" Marietta asked.

Mira shook her head as if to say no. Her sister stepped forward. She slammed her hands on the table. "If we're going to hear the truth then we have to hear the entire truth."

Gemma glanced to Zia and Catalina. Mira wasn't sure why their presence made her uncomfortable but it was evident she struggled with the story she had to tell partly because they were part of her audience. "Before James went to prison Manny made a move on Lisa. She literally had to fight him off her and escape the club. James was furious. He came back and told Manny he'd kill him if he tried it again. At first we all thought Manny would cut his throat or have one of his men do it. Instead he promoted him. Which for that time, that place, with those men it was unheard of. James never knew what hit him. Manny set the trap and he and Lisa walked right into it."

"She told you this?" Mira asked.

"I saw it firsthand. We were friends at this point. Lisa didn't have many. She was scared by the gifts Manny sent her but James told her it was the way of the Sicilians. That Manny was sincere. He was. Sincerely obsessed with your mother." Gemma's gaze lowered to her hands. She shared the rest of her tale that way. "Manny had a job for James. According to Lisa, James was really excited about it. The payout would be enough for them to leave Philadelphia for good."

"It was a setup," Marietta said.

Gemma nodded her head yes slowly. "Lisa waited all night for him to come home. He never did. In the morning there was a knock to the door and it was Manny's men. They told her she had to come with them. She feared James was hurt or in trouble so she went. They brought her to Manny. He told her James had killed a man, a white businessman that owned a rival club. Several men died in a fire and it was all pinned on James. It was a lie. He never had a chance to prove his innocence. Lisa begged Manny to help him. He told her the price." Gemma looked up. "She paid the price."

"I don't want to hear anymore." Mira said feeling sick.

"I do!" Marietta said, shaking with rage. "He raped her! The dirty bastard!"

Gemma nodded yes. "I found her afterwards in the bathroom throwing up. Never seen a kid so hurt and confused. She never saw James again. She knew the moment she agreed to be Manny's it was all a lie. That's how your mother became part of our world."

"What world was that?" Mira frowned.

"Whores!" Zia snapped. Her voice cracked like a whip. "I know who you are." She leveled a finger at her. "You're part of *la Abandonato*."

"Who?" Marietta asked. "What?"

Zia explained. "*Abandonato* is derived from the word forsaken. In the *Campania* there were many of these women, whores that provided services under the protection and for the profit of the *Camorra*. All of it was legal up until around…"

"1958," Gemma said sadly. "*Sfruttamento della prostituzione* was established to outlaw pimping. Targeted more toward the mob bosses who were exploiting us. It was the Battaglias in the *Camorra* and the Mancinis in the Mafia who jointly ran the business out of the *Campania*. I was one of those girls who got passed between."

Zia nodded. "When it was illegal for the brothels the *Camorra* and Mafia expanded their business beyond Italia and *Sicilia*."

"To America." Gemma cut in. "It was a miserable life here. Not much better in the States. I lived in America for many years illegally."

"Don't trust this woman, Mira. She wasn't your mother's friend. She was a whore to your father. Weren't you?" Zia asked.

Gemma's gaze lifted. Marietta drew back in surprise. "Wait? Are you saying you were involved with this Manny Cigars too?"

"No," Gemma denied it. "I was just a girl who he exploited like your mother. I was his victim."

"She's a liar! A whore! The kind our husbands keep on the side!" Zia shouted. "Don't trust her."

Mira grabbed Zia's hand. She kissed it. "Please, let her finish, Zia. Then we will decide what is fact and what is fiction. Okay?"

Gemma gave Zia a hateful look. But it passed over her face quickly. She looked back down to her hands. "After a few days Lisa was told that James was dead. Killed in jail. To this day I'm not sure if it was true. But Lisa believed it. Manny, who you know as Mancini, kept her with him always. Locked away at his apartment. We saw her only briefly, dressed beautifully, shyly regulated to a corner he'd post her in under guard of his men. She was so beautiful, so sad, so young. I was her once. I knew what she endured."

"So you two became friends?" Mira asked.

"Yes." Gemma smiled. "And unfortunately I was not a good friend to her. What I'm about to tell you is my greatest sin." Gemma lifted her face and looked to Marietta with weepy eyes. "It's why I tried to protect you, to save you from your father and the Battaglias by keeping your birth a secret. I did it because I owed it to your mother. I failed her twice in life. The first time was soon after we became friends. Mancini would often have to go on these long trips to Sicily to deal with his father. I was chosen to be her companion, more like her jailor. She was so miserable at first. She suffered such guilt over her lover James, and the life she lost with him. And she was so naïve. She started to blame herself. And then she... actually began to fall in love with the evil bastard."

"What did you do, Gemma?" Marietta demanded. "Stop stalling and tell us."

"I turned her on to opium, and then to heroin."

Before Mira could digest the news her sister flew across the table. Gemma was slammed back into the floor. Marietta was all fists. She beat on Gemma savagely. It took for Mira and Catalina to drag her off the poor woman.

"Let me go! Let me go!" Marietta screamed. "I'll kill her!"

"Help me get her into the other room. Please!" Mira said, as she suffered a few smacks and blows to her sensitive stomach area. Winded she thought she'd lose the battle. But Catalina proved stronger than Mira imagined. She grabbed Marietta by the neck and dragged her with the tight hold beyond the door to the bedroom. Mira was quick to close it. When she turned around Catalina and Marietta were fighting.

"Stop it! Stop it dammit!" Mira yelled.

Catalina pinned Marietta to the floor. The women panted and snarled at each other. Both were so angry neither could verbalize anything beyond vicious curse words. Mira couldn't believe the scene before her. She held her stomach. She suffered cramps and soreness to her midriff from the tussle and remained cautious not to get any closer. "Let her go, Catalina. It's over."

Catalina did so and Marietta got to her feet.

"You have to calm down," she said to her sister.

"Shut up!" Marietta leveled a finger at Mira. "Don't you tell me what to do! You have no idea the betrayal of that evil bitch!"

"Don't I?" Mira asked. "Whether you thought she was your godmother or not she poisoned my mother too with those drugs. I'm just as pissed as you!" Mira shouted.

"You don't look it to me." Marietta spat and turned away with her hands in her hair.

"We brought her here for the truth and we haven't heard it all." Mira reasoned.

"I've heard enough! If I go back out there I'll kill the bitch!" Marietta said. Mira looked to Catalina who shrugged and paced herself trying to calm down. It was all falling apart. Mira had to question her own sanity. Why did she think that speaking with this woman would give her the freedom to deal with her husband? If anything she felt more hopeless.

"Let me think," Mira panted. She closed her eyes. She had no choice but to see this through. She opened her eyes and found both Marietta and Catalina staring at her. "Stay in here. I'll talk to Gemma. Then we decide what to do. Agreed?"

Marietta rolled her eyes and flopped down on the bed. Catalina nodded that she'd stay with Marietta. Mira wasn't sure that was a good idea after witnessing the violence between them.

"We'll be fine," Marietta mumbled as if she read Mira's mind.

Without further delay Mira left them both and closed the door behind her. Zia was applying ice wrapped in a cloth to Gemma's face. They both looked up when she approached. "I didn't bring you here for violence. I am sorry for what my sister did."

"And you? Do you want to strike me too?" Gemma asked.

"Even if I did, and I don't, it would solve nothing. What I want to know is the truth. All of it. You turned my mother on drugs. Not Manny Cigars?"

Gemma lowered her towel. "At first we concealed it from him. But he found out she was using. Lisa didn't want me hurt. So she lied and blamed it on another of his men. Neither of us expected the outcome. I'll spare you the details. Manny killed him with his bare hands." Gemma glanced to Zia and then averted her gaze. "Our lives weren't our own back then. We were trying to survive. Lisa fell into the role of mistress. She struggled with her addiction, but she believed the lies Manny fed her. He put her up in a fancy penthouse. It was still very segregated in Philadelphia at the time. Blacks on one side, and whites on the other. America with all its false dreams nurtures the root of separatism to this day. The country itself is big fat hypocrisy." Gemma spat with disgust. She continued. "But with Manny's connections, wealth and reputation he got Lisa through doors closed to brown women. And then she was pregnant."

Mira returned to her chair. "With us?"

"With you two, yes." Gemma smiled. "She wanted to do things right. Be a good mother. She thought Manny would leave his wife and marry her. He vowed he would. And she soon learned that too was a lie. So I helped her pack up her things. She was going to return to Virginia and leave Manny for good. She was going to try to bring you girls into the world clean and sober. Do it the right way. She ran away."

"She went home?" Mira frowned. "To my grandparents? Are you sure?"

"Yes." Gemma nodded. "They took one look at her and closed the door on her. I guess Lisa being swollen with babies from a Sicilian mobster wasn't something her father could accept."

"My grandfather wasn't like that. He was a good man," Mira said.

"He was not always a good man to Lisa. I'm sorry," Gemma said.

Mira wiped at her tears. "What happened to her?" Mira asked.

"She contacted me. She didn't want to return to Manny. She didn't trust him. But she had nowhere to go. She was an unwed mother in her third trimester. She had very little options. And by then Manny had found out she was gone. He was coming to America to find her. None of us thought he would. But he did."

"Did you help her?" Mira asked.

"I tried. I swear to you I tried. I hid her at a friend's place in Philadelphia. It was a roach infested dump. But at least she was free. We were going to wait out the babies' delivery and then when you twins were stronger she would get a job, save up enough money and move to New York where work was good for her kind."

"Her kind?" Mira asked.

"Forgive me?" Gemma sighed. She nursed her side of her head. "I don't mean it as disrespect. Lisa was different. I was different. That's all I'm saying. Jobs were better in New York for black people."

Mira nodded. "How did we get separated? Me and Marietta?"

Gemma glanced up. "Manny found her. And it was a good thing he did."

"Why?" Mira asked.

"She had some complications. Her blood pressure when she delivered. She had a stroke."

The news hit Mira hard. She blinked at Gemma twice. Then looked up at Zia confused. "My mother, had a stroke? Like me?"

"She was in a coma for several days after the delivery. If he hadn't found her when he did she would have died. You all would have died. And he never left her side. He was determined to help her. Got her into the best hospital and saw to her recovery. I will admit that."

"Like Giovanni," Mira said. She shook her head at the comparison. Zia put her hand to Mira's shoulder. She was weak from the truth, but she had to see it through. "So what happened next?"

"It was too late. Lisa despised him. He had told her too many lies. And she was wiser now. She knew his men weren't fond of her. No one believed in their affair. Most mocked Manny and made fun of him behind his back. They didn't give a shit about saying it to Lisa's face. And Manny's father was growing angrier with him leaving his wife and son behind to chase after Lisa. We all felt it. Something brewing."

"Did she run away again?"

"Not at first. There was no way to do so at first. She had to do things Manny's way. He had her in another place, this time in New York. And Capriccio was her warden. After the first few months of living there with you babies she convinced Manny to let me move in as .your caregivers. Lisa and I plotted daily on her escape. We thought of everything but nothing we considered could work. Manny had the resources to find her no matter what she did," Gemma sighed. She looked haggard. The vibrant woman that arrived aged within the hour of sharing her mother's sad story. And though it tore at her heart Mira had to hear it all.

"Please continue. What happened in New York?"

"Capriccio. He said a contract was put on her life and the life of her daughters."

"By Tomosino Battaglia?" Mira asked. She looked at Zia and then back at Gemma. "It was him?"

"Yes." Gemma nodded. "There was some nasty business going on with the Sicilians and the *Camorra*. Tomosino wanted her dead to end Manny going back and forth with her. Capriccio said he'd help her. Lisa had to leave. The babies needed to be hidden. Lisa didn't think her poor mother and father could take care of both babies. She wasn't sure what to do. And I..." Gemma's voice faltered. "I wanted Marietta. I loved you both, but Marietta, I adored her. So I told Lisa to go home with you and I'd follow with Marietta. We'd split up in case someone was after her. She didn't like the plan. Maybe she knew my fondness for her daughter made me untrustworthy. Capriccio told her she had to do something and decide quickly. Reluctantly she agreed."

"She went back to my grandparents.," Mira said.

Gemma nodded. "I ran with Marietta. I didn't keep my promise. She couldn't find us, and she couldn't contact Capriccio. After nearly a year with Marietta and staying with my friends in Chicago I knew I had done her wrong. So I contacted her. She agreed to meet me in Chicago and..."

"That's a lie!" Marietta said.

Mira glanced back. Her sister walked out. "You're lying now. Why are you lying?"

"I'm not," Gemma said.

"You are, bitch! You think I can't tell? I lived with the Leones. You never wanted to take me out of there. You breezed in and out of my life and watched me suffer without hesitation."

Gemma sighed. She looked to Mira and then Marietta. "The Leones weren't my friends. They were related to Capriccio. His sister is Teresa Leone."

"Tell us the truth." Mira said.

Gemma sighed, "I did lie. Lisa woke one morning and Marietta and I were gone. Capriccio made me take you to them. He said he'd spare Lisa and her other baby if I did as he asked. If Manny knew what we conspired to do he'd kill us both."

"Why?" Marietta cringed. "Why did he do that?"

"He wanted to give his sister a baby to help her with her mean husband. You were so fair. You looked white to us. Mira was a brown baby. Teresa Leone was near madness after having several miscarriages."

"What did my mother do?" Mira asked.

"With Manny gone and Capriccio telling her there was a contract on both of your lives she ran back to Virginia."

"Then what?" Marietta pressed.

Gemma continued. "I went back to Philly to work. Manny didn't return. It was as if he didn't care anymore what became of

Lisa. And then one day, after two years of not seeing her Lisa walked into the club. Shocked us all. She pulled me aside. She demanded to know where Marietta was. Said she was going to the police and she would name, names." Gemma breathed out a long breath. "I panicked. I knew Capriccio would silence her. I knew more of the truth then. So she and I went to Chicago. I was going to help her to get you, but one of the girls tipped Capriccio off to Lisa's return. He figured it out. He had to cover his trail. You see, Capriccio had lied to us all. He approached the Battaglias and gave them information on Mancini. Offered to kill Lisa. Tomosino refused to put an order out on a woman and child. Cappriccio would have to act alone. And he was too much of a coward then. But things had changed in reagards to his courage when Lisa returned. .He didn't want any of Lisa's allegations to get out through the mob. The mobsters in America, Italy, Sicily, would have killed us all for the games we played. Not to mention what Manny would have done." Gemma wiped at her tears. "Lisa was discarded and so were you because that's what those men do to their whores. They always go home to their wives."

"Who killed my mother?" Mira asked.

"When Lisa and I showed up in Chicago at the Leones to demand her daughter they learned that you were half black Marietta. And Lisa learned the truth about my role in it all."

"Capriccio killed her?" Mira asked, cutting to the real truth.

"Yes. His sister and Lisa got into an ugly argument. She had Lisa arrested. Capriccio bailed Lisa out. It was the last time she was seen alive. Two weeks later her body was found. They said she had died of a heroin overdose, but it was another lie. A Capriccio lie." Gemma looked directly at Marietta. "When I found out the truth and that her body was unclaimed I contacted Marsuvio Mancini. He came to America. I hated him for what he did so I told him you were dead too. I truly believed that it was best. He had Lisa's body brought to her parents. And he left you, Mira, behind."

"Why was Capriccio's name on my birth certificate?" Marietta asked.

"Octavio wanted his name off your fake certificate. And Capriccio couldn't risk Manny learning the truth about you. So he put his name on it, in case it ever surfaced. If Manny learned the truth he'd kill Capriccio and all of his sons."

"Or maybe not, since he left his daughters behind." Mira said.

"That's it right there!" Marietta pointed a finger at her "That's the truth, Mira. Right there. See, Gemma didn't call Mancini,

Manny, whoever the hell he is. I guarantee he never knew she was involved. Capriccio probably told his boss about our mother's death and blamed it on her addiction. They kept me a secret to protect their asses. They hid me to cover up our mother's murder." Marietta leaned forward with her hands flat to the table. "You know what I think? I think you were never my mother's friend. I think you conveniently spun this story to hide the truth. That it was your fault she's dead. I believe it with everything in me. I hate you."

Gemma wept.

"I've heard enough. If what you say is true, it wasn't Tomosino who killed my mother. It was you and Capriccio. Marietta's right. When Mama came back and confronted the mob and threatened to go to the police that signed her death warrant. I don't know this Mancini, but I know my husband. There is no way any man in this life would have let you two live if he knew what you had done."

"What do we do now?" Zia asked.

"You should see Mancini," Catalina said to the shock of them all. "My Patri was a cruel man, but I can't believe he had your mother killed. You're right. This woman tells you only part of the truth. You need to see Mancini yourself."

"No! No!" Zia said. "We can't go to him. It's too dangerous."

"Yes. We should see our father. You're coming with us, Gemma. You try to leave the villa you will be stopped," Mira said.

"I won't leave." Gemma looked to Marietta and gave her a sad smile. "I'm sorry, for the lies. I didn't want you to hate me."

"Too late. I already do," Marietta said.

* B *

Rosetta answered the phone on the first ring. "Domi?"

"It's me. What's the emergency, Rosie?" Dominic said.

"Thank you for calling, Domi. I didn't know what to do. If the *Donna* knows I called you, she'd never forgive me."

"What's the problem?" Dominic asked.

"They have a woman here. She is pretending to be my cousin Ines. Her real name is Gemma. The *Donna* called a meeting with all of us to help convince the men to let her inside. She had Zia lie to the men. Renaldo hasn't returned and well… they have her out in the beach villa. She's supposed to tell them the truth about the *Donna* and her sister. What happened to their mother."

The line went silent.

"Domi?"

"It's good you called me. Don't worry. No one will know. I'll take care of it."

Rosetta hung up the line. She sat back on the pillows and smiled. Cecilia returned in the room. The twins were sleeping. Cecilia had Evie who had just completed her bath.

"Was that the phone?" Cecilia asked.

"Nope." Rosetta lied.

Cecilia glanced up at Rosetta who met her stare with a challenging one of her own. Cecilia ignored her and began to dress Eve. Rosetta was sure she was making progress with Domi.

* B *

"Rispondetemi!"

Giovanni paced before Mottola. His sleeves rolled up to his elbows, his fists both bloodied and bruised. Mottola had been beaten to his knees. Mottola looked up with his good eye. He dropped his head in defeat.

"This has to stop!" Dominic tried to push past Lorenzo.

Lo turned and blocked his pass. "Giovanni needs this."

"No. He doesn't. He's out of control." Dominic warned.

Lorenzo smirked. "Looks fine to me."

Dominic could not get to Giovanni without making a scene with Lorenzo. After Mottola was dragged in, the torture and beatings were done with Giovanni taking the lead. He knew his brother. The darker he sank into this madness the harder it would be for him to come out of it. They had left these days behind with the Calderones. They were now close to being legitimate. And it was never what Lorenzo wanted. This is all Lorenzo wanted.

"We have to get you both back to Sicily," Dominic said.

Lorenzo's brows lowered. He shoved Dominic back out of the earshot of the other men. "Why?"

"Mira and Marietta have found a woman named Gemma. Know her?"

Lorenzo's eyes widened.

"They have her at Villa Mare Blu. Interrogating her."

"How the hell did they get her past the men?" Lorenzo asked.

"Renaldo went on some errand in Palermo. Every man of any use is here, doing this!" Dominic hissed. "It's time to end it. Now!"

Lorenzo nodded. "I agree."

Dominic felt a sliver of relief. The men all around observed as Giovanni yanked back the head of Mottola and whispered in the man's ear his fate. Dominic and Lorenzo waited for the moment to end the macabre show.

"Kill me!" Mottola said in defiance.

Giovanni let him go. Mottola was worth more to him alive. But he had reached his limit. "Stand him up!" Giovanni ordered.

Three of his men rushed Mottola and forced him to stand. Covered in sweat and fueled with adrenaline, Giovanni wiped his brow with the back of his bruised bloody hand. He glanced back at Lorenzo and Dominic then started to the door. Mottola was dragged behind him. He tossed it open and walked inside. Immediately Mottola wept and cried out in horror. What was left of his sons and nephews was a ghastly sight. Only two of them remained alive. The Armenians had gone beyond the limits and even Giovanni had a hard time looking upon their cruelty.

"Noooo!" Mottola begged. "No!" he slobbered.

"Shall I send them home crippled with your body to bury? Or should I bury them with their mothers and wives?" Giovanni asked.

Mottola looked up confused.

Yeremian hollered for his men to bring out their hostages. The women, old and young were brought out of the back room with their hands tied and mouths taped. The fear for his loved ones broke the man. He fell forward on his hands and knees. He literally crawled to Giovanni for mercy.

"I will do it. Spare my daughters and wife and I'll do it." Mottola begged. He took Giovanni's hand and smeared his own blood over his fist and knuckles with his kiss of respect.

Giovanni stroked the back of his head and smiled. "Very good. And to show you that I too own responsibility in the failure of our clans to protect the *Camorra* I will make a sacrifice as well."

Santo was forced into the room at gunpoint. He looked around at men he considered brothers, bewildered. "Giovanni? What is this? What the hell is going on?"

Carlo hit Santo to the back of his head so hard the man crumbled and fell to his hands and knees. Dazed, Santo's head bowed as he groaned and tried to keep from collapsing. Giovanni walked over to his childhood friend and trusted confidant. He had no doubt that Santo worked for his own purposes and had no reason to seek proof of his indictment. Giovanni had judged him guilty and that was all that was needed.

Santo looked up at him and shook his head slowly. "I have not betrayed you, brother. I'll prove it. Give me a chance and I'll prove it."

Giovanni smiled. "I will give you a chance. In the morning you will meet with the `Ndrangheta. But the meeting will be for the benefit of the *Polizi di Stato*. They will seize everything and you will confess to working for them solely. Against my family and our wishes. With your testimony the war of our clans ends."

"I will be a marked man in prison. A dog. I can't go back to prison. I can't!" Santo said.

"You do this, Santo, and it proves your loyalty. I will work out your release. You failed me. You let this happen. This is on your head. Prove to me that your alliance to our *famiglia* is the only one you serve."

"But I have, Gio. I've spent years in prison to prove my loyalty. I've lost my family, everything. For you! For our clan."

"So this sacrifice should be even easier to withstand. No?"

Santo looked to Mottola who had all but collapsed in his grief over his sons. He glanced back to Lorenzo and Carlo who sneered in return. And lastly he looked to Giovanni. *"Sì."*

"Andiamo," Giovanni said to his men. Yeremian followed him as the men dealt with preparing Santo and Mottola for their debut. He glanced over to Yeremian. "Let the women go. Drop the men off at the church doorstep."

"Are you sure? It's easier to bury them all." Yeremian said.

Giovanni nursed his bruised hand. He looked over to Dominic whose wishes were clear in his eyes. He looked to Lorenzo who desired the opposite. And though he came home to release his demons, the evening had drained him of too much of his soul. "Let them go." Giovanni addressed Yeremian. *"Grazie."*

Yeremian smiled. They embraced. Giovanni continued to the car. Once inside the back of the vehicle he groaned and inspected his hand. The right hand had swollen. He feared that at least one of his knuckles was broken.

Lorenzo got in the back seat with him. "We have to catch a flight out now."

"What? What's wrong? Is it Bella? The babies?"

"Yes." Lorenzo said. "Our wives have decided to do their own little interrogation. They've brought a woman named Gemma into the villa. Got her inside around Renaldo and the men by saying she was Ines. Dominic has already called ahead to have our plane ready. We will be there in two hours."

486

Giovanni grunted. He exhaled a deep breath of frustration. "Who is this woman?"

"Gemma Scafidi. She is the one that told Marietta the truth of Mancini. Not sure if she works for him or not. Don't worry. We'll get to the bottom of it."

"That's it. We're coming out of Mondello. After tonight there is no reason to keep the family in Sicily."

"Agreed." Lorenzo said.

Later –

"She's your *Donna*. Who are you to keep us locked up in here like this?" Marietta shouted.

Renaldo glanced to Mira and then to Marietta, he shrugged but didn't answer. Out of all of Giovanni's men he was the most unshakable to his convictions. A man of orders. And someone had given him the order to keep them all under his watch until Giovanni returned.

Mira looked over to Gemma. Her plan had nearly worked. Zia provided the distraction for the men by claiming to have fallen off the bottom step. Gemma and Marietta got to the car first. Mira arrived last after locating her gun for protection.

However by the time she crept around the house Renaldo was there. He had returned from wherever he had been and marched them all back inside. Renaldo informed them that Giovanni was on his way and no one was to leave. And for two hours they were kept downstairs to wait. Mira knew that the moment her husband walked through the door there would be no way to convince him of what she needed.

She glanced to Gemma who sat there stone cold silent, as if sentenced to death. She glanced to Marietta who paced. The gun she carried remained concealed by her jacket pocket. She could never pull it out on Renaldo. He was family to her. As were all these men. But she had to do something. And do it quick.

"I need to go check on the babies." Mira stood.

Renaldo glanced up. "Forgive me, *Donna*, but I've been told for you to not leave my sight," he said in Italian. Renaldo spoke broken English and not very well.

"It can't wait. They're babies idiot!" Marietta said.

Mira smiled at Renaldo. "I won't be long."

Renaldo stepped forward to stop Mira and from behind a vase

was smashed over his head. The blow was so severe the six foot three tall man dropped immediately. Mira gasped. Marietta wielded the weapon.

"What the hell are you doing?"

"Getting us out of here!" Marietta said, panting hard. "I had to think of something."

"I was going to distract him. Come up with something! Not this!" Mira shouted at her. "My God. Is he okay?" Mira went to her knees. She touched him and turned him. He was breathing.

"Let's go!" Marietta said to Gemma. "Now!"

Mira got a pillow from the sofa and put it under Renaldo's head. There was no blood. He groaned a bit but didn't fully wake.

"Get his keys!" Marietta said. When Mira ignored her she dropped to her knees and removed his keys. "He drives the black truck. Let's go! Now damn it!"

Mira did as she was told. The gun in her pocket felt heavy as her guilt over their actions. She had no time to think about it. They were going to have to see this one through. And Marietta was the only one bold enough to make sure of it. When they raced out of the front door three men stopped them. Mira did the unthinkable. She removed the gun that Giovanni had given her and turned it on the men. Leo was the first to look at her with surprise.

"Let us go," she said.

"We can't. The boss…"

"Do it, Leo! Now!" Mira leveled the gun. Marietta and Gemma never knew she had the weapon. They both looked at her with surprise. The men stepped aside. Marietta bolted for the truck and Mira gave Leo an apologetic smile. "I'll take the blame for this, Leo. Giovanni won't punish you."

Leo looked on as if he didn't believe her. They piled in the truck and reversed out. Marietta sprayed dirt and rocks in a cloud of dust in their wake. Mira felt a pang of guilt for leaving her babies. "I'm not sure how we should do this."

"Huh?" Marietta glanced over at her. "Are you for real? You say that now?"

"I just… didn't think it through," Mira said.

Marietta accelerated. "This is it, Mira. We either take a stand and end this or we let our husbands tell us what to believe."

Mira chewed over the reasoning and held to the inside of the door as they drove dangerously fast around the mountain. "We can't go this way."

"Why?" Marietta asked.

"She's right," Gemma spoke up. "If your husbands are coming then you have to get off the main road. They'll see you."

Mira nodded. She glanced up at the moon. She had no idea if Giovanni had left Italy or not but her gut said he had. "Do you know another way?"

"I do. It'll take longer, but get us there. Take this road." Gemma pointed. Mira squinted at the road that was covered in dense forest. As soon as Marietta made the turn Mira suspected it was a mistake. The isolation of the road and absence of moonlight made it very hazardous for the large truck.

Marietta decreased speed.

"I don't like this," Mira cast Gemma a suspicious look. She removed her gun and put it on her lap so Gemma could see it in the dark. "This better not be a trap."

Gemma shook her head. "I swear it. I'll get you to Mancini. I only ask that you help me in return."

"Help you how?" Marietta asked.

"Keep your husbands from retaliating against me. We get to Mancini and you let me go. If he sees me... I can't see him. I've done my part in this. I gave you the truth and your father. Spare my life by letting me go."

Marietta glanced to Mira, and Mira glanced to her. They both nodded that they would. But neither meant it.

* B *

Giovanni was out of the car before it came to a full stop. Renaldo walked out to meet them. "Where are they?" Giovanni demanded.

"You just missed them, Boss. You had to have passed them on the road," Renaldo said with an ice pack to the side of his head.

"What the fuck do you mean I missed them?" Giovanni checked his watch. Before he boarded the plane he called and confirmed that the women were being watched. That was barely two hours ago. "How the fuck did they leave?"

"It was my fault," Renaldo said, standing up for his men. "Marietta hit me from behind. I was only out for a few minutes but they got to my truck and left."

The confession confounded Giovanni. Mira wasn't prone to this kind of deception. And for what? He looked to Lorenzo. "Where would they go?"

"Only one place, Gio, to see Mancini."

Giovanni's right hand was useless. The pain had been unmerciful. He couldn't strike Renaldo even if he wanted to.

"I'll go after them," Lorenzo said.

"No. We'll go." Giovanni said. They're off the main road so that means we can catch them. He glanced back to Nico who was out of their vehicles. "Nico will stay with the women. Renaldo you come with us."

"Boss?"

"What is it?" Giovanni demanded.

"The *Donna*, she… the men tell me she has her gun with her."

Giovanni frowned. "She drew her weapon on you?"

"On Leo, sir," Renaldo said.

He looked to Lorenzo shocked. "Have they lost their fucking minds?"

Lorenzo chuckled. Giovanni found none of it funny. He walked back to the car and got inside. His only prayer was he got to them before they reached Mancini.

* B *

At first Mira feared her concerns were true. The road was dark, and the small village they drove through looked deserted. But after another fifteen minutes on the road the land opened and the half-moon and stars relaxed her fears. She checked her watch. It was close to five in the morning.

"So how will you do it, girls?" Gemma asked.

"Do what?" Mira asked.

"You can't drive up to Mancini's gates with that gun. How do you plan to get inside? And out."

"You said he didn't want us dead. You said he was looking for us," Marietta said.

"Possibly. But you have a brother too. No matter what his father wants he surely isn't open to acknowledging either of you," Gemma said.

"Why is that?" Mira asked for the sake of conversation. Though she knew fully why.

"There's a lot of history between your families. He's the sole heir to the Mancini fortune unless you two decide to contest it."

"We don't want his money," Marietta said with disgust, keeping her eyes on the road.

Mira had to agree. She glanced back out the window at the stars. Her mother's death wasn't on her husband's shoulders, and tonight she'd prove it by making Mancini confess. After it was done she wanted to leave Sicily and never return. There was nothing remotely familiar or comforting to her about this place. She found it ironic that Giovanni had hoped their visit to the island would make her love the island. She loathed it instead.

"Heads up!" Marietta said.

Mira's gaze swung to the road. Cars approached fast, four of them with bright lights beaming.

"Do you think it's Mancini's men?" Marietta asked. "Are we near his villa?"

"No, we aren't," Gemma frowned with worry. "Can't be his men."

Mira picked up her gun. It could be a set up. She glanced to Gemma. "If you did this."

"I swear I did not. I don't know who it is, but we can't outrun them on this road. It's too narrow." Gemma warned.

"What do I do?" Marietta asked.

"Stop. We have no choice." Mira checked the chamber of the gun. She prayed she didn't have to use it. Target practice was one thing but if she had to shoot armed thugs in the night she didn't know what would be the outcome.

Marietta slowed the car to a stop. The car ahead of them parked in front of theirs. The high beams made it impossible for them to see who was inside. The cars circled around. Their dark tented windows in the night made it impossible to make out the drivers or passengers. They were blocked in on all sides.

"Somebody is getting out," Marietta said. She glanced to Mira who held the gun.

Mira squinted. Even in the glare her husband's imposing form could clearly be seen. Relief filled her to the brim. She nearly smiled. Gemma grabbed her wrist. "Please. Remember your promise. That you'll let me go," Gemma pleaded. "I know I don't deserve to ask for anything, but I did come to you to tell you the truth."

"I didn't make that promise," Marietta said.

"Me either," Mira said.

"What? You two can't... they'll kill me!" Gemma said.

Marietta looked to Mira. Mira looked to her sister. She then looked to Gemma. "We will show you as much mercy as you showed our mother."

"No! Wait!"

"Stay inside. Marietta, don't get out. Let me speak to Giovanni." Mira opened the door and exited the truck. She thought to leave the gun behind but decided to take it with her. As soon as she stepped out into the night she realized that the men were out of their cars as well, staring at her. Mira approached her husband and the steely look of anger in his eyes made her bravery slip. His gaze lowered from her face to the gun in her hand. He narrowed his eyes on it. Mira couldn't believe the sight of him. He hadn't shaved in days, and yes she knew he had been drinking. But he looked wild to her, and was that blood on his suit? She couldn't be sure. He raised a hand and she saw how swollen and bruised his knuckles were.

"In the car," he said and pointed to the waiting vehicle.

"Gio—"

"GET IN THE FUCKING CAR!" he shouted at her.

His voice boomed louder than thunder. There was no room for discussion by the hard unforgiving look of madness in his eyes. She glanced back to Marietta and Gemma in the truck. Lorenzo walked past her and went to Marietta's side of the car.

"NOW!" Giovanni shouted and took a step toward her.

Mira went to the car where the door was held open for her. She was inside the back of the car waiting when Giovanni joined her. He slammed the door so hard she jumped.

"Are you going to let me explain?" she asked.

Giovanni hit the passenger glass of his window so hard with his closed fist it cracked. Mira looked at him with disbelief. "You left my children in the night? You pulled a gun on my men? You let a stranger into our home."

"I'm sorry."

"Sorry? You're fucking sorry!" he seethed. The mask of anger and contempt on his face was grave. She was grateful when he looked away.

"Do you want to go on like this? Do you?" she asked and her voice wavered. She knew he was on edge. Hell they both were. Guilt skewered through her. The past had come back to haunt them. It threatened to rob them both of the future they desired. She had to do something. "Let me explain myself to you. Please," she pleaded.

"Mira," he breathed in and out deeply. His rage burned his face and neck red. Though his hand looked like it was broken he kept pounding it against his thigh. Each time he did she winced.

"Please, give me a chance to explain. One chance." She reached over and touched the top of his hand to stop him from inflicting pain on himself.

He stilled.

"What's become of us? I can't... I can't tell you how badly I feel about all of it... there's so much anger between us now," her voice choked on emotion. With her anger and disappointment in him came fresh memories of how he'd massage her feet and feed her in bed. How he'd wake in the night and readjust her pillows to make sure she was comfortable. Flashes of him with Eve and their bond surfaced. The first time she saw him hold their sons. Fresh tears welled in her eyes. Zia was right. She had lost focus. She turned her back and hid from their problems instead of facing them. She played an equal role in the state they found themselves in.

Mira opened her mouth to speak and emotion clogged her throat. She had to clear it to be heard. "You said to me that you could never stay angry at the woman you love. Did you mean it?" she asked

His gaze slipped over to her.

Mira continued. "You spent weeks protecting me and our children. Longer than that if you count Switzerland. You were at my side. You took care of me through my anxiety; and there was plenty. Left your business affairs to others to hold my hand..." she bit on her quivering lip. Her nerves were frayed. "The doctors told you I could lose the babies to stress and you put it all on the line to keep me from stress. The moment I had to do the same I put us in jeopardy. My babies, they could have died. I lost focus on what was important for a split second and everything fell apart," she wiped at her tears. She dropped her head and cried. Giovanni didn't touch or comfort her as he had in the past. That was different. One tear from her and he'd bring her through it. Now he sat at her side silent and withdrawn. That hurt her deeply. She collected herself and tried to continue.

"I'll bend."

She lifted her gaze to his face. His brows creased. He stared at her. For a moment there was complete silence. And then he spoke to her. "Bend? What does that mean?"

For the first time since their fighting began she had clarity. She wanted her husband back. She wanted peace in her heart and in her marriage. Fabiana was right. She shielded herself from the bad and pretended at the good. She did it with Kei, and she did it in her other disasterous relationships. It was time to open her eyes and face her choices. He was her choice. The good and the bad.

"Bella? What do you mean by *bend*?" he asked again.

"From the very beginning of this you have been selective with the truth, Giovanni. And I have been willfully blind. And I know why. You thought that your father and what he did would drive me from you. And I gave you reason to, because I do run from my problems. I've run all my life from one thing or person to the next," she looked up at him. "There are things about me, Giovanni, you don't know. A past I pretend never happened. Bad choices I've made that I ignore. Some of it explains why I am the way I am. Why I am capbable of loving a man as complicated as you. None of it is an excuse. Now you don't have any faith left in us," she sighed. "And that's my fault. I told you that I would never abandon you. I swore it. And it's exactly what I did. You wanted to talk it out, to fight about it. I... I... I wanted to punish you instead."

Giovanni sighed. "It's done—"

Mira kept going. "No it's not. Because I never truly accepted this life of guns, violence, deception, the man you are for them out there. I couldn't conceive it at first, because with me you were just the man I love..."

"Bella—"

"Stop! Let me finish. You knew I ignored the truth of what we do in this family. And you let me create this bubble for us. Float through our marriage with my eyes closed. Because you didn't believe that I'm strong enough, that I love you enough, that I can handle any of it. That's not on you, baby, it's on me." Mira began to cry. It was hard. She sucked down her tears and tried. "I'll bend, because I love you. I made a promise to you. I broke it. You made a promise to me and you broke it. One of his has to bend. I'll do it." She looked up at him. "Because in this life we have, someone has to. And it can't be you," she wept.

He pulled her to him. She hugged him tightly grateful for his love. She clung to him and let go of her fear of losing him. She felt a bit stronger, but not much. "I lied to you," he said. "I could have handled things differently."

She looked up at him. "Someone has to give in. If it's what you need to stop pushing me away, let me be the one," she touched his face. "I want all of you, Don Giovanni Battaglia. Even the parts that scare me. And I'll learn to be the wife you need. Even if I make mistakes, I'll learn. I swear it. And I'll trust you. I'll bend for you, baby, because you have to be strong for all of us. We're a family. And our family means everything to me."

She brought her lips closer to his. "I'm sorry I hurt you," she said softy. He brought her over to him and she straddled his lap. She kissed him softly at first, and then released her forgiveness and passion for him, because it was the only way to release his.

"I'm sorry, Bella," he panted when their lips parted. "I'm sorry for everything I've done to you." Giovanni held her with crushingly tight strength and she allowed it. He kissed her face, and neck, and she allowed it.

"I want you to take me to see my father," she whispered in his ear.

He stopped kissing her neck.

She lifted her face and looked down into his eyes. "Tonight we end it. Together. I swear to you it's all I need. My mother died because she was lost in this world. Forced into by that man, and then discarded like trash. I don't blame Tomosino or you. I blame him. And I want my closure." She kissed his lips. "Let go of your anger, Giovanni, and give me what I need. I need this."

He cut his gaze away and for a minute she thought he'd refuse her. "And then it's over?" he asked. "You'll be mine again? My Bella?"

"Yes, its over. I'll face your men and apologize for my actions. I'm your wife. I'm their *Donna*. I haven't forgotten," she smiled. "Be my husband and stand at my side, not in front of me. I need you too. Help me."

He looked up into her eyes. He dropped his head back. "You're killing me."

"We'll work it out. Together. I promise." She kissed his brow, his nose, his lips.

Mira heard a woman's screams. She looked to the window but couldn't see her from the position in the back of the car. She looked to Giovanni. "Please. Take us. Now."

He moved her off his lap and got out of the car. Mira got out behind him in time to see the men dragging Gemma to another car.

"They're going to kill me!" Gemma screeched. "They'll do it."

Mira grabbed Giovanni's hand. He looked at her. He expected her to plead for Gemma's life. Mira glanced back to Gemma again. She remained silent.

Giovanni nodded. "We're taking them all to Mancini." Giovanni announced to his men. Lorenzo and the others looked on. "Take the woman as well. Armando Mancini can decide on what to do with her."

"Marietta! Please help me!" Gemma begged.

Lorenzo pulled Marietta by the hand to the car. Whatever he said in her ear calmed her down. Mira was brought back to the car and she re-entered the vehicle. Lorenzo behind the wheel drove faster in the night than they had in Renaldo's truck. The troupe of cars followed.

495

Mira reached over and took Giovanni's bruised hand in hers. She kissed his bloody knuckles tenderly. He looked at her with a sliver of distrust in his eyes. She understood it. She smiled. She stroked his battered knuckles afraid to ask the cause. No one spoke. She could barely hear herself breathe. They drove through the city of Palermo in silence out to the neighboring township that brought them to their father. And as soon as they approached the gates Mira's breath hitched in her lungs. She was actually going to face the man. What would she say? What would he say?

In the dark she could see so little. But she felt the expanse of the estate and wondered if it was as vast as Melanzana.

The window rolled down. Lorenzo spoke to the men in Italian. The man outside of the car shouted at him.

"Tell Marsuvio both of his daughters are here!" Lorenzo insisted.

That seemed to silence the man. There was activity around the car. Giovanni didn't seem fazed by it. Mira however felt the tension coil tighter around her gut. Her husband stared out of his window lost in his thoughts. After ten minutes they were waved through the gates. All of the cars were allowed access.

"How do you want to handle it, Gio?" Lorenzo asked.

Mira looked into her husband's eyes. He took a moment before he responded. "We will go in there and let you see the man. I want two things, Bella."

"Name it?" Mira asked.

"You agree to nothing without discussing it with me first."

"Okay, and the other thing?" Mira asked. She looked up at Marietta who sat silently next to Lorenzo. She looked to her husband again. "What else?"

"If I say the visit is over, we leave. We do so without question."

"That's all?" Mira teased him with a smile.

He cut his eyes unable to smile at the moment. Mira pulled on his hand gently. "I can do whatever you ask. Without question. I swear it."

He tossed open the door and reached back to help her out. As soon as she emerged from the car she could hear the fast approach of men. Mira looked past her husband to the tall man with silky hair that dusted his shoulders. He locked eyes with her and then switched his gaze over to her husband.

"Giovanni? You got my message?" the man asked.

Mira was now shoulder to shoulder with her sister. Their husbands stood on either side of them. The man glanced over at the others in their group and then addressed Giovanni again.

"What message?" Giovanni answered in a flat tone.

"Then how did you know?" Armando frowned.

"Know what?" Giovanni asked.

Armando wiped his hand back over his head. He glanced to Mira and then Marietta. "My father isn't well. They don't expect him to make it through the night. He's asked for you both. I thought you came because of my request."

Mira glanced to her husband. She had no idea Mancini was ill. She looked to Marietta who stood next to Lorenzo holding his hand. There was no emotion on her face. "Can we see him?" Mira asked.

"You must be Mirabella?" Armando said. He extended his hand. Mira looked to Giovanni and his agreement was reluctantly slow. She extended her hand and shook her brother's. "*Armando Mancini. I'm your brother*," he said with a sly smile. He then turned his attention to Marietta. "Ah, and you are Marietta. My long lost sister." He took Marietta's hand and kissed it. She pulled it away.

"Come with me. It's time." Armando said.

Mira was helped up the stairs by Giovanni. She knew his hands pained him so she tried hard not to hold too tightly or draw attention to them. The inside of the Mancini villa was quite lavish with marble floors and a wide-open foyer under a huge crystal chandelier.

"I can escort the ladies from here," Armando said.

"I won't be separated from my husband," Mira replied.

"Me either," Marietta echoed.

Armando looked them both over. He smiled. "Certainly."

The men came forward and patted Lorenzo and Giovanni down. Armando started off. "Come this way," he said.

They walked to the back left of the estate and then went up the stairs. With each step Mira felt her stomach muscles clench tighter and tighter. She only remembered recently that Gemma was supposed to be with them, but when she looked back she only saw Marietta and Lorenzo following.

Mira cleared her throat. "Can I ask what is wrong with him?"

Armando glanced her way. "He has pneumonia. He's been living with an iron lung for several years now. The doctors have done all they can."

They arrived before a closed door. It opened and Carmella stepped out. She carried a tray with her that looked to have been someone's half eaten dinner. When she looked at Mira and Giovanni she froze. Mira glanced to her husband for a reaction. He stared directly at Carmella. The woman shyly looked to Armando who seemed dismissive of the awkward moment. *"Ciao, Giovanni, Donna,"* Carmella nodded to Marietta and Lorenzo.

"Is Papa awake?" Armando asked.

"He is. He's awake." She said. *"Scusi."* She quickly made an exit.

"I will let him know you are here," Armando said. Mira nodded and he disappeared inside the room.

21.

The respiration sounded labored and phlegmy in his chest but he felt stronger. The sharp contrast between his pathetic reality and his numbing state was possibly due to the heavy regimens of morphine the doctors had introduced into his bloodstream. Death had never been a consequence of his in life. He had done so many things and overcome so many obstacles that he truly believed himself invincible. Until now.

The door opened as his eyes closed. The morphine made it so much easier to accept his fate. "Turn off the light he mumbled," slipping deeper into the numbness.

"Papa, you have visitors."

Mancini opened his eyes and his vision cleared. His son stood over him. "What visitors?" he eased up on his pillows and Armando made sure to adjust the stack behind him.

"Your daughters."

He tried to focus on the words his son spoke but his mind fogged over. He almost believed that his son said his daughters had come.

"Did you hear me, Papa? They're here."

"Who?"

"Mirabella and Marietta. They want to see you," Armando said. Mancini double blinked. His head cleared, as did his hearing. He wheezed instead of answering. Taking the time to practice his breathing he couldn't help but smile.

"You brought them?" he asked.

"Yes, Papa. I brought them." Armando smiled.

He walked away from the bed and opened the door. Mancini waited for what seemed like an eternity for his girls to step through. First came Mirabella. She looked as beautiful as her pictures. Her hair was straight with bangs that covered her brows. She wore pants and a blouse. His daughter Marietta appeared. She was a bit fairer but equally as beautiful as her sister. The girls looked at him in the bed and didn't speak. He'd lived this moment in his head many times over the years.

"Come closer," he gestured.

The women stepped further inside and their husbands appeared next. Mancini's weak beating heart froze. He hadn't anticipated the audience. The look from Giovanni and Lorenzo indicated there would be one whether he wanted it or not. He smiled at his girls.

Marietta stared at her father, taking him in. He was older than she remembered, and much more fragile. Yet his eyes told the true story. She looked to her sister and her gaze swung back to Mancini. The three of them all had the same eyes. Though their father's eyes were cast under a brooding brow the resemblance shared by the three of them was hard not to see.

He wore a dark cranberry red smoking jacket trimmed in black. And his thinning gray hair was combed back over his balding scalp. A hint of his fading youth was evident by the dark streaks of hair that hadn't turned silver. He breathed with assistance, a tube connected to his nose and hooked around both of his ears.

"I have waited a long time for this moment," he said.

"Papa, this is…" Armando began.

"I know who they are, boy. My baby girls," he glanced from one to the other.

Marietta stepped closer. The lump in her throat was so large that she found it hard to swallow, but she opened her mouth to speak anyway.

"You think we came here for you. We came here because Gemma told us everything."

Mancini's smile faded. "Gemma?"

"She told us how you tricked our mother, raped her, turned her out like the stable of whores you imported into America. Except you made her your dirty little secret."

"Gemma told you this?" Mancini asked. He glanced to Lorenzo as if the accusation lied there.

"Yes! Because it was Gemma who hid me from you all these years. It was Gemma who put our mother on drugs right under your nose. It was Gemma who helped her run away from you more than once!" Marietta fired off. She felt a hand touch hers and she saw it was Mira. She gripped her hand for support. Mancini didn't deny a word. He just absorbed all she said. It was a good thing because if he denied a word of it Marietta wasn't sure what she'd do next.

"Gemma told us after we were born you deposited our mother in New York and promised her you'd return. You didn't. You left her behind for your Sicilian family." Marietta tossed a look to Armando who observed from the corner in the room. "And even if I were to believe there is a heart in that rotten chest of yours there is no way I will ever believe it beats for me and my sister."

The man swallowed back a rising coughing attack. Marietta was surprised at how harsh it sounded coming from him considering his fragile state. Mancini put up his withered left hand like a stop sign. Marietta glanced back to see Armando had stepped closer. Mancini closed his eyes and breathed in slow. "Hear my side of things, *cara*," he pleaded softly. "Alone?"

"No." Marietta said.

"We should talk to him alone," Mira said. Marietta looked at her surprised. Mira looked back to her husband. "If it's okay with you, Giovanni?"

He glanced from his wife to Mancini. A blind man could see Mancini was dying and the sight of him this way did affect Marietta. But not more than her anger and hurt. Nothing the bastard said could make up for how badly she hurt.

Giovanni approached Mira. He kissed her and whispered something in her ear. Mira let go of Marietta's hand and hugged her husband. She kissed him on the mouth more passionately in front of everyone. Marietta wasn't sure how but something had changed with the two of them. They were again wrapped up in their private world. Invincible. She glanced to Lorenzo who winked at her. Fighting back her tears she went to him and he immediately wrapped her up on his big arms. "It's your father, Marie," Lorenzo whispered. "Cut the bullshit tanturms. This is the moment you wanted. Take it, *cara*."

She looked up into his eyes. "I love you, Lorenzo. I don't need him."

"I love you too." He kissed her brow.

Mira let go of her husband and the men all left the room. She looked over to the dying man and felt nothing but pity. The horrors her mother endured because of him broke her heart. Still she couldn't hate him. And she was so tired of her sister's angry outbursts. Marietta didn't appear to have coping skills. Whenever she was hurt or backed in a corner she fought to hurt everyone around her. And that too broke Mira's heart. She heard the story of her suffering with the Leones. It would take a long time before those wounds were healed.

"Mirabella," Mancini said softly. "Marietta, I have so much to tell you."

She glanced back to the bed. He lifted his hand. Mira stared at it for a moment. She knew Marietta watched her. If there were any steps toward forgiveness to be made it would have to be by her. She accepted his hand with hers. He brought it to his lips and kissed it softly. "Mirabella," he said as he brushed it over his cheek. "You look like her."

Mira removed her hand from his. She found her voice but it wavered. "Tell us your story. Why did you take my mother and abandon her?"

"Lisa, was everything to me," Mancini smiled. "The first time I saw her she was at a piano, playing, singing like an angel. Did you know she could sing? She loved music. Loved to dance."

Marietta broke. She put her hands to her face.

Mira wasn't expecting her to fall apart so soon. She prayed she held on. "Go on," Mira said to their father.

"She was young, very young. And I had no respect for that. I wanted her because she was different, innocent, and not the least bit interested in me." Mancini wheezed. "Now that you tell me Gemma is at fault. It all makes sense to me. Gemma and I have a very bad history. And I should have never trusted her around Lisa."

"Is what she said true? Did you rape my mother?" Mira asked. Marietta stepped closer to the bed. At last her sister calmed enough to join the conversation.

"Rape?" Mancini shook his head. "What I did was far worse. I didn't take her by force. I took everything from her to make her mine. Every option she had, until..." he wheezed. "Until she had no other choice. So yes, I'm sorry."

"I don't understand how she didn't put a knife in you," Marietta said.

Mancini nodded. "Your mother was very... forgiving. I know that sounds bad. I can't... I don't have the strength to make it anything more than what it was. She shared her life with me. How she grew up, what her dreams were. She was so beautiful. She changed me. I loved her," he said.

"How? How did my mother love the man who abused and destroyed her?" Mira asked. "It doesn't make sense. I don't think she loved you at all."

"She did. I have proof," he coughed. "Bible," he said.

They both looked to each other in confusion.

He pointed. "Psalm 51."

Marietta stepped around them and picked up his bible. She opened it to remove an old Polaroid. Her mother and Mancini posed in a picture with her mother smiling.

"Be merciful to me oh God, because of your constant love. Because of your great mercy wipe away my sins! Wash away all my evil and make me clean from sin…" he began.

Mira cut in and began to recite the psalm for him. "I recognize my faults; I am always conscious of my sins. I have sinned against you—only you—and done what you considered evil."

Mancini nodded and finished the psalm. "So you are right in judging me. You are justified in condemning me. I have been evil from the day I was born. From the time I was conceived I have been sinful."

Marietta dropped the Bible. She wept. She stared at the photo of her mother, clasped the image with shaking hands. She wept. Mira shook her head sadly. "My grandfather used to recite Psalm 51 in his prayers at night. My grannie said he felt a lot of guilt for my mother, for sending her away, for her death."

"Your mother taught me that psalm, when my guilt became too much," Mancini said. "I was raised in the Catholic church but never learned the principles I should have. Whenever I came to her, weak from the burdens my father put upon me, with the blood of my friends and ex-associates on my hands, she'd tell me to pray. And when I refused she'd pray for me. She'd recite that psalm. That psalm is for forgivness. She forgave me. It was who she was. Pure, loving." He coughed. "Until I corrupted her. I took so much from her." He wheezed down a breath and Mira looked at him with concern. She didn't know what to do to make him comfortable. He then stabilized and began again. "That's why I left her behind in New York. I forced her out of that hospital. I took her there to set her up. To keep her from returning home. I knew if she did I'd lose her. But my life had other demands. I had to come back to Sicily."

"You left her."

"When I tried to find her she had run away. Capriccio told me she was back in Virginia with her parents. I could have come back, and forced her to return to New York but I knew it was time to let her go. So I believed him. I swear I didn't know. I still don't know how Cappricio and Gemma separated you girls. When I learned the truth Lisa was dead. I was told you were dead, Marietta. And you were with your grandparents Mirabella."

Marietta walked over to the bed holding the picture. "Did she want me?"

Mancini smiled. "She loved you both. I named you. I remember when they told us we were having girls. I returned to Sicily, had bracelets made for you. I had every intention of being a father to you—at least I thought I did."

"Did you know there was a contract on her life?" Mira asked.

"No. Why would my father do such a thing, he didn't believe in hurting women or children? It's not our way. I can't even think that Tomosino would. It's not our way."

"He didn't see her as a woman, a daughter, a mother, he saw her as something to be discarded like you did!" Marietta said.

Mancini closed his eyes. "I didn't know it was Gemma. But now that I think on it Giovanni was right." He opened his eyes and looked to Mira. "I never tried to know what happened to Lisa. I've been hiding from the truth of her death for years."

"What did you think happened?" Mira asked.

"When Capriccio called me and told me that she was dead…"

"Wait? Capriccio told you?" Marietta asked. "Not Gemma?"

Mancini nodded. "Capriccio said he had contacts in Chicago who told him she and an infant were dead. I have no idea why she went to Chicago. It had been two years and she had cut off all communication with me. I came immediately, but there was no body for my baby girl, just Lisa's. And I took her home and discovered you were alive, Mirabella. I asked your grandfather why she left you behind. He said she was back on drugs. I told him of your death, Marietta. He cursed me. Said I should stay away from you, Mirabella. But…" he smiled. "Your grandmother, she understood."

"Understood?" Mira frowned.

He nodded. Mancini pointed at the cigar box over on the chair. "There. The box."

Mira stood. She walked over and opened it. Inside she found momentos of her childhood. Pictures from elementary up to her thirteenth birthday before her grandmother died.

"Your grandmother sent me cards, and pictures over the years. When they stopped I knew it must have meant she had died," Mancini said.

"Why did you come for me?" Mira asked again. "If you had your life in Sicily and your new family. If my mother was dead and you had given me to my grandparents. Why come back?"

"My guilt was with me everyday. You have to understand. I didn't think I failed just Lisa, but Marietta too. I thought she was dead." He looked over to Marietta. "I thought you were murdered with your mother. I had no idea who had you, Marietta."

"His name was Octavio Leone. And he pretty much abused me from the moment he could," Marietta said.

"And if I could rise from this bed I would get you justice. I swear it." Mancini grunted.

"I don't want your justice. It's too late!" Marietta said. "I don't want to know why you abandoned us, why you tossed our mother aside like garbage. I want to know why you think now we owe you anything!"

Mancini nodded. "I'm dying. I've been dying for years. I want forgiveness." He reached for the drawer and Mira thought to help him. But he removed the folder without assistance. "I've kept them hidden, until now," he said. He removed from the folder two original birth certificates. He smiled at them and passed them to Mira. She stared down at the little stamped prints of her and Marietta's feet.

"I want Lisa," Mancini wheezed. "I know my soul will never make it past purgatory or the lakes of fire in hell to see her without your forgiveness." He looked up at Mira. "I watched you for years. I promised your grandparents I would never interfere. I had no right to know you. But I did interfere. When you were seventeen and your grandfather died, you applied to Parsons for a scholarship."

Mira blinked at him. "Yes. How did you know?"

Mancini smiled. "I paid the tuition, set up the scholarship. I had regular reports on your life."

Mira couldn't believe it.

Mancini sighed. "When I learned I was dying I couldn't keep that promise to stay away any longer. I used your attorney Theodore Tate to bring you to me, and then you met... Giovanni." Mancini closed his eyes. "I'm not a good man, girls. And I did hurt your mother. In ways I can never forgive myself. But through it all she found a way to love me. And that love saved me. And that love created you," Mancini said.

Mira sat on the edge of the bed. She put a hand to his chest. "I can't forgive you for what you did to my mother. But I can see, in your warped mind you do think you loved her."

"I did!" Mancini insisted. "I'm not so different from Giovanni. If I can't love neither can he," Mancini said.

Mira shook her head. "He believes that. He thinks he's his father. He thinks he's a man like you. And I'm not blind to his faults so don't throw them in my face. What Giovanni and I have is nothing like what you had with my mother." Mira glanced to Marietta who continued to stare at the photo. "What she has with Lorenzo is nothing like it either."

"This is not the life for you, Mira, or you, Marietta. I have money. You have an inheritance I plan to leave to you. Armando is your brother. He'll help you escape them. Claim your life. Be that great fashion designer. That was your dream. I want you both to have your dreams."

Mira removed her hand from his chest. She frowned. "I don't want your money, I don't want your legacy. My children will be raised as Battaglia. If you want forgiveness I'll try to give it. But you won't get anything else. And as for my dream, I have my dream. Her name is Eve. And I have sons, their names are Gianni and Gino. I have a husband who is part of me. That's my dream."

Mancini gripped her wrist. His eyes began to tear and she saw he struggled to appear strong. "Lisa," he said staring at her. "You're my Lisa."

Marietta walked over to the bed. She pulled her sister free from his grasping. "It's time to go. We've come for what we wanted. Let's go!"

In that moment Mira knew, this would be the last time she saw her father. He stared at her with such pain in his eyes.

"Mira! Let's go! He should suffer! After what he did to her, he should suffer."

"Don't you see it, Marietta?" Mira looked to her sister, and tears slipped down her cheeks. "He's suffering. Just like you. The past can't change. So you both have to let it go." She looked back at Mancini. She leaned over and kissed his brow.

Mancini wept. "Lisa…"

She kissed his cheek. *"Mi Papa, andate in pace."*

And in her heart she had released him. Mancini whispered his love for her mother. She let up and let him go. Mira stood. She reached for Marietta to encourage her to say goodbye but her sister dodged her touch. She looked at Mancini with disgust. Mira feared she'd one day regret this moment between them, but she couldn't force it.

"However you want to do it. Say goodbye," Mira said.

"Goodbye," Marietta said and walked to the door, opened it, and walked out of it. Mira picked up the cigar box. She put their birth certificates inside and stepped back from the bed. Mancini closed his eyes and continued to sob. There were no more answers to be found with him. Just the cold-hearted resolution she needed. She followed her sister out.

Giovanni looked up. Marietta stepped out of the door first. Mira followed soon after carrying a cigar box. His wife had tears on her cheeks. She smiled at him. She then cast her gaze to Armando. Giovanni watched as she walked over to him. Armando frowned, but didn't object when Mira embraced him. "Thank you for letting us see him," she said.

He kissed Mira on both cheeks. "Will you call us to let us know, when..." she glanced back to the room. "I'd like to pay my respects."

"I will," Armando said.

She smiled.

When she returned to Giovanni he could breathe again. "Take me out of this place please," she said softy.

Giovanni eased his arm around her waist and they followed Lorenzo and Marietta down the stairs. They left the Mancini gates without incident. It wasn't until they were half way home did she think of Gemma.

"Where's Gemma?" Mira asked.

"She's Mancini's problem now," he replied. Giovanni cast his eyes to Mira. He studied her reaction. The answer seemed to satisfy her. When the men left the room Giovanni informed Armando of the facts. The ones he wanted him to know. Gemma was responsible for the girls learning the truth. Armando said he'd been looking for her. They had unfinished business. Giovanni didn't inquire further. She was Mancini's problem now. He also let him know that if there were any further attempts to harm their wives, he'd pay with his life. Armando smirked and nodded to the threat. A clear challenge.

"What happened to your hand?" Mira asked. She picked it up again. "Giovanni, it looks broken."

"It's fine. I'll have someone take a look at it in the morning," he replied as he went through the cigar box of momentos. The pictures of his Bella as a little girl riveted him. She was right. There wasn't much he knew about her past. Only her mother's fate was told to him. Who was her first love? How did she grow up? What made her become a fashion designer? All of the questions flooded his brain.

"No. No. Lorenzo, take us to the hospital," Mira said.

"I said it's fine." Giovanni tried to pull his hand away. But she held firmly to it.

"Take us to the hospital please." She stroked his hand and smiled. "I'm going to take care of you." She leaned over and kissed his cheek.

Giovanni stiffened. He was still very gun-shy of her affection. But the melting softness in her smile made him want to believe her sincerity.

"Do as my wife said," Giovanni forced a smile. "I want her to take care of me."

* B *

Mancini pushed up on the pillows. The door was open when Armando walked Gemma inside. He hadn't seen her in over twenty years. The accusations Marietta threw at him burned his heart. How could he have been so blind?

"It was you. All this time I blamed Capriccio and it was you."

"You did this. Don't blame me," Gemma said. She held her head high. "I was her friend."

"Liar!" Mancini said. He began to cough. So harsh and chokingly tight was this coughing fit he spit up blood. Armando returned to his side. He helped him. Mancini didn't want help. With the last of his strength he wanted truth. "You set it in motion and I was a fool. You were doing this under my nose and I never suspected."

"Yes!" Gemma said. "I loved you, Marsuvio. I was good enough for you until you saw Lisa. And then you made me watch as you treated her like your woman. I was the one who put her on drugs!" Gemma proclaimed with pride. Mancini sat upright. She nodded. "Just like you were the one that led me to them. I was the one that kept feeding her fears, telling her to run from you. I was the one who convinced Capriccio to give your daughter to that sadist brother in-law of his. I was the one that held Lisa down while Capriccio put a needle in her arm filled with heroin so she could overdose. I wanted to destroy her after years of watching you give her what was mine!"

Mancini couldn't speak.

Gemma let go a mad laugh. "When Isabella told me what she wanted to do to you I was glad. I wanted you to pay. And I wanted you to find out that Marietta was alive after all these years. So you would know what is like to lose a child. How badly it hurt. Just like it hurt when I lost the child I carried for you!"

Marsuvio reclined back into his pillows.

"Was there ever a contract on Lisa's life?" he asked.

"No, it was something Flavio tried to convince Tomosino to do. He hated you. Did you know that? Flavio hated you and Capriccio worked with him for years. But Tomosino never okayed it. Lisa died when she came back for Marietta and threatened to expose Capriccio and me."

508

Mancini closed his eyes. He drowned in the bottomless depths of his sins. He could deny nothing anymore. There was no point. Gemma was his whore before Lisa, and in his arrogance he turned his beloved Lisa over to her killers.

"I spared your daughters that truth. It's ugly enough what happened to their mother. I can live with my part in it. But Marietta doesn't need to know that her suffering was the sentence I gave her for being your favorite. I chose her, because I remember seeing you at her crib. Telling her how much you loved her. How you would protect her. She got none of that love or protection! I saw to it."

He nodded. "I will see you in hell."

Gemma spat at him.

Armando grabbed her by the arm. Gemma began to shout at him. "Rot in hell! I don't care what you do to me! Rot in hell!"

Mancini said nothing. He didn't look her way as she screamed at him. She was dragged from the room screaming and pleading. He closed his eyes.

"Are they sleeping?" Mancini asked.

Lisa turned and smiled at him. "Look at them, Manny. They hold hands when they sleep." He walked over to the crib. He folded his arms around Lisa and held her to him. The moonlight poured in over the crib. The girls slept side by side on their small stomachs. Marietta's hand covered Mira's tightly balled fist. He'd never been into children. He'd only held his son twice and that was once at his christening. But his girls were beyond beautiful.

"I like their names now, Mirabella and Marietta. I think they're perfect for them." Lisa said. "I'll be a good mother, like my mother. I'll do whatever it takes to protect them."

"You already are a good mother. A good woman. No longer the girl who was afraid of her shadow."

Lisa turned in his arms. She took his face. "And you're a good man, Manny. I love you. No matter what happens between us, always remember that."

He chuckled. "You act as if things will change. I swear to you, Lisa, I won't abandon you and my daughters. Never."

"Shh... don't make promises to me. I don't need them. Not anymore." She kissed him softly. The softest sweetest kisses he'd ever imagined possible. And he believed in them.

Mancini opened his eyes. His tears blurred his vision. There was someone in the room. He struggled to focus on the identity. "Mirabella?" he asked at first. The person moved to the bed and his vision cleared.

"Lisa?"

His beloved sat on the side of the bed. Her fragrance bloomed in his nostrils. She was as beautiful as the day he met her. She leaned in and kissed him again with those petal soft lips of hers. *"It's me, Manny. I'm here."*

Armando walked back down the hall. His head swam from the events of the night. He'd learned too much of his father for his liking. Surprisingly he'd learned even more of the women who were his sisters. How fragile and unsuspecting they were of their connection. He had to admit his father had been right to bring them back. But what was he to do now?

"Papa?" he opened his father's door.

Mancini lay still in his bed. His eyes closed. Armando walked over to the bed. "Papa, I sent them away. Giovanni and I have a new understanding. I don't think peace is possible if you won't give me full control. Papa?"

Armando put his hand to his father's chest. He felt no heartbeat. "Papa!"

He put his finger under his nose and checked for breathing.

There was none.

Marsuvio Mancini was dead.

"Papa!" He dropped to his knees. He took his hand. He kissed his ring. "Papa, no. Not yet. No!"

* B *

"Are you okay?" Lorenzo asked.

Marietta buried her face against his neck. She sat on his lap in the waiting room area while the doctors saw to Giovanni. She cried and held to him from the moment they arrived. Lorenzo tried several times to talk to her but all she could do was cry.

"Marie? Talk to me. Please. What did he say?"

She lifted her face from his neck. She wiped at her tears and snot with her jacket sleeve and then reached in her pocket and removed the Polaroid. "This is my mother," she said.

Lorenzo stared down at the image of a smiling dark skinned

woman with a younger Marsuvio Mancini. "She's beautiful."

"How old do you think she is in that picture?" she asked.

"I'm not sure. Not very old. Early twenties."

"I think she was pregnant with us. See, her face is full. Her breasts. She looks pregnant doesn't she?"

Lorenzo looked to Marietta. He turned her chin so he could look into her eyes. "Talk to me. What is it?"

"I thought…" Marietta's words choked in her throat. "I thought if I found the truth, found her, I would feel different. But you are right. The truth makes it worse. She died because of me. If she hadn't come back for me she would be alive. I killed her."

"No. She died because she loved you. I had a mother who was incapable of love. You, my beautiful wife, had the opposite. She made the greatest sacrifice for you. There is nothing greater."

Marietta smiled. She nodded smiling.

"See. The truth does make it better. For you, for us all." Lorenzo kissed her. "Mmm, I want to fuck you." He groaned.

She laughed. She hit his chest playfully and then hugged his neck. "I'll let you. I promise!"

* B *

"How bad is it, doctor?" Mira asked.

"Three fingers and a knuckle. Unfortunately, *signor*, your hand will need to be in this cast for eight weeks."

Mira looked at him alarmed. "How did you do this?"

"I closed it in a car door," he smiled.

The doctor looked up in disbelief. He lowered his gaze and continued to wrap Giovanni's hand. Mira felt so tired, and emotionally drained. Worst of all her breasts were engorged and pained her. The doctor finished and Giovanni's hand was fitted with a glove. When he left the room she stared at her husband.

"It's been a helluva day hasn't it?" she said.

"Yes. Are you okay?" he asked.

"I am now." She walked over and touched him. "Your father didn't kill my mother. Even if what you believe is true and he considered it the contract was never carried out. My mother lived a very complicated, sad life, but it was her life. There is nothing in the past between us, Giovanni, only our own insecurities and mistakes. We're married. It's a partnership and it can't survive this life without trust. I want to trust you again. I want you to trust me. Tell me you want the same thing?"

511

"I do. I'll never let you down again. I swear it," he kissed her hand. "On my life."

She smiled. She kissed his brow. "Let's go home, sweetheart. Our children need us."

* B *

The family was awake when they arrived. Everyone had gathered inside of the parlor. Mira held Giovanni's good hand as she walked in with him. Rocco and Zia looked up first. Catalina held a sleeping Eve in her arms. Apparently her daughter had risen in the night. Rosetta and Cecilia sat next to each other and all of the men who weren't on patrol were inside waiting.

"I need to say something," Mira said. She looked at Giovanni and then to her sister. She smiled at the family. "I'm sorry. Tonight shouldn't have happened. Zia, I shouldn't have asked you to lie for me. Any of you," Mira looked to Catalina and the other girls. She then turned her gaze to Leo, David, and lastly Renaldo. "I drew a gun tonight and I'm ashamed of my actions. I won't ever turn a gun on any member of this family again." She looked to Marietta. Her sister picked up on her cue.

"Renaldo," Marietta said. "I'm sorry for hitting you."

He nodded to her.

Mira smiled. "It's over. Our time in Sicily is over." Mira hugged Giovanni. "We're going home."

Everyone clapped. Mira turned her chin up and kissed Giovanni. He put his arm around her shoulders. "So get packed and be ready. Good night."

Catalina walked over and gave her a sleeping Eve.

Cecilia came over and gave her the baby monitor. Mira said her goodnights to everyone and passed her daughter to her husband before they climed the stairs.

"How was that?" she whispered to Giovanni.

He chuckled. "You did fine."

Later –

Giovanni opened his eyes. The pain medicine had worn off. The discomfort extended up his arm. There was little night left to them for sleep. He looked over to his sleeping wife. The bed they shared

512

in the nursery was smaller than their own. But he didn't mind. Her warm body was pressed against his. It felt as if he hadn't held her in an eternity. Giovanni stared up at the ceiling. He cast the cover aside and eased from the bed, careful not to hit his hand. He had joined her in nothing but his boxers. He found his pants and pulled them on.

After spending weeks without sleep he thought tonight he'd crash and possibly never wake up. But he was restless with excitement, relief, and happiness. He had his girl back. And he couldn't keep from reflecting on how close he came to driving her away.

Giovanni approached the crib. Both of his boys slept. The sight of the boys filled him with pride. Giovanni leaned on the crib. He was careful with his right hand that was now useless. He stared at his boys.

"What are you doing?" Mira groaned awake.

He glanced back. "Go back to sleep."

She sat up and stared at him. She smiled. "They are cute aren't they?"

He nodded. "Was Eve this small?" he asked

"She was six pounds when she was born. A little bigger than them." Mira left the bed. She wore just a shirt and her panties. She walked over to the crib and rubbed his back. "She didn't sleep a lot. I remember going days with only two hours of sleep."

"Why is your shirt in the crib?" Giovanni frowned.

"Zia," Mira whispered. "She told me to lay my shirt down for the twins to sleep on. She said my scent would soothe them. Make them sleep longer. It works."

Giovanni nodded. He glanced over to Mira and she looked at him. "What is it, Bella? Why are you looking at me like that?"

"A shave, you need one. I hate when you grow the beard." She touched his cheek.

"Will you shave me?" he asked.

"Yes. Go in our room. Wait for me."

He kissed her brow and did as she told him. He entered the quiet hall. He had sent Leo away from his post. The days of him fearing Bella couldn't take care of herself were now over. His wife proved to be quite resourceful.

In his room he inhaled and exhaled. True to her word she came in shortly after. "Are the men in trouble?" she asked.

"For what?" he frowned.

She took his hand and walked him into the bathroom. "For me getting out of here against your orders. I feel really bad about

Renaldo. And the gun, I hate I pulled it on the men. I'm embarrassed."

"You apologized to them. It made all the difference," Giovanni chuckled. "We all learned a lesson from your great escape, Bella. No, they aren't in trouble. But I admit I've underestimated my wife one too many times. I won't make that mistake again."

"Sit." She gestured to the closed *toilette* lid. He sat down obediently.

"Your father doesn't have much longer. You do realize that, Bella? Don't you?"

"Yes," she answered softly.

"He told me he put you in his will." Giovanni said.

"I know. He told me too," Mira said. She tilted his chin and began to lather his jaw with the shaving cream brush. He picked up the straight razor and ran it under a cool tap.

"And what did you tell him?" Giovanni asked. He peeked at her with one eye closed. She avoided looking into his eyes. Instead she focused on running the blade smoothly up his jawline.

"That I don't want his money. I told him my children are Battaglia. They have their legacy." She looked over at him. "I do want to pay my respects, when... he dies. Can you arrange it?"

"Yes."

She smoothly slid the razor up over his jaw and dropped globs of suds and hair into the sink. Giovanni loved her touch.

"Can I ask you a question?" Giovanni opened his eyes. Mira looked down at him with her wide expressive brown orbs glistening. He smiled up at her.

"Yes?" she said.

"How long before we can have sex?" he ran his left hand along her thigh.

She chuckled. "Six weeks, and I'm not ready. My body... I need to lose some weight."

"Nonsense. I like your weight," he grinned.

"Well say what you want but I plan to start working out immediately." She informed him. "And then I'll feel sexy enough to spread my legs."

"I can't wait." He pulled her down to his lap. "I have been so afraid, for you, Bella. You had a stroke, like your mother when she gave birth to you," Giovanni said. "I didn't know if you would wake up. And then... I had to wonder if I could ever get my wife back. Get us back on track."

"So you closed my company? Nice." She half-joked.

"Your love keeps me grounded and the doors to your company open," he teased.

She brushed her nose over his. "Dominic said I needed to learn my purpose, my place in this family. To keep us all safe. I know what my mother went through, what your mother went through. I won't suffer their fate. Because we won't ever be them."

"I agree." Giovanni said.

"Then you agree to open my company back up?" she asked.

"Our company," he grinned.

She shook her head smiling. She rose from his lap and he smacked her on the ass. She went to the sink and washed her hands. He found that curious since she hadn't finished his shave. When she looked at him he saw something in her eyes, something akin to desire. And then she returned to him on her knees.

Mira ran his zipper down. From that action alone his cock bulked. She looked up at him and smiled. She eased it out into her hand and fisted it at the root. She stroked and brought his erection forth with a tightening grip. Giovanni's head dropped back.

Mira took him down her throat, and in response his fingers dug into her scalp, relaxed, scraped, and threaded through her hair to get a good grip. She sank forward on his cock and drew back sucking him hard with her tongue flat and rolling up and down on the thick center vein of his dick. Over and over she stroked her tongue along his dick and she loved the hard yet satiny feel of raw muscle in her mouth.

She released his cock from her mouth and he gasped. But she was far from done. Determined to take him to the brink and force him over she jacked her hands up and down with hard strokes. Her husband groaned and the veins thickened in his neck as his jaw went rigid tight. She kept going with an increase and decrease in pressure with every long pull. And soon his will collapsed. He ejaculated a long stream of essence that created their babies and filled her happiness.

Mira smiled.

Mira didn't stop. She worked her hand and loved him down until he lost the battle and was hers.

22.

Lorenzo closed he door on a sleeping Marietta. He buttoned his shirt as he made his way down the hall. The only noise he heard was from the direction of the kitchen. He turned down the opposite hall. He opened the door to Giovanni's office. His cousin was seated behind the desk. Eve was on the floor in her night jumper. She blinked up at him and then continued to play with her bear. He recognized the kid had been without her pacifier lately.

"Morning," Lorenzo said.

Giovanni gestured for him to enter. Lorenzo picked up Eve and came over to the chair. He sat with her on his lap. Eve looked at him with a curious stare. He couldn't wait to have a baby of his own. He tickled her and kissed her until she giggled with delight. Eve scooted off of Lorenzo's lap and walked around the desk to her father. Lorenzo watched as he put her on his desk and kissed her face. He looked like a father now, not the ferocious madman he unleashed last night.

"I take it you and the *Donna* are well?" Lorenzo asked.

"We're getting there," Giovanni smiled.

"About last night. I had a long talk with Marietta. She understands that it can't happen again," Lorenzo said. "She apologized. Did you notice?"

"I noticed. My wife and I understand each other. Let's drop it. The secret is exposed and so is Mancini. There is nothing to worry about any longer." Giovanni blew kisses against Eve's neck and the toddler kicked her feet with celebration. The phone rang. Giovanni switched it to speakerphone. *"Pronto?"* he answered.

"It's Armando," a voice replied.

"What is it?" Giovanni asked. He glanced up to Lorenzo.

"You should tell your wife that my... our father died last night," Armando said. Giovanni's brows lowered. He looked to the phone.

"Condolences." Giovanni said.

"We will bury him tomorrow. The family doesn't know about the women. I want my father buried in peace with respect."

"Of course. We can be discreet when we pay ours. My wife has told me she wants to attend," Giovanni said. "May I suggest she and her sister be witness to the burial without disturbing your family."

Armando sighed. "Papa would want them there, if they wish it. Yes. That will work instead."

"My wife tells me that your father wanted... decided to include her in his will?"

Armando didn't respond.

"There is no good blood between us. I am not sure how I feel we can settle the matter of you attempting to poison my wife."

"I never gave that order," Armando replied.

"Of course you didn't. Needless to say I see no reason for us to do anything to undue the truce we've shared for the past thirty years. I have a proposal."

"I'm listening," Armando said.

"We sever ties. I will have Mira sign over whatever has been willed to her. In return you will stay away from my wife and we will continue to respect boundaries. Far as you are concerned she is not your sister, blood, *famiglia*."

"And Marietta? Will she do the same?" Armando asked.

Giovanni looked at Lorenzo.

"No," Lorenzo spoke up.

Giovanni frowned.

"Marietta is owed, what she is owed. And I intend to make sure she has it," Lorenzo told them both.

"Then that changes everything," Armando replied. He hung up.

"Why are you refusing?" Giovanni asked.

"Why did you agree to surrender what is possibly a fortune?" Lorenzo asked. "My wife has gotten the shit end of this from the beginning. I mean no disrespect, Gio, but this is her legacy. And that slimy bastard owes her this and more."

"Her legacy is the one you and she create, Lorenzo." Giovanni reminded him.

"Whatever is left to Marietta she will claim. And Armando Mancini better be wise to stay out of my way."

"But that's the point, Lorenzo. He isn't going to stay out of your way or mine if we are in bed with his business affiars."

Lorenzo shrugged. He didn't give a shit about having to deal with the Mancinis. What he cared about was Marietta and getting her justice.

"If I insist you will sign it over. To sever the tie between our families?" Giovanni asked.

"The last time I did as you wished against my wife's interests it ended badly. Do we travel this road again, Gio? You have it all. Mottola's men now bow at your feet. The clan bosses are celebrating your victory of stopping the investigation into our business deals. The entire region is yours. The blow we strike against the *'Ndrangheta* will be felt through the triangle. And I will do whatever it takes to make sure you remain the *capo di tutti capi*. Give me this. For my wife. For my family. For my own legacy."

"You think Armando will step aside and hand over three hundred years of wealth to you?" Giovanni chuckled.

"Who knows what the future brings. And who says he has to step aside. I can step on him to get what is owed to Marietta." Lorenzo sighed. "I have another request."

"I'm listening," Giovanni said. He brought Eve down from the desk to his lap.

"I want to send Renaldo to Chicago. America."

"Why?" Giovanni frowned.

"Marietta. The man who raised her was as evil as Micheli Esposito, Dominic's father. I owe her a wedding present," Lorenzo said. "I'd go personally but…"

"No. I need you here. Send Renaldo. Keep it clean."

Lorenzo smirked. "*Grazie.*"

"I am confused about one thing," Givoanni said. "Bella says that Patri never gave the okay to put a contract out on her mother. Why did Rocco tell us he did?"

"We should ask him. Rocco has been out of the family for years. Maybe he misunderstood the facts."

Giovanni pondered it bit. "I want it clarified."

* B *

Marietta knocked lightly on the door. She eased the door open. Cecilia was in with Mira. She fed one of the babies and Mira fed the other. "Come in."

"Morning," Marietta said.

"How did you sleep?" Mira asked with concern.

Marietta knew how she looked. Her eyes were nearly swollen shut. She hadn't even bothered to brush her teeth or comb her hair. She rolled out of bed and came to the nursery first. To her surprise

518

Mira looked fresh and lovely. She wore a housedress for the tropics that outlined her full figure and deflating belly.

"Marietta?" Mira said.

"Huh? Oh… yeah, I just wanted to check in with you. Some night huh?" she asked.

Mira stood and put her baby on her shoulder. She soothed his back encouraging him to burp. "Why don't you shower, and after I get the boys fed we share a cup of coffee together?"

"Yeah, yeah okay." she smiled. She turned and Catalina appeared in the door. She walked in the room.

"What happened last night? My God it was chaos in here. We were damn near jailed. And then you and Giovanni walk in the door holding hands? Kissing?"

"I'll explain it to you. I promise." Mira smiled. "It's a long story. Right?" she said to Marietta.

"Yeah. A long story."

"Where is Rosetta?" Mira asked.

"In her room I suppose." Catalina replied.

Mira nodded. "I need to pay her a visit."

* B *

Lorenzo found Marietta in the room changing. She had freshly showered. Her hair was combed back into a single braid. When she turned she looked up at him and smiled. "Hi, baby."

"Sorry I left so early." He walked over and stopped her from fastening her pants. "Come here. I want to talk to you."

"Hey, stop pulling on me." She laughed. "Seriously, Lo, I can't. I told Mira I would meet her downstairs for coffee."

Lorenzo chuckled. He picked her up and carried her to bed. And he understood why she misread his intentions. Typically he seized any moment or reason to undress her and make love to her. He never tired of her physically.

"I only want to talk," he said. He sat her down on the bed. He sat next to her. "Your brother called."

"Brother?" Marietta frowned. "I don't want to see him or that—"

"Your father's dead," Lorenzo said. "I'm sorry, *cara*. Truly sorry. He's dead."

"But we just saw him," Marietta said.

"He was a sick man." Lorenzo took her hand and kissed it.

"They will bury him tomorrow. Armando has agreed to give you permission to pay respects as long as we keep our distance."

"I don't need his permission!" Marietta stood. She crossed her arms. "He was my father too. I can go to the damn funeral and sit in the front row if I want!"

"Marie... you can't and you won't," Lorenzo said firmly.

"I don't care! I wished he was dead the moment I saw him. The moment I knew the truth. I hope he suffered. I... I don't care!" She put her hands to her hips. "I don't care."

Lorenzo stood and drew her into his arms. He held her. Protected her with his embrace while she cried. "We'll pay our respects."

She hugged him. "He was a horrible man."

"We all are. Remember?"

She looked up at him and he smiled.

"No. You aren't. Stop saying that. You would never do what he did to my mother."

"Agreed. I could never hurt anyone I love," Lorenzo said.

"Can we leave Sicily? I want to go and I want to stay gone. For good," she said. "Maybe we can go back to Bellagio. Or find us a place in Milano?"

"I promise. We'll leave." Lorenzo nodded.

She hugged him once more. "I can't wait."

* B *

"*Donna?*" Cecilia said.

Mira looked up from changing Eve's diaper. "Yes?"

"There's something you should know."

The tone Cecilia used gave her pause. "What is it? Is it the boys?"

"It's Rosetta, ah, I wanted to tell you that I heard her," Cecilia said.

"Heard her do what?" Mira asked.

"She called Dominic and told him that you and *Signora* Marietta brought Gemma here. That is how Giovanni knew to return home. I heard her tell him everything."

Mira figured it was Rosetta. She had intended to dig into the matter deeper. Now she had proof. "Thanks for telling me, Cecilia."

"There's more. I am sorry, I don't want to speak ill against any member of the Battaglia family." Cecilia cast her gaze away. "The wedding, my fall? I was pushed. By Rosetta. She threatened me. She wanted to be the one to be close to you and Eve. To travel with you on your honeymoon to Capri. I let the incident go because I didn't want trouble. But now I see her, she sneaks into Catalina's room, tries on her dresses and things. She follows Dominic around the house and tells him the private conversations she eavesdrops on. I've seen all of this."

"Cecilia! You should have come to me." Mira stepped to the young woman. She took her hands. "My God you could have been killed. I am so sorry you felt the need to hide this. But I promise you no one in this family will ever hurt you again." She pulled her into her arms and hugged her. "I'm so sorry."

* B *

Mira sat with Eve on her lap. She cradled her daughter to her breast. She couldn't shed another tear for Marsuvio Mancini. To her the darkness was gone. She glanced over to Zia, and Catalina. They had joined because of her request. There was no need for any secrets. "When is the funeral?"

"Tomorrow." Giovanni said.

Mira nodded. "We should send flowers. It's what's done? Right?"

Giovanni stared at her. They all stared at her expecting something more. She shifted Eve on her lap. "After we pay respects I want to go home. Back to Sorrento."

"Agreed," Giovanni smiled.

"Mama?" Eve patted her breast. "Me too," Eve said.

Everyone laughed. She squeezed Eve. She looked to her husband who winked. The darkness was gone. She could see nothing but their future and it was full of promise ahead.

* B *

Mira knocked twice. The day was filled with packing. Everyone at Villa Mare Blu began to prepare for his or her return home. After the funeral they'd fly out. She was at Rosetta's door. When she opened it the young girl was running around gathering her things. She glanced back. "Ciao, *Donna!* I'm so excited. I can't wait to see *Fabiana's.*"

521

Mira closed the door. "You won't be coming with us," she said.

Rosetta paused. "Huh? I don't understand."

"I've called your father. He's coming to pick you up and take you back to Palermo."

"Why?" Rosetta gasped.

Mira walked in the room. She crossed her arms. "I know you called Dominic and told him to tell Giovanni about my plans. After I specifically told you how important it was to stand with me."

"I... no... I only did it because I was afraid."

"No." Mira smiled. "You did it to score points with Dominic. I've watched you play games around this house. Keep little fires going. I had hoped you would mature and focus on being part of this family. And now I learn that you aren't only selfish and spoiled but dangerous. I should tell Giovanni about what you did to Cecilia."

"No Donna! It was an accident."

"Hush now! You and I both know it wasn't. And to think I trusted you with Eve. I am so disappointed in you Rosetta."

"Please," Rosetta rushed to her. "Please don't send me away. Please!"

Mira shook her head and pushed her off her. "I don't want anyone in this family I can't trust. And until I feel otherwise about you, don't come to Melanzana without permission from me."

"But you said last night that you were wrong to make Zia lie. That you should have never asked any of us to lie." Rosetta reasoned. "It's Cecilia word against mine. I only called Dominic because I was worried for you."

"I'm your *Donna*. What I say and what I do are two different things entirely." Mira imformed her.

"No. You can't send me home to Papa! I'll die!" Rosetta wept.

"He'll be here to pick you up. Save your false tears for him. You better hurry and finish packing." Mira said.

She walked out to Rosetta's screaming wails.

* B *

Rocco shuffled with his cup to the table. Giovanni watched his uncle. For years his uncle was at his fathers' side. Until one day he was banished to the vineyard. No one knew the true story. But from what he did know Rocco was once as ruthless and conniving as Tomosino and Marsuvio. Maybe he still was.

"Zio?" Giovanni walked in.

"I see you staring, Gio. I was waiting for you to join me," Rocco exhaled. "I'm sorry I wasn't here last night to stop the women. I was in Bagheria visiting my brother. I had no idea Zia would pull a stunt like this. I've spoken with her. It won't happen again."

"It's done. Let's not rehash it."

"Sit. It's time we talk." Rocco sipped from his cup.

"So you know I wanted to talk." Giovanni asked. He walked over and pulled out a chair.

"I thought you might, when I heard this morning that you paid a visit to Mancini."

"He's dead," Giovanni replied.

"I know," Rocco replied.

Giovanni sighed. "You told me that Patri put a contract on Mira's mother's life. We now know that it's not true. Why did you lie to me?"

Rocco set his mug down. "Your father kept trying to reason with Mancini. Bargain with the Five Dons. Flavio and I knew something more decisive needed to happen. At the time I served as your father's left hand. He gave me power neded to do the difficult things. As you do with Lorenzo," Rocco glanced over to Giovanni and held his stare. "When Capriccio shared Mancini's weakness, he asked for permission to kill the black whore that made his boss so weak. Flavio didn't agree to it. At first. But I…" Rocco looked up. "I did."

"You?" Giovanni said.

Rocco picked up his cup and sipped. He set it down on the saucer. "Tomosino discussed it with Mancini's father. They agreed that killing a mother and child was disgraceful. Neither would approve of it. But I had aleady set it in motion. Tomosino was advised. If the kill order had happened and Mancini discovered the truth, Tomosino's brotherhood with Mancini would have been over. Apparently that friendship meant more to him than me, his own brother. He humiliated me for it. Put me on my knees in front of Cappriccio and the other men. One of many times he took pleasure in breaking me. As you do with Lorenzo," Rocco said.

"Not true." Giovanni scowled.

"It is true son. Cappricio was sent back to America with nothing more than a mission to report on Mancini's affairs. How the poor woman died is not something I know. But my role in it I had to conceal. I love Mira. I was shocked and sick over learning she is the long lost daughter of Marsuvio. That she is the baby I almost had murdered," Rocco sighed. "My final punishment was a more public shaming. My brother banished me to be a farmer. Stripping me of my rank. He let Flavio's role in the matter pass and I was the only one punished for conspiring to go against his wishes." Rocco chuckled. "I didn't want to clear Tomosino's name. But I knew if you pursued this somehow the truth would surface." Rocco looked up at him. "I warned you against being rash. Acting out without cause. Betraying *omerta*. I warn you of these things because I was the one foolish enough to do these things."

Giovanni stroked his jaw. "I don't really know you, do I Rocco?"

Rocco shrugged. "No son, you don't."

"Mira doesn't have to know you in any way other than as Zio Rocco. *Capice?*"

Rocco picked up Giovanni's hand and kissed his ring. "*Capice.*"

The Next Day –

From a distance Carmella watched them. Mirabella Battaglia stood next to Marietta. The ceremonial burial service at the gravesite was now over. The Battaglias had kept a respectful distance during the funeral. The *Donna,* however, was hard to miss. She wore a slimming black skirt with a black silk blouse. Carmella marveled at how nicely polished and trim her figure looked from afar after delivering twins. Her large oval shaped sunglasses covered her eyes. Her sister wore a veil over her face. To everyone else their presence was easily explained by their husbands' presence. Afterall it was a matter of respect that the Battaglias attend.

The Mancini family left the grave first. Two of the women in the family were on the arms of Armando to comfort him. Of course Armando showed no emotion. Carmella hadn't seen him shed a tear since they carried his father out the front door. And when she tried to be supportive he sent her away.

There was nothing left between them. She accepted that fact now. She glanced up once more to see the Battaglia wives, Marietta and Mirabella, walk hand in hand to the open grave. They both held long stem blue roses. Carmella assumed they had come from Eve's garden. They said something she couldn't hear and then tossed in the roses in for their father. Carmella had seen enough. She turned and walked away. She'd collect her things and leave Sicily. Maybe go to Greece, or Spain. Anywhere.

She walked through the prickly tall grass toward her car. If she had been paying attention she would have seen the man standing in the shadows of leaving mourners watching her. She didn't. Numb to everything in her life she opened the door and got inside.

The passenger door opened. Carlo eased in to the passenger seat.

"What are you doing? Why are you in my car?" Carmella gasped.

Carlo dropped the seat back and made himself comfortable.

"Carlo? I asked you a question. Why are you in my car?" she repeated.

Carlo cut her a sideways look. "Drive."

"No."

He stared at her.

With a shaky hand she turned over the ignition and drove out of the graveyard.

* B *

Mira and Giovanni arrived in their own car. Her sister and Lorenzo had decided to drive themselves to the funeral. As they travelled out of the graveyard they headed for the airport. The family was there waiting.

"Are you okay, Bella," he asked.

"I'm fine," she said. She kept her sunglasses on to cover her tears. Why she cried for a father she never knew was beyond her, especially a man as despicable as Marsuvio Mancini. She should hate him for what he'd done to her mother. She didn't.

"Giovanni?"

"Yes," he said.

"Do you think it's possible for Marietta and me to get to know Armando?" she asked. She glanced over to him. "In a matter of weeks I've learned I have a brother and sister. It seems strange to leave it there."

"There's something you should know," Giovanni began. "Armando isn't interested in a relationship with you, Bella. He paid Carmella to try to poison you."

"Poison me?" Mira double blinked. She couldn't fathom that Carmella had been fixing their food and trying to poison her.

"Yes. Carmella was stopped. Armando denies it, but we are clear that it was him." He kept his focus on the road as he spoke.

"It's not safe for you to trust him, or reach out to him. Do you understand?"

"Completely. I guess he's like his father." Mira said. A numbing feeling of bleakness went though her.

"We men are all like our fathers, unfortunately," Giovanni said.

Mira extended her hand and placed it over his leg. She watched the last of Sicily pass by her window. And she felt nothing.

* B *

"You okay, Marie?" Lorenzo asked.

"I guess," she removed her hat and tossed it to the back seat. They were following Mira and Giovanni out of the graveyard. "I didn't feel anything. He was a stranger to me."

"For the best." Lorenzo nodded. "After hearing what he did to your mother it's understandable."

"Yeah," Marietta turned her gaze toward the window and blinked away her tears. Part of her did feel something. She just didn't know what to name the emotion. Until she did she wouldn't discuss it.

"There's something you should know." Lorenzo said. "I told Giovanni that we would keep the inheritance. It's your money, and property."

"I don't want anything from him," Marietta said.

"What abour our children? We need to think of our future, Marie. Their legacy." Lorenzo said.

Marietta closed her eyes. He'd been mentioning children more and more. The man wasn't even aware she was on birth control pills. She hadn't found the right moment to tell him. "Can we not discuss it now?" she asked.

"I'm your husband. A decision like this is mine to make. I've made it."

Marietta frowned. She glanced over at him. "Why? Why do you want the money?"

Lorenzo smirked and said nothing. She rolled her eyes away. "I don't want anything to do with him. Ever."

EPILOGUE

Six Weeks Later –

"Wait up!" Marietta panted. She stopped and bent over with her hands gripping her knees she tried to catch a breath. Her hands were pressed to her knees. They'd run for two miles and Mira was ahead of her. She had no choice but to push onward.

Sorrento at the end of summer had beautiful clear skies and nicely warm weather. Marietta and her sister ran the path out from behind Melanzana that circled to the east side of *Villa Rosso*. Mira wore her hair in a ponytail that swayed and reached just to the bottom of her neck. She made jogging look easy. With the burn of the run achingly strong at the back of her thighs, Marietta raced ahead with unwavering determination. She had to squint whenever the sun's glare became too much.

She caught up to find Mira pacing. She cooled down as she waited for her.

"What the hell man? It's a jog not a sprint!" Marietta wheezed.

Mira swung her arms left and right twisting the top of her torso at the waist. "You used to out run me, now look at you," she chuckled.

"Whatever, wonder woman." Marietta smiled. As she gulped down the cool air into her lungs she let her gaze wash over Mira from head to toe. The baby weight had peeled from her middle section. She had some left in her breasts, hips and ass. Everything looked to be tucked into the right place. "You look good, girl."

Mira looked down at herself. She smiled. "Thanks to you. Fastest weight loss diet of my life. I'd cut off my right arm for a cheeseburger though."

Marietta chuckled. She looked at her watch. "We got to get you ready. Lorenzo said they'd be back before dinner."

Mira nodded. She and Marietta started walking toward the house. "So what have you decided?" Mira asked. "About my offer."

It was the question Marietta had hoped to avoid. She knew what her husband wanted. But she'd had other desires. She looked over to Mira. "I love my life. Who knew I'd like living here in Melanzana—with your clan."

Mira chuckled. "Then join my clan. Work with Catalina to get *Fabiana's* going strong. In a few months I will need you both to deal with expansion. I'm thinking of closing New York and moving that office to Paris."

"I'm not a fashion designer, Mira," Marietta sighed.

"But you're talented. You ran your own business."

"Yep, ran it into the ground," she half joked.

"Be serious. The sky is the limit. We can do something more commercial. Who knows?" Mira said.

"It feels weird. Working for a company named after my husband's dead girlfriend." Marietta admitted. She peeked over at Mira to see if she offended her.

Mira waved off the comment. "That's not your reason for holding back. What is it?"

"I'm not holding back," she chuckled. "My husband wants his own dynasty. We have to meet with Armando next week. He's still negotiating with the man. He wants me to take the money, the property, all of it."

"And?" Mira asked.

"You don't want to keep it?" Marietta asked.

"Giovanni and I already discussed it. We don't need the Mancini fortune. The only reason I haven't signed it over is because of this feud between my husband and Armando." Mira panted. "I think Lorenzo is influencing Giovanni on this. They might want to take over control of Mancini's interests. I'm not sure how I feel about that."

"He's our brother," Marietta said. "We should acknowledge it."

Mira stopped. Marietta looked back. "Well he is," Marietta shrugged.

"He doesn't see it that way, Marietta." Mira reminded her. "He did try to poison me."

"Yeah. There's that. But that was before he met us, and he feels really remorseful for it." Marietta reasoned.

"And how would you know how he feels?" Mira asked.

Marietta looked away. Mira stepped to her. "Have you been in contact with Armando Mancini?"

"He wants to get to know me. We're the only siblings he's got. I know how that feels," Marietta said. "To be alone in the world."

"Absolutely not. It won't work. It can't work. And you should never have discussions with him behind Lorenzo's back. It's dangerous."

"It will work if you talk to your husband. Ask Giovanni to let us try. If we both keep our inheritance then Armando and us will have to work together. Get to know each other."

"I stand with my husband, Marietta," Mira said. "It's not a battle I want to fight."

"Well Lorenzo wants the inheritance because of greed."

"What do you want?" Mira asked.

"I want to know my brother the same way I got to know you. I want a family."

Mira smiled. She dropped her arm around Mira's shoulder. "When are you going to see it, Marietta? You already have one."

She hugged her. Marietta hugged her tightly. Even Mira's sweat smelled sweet. Marietta shook her head and released her. "Enough talk. Let's do your hair. Everything is ready for you tonight."

Mira laughed. She started to jog back and Marietta fell in step at her side. They ran silently for a moment. "Hey, can I ask you a question?" Mira asked.

"Sure," Marietta panted.

"Do you strip and dance for Lorenzo?"

Marietta stopped with a burst of laughter. She laughed so hard she dropped to her hands and knees. She looked up grinning. "Why did you ask me that?"

"I wasn't invading your privacy. I swear. But..." Mira chewed on her lips. "The other day I was on your hall and I passed your room. The music was playing. I couldn't help but be curious from the sounds of that music."

Marietta chuckled. "When my husband is agitated it helps him unwind. You want some lessons?"

"Me? No! I just, its just you two are... you're perfect for each other," Mira said.

"Thank you, Queen B."

Mira paused. "On second thought. If you could teach me a few moves, I wouldn't mind." She then started to jog away.

"Sure! That's what sisters are for!" Marietta yelled after her. She got up, dusted her hands and tried to catch up.

* B *

Lorenzo reclined in the chair. His office was on the same hall as Giovanni's. He expected his cousin to return that afternoon. He didn't feel good about the prison visit Giovanni insisted upon making. Why pay Santo any kind of visit? Why show him any mercy?

Carlo knocked on his door and entered.

"I thought you'd be in here," said Carlo.

"Giovanni isn't back yet," Lorenzo grumbled. Carlo closed the door. He chose the seat on the sofa instead of the one in front of his desk.

"It's a good thing. We convicted Santo with no proof. If there is a chance that he didn't betray us, he deserves the benefit of *famiglia* protection," Carlo said.

Lorenzo grimaced. "He deserves shit."

Carlo shook his head. "I've done everything you asked, Lo. Dr. Buhari? I gutted him after Armando Mancini's men roughed him up. Killed the two-faced bastard. Your orders. And Carmella, I got rid of her so Giovanni wouldn't have to consider doing it himself." Carlo shook his head. "I've done everything you wanted. Now it's time for you and I to stand down. Let Giovanni lead us."

"I'm only helping him," Lorenzo said. "Gio was too distracted to deal with those two. Dominic's too weak. That's why I'm his left hand. That's why I do what is necessary, before he conceives it. And I tell you Santo isn't to be trusted."

Carlo stared at him. "It's not your call, Lo."

"Beh!" Lorenzo shot his hand up in a dismissive manner. "Renaldo returned a week ago." Lorenzo smiled. He removed the folder. He opened it and pulled out the images. A dead Octavio Leone was on each photo. "My wife's nightmares are over."

"You plan to tell her?" Carlo asked.

"No. Not unless she mentions the bastard. Or maybe I'll save it for her birthday," he chuckled.

"How is she?" Carlo asked.

Lorenzo reclined in his chair. "Marietta is happy. She's adjusting. Right now her priority is getting pregnant."

"Pregnant?" Carlo asked.

"Yes. Of course, we want kids. Why do you say it like that?" Lorenzo snapped.

Carlo shrugged. "No reason. Just didn't know you wanted a kid this soon. I'll go make a few pickups. I'll... uh, come back later this evening to see Gio. *Ciao.*" He stood. He nodded to Lorenzo and walked out. Lorenzo rocked back in his chair. He frowned at the tone Carlo used in his voice. His friend seemed to be unsettled. Maybe he should find a woman and settle down.

Outside in the hall Carlo started to walk away. And then he saw her. She wore a runner's suit, the pants tight as skin on her shapely legs. The white shirt she wore was open. A ring of sweat was around the collar. She'd been excercising he supposed. Her ample breasts and trim waist drew his eyes. She drank down a cool drink in a plastic bottle.

His gaze travelled up to hers. Marietta stopped and lowered the bottle. He'd kept his promise. He stayed away. This was the first he had seen of her in weeks.

Carlo approached her.

"Hi," she said.

"*Ciao,*" he said and started to walk past her.

She blocked him. "Carlo, we can be friends can't we?" she asked.

He looked down at her. "Sure. Friends. Congratulations."

"For what?" Marietta asked.

"Lorenzo told me you are trying to have a baby," Carlo said. He studied her reaction. Marietta lowered her gaze. She mumbled something he didn't quite hear. He lifted his chin. "You'd make a good mother, *cara*. The kid woud be tough like you," he smiled.

She grinned at him. "Thanks, Carlo."

"See you later," he said.

She stepped aside. He forced himself to continue without looking back.

Marietta watched Carlo go. She hated the awkwardness between them. She feared it even more when he was kind. What if Lorenzo picked up on how Carlo avoided her, or the way he stared at her? She wiped her hand back over her brow. And a baby? She and Lorenzo needed to talk. She went to her husband's office. When she opened his door she found him sitting behind his desk.

"Hi, baby," she said.

Lorenzo looked up. "Hello, beautiful."

"Working still?" she asked.

"Just started," he said.

Marietta came inside. "I was about to shower. Wanted to know if you wanted to watch?" she sipped her water. Lorenzo chuckled. Marietta smiled. "I think I will accept Mira's offer and start to work with Catalina at *Fabiana's*."

"You sure? You had your concerns," Lorenzo said.

"I want to work with my sister, and my husband. Who says I can't do both." Marietta smiled.

Lorenzo pushed back from his desk. He walked around and sat on the front of it. "I will handle Mancini and our affairs. You trust me right?"

"With my life," she walked over to him and he opened his arms to hug her. She was pulled in between his legs. He gripped her ass.

"I want children, Marie," Lorenzo said.

Marietta closed her eyes, "I know you do. But we should wait, Lorenzo. Get things settled between us first."

"When? When will you be ready?" Lorenzo asked.

Marietta sighed, "I don't know."

He lifted her chin from his chest so he could look into her eyes. "Maybe I should join you in that shower to convince you?"

Marietta grinned. "A little practice may help."

Lorenzo stood. He grabbed her and threw her over his shoulder. Marietta laughed. She grinned as he carried her out of his office.

* B *

Santo was brought into the private room after an hour of waiting. Giovanni looked up at his childhood friend and saw the battle scars of a prison beating swollen on his face and neck. Giovanni stood and greeted Santo with a brotherly hug. "Sit," he told him.

Santo did so in silence. Dominic stood off in the corner. No one spoke. Giovanni smoothed his hand across the surface of the table. "You will be moved. Protetcted." Giovanni's gaze lifted. "It troubles me that it has taken this long to arrange it."

Santo stared at him.

"I've spoken with the attorneys. They have a deal on the table for the prosecutors. Because of your testimony you will be granted early release. In a few weeks you will be a free man again," Giovanni advised.

"I testify and I'm a marked man," Santo said. "No one will ever take me serious again, Gio."

"It's a sacrifice I want you to make. For the greater good," Giovanni smiled.

"Can I ask you why, Gio? Why is it you are so blind to Lorenzo?" Santo asked. He glanced to Dominic. "You know I didn't betray you. Can you say that Lorenzo is more trustworthy than me?"

"Lorenzo is my blood. I don't have to say anything about his loyalties."

Santo nodded. "True. But even after my release I can never start my own clan with this on my reputation. Why am I even needed to testify? Mottola hung himself in his cell." Santo looked up. "Or at least that is what the authorities want the press to believe."

"It's the way things are done. The 'Ndrangheta are on trial, as are the members of Mottola's clan. You are a key witness. You will only testify regarding our business deals. Dominic and the attorneys will help you." Giovanni leaned forward. He lowered his voice. "Nothing regarding la famiglia will ever part your lips. Do we understand each other?"

"Sí," he nodded. "Perfectly."

Giovanni stood. He walked around the table and patted Santo on the shoulder. He glanced to Dominic and nodded he was done. "Be well. See me again when you are free."

"Grazie," Santo said through clenched teeth.

Santo was escorted to his cell. Giovanni had kept his word. He had him moved. But the trap set by Lorenzo still burned Santo's gut. If he did nothing, he'd make sure that Lorenzo was made to pay.

"Santo! You have a visitor!" The guard announced.

Santo turned in his cell. Had Giovanni forgotten something? Was it his attorneys visiting so soon after his boss? He nodded and walked out of his cell. The guard again clamped down handcuffs on his wrists and forced him to walk out into the hall. When he turned the corner to the private room he stopped in surprise.

"Isabella? What are you doing here?"

She smiled sweetly. Santo was unchained. Isabella walked over to him. "How are you, Santo?" she took his face in her hands. "What happed to you? Did they attack you?"

"I'm fine," he said. Her sweet floral scent filled his nostrils. He hugged her and she was soft and feminine. Isabella was only someone he briefly met. She made a few proposals to him for Giovanni. But he hadn't truly had a chance to present them. Her visit was kind, and a bit strange considering their unfamiliar history.

"Why are you here?" he asked.

"You look like you need a friend." Isabella smiled. "I'd like to be one."

Mira checked her appearance in the mirror. The dress, her hair, down to the color of the polish on her nails had all been done with care. The door below her had closed. *Villa Rosso* was forbidden territory. But she had made sure this night it was their sanctuary. She hurried down the stairs, careful of the hem of her dress.

Giovanni stood in the center of the room. He looked as yummy as ever. His tall hard-bone muscular frame was richly outlined in a black silk tailored suit with a crisp white shirt and black and white striped tie. Raven dark hair tapered low to his thick sideburns and nape contrasted with his deep olive brown skin that spoke to his Sicilian heritage. And of course it was his eyes that made her love for him deepen. The intensity of their hue often left her light headed and giddy when she stared into them too long.

Violet-blue, his steely gaze swept the room and his silky dark brows drew together with concern. The ambiance had to have startled him. Afterall this was his territory. A place where deals were made, and lives were controlled or broken. On a rare occaision or two she'd joined him here. Today she had the place cleaned and scrubbed of the stench of tobacco, leather, and vino. Candles were left on tall and short pedestals around the place giving off a dim yellow glow. She'd gotten a tape cassette of Sade and put it in his stereo to set the mood. The sultry words Sade sang, professing her love and vow to by her man's side filled the room.

His man cave was now their love shack.

"Hi, baby," she said.

His gaze swung her way and she felt a throb of response intimately. He regarded her between narrowed lids. It was time for her seduction and she was as nervous as she was the first time he had laid his hands on her. She gave him a moment to take her all in. She'd chosen one of her special creations. A wrap around silk dress with a low cut front and a side split of the fabric that reached her hipbone. It was midnight blue and had a short train that rippled across the floor as she walked toward him. It was taboo for a designer with a collection as vast as hers to repeat the same design of dress over and over again. But her man liked dresses that unwrapped easily. So she wore this one special for him.

"Welcome home," she said.

She untied the belt to her dress with a slow erotic striptease like the one she practiced with Marietta. Giovanni smiled as she let the fabric peel away from her skin. Their eyes met. She moved her hips in a slow roll to Sade's seductive voice. She wore a black lace half bra that barely covered her nipples in the cups that heaved her bosom upward. She'd chosen a matching high-wasted thong panty. For weeks she'd kept her figure hidden under baggy clothes. She didn't shower with him. She had to make sure to wear pajama pants and oversized t-shirts to bed. She wanted this moment.

She earned this moment. Mira danced for her husband. She moved as she hooked her thumbs into the sides of her panty and started to work them off her hips and thighs until they dropped to her knees and then ankles so she could step out of them. She closed her eyes and felt the music move through her. Let the lyrics and sexy rhythm consume her. She unhooked her bra and tossed it. Her eyes opened. Giovanni stood there watching.

"For me?" he asked, his gaze sweeping every inch of her curves.

"For you," she said and approached him. She ran her hand down his tie and then slid both of her hands under his suit jacket to either side of his shoulders so she could help him out of the jacket. "You want to know why I chose Villa Rosso? Why I invaded your sanctuary?"

Giovanni's left brow winged up with curiosity.

"Because this is a part of you. The part of you that's kept unseen." She brushed her lips over his. "I want to start again here. Love you," she kissed his lips. "Here."

Mira began to loosen his tie and then slid it out of its knot. She unraveled it from around his neck. "Tonight I'm yours. And you're mine. Tonight I fuck *Don* Giovanni."

He chuckled.

She squeezed his cock and flicked her tongue at his lip, before drawing it into her mouth.

"Mmm…. It's going to get rough, Bella," he whispered.

"I can take it," she said rubbing her body up against him. "If you do one thing for me?"

"Name it," he said.

"My pussy," she whispered in his ear.

Giovanni swept her up in his arms. She giggled and held to his neck, kissing his face. He carried her into his office instead of upstairs to the bed. "You want to fuck the *Don,* you fuck him in here," he said.

He put her on the sofa. Mira parted her legs. She touched her pussy for him with one hand and pinched her nipple with the other.

As if under her spell he shed his shirt obdiently. He went to his knees. Mira closed her eyes.

The sight of her sex both flush and pink brought him to his knees. He had missed her desperately. She parted the dark lips at her center and revealed her hot pink flower. Moisture glazed the walls of her cunt. Giovanni swiped a finger across her silken walls and brought the finger to his mouth and tasted her. Mira smiled. His head lowered as he tongued her opening and fucked her hole with the tip of his tongue.

Mira's breathing went uneven.

He rubbed his hand up and stroked her belly, reached and pinched her nipple. He used his other hand to lift the top hood of her pussy to release her clit. His tongue swiped up out of her hole to toy with the nub.

"Yes!" Mira cried out.

Giovanni groaned and sank his face, mouth deeper into her pussy as he sucked her clit and rubbed his nose over the curly hairs covering her mons. She gasped loudly bucking her ass up off the sofa seat. He used his tongue to soothe her clit with gentle glides up and down it, before going low. She neared her climax and pumped her pussy up against his mouth, beating her fist against the back cushion of the sofa.

"Giovanni! Yes, please!" she cried out.

Using his thumb and forefinger to hold her open he feasted on her pussy until she reached her earth shattering release.

He drew away licking his lips. He undid his belt buckle and ripped his zipper down. "Get on your knees. Now."

She wheezed for a breath, and shakily sunk to the floor. She turned in front of him and got on her hands and knees. Giovanni's entire body hardened at the sight of her. She tossed him a look over her shoulder. Wild excitement glittered in her eyes. His jaw tightened and he closed the distance between them. He caressed the curve of her ass.

The head of his cock nudged her her pussy until he found her entrance. He flexed his hips and drove himself deep with one hard stroke.

"Ugh!" she gasped.

The sweet hot tightness clenching and releasing his dick had left him struggling for a breath. He gripped both sides of her hips and relaxed himself to savor the moment.

"Tell me you need me," he said.

"I need you," she answered and moved back against his push.

"Tell me you need only me," he said and slammed into her pussy harder and faster.

Mira gasped.

"Say it!" he demanded.

"Only… you…" she gasped.

He forced her down by pushing at the center of her spine. Her pussy opened up fully to him. Her ass beat against his pelvis. His dick slammed in harder, and harder, relentless and he felt himself near the edge. Giovanni stopped himself. He withdrew. Mira collapsed and he dragged her under him, forcing her to her back. Her soft thighs closed around his hips. His erection found her creamy tightness and sank into her. The feel of her soft curves beneath him made him pause. She licked his neck, his chin, sought his mouth and dragged his tongue down into a kiss. He began to move again. His cock surged, his balls throbbed, he whirled his hips screwing her good.

Mira moved under him whimpering her pleasure. He loved her gently for the moment. Savoring every emotion straining and changing her pretty features.

"So beautiful. That's why you are my Bella," he said kissing her pouty swollen lips and then tasting her neck before sucking the tender skin between his teeth.

His ass rose and fell with each gentle push and withdrawal of his cock. Mira gripped both of his ass cheeks. She squeezed. His pants and boxers were still gathered at his knees. He hadn't bothered to remove them.

"Please fuck me," she whispered to him.

He lifted from her but his cock remained buried deep. He lifted her left leg and crossed it over her right. On his knees with his hands holding her leg down he thrust with rapid succession.

Heaven, was his single thought as he reached depths he hadn't imagined. Mira cried out loudly, clawing at him to slow his rhythm. He brough her left leg straight up against his chest and put her into a scissor position without a break in his stride.

"Oh, Gio, too deep," she panted.

"Shh… you can take it," he teased. Giovanni pulled out and thrust forward. Her cunt rippled and pulsed around him. Sweat rained down his brow dripping to his chest as his body temperature reached a feverish pitch. Her body shook with each downward thrust.

It wasn't enough. He needed more.

He withdrew and let her legs go down. Mira groaned. He lifted her beautiful body and sat back on his hunches. She was now seated on his lap. Like a demon possessed he gave her no time to catch her breath. He gripped her by the hips and she held to his neck as he helped her rise and fall on his dick hard and fast. Tension sung through him and with great effort he tried to control the pace. Bella squeezed his neck tightly and moved with her own purpose taking over.

She moved back and forth, up and down, rolled her sweet pussy and he was lost. The mounting pressure in his chest imploded and shockwaves crippled him. The rush of pleasure was so extreme he fell back, awkwardly pinned with his pants trapped at his knees. She allowed him to move his legs, straighten them and she was back on top.

His entire body seized as she rode his cock wild and free. Giovanni felt his heart reach an unattainable beat. "Bella!" he cried out.

"Shhh… you can take it," she teased.

He gripped her thighs for support and slammed his hips up to deliver decisive strikes before he broke and released.

"Mmmm," he said. "I want to fuck you on my desk next," he mumbled.

She chuckled and lay on him. "You can fuck me any way you please."

Giovanni woke with Mira in his arms. After a night of loving her, drinking and laughing they ended upstairs in his bed. He had lost track of time. He had no concept of it. The room they occupied had no windows. He lay with her sweet body pressed against his.

"You awake?" he asked.

"Mmm… what's wrong?" she groaned.

"Nothing, I… *ti amo*," he said. *"Amore mia."*

"Yes, Giovanni, you're my love,"

He closed his eyes and focused on the feel of his wife in his arms. Before he slipped back into bliss he whispered to her. "I adore you."

Book Club Questions

Are you a fan of the series thus far? Do you and your friends chat over the drama and romantic tales of the Battaglias? The author has provided twenty book club questions for you to further the discussion!

1. At the beginning of La Famiglia Giovanni and Mirabella adjust to marital bliss. They visit Milan and he gives her an immortalizing portrait of the woman she once was. Who do you think Giovanni wants as a wife: the uptight businesswoman who loves deeply but is blind to his criminal exploits, or the disciplined Donna who accepts his darkness and learns day-by-day how to wield the ultimate power over his heart? Also, was Flavio right in saying that the love of a woman is the weakness that could destroy him?

2. Marietta agrees to sail the Mediterranean with Lorenzo. After four months they are in love. Is that too fast for this complicated couple? Do you think that their passion and impulsive nature will bind them or destroy them?

3. Dominic is an orphan that Giovanni helped raise with his father. You learn the sad story of his arrival to the Battaglia family. Do you agree with Giovanni that their brotherhood should have never allowed him to cross the line with Catalina? Or do you understand what Dominic to be so passionate about his love for Catalina and Giovanni?

4. Catalina matures in La Famiglia. She is devoted to her family but she is also excited about her future. Should the Battaglia women be allowed to have independent lives from the famiglia? Or is their lifestyle to dangerous to allow such freedom?

5. Will Catalina and Dominic's love survive her passion for a career?

6. Giovanni kept a secret from his wife. Discuss his choice. Could you forgive a mafia husband for deceiving you? Was Mira's reaction to his deception founded or as many of the family believed unnecessarily punishing?

7. What do you think of Mira's reaction to her husbands lies compared to her sisters' ability to forgive and move on?

8. Marietta and Carlo have a dangerous connection. The

love/hate dynamic between them was ultimately bond to implode. How do you feel about Carlo's affections toward Marietta? Do you think they will ever cross the line again in the future?

9. Lorenzo loves his wife. What do you think he would do if he discovered their indiscretion?

10. Giovanni revealed his vulnerability. But not like most alpha men you read about in romance novels. His hard-edged madness and retaliation may not be appealing for a hero. As a reader would you have preferred he 'bend' to Mira's will, or were you accepting of her choice to 'bend' for him?

11. Dominic is truly a consigliere. He learned and trained under Flavio. He also feels the family should move toward more legitimate pursuits. Do you think Lorenzo's approach to keeping them strong and deadly is the better way to secure their legacy, or is Dominic's approach best?

12. What are you thoughts on Gemma?

13. Many stories have been shared about Melissa 'Lisa' Ellison. Which story do you believe? Gemma's or Mancini's? Was 'Lisa' Mancini's victim or just a young lady controlled by her drug addiction and love for a complicated man?

14. Armando and Mancini had a complicated relationship. Do you think he can set aside his prejudices and pride to get to know his sisters or will he be a threat to the women in the future?

15. What do you think happened to Carmella? Did Carlo kill her or give her money and send her away in the same manner he offered to do for Marietta?

16. Rocco appears to have more Battaglia secrets. Have we heard everything in the story of Tomosino and Rocco? Do you see any comparisons now with Rocco's actions to Lorenzo's?

17. Isabella lives. Why did she fake her death? And what do you think she has planned for Santo?

18. What was the most unforgettable moment in La Famiglia?

19. What would you have done differently in the story?

20. Can Mira evolve into the Bella Mafia Donna that the family needs? And at what cost?

Thank you for reading....

Coming next in 2014!

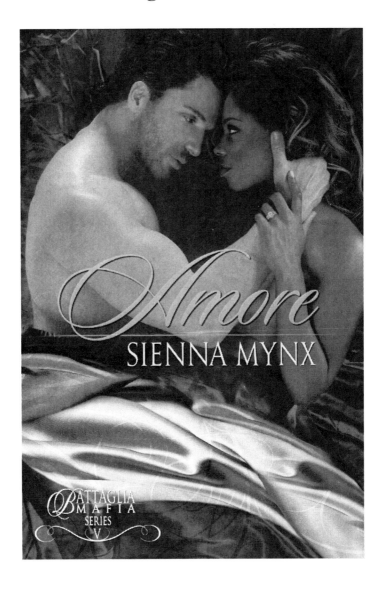

CPSIA information can be obtained at www.ICGtesting.com
Printed in the USA
BVOW02s2018290815

415724BV00013B/156/P